FORGOTTEN REALMS®

R.A. SALVATORE

THE LEGEND OF DRIZZT® COLLECTOR'S EDITION · BOOK II

THE CRYSTAL SHARD

STREAMS OF SILVER

THE HALFLING'S GEM

Wizards OF THE COAST®

The Legend of Drizzt
Collector's Edition, Book II

©2010 Wizards of the Coast LLC

Published by Wizards of the Coast LLC. FORGOTTEN REALMS, WIZARDS OF THE COAST, and their respective logos, and THE LEGEND OF DRIZZT are trademarks of Wizards of the Coast LLC in the U.S.A. and other countries.

Printed in the U.S.A.

Cover art by Todd Lockwood
Collector's Edition First Hardcover Printing: March 2008
This Edition First Printing: May 2010

This book collects the complete text from the January 2007 edition of *The Crystal Shard*, the May 2007 edition of *Streams of Silver*, and the August 2007 edition of *The Halfling's Gem*.

9 8 7 6 5 4 3 2 1

ISBN: 978-0-7869-5487-2
620-25381000-001-EN

U.S., CANADA,
ASIA, PACIFIC, & LATIN AMERICA
Wizards of the Coast LLC
P.O. Box 707
Renton, WA 98057-0707
+1-800-324-6496

EUROPEAN HEADQUARTERS
Hasbro UK Ltd
Caswell Way
Newport, Gwent NP9 0YH
GREAT BRITAIN
Save this address for your records.

Visit our web site at www.wizards.com

THE CRYSTAL SHARD

TO MY WIFE, DIANE
AND TO BRYAN, GENO, AND CAITLIN
FOR THEIR SUPPORT AND PATIENCE
THROUGH THIS EXPERIENCE.

AND TO MY PARENTS, GENO AND IRENE,
FOR BELIEVING IN ME EVEN WHEN I DIDN'T.

Whenever an author takes on a project like this, especially if it is his first novel, there are invariably a number of people who help him accomplish the task. The writing of The Crystal Shard was no exception.

Publishing a novel involves three elements: a degree of talent; a lot of hard work; and a good measure of luck. The first two elements can be controlled by the author, but the third involves being in the right place at the right time and finding an editor who believes in your ability and dedication to the task at hand.

Therefore, my greatest thanks go to TSR, and especially to Mary Kirchoff, for taking a chance on a first time author and guiding me throughout the process.

Writing in the 1980s has become a high-tech chore as well as an exercise in creativity. In the case of The Crystal Shard, luck once again worked on my side. I consider myself lucky to have a friend like Brian P. Savoy, who loaned me his software expertise in smoothing out the rough edges.

My thanks also to my personal opinion-givers, Dave Duquette and Michael LaVigueur, for pointing out strengths and weaknesses in the rough draft, to my brother, Gary Salvatore, for his work on the maps of Icewind Dale, and to the rest of my AD&D® game group, Tom Parker, Daniel Mallard, and Roland Lortie, for their continued inspiration through the development of eccentric characters fit to wear the mantle of a hero in a fantasy novel.

And finally; to the man who truly brought me into the world of the AD&D game, Bob Brown. Since you moved away (and took the pipe smoke with you) the atmosphere around the gaming table just hasn't been the same.

—R.A. Salvatore, 1988

⚔

STREAMS OF SILVER

As with everything I do,
to my wife, Diane,
and to the most important people
in our lives,
Bryan, Geno, and Caitlin.

⚔

THE HALFLING'S GEM

To my sister Susan,
who'll never know how much her support
has meant to me over the last few years

Icewind Dale

Mac Dualdoon

Bremen's Run

Kelvin's Cairn

Lonelywood

Termalaine

Bremen

Targos

Icewind Pass

Caer Konig

Lac Dinnesh

Caer Dineval

Bryn Shander

The Eastway

Easthaven

Good Mead

Dougan's Hole

Redwaters

The demon sat back on the seat it had carved in the stem of the giant mushroom. Sludge slurped and rolled around the rock island, the eternal oozing and shifting that marked this layer of the Abyss.

Errtu drummed its clawed fingers, its horned, apelike head lolling about on its shoulders as it peered into the gloom. "Where are you, Telshazz?" the demon hissed, expecting news of the relic. Crenshinibon pervaded all of the demon's thoughts. With the shard in its grasp, Errtu could rise over an entire layer, maybe even several layers.

PRELUDE

And Errtu had come so close to possessing it!

The demon knew the power of the artifact; Errtu had been serving seven lichs when they combined their evil magics and made the Crystal Shard. The lichs, undead spirits of powerful wizards that refused to rest when their mortal bodies had passed from the realms of the living, had gathered to create the most vile artifact ever made, an evil that fed and flourished off of that which the purveyors of good considered most precious—the light of the sun.

But they had gone beyond even their own considerable powers. The forging actually consumed the seven, Crenshinibon stealing the magical strength that preserved the lichs' undead state to fuel its own first flickers of life. The ensuing bursts of power had hurtled Errtu back to the Abyss, and the demon had presumed the shard destroyed.

But Crenshinibon would not be so easily destroyed. Now, centuries later, Errtu had stumbled upon the trail of the Crystal Shard again; a crystal tower, Cryshal-Tirith, with a pulsating heart the exact image of Crenshinibon.

Errtu knew the magic was close by; the demon could sense the powerful presence of the relic. If only it could have found the thing earlier . . . if only it could have grasped. . . .

But then Al Dimeneira had arrived, an angelic being of tremendous power. Al Dimeneira banished Errtu back to the Abyss with a single word.

Errtu peered through the swirling smoke and gloom when it heard the sucking footsteps.

"Telshazz?" the demon bellowed.

"Yes, my master," the smaller demon answered, cowering as it approached the mushroom throne.

"Did he get it?" Errtu roared. "Does Al Dimeneira have the Crystal Shard?"

Telshazz quivered and whimpered, "Yes, my lord . . . uh, no, my lord!"

Errtu's evil red eyes narrowed.

"He could not destroy it," the little demon was quick to explain. "Crenshinibon burned his hands!"

"Hah!" Errtu snorted. "Beyond even the power of Al Dimeneira! Where is it, then? Did you bring it, or does it remain in the second crystal tower?"

Telshazz whimpered again. It didn't want to tell its cruel master the truth, but it would not dare to disobey. "No, master, not in the tower," the little demon whispered.

"No!" Errtu roared. "Where is it?"

"Al Dimeneira threw it."

"Threw it?"

"Across the planes, merciful master!" Telshazz cried. "With all of his strength!"

"Across the very planes of existence!" Errtu growled.

"I tried to stop him, but . . ."

The horned head shot forward. Telshazz's words gurgled indecipherably as Errtu's canine maw tore its throat out.

⋈ ⋈ ⋈ ⋈ ⋈

Far removed from the gloom of the Abyss, Crenshinibon came to rest upon the world. Far up in the northern mountains of Faerûn the Crystal Shard, the ultimate perversion, settled into the snow of a bowl-shaped dell.

And waited.

PART ONE

If I could choose what life would be mine, it would be this life that I now have, at this time. I am at peace, and yet, the world around me swirls with turmoil, with the ever-present threat of barbarian raids and goblin wars, with tundra yetis and gigantic polar worms. The reality of existence here in Icewind Dale is harsh indeed, an environment unforgiving, where one mistake will cost you your life.

TEN-TOWNS

That is the joy of the place, the very edge of disaster, and not because of treachery, as I knew in my home of Menzoberranzan. I can accept the risks of Icewind Dale; I can revel in them and use them to keep my warrior instincts finely honed. I can use them to remind me every day of the glory and joy of life. There is no complacency here, in this place where safety cannot be taken for granted, where a turn of the wind can pile snow over your head, where a single misstep on a boat can put you into water that will steal your breath away and render muscles useless in mere seconds, or a simple lapse on the tundra can put you in the belly of a fierce yeti.

When you live with death so close, you come to appreciate life all the more.

And when you share that life with friends like those that I have come to know these last years, then you know paradise. Never could I have imagined in my years in Menzoberranzan, or in the wilds of the Underdark, or even when I first came to the surface world, that I would ever surround myself with such friends as these. They are of different races, all three, and all three different from my own, and yet, they are more alike what is in my heart than anyone I have ever known, save, perhaps, my father Zaknafein and the ranger, Montolio, who trained me in the ways of Mielikki.

I have met many folk up here in Ten-Towns, in the savage land of Icewind Dale, who accept me despite my dark elf heritage, and yet, these three, above all others, have become as family to me.

Why them? Why Bruenor, Regis, and Cattibrie above all others, three friends whom I treasure as much as Guenhwyvar, my companion for all these years?

Everyone knows Bruenor as blunt—that is the trademark of many dwarves, but in Bruenor, the trait runs pure. Or so he wants all to believe. I know better. I know the other side of Bruenor, the hidden side, that soft and warm place. Yes, he has a heart, though he tries hard to bury it! He is blunt, yes, particularly with criticism. He speaks of errors without apology and without judgment, simply telling the honest truth and leaving it up to the offender to correct, or not correct the situation. Bruenor never allows tact or empathy to get in the way of his telling the world how it can be better!

But that is only half of the tale concerning the dwarf, on the other side of the coin, he is far from blunt. Concerning compliments, Bruenor is not dishonest, just quiet.

Perhaps that is why I love him. I see in him Icewind Dale itself, cold and harsh and unforgiving, but ultimately honest. He keeps me at my best, all the time, and in doing that, he helps me to survive in this place. There is only one Icewind Dale, and only one Bruenor Battlehammer, and if ever I met a creature and a land created for each other . . .

Conversely, Regis stands (or more appropriately, reclines), as a reminder to me of the goals and rewards of a job well done—not that Regis is ever the one who does that job. Regis reminds me, and Bruenor, I would guess, that there is more to life than responsibility, that there are times for personal relaxation and enjoyment of the rewards brought about by good work and vigilance. He is too soft for the tundra, too round in the belly and too slow on his feet. His fighting skills are lacking and he could not track a herd of caribou on fresh snow. Yet he survives, even thrives up here with wit and attitude, with an understanding, better than Bruenor's surely, and even better than my own, of how to appease and please those around him, of how to anticipate, rather than just react to the moves of others. Regis knows more than just what people do, he knows why they do it, and that ability to understand motivation allowed him to see past the color of my skin and the reputation of my people. If Bruenor is honest in expressing his observations, then Regis is honest in following the course of his heart.

And finally there is Catti-brie, wonderful and so full of life. Catti-brie is the opposite side of the same coin to me, a different reasoning to reach the same conclusions. We are soulmates who see and judge different things in the world to arrive at the same place. Perhaps we thus validate each other. Perhaps in seeing Catti-brie arriving at the same place as myself, and knowing that she arrived there along a different road, tells me that I followed my heart truly. Is that it? Do I trust her more than I trust myself?

That question is neither indictment of my feelings, nor any self-incrimination. We share beliefs about the way of the world and the way the world should be. She is akin to my heart as is Mielikki, and if I found my goddess by looking honestly into my own heart, then so I have found my dearest friend and ally.

They are with me, all three, and Guenhwyvar, dear Guenhwyvar, as well. I am living in a land of stark beauty and stark reality, a place where you have to be wary and alert and at your very best at all times.

I call this paradise.

—Drizzt Do'Urden

I

THE STOOGE

When the wizards' caravan from the Hosttower of the Arcane saw the snow-capped peak of Kelvin's Cairn rising from the flat horizon, they were more than a little relieved. The hard journey from Luskan to the remote frontier settlement known as Ten-Towns had taken them more than three tendays.

The first tenday hadn't been too difficult. The troop held close to the Sword Coast, and though they were traveling along the northernmost reaches of the Realms, the summer breezes blowing in off the Trackless Sea were comfortable enough.

But when they rounded the westernmost spurs of the Spine of the World, the mountain range that many considered the northern boundary of civilization, and turned into Icewind Dale, the wizards quickly understood why they had been advised against making this journey. Icewind Dale, a thousand square miles of barren, broken tundra, had been described to them as one of the most unwelcoming lands in all the Realms, and within a single day of traveling on the northern side of the Spine of the World, Eldeluc, Dendybar the Mottled, and the other wizards from Luskan considered the reputation well-earned. Bordered by impassable mountains on the south, an expanding glacier on the east, and an unnavigable sea of countless icebergs on the north and west, Icewind Dale was attainable only through the pass between the Spine of the World and the coast, a trail rarely used by any but the most hardy of merchants.

For the rest of their lives, two memories would ring clear in the wizards' minds whenever they thought about this trip, two facts of life on Icewind Dale that travelers here never forgot. The first was the endless moaning of the wind, as though the land itself was continuously groaning in torment. And the second was the emptiness of the dale, mile after mile of gray and brown horizon lines.

The caravan's destination marked the only varying features in all the dale—ten small towns positioned around the three lakes of the region, under the shadow of the only mountain, Kelvin's Cairn. Like everyone else who came to this harsh land the wizards sought Ten-Towns' scrimshaw, the fine ivory carvings made from the headbones of the knucklehead trout which swam in the waters of the lakes.

Some of the wizards, though, had even more devious gains in mind.

⚔ ⚔ ⚔ ⚔

The man marveled at how easily the slender dagger slipped through the folds in the older man's robe and then cut deeper into the wrinkled flesh.

Morkai the Red turned on his apprentice, his eyes locked into a widened, amazed set at the betrayal by the man he had raised as his own son for a quarter of a century.

Akar Kessell let go of the dagger and backed away from his master, horrified that the mortally wounded man was still standing. He ran out of distance for his retreat, stumbling into the rear wall of the small cabin the wizards of Luskan had been given as temporary quarters by the host city of Easthaven. Kessell trembled visibly, pondering the grisly consequences he would face in light of the growing possibility that the magical expertise of the old mage had found a way to defeat even death itself.

What terrible fate would his mighty mentor impose upon him for his betrayal? What magical torments could a true and powerful wizard such as Morkai conjure that would outdo the most agonizing of the tortures common throughout the land?

The old man held his gaze firmly on Akar Kessell, even as the last light began to fade from his dying eyes. He didn't ask why, he didn't even outwardly question Kessell about the possible motives. The gain of power was involved somewhere, he knew—that was always the case in such betrayals. What confused him was the instrument, not the motive. Kessell? How could Kessell, the bumbling apprentice whose stuttering lips could barely call out the simplest of cantrips, possibly hope to profit from the death of the only man who had ever shown him more than basic, polite consideration?

Morkai the Red fell dead. It was one of the few questions he had never found the answer to.

Kessell remained against the wall, needing its tangible support, and continued to shake for long minutes. Gradually, the confidence that had put him in this dangerous position began to grow again within him. He was the boss now—Eldeluc, Dendybar the Mottled, and the other wizards who had made the trip had said so. With his master gone, he, Akar Kessell, would be rightfully awarded his own meditation chamber and alchemy lab in the Hosttower of the Arcane in Luskan.

Eldeluc, Dendybar the Mottled, and the others had said so.

⚔ ⚔ ⚔ ⚔ ⚔

"It is done, then?" the burly man asked when Kessell entered the dark alley designated as the meeting place.

Kessell nodded eagerly. "The red-robed wizard of Luskan shan't cast again!" he proclaimed too loudly for the likes of his fellow conspirators.

"Speak quietly, fool," Dendybar the Mottled, a frail-looking man tucked defensively within the alleyway's shadows, demanded in the same monotonous voice that he always used. Dendybar rarely spoke at all and never displayed any semblance of passion when he did. Ever was he hidden beneath the low-pulled cowl of his robe. There was something cold-blooded about Dendybar that unnerved most people who met him. Though the wizard was physically the smallest and least imposing man on the merchant caravan that had made the four-hundred mile journey to the frontier settlement of Ten-Towns, Kessell feared him more than any of the others.

"Morkai the Red, my former master, is dead," Kessell reiterated softly.

"Akar Kessell, this day forward known as Kessell the Red, is now appointed to the Wizard's Guild of Luskar!"

"Easy, friend," said Eldeluc, putting a comforting hand on Kessell's nervously twitching shoulder. "There will be time for a proper coronation when we return to the city." He smiled and winked at Dendybar from behind Kessell's head.

Kessell's mind was whirling, lost in a daydream search through all of the ramifications of his pending appointment. Never again would he be taunted by the other apprentices, boys much younger than he who climbed through the ranks in the guild step by tedious step. They would show him some respect now, for he would leap beyond even those who had passed him by in the earliest days of his apprenticeship, into the honorable position of wizard.

As his thoughts probed every detail of the coming days, though, Kessell's radiant face suddenly grayed over. He turned sharply on the man at his side, his features tensed as though he had discovered a terrible error. Eldeluc and several of the others in the alley became uneasy. They all fully understood the consequences if the archmage of the Hosttower of the Arcane ever learned of their murderous deed.

"The robe?" Kessell asked. "Should I have brought the red robe?"

Eldeluc couldn't contain his relieved chuckle, but Kessell merely took it as a comforting gesture from his new-found friend.

I should have known that something so trivial would throw him into such a fit, Eldeluc told himself, but to Kessell he merely said, "Have no fear about it. There are plenty of robes in the Hosttower. It would seem a bit suspicious, would it not, if you showed up at the archmage's doorstep claiming the vacated seat of Morkai the Red and holding the very garment that the murdered wizard was wearing when he was slain?"

Kessell thought about it for a moment, then agreed.

"Perhaps," Eldeluc continued, "you should not wear the red robe."

Kessell's eyes squinted in panic. His old self-doubts, which had haunted him for all of his days since his childhood, began to bubble up within him. What was Eldeluc saying? Were they going to change their minds and not award him the seat he had rightfully earned?

Eldeluc had used the ambiguity of his statement as a tease, but he didn't want to push Kessell into a dangerous state of doubt. With a second wink at Dendybar, who was inwardly thoroughly enjoying this game, he answered the poor wretch's unspoken question. "I only meant that perhaps a different color would better suit you. Blue would compliment your eyes."

Kessell cackled in relief. "Perhaps," he agreed, his fingers nervously twiddling.

Dendybar suddenly grew tired of the farce. He motioned for his burly companion to be rid of the annoying little wretch.

Eldeluc obediently led Kessell back down the alleyway. "Go on, now, back to the stables," he instructed. "Tell the master there that the wizards shall be leaving for Luskan this very night."

"But what of the body?" Kessell asked.

Eldeluc smiled evilly. "Leave it. That cabin is reserved for visiting merchants and dignitaries from the south. It will most probably remain vacant until next spring. Another murder in this part of the world will cause little excitement, I assure you, and even if the good people of Easthaven were to decipher what had truly happened, they are wise enough to tend to their own business and leave the affairs of wizards to wizards!"

The group from Luskan moved out into the waning sunlight on the street. "Now be off!" Eldeluc commanded. "Look for us as the sun sets." He watched as Kessell, like some elated little boy, scurried away.

"How fortunate to find so convenient a tool," Dendybar noted. "The wizard's stupid apprentice saved us much trouble. I doubt that we would have found a way to get at that crafty old one. Though the gods alone know why, ever did Morkai have a soft spot for his wretched little apprentice!"

"Soft enough for a dagger's point!" laughed a second voice.

"And so convenient a setting," remarked yet another. "Unexplained bodies are considered no more than an inconvenience to the cleaning wenches in this uncivilized outpost."

The burly Eldeluc laughed aloud. The gruesome task was at last completed; they could, finally, leave this barren stretch of frozen desert and return home.

⚔ ⚔ ⚔ ⚔ ⚔

Kessell's step was sprightly as he made his way across the village of Easthaven to the barn where the wizards' horses had been stabled. He felt as though becoming a wizard would change every aspect of his daily life, as if some mystical strength had somehow been infused into his previously incompetent talents.

He tingled in anticipation of the power that would be his. An alleycat crossed before him, casting him a wary glance as it pranced by.

Slit-eyed, Kessell looked around to see if anyone was watching. "Why not?" he muttered. Pointing a deadly finger at the cat, he uttered the command words to call forth a burst of energy. The nervous feline bolted away at the spectacle, but no magical bolts struck it, or even near it.

Kessell looked down at his singed fingertip and wondered what he had done wrong.

But he wasn't overly dismayed. His own blackened nail was the strongest effect he had ever gotten from that particular spell.

2
ON THE BANKS OF MAER ĐUALĐON

Regis the halfling, the only one of his kind for hundreds of miles in any direction, locked his fingers behind his head and leaned back against the mossy blanket of the tree trunk. Regis was short, even by the standards of his diminutive race, with the fluff of his curly brown locks barely cresting the three-foot mark, but his belly was amply thickened by his love of a good meal, or several, as the opportunities presented themselves.

The crooked stick that served as his fishing pole rose up above him, clenched between two of his furry toes, and hung out over the quiet lake, mirrored perfectly in the glassy surface of Maer Dualdon. Gentle ripples rolled down the image as the red-painted wooden bobber began to dance slightly. The line had floated in toward shore and hung limply in the water, so Regis couldn't feel the fish nibbling at the bait. In seconds, the hook was cleaned with no catch to show for it, but the halfling didn't know, and it would be hours before he'd even bother to check. Not that he'd have cared, anyway.

This trip was for leisure, not work. With winter coming on, Regis figured that this might well be his last excursion of the year to the lake; he didn't go in for winter fishing, like some of the fanatically greedy humans of Ten-Towns. Besides, the halfling already had enough ivory stocked up from other people's catches to keep him busy for all seven months of snow. He was truly a credit to his less-than-ambitious race, carving out a bit of civilization in a land where none existed, hundreds of miles from the most remote settlement that could rightly be called a city. Other halflings never came this far north, even during the summer months, preferring the comfort of the southern climes. Regis, too, would have gladly packed up his belongings and returned to the south, except for a little problem he had with a certain guildmaster of a prominent thieves' guild.

A four-inch block of the "white gold" lay beside the reclining halfling, along with several delicate carving instruments. The beginnings of a horse's muzzle marred the squareness of the block. Regis had meant to work on the piece while he was fishing.

Regis meant to do a lot of things.

"Too fine a day," he had rationalized, an excuse that never seemed to grow stale for him. This time, though, unlike so many others, it truly bore credibility. It seemed as though the weather demons that bent this harsh land to their iron will had taken a holiday, or perhaps they were just gathering their strength for a brutal winter. The result was an autumn day fitting for the civilized lands to the south. A rare day indeed for the land that had come to be called Icewind Dale, a name well-earned by the eastern breezes that always seemed to blow in, bringing with them the chilled air of Reghed Glacier. Even on the few days that the wind shifted there was little relief, for Ten-Towns was bordered on the north and west by miles of empty tundra and then more ice, the Sea of Moving Ice. Only southern breezes promised any relief, and any wind that tried to reach this desolate area from that direction was usually blocked by the high peaks of the Spine of the World.

Regis managed to keep his eyes open for a while, peering up through the fuzzy limbs of the fir trees at the puffy white clouds as they sailed across the sky on the mild breezes. The sun rained down golden warmth, and the halfling was tempted now and then to take off his waistcoat. Whenever a cloud blocked out the warming rays, though, Regis was reminded that it was Eleint on the tundra. In a month there would be snow. In two, the roads west and south to Luskan, the nearest city to Ten-Towns, would be impassable to any but the sturdy or the stupid.

Regis looked across the long bay that rolled in around the side of his little fishing hole. The rest of Ten-Towns was taking advantage of the weather, too; the fishing boats were out in force, scrambling and weaving around each other to find their special "hitting spots." No matter how many times he witnessed it, the greed of humans always amazed Regis. Back in the southern land of Calimshan, the halfling had been climbing a fast ladder to Associate Guildmaster in one of the most prominent thieves' guilds in the port city of Calimport. But as he saw it, human greed had cut short his career. His guild-master, the Pasha Pook, possessed a wonderful collection of rubies—a dozen, at least—whose facets were so ingeniously cut that they seemed to cast an almost hypnotic spell on anyone who viewed them. Regis had marveled at the scintillating stones whenever Pook put them out on display, and after all, he'd only taken one. To this day, the halfling couldn't figure out why the Pasha, who had no less than eleven others, was still so angry with him.

"Alas for the greed of humans," Regis would say whenever the Pasha's men showed up in another town that the halfling had made his home, forcing him to extend his exile to an even more remote land. But he hadn't needed that phrase for a year-and-a-half now, not since he had arrived in Ten-Towns. Pook's arms were long, but this frontier settlement, in the middle of the most inhospitable and untamed land imaginable, was a longer way still, and Regis was quite content in the security of his new sanctuary. There was wealth here, and for those nimble and talented enough to be a scrimshander, someone who could transform the ivorylike bone of a knucklehead trout into an artistic carving, a comfortable living could be made with a minimum amount of work.

And with Ten-Towns' scrimshaw fast becoming the rave of the south, the halfling meant to shake off his customary lethargy and turn his new-found trade into a booming business.

Someday.

⚔ ⚔ ⚔ ⚔ ⚔

Drizzt Do'Urden trotted along silently, his soft, low-cut boots barely stirring the dust. He kept the cowl of his brown cloak pulled low over the flowing waves of his stark white hair and moved with such effortless grace that an onlooker might have thought him to be no more than an illusion, an optical trick of the brown sea of tundra.

The dark elf pulled his cloak tighter about him. He felt as vulnerable in the sunlight as a human would in the dark of night. More than half a century of living many miles below ground had not been erased by several years on the sunlit surface. To this day, sunlight drained and dizzied him.

But Drizzt had traveled right through the night and was compelled to continue. Already he was overdue for his meeting with Bruenor in the dwarf's valley, and he had seen the signs.

The reindeer had begun their autumn migration southwest to the sea, yet no human track followed the herd. The caves north of Ten-Towns, always a stopover for the nomadic barbarians on their way back to the tundra, had not even been stocked to re-provision the tribes on their long trek. Drizzt understood the implications. In normal barbarian life, the survival of the tribes depended on their following the reindeer herd. The apparent abandonment of their traditional ways was more than a little disturbing.

And Drizzt had heard the battle drums.

Their subtle rumblings rolled over the empty plain like distant thunder, in patterns usually recognizable only to the other barbarian tribes. But Drizzt knew what they foretold. He was an observer who understood the value of knowledge of friend or foe, and he had often used his stealth prowess to observe the daily routines and traditions of the proud natives of Icewind Dale, the barbarians.

Drizzt picked up his pace, pushing himself to the limits of his endurance. In five short years, he had come to care for the cluster of villages known as Ten-Towns and for the people who lived there. Like so many of the other outcasts who had finally settled there, the drow had found no welcome anywhere else in the Realms. Even here he was only tolerated by most, but in the unspoken kinship of fellow rogues, few people bothered him. He'd been luckier than most; he'd found a few friends who could look beyond his heritage and see his true character.

Anxiously, the dark elf squinted at Kelvin's Cairn, the solitary mountain that marked the entrance to the rocky dwarven valley between Maer Dualdon and Lac Dinneshere, but his violet-colored almond eyes, marvelous orbs that could rival an owl's in the night, could not penetrate the blur of daylight enough to gauge the distance.

Again he ducked his head under the cowl, preferring a blind run to the dizziness of prolonged exposure to the sun, and sank back into the dark dreams of Menzoberranzan, the lightless underworld city of his ancestors. The drow elves had actually once walked on the surface world, dancing beneath the sun and the stars with their fair-skinned cousins. Yet the dark elves were malicious, passionless killers beyond the tolerance of even their normally unjudging kin. And in the inevitable war of the elven nations, the drow were driven into the bowels of the ground. Here they found a world of dark secrets and dark magics and were content to remain. Over the centuries, they had flourished and grown strong once more, attuning themselves to the ways of mysterious magics. They became more powerful than even their surface-dwelling cousins, whose dealings with the arcane arts under the life-giving warmth of the sun were hobby, not necessity.

As a race, though, the drow had lost all desire to see the sun and the stars. Both their bodies and minds had adapted to the depths, and luckily for all who dwelt under the open sky, the evil dark elves were content to remain where they were, only occasionally resurfacing to raid and pillage. As far as Drizzt knew, he was the only one of his kind living on the surface. He had learned some tolerance of the light, but he still suffered the hereditary weaknesses it imparted upon his kind.

Yet even considering his disadvantage under daytime conditions, Drizzt was outraged by his own carelessness when the two bearlike tundra yetis, their camouflaging coats of shaggy fur still colored in summer brown, suddenly rose up before him.

× × × × ×

A red flag rose from the deck of one of the fishing boats, signaling a catch. Regis watched as it moved higher and higher. "A four-footer, or better," the halfling mumbled approvingly when the flag topped out just below the mast's crosspiece. "There'll be singing in one house tonight!"

A second ship raced up beside the one that had signaled the catch, banging into the anchored vessel in its rush. The two crews immediately drew weapons and faced off, though each remained on its respective ship.

With nothing between him and the boats but empty water, Regis clearly heard the shouts of the captains.

"Ere, ye stole me catch!" the captain of the second ship roared.

"You're water-weary!" the captain of the first ship retorted. "Never it was! It's our fish fairly hooked and fairly hauled! Now be gone with your stinking tub before we take you out of the water!"

Predictably, the crew of the second ship was over the rail and swinging before the captain of the first ship had finished speaking.

Regis turned his eyes back to the clouds; the dispute on the boats did not hold any interest for him, though the noises of the battle were certainly disturbing. Such squabbles were common on the lakes, always over the fish, especially if someone landed a big one. Generally they weren't too serious, more bluster and parrying than actual fighting, and only rarely did someone get badly wounded or killed. There were exceptions, though. In one skirmish involving no less than seventeen boats, three full crews and half of a fourth were cut down and left floating in the bloodied water. On that same day, that particular lake, the southernmost of the three, had its name changed from Dellon-lune to Redwaters.

"Ah little fishes, what trouble you bring," Regis muttered softly, pondering the irony of the havoc the silvery fish wreaked on the lives of the greedy people of Ten-Towns. These ten communities owed their very existence to the knucklehead trout, with their oversized, fist-shaped heads and bones the consistency of fine ivory. The three lakes were the only spots in the world where the valuable fish were known to swim, and though the region was barren and wild, overrun with humanoids and barbarians and sporting frequent storms that could flatten the sturdiest of buildings, the lure of quick wealth brought in people from the farthest reaches of the Realms.

As many inevitably left as came in, though. Icewind Dale was a bleak, colorless wasteland of merciless weather and countless dangers. Death was a common visitor to the villagers, stalking any who could not face the harsh realities of Icewind Dale.

Still, the towns had grown considerably in the century that had passed since the knuckleheads were first discovered. Initially, the nine villages on the lakes were no more than the shanties where individual frontiersmen had staked out a claim on a particularly good fishing hole. The tenth village, Bryn Shander, though now a walled, bustling settlement of several thousand people, had been merely an empty hill sporting a solitary cabin where the fishermen would meet once a year, exchanging stories and goods with the traders from Luskan.

Back in the early days of Ten-Towns a boat, even a one-man rowboat, out on the lakes, whose waters year-round were cold enough to kill in minutes anyone unfortunate enough to fall overboard, was a rare sight, but now every town on the lakes had a fleet of sailing vessels flying its flag. Targos alone, largest of the fishing towns, could put over a hundred vessels onto Maer Dualdon, some of them two-masted schooners with crews of ten or more.

A death cry sounded from the embattled ships, and the clang of steel on steel rang out loudly. Regis wondered, and not for the first time, if the people of Ten-Towns would be better off without the troublesome fish.

The halfling had to admit that Ten-Towns had been a haven for him, though. His practiced, nimble fingers adapted easily to the instruments of the scrimshander, and he had even been elected as the council spokesman of one of the villages. Granted, Lonelywood was the smallest and northernmost of the ten towns, a place where the rogues of rogues hid out, but Regis still considered his appointment an honor. It was convenient as well. As the only true scrimshander in Lonelywood, Regis was the sole person in the town with reason or desire to travel regularly to Bryn Shander, the principal settlement and market hub of Ten-Towns. This had proved to be quite a boon to the halfling. He became the primary courier to bring the catches of Lonelywood's fishermen to market, for a commission equaling a tenth-piece of the goods. This alone kept him deep enough in ivory to make an easy living.

Once a month during the summer season and once every three in the winter, weather permitting, Regis had to attend council meetings and fulfill his duties as spokesman. These meetings took place in Bryn Shander, and though they normally broke down into nothing more than petty arguments over fishing territories between villages, they usually lasted only a few hours. Regis considered his attendance a small price to pay for keeping his monopoly on trips to the southern marketplace.

The fighting on the boats soon ended, only one man dead, and Regis drifted back into quiet enjoyment of the sailing clouds. The halfling looked back over his shoulder at the dozens of low wooden cabins dotting the thick rows of trees that comprised Lonelywood. Despite the reputation of its inhabitants, Regis found this town to be the best in the region. The trees provided a measure of protection from the howling wind and good corner posts for the houses. Only its distance from Bryn Shander had kept the town in the wood from being a more prominent member of Ten-Towns.

Abruptly, Regis pulled the ruby pendant out from under his waistcoat and stared at the wondrous gem he had appropriated from his former master a thousand miles and more to the south, in Calimport.

"Ah, Pook," he mused, "if only you could see me now."

⚔ ⚔ ⚔ ⚔

The elf went for the two scimitars sheathed on his hips, but the yetis closed quickly. Instinctively, Drizzt spun to his left, sacrificing his opposite flank to accept the rush of the closest monster. His right arm became helplessly pinned to his side as the yeti wrapped its great arms around him, but he managed to keep his left arm free enough to draw his second weapon. Ignoring the pain of the yeti's squeeze, Drizzt set the hilt of the scimitar firmly against his hip and allowed the momentum of the second charging monster to impale it on the curving blade.

In its frenzied death throes, the second yeti pulled away, taking the scimitar with it.

The remaining monster bore Drizzt to the ground under its weight. The drow worked his free hand frantically to keep the deadly teeth from gaining a hold on his throat, but he knew that it was only a matter of time before his stronger foe finished him.

Suddenly Drizzt heard a sharp crack. The yeti shuddered violently. Its head contorted weirdly, and a gout of blood and brains poured over its face from above its forehead.

"Yer late, elf!" came the rough edge of a familiar voice. Bruenor

Battlehammer walked up the back of his dead foe, disregarding the fact that the heavy monster lay on top of his elven friend. In spite of the added discomfort, the dwarf's long, pointed, often-broken nose and gray-streaked though still-fiery red beard came as a welcome sight to Drizzt. "Knew I'd find ye in trouble if I came out an' looked for ye!"

Smiling in relief, and also at the mannerisms of the ever-amazing dwarf, Drizzt managed to wriggle out from under the monster while Bruenor worked to free his axe from the thick skull.

"Head's as hard as frozen oak," grumbled the dwarf. He planted his feet behind the yeti's ears and pulled the axe free with a mighty jerk. "Where's that kitten o' yers, anyway?"

Drizzt fumbled around in his pack for a moment and produced a small onyx statue of a panther. "I'd hardly label Guenhwyvar a kitten," he said with fond reverence. He turned the figurine over in his hands, feeling the intricate details of the work to ensure that it had not been damaged in the fall under the yeti.

"Bah, a cat's a cat!" insisted the dwarf. "An' why isn't it here when ye needed it?"

"Even a magical animal needs its rest," Drizzt explained.

"Bah," Bruenor spouted again. "It's sure to be a sorry day when a drow—and a ranger, what's more—gets taken off 'is guard on an open plain by two scab tundra yetis!" Bruenor licked his stained axe blade, then spat in disgust.

"Foul beasts!" he grumbled. "Can't even eat the damn things!" He pounded the axe into the ground to clean the blade and stomped off toward Kelvin's Cairn.

Drizzt put Guenhwyvar back into the pack and went to retrieve his scimitar from the other monster.

"Come on, elf," scolded the dwarf. "We've five miles an' more of road to go!"

Drizzt shook his head and wiped the bloodstained blade on the felled monster's fur. "Roll on, Bruenor Battlehammer," he whispered under his smile. "And know to your pleasure that every monster along our trail will mark well your passing and keep its head safely hidden!"

3

THE MEAD HALL

Many miles north of Ten-Towns, across the trackless tundra to the northernmost edge of land in all the Realms, the frosts of winter had already hardened the ground in a white-tipped glaze. There were no mountains or trees to block the cold bite of the relentless eastern wind, carrying the frosty air from Reghed Glacier. The great bergs of the Sea of Moving Ice drifted slowly past, the wind howling off of their high-riding tips in a grim reminder of the coming season. And yet, the nomadic tribes who summered there with the reindeer had not journeyed with the herd's migration southwest along the coast to the more hospitable sea on the south side of the peninsula.

The unwavering flatness of the horizon was broken in one small corner by a solitary encampment, the largest gathering of barbarians this far north in more than a century. To accommodate the leaders of the respective tribes, several deerskin tents had been laid out in a circular pattern, each encompassed in its own ring of campfires. In the center of this circle, a huge deerskin hall had been constructed, designed to hold every warrior of the tribes. The tribesmen called it Hengorot, "The Mead Hall," and to the northern barbarians this was a place of reverence, where food and drink were shared in toasts to Tempus, the God of Battle.

The fires outside the hall burned low this night, for King Heafstaag and the Tribe of the Elk, the last to arrive, were expected in the camp before moonset. All the barbarians already in the encampment had assembled in Hengorot and begun the pre-council festivities. Great flagons of mead dotted every table, and good-natured contests of strength sprang up with growing frequency. Though the tribes often warred with each other, in Hengorot all differences were put aside.

King Beorg, a robust man with tousled blond locks, a beard fading to white, and lines of experience etched deeply into his tanned face, stood solemnly at the head table. Representing his people, he stood tall and straight, his wide shoulders proudly squared. The barbarians of Icewind Dale stood a full head and more above the average inhabitant of Ten-Towns, sprouting as though to take advantage of the wide and roomy expanses of empty tundra.

They were indeed much akin to their land. Like the ground they roamed over, their often-bearded faces were browned from the sun and cracked by the constant wind, giving them a leathery, toughened appearance, a foreboding, expressionless mask that did not welcome outsiders. They despised the people of Ten-Towns, whom they considered weak wealth-chasers possessed of no spiritual value whatsoever.

Yet one of those wealth-chasers stood among them now in their most revered hall of meeting. At Beorg's side was deBernezan, the dark-haired southerner, the only man in the room who was not born and bred of the barbarian tribes. The mousey deBernezan kept his shoulders defensively hunched as he glanced nervously about the hall. He was well aware that the barbarians were not overly fond of outsiders and that any one of them, even the youngest attendant, could break him in half with a casual flick of his huge hands.

"Hold steady!" Beorg instructed the southerner. "Tonight you hoist mead flagons with the Tribe of the Wolf. If they sense your fear." He left the rest unspoken, but deBernezan knew well how the barbarians dealt with weakness. The small man took a steadying deep breath and straightened his shoulders.

Yet Beorg, too, was nervous. King Heafstaag was his primary rival on the tundra, commanding a force as dedicated, disciplined, and numerous as his own. Unlike the customary barbarian raids, Beorg's plan called for the total conquest of Ten-Towns, enslaving the surviving fishermen and living well off of the wealth they harvested from the lakes. Beorg saw an opportunity for his people to abandon their precarious nomadic existence and find a measure of luxury they had never known. Everything now hinged on the assent of Heafstaag, a brutal king interested only in personal glory and triumphant plunder. Even if the victory over Ten-Towns was achieved, Beorg knew that he would eventually have to deal with his rival, who would not easily abandon the fervent bloodlust that had put him in power. That was a bridge the King of the Tribe of the Wolf would have to cross later; the primary issue now was the initial conquest, and if Heafstaag refused to go along, the lesser tribes would split in their alliances among the two. War might be joined as early as the next morning. This would prove devastating to all their people, for even the barbarians who survived the initial battles would be in for a brutal struggle against winter. The reindeer had long since departed for the southern pastures, and the caves along the route had not been stocked in preparation. Heafstaag was a cunning leader; he knew that at this late date the tribes were committed to following the initial plan, but Beorg wondered what terms his rival would impose.

Beorg took comfort in the fact that no major conflicts had broken out among the assembled tribes, and this night, when they all met in the common hall, the atmosphere was brotherly and jovial, with every beard in Hengorot lathered in foam. Beorg's gamble had been that the tribes could be united by a common enemy and the promise of continued prosperity. All had gone well . . . so far.

But the brute, Heafstaag, remained the key to it all.

⚔ ⚔ ⚔ ⚔ ⚔

The heavy boots of Heafstaag's column shook the ground beneath their determined march. The huge, one-eyed king himself led the procession, his great, swinging strides indicative of the nomads of the tundra. Intrigued by Beorg's proposal and wary of winter's early onset, the rugged king had chosen to march straight through the cold nights, stopping only for short periods of food and rest. Though primarily known for his ferocious proficiency in battle, Heafstaag was a leader who carefully weighed his every move. The impressive march would add to the initial respect given his people by the warriors of the other tribes, and Heafstaag was quick to pounce on any advantage he could get.

Not that he expected any trouble at Hengorot. He held Beorg in high respect. Twice before he had met the King of the Tribe of the Wolf on the field of honor with no victory to show for it. If Beorg's plan was as promising as it initially seemed, Heafstaag would go along, insisting only on an equal share in the leadership with the blond king. He didn't care for the notion that the tribesmen, once they had conquered the towns, could end their nomadic lifestyle and be contented with a new life trading knucklehead trout, but he was willing to allow Beorg his fantasies if they delivered to him the thrill of battle and easy victory. Let the plunder be taken and warmth secured for the long winter before he changed the original agreement and redistributed the booty.

When the lights of the campfires came into view, the column quickened its pace. "Sing, my proud warriors!" Heafstaag commanded. "Sing hearty and strong! Let those gathered tremble at the approach of the Tribe of the Elk."

✕ ✕ ✕ ✕ ✕

Beorg had an ear cocked for the sound of Heafstaag's arrival. Knowing well the tactics of his rival, he was not surprised in the least when the first notes of the Song of Tempus rolled in from the night. The blond king reacted at once, leaping onto a table and calling silence to the gathering. "Harken, men of the north!" he cried. "Behold the challenge of the song!"

Hengorot immediately burst into commotion as the men dashed from their seats and scrambled to join the assembling groups of their respective tribes. Every voice was lifted in the common refrain to the God of Battle, singing of deeds of valor and of glorious deaths on the field of honor. This verse was taught to every barbarian boy from the time he could speak his first words, for the Song of Tempus was actually considered a measure of a tribe's strength. The only variance in the words from tribe to tribe was the refrain that identified the singers. Here the warriors sang at crescendo pitch, for the challenge of the song was to determine whose call to the God of Battle was most clearly heard by Tempus.

Heafstaag led his men right up to the entrance of Hengorot. Inside the hall the calls of the Tribe of the Wolf were obviously drowning out the others, but Heafstaag's warriors matched the strength of Beorg's men.

One by one, the lesser tribes fell silent under the dominance of the Wolf and the Elk. The challenge dragged on between the two remaining tribes for many more minutes, neither willing to relinquish superiority in the eyes of their deity. Inside the mead hall, men of the beaten tribes nervously put their hands to their weapons. More than one war had erupted on the plains because the challenge of the song could determine no clear winner.

Finally, the flap of the tent opened admitting Heafstaag's standard bearer, a youth, tall and proud, with observing eyes that carefully weighed everything about him and belied his age. He put a whalebone horn to his lips and blew a clear note. Simultaneously, according to tradition, both tribes stopped their singing.

The standard bearer walked across the room toward the host king, his eyes never blinking or turning away from Beorg's imposing visage, though Beorg could see that the youth marked the expressions that were upon him. Heafstaag had chosen his herald well, Beorg thought.

"Good King Beorg," the standard bearer began when all commotion had ceased, "and other assembled kings. The Tribe of the Elk asks leave to enter Hengorot and share mead with you, that we might join together in toast to Tempus."

Beorg studied the herald a bit longer, testing to see if he could shake the youth's composure with an unexpected delay.

But the herald did not blink or turn aside his penetrating stare, and the set of his jaw remained firm and confident.

"Granted," answered Beorg, impressed. "And well met." Then he mumbled under his breath, "A pity that Heafstaag is not possessed of your patience."

"I announce Heafstaag, King of the Tribe of the Elk," the herald cried out in a clear voice, "son of Hrothulf the Strong, son of Angaar the Brave; thrice

killer of the great bear; twice conqueror of Termalaine to the south; who slew
Raag Doning, King of the Tribe of the Bear, in single combat in a single
stroke . . ." (this drawing uneasy shuffles from the Tribe of the Bear, and
especially their king, Haalfdane, son of Raag Doning). The herald went on
for many minutes, listing every deed, every honor, every title, accumulated
by Heafstaag during his long and illustrious career.

As the challenge of the song was competition between the tribes,
the listing of titles and feats was a personal competition between men,
especially kings, whose valor and strength reflected directly upon their
warriors. Beorg had dreaded this moment, for his rival's list exceeded even
his own. He knew that one of the reasons Heafstaag had arrived last was
so that his list could be presented to all in attendance, men who had heard
Beorg's own herald in private audience upon their arrival days before.
It was the advantage of a host king to have his list read to every tribe in
attendance, while the heralds of visiting kings would only speak to the
tribes present upon their immediate arrival. By coming in last, and at a
time when all the other tribes would be assembled together, Heafstaag had
erased that advantage.

At length, the standard bearer finished and returned across the hall to
hold open the tent flap for his king. Heafstaag strode confidently across
Hengorot to face Beorg.

If men were impressed with Heafstaag's list of valor, they were certainly
not disappointed by his appearance. The red-bearded king was nearly
seven feet tall, with a barrel-shaped girth that dwarfed even Beorg's. And
Heafstaag wore his battle scars proudly. One of his eyes had been torn out
by the antlers of a reindeer, and his left hand was hopelessly crumpled from
a fight with a polar bear. The King of the Tribe of the Elk had seen more
battles than any man on the tundra, and by all appearances he was ready
and anxious to fight in many more.

The two kings eyed each other sternly, neither blinking or diverting his
glance for even a moment.

"The Wolf or the Elk?" Heafstaag asked at length, the proper question
after an undecided challenge of the song.

Beorg was careful to give the appropriate response. "Well met and well fought," he said. "Let the keen ears of Tempus alone decide, though the god himself will be hard-pressed to make such a choice!"

With the formalities properly carried out, the tension eased from Heafstaag's face. He smiled broadly at his rival. "Well met, Beorg, King of the Tribe of the Wolf. It does me well to face you and not see my own blood staining the tip of your deadly spear!"

Heafstaag's friendly words caught Beorg by surprise. He couldn't have hoped for a better start to the war council. He returned the compliment with equal fervor. "Nor to duck the sure cut of your cruel axe!"

The smile abruptly left Heafstaag's face when he took notice of the dark-haired man at Beorg's side. "What right, by valor or by blood, does this weakling southerner have in the mead hall of Tempus?" the red-bearded king demanded. "His place is with his own, or with the women at best!"

"Hold to faith, Heafstaag," Beorg explained. "This is deBernezan, a man of great import to our victory. Valuable is the information he has brought to me, for he has dwelt in Ten-Towns for two winters and more."

"Then what role does he play?" Heafstaag pressed.

"He has informed," Beorg reiterated.

"That is past," said Heafstaag. "What value is he to us now? Certainly he cannot fight beside warriors such as ours."

Beorg cast a glance at deBernezan, biting back his own contempt for the dog who had betrayed his people in a pitiful attempt to fill his own pockets. "Plead your case, southerner. And may Tempus find a place in his field for your bones!"

deBernezan tried futilely to match the iron gaze of Heafstaag. He cleared his throat and spoke as loudly and confidently as he could. "When the towns are conquered and their wealth secured, you shall need one who knows the southern marketplace. I am that man."

"At what price?" growled Heafstaag.

"A comfortable living," answered deBernezan. "A respected position, nothing more."

"Bah!" snorted Heafstaag. "He would betray his own, he would betray us!" The giant king tore the axe from his belt and lurched at deBernezan. Beorg grimaced, knowing that this critical moment could defeat the entire plan.

With his mangled hand Heafstaag grabbed deBernezan's oily black hair and pulled the smaller man's head to the side, exposing the flesh of his neck. He swung his axe mightily at the target, his gaze locked onto the southerner's face. But even against the unbending rules of tradition, Beorg had rehearsed deBernezan well for this moment. The little man had been warned in no uncertain terms that if he struggled at all he would die in any case. But if he accepted the stroke and Heafstaag was merely testing him, his life would probably be spared. Mustering all of his willpower, deBernezan steeled his gaze on Heafstaag and did not flinch at the approach of death.

At the very last moment, Heafstaag diverted the axe, its blade whistling within a hair's breadth of the southerner's throat. Heafstaag released the man from his grasp, but he continued to hold him in the intense lock of his single eye.

"An honest man accepts all judgments of his chosen kings," deBernezan declared, trying to keep his voice as steady as possible.

A cheer erupted from every mouth in Hengorot, and when it died away, Heafstaag turned to face Beorg. "Who shall lead?" the giant asked bluntly.

"Who won the challenge of the song?" Beorg answered.

"Well settled, good king." Heafstaag saluted his rival. "Together, then, you and I, and let no man dispute our rule!"

Beorg nodded. "Death to any who dare!"

deBernezan sighed in deep relief and shifted his legs defensively. If Heafstaag, or even Beorg, ever noticed the puddle between his feet, his life would certainly be forfeit. He shifted his legs again nervously and glanced around, horrified when he met the gaze of the young standard bearer. deBernezan's face blanched white in anticipation of his coming humiliation and death. The standard bearer unexpectedly turned away and smiled in amusement but in an unprecedented merciful act for his rough people, he said nothing.

Heafstaag threw his arms above his head and raised his gaze and axe to the ceiling. Beorg grabbed his axe from his belt and quickly mimicked the movement. "Tempus!" they shouted in unison. Then, eyeing each other once more, they gashed their shield arms with their axes, wetting the blades with their own blood. In a synchronous movement, they spun and heaved the weapons across the hall, each axe finding its mark in the same keg of mead. Immediately, the closest men grabbed flagons and scrambled to catch the first drops of spilling mead that had been blessed with the blood of their kings.

"I have drawn a plan for your approval," Beorg told Heafstaag.

"Later, noble friend," the one-eyed king replied. "Let tonight be a time of song and drink to celebrate our coming victory." He clapped Beorg on the shoulder and winked with his one eye. "Be glad of my arrival, for you were sorely unprepared for such a gathering," he said with a hearty laugh. Beorg eyed him curiously, but Heafstaag gave him a second grotesque wink to quench his suspicions.

Abruptly, the lusty giant snapped his fingers at one of his field lieutenants, nudging his rival with his elbow as if to let him in on the joke.

"Fetch the wenches!" he commanded.

4

THE CRYSTAL SHARD

There was only blackness. Mercifully, he couldn't remember what had happened, where he was. Only blackness, comforting blackness.

Then a chilling burn began to grow on his cheeks, robbing him of the tranquility of unconsciousness. Gradually, he was compelled to open his eyes, but even when he squinted, the blinding glare was too intense.

He was face down in the snow. Mountains towered all about him, their jagged peaks and deep snow caps reminding him of his location. They had dropped him in the Spine of the World. They had left him to die.

Akar Kessell's head throbbed when he finally managed to lift it. The sun was shining brightly, but the brutal cold and swirling winds dispelled any warmth the bright rays could impart. Ever was it winter in these high places, and Kessell wore only flimsy robes to protect him from the cold's killing bite.

They had left him to die.

He stumbled to his feet, knee deep in white powder, and looked around. Far below, down a deep gorge and moving northward, back toward the tundra and the trails that would take them around the foreboding range of impassable mountains, Kessell saw the black specks that marked the wizards' caravan beginning its long journey back to Luskan. They had deceived him.

He understood now that he had been no more than a pawn in their devious designs to rid themselves of Morkai the Red.

Eldulac, Dendybar the Mottled, and the others.

They'd never had any intentions of granting him the title of wizard.

"How could I have been so stupid?" Kessell groaned. Images of Morkai, the only man who had ever granted him any measure of respect, flashed across his mind in a guilt-driven haze. He remembered all the joys that the wizard had allowed him to experience. Morkai had once turned him into a bird so that he could feel the freedom of flight; and once a fish, to let him experience the blurry world of the undersea.

And he had repaid that wonderful man with a dagger.

Far down the trails, the departing wizards heard Kessell's anguished scream echoing off the mountain walls.

Eldulac smiled, satisfied that their plan had been executed perfectly, and spurred his horse on.

⚔ ⚔ ⚔ ⚔ ⚔

Kessell trudged through the snow. He didn't know why he was walking—he had nowhere to go. Kessell had no escape. Eldulac had dropped him into a bowl-shaped, snow-filled depression, and with his fingers numbed beyond feeling, he had no chance of climbing out.

He tried again to conjure a wizard's fire. He held his outstretched palm skyward and through chattering teeth uttered the words of power.

Nothing.

Not even a wisp of smoke.

So he started moving again. His legs ached; he almost believed that several of his toes had already fallen away from his left foot. But he didn't dare remove his boot to verify his morbid suspicion.

He began to circumnavigate the bowl again, following the same trail he had left behind on his first pass. Abruptly, he found himself veering toward the middle. He didn't know why, and in his delirium, he didn't pause to try and figure it out. All the world had become a white blur. A frozen white blur. Kessell felt himself falling. He felt the icy bite of the snow on his face again. He felt the tingling that signaled the end of the life of his lower extremities.

Then he felt . . . warmth.

Imperceptible at first, but growing steadily stronger. Something was beckoning to him. It was beneath him, buried under the snow, yet even through the frozen barrier, Kessell felt the life-giving glow of its warmth.

He dug. Visually guiding hands that could not feel their work, he dug for his life. And then he came upon something solid and felt the heat intensify. Scrambling to push the remaining snow away from it, he managed at last to pull it free. He couldn't understand what he was seeing. He blamed it on delirium. In his frozen hands, Akar Kessell held what appeared to be a square-sided icicle. Yet its warmth flowed through him, and he felt the tingles again, this time signaling the rebirth of his extremities.

Kessell had no idea what was happening, and he didn't care in the least. For now, he had found hope for life, and that was enough. He hugged the Crystal Shard to his chest and moved back toward the rocky wall of the dell, searching out the most sheltered area he could find.

Under a small overhang, huddled in a small area where the heat of the crystal had pushed the snow away, Akar Kessell survived his first night in the Spine of the World. His bedfellow was the Crystal Shard, Crenshinibon, an ancient, sentient relic that had waited throughout ages uncounted for one such as he to appear in the bowl. Awakened again, it was even now pondering the methods it would use to control the weak-willed Kessell. It was a relic enchanted in the earliest days of the world, a perversion that had been lost for centuries, to the dismay of those evil lords who sought its strength.

Crenshinibon was an enigma, a force of the darkest evil that drew its strength from the light of day. It was an instrument of destruction, a tool for scrying, a shelter and home for those who would wield it. But foremost among the powers of Crenshinibon was the strength it imparted to its possessor.

Akar Kessell slept comfortably, unaware of what had befallen him. He knew only—and cared only—that his life was not yet at an end. He would learn the implications soon enough. He would come to understand that he would never again play the role of stooge to pretentious dogs like Eldulac, Dendybar the Mottled, and the others.

He would become the Akar Kessell of his own fantasies, and all would bow before him.

"Respect," he mumbled from within the depths of his dream, a dream that Crenshinibon was imposing upon him.

Akar Kessell, the Tyrant of Icewind Dale.

⚔ ⚔ ⚔ ⚔

Kessell awakened to a dawn that he thought he would never see. The Crystal Shard had preserved him through the night, yet it had done much more than simply prevent him from freezing. Kessell felt strangely changed that morning. The night before, he had been concerned only with the quantity of his life, wondering how long he could merely survive. But now he pondered the quality of his life. Survival was no longer a question; he felt strength flowing within him.

A white deer bounded along the rim of the bowl.

"Venison," Kessell whispered aloud. He pointed a finger in the direction of his prey and spoke the command words of a spell, tingling with excitement as he felt the power surge through his blood. A searing white bolt shot out from his hand felling the hart where it stood.

"Venison," he declared, mentally lifting the animal through the air toward him without a second thought to the act, though telekinesis was a spell that hadn't even been in the considerable repertoire of Morkai the Red, Kessell's sole teacher. Though the shard would not have let him, Kessell the greedy did not stop to ponder the sudden appearance of abilities he'd felt long overdue him.

Now he had food and warmth from the shard. Yet a wizard should have a castle, he reasoned. A place where he might practice his darkest secrets undisturbed. He looked to the shard for an answer to his dilemma and found a duplicate crystal laying next to the first. Instinctively, so he presumed (though, in reality, it was another subconscious suggestion from Crenshinibon that guided him), Kessell understood his role in fulfilling his own request. He knew the original Shard at once from the warmth and strength that it exuded, but this second one intrigued him as well, holding an impressive aura of power of its own. He took up the copy of the shard and carried it to the center of the bowl, setting it down on the deep snow.

"Ibssum dal abdur," he mumbled without knowing why, or even what it meant.

Kessell backed away as he felt the force within the image of the relic begin to expand. It caught the rays of the sun and drew them within its depths. The area surrounding the bowl fell into shadow as it stole the very light of day. It began to pulse with an inner, rhythmic light.

And then it began to grow.

It widened at the base, nearly filling the bowl, and for a while Kessell feared that he would be crushed against the rocky walls. And in accordance with the crystal's widening, its tip rose up into the morning sky, keeping the dimensions aligned with its power source. Then it was complete, still an exact image of Crenshinibon, but now of mammoth proportions.

A crystalline tower. Somehow—the same way Kessell knew anything about the Crystal Shard—he knew its name.

Cryshal-Tirith.

☒ ☒ ☒ ☒ ☒

Kessell would have been contented, for the time being, at least, to remain in Cryshal-Tirith and feast off of the unfortunate animals that wandered by. He had come from a meager background of unambitious peasants, and though he outwardly boasted of aspirations beyond his station, he was intimidated by the implications of power. He didn't understand how or why those who had gained prominence had risen above the common rabble, and even lied to himself, passing off the accomplishments of others, and conversely, the lack of his own, as a random choice of fate.

Now that he had power within his grasp he had no notion of what to do with it.

But Crenshinibon had waited too long to see its return to life wasted as a hunting lodge for a puny human. Kessell's wishy-washiness was actually a favorable attribute from the relic's perspective. Over a period of time, it could persuade Kessell to follow almost any course of action with its nighttime messages.

And Crenshinibon had the time. The relic was anxious to again taste the thrill of conquest, but a few years did not seem long to an artifact that had been created at the dawn of the world. It would mold the bumbling Kessell into a proper representative of its power, nurture the weak man into an iron-fisted glove to deliver its message of destruction. It had done likewise a hundred times in the initial struggles of the world, creating and nurturing some of the most formidable and cruel opponents of law across any of the planes.

It could do so again.

That very night, Kessell, sleeping in the comfortably adorned second level of Cryshal-Tirith, had dreams of conquest. Not violent campaigns waged against a city such as Luskan, or even on the scale of battle against a frontier settlement, like the villages of Ten-Towns, but a less ambitious and more realistic start to his kingdom. He dreamed that he had forced a tribe of goblins into servitude, using them to assume the roles as his personal staff, catering to his every need. When he awakened the next morning, he remembered the dream and found that he liked the idea.

Later that morning, Kessell explored the third level of the tower, a room like all the others, made of smooth yet stone-strong crystal, this particular one filled with various scrying devices. Suddenly, an urge came over him to make a certain gesture and speak an arcane word of command that he assumed he must have heard in the presence of Morkai. He complied with the feeling and watched in amazement as the dimension within the depths of one of the mirrors in the room suddenly swirled in a gray fog. When the fog cleared, an image came into focus.

Kessell recognized the area depicted as a valley he had passed a short distance down the trail when Eldulac, Dendybar the Mottled, and the others had left him to die.

The image of the region was bustling with a tribe of goblins at work constructing a campsite. These were nomads, probably, for war bands rarely brought females and young ones along on their raids. Hundreds of caves dotted the sides of these mountains, but they weren't numerous enough to hold the tribes of orcs, goblins, ogres, and even more powerful monsters. Competition for lairs was fierce, and the lesser goblin tribes were usually forced above ground, enslaved, or slaughtered.

"How convenient," Kessell mused, wondering if the subject of his dream had been a coincidence or a prophecy. On another sudden impulse, he sent his will through the mirror toward the goblins. The effect startled him.

As one, the goblins turned, apparently confused, in the direction of the unseen force. The warriors apprehensively drew their clubs and stone-headed axes, and the females and children huddled in the back of the group.

One larger goblin, the leader presumably, holding its club defensively before it, took a few cautious steps ahead of its soldiers.

Kessell scratched his chin, pondering the extent of his new-found power.

"Come to me," he called to the goblin chieftain. "You cannot resist!"

⚔ ⚔ ⚔ ⚔

The tribe arrived at the bowl a short time later, remaining a safe distance away while they tried to figure out exactly what the tower was and where it had come from. Kessell let them marvel over the splendor of his new home, then called again to the chieftain, compelling the goblin to approach Cryshal-Tirith.

Against its own will, the large goblin strode from the ranks of the tribe. Fighting every step, it walked right up to the base of the tower. It couldn't see any door, for the entrance to Cryshal-Tirith was invisible to all except denizens of foreign planes and those that Crenshinibon, or its wielder, allowed to enter.

Kessell guided the terrified goblin into the first level of the structure. Once inside, the chieftain remained absolutely motionless, its eyes darting around nervously for some indication of the overpowering force that had summoned it to this structure of dazzling crystal.

The wizard (a title rightfully imparted to the possessor of Crenshinibon, even if Kessell had never been able to earn it by his own deeds) let the miserable creature wait for a while, heightening its fear. Then he appeared at the top of the stairwell through a secret mirror door. He looked down upon the wretched creature and cackled with glee.

The goblin trembled visibly when it saw Kessell. It felt the wizard's will imposing upon it once again, compelling the creature to its knees.

"Who am I?" Kessell asked as the goblin groveled and whimpered.

The chieftain's reply was torn from within by a power that it could not resist.

"Master."

5

SOMEĐAY

Bruenor walked up the rocky slope with measured steps, his boots finding the same footholds he always used when he ascended to the high point of the southern end of the dwarven valley. To the people of Ten-Towns, who often saw the dwarf standing meditatively on the perch, this high column of stones in the rocky ridge that lined the valley had come to be known as Bruenor's Climb. Just below the dwarf, to the west, were the lights of Termalaine, and beyond them the dark waters of Maer Dualdon, spotted occasionally by the running lights of a fishing boat whose resolute crew stubbornly refused to come ashore until they had landed a knucklehead.

The dwarf was well above the tundra floor and the lowest of the countless stars that sparkled the night. The celestial dome seemed polished by the chill breeze that had blown since sunset, and Bruenor felt as though he had escaped the bonds of earth.

In this place he found his dreams, and ever they took him back to his ancient home. Mithral Hall, home of his fathers and theirs before them, where rivers of the shining metal ran rich and deep and the hammers of dwarven smiths rang out in praise to Moradin and Dumathoin. Bruenor was merely an unbearded boy when his people had delved too deep into the bowels of the world and had been driven out by the dark things in dark holes. He was now the eldest surviving member of his small clan and the only one among them who had witnessed the treasures of Mithral Hall.

They had made their home in the rocky valley between the two northernmost of the three lakes long before any humans, other than the barbarians, had come to Icewind Dale. They were a poor remnant of what had once been a thriving dwarven society, a band of refugees beaten and broken by the loss of their homeland and heritage. They continued to dwindle in numbers, their elders dying as much of sadness as old age. Though the mining under the fields of the region was good, the dwarves seemed destined to fade away into oblivion.

When Ten-Towns had sprung up, though, the luck of the dwarves rose considerably. Their valley was just north of Bryn Shander, as close to the principal city as any of the fishing villages, and the humans, often warring with each other and fighting off invaders, were happy to trade for the marvelous armor and weapons that the dwarves forged.

But even with the betterment of their lives, Bruenor, particularly, longed to recover the ancient glory of his ancestors. He viewed the arrival of Ten-Towns as a temporary stay from a problem that would not be resolved until Mithral Hall had been recovered and restored.

"A cold night for so high a perch, good friend," came a call from behind.

The dwarf turned around to face Drizzt Do'Urden, though he realized that the drow would be invisible against the black backdrop of Kelvin's Cairn. From this vantage point, the mountain was the only silhouette that broke the featureless line of the northern horizon. The cairn had been so named because it resembled a mound of purposely piled boulders; barbarian legend claimed that it truly served as a grave. Certainly the valley where the dwarves now made their home did not resemble any natural landmark. In every direction the tundra rolled on, flat and earthen. But the valley had only sparse patches of dirt sprinkled in among broken boulders and walls of solid stone. It, and the mountain on its northern border, were the only features in all of Icewind Dale with any mentionable quantities of rock, as if they had been misplaced by some god in the earliest days of creation.

Drizzt noted the glazed look of his friend's eyes. "You seek the sights that only your memory can see," he said, well aware of the dwarf's obsession with his ancient homeland.

"A sight I'll see again!" Bruenor insisted. "We'll get there, elf."

"We do not even know the way."

"Roads can be found," said Bruenor. "But not until ye look for them."

"Someday, my friend," Drizzt humored. In the few years that he and Bruenor had been friends, the dwarf had constantly badgered Drizzt about accompanying him on his adventure to find Mithral Hall. Drizzt thought the idea foolish, for no one that he had ever spoken with had even a clue as to the location of the ancient dwarven home, and Bruenor could only remember disjointed images of the silvery halls. Still, the drow was sensitive to his friend's deepest desire, and he always answered Bruenor's pleas with the promise of "someday."

"We have more urgent business at the moment," Drizzt reminded Bruenor. Earlier that day, in a meeting in the dwarven halls, the drow had detailed his findings to the dwarves.

"Yer sure they'll be comin' then?" Bruenor asked now.

"Their charge will shake the stones of Kelvin's Cairn," Drizzt replied as he left the darkness of the mountain's silhouette and joined his friend. "And if Ten-Towns does not stand united against them, the people are doomed."

Bruenor settled into a crouch and turned his eyes to the south, toward the distant lights of Bryn Shander. "They'll not, the stubborn fools," he muttered.

"They might, if your people went to them."

"No," growled the dwarf. "We'll fight beside them if they choose to stand together, an' pity then to the barbarians! Go to them, if ye wish, an' good luck to ye, but nothing o' the dwarves. Let us see what grit an' guts the fisherfolk can muster."

Drizzt smiled at the irony of Bruenor's refusal. Both of them knew well that the drow was not trusted, not even openly welcomed, in any of the towns other than Lonelywood, where their friend Regis was spokesman. Bruenor marked the drow's look, and it pained him as it pained Drizzt, though the elf stoically pretended otherwise.

"They owe ye more than they'll ever know," Bruenor stated flatly, turning a sympathetic eye on his friend.

"They owe me nothing!"

Bruenor shook his head. "Why do ye care?" he growled. "Ever yer watchin' over the folk that show ye no good will. What do ye owe to them?"

Drizzt shrugged, hard-pressed to find an answer. Bruenor was right. When the drow had first come to this land the only one who had shown him any friendship at all was Regis. He often escorted and protected the halfling through the dangerous first legs of the journey from Lonelywood, around the open tundra north of Maer Dualdon and down toward Bryn Shander, when Regis went to the principal city for business or council meetings. They had actually met on one such trek: Regis tried to flee from Drizzt because he'd heard terrible rumors about him. Luckily for both of them, Regis was a halfling who was usually able to keep an open mind about people and make his own judgments concerning their character. It wasn't long before the two were fast friends.

But to this day, Regis and the dwarves were the only ones in the area who considered the drow a friend. "I do not know why I care," Drizzt answered honestly. His eyes turned back to his ancient homeland where loyalty was merely a device to gain an advantage over a common foe. "Perhaps I care because I strive to be different from my people," he said, as much to himself as to Bruenor. "Perhaps I care because I am different from my people. I may be more akin to the races of the surface . . . that is my hope at least. I care because I have to care about something. You are not so different, Bruenor Battlehammer. We care lest our own lives be empty."

Bruenor cocked a curious eye.

"You can deny your feelings for the people of Ten-Towns to me, but not to yourself."

"Bah!" Bruenor snorted. "Sure that I care for them! My folk need the trade!"

"Stubborn," Drizzt mumbled, smiling knowingly. "And Catti-brie?" he pressed. "What of the human girl who was orphaned in the raid those years ago on Termalaine? The waif that you took in and raised as your own child?" Bruenor was glad that the cover of night offered some protection from his revealing blush. "She lives with you still, though even you would have to admit that she is able to go back to her own kind. Might it be, perhaps, that you care for her, gruff dwarf?"

"Aw, shut yer mouth," Bruenor grumbled. "She's a servin' wench and makes my life a bit easier, but don't ye go gettin' sappy about her!"

"Stubborn," Drizzt reiterated more loudly this time. He had one more card to play in this discussion. "What of myself, then? Dwarves are not overly fond of the light elves, let alone the drow. How do you justify the friendship you have shown me? I have nothing to offer you in return but my own friendship. Why do you care?"

"Ye bring me news when—" Bruenor stopped short, aware that Drizzt had cornered him.

But the drow didn't press the issue any further.

So the friends watched in silence as the lights of Bryn Shander went down, one by one. Despite his outward callousness, Bruenor realized how true some of the drow's accusations had rung; he had come to care for the people who had settled on the banks of the three lakes.

"What do ye mean to do then?" the dwarf asked at length.

"I mean to warn them," Drizzt replied. "You underestimate your neighbors, Bruenor. They're made of tougher stuff than you believe."

"Agreed," said the dwarf, "but my questions are of their character. Every day we see fightin' on the lakes, an' always over the damned fish. The people cling to their own towns an' goblins take the others, for all they care! Now they've to show me an' mine that they've the will to fight together!"

Drizzt had to admit the truth of Bruenor's observations. The fishermen had grown more competitive over the last couple of years as the knucklehead trout took to the deeper waters of the lakes and became harder to catch. Cooperation among the towns was at a low point as each town tried to gain an economic advantage over the rival towns on its lake.

"There is a council in Bryn Shander in two days," Drizzt continued. "I believe that we still have some time before the barbarians come. Though I fear for any delays, I do not believe that we would be able to bring the spokesmen together any sooner. It will take me that long to properly instruct Regis on the course of action that he must take with his peers, for he must carry the tidings of the coming invasion."

"Rumblebelly?" snorted Bruenor, using the name he had tagged on Regis for the halfling's insatiable appetite. "He sits on the council for no better reason than t'keep his stomach well-stocked! They'll hear 'im less than they'd hear yerself, elf."

"You underestimate the halfling, moreso even than you underestimate the people of Ten-Towns," answered Drizzt. "Remember always that he carries the stone."

"Bah! A fine-cut gem, but no more!" Bruenor insisted. "I've seen it meself, an' it holds no spell on me."

"The magic is too subtle for the eyes of a dwarf, and perhaps not strong enough to penetrate your thick skull," laughed Drizzt. "But it is there—I see it clearly and know the legend of such a stone. Regis may be able to influence the council more than you would believe—and certainly more than I could. Let us hope so, for you know as well as I that some of the spokesmen might be reluctant to pursue any plan of unity, whether in their arrogant independence, or in their belief that a barbarian raid upon some of their less protected rivals might actually help their own selfish ambitions. Bryn Shander remains the key, but the principal city will only be spurred to action if the major fishing towns, Targos in particular, join in."

"Ye know that Easthaven'll help," said Bruenor. "They're ever ones for bringing all o' the towns together."

"And Lonelywood, too, with Regis speaking for them. But Kemp of Targos surely believes that his walled city is powerful enough to stand alone, whereas its rival, Termalaine, would be hard-pressed to hold back the horde."

"He's not likely to join anythin' that includes Termalaine. An' yer in for more trouble then, drow, for without Kemp ye'll never get Konig and Dineval to shut up!"

"But that is where Regis comes in," Drizzt explained. "The ruby he possesses can do wondrous things, I assure you!"

"Again ye speak of the power o' the stone," Bruenor. "But Rumblebelly claims that his master o' old had twelve o' the things," he reasoned. "Mighty magics don't come in dozens!"

"Regis said that his master had twelve similar stones," Drizzt corrected. "In truth, the halfling had no way of knowing if all twelve, or any of the others, were magical."

"Then why would the man have given the only one o' power to Rumblebelly?"

Drizzt left the question unanswered, but his silence soon led Bruenor to the same inescapable conclusion. Regis had a way of collecting things that didn't belong to him, and though the halfling had explained the stone as a gift. . . .

6
BRYN SHANDER

Bryn Shander was unlike any of the other communities of Ten-Towns. Its proud pennant flew high from the top of a hill in the middle of the dry tundra between the three lakes, just south of the southern tip of the dwarven valley. No ships flew the flags of this city, and it had no docks on any of the lakes, yet there was little argument that it was not only the geographical hub of the region but the center of activity as well.

This was where the major merchant caravans from Luskan put in, where the dwarves came to trade, and where the vast majority of craftsmen, scrimshanders, and scrimshaw evaluators were housed. Proximity to Bryn Shander was second only to the quantity of fish hooked in determining the success and size of the fishing towns. Thus, Termalaine and Targos on the southeastern banks of Maer Dualdon, and Caer-Konig and Caer-Dineval on the western shores of Lac Dinneshere, four towns less than a day's journey from the principal city, were the dominant towns on the lakes.

High walls surrounded Bryn Shander, as much protection from the biting wind as from invading goblins or barbarians. Inside, the buildings were similar to those of the other towns: low, wooden structures, except that in Bryn Shander they were more tightly packed together and often subdivided to house several families. Congested as it was, though, there was a measure of comfort and security in the city, the largest taste of civilization a person could find for four hundred long and desolate miles.

Regis always enjoyed the sounds and smells that greeted him when he walked through the iron-bound wooden gates on the northern wall of the principal city. Though on a smaller scale than the great cities of the south, the bustle and shouts of Bryn Shander's open markets and plentiful street vendors reminded him of his days back in Calimport. And as in Calimport, the people of Bryn Shander's streets were a cross-section of every heritage that the Realms had to offer. Tall, dark-skinned desert folk mingled among fair-skinned travelers from the Moonshaes. The loud boasts of swarthy southerners and robust mountain men trading fanciful tales of love and battle in one of the many taverns echoed on nearly every street corner.

And Regis took it all in, for though the location was changed, the noise remained the same. If he closed his eyes as he skipped along down one of the narrow streets he could almost recapture the zest for life that he had known those years before in Calimport.

This time, though, the halfling's business was so grave that it dampened even his ever-lifted spirits. He had been horrified at the drow's grim news and was nervous about being the messenger who would deliver it to the council.

Away from the noisy market section of the city, Regis passed the palatial home of Cassius, the spokesman of Bryn Shander. This was the largest and most luxurious building in all of Ten-Towns, with a columned front and bas-relief artwork adorning all its walls. It had originally been built for the meetings of the ten spokesmen, but as interest in the councils had died away, Cassius, skilled in diplomacy and not above using strong-arm tactics, had appropriated the palace as his official residence and moved the council hall to a vacant warehouse tucked away in a remote corner of the city. Several of the other spokesmen had complained about the change, but though the fishing towns could often exert some influence on the principal city in matters of public concern, they had little recourse in an issue as trivial to the general populace as this. Cassius understood his city's position well and knew how to keep most of the other communities under his thumb. The militia of Bryn Shander could defeat the combined forces of any five of the other nine towns combined, and Cassius's officers held a monopoly on connections to the necessary marketplaces in the south. The other spokesmen might grumble about the change in the meeting place, but their dependence on the principal city would prevent them from taking any actions against Cassius.

Regis was the last to enter the small hall. He looked around at the nine men who had gathered at the table and realized how out of place he truly was. He had been elected spokesman because nobody else in Lonelywood cared enough to want to sit on the council, but his peers had attained their positions through valorous and heroic deeds. They were the leaders of their communities, the men who had organized the structure and defenses of the towns. Each of these spokesmen had seen a score of battles and more, for goblin and barbarian raiders descended upon Ten-Towns more often than sunny days. It was a simple rule of life in Icewind Dale that if you couldn't fight, you couldn't survive, and the spokesmen of the council were some of the most proficient fighters in all of Ten-Towns.

Regis had never been intimidated by the spokesmen before because normally he had nothing to say at council. Lonelywood, a secluded town hidden away in a small, thick wood of fir trees, asked for nothing from anyone. And with an insignificant fishing fleet, the other three towns it shared Maer Dualdon with imposed no demands upon it. Regis never offered an opinion unless pressed and had been careful always to cast his vote on an issue in the way of the general consensus. And if the council was split on an issue, Regis simply followed the lead of Cassius. In Ten-Towns, one couldn't go wrong by following Bryn Shander.

This day, though, Regis found that he was intimidated by the council. The grim news that he bore would make him vulnerable to their bullying tactics and often angry reprisals. He focused his attention on the two most powerful spokesmen, Cassius of Bryn Shander and Kemp of Targos, as they sat at the head of the rectangular table and chatted. Kemp looked the part of rugged frontiersman: not too tall but barrel-chested, with gnarled and knotted arms, and a stern demeanor that frightened friend and foe alike.

Cassius, though, hardly seemed a warrior. He was small of frame, with neatly trimmed gray hair and a face that never showed a hint of stubble. His big, bright blue eyes forever seemed locked into an inner contentment. But anyone who had ever seen the spokesman from Bryn Shander raise a sword in battle or maneuver his charge on the field had no doubts concerning his fighting prowess or his bravery. Regis truly liked the man, yet he was careful not to fall into a situation that left him vulnerable. Cassius had earned a reputation for getting what he wanted at another's expense.

"Come to order," Cassius commanded, rapping his gavel on the table. The host spokesman always opened the meeting with the Formalities of Order, readings of titles and official proposals that had originally been intended to give the council an aura of importance, impressing especially the ruffians that sometimes showed up to speak for the more remote communities. But now, with the degeneration of the council as a whole, the Formalities of Order served only to delay the end of the meeting, to the regret of all ten spokesmen. Consequently, the Formalities were pared down more and more each time the group gathered, and there had even been talk of eliminating them altogether.

When the list had finally been completed, Cassius turned to the important issues. "The first item on the agenda," he said, hardly glancing at the notes that were laid out before him, "concerns the territorial dispute between the sister cities, Caer-Konig and Caer-Dineval, on Lac Dinneshere. I see that Dorim Lugar of Caer-Konig has brought the documents that he promised at the last meeting, so I turn the floor over to him. Spokesman Lugar."

Dorim Lugar, a gaunt, dark-complected man whose eyes never seemed to stop darting about nervously, nearly leaped out of his chair when he was introduced.

"I have in my hand," he yelled, his upraised fist closed about an old parchment, "the original agreement between Caer-Konig and Caer-Dineval, signed by the leaders of each town," he shot an accusing finger in the direction of the spokesman from Caer-Dineval, "including your own signature, Jensin Brent!"

"An agreement signed during a time of friendship and in the spirit of good will," retorted Jensin Brent, a younger, golden-haired man with an innocent face that often gave him an advantage over people who judged him naive. "Unroll the parchment, Spokesman Lugar, and let the council view it. They shall see that it makes no provisions whatsoever for Easthaven." He looked around at the other spokesmen. "Easthaven could hardly be called even a hamlet when the agreement to divide the lake in half was signed," he explained, and not for the first time. "They had not a single boat to put in the water."

"Fellow spokesmen!" Dorim Lugar yelled, jolting some of them from the lethargy that had already begun to creep in. This same debate had dominated the last four councils with no ground gained by either side. The issue held little importance or interest for any but the two spokesmen and the spokesman from Easthaven.

"Surely Caer-Konig cannot be blamed for the rise of Easthaven," pleaded Dorim Lugar. "Who could have foreseen the Eastway?" he asked, referring to the straight and smooth road that Easthaven had constructed to Bryn Shander. It was an ingenious move and proved a boon to the small town on the southeastern corner of Lac Dinneshere. Combining the appeal of a remote community with easy access to Bryn Shander had made Easthaven the fastest growing community in all of Ten-Towns, with a fishing fleet that had swelled to nearly rival the boats of Caer-Dineval.

"Who indeed?" retorted Jensin Brent, now a bit of fluster showing through his calm facade. "It is obvious that Easthaven's growth has put Caer-Dineval in stiff competition for the southern waters of the lake, while Caer-Konig sails freely in the northern half. Yet Caer-Konig has flatly refused to renegotiate the original terms to compensate for the imbalance! We cannot prosper under such conditions!"

Regis knew that he had to act before the argument between Brent and Lugar got out of control. Two previous meetings had been adjourned because of their volatile debates, and Regis couldn't let this council disintegrate before he had told them of the impending barbarian attack.

He hesitated, having to admit to himself once again that he had no options and could not back away from this urgent mission; his haven would be destroyed if he said nothing. Although Drizzt had reassured him of the power he possessed, he retained his doubts about the true magic of the stone. Yet due to his own insecurity, a trait common among little folk, Regis found himself blindly trusting in Drizzt's judgment. The drow was possibly the most knowledgeable person he had ever known, with a list of experiences far beyond the tales that Regis could tell. Now was the time for action, and the halfling was determined to give the drow's plan a try.

He closed his fingers around the little wooden gavel that was set out on the table before him. It felt unfamiliar to his touch, and he realized then that this was the first time that he had ever used the instrument. He tapped it lightly on the wooden table, but the others were intent on the shouting match that had erupted between Lugar and Brent. Regis reminded himself of the urgency of the drow's news once again and boldly pounded the gavel down.

The other spokesmen turned immediately to the halfling, blank expressions stamped upon their faces. Regis rarely spoke at the meetings, and then only when cornered with a direct question.

Cassius of Bryn Shander brought his heavy gavel down. "The council recognizes Spokesman . . . uh . . . the spokesman from Lonelywood," he said, and from his uneven tone Regis could guess that he had struggled to address the halfling's request for the floor seriously.

"Fellow spokesmen," Regis began tentatively, his voice cracking into a squeak. "With all due respect to the seriousness of the debate between the spokesmen from Caer-Dineval and Caer-Konig, I believe that we have a more urgent problem to discuss." Jensin Brent and Dorim Lugar were livid at being interrupted, but the others eyed the halfling curiously. Good start, Regis thought, I've got their full attention.

He cleared his throat, trying to steady his voice and sound a bit more impressive. "I have learned beyond doubt that the barbarian tribes are gathering for a united attack on Ten-Towns!" Though he tried to make the announcement dramatic, Regis found himself facing nine apathetic and confused men.

"Unless we form an alliance," Regis continued in the same urgent tones, "the horde will overrun our communities one by one, slaughtering any who dare to oppose them!"

"Certainly, Spokesman Regis of Lonelywood," said Cassius in a voice he meant to be calming but was, in effect, condescending, "we have weathered barbarian raids before. There is no need for—"

"Not like this one!" Regis cried. "All the tribes have come together. The raids before matched one tribe against one city, and usually we fared well.

But how would Termalaine or Caer-Konig—or even Bryn Shander—stand against the combined tribes of Icewind Dale?" Some of the spokesmen settled back into their chairs to contemplate the halfling's words; the rest began talking among themselves, some in distress, some in angry disbelief. Finally Cassius pounded his gavel again, calling the hall to silence.

Then, with familiar bravado, Kemp of Targos slowly rose from his seat. "May I speak, friend Cassius?" he asked with unnecessary politeness. "Perhaps I may be able to put this grave pronouncement in the proper light."

Regis and Drizzt had made some assumptions about alliances when they had planned the halfling's actions at this council. They knew that Easthaven, founded and thriving on the principle of brotherhood among the communities of Ten-Towns, would openly embrace the concept of a common defense against the barbarian horde. Likewise Termalaine and Lonelywood, the two most accessible and raided towns of the ten, would gladly accept any offers of help.

Yet even Spokesman Agorwal of Termalaine, who had so much to gain from a defensive alliance, would hedge and hold his silence if Kemp of Targos refused to accept the plan. Targos was the largest and mightiest of the nine fishing villages, with a fleet more than twice the size of the second largest.

"Fellow members of the council," Kemp began, leaning forward over the table to loom larger in the eyes of his peers. "Let us learn more of the half-ling's tale before we begin to worry. We have fought off barbarian invaders and worse enough times to be confident that the defenses of even the smallest of our towns are adequate."

Regis felt his tension growing as Kemp rolled into his speech, building on points designed to destroy the halfling's credibility. Drizzt had decided early on in their planning that Kemp of Targos was the key, but Regis knew the spokesman better than the drow and knew that Kemp would not be easily manipulated. Kemp illustrated the tactics of the powerful town of Targos in his own mannerisms. He was large and bullying, often taking to sudden fits of violent rage that intimidated even Cassius. Regis had tried to steer Drizzt away from this part of their plan, but the drow was adamant.

"If Targos agrees to accept the alliance with Lonelywood," Drizzt had reasoned, "Termalaine will gladly join and Bremen, being the only other village on the lake, will have no choice but to go along. Bryn Shander will certainly not oppose a unified alliance of the four towns on the largest and most prosperous lake, and Easthaven will make six in the pact, a clear majority."

The rest would then have no choice but to join in the effort. Drizzt had believed that Caer-Dineval and Caer-Konig, fearing that Easthaven would receive special consideration in future councils, would put on a blusterous show of loyalty, hoping themselves to gain favor in the eyes of Cassius. Good Mead and Dougan's Hole, the two towns on Redwaters, though relatively safe from an invasion from the north, would not dare to stand apart from the other eight communities.

But all of this was merely hopeful speculation, as Regis clearly realized when he saw Kemp glaring at him from across the table. Drizzt had conceded the point that the greatest obstacle in forming the alliance would be Targos. In its arrogance, the powerful town might believe that it could withstand any barbarian raid. And if it did manage to survive, the destruction of some of its competitors might actually prove profitable.

"You say only that you have learned of an invasion," Kemp began. "Where could you have gathered this valuable and no doubt, hard to find information?"

Regis felt sweat beading on his temples. He knew where Kemp's question would lead, but there was no way that he could avoid the truth. "From a friend who often travels the tundra," he answered honestly.

"The drow?" Kemp asked.

With his neck bent up and Kemp towering over him, Regis found himself quickly placed on the defensive. The halfling's father had once warned him that he would always be at a disadvantage when dealing with humans because they physically had to look down when speaking to him, as they would to their own children. At times like this, the words of his father rang painfully true to Regis. He wiped a bead of moisture from his upper lip.

"I cannot speak for the rest of you," Kemp continued, adding a chuckle to place the halfling's grave warning in an absurd light, "but I have too much serious work to do to go into hiding on the words of a drow elf!" Again the burly spokesman laughed, and this time he was not alone.

Agorwal of Termalaine offered some unexpected assistance to the halfling's failing cause. "Perhaps we should let the spokesman from Lonelywood continue. If his words are true—"

"His words are the echoes of a drow's lies!" Kemp snarled. "Pay them no heed. We have fought off the barbarians before, and—"

But then Kemp, too, was cut short as Regis suddenly sprang up on the council table. This was the most precarious part of Drizzt's plan. The drow had shown faith in it, describing it matter-of-factly, as though it would pose no problems. But Regis felt impending disaster hovering all about him. He clasped his hands behind his back and tried to appear in control so that Cassius wouldn't take any immediate actions against his unusual tactics.

During Agorwal's diversion, Regis had slipped the ruby pendant out from under his waistcoat. It sparkled on his chest as he walked up and down, treating the table as though it were his personal stage.

"What do you know of the drow to jest of him so?" he demanded of the others, pointedly Kemp. "Can any of you name a single person that he has harmed? No! You chastise him for the crimes of his race, yet have none of you ever considered that Drizzt Do'Urden walks among us because he has rejected the ways of his people?" The silence in the hall convinced Regis that he had either been impressive or absurd. In any case, he was not so arrogant or foolish to think his little speech sufficient to accomplish the task.

He walked over to face Kemp. This time he was the one looking down, but the spokesman from Targos seemed on the verge of exploding into laughter.

Regis had to act quickly. He bent down slightly and raised his hand to his chin, by appearance to scratch an itch though in truth to set the ruby pendant spinning, tapping it with his arm as it passed. He then held the silence of the moment patiently and counted as Drizzt had instructed. Ten seconds passed and Kemp had not blinked. Drizzt had said that this would be enough, but Regis, surprised and apprehensive at the ease with which he had accomplished the task, let another ten go by before he dared begin testing the drow's beliefs.

"Surely you can see the wisdom of preparing for an attack," Regis suggested calmly. Then in a whisper that only Kemp could hear he added, "These people look to you for guidance, great Kemp. A military alliance would only enhance your stature and influence."

The effect was dazzling.

"Perhaps there is more to the halfling's words than we first believed," Kemp said mechanically, his glazed eyes never leaving the ruby.

Stunned, Regis straightened up and quickly slipped the stone back under his waistcoat. Kemp shook his head as though clearing a confusing dream from his thoughts, and he rubbed his dried eyes. The spokesman from Targos couldn't seem to recall the last few moments, but the halfling's suggestion was planted deeply into his mind. Kemp found, to his own amazement, that his attitudes had changed.

"We should hear well the words of Regis," he declared loudly. "For we shall be none the worse from forming such an alliance, yet the consequences of doing nothing may prove to be grave, indeed!"

Quick to seize an advantage, Jensin Brent leaped up from his chair. "Spokesman Kemp speaks wisely," he said. "Number the people of Caer-Dineval, ever proponents of the united efforts of Ten-Towns, among the army that shall repel the horde!"

The rest of the spokesmen lined up behind Kemp as Drizzt had expected, with Dorim Lugar making an even bigger show of loyalty than Brent's.

Regis had much to be proud of when he left the council hall later that day, and his hopes for the survival of Ten-Towns had returned. Yet the halfling found his thoughts consumed by the implications of the power he had discovered in his ruby. He worked to figure the most fail-safe way in which he could turn this new-found power of inducing cooperation into profit and comfort.

"So nice of the Pasha Pook to give me this one!" he told himself as he walked through the front gate of Bryn Shander and headed for the appointed spot where he would meet with Drizzt and Bruenor.

7

THE COMING STORM

They started at dawn, charging across the tundra like an angry whirlwind. Animals and monsters alike, even the ferocious yetis, fled before them in terror. The frozen ground cracked beneath the stamp of their heavy boots, and the murmur of the endless tundra wind was buried under the strength of their song, the song to the God of Battle.

They marched long into the night and were off again before the first rays of dawn, more than two thousand barbarian warriors hungry for blood and victory.

✕ ✕ ✕ ✕

Drizzt Do'Urden sat nearly halfway up on the northern face of Kelvin's Cairn, his cloak pulled tight against the bitter wind that howled through the boulders of the mountain. The drow had spent every night up here since the council in Bryn Shander, his violet eyes scanning the blackness of the plain for the first signs of the coming storm. At Drizzt's request, Bruenor had arranged for Regis to sit beside him. With the wind nipping at him like an invisible animal, the halfling squeezed in between two boulders as further protection from the unwelcoming elements.

Given a choice, Regis would have been tucked away into the warmth of his own soft bed in Lonelywood, listening to the quiet moan of the swaying tree branches beyond his warm walls. But he understood that as a spokesman everyone expected him to help carry out the course of action he had suggested at the council. It quickly became obvious to the other spokesmen and to Bruenor, who had joined in the subsequent strategy meetings as the representative of the dwarves, that the halfling wouldn't be much help in organizing the forces or drawing any battle plans, so when Drizzt told Bruenor that he would need a courier to sit watch with him, the dwarf was quick to volunteer Regis.

Now the halfling was thoroughly miserable. His feet and fingers were numbed from the cold, and his back ached from sitting against the hard stone. This was the third night out, and Regis grumbled and complained constantly, punctuating his discomfort with an occasional sneeze. Through it all, Drizzt sat unmoving and oblivious to the conditions, his stoic dedication to duty overriding any personal distress.

"How many more nights do we have to wait?" Regis whined. "One morning, I'm sure—maybe even tomorrow—they'll find us up here, dead and frozen to this cursed mountain!"

"Fear not, little friend," Drizzt answered with a smile. "The wind speaks of winter. The barbarians will come all too soon, determined to beat the first snows." Even as he spoke, the drow caught the tiniest flicker of light in the corner of his eye. He rose from his crouch suddenly, startling the halfling, and turned toward the direction of the flicker, his muscles tensed with reflexive wariness, his eyes straining to spot a confirming sign.

"What's—" Regis began, but Drizzt silenced him with an outstretched palm. A second dot of fire flashed on the edge of the horizon.

"You have gotten your wish," Drizzt said with certainty.

"Are they out there?" Regis whispered. His vision wasn't nearly as keen as the drow's in the night.

Drizzt stood silently in concentration for a few moments, mentally trying to measure the distance of the campfires and calculate the time it would take the barbarians to complete their journey.

"Go to Bruenor and Cassius, little friend," he said at length. "Tell them that the horde will reach Bremen's Run when the sun peaks tomorrow."

"Come with me," said Regis. "Surely they'll not put you out when you bear such urgent news."

"I have a more important task at hand," Drizzt answered. "Now be off! Tell Bruenor—and Bruenor alone—that I shall meet him on Bremen's Run at the first light of dawn." And with that, the drow padded off into the darkness. He had a long journey before him.

"Where are you going?" Regis called after him.

"To find the horizon's horizon!" came a cry from the black night.

And then there was only the murmur of the wind.

⚔ ⚔ ⚔ ⚔ ⚔

The barbarians had finished setting up their encampment shortly before Drizzt reached its outer perimeter. This close to Ten-Towns, the invaders were on their guard; the first thing Drizzt noticed was that they had set many men on watch. But alert as they were, their campfires burned low and this was the night, the time of the drow. The normally effective watchmen were outmatched by an elf from a world that knew no light, one who could conjure a magical darkness that even the keenest eyes could not penetrate and carry it beside him like a tangible cloak. Invisible as a shadow in the darkness, with footfalls as silent as a stalking cat's, Drizzt passed by the guards and entered the inner rings of the camp.

Just an hour earlier, the barbarians had been singing and talking of the battle they would fight the next day. Yet even the adrenaline and bloodlust that pumped through their veins could not dispel the exhaustion from their hard march. Most of the men slept soundly, their heavy, rhythmic breathing comforting Drizzt as he picked his way among them in search of their leaders, who would no doubt be finalizing the battle plans.

Several tents were grouped together within the encampment. Only one, though, had guards posted outside its entrance. The flap was closed, but Drizzt could see the glow of candles within, and he could hear gruff voices, often raised in anger. The drow slipped around to the back. Luckily, no warriors had been permitted to make their beds close to the tent, so Drizzt was fairly secluded. As a precaution, he pulled the panther figurine out of his pack. Then, taking out a slender dagger, he poked a tiny hole in the deerskin tent and peeked in.

There were eight men inside, the seven barbarian chiefs and a smaller dark-haired man that Drizzt knew could not have been from northern stock. The chiefs sat on the ground in a semicircle around the standing southerner, asking him questions about the terrain and forces they would encounter the next day.

"We should destroy the town in the wood first," insisted the largest man in the room, possibly the largest man Drizzt had ever seen, who bore the symbol of the Elk. "Then we can follow your plan to the town called Bryn Shander."

The smaller man appeared absolutely flustered and outraged, though Drizzt could see that fear of the huge barbarian king would temper his response. "Great King Heafstaag," he answered tentatively, "if the fishing fleets sight trouble and land before we get to Bryn Shander, we shall find an army that outnumbers our own waiting for us within the solid walls of that city."

"They are only weakly southerners!" growled Heafstaag, thrusting out his barrel chest in pride.

"Mighty king, I assure you that my plan will satisfy your hunger for southern blood," said the dark-haired man.

"Then speak, deBernezan of Ten-Towns. Prove your worth to my people!"

Drizzt could see that the last statement rattled the one called deBernezan, for the undertones of the barbarian king's demand clearly showed his contempt for the southerner. Knowing how barbarians generally felt about outsiders, the drow realized that the slightest error during any part of this campaign would probably cost the little man his life.

deBernezan reached down into the side of his boot and produced a scroll. He unrolled it and held it out for the barbarian kings to see. It was a poor map, roughly drawn, its lines further blurred by the slight tremble of the southern man's hand but Drizzt could clearly make out many of the distinctive features that marked Ten-Towns on the otherwise featureless plain.

"To the west of Kelvin's Cairn," deBernezan explained, running his finger along the western bank of the largest lake on the map, "there is a clear stretch of high ground called Bremen's Run that goes south between the mountain and Maer Dualdon. From our location, this is the most direct route to Bryn Shander and the path that I believe we should take."

"The town on the banks of the lake," Heafstaag reasoned, "should then be the first that we crush!"

"That is Termalaine," replied deBernezan. "All of its men are fishermen and will be out on the lake as we pass. You would not find good sport there!"

"We will not leave an enemy alive behind us!" Heafstaag roared, and several other kings cried out their agreement.

"No, of course not," said deBernezan. "But it will not take many men to defeat Termalaine when the boats are out. Let King Haalfdane and the Tribe of the Bear sack the town while the rest of the force, led by yourself and King Beorg, presses on to Bryn Shander. The fires of the burning town should bring the entire fleet, even the ships from the other towns of Maer Dualdon, into Termalaine where King Haalfdane can destroy them on the docks. It is important that we keep them away from the stronghold of Targos. The people of Bryn Shander will receive no aid from the other lakes in time to support them and will have to stand alone against your charge. The Tribe of the Elk will flank around the base of the hill below the city and cut off any possible escape or any last-minute reinforcements."

Drizzt watched closely as deBernezan described this second division of the barbarian forces on his map. Already the drow's calculating mind was formulating initial defense plans. Bryn Shander's hill wasn't very high but its base was thick, and the barbarians who were to swing around the back of the hill would be a long way from the main force.

A long way from reinforcements.

"The city will fall before sunset!" deBernezan declared triumphantly. "And your men will feast on the finest booty in all of Ten-Towns!" A sudden cheer went up on cue from the seated kings at the southerner's declaration of victory.

Drizzt put his back to the tent and considered what he had heard. This dark-haired man named deBernezan knew the towns well and understood their strengths and weaknesses. If Bryn Shander fell, no organized resistance could be formed to drive off the invaders. Indeed, once they held the fortified city, the barbarians would be able to strike at their leisure at any of the other towns.

"Again you have shown me your worth," Drizzt heard Heafstaag tell the southerner, and the ensuing of conversations told the drow that the plans had been accepted as final. Drizzt then focused his keen senses on the encampment around him, seeking the best path for his escape. He noticed suddenly that two guards were walking his way and talking. Though they were too far away for their human eyes to see him as anything but a shadow on the side of the tent, he knew that any movement on his part would surely alert them.

Acting immediately, Drizzt dropped the black figurine to the ground. "Guenhwyvar," he called softly. "Come to me, my shadow."

✕ ✕ ✕ ✕ ✕

Somewhere in a corner of the vast astral plane, the entity of the panther moved in sudden, subtle steps as it stalked the entity of the deer. The beasts of this natural world had played out this scenario countless times, following the harmonious order that guided the lives of their descendents. The panther crouched low for the final spring, sensing the sweetness of the upcoming kill. This strike was the harmony of natural order, the purpose of the panther's existence, and the meat its reward.

It stopped at once, though, when it heard the call of its true name, compelled above any other directives to heed the call of its master.

The great cat's spirit rushed down the long, darkened corridor that marked the void between the planes, seeking the solitary speck of light that was its life on the material plane. And then it was beside the dark elf, its soulmate and master, crouching in the shadows by the hanging skins of a human dwelling.

It understood the urgency of its master's call and quickly opened its mind to the drow's instructions.

The two barbarian guards approached cautiously, trying to make out the dark forms that stood beside their kings' tent. Suddenly Guenhwyvar sprang toward them and soared in a mighty leap past their drawn swords. The guards swung the weapons futilely and charged off after the cat, screaming an alert to the rest of the camp.

In the excitement of the diversion, Drizzt moved calmly and stealthily away in a different direction. He heard the shouts of alarm as Guenhwyvar darted through the campsites of the sleeping warriors and couldn't help but smile when the cat crossed through one particular group. Upon sighting this feline, who moved with so much grace and speed that it appeared as no more than a cat's spirit, the Tribe of the Tiger, instead of giving chase, fell to their knees and raised their hands and voices in thanks to Tempus.

Drizzt had little trouble escaping the perimeter of the camp, as all of the sentries were rushing off in the direction of the commotion. When the drow gained the blackness of the open tundra, he turned south toward Kelvin's Cairn and sped off across the lonely plain in full flight, all the while concentrating on finalizing a deadly counter-plan of defense. The stars told him that there were less than three hours left before dawn, and he knew that he mustn't be late for his meeting with Bruenor if the ambush were to be properly set.

The noise of the surprised barbarians soon died away, except for the prayers of the Tribe of the Tiger, which would continue until dawn. A few minutes later, Guenhwyvar was trotting easily by Drizzt's side.

"A hundred times you have saved my life, trusted friend," Drizzt said as he patted the great cat's muscled neck. "A hundred times and more!"

⚔ ⚔ ⚔ ⚔ ⚔

"They've been arguin' and scufflin' for two days now," Bruenor remarked disgustedly. "A blessing it is that the greater enemy has finally arrived!"

"Better to name the coming of barbarians in a different way," Drizzt replied, though a smile had found its way onto his normally stoic features. He knew that his plan was solid and that the battle this day would belong to the people of Ten-Towns. "Go now and lay the trap—you've not much time."

"We began loadin' the womenfolk and children onto the boats as soon as Rumblebelly told us yer news," Bruenor explained. "We'll chase the vermin from our borders before the day is through!" The dwarf spread his feet wide in his customary battle stance and banged his axe onto his shield to emphasize his point. "Ye've a good eye for battle, elf. Yer plan'll turn the surprise on the barbarians and it still splits the glory evenly among them that needs glory."

"Even Kemp of Targos should be pleased," Drizzt agreed.

Bruenor clapped his friend on the arm and turned to leave. "Ye'll fight beside me, then?" he asked over his shoulder, though he already knew the answer.

"As it should be," Drizzt assured him.

"An' the cat?"

"Guenhwyvar has already played its part in this battle," replied the drow. "I'll be sending my friend home soon."

Bruenor was pleased with the answer; he didn't trust the drow's strange beast. "It ain't natural," he said to himself as he trekked down Bremen's Run toward the gathered hosts of Ten-Towns.

Bruenor was too far away for Drizzt to make out his final words, but the drow knew the dwarf well enough to gather the general meaning of his grumblings. He understood the uneasiness that Bruenor, and many others, felt around the mystical cat. Magic was a prominent part of the underworld of his people, a necessary fact of their everyday existence, but it was much rarer and less understood among the common folk of the surface. Dwarves in particular were usually uncomfortable with it, except for the crafted magical weapons and armor they often made themselves.

The drow, though, had no anxiety around Guenhwyvar from the very first day he had met the cat. The figurine had belonged to Masoj Hun'ett, a drow of high standing in a prominent family of the great city of Menzoberranzan, a gift from a demon lord in exchange for some assistance that Masoj had given him in a matter concerning some troublesome gnomes. Drizzt and the cat had crossed paths many times over the years in the dark city, often in planned meetings. They shared an empathy with each other that transcended the relationship that the cat felt with its then-master.

Guenhwyvar had even rescued Drizzt from certain death, uncalled for, as if the cat had been watching protectively over the drow who was not yet its master. Drizzt had struck out alone from Menzoberranzan on a journey to a neighboring city when he fell prey to a cave fisher, a crablike denizen of the dark caverns that customarily found a niche high above the floor of a tunnel and dropped an invisible, sticky line of webbing. Like an angler, this cave fisher had waited, and like a fish, Drizzt had fallen into its trap. The sticky line entangled him completely, rendering him helpless as he was dragged up the side of the corridor's stone wall.

He saw no hope for surviving this encounter and vividly understood that a terrible death certainly awaited him.

But then Guenhwyvar had arrived, leaping among the broken clefts and ridges along the wall at the same level as the monster. Without any regard to its own safety and following no orders, the cat charged right in on the fisher, knocking it from its perch. The monster, seeking only its own safety, tried to scramble away, but Guenhwyvar pounced upon it vindictively, as if to punish it for attacking Drizzt.

Both the drow and the cat knew from that day on that they were destined to run together. Yet the cat had no power to disobey the will of its master, and Drizzt had no right to claim the figurine from Masoj, especially since the house of Hun'ett was much more powerful than Drizzt's own family in the structured hierarchy of the underworld.

And so the drow and the cat continued their casual relationship as distant comrades.

Soon after, though, came an incident that Drizzt could not ignore. Guenhwyvar was often taken on raids with Masoj, whether against enemy drow houses or other denizens of the underworld. The cat normally carried out its orders efficiently, thrilled to aid its master in battle. On one particular raid, though, against a clan of svirfnebli, the deep mining, unassuming gnomes that often had the misfortune of running up against the drow in their common habitat, Masoj went too far in his maliciousness.

After the initial assault on the clan, the surviving gnomes scattered down the many corridors of their mazework mines. The raid had been successful; the treasures that had been sought were taken, and the clan had been dispatched, obviously never to bother the drow again. But Masoj wanted more blood.

He used Guenhwyvar, the proud, majestic hunter, as his instrument of murder. He sent the cat after the fleeing gnomes one by one until they were all destroyed.

Drizzt and several other drow witnessed the spectacle. The others, in their characteristic vileness, thought it great sport, but Drizzt found himself absolutely disgusted. Furthermore, he recognized the humiliation painfully etched on the proud cat's features. Guenhwyvar was a hunter, not an assassin, and to use it in such a role was criminally degrading, to say nothing of the horrors that Masoj was inflicting upon the innocent gnomes.

This was actually the final outrage in a long line of outrages which Drizzt could no longer bear. He had always known that he was unlike his kin in many ways, though he had many times feared that he would prove to be more akin to them than he believed. Yet he was rarely passionless, considering the death of another more important than the mere sport it represented to the vast majority of drow. He couldn't label it, for he had never come across a word in the drow language that spoke of such a trait, but to the surface-dwellers that later came to know Drizzt, it was called conscience.

One day the very next tenday, Drizzt managed to catch Masoj alone outside the cluttered grounds of Menzoberranzan. He knew that there could be no turning back once the fatal blow had been struck, but he didn't even hesitate, slipping his scimitar through the ribs of his unsuspecting victim. That was the only time in his life that he had ever killed one of his own race, an act that thoroughly revolted him despite his feelings toward his people.

Then he took the figurine and fled, meaning only to find another of the countless dark holes in the vast underworld to make his home, but eventually winding up on the surface. And then, unaccepted and persecuted for his heritage in city after city in the populated south, he had made his way to the wilderness frontier of Ten-Towns, a melting pot of outcasts, the last outpost of humanity, where he was at least tolerated.

He didn't care much about the shunning he usually received even here. He had found friendship with the halfling, and the dwarves, and Bruenor's adopted daughter, Catti-brie.

And he had Guenhwyvar by his side.

He patted the great cat's muscled neck once again and left Bremen's Run to find a dark hole where he could rest before the battle.

8

BLOODY FIELDS

The horde entered the mouth of Bremen's Run just before midday. They longed to announce their glorious charge with a song of war, but they understood that a certain degree of stealth was vital to the ultimate success of deBernezan's battle plan.

deBernezan was comforted by the familiar sight of sails dotting the waters of Maer Dualdon as he jogged beside King Haalfdane. The surprise would be complete, he believed, and then with ironic amusement he noted that some of the ships already flew the red flags of the catch. "More wealth for the victors," he hissed under his breath. The barbarians had still not begun their song when the Tribe of the Bear split away from the main group and headed toward Termalaine, though the cloud of dust that followed their run would have told a wary observer that something out of the ordinary was happening. They rolled on toward Bryn Shander and cried out their first cheer when the pennant of the principal city came into sight.

The combined forces of the four towns of Maer Dualdon lay hidden in Termalaine. Their goal was to strike fast and hard at the small tribe that attacked the city, overrunning them as quickly as possible, then charge to the aid of Bryn Shander, trapping the rest of the horde between the two armies. Kemp of Targos was in command of this operation, but he had conceded the first blow to Agorwal, spokesman of the home city.

Torches set the first buildings of the city ablaze as Haalfdane's wild army rushed in. Termalaine was second only to Targos among the nine fishing villages in population, but it was a sprawling, uncluttered town, with houses spread out over a large area and wide avenues running between them. Its people had retained their privacy and a measure of breathing room, giving the town an air of solitude that belied its numbers. Still, deBernezan sensed that the streets seemed unusually deserted. He mentioned his concern to the barbarian king at his side, though Haalfdane assured him that the rats had gone into hiding at the approach of the Bear.

"Pull them out of their holes and burn their houses!" the barbarian king roared. "Let the fishermen on the lake hear the cries of their women and see the smoke of their burning town!"

But then an arrow thudded into Haalfdane's chest, burying itself deep within his flesh and biting through, tearing into his heart. The shocked barbarian looked down in horror at the vibrating shaft, though he couldn't even utter a final cry before the blackness of death closed in around him.

With his ashwood bow, Agorwal of Termalaine had silenced the King of the Tribe of the Bear. And on signal from Agorwal's strike, the four armies of Maer Dualdon sprang to life.

They leaped from the rooftops of every building, from the alleys and doorways of every street. Against the ferocious assault of the multitude, the confused and stunned barbarians realized immediately that their battle would soon be at an end. Many were cut down before they could even ready their weapons.

Some of the battle-hardened invaders managed to form into small groups, but the people of Ten-Towns, fighting for their homes and the lives of their loved ones and armed with crafted weapons and shields forged by dwarven smiths, pressed in immediately. Fearlessly, the defenders bore the remaining invaders down under the weight of their greater numbers.

In an alley on the edge of Termalaine, Regis dived behind the conceal-ment of a small cart as two fleeing barbarians passed by. The halfling fought with a personal dilemma: He didn't want to be labeled a coward, but he had no intention of jumping into the battle of big folk. When the danger had passed, he walked back around the cart and tried to figure out his next move.

Suddenly a dark-haired man, a member of Ten-Towns' militia, Regis supposed, entered the alley and spotted the halfling. Regis knew that his little game of hiding was over, the time had come for him to make his stand. "Two of the scum just passed this way," he called boldly to the dark-haired southerner. "Come, if we're quick we can catch them yet!"

deBernezan had different plans, though. In a desperate attempt to save his own life, he had decided to slip down one alley and emerge from another as a member of the Ten-Towns' force. He had no intention of leaving any witnesses to his treachery. Steadily he walked toward Regis, his slender sword at the ready.

Regis sensed that the mannerisms of the closing man weren't quite right. "Who are you?" he asked, though he somehow expected no reply. He thought that he knew nearly everyone in the city, though he didn't believe that he had ever seen this man before. Already, he had the uncomfortable suspicion that this was the traitor Drizzt had described to Bruenor. "How come I didn't see you come in with the others earli—"

deBernezan thrust his sword at the halfling's eye. Regis, dexterous and ever-alert, managed to lurch out of the way, though the blade scratched the side of his head and the momentum of his dodge sent him spinning to the ground. With an unemotional, disturbingly cold-blooded calm, the dark-haired man closed in again.

Regis scrambled to his feet and backed away, step for step with his assailant. But then he bumped up against the side of the small cart. deBernezan advanced methodically. The halfling had nowhere left to run.

Desperate, Regis pulled the ruby pendant from under his waistcoat. "Please don't kill me," he pleaded, holding the sparkling stone out by its chain and letting it dance seductively. "If you let me live, I'll give you this and show you where you can find many more!" Regis was encouraged by deBernezan's slight hesitation at the sight of the stone. "Surely, it's a beautiful cut and worth a dragon's hoard of gold!"

deBernezan kept his sword out in front of him, but Regis counted as the seconds passed and the dark-haired man did not blink. The halfling's left hand began to steady, while his right, concealed behind his back, clasped firmly onto the handle of the small but heavy mace crafted for him personally by Bruenor.

"Come, look closer," Regis suggested softly. deBernezan, firmly under the spell of the sparkling stone, stooped low to better examine its fascinating dance of light.

"This isn't really fair," Regis lamented aloud, confident that deBernezan was oblivious to anything he might say at that moment. He cracked the spiked ball of the mace onto the back of the bending man's head.

Regis eyed the result of his dirty work and shrugged absently. He had only done what was necessary.

The sounds of the battle in the street rang closer to his alley sanctuary and dispelled his contemplation. Again the halfling acted on instinct. He crawled under the body of his felled enemy, then twisted around underneath to make it look as if he had gone down under the weight of the larger man.

When he inspected the damage of deBernezan's initial thrust, he was glad that he hadn't lost his ear. He hoped that his wound was serious enough to give credence to this image of a death struggle.

⚔ ⚔ ⚔ ⚔ ⚔

The main host of the barbarian force reached the long, low hill that led up to Bryn Shander unaware of what had befallen their comrades in Termalaine. Here they split again, with Heafstaag leading the Tribe of the Elk around the eastern side of the hill and Beorg taking the rest of the horde straight toward the walled city. Now they took up their song of battle, hoping to further unnerve the shocked and terrified people of Ten-Towns.

But behind the wall of Bryn Shander was a very different scene than the barbarians imagined. The army of the city, along with the forces of Caer-Konig and Caer-Dineval, sat ready with bows and spears and buckets of hot oil.

In a dark twist of irony, the Tribe of the Elk, out of sight of the front wall of the city, took up a cheer when the first screams of death rang out on the hill, thinking the victims to be the unprepared people of Ten-Towns. A few seconds later, as Heafstaag led his men around the easternmost bend in the hill, they too met with disaster. The armies of Good Mead and Dougan's Hole were firmly dug in and waiting, and the barbarians were hard-pressed before they even knew what had hit them.

After the first few moments of confusion, though, Heafstaag managed to regain control of the situation. These warriors had been through many battles together, seasoned fighting men who knew no fear. Even with the losses of the initial attack, they were not outnumbered by the force before them, and Heafstaag was confident that he could overrun the fishermen quickly and still get his men into position.

But then, shouting as they came, the army of Easthaven charged down the Eastway and pressed the barbarians on their left flank. And Heafstaag, still unshaken, had just ordered his men to make the proper adjustments to protect against the new foe when ninety battle-hardened and heavily armored dwarves tore into them from behind. The grim-faced dwarven host attacked in a wedge formation with Bruenor as its deadly tip. They cut into the Tribe of the Elk, felling barbarians like a low-swinging scythe through tall grass.

The barbarians fought bravely, and many fishermen died on the eastern slopes of Bryn Shander. But the Tribe of the Elk was outnumbered and out-flanked, and barbarian blood ran freer than the blood of their foes. Heafstaag worked wildly to rally his men, but all semblance of formation and order disintegrated around him. To his worst horror and disgrace, the giant king realized that every one of his warriors would die on this field if they didn't find a way to escape the ring of enemies and flee back to the safety of the tundra.

Heafstaag himself, who had never before retreated in battle, led the desperate break. He and as many warriors as he could gather together rushed around the dwarven host, seeking a route between them and the army of Easthaven. Most of the tribesmen were cut down by the blades of Bruenor's people, but some managed to break free of the ring and bolt away toward Kelvin's Cairn.

Heafstaag got through the gauntlet, killing two dwarves as he passed, but suddenly the giant king was engulfed in an impenetrable globe of absolute

blackness. He dived headlong through it and emerged back into the light only to find himself face to face with a dark elf.

✕ ✕ ✕ ✕ ✕

Bruenor had seven notches to put on his axe-handle and he bore down on number eight, a tall, gangly barbarian youth, too young even to show any stubble on his tanned face, but bearing the standard of the Tribe of the Elk with the composure of an experienced warrior. Bruenor curiously considered the engaging stare and calm visage as he closed in on the youth. It surprised him that he did not find the savage fire of barbarian bloodlust contorting the youth's features, but rather an observant, understanding depth. The dwarf found himself truly lamenting having to kill one so young and unusual, and his pity caused him to hesitate slightly as the two joined battle.

Ferocious as his heritage dictated, though, the youth showed no fear, and Bruenor's hesitation had given him the first swing. With deadly accuracy, he slammed his standard pole down onto his foe, snapping it in half. The amazingly powerful blow dented Bruenor's helm and jolted the dwarf into a short bounce. Tough as the mountain stone he mined, Bruenor put his hands on his hips and glared up at the barbarian, who nearly dropped his weapon, so shocked was he that the dwarf still stood.

"Silly boy," Bruenor growled as he cut the youth's legs out from under him. "Ain't ye never been told not to hit a dwarf on the head?" The youth desperately tried to regain his footing, but Bruenor slammed an iron shield into his face.

"Eight!" roared the dwarf as he stormed away in search of number nine. But he looked back for a moment over his shoulder to consider the fallen youth, shaking his head at the waste of one so tall and straight, with intelligent eyes to match his physical prowess, a combination uncommon among the wild and ferocious natives of Icewind Dale.

✕ ✕ ✕ ✕ ✕

Heafstaag's rage doubled when he recognized his newest opponent as a drow elf. "Sorcerous dog!" he bellowed, raising his huge axe high into the sky.

Even as he spoke, Drizzt flicked a finger and purple flames limned the tall barbarian from head to toe. Heafstaag roared in horror at the magical fire, though the flames did not burn his skin. Drizzt bore in, his two scimitars whirling and jabbing, thrusting high and low too quickly for the barbarian king to deflect both.

Blood trickled from many small wounds, but Heafstaag seemed able to shake off the punctures of the slender scimitars as no more than a discomfort. The great axe arced down, and though Drizzt was able to deflect its path, the effort numbed his arm. Again the barbarian swung his axe. This time Drizzt was able to spin out of its killing sweep, and the completion of the drow's rotation left the overbalanced Heafstaag stumbling and open to a counter. Drizzt didn't hesitate, driving one of his blades deep into the barbarian king's side.

Heafstaag howled in agony and launched a backhand swing in retaliation. Drizzt thought his last thrust to be fatal, and his surprise was total when the flat head of Heafstaag's axe smashed into his ribs and launched him through the air. The barbarian charged quickly after, meaning to finish this dangerous opponent before he could regain his footing.

But Drizzt was as nimble as a cat. He landed in a roll and came up to meet Heafstaag's charge with one of his scimitars firmly set. His axe helplessly poised above his head, the surprised barbarian couldn't stop his momentum before he impaled his belly on the wicked point. Still, he glared at the drow and began to swing his axe. Already convinced of the superhuman strength of the barbarian, Drizzt had kept up his guard this time. He knifed his second blade just under the first, opening the lower part of Heafstaag's abdomen from hip to hip.

Heafstaag's axe fell harmlessly to the ground as he grabbed at the wound, desperately trying to keep his belly from spilling out. His huge head lolled from side to side, the world spun about him, and he felt himself endlessly falling.

Several other tribesmen, in full flight and with dwarves hot on their heels, came by at that moment and caught their king before he hit the ground. So great was their dedication to Heafstaag that two of them lifted him and carried him away while the others turned to face the coming tide of dwarves, knowing that they would certainly be cut down, but hoping only to give their comrades enough time to bear their king to safety.

Drizzt rolled away from the barbarians and leaped to his feet, meaning to give chase to the two who bore Heafstaag. He had a sickening feeling that the terrible king would survive even the last grievous wounds, and he was determined to finish the job. But when he rose, he, too, found the world spinning. The side of his cloak was stained with his own blood, and he suddenly found it difficult to catch his breath. The blazing midday sun burned into his night eyes, and he was lathered in sweat.

Drizzt collapsed into darkness.

⚔ ⚔ ⚔ ⚔ ⚔

The three armies waiting behind Bryn Shander's wall had quickly dispatched the first line of invaders and then driven the remaining barbarian host halfway back down the hill. Undaunted and thinking that time would play in their favor, the ferocious horde had regrouped around Beorg and begun a steady, cautious march back toward the city.

When the barbarians heard the charge coming up the eastern slope, they assumed that Heafstaag had finished his battle on the side of the hill, had learned of the resistance at the front gate, and was returning to help them smash into the city. Then Beorg spotted tribesmen fleeing to the north toward Icewind Pass, the stretch of ground opposite Bremen's Run that passed between Lac Dinneshere and the western side of Kelvin's Cairn. The king of the Tribe of the Wolf knew that his people were in trouble. Offering no explanation beyond the promised thrust of the tip of his spear to any who questioned his orders, Beorg started to turn his men around to head away from the city, hoping to regroup with Haalfdane and the Tribe of the Bear and salvage as many of his people as he could.

Before he had even completed the reversal of the march, he found Kemp and the four armies of Maer Dualdon behind him, their deep ranks barely thinned by the slaughter in Termalaine. Over the wall came the armies of Bryn Shander, Caer-Konig, and Caer-Dineval, and around the hill came Bruenor, leading the dwarven clan and the last three armies of Ten-Towns.

Beorg ordered his men into a tight circle. "Tempus is watching." he yelled at them. "Make him proud of his people!"

Nearly eight hundred barbarians remained, and they fought with the confidence of the blessing of their god. They held their formation for almost an hour, singing and dying, before the lines broke down and chaos erupted.

Less than fifty escaped with their lives.

⚔ ⚔ ⚔ ⚔

After the final blows had at last been swung, the exhausted warriors of Ten-Towns set about the grim task of sorting out their losses. More than five hundred of their companions had been killed and two hundred more would eventually die of their wounds, yet the toll wasn't heavy considering the two thousand barbarians who lay dead in the streets of Termalaine and on the slopes of Bryn Shander.

Many heroes had been made that day, and Bruenor, though anxious to get back to the eastern battlefields to search for missing companions, paused for a long moment as the last of them was carried in glory up the hill to Bryn Shander.

"Rumblebelly?" exclaimed the dwarf.

"The name is Regis," the halfling retorted from his high perch, proudly folding his arms across his chest.

"Respect, good dwarf," said one of the men carrying Regis. "In single combat Spokesman Regis of Lonelywood slew the traitor that brought the horde upon us, though he was wickedly injured in the battle!"

Bruenor snorted in amusement as the procession passed. "There's more to that tale than what's been told, I'll wager!" he chuckled to his equally amused companions. "Or I'm a bearded gnome!"

⚔ ⚔ ⚔ ⚔

Kemp of Targos and one of his lieutenants were the first to come upon the fallen form of Drizzt Do'Urden. Kemp prodded the dark elf with the toe of his blood-stained boot, drawing a semiconscious groan in response.

"He lives," Kemp said to his lieutenant with an amused smile. "A pity." He kicked the injured drow again, this time with more enthusiasm. The other man laughed in approval and lifted his own foot to join in the fun.

Suddenly, a mailed fist slammed into Kemp's kidney with enough force to carry the spokesman over Drizzt and send him bouncing down the long decline of the hill. His lieutenant whirled around, conveniently ducking low to receive Bruenor's second swing square in the face.

"One for yerself, too!" the enraged dwarf growled as he felt the man's nose shatter under his blow.

Cassius of Bryn Shander, viewing the incident from higher up on the hill, screamed in anger and rushed down the slope toward Bruenor. "You should be taught some diplomacy!" he scolded.

"Stand where y' are, son of a swamp pig!" was Bruenor's threatening response. "Ye owe the drow yer stinkin' lives and homes," he roared to all around who could hear him, "and ye treat him as vermin!"

"Ware your words, dwarf!" retorted Cassius, tentatively grabbing at his sword hilt. The dwarves formed a line around their leader, and Cassius's men gathered around him.

Then a third voice sounded clearly. "Ware your own, Cassius," warned Agorwal of Termalaine. "I would have done the same thing to Kemp if I was possessed of the courage of the dwarf!" He pointed to the north. "The sky is clear," he yelled. "Yet were it not for the drow, it would be filled with the smoke of burning Termalaine!" The spokesman from Termalaine and his companions moved over to join Bruenor's line. Two of the men gently lifted Drizzt from the ground.

"Fear not for your friend, valiant dwarf," said Agorwal. "He will be well tended in my city. Never again shall I, or my fellow men of Termalaine, prejudge him by the color of his skin and the reputation of his kin!"

Cassius was outraged. "Remove your soldiers from the grounds of Bryn Shander!" he screamed at Agorwal, but it was an empty threat, for the men of Termalaine were already departing.

Satisfied that the drow was in safe hands, Bruenor and his clan moved on to search the rest of the battleground.

"I'll not forget this!" Kemp yelled at him from far down the hill.

Bruenor spat at the spokesman from Targos and continued on unshaken.

And so it went that the alliance of the people of Ten-Towns lasted only as long as their common enemy.

Epilogue

All along the hill, the fishermen of Ten-Towns moved among their fallen enemies, looting the barbarians of what small wealth they possessed and putting the sword to the unfortunate ones who were not quite dead.

Yet amid the carnage of the bloody scene, a finger of mercy was to be found. A man from Good Mead rolled the limp form of an unconscious young barbarian over onto its back, preparing to finish the job with his dagger. Bruenor came upon them then and recognizing the youth as the standard bearer who had dented his helmet, stayed the fisherman's thrust. "Don't kill 'im. He's nothing but a boy, and he can't have known truly what he an' his people did."

"Bah!" huffed the fisherman. "What mercy would these dogs have shown to our children, I ask you? He's half in the grave anyway."

"Still I ask ye to let him be!" Bruenor growled, his axe bouncing impatiently against his shoulder. "In fact, I insist!"

The fisherman returned the dwarf's scowl, but he had witnessed Bruenor's proficiency in battle and thought the better of pushing him too far. With a disgusted sigh, he headed off around the hill to find less protected victims.

The boy stirred on the grass and moaned.

"So ye've a bit of life left in ye yet," said Bruenor. He knelt beside the lad's head and lifted it by the hair to meet his eyes. "Hear me well, boy. I saved yer life here—why, I'm not quite knowin'—but don't ye think ye've been pardoned by the people of Ten-Towns. I want ye to see the misery yer people have brung. Maybe killing is in yer blood, and if it is, then let the fisherman's blade end ye here and now! But I'm feelin' there's more to ye, and ye'll have the time to show me right.

"Ye're to serve me and me people in our mines for five years and a day to prove yourself worthy of life and freedom."

Bruenor saw that the youth had slumped back into unconsciousness. "Never mind," he muttered. "Ye'll hear me well before all's done, be sure o' that!" He moved to drop the head back to the grass, but laid it down gently instead.

Onlookers to the spectacle of the gruff dwarf showing kindness to the barbarian youth were indeed startled, but none could guess the implications of what they had witnessed. Bruenor himself, for all of his assumptions of this barbarian's character, could not have foreseen that this boy, Wulfgar, would grow into the man who would reshape this harsh region of the tundra.

⚔ ⚔ ⚔ ⚔

Far to the south, in a wide pass among the towering peaks of the Spine of the World, Akar Kessell languished in the soft life that Crenshinibon had provided for him. His goblin slaves had captured yet another female from a merchant caravan for him to play with, but now something else had caught his eye. Smoke, rising into the empty sky from the direction of Ten-Towns.

"Barbarians," Kessell guessed. He had heard rumors that the tribes were gathering when he and the wizards from Luskan had been visiting Easthaven. But it didn't matter to him, and why should it? He had all that he needed right here in Cryshal-Tirith and had no desire to travel anywhere else.

No desires that were wrought of his own will.

Crenshinibon was a relic that was truly alive in its magic. And part of its life was the desire to conquer and command. The Crystal Shard was not content with an existence in a desolate mountain range, where the only servants were lowly goblins. It wanted more. It wanted power.

Kessell's own subconscious recollections of Ten-Towns when he had spotted the column of smoke had stirred the relic's hunger, so it now used the same empathetic power of suggestion on Kessell.

A sudden image grasped at the wizard's deepest needs. He saw himself seated on a throne in Bryn Shander, immeasurably wealthy and respected by all in his court. He imagined the response from the Hosttower of the Arcane in Luskan when the mages there, especially Eldulac and Dendybar, learned of Akar Kessell, Lord of Ten-Towns and Ruler of all Icewind Dale! Would they offer him a robe in their puny order then?

Despite Kessell's true enjoyment of the leisurely existence he had found, the thought appealed to him. He let his mind continue through the fantasy, exploring the paths that he might take to accomplish such an ambitious goal.

He ruled out trying to dominate the fisherfolk as he had dominated this goblin tribe, for even the least intelligent of the goblins had held out against his imposing will for quite a long time. And when any of these had gotten away from the immediate area of the tower, they regained their ability to determine their own actions and had fled into the mountains. No, simple domination would not work against the humans.

Kessell pondered using the power that he felt pulsing within the structure of Cryshal-Tirith, destructive forces beyond anything he had ever heard of, even in the Hosttower. This would help, but it wouldn't be enough. Even the strength of Crenshinibon was limited, requiring lengths of time under the sun to gather new power to replace expended energy. Furthermore, in Ten-Towns there were too many people too widely scattered to be corralled by a single sphere of influence, and Kessell didn't want to destroy them all. Goblins were convenient; but the wizard longed to have humans bowing before him, real men like the ones who had persecuted him for all of his life.

For all of his life before he had gained the shard.

His ponderings eventually led him inevitably down the same line of reasoning. He would need an army.

He considered the goblins he presently commanded. Fanatically devoted to his every wish, they would gladly die for him (in fact, several had). Yet even they weren't nearly numerous enough to engulf the wide region of the three lakes with any semblance of strength.

And then an evil thought, again covertly insinuated into his will by the Crystal Shard, came upon the wizard. "How many holes and caves," Kessell cried aloud, "are there in this vast and rugged mountain range? And how many goblins, ogres, even trolls and giants, do they harbor?" The beginnings of a devious vision took shape in his mind. He saw himself at the head of a huge goblin and giant army, sweeping across the plains, unstoppable and irresistible.

How he would make men tremble!

He lay back on a soft pillow and called for the new harem girl. He had another game in mind, one that had also come to him in a strange dream; it called for her to beg and whimper, and finally, to die. The wizard decided, though, that he would certainly consider the possibilities of lordship over Ten-Towns that had opened wide before him. But there was no need to hurry; he had time. The goblins could always find him another plaything.

Crenshinibon, too, seemed to be at peace. It had placed the seed within Kessell's mind, a seed that it knew would germinate into a plan of conquest. But like Kessell, the relic had no need for haste.

The Crystal Shard had waited ten thousand years to return to life and see this opportunity of power flicker again. It could wait a few more.

PART TWO

Tradition

The very sound of the word invokes a sense of gravity and solemnity. Tradition. Suuz'chok in the drow language, and there, too, as in every language that I have heard, the word rolls off of one's tongue with tremendous weight and power.

WULFGAR

Tradition. It is the root of who we are, the link to our heritage, the reminder that we as a people, if not individually, will span the ages. To many people and many societies, tradition is the source of structure and of law, the abiding fact of identity that denies the contrary claims of the outlaw, or the misbehavior of the rogue. It is that echoing sound deep in our hearts and our minds and our souls that reminds us of who we are by reinforcing who we were. To many it is even more than the law; it is the religion, guiding faith as it guides morality and society.

To many, tradition is a god itself, the ancient rituals and holy texts, scribbled on unreadable parchments yellowed with age or chiseled into eternal rocks.

To many, tradition is all.

Personally, I view it as a double-edged sword, and one that can cut even more deeply in the way of error.

I saw the workings of tradition in Menzoberranzan, the ritualistic sacrifice of the third male child (which was almost my own fate), the workings of the three drow schools. Tradition justified my sister's advances toward me in the graduation of Melee-Magthere, and denied me any claims against that wretched ceremony. Tradition holds the Matrons in power, limiting the ascent of any males. Even the vicious wars of Menzoberranzan, house against house, are rooted in tradition, are justified because that is the way it has always been.

Such failings are not exclusive to the drow. Often I sit on the northern face of Kelvin's Cairn looking out over the empty tundra and the twinkling lights of the campfires in the vast barbarian encampments. There, too, is a people wholly consumed by tradition, a people clinging to ancient codes and ways that once allowed them to survive as a society in an inhospitable land but that now hinder them as much as, or more than, helps them. The barbarians of Icewind Dale follow the caribou herd from one end of the dale to the other. In days long past that was the only way they could have survived up here, but how much easier might their existence be now if they only traded with the folk of Ten-Towns, offering pelts and good meat in exchange for stronger materials brought up from the south so they might construct more permanent homes for themselves?

In days long past, before any real civilization crept this far to the north, the barbarians refused to speak with, or even to accept, anyone else within Icewind Dale, the various tribes often joining for the sole purpose of driving out any intruders. In those past times, any newcomers would inevitably become rivals for the meager food and other scarce supplies, and so such xenophobia was necessary for basic survival.

The folk of Ten-Towns, with their advanced fishing techniques, and their rich trade with Luskan, are not rivals of the barbarians—most have never even eaten venison, I would guess. And yet, tradition demands of the barbarians that they do not make friends with those folk, and indeed, often war upon them.

Tradition.

What gravity indeed does that word impart! What power it wields! As it roots us and grounds us and gives us hope for who we are because of who we were, so it also wreaks destruction and denies change.

I would never pretend to understand another people well enough to demand that they change their traditions, yet how foolish it seems to me to hold fast and unyieldingly to those mores and ways without regard for any changes that have taken place in the world about us.

For that world is a changing place, moved by advancements in technology and magic, by the rise and fall of populations, even by the blending of races, as in the half-elf communities. The world is not static, and if the roots of our perceptions, traditions, hold static, then we are doomed, I say, into destructive dogma.

Then we fall upon the darker blade of that double-edged sword.

—Drizzt Do'Urden

9
NO MORE A BOY

Regis stretched out lazily against his favorite tree and enjoyed a drawn-out yawn, his cherubic dimples beaming in the bright ray of sunlight that somehow found its way to him through the thickly packed branches. His fishing pole stood poised beside him, though its hook had long since been cleaned of any bait. Regis rarely caught any fish, but he prided himself on never wasting more than one worm.

He had come out here every day since his return to Lonelywood. He wintered in Bryn Shander now, enjoying the company of his good friend, Cassius. The city on the hill didn't compare to Calimport, but the palace of its spokesman was the closest thing to luxury in all of Icewind Dale. Regis thought himself quite clever for persuading Cassius to invite him to spend the harsh winters there.

A cool breeze wafted in off Maer Dualdon, drawing a contented sigh from the halfling. Though Kythorn had already passed its midpoint, this was the first hot day of the short season. And Regis was determined to make the most of it. For the first time in over a year he had been out before noon, and he planned to stay in this spot, stripped of his clothes, letting the sun sink its warmth into every inch of his body until the last red glow of sunset.

An angry shout out on the lake caught his attention. He lifted his head and half-opened one heavy eyelid. The first thing he noticed, to his complete satisfaction, was that his belly had grown considerably over the winter, and from this angle, lying flat on his back, he could see only the tips of his toes.

Halfway across the water, four boats, two from Termalaine and two from Targos, jockeyed for position, running past each other with sudden tacks and turns, their sailors cursing and spitting at the boats that flew the flag of the other city. For the last four and a half years, since the Battle of Bryn Shander, the two cities had virtually been at war. Though their battles were more often fought with words and fists than weapons, more than one ship had been rammed or driven into rocks or up to beach in shallow waters.

Regis shrugged helplessly and dropped his head back to his folded waistcoat. Nothing had changed much around Ten-Towns in the last few years. Regis and some of the other spokesmen had entertained high hopes of a united community, despite the heated argument after the battle between Kemp of Targos and Agorwal of Termalaine over the drow.

Even on the banks of the lake across the way, the period of good will was short-lived among the long-standing rivals. The truce between Caer-Dineval and Caer-Konig had lasted only until the first time one of Caer-Dineval's boats landed a valuable and rare five-footer, on the stretch of Lac Dinneshere that Caer-Konig had relinquished to her as compensation for the waters she had lost to Easthaven's expanding fleet.

Furthermore, Good Mead and Dougan's Hole, the normally unassuming and fiercely independent towns on the southernmost lake, Redwaters, had boldly demanded compensation from Bryn Shander and Termalaine. They had suffered staggering casualties in the battle on Bryn Shander's slopes, though they had never even considered the affair their business. They reasoned that the two towns which had gained the most from the united effort should be made to pay. The northern cities, of course, balked at the demand.

And so the lesson of the benefits of unification had gone unheeded. The ten communities remained as divided as ever before.

In truth, the town which had benefited the most from the battle was Lonelywood. The population of Ten-Towns as a whole had remained fairly constant. Many fortune hunters or hiding scoundrels continued to filter into the region, but an equal number were killed or grew disenchanted with the brutal conditions and returned to the more hospitable south.

Lonelywood, though, had grown considerably. Maer Dualdon, with its consistent yield of knucklehead, remained the most profitable of the lakes, and with the fighting between Termalaine and Targos, and Bremen precariously perched on the banks of the unpredictable and often flooding Shaengarne River, Lonelywood appeared the most appealing of the four towns. The people of the small community had even launched a campaign to draw newcomers, citing Lonelywood as the "Home of the Halfling Hero," and as the only place with shade trees within a hundred miles.

Regis had given up his position as spokesman shortly after the battle, a choice mutually arrived at by himself and the townsfolk. With Lonelywood growing into greater prominence and shaking off its reputation as a melting pot of rogues, the town needed a more aggressive person to sit on the council. And Regis simply didn't want to be bothered with the responsibility anymore.

Of course, Regis had found a way to turn his fame into profit. Every new settler in the town had to pay out a share of his first catches in return for the right to fly Lonelywood's flag, and Regis had persuaded the new spokesman and the other leaders of the town that since his name had been used to help bring in the new settlers, he should be cut in for a portion of these fees.

The halfling wore a broad smile whenever he considered his good fortune. He spent his days in peace, coming and going at his leisure, mostly just lying against the moss of his favorite tree, putting a line in the water once and letting the day pass him by.

His life had taken a comfortable turn, though the only work he ever did now was carving scrimshaw. His crafted pieces carried ten times their old value, the price partially inflated by the halfling's small degree of fame, but moreso because he had persuaded some connoisseurs who were visiting Bryn Shander that his unique style and cut gave his scrimshaw a special artistic and aesthetic worth.

Regis patted the ruby pendant that rested on his bare chest. It seemed that he could "persuade" almost anyone of almost anything these days.

✕ ✕ ✕ ✕ ✕

The hammer clanged down on the glowing metal. Sparks leaped off the anvil platform in a fiery arc, then died into the dimness of the stone chamber. The heavy hammer swung again and again, guided effortlessly by a huge, muscled arm.

The smith wore only a pair of pants and a leather apron tied about his waist in the small, hot chamber. Black lines of soot had settled in the muscular grooves across his broad shoulders and chest, and he glistened with sweat in the orange glow of the forge. His movements were marked by such rhythmic, tireless ease that they seemed almost preternatural, as though he were the god who had forged the world in the days before mortal man.

An approving grin spread across his face when he felt the rigidity of the iron finally give a bit under the force of his blows. Never before had he felt such strength in the metal; it tested him to the limits of his own resilience, and he felt a shiver as alluring as the thrill of battle when he had at last proven himself the stronger.

"Bruenor will be pleased."

Wulfgar stopped for a moment and considered the implications of his thoughts, smiling in spite of himself as he remembered his first days in the mines of the dwarves. What a stubborn, angry youth he had been then, cheated out of his right to die on the field of honor by a grumbling dwarf who justified unasked-for compassion by labeling it "good business."

This was his fifth and final spring indentured to the dwarves in tunnels that kept his seven-foot frame continually hunched. He longed for the freedom of the open tundra, where he could stretch his arms up high to the warmth of the sun or to the intangible pull of the moon. Or lie flat on his back with his legs unbent, the ceaseless wind tickling him with its chill bite and the crystalline stars filling his mind with mystical visions of unknown horizons.

And yet, for all of their inconveniences, Wulfgar had to admit that he would miss the hot drafts and constant clatter of the dwarven halls. He had clung to the brutal code of his people, which defined capture as disgrace, during the first year of his servitude, reciting the Song of Tempus as a litany of strength against the insinuation of weakness in the company of the soft, civilized southerners.

Yet Bruenor was as solid as the metal he pounded. The dwarf openly professed no love for battle, but he swung his notched axe with deadly accuracy and shrugged off blows that would fell an ogre.

The dwarf had been an enigma to Wulfgar in the early days of their relationship. The young barbarian was compelled to grant Bruenor a degree of respect, for Bruenor had bested him on the field of honor. Even then, with the battlelines firmly defining the two as enemies, Wulfgar had recognized a genuine and deeply rooted affection in the eyes of the dwarf that had confused him. He and his people had come to pillage Ten-Towns, yet Bruenor's underlying attitude seemed more the concern of a stern father than the callous perspective of a slave's master. Wulfgar always remembered his rank in the mines, however, for Bruenor was often gruff and insulting, working Wulfgar at menial, sometimes degrading, tasks.

Wulfgar's anger had dissipated over the long months. He came to accept his penance with stoicism, heeding Bruenor's commands without question or complaint. Gradually, conditions had improved.

Bruenor had taught him to work the forge, and later, to craft the metal into fine weapons and tools. And finally, on a day that Wulfgar would never forget, he had been given his own forge and anvil where he could work in solitude and without supervision—though Bruenor often stuck his head in to grumble over an inexact strike or to spout a few pointers. More than the degree of freedom, though, the small workshop had restored Wulfgar's pride. Since the first time he lifted the smithy hammer he called his own, the methodical stoicism of a servant had been replaced by the eagerness and meticulous devotion of a true craftsman. The barbarian found himself fretting over the smallest burr, sometimes reworking an entire piece to correct a slight imperfection. Wulfgar was pleased about this change in his perspective, viewing it as an attribute that might serve him well in the future, though he didn't as yet understand how.

Bruenor called it "character."

The work paid dividends physically as well. Chopping stone and pounding metal had corded the barbarian's muscles, redefining the gangly frame of his youth into a hardened girth of unrivaled strength. And he possessed great stamina, for the tempo of the tireless dwarves had strengthened his heart and stretched his lungs to new limits.

Wulfgar bit his lip in shame as he vividly remembered his first conscious thought after the Battle of Bryn Shander. He had vowed to pay Bruenor back in blood as soon as he had fulfilled the terms of his indenture. He understood now, to his own amazement, that he had become a better man under the tutelage of Bruenor Battlehammer, and the mere thought of raising a weapon against the dwarf sickened him.

He turned his sudden emotion into motion, slamming his hammer against the iron, flattening its incredibly hard head more and more into the semblance of a blade. This piece would make a fine sword.

Bruenor would be pleased.

10
THE GATHERING GLOOM

Torga the orc faced Grock the goblin with open contempt. Their respective tribes had been warring for many years, as long as any living member of either group could remember. They shared a valley in the Spine of the World and competed for ground and food with the brutality indicative of their warlike races.

And now they stood on common ground with no weapons drawn, compelled to this spot by a force even greater than their hatred for each other. In any other place, at any other time, the tribes could never have been this close without joining in fierce battle. But now, they had to be content with idle threats and dangerous glares, for they had been commanded to put aside their differences.

Torga and Grock turned and walked, side by side, to the structure that held the man who would be their master.

They entered Cryshal-Tirith and stood before Akar Kessell.

☒ ☒ ☒ ☒

Two more tribes had joined his swelling ranks. All about the plateau that harbored his tower were the standards of various bands of goblins: the Goblins of Twisting Spears, Slasher Orcs, the Orcs of the Severed Tongue, and many others, all come to serve the master. Kessell had even pulled in a large clan of ogres, a handful of trolls, and two score rogue verbeeg, the least of the giants but giants nonetheless.

But his crowning achievement was a group of frost giants that had simply wandered in, desiring only to please the wielder of Crenshinibon.

Kessell had been quite content with his life in Cryshal-Tirith, with all of his whims obediently served by the first tribe of goblins that he had encountered. The goblins had even been able to raid a trading caravan and supply the wizard with a few human women for his pleasures. Kessell's life had been soft and easy, just the way that he liked it.

But Crenshinibon was not contented. The relic's hunger for power was insatiable. It would settle for small gains for a short time, and then demand that its wielder move on to greater conquests. It wouldn't openly oppose Kessell, for in their constant war of wills Kessell ultimately held the power of decision. The small crystal shard bridled a reserve of incredible power, but without a wielder, it was akin to a sheathed sword with no hand to draw it. Thus Crenshinibon exerted its will through manipulation, insinuating illusions of conquest into the wizard's dreams, allowing Kessell to view the possibilities of power. It dangled a carrot before the nose of the once-bumbling apprentice that he could not refuse—respect.

Kessell, ever a spit bucket for the pretentious wizards in Luskan—and everyone else, it seemed—was easy prey for such ambitions. He, who had been down in the dirt beside the boots of the important people, ached for the chance to reverse the roles.

And now he had the opportunity to turn his fantasies into reality, Crenshinibon often assured him. With the relic close to his heart, he could become the conqueror; he could make people, even the wizards in the Hosttower, tremble at the mere mention of his name.

He had to remain patient. He had spent several years learning the subtleties of controlling one, and then a second, goblin tribe. Yet the task of bringing together dozens of tribes and bending their natural enmity into a common cause of servitude to him was far more challenging. He had to bring them in, one at a time at first, and ensure that he had enslaved them to his will wholeheartedly before he dared summon another group.

But it was working, and now he had brought in two rival tribes simultaneously with positive results. Torga and Grock had entered Cryshal-Tirith each searching for a way to kill the other without bringing on the wrath of the wizard. When they left, though, after a short discussion with Kessell, they were chatting like old friends about the glory of their coming battles in the army of Akar Kessell.

Kessell lounged back on his pillows and considered his good fortune. His army was indeed taking shape. He had frost giants for his field commanders, ogres as his field guard, verbeeg as a deadly strike force, and trolls, wretched, fear-inspiring trolls, as his personal bodyguard. And by his count thus far, ten thousand fanatically loyal goblin kin troops to carry out his swath of destruction.

"Akar Kessell!" he shouted to the harem girl that manicured his long fingernails as he sat in contemplation, though the girl's mind had long ago been destroyed by Crenshinibon. "All glory to the Tyrant of Icewind Dale!"

⚔ ⚔ ⚔ ⚔ ⚔

Far to the south of the frozen steppes, in the civilized lands where men had more time for leisure activities and contemplation and every action wasn't determined by sheer necessity, wizards and would-be wizards were less rare. The true mages, lifelong students of the arcane arts, practiced their trade with due respect for the magic, ever wary of the potential consequences of their spellcastings.

Unless consumed by the lust for power, which was a very dangerous thing, the true mages tempered their experiments with caution and rarely caused disasters.

The would-be mages, however, men who somehow had come into a degree of magical prowess, whether they had found a scroll or a master's spellbook or some relic, were often the perpetrators of colossal calamities.

Such was the case that night in a land a thousand miles from Akar Kessell and Crenshinibon. A wizard's apprentice, a young man who had shown great promise to his master, came into possession of a diagram of a powerful magic circle, and then sought and found a spell of summoning.

The apprentice, lured by the promise of power, managed to extract the true name of a demon from his master's private notes.

Sorcery, the art of summoning entities from other planes into servitude, was this young man's particular love. His master had allowed him to bring midges and manes through a magical portal—closely supervised—hoping to demonstrate the potential dangers of the practice and reinforce the lessons of caution. Actually, the demonstrations had only served to heighten the young man's appetite for the art. He had begged his master to allow him to try for a true demon, but the wizard knew that he wasn't nearly ready for such a test.

The apprentice disagreed.

He had completed inscribing the circle that same day. So confident was he in his work that he didn't spend an extra day (some wizards would spend a tenday) checking the runes and symbols or bother to test the circle on a lesser entity, such as a mane.

And now he sat within it, his eyes focused on the fire of the brazier that would serve as the gate to the Abyss. With a self-assured, overly proud smile, the would-be sorcerer called the demon.

Errtu, a major demon of catastrophic proportions, faintly heard its name being uttered on the faraway plane. Normally, the great beast would have ignored such a weak call; certainly the summoner hadn't demonstrated any ability of sufficient strength to compel the demon to comply.

Yet Errtu was glad of the fateful call. A few years before, the demon had felt a surge of power on the material plane that it believed would culminate a quest it had undertaken a millennium ago. The demon had suffered through the last few years impatiently, eager for a wizard to open a path for it so that it could come to the material plane and investigate.

The young apprentice felt himself being drawn into the hypnotic dance of the brazier's fire. The blaze had unified into a single flame, like the burn of a candle only many times larger, and it swayed tantalizingly, back and forth, back and forth.

The mesmerized apprentice wasn't even aware of the growing intensity of the fire. The flame leaped higher and higher, its flickering sped up, and its color moved through the spectrum toward the ultimate heat of whiteness.

Back and forth. Back and forth.

Faster, now, wagging wildly and building its strength to support the mighty entity that waited on the other side.

Back and forth. Back and forth.

The apprentice was sweating. He knew that the power of the spell was growing beyond his bounds, that the magic had taken over and was living a life of its own. That he was powerless to stop it.

Back and forth. Back and forth.

Now he saw the dark shadow within the flame, the great clawed hands, and the leathery, batlike wings. And the size of the beast! A giant even by the standards of its kind.

"Errtu!" the young man called, the words forced from him by the demands of the spell. The name hadn't been completely identified in his master's notes, but he saw clearly that it belonged to a mighty demon, a monster ranking just below the demon lords in the hierarchy of the Abyss.

Back and forth. Back and forth.

Now the grotesque, monkeylike head, with the maw and muzzle of a dog and the oversized incisors of a boar, was visible, the huge, blood-red eyes squinting from within the brazier's flame. The acidic drool sizzled as it fell to the fire.

Back and forth. Back and forth.

The fire surged into a final climax of power, and Errtu stepped through. The demon didn't pause at all to consider the terrified young human that had foolishly called its name. It began a slow stalk around the magic circle in search of clues to the extent of this wizard's power.

The apprentice finally managed to steady himself. He had summoned a major demon! That fact helped him to reestablish his confidence in his abilities as a sorcerer. "Stand before me!" he commanded, aware that a firm hand was necessary to control a creature from the chaotic lower planes.

Errtu, undisturbed, continued its stalk.

The apprentice grew angry. "You will obey me!" he screamed. "I brought you here, and I hold the key to your torment! You shall obey my command and then I shall release you, mercifully, back to your own filthy world! Now, stand before me!"

The apprentice was defiant. The apprentice was proud.

But Errtu had found an error in the tracing of a rune, a fatal imperfection in a magic circle that could not afford to be almost perfect.

The apprentice was dead.

× × × × ×

Errtu felt the familiar sensation of power more distinctly on the material plane and had little trouble discerning the direction of the emanations. It soared on its great wings over the cities of the humans, spreading a panic wherever it was noticed, but not delaying its journey to savor the erupting chaos below.

Arrow-straight and with all speed Errtu soared, over lakes and mountains, across great expanses of empty land. Toward the northernmost range in the Realms, the Spine of the World, and the ancient relic that it had spent centuries searching for.

× × × × ×

Kessell was aware of the approaching demon long before his assembled troops began scattering in terror from under the swooping shadow of darkness. Crenshinibon had imparted the information to the wizard, the living relic anticipating the movements of the powerful creature from the lower planes that had been pursuing it for ages uncounted.

Kessell wasn't worried, though. Inside his tower of strength he was confident that he could handle even a nemesis as mighty as Errtu. And he had a distinct advantage over the demon. He was the rightful wielder of the relic. It was attuned to him, and like so many other magical artifacts from the dawn of the world, Crenshinibon could not be wrested from its possessor by sheer force. Errtu desired to wield the relic and therefore, would not dare to oppose Kessell and invoke Crenshinibon's wrath.

Acid drool slipped freely from the demon's mouth when it saw the tower image of the relic. "How many years?" it bellowed victoriously. Errtu saw the tower's door clearly, for the demon was a creature not of the material plane, and approached at once. None of Kessell's goblins, or even giants, stood to hinder the demon's entrance.

Flanked by his trolls, the wizard was waiting for Errtu in Cryshal-Tirith's main chamber, the tower's first level. The wizard understood that the trolls would be of little use against a fire-wielding demon, but he wanted them present to enhance the demon's first impression of him. He knew that he held the power to send Errtu away easily enough, but another thought, again implanted through a suggestion of the Crystal Shard, had come to him.

The demon could be very useful.

Errtu pulled up short when it passed through the narrow entryway and came upon the wizard's entourage. Because of the remote location of the tower, the demon had expected to find an orc, or perhaps a giant, holding the shard. It had hoped to intimidate and trick the slow-witted wielder into surrendering the relic, but the sight of a robed human, probably even a mage, threw a snag into its plans.

"Greetings, mighty demon," Kessell said politely, bowing low. "Welcome to my humble home."

Errtu growled in rage and started forward, forgetting the drawbacks of destroying the possessor in its all-consuming hatred and envy for the smug human.

Crenshinibon reminded the demon.

A sudden flare of light pulsed from the tower walls, engulfing Errtu in the painful brightness of a dozen desert suns. The demon halted and covered its sensitive eyes. The light dissipated soon enough, but Errtu held its ground and did not approach the wizard again.

Kessell smirked. The relic had supported him. Brimming with confidence, he addressed the demon again, this time a stern edge in his voice. "You have come to take this," he said, reaching within the folds of his robe to produce the shard. Errtu's eyes narrowed and locked onto the object it had pursued for so long.

"You cannot have it," Kessell said flatly, and he replaced it under his robe. "It is mine, rightfully found, and you have no claim over it that it would honor!" Kessell's foolish pride, the fatal flaw in his personality that had always pushed him down a road of certain tragedy, wanted him to continue his taunting of the demon in its helpless situation.

"Enough," warned a sensation within him, the silent voice he had come to suspect was the sentient will of the shard.

"This is none of your affair," Kessell shot back aloud. Errtu looked around the room, wondering who the wizard was addressing. Certainly the trolls had paid him no heed. As a precaution, the demon invoked various detection spells, fearing an unseen assailant.

"You taunt a dangerous foe," the shard persisted. "I have protected you from the demon, yet you persist in alienating a creature that would prove a valuable ally!"

As was usually the case when Crenshinibon communicated with the wizard, Kessell began to see the possibilities. He decided upon a course of compromise, an agreement mutually beneficial to both himself and the demon.

Errtu considered its predicament. It couldn't slay the impertinent human, though the demon would have truly savored such an act. Yet leaving without the relic, putting off the quest that had been its primary motivation for centuries, was not an acceptable option.

"I have a proposal to offer, a bargain that might interest you," Kessell said temptingly, avoiding the death-promising glare that the demon was throwing him. "Stay by my side and serve as commander of my forces! With you leading them and the power of Crenshinibon and Akar Kessell behind them, they shall sweep through the northland!"

"Serve you?" Errtu laughed. "You have no hold over me, human."

"You view the situation incorrectly," retorted Kessell. "Think of it not as servitude but as an opportunity to join in a campaign that promises destruction and conquest! You have my utmost respect, mighty demon. I would not presume to call myself your master."

Crenshinibon, with its subconscious intrusions, had coached Kessell well. Errtu's less-threatening stance showed that it was intrigued by the wizard's proposition.

"And consider the gains that you shall someday make," Kessell continued. "Humans do not live a very long time by your ageless estimations. Who, then, shall take the Crystal Shard when Akar Kessell is no more?"

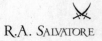
Errtu smiled wickedly and bowed before the wizard. "How could I refuse such a generous offer?" the demon rasped in its horrible, unearthly voice. "Show me, wizard, what glorious conquests lie in our path."

Kessell nearly danced with joy. His army was, in effect, complete.

He had his general.

II

AEGIS-FANG

Sweat beaded on Bruenor's hand as he put the key into the dusty lock of the heavy wooden door. This was the beginning of the process that would put all of his skill and experience to the ultimate trial. Like all master dwarven smiths, he had been waiting for this moment with excitement and apprehension since the beginning of his long training.

He had to push hard to swing the door in on the small chamber. Its wood creaked and groaned in protest, having warped and settled since it was last opened many years before. This was a comfort to Bruenor, though, for he dreaded the thought of anyone looking in on his most prized possessions. He glanced around at the dark corridors of this little-used section of the dwarven complex, making sure once more that he hadn't been followed, then he entered the room, putting his torch in before him to burn away the hanging fringes of many cobwebs.

The only piece of furniture in the room was a wooden, iron-bound box, banded by two heavy chains joined by a huge padlock. Spiderwebs criss-crossed and flowed from every angle of the chest, and a thick layer of dust covered its top. Another good sign, Bruenor noted. He looked out into the hall again, then shut the wooden door as quietly as he could.

He knelt before the chest and placed his torch on the floor beside him. Several webs, licked by its flame, puffed into orange for just an instant, then died away. Bruenor took a small block of wood from his belt pouch and removed a silver key that hung on a chain about his neck. He held the wood block firmly in front of him and keeping the fingers of his other hand below the level of the padlock as much as possible, gently slid the key into the lock.

Now came the delicate part. Bruenor turned the key slowly, listening. When he heard the tumbler in the lock click, he braced himself and quickly pulled his hand from the key, allowing the mass of the padlock to drop away from its ring, releasing a spring-loaded lever that had been pressed between it and the chest. The small dart knocked into the block of wood, and Bruenor breathed a sigh of relief. Though he had set the trap nearly a century before, he knew that the poison of the Tundra Widowmaker snake had kept its deadly sting.

Sheer excitement overwhelmed Bruenor's reverence of this moment, and he hurriedly threw the chains back over the chest and blew the dust from its lid. He grasped the lid and started to lift it but suddenly slowed again, recovering his solemn calm and reminding himself of the importance of every action.

Anyone who had come upon this chest and managed to get by the deadly trap would have been pleased with the treasures he found inside. A silver goblet, a bag of gold, and a jeweled though poorly balanced dagger were mixed in among other more personal and less valuable items: a dented helm, old boots, and other similar pieces that would hold little appeal for a thief.

Yet these items were merely a foil. Bruenor pulled them out and dropped them on the dirty floor without a second thought.

The bottom of the heavy chest sat just above the level of the floor, giving no indication that anything more was to be found here. But Bruenor had cunningly cut the floor lower under the chest, fitting the box into the hole so perfectly that even a scrutinizing thief would swear that it sat on the floor. The dwarf poked out a small knothole in the box's bottom and hooked a stubby finger through the opening. This wood, too, had settled over the years, and Bruenor had to tug mightily to finally pull it free. It came out with a sudden snap, sending Bruenor tumbling backward. He was back at the chest in an instant, peering cautiously over its edge at his greatest treasures.

A block of the purest mithral, a small leather bag, a golden coffer, and a silver scroll tube capped on one end by a diamond were spaced exactly as Bruenor had lain them so long ago.

Bruenor's hands trembled, and he had to stop and wipe the perspiration from them several times as he removed the precious items from the chest, placing those that would fit in his pack and laying the mithral block on a blanket he had unrolled. Then he quickly replaced the false bottom, taking care to fit the knothole back into the wood perfectly, and put his phony treasure back in place. He chained and locked the box, leaving everything exactly as he had found it, except that he saw no reason to chance accidents by rearming the needle trap.

⚔ ⚔ ⚔ ⚔ ⚔

Bruenor had constructed his outdoor forge in a hidden nook tucked away at the base of Kelvin's Cairn. This was a seldom-traveled portion of the dwarven valley, the northern end, with Bremen's Run widening out into the open tundra around the western side of the mountain, and Icewind Pass doing likewise on the east. To his surprise, Bruenor found that the stone here was hard and pure, deeply imbued with the strength of the earth, and would serve his small temple well.

As always, Bruenor approached this sacred place with measured, reverent steps. Carrying now the treasures of his heritage, his mind drifted back over the centuries to Mithral Hall, ancient home of his people, and to the speech his father had given him on the day he received his first smithy hammer.

"If yer talent for the craft is keen," his father had said, "and ye're lucky enough to live long and feel the strength of the earth, ye'll find a special day. A special blessin'—some would say a curse—has been placed upon our people, for once, and only once, the very best of our smiths may craft a weapon of their choosing that outdoes any work they'd ever done. Be wary of that day, son, for ye'll put a great deal of yerself into that weapon.

Ye'll never match its perfection in yer life again and knowing this, ye'll lose a lot of the craftsman's desire that drives the swing of yer hammer. Ye may find an empty life after yer day, but if yer good as yer line says ye'll be, ye'll have crafted a weapon of legend that will live on long after yer bones are dust."

Bruenor's father, cut down in the coming of the darkness to Mithral Hall, hadn't lived long enough to find his special day, though if he had, several of the items that Bruenor now carried would have been used by him. But the dwarf saw no disrespect in his taking the treasures as his own, for he knew that he would craft a weapon to make the spirit of his father proud.

Bruenor's day had come.

‖ ‖ ‖ ‖ ‖

The image of a two-headed hammer hidden within the block of mithral had come to Bruenor in a dream earlier that tenday. The dwarf had understood the sign at once and knew that he would have to move quickly to get everything ready for the night of power that was fast approaching. Already the moon was big and bright in the sky. It would reach its fullness on the night of the solstice, the gray time between the seasons when the air tingled with magic. The full moon would only enhance the enchantment of that night, and Bruenor believed that he would capture a mighty spell indeed when he uttered the dweomer of power.

The dwarf had much work before him if he was to be prepared. His labor had begun with the construction of the small forge. That had been the easy part and he went about it mechanically, trying to hold his thoughts to the task at hand and away from the disrupting anticipation of crafting the weapon.

Now the time he had waited for was upon him. He pulled the heavy block of mithral from his pack, feeling its pureness and strength. He had held similar blocks before and grew apprehensive for a moment. He stared into the silvery metal.

For a long moment, it remained a squared block. Then its sides appeared to round as the image of the marvelous warhammer came clear to the dwarf. Bruenor's heart raced, and he breathed in short gasps.

His vision had been real.

He fired up the forge and began his work at once, laboring through the night until the light of dawn dispelled the charm that was upon him. He returned to his home that day only to collect the adamantite rod he had set aside for the weapon, returning to the forge to sleep and later to pace nervously while he waited for darkness to fall.

As soon as daylight faded, Bruenor eagerly went back to work. The metal molded easily under his skilled manipulations, and he knew that before the dawn could interrupt him, the head of the hammer would be formed. Though he still had hours of work ahead of him, Bruenor felt a surge of pride at that moment. He knew that he would meet his demanding schedule. He would attach the adamantite handle the next night, and all would be ready for the enchantment under the full moon on the night of the summer solstice.

⚔ ⚔ ⚔ ⚔

The owl swooped silently down on the small rabbit, guided toward its prey by senses as acute as any living creature's. This would be a routine kill, with the unfortunate beast never even aware of the coming predator. Yet the owl was strangely agitated, and its hunter's concentration wavered at the last moment. Seldom did the great bird miss, but this time it flew back to its home on the side of Kelvin's Cairn without a meal.

Far out on the tundra, a lone wolf sat as still as a statue, anxious but patient as the silver disk of the huge summer moon broke the flat rim of the horizon. It waited until the alluring orb came full in the sky, then it took up the ancient howling cry of its breed. It was answered, again and again, by distant wolves and other denizens of the night, all calling out to the power of the heavens.

The night of the summer solstice, when magic tingled in the air, exciting all but the rational beings who had rejected such base instinctual urges, had begun.

In his emotional state, Bruenor felt the magic distinctly. But absorbed in the culmination of his life's labors, he had attained a level of calm concentration. His hands did not tremble as he opened the golden lid of the small coffer.

The mighty warhammer lay clamped to the anvil before the dwarf. It represented Bruenor's finest work, powerful and beautifully crafted even now, but waiting for the delicate runes and intonations that would make it a weapon of special power.

Bruenor reverently removed the small silver mallet and chisel from the coffer and approached the warhammer. Without hesitation, for he knew that he had little time for such intricate work, he set the chisel on the mithral and solidly tapped it with the mallet. The untainted metals sang out a clear, pure note that sent shivers through the appreciative dwarf's spine. He knew in his heart that all of the conditions were perfect, and he shivered again when he thought of the result of this night's labors.

He did not see the dark eyes peering intently at him from a ridge a short distance away.

Bruenor needed no model for the first carvings; they were symbols etched into his heart and soul. Solemnly, he inscribed the hammer and anvil of Moradin the Soulforger on the side of one of the warhammer's heads, and the crossed axes of Clangeddin, the dwarven God of Battle, across from the first on the side of the other head. Then he took the silver scroll tube and gently removed its diamond cap. He sighed in relief when he saw that the parchment inside had survived the decades. Wiping the oily sweat from his hands, he removed the scroll and slowly unrolled it, laying it on the flat of the anvil. At first, the page seemed blank, but gradually the rays of the full moon coaxed its symbols, the secret runes of power, to appear.

These were Bruenor's heritage, and though he had never seen them before, their arcane lines and curves seemed comfortably familiar to him. His hand steady with confidence, the dwarf placed the silver chisel between the symbols he had inscribed of the two gods and began etching the secret runes onto the warhammer. He felt their magic transferring from the parchment through him to the weapon and watched in amazement as each one disappeared from the scroll after he had inscribed it onto the mithral.

Time had no meaning to him now as he fell deeply into the trance of his work, but when he had completed the runes, he noticed that the moon had passed its peak and was on the wane.

The first real test of the dwarf's expertise came when he overlaid the rune carvings with the gem inside the mountain symbol of Dumathoin, the Keeper of Secrets. The lines of the god's symbol aligned perfectly with those of the runes, obscuring the secret tracings of power.

Bruenor knew then that his work was nearly complete. He removed the heavy warhammer from its clamp and took out the small leather bag. He had to take several deep breaths to steady himself, for this was the final and most decisive test of his skill. He loosened the cord at the top of the bag and marveled at the gentle shimmering of the diamond dust in the soft light of the moon.

From behind the ridge, Drizzt Do'Urden tensed in anticipation, but he was careful not to disturb his friend's complete concentration.

Bruenor steadied himself again, then suddenly snapped the bag into the air, releasing its contents high into the night. He tossed the bag aside, grasped the warhammer in both hands, and raised it above his head. The dwarf felt his very strength being sucked from him as he uttered the words of power, but he would not truly know how well he had performed until his work was complete. The level of perfection of his carvings determined the success of his intonations, for as he had etched the runes onto the weapon, their strength had flowed into his heart. This power then drew the magical dust to the weapon and its power, in turn, could be measured by the amount of shimmering diamond dust it captured.

A fit of blackness fell over the dwarf. His head spun, and he did not understand what kept him from toppling. But the consuming power of the words had gone beyond him. Though he wasn't even conscious of them, the words continued to flow from his lips in an undeniable stream, sapping more and more of his strength. Then, mercifully, he was falling, though the void of unconsciousness took him long before his head hit the ground.

Drizzt turned away and slumped back against the rocky ridge; he, too, was exhausted from the spectacle. He didn't know if his friend would survive this night's ordeal, yet he was thrilled for Bruenor. For he had witnessed the dwarf's most triumphant moment, even if Bruenor had not, as the hammer's mithral head flared with the life of magic and pulled in the shower of diamond.

And not a single speck of the glittering dust had escaped Bruenor's beckon.

12

THE GIFT

Wulfgar sat high up on the northern face of Bruenor's Climb, his eyes trained on the expanse of the rocky valley below, intently seeking any movement that might indicate the dwarf's return. The barbarian came to this spot often to be alone with his thoughts and the mourn of the wind. Directly before him, across the dwarven vale, were Kelvin's Cairn and the northern section of Lac Dinneshere. Between them lay the flat stretch of ground known as Icewind Pass that led to the northeast and the open plain.

And for the barbarian, the pass that led to his homeland.

Bruenor had explained that he would be gone for a few days, and at first Wulfgar was happy for the relief from the dwarf's constant grumbling and criticism. But he found his relief short-lived.

"Worried for him, are you?" came a voice behind him. He didn't have to turn to know that it was Catti-brie.

He left the question unanswered, figuring that she had asked it rhetorically anyway and would not believe him if he denied it.

"He'll be back," Catti-brie said with a shrug in her voice. "Bruenor's as hard as mountain stone, and there is nothing on the tundra that can stop him."

Now the young barbarian did turn to consider the girl. Long ago, when a comfortable level of trust had been reached between Bruenor and Wulfgar, the dwarf had introduced the young barbarian to his "daughter," a human girl the barbarian's own age.

She was an outwardly calm girl, but packed with an inner fire and spirit that Wulfgar had been unaccustomed to in a woman. Barbarian girls were raised to keep their thoughts and opinions, unimportant by the standards of men, to themselves. Like her mentor, Catti-brie said exactly what was on her mind and left little doubt as to how she felt about a situation. The verbal sparring between her and Wulfgar was nearly constant and often heated, but still, Wulfgar was glad to have a companion his own age, someone who didn't look down at him from a pedestal of experience.

Catti-brie had helped him through the difficult first year of his indenture, treating him with respect (although she rarely agreed with him) when he had none for himself. Wulfgar even had the feeling that she had something indirectly to do with Bruenor's decision to take Wulfgar under his tutorship.

She was his own age, but in many ways Catti-brie seemed much older, with a solid inner sense of reality that kept her temperament on an even level. In other ways, however, such as the skipping spring in her step, Catti-brie would forever be a child. This unusual balance of spirit and calm, of serenity and unbridled joy, intrigued Wulfgar and kept him off-balance whenever he spoke with the girl.

Of course, there were other emotions that put Wulfgar at a disadvantage when he was with Catti-brie. Undeniably, she was beautiful, with thick waves of rich, auburn hair rolling down over her shoulders and the darkest blue, penetrating eyes that would make any suitor blush under their knowing scrutiny. Still, there was something beyond any physical attraction that interested Wulfgar. Catti-brie was beyond his experience, a young woman who did not fit the role as it had been defined to him on the tundra. He wasn't sure if he liked this independence or not. But he found himself unable to deny the attraction that he felt for her.

"You come up here often, do you not?" Catti-brie asked. "What is it you look for?"

Wulfgar shrugged, not fully knowing the answer himself.

"Your home?"

"That, and other things that a woman would not understand."

Catti-brie smiled away the unintentional insult. "'Tell me, then," she pressed, hints of sarcasm edging her tone. "Maybe my ignorance will bring a new perspective to these problems." She hopped down the rock to circle the barbarian and take a seat on the ledge beside him.

Wulfgar marveled at her graceful movements. Like the polarity of her curious emotional blend, Catti-brie also proved an enigma physically. She was tall and slender, delicate by all appearances, but growing into womanhood in the caverns of the dwarves, she was accustomed to hard and heavy work.

"Of adventures and an unfulfilled vow," Wulfgar said mysteriously, perhaps to impress the young girl, but moreso to reinforce his own opinion about what a woman should and should not care about.

"A vow you mean to fulfill," Catti-brie reasoned, "as soon as you're given the chance."

Wulfgar nodded solemnly. "It is my heritage, a burden passed on to me when my father was killed. The day will come . . ." He let his voice trail away, and he looked back longingly to the emptiness of the open tundra beyond Kelvin's Cairn.

Catti-brie shook her head, the auburn locks bouncing across her shoulders. She saw beyond Wulfgar's mysterious facade enough to understand that he meant to undertake a very dangerous, probably suicidal, mission in the name of honor. "What drives you, I cannot tell. Luck to you on your adventure, but if you're taking it for no better reason than you have named, you're wasting your life."

"What could a woman know of honor?" Wulfgar shot back angrily.

But Catti-brie was not intimidated and did not back down. "What indeed?" she echoed. "Do you think that you hold it all in your oversized hands for no better reason than what you hold in your pants?"

Wulfgar blushed a deep red and turned away, unable to come to terms with such nerve in a woman.

"Besides," Catti-brie continued, "you can say what you want about why you have come up here this day. I know that you're worried about Bruenor, I'll hear no denying."

"You know only what you desire to know!"

"You are a lot like him," Catti-brie said abruptly, shifting the subject and disregarding Wulfgar's comments. "More akin to the dwarf than you'd ever admit." She laughed. "Both stubborn, both proud, and neither about to admit an honest feeling for the other. Have it your own way, then, Wulfgar of Icewind Dale. To me you can lie, but to yourself . . . there's a different tale!" She hopped from her perch and skipped down the rocks toward the dwarven caverns.

Wulfgar watched her go, admiring the sway of her slender hips and the graceful dance of her step, despite the anger that he felt. He didn't stop to think of why he was so mad at Catti-brie.

He knew that if he did, he would find, as usual, that he was angry because her observations hit the mark.

⚔ ⚔ ⚔ ⚔

Drizzt Do'Urden kept a stoic vigil over his unconscious friend for two long days. Worried as he was about Bruenor and curious about the wondrous warhammer, the drow remained a respectful distance from the secret forge.

Finally, as morning dawned on the third day, Bruenor stirred and stretched. Drizzt silently padded away, moving down the path he knew the dwarf would take. Finding an appropriate clearing, he hastily set up a small campsite.

The sunlight came to Bruenor as only a blur at first, and it took him several minutes to reorient himself to his surroundings. Then his returning vision focused on the shining glory of the warhammer.

Quickly, he glanced around him, looking for signs of the fallen dust. He found none, and his anticipation heightened. He was trembling once again as he lifted the magnificent weapon, turning it over in his hands, feeling its perfect balance and incredible strength. Bruenor's breath flew away when he saw the symbols of the three gods on the mithral, diamond dust magically fused into their deeply etched lines. Entranced by the apparent perfection of his work, Bruenor understood the emptiness his father had spoken of. He knew that he would never duplicate this level of his craft, and he wondered if, knowing this, he would ever be able to lift his smithy hammer again.

Trying to sort through his mixed emotions, the dwarf put the silver mallet and chisel back into their golden coffer and replaced the scroll in its tube, though the parchment was blank and the magical runes would never reappear. He realized that he hadn't eaten in several days, and his strength hadn't fully recovered from the drain of the magic. He collected as many things as he could carry, hoisted the huge warhammer over his shoulder, and trudged off toward his home.

The sweet scent of roasting coney greeted him as he came upon Drizzt Do'Urden's camp.

"So, yer back from yer travels," he called in greeting to his friend.

Drizzt locked his eyes onto the dwarf's, not wanting to give away his overwhelming curiosity for the warhammer. "At your request, good dwarf," he said, bowing low. "Surely you had enough people looking for me to expect that I'd return."

Bruenor conceded the point, though for the present he only offered absently, "I needed ye," as an explanation. A more pressing need had come over him at the sight of the cooking meat.

Drizzt smiled knowingly. He had already eaten and had caught and cooked this coney especially for Bruenor. "Join me?" he asked.

Before he had even finished the offer, Bruenor was eagerly reaching for the rabbit. He stopped suddenly, though, and turned a suspicious eye upon the drow.

"How long have ye been in?" the dwarf asked nervously.

"Just arrived this morning," Drizzt lied, respecting the privacy of the dwarf's special ceremony. Bruenor smirked at the answer and tore into the coney as Drizzt set another on the spit.

The drow waited until Bruenor was engrossed with his meal, then quickly snatched up the warhammer. By the time Bruenor could react, Drizzt had already lifted the weapon.

"Too big for a dwarf," Drizzt remarked casually. "And too heavy for my slender arms." He looked at Bruenor, who stood with his forearms crossed and his foot stamping impatiently. "Who then?"

"Ye've a talent for puttin' yer nose where it don't belong, elf," the dwarf answered gruffly.

Drizzt laughed in response. "The boy, Wulfgar?" he asked in mock disbelief. He knew well that the dwarf harbored strong feelings for the young barbarian, though he also realized that Bruenor would never openly admit it. "A fine weapon to be giving a barbarian. Did you craft it yourself?"

Despite his chiding, Drizzt was truly awe-stricken by Bruenor's workmanship. Though the hammer was far too heavy for him to wield, he could clearly feel its incredible balance.

"Just an old hammer, that's all," Bruenor mumbled. "The boy lost 'is club; I couldn't well turn 'im loose in this wild place without a weapon!"

"And its name?"

"Aegis-fang," Bruenor replied without thinking, the name flowing from him before he even had time to consider it. He didn't remember the incident, but the dwarf had determined the name of the weapon when he had enchanted it as part of the magical intonations of the ceremony.

"I understand," Drizzt said, handing the hammer back to Bruenor. "An old hammer, but good enough for the boy. Mithral, adamantite, and diamond will simply have to do."

"Aw, shut yer mouth," snapped Bruenor, his face flushed red with embarrassment. Drizzt bowed low in apology.

"Why did you request my presence, friend?" the drow asked, changing the subject.

Bruenor cleared his throat. "The boy," he grumbled softly. Drizzt saw the uncomfortable lump well in Bruenor's throat and buried his next taunt before he spoke it.

"He comes free afore winter," continued Bruenor, "an' he's not rightly trained. Stronger than any man I've ever seen and moves with the grace of a fleeing deer, but he's green to the ways o' battle."

"You want me to train him?" Drizzt asked incredulously.

"Well, I can't do it!" Bruenor snapped suddenly. "He's seven foot and wouldn't be takin' well to the low cuts of a dwarf!"

The drow eyed his frustrated companion curiously. Like everyone else who was close to Bruenor, he knew that a bond had grown between the dwarf and the young barbarian, but he hadn't guessed just how deep it ran.

"I didn't take 'im under me eye for five years just to let him get cut down by a stinkin' tundra yeti!" Bruenor blurted, impatient with the drow's hesitance, and nervous that his friend had guessed more than he should. "Will ye do it, then?"

Drizzt smiled again, but there was no teasing in it this time. He remembered his own battle with tundra yetis nearly five years before. Bruenor had saved his life that day, and it hadn't been the first and wouldn't be the last time that he had fallen into the dwarf's debt. "The gods know that I owe you more than that, my friend. Of course I'll train him."

Bruenor grunted and grabbed the next coney.

⚔ ⚔ ⚔ ⚔ ⚔

The ring of Wulfgar's pounding echoed through the dwarven halls. Angered by the revelations he had been forced to see in his discussion with Catti-brie, he had returned to his work with fervor.

"Stop yer hammerin', boy," came a gruff voice behind him. Wulfgar spun on his heel. He had been so engrossed in his work that he hadn't heard Bruenor enter. An involuntary smile of relief widened across his face. But he caught the show of weakness quickly and repainted a stern mask.

Bruenor regarded the young barbarian's great height and girth and the scraggly beginnings of a blond beard upon the golden skin of his face. "I can't rightly be callin' ye 'boy' anymore," the dwarf conceded.

"You have the right to call me whatever you wish," retorted Wulfgar. "I am your slave."

"Ye've a spirit as wild as the tundra," Bruenor said, smiling. "Ye've ne'er been, nor will ye ever be, a slave to any dwarf or man!"

Wulfgar was caught off guard by the dwarf's uncharacteristic compliment. He tried to reply but could find no words.

"Never have I seen ye as a slave, boy," Bruenor continued. "Ye served me to pay for the crimes of yer people, and I taught ye much in return. Now put yer hammer away." He paused for a moment to consider Wulfgar's fine workmanship.

"Yer a good smith, with a good feel for the stone, but ye don't belong in a dwarf's cave. It's time ye felt the sun on yer face again."

"Freedom?" Wulfgar whispered.

"Get the notion outta yer head!" Bruenor snapped. He pointed a stubby finger at the barbarian and growled threateningly. "Yer mine 'til the last days of fall, don't ye forget that!"

Wulfgar had to bite his lip to stem a laugh. As always, the dwarf's awkward combination of compassion and borderline rage had confused him and kept him off balance. It no longer came as a shock, though. Four years at Bruenor's side had taught him to expect—and disregard—the sudden outbursts of gruffness.

"Finish up whatever ye got here to do," Bruenor instructed. "I take ye out to meet yer teacher tomorrow morning, and by yer vow, ye'll heed to him as ye would to me!"

Wulfgar grimaced at the thought of servitude to yet another, but he had accepted his indenture to Bruenor unconditionally for a period of five years and a day, and he would not dishonor himself by going back on his oath. He nodded his consent.

"I won't be seein' much more o' ye," Bruenor continued, "so I'll have yer oath now that ye'll never again raise a weapon against the people o' Ten-Towns."

Wulfgar set himself firmly. "That you may not have," he replied boldly. "When I have fulfilled the terms you set before me, I shall leave here a man of free will!"

"Fair enough," Bruenor conceded, Wulfgar's stubborn pride actually enhancing the dwarf's respect for him. He paused for a moment to look over the proud young warrior and found himself pleased at his own part in Wulfgar's growth.

"Ye broke that stinkin' pole o' yers on me head," Bruenor began tentatively. He cleared his throat. This final order of business made the tough dwarf uncomfortable. He wasn't quite sure of how he could get through it without appearing sentimental and foolish. "Winter'll be fast upon ye after yer term to me is ended. I can't rightly send ye out into the wild without a weapon." He reached back into the hallway quickly and grabbed the warhammer.

"Aegis-fang," he said gruffly as he tossed it to Wulfgar. "I'll place no bonds on yer will, but I'll have yer oath, for me own good conscience, that ye'll never raise this weapon against the people o' Ten-Towns!

As soon as his hands closed around the adamantite handle, Wulfgar sensed the worth of the magical warhammer. The diamond-filled runes caught the glow of the forge and sent a myriad of reflections dancing about the room. The barbarians of Wulfgar's tribe had always prided themselves on the fine weapons they kept, even measuring the worth of a man by the quality of his spear or sword, but Wulfgar had never seen anything to match the exquisite detail and sheer strength of Aegis-fang. It balanced so well in his huge hands and its height and weight fit him so perfectly that he felt as if he had been born to wield this weapon. He told himself at once that he would pray for many nights to the gods of fate for delivering this prize unto him. Certainly they deserved his thanks.

As did Bruenor.

"You have my word," Wulfgar stammered, so overcome by the magnificent gift that he could hardly speak. He steadied himself so that he could say more, but by the time he was able to pull his gaze from the magnificent hammer, Bruenor was gone.

The dwarf stomped through the long corridors toward his private chambers, mumbling curses at his weakness, and hoping that none of his kin came upon him. With a cautious look around, he wiped the moisture from his gray eyes.

13

As the Wielder Bids

"Gather together your people and go, Biggrin," the wizard told the enormous frost giant that stood before him in Cryshal-Tirith's throne room. "Remember that you represent the army of Akar Kessell. You are the first group to go into the area, and secrecy is the key to our victory! Do not fail me! I shall be watching over your every move."

"We'll not fail ye, master," the giant responded. "The lair'll be set and readied for your coming!"

"I have faith in you," Kessell assured the huge commander. "Now be off."

The frost giant lifted the blanketed mirror that Kessell had given it, gave one final bow to its master, and walked out of the room.

"You should not have sent them," hissed Errtu, who had been standing invisibly beside the throne during the conversation. "The verbeeg and their frost giant leader will be easy to mark in a community of humans and dwarves."

"Biggrin is a wise leader," Kessell shot back, angered at the demon's impertinence. "The giant is cunning enough to keep troops out of sight!"

"Yet the humans would have been better suited for this mission, as Crenshinibon has shown you."

"I am the leader!" screamed Kessell. He pulled the Crystal Shard out from under his robes and waved it menacingly at Errtu, leaning forward in an attempt to emphasize the threat. "Crenshinibon advises, but I decide! Do not forget your place, mighty demon. I am the wielder of the shard, and I shall not tolerate your questioning my every move."

Errtu's blood-red eyes narrowed dangerously, and Kessell straightened back in his throne, suddenly reconsidering the wisdom of threatening the demon. But Errtu calmed quickly, accepting the minor inconveniences of Kessell's foolish outbursts for the long-term gains it stood to make.

"Crenshinibon has existed since the dawn of the world," the demon rasped, making one final point. "It has orchestrated a thousand campaigns much grander than the one you are about to undertake. Perhaps you would be wise to give more credence to its advice."

Kessell twitched nervously. The shard had indeed counseled him to use the humans he would soon command in the first excursion into the region. He had been able to create a dozen excuses to validate his choice of sending the giants, but in truth, he had sent Biggrin's people more to illustrate his undeniable command to himself, to the shard, and to the impertinent demon, than for any possible military gains.

"I shall follow Crenshinibon's advice when I deem it appropriate," he told Errtu. He pulled a second crystal, an exact duplicate of Crenshinibon and the crystal he had used to raise this tower, out from one of the many pockets of his robe. "Take this to the appropriate spot and perform the ceremony of raising," he instructed. "I shall join you through a mirror door when all is ready."

"You wish to raise a second Cryshal-Tirith while the first still stands?" Errtu balked. "The drain on the relic shall be enormous!"

"Silence!" Kessell ordered, trembling visibly, "Go and perform the ceremony! Let the shard remain my concern!"

Errtu took the replica of the relic and bowed low. Without a further word, the demon stalked out of the room. It understood that Kessell was foolishly demonstrating his control over the shard at the expense of proper restraint and wise military tactics. The wizard did not have the capacity or the experience to orchestrate this campaign, yet the shard continued to back him.

Errtu had made a secret offer to it to dispose of Kessell and take over as wielder. But Crenshinibon had refused the demon. It preferred the demonstrations that Kessell demanded of it to appease his own insecurities over the constant struggle of control it would face against the powerful demon.

⚔ ⚔ ⚔ ⚔

Though he walked among giants and trolls, the proud barbarian king's stature was not diminished. He strode defiantly through the iron door of the black tower and pushed through the wretched troll guards with a threatening growl. He hated this place of sorcery and had decided to ignore the calling when the singular spinet of the tower appeared on the horizon like an icy finger risen from the flat ground. Yet in the end he could not resist the summons of the master of Cryshal-Tirith.

Heafstaag hated the wizard. By all measures of a tribesman Akar Kessell was weak, using tricks and demonic callings to do the work of muscle. And Heafstaag hated him even more because he could not refute the power that the wizard commanded.

The barbarian king threw aside the dangling, beaded strands that sectioned off Akar Kessell's private audience hall on the tower's second level. The wizard reclined on a huge, satin pillow in the middle of the room, his long, painted fingernails tapping impatiently on the floor. Several nude slave girls, their minds bent and broken under the shard's domination, waited on every whim of the shard's wielder.

It angered Heafstaag to see women enslaved to such a puny, pitiful shell of a man. He considered, and not for the first time, a sudden charge, burying his great axe deep into the wizard's skull. But the room was filled with strategically located screens and pillars, and the barbarian knew, even if he refused to believe that the wizard's will could deny his rage, that Kessell's pet demon wouldn't be far from its master.

"So good that you could join me, noble Heafstaag," said Kessell in a calm, disarming way. Errtu and Crenshinibon were close at hand. He felt quite secure, even in the presence of the rugged barbarian king. He fondled one of the slaves absently, showing off his absolute rule. "Really, you should have come sooner. Already many of my forces are assembled; the first group of scouts has already departed."

He leaned forward toward the barbarian to emphasize his point. "If I can find no room for your people in my plans," he said with an evil snicker, "then I shall have no need for your people at all."

Heafstaag didn't flinch or change his expression in the least.

"Come now, mighty king," the wizard crooned, "sit and share in the riches of my table."

Heafstaag clung to his pride and remained unmoving.

"Very well!" snapped Kessell. He clenched his fist and uttered a command word. "To whom do you owe your fealty?" he demanded.

Heafstaag's body went rigid. "To Akar Kessell!" he responded, to his own repulsion.

"And tell me again who it is that commands the tribes of the tundra."

"They follow me," Heafstaag replied, "and I follow Akar Kessell. Akar Kessell commands the tribes of the tundra!"

The wizard released his fist, and the barbarian king slumped back.

"I take little joy in doing that to you," said Kessell, rubbing a burr in one of his painted nails. "Do not make me do it again." He pulled a scroll out from behind the satin pillow and tossed it to the floor. "Sit before me," be instructed Heafstaag. "Tell me again of your defeat."

Heafstaag took his place on the floor in front of his master and unrolled the parchment.

It was a map of Ten-Towns.

14
LAVENDER EYES

Bruenor had regained his dour visage by the time he called on Wulfgar the following morning. Still, it touched the dwarf deeply, though he was able to hide the fact, to see Aegis-fang casually slung over the young barbarian's shoulder as if it had always been there—and always belonged there.

Wulfgar, too, was wearing a sullen mask. He passed it off as anger at being put into the service of another, but if he had examined his emotions more closely, he would have recognized that he was truly saddened about separating from the dwarf.

Catti-brie was waiting for them at the junction of the final passage that led to the open air.

"Sure that you're a sour pair this fine morning!" she said as they approached. "But not to mind, the sun will put a smile on your faces."

"You seemed pleased at this parting," Wulfgar answered, a bit perturbed though the sparkle in his eyes at the sight of the girl belied his anger. "You know, of course, that I am to leave the dwarven town this day?"

Catti-brie waved her hand nonchalantly. "You will be back soon enough," She smiled. "And be happy for your going! Consider the lessons you will soon learn needed if you're ever to reach your goals."

Bruenor turned toward the barbarian. Wulfgar had never spoken with him about what lay ahead after the term of indenture, and the dwarf, though he meant to prepare Wulfgar as well as he could, hadn't honestly come to terms with Wulfgar's resolve to leave.

Wulfgar scowled at the girl, showing her beyond doubt that their discussion of the unfulfilled vow was a private matter. Of her own discretion, Catti-brie hadn't intended to discuss the issue any further anyway. She simply enjoyed teasing some emotion out of Wulfgar. Catti-brie recognized the fire that burned in the proud young man. She saw it whenever he looked upon Bruenor, his mentor whether he would admit it or not. And she marked it whenever Wulfgar looked at her.

"I am Wulfgar, son of Beornegar," he boasted proudly, throwing back his broad shoulders and straightening his firm jaw. "I have grown among the Tribe of the Elk, the finest warriors in all of Icewind Dale! I know nothing of this tutor, but he will be hard-pressed indeed to teach me anything of the ways of battle!"

Catti-brie exchanged a knowing smile with Bruenor as the dwarf and Wulfgar passed her. "Farewell, Wulfgar, son of Beornegar," she called after them. "When next we meet, I'll mark well your lessons of humility!"

Wulfgar looked back and scowled again, but Catti-brie's wide smile diminished not at all.

The two left the darkness of the mines shortly after dawn, traveling down through the rocky valley to the appointed spot where they were to meet the drow. It was a cloudless, warm summer day, the blue of the sky paled by the morning haze. Wulfgar stretched high into the air, reaching to the limits of his long muscles. His people were meant to live in the wide expanses of the open tundra, and he was relieved to be out of the stifling closeness of the dwarven-made caverns.

Drizzt Do'Urden was at the spot waiting for them when they arrived. The drow leaned against the shadowed side of a boulder, seeking relief from the glare of the sun. The hood of his cloak was pulled low in front of his face as further protection. Drizzt considered it the curse of his heritage that no matter how many years he remained among the surface dwellers his body would never fully adapt to the sunlight.

He held himself motionless, though he was fully aware of the approach of

Bruenor and Wulfgar. Let them make the first moves, he thought, wanting to judge how the boy would react to the new situation.

Curious about the mysterious figure who was to be his new teacher and master, Wulfgar boldly walked over and stood directly in front of the drow. Drizzt watched him approach from under the shadows of his cowl, amazed at the graceful interplay of the huge man's corded muscles. The drow had originally planned to humor Bruenor in his outrageous request for a short while, then make some excuse and be on his way. But as he noted the smooth flow and spring of the barbarian's long strides, an ease unusual in someone his size, Drizzt found himself growing interested in the challenge of developing the young man's seemingly limitless potential.

Drizzt realized that the most painful part of meeting this man, as it was with everyone he met, would be Wulfgar's initial reaction to him. Anxious to get it over with, he pulled back his hood and squarely faced the barbarian.

Wulfgar's eyes widened in horror and disgust. "A dark elf!" he cried incredulously. "Sorcerous dog!" He turned on Bruenor as though he had been betrayed. "Surely you cannot ask this of me! I have no need nor desire to learn the magical deceits of his decrepit race!"

"He'll teach ye to fight—no more," Bruenor said. The dwarf had expected this. He wasn't worried in the least, fully aware, as was Catti-brie, that Drizzt would teach the overly proud young man some needed humility.

Wulfgar snorted defiantly. "What can I learn of fighting from a weakling elf? My people are bred as true warriors!" He eyed Drizzt with open contempt. "Not trickster dogs like his kind!"

Drizzt calmly looked to Bruenor for permission to begin the day's lesson. The dwarf smirked at the barbarian's ignorance and nodded his consent.

In an eyeblink, the two scimitars leaped from their sheaths and challenged the barbarian. Instinctively, Wulfgar raised his warhammer to strike.

But Drizzt was the quicker. The flat sides of his weapons slapped in rapid succession against Wulfgar's cheeks, drawing thin streaks of blood. Even as the barbarian moved to counter, Drizzt spun one of the deadly blades in a declining arc, its razor edge diving at the back of Wulfgar's knee. Wulfgar managed to slip his leg out of the way, but the action, as Drizzt had anticipated, put him off-balance. The drow casually slipped the scimitars back into their leather scabbards as his foot slammed into the barbarian's stomach, sending him sprawling into the dust, the magical hammer flying from his hands.

"Now that ye understand each other," declared Bruenor, trying to hide his amusement for the sake of Wulfgar's fragile ego, "I'll be leavin' ye!" He looked questioningly at Drizzt to make sure that the drow was comfortable with the situation.

"Give me a few tendays," Drizzt answered with a wink, returning the dwarf's smile.

Bruenor turned back to Wulfgar, who had retrieved Aegis-fang and was resting on one knee, eyeing the elf with blank amazement. "Heed his words, boy," the dwarf instructed one last time. "Or he'll cut ye into pieces small enough for a vulture's gullet."

✄ ✄ ✄ ✄ ✄

For the first time in nearly five years, Wulfgar looked out beyond the borders of Ten-Towns to the open stretch of Icewind Dale that spread wide before him. He and the drow had spent the remainder of their first day together hiking down the length of the valley and around the eastern spurs of Kelvin's Cairn. Here, just above the base of the northern side of the mountain, was the shallow cave where Drizzt made his home.

Sparsely furnished with a few skins and some cooking pots, the cave had no luxuries to speak of. But it served the unpretentious drow ranger well, allowing him the privacy and seclusion that he preferred above the taunts and threats of the humans. To Wulfgar, whose people rarely stayed in any place longer than a single night, the cave itself seemed a luxury.

As dusk began to settle over the tundra, Drizzt, in the comfortable shadows deeper in the cave, stirred from his short nap. Wulfgar was pleased that the drow had trusted him enough to sleep easily, so obviously vulnerable, on their first day together. This, coupled with the beating Drizzt had given him earlier, had caused Wulfgar to question his initial outrage at the sight of a dark elf.

"Do we begin our sessions this night, then?" Drizzt asked.

"You are the master," Wulfgar said bitterly. "I am only the slave!"

"No more a slave than I," replied Drizzt. Wulfgar turned to him curiously.

"We are both indebted to the dwarf," Drizzt explained. "I owe him my life many times over and thus have agreed to teach you my skill in battle. You follow an oath that you made to him in exchange for your life. Thus you are obliged to learn what I have to teach. I am no man's master, nor would I ever want to be."

Wulfgar turned back to the tundra. He didn't fully trust Drizzt yet, though he couldn't figure out what ulterior motives the drow could possibly be pursuing with the friendly facade.

"We fulfill our debts to Bruenor together," said Drizzt. He empathized with the emotions Wulfgar was feeling as the young man gazed out over the plains of his homeland for the first time in years. "Enjoy this night, barbarian. Go about as you please and remember again the feel of the wind on your face. We shall begin at the fall of tomorrow's night." He left then to allow Wulfgar the privacy he desired.

Wulfgar could not deny that he appreciated the respect the drow had shown him.

※ ※ ※ ※

During the daytime, Drizzt rested in the cool shadows of the cave while Wulfgar acclimated himself to the new area and hunted for their supper.

By night, they fought.

Drizzt pressed the young barbarian relentlessly, slapping him with the flat of a scimitar every time he opened a gap in his defenses. The exchanges often escalated dangerously, for Wulfgar was a proud warrior and grew enraged and frustrated at the drow's superiority. This only put the barbarian at a further disadvantage, for in his rage all semblance of discipline flew from him. Drizzt was ever quick to point this out with a series of slaps and twists that ultimately left Wulfgar sprawled on the ground.

To his credit, though, Drizzt never taunted the barbarian or tried to humiliate him. The drow went about his task methodically, understanding that the first order of business was to sharpen the barbarian's reflexes and teach him some concern for defense.

Drizzt was truly impressed with Wulfgar's raw ability. The incredible potential of the young warrior staggered him. At first he feared that Wulfgar's stubborn pride and bitterness would render him untrainable, but the barbarian had risen to the challenge. Recognizing the benefits he could reap from one as adept with weapons as Drizzt, Wulfgar listened attentively. His pride, instead of limiting him into believing that he was already a mighty warrior and needed no further instruction, pushed him to grab at every advantage he could find that would help him to achieve his ambitious goals. By the end of the first tenday, during those times he could control his volatile temper, he was already able to deflect many of Drizzt's cunning attacks.

Drizzt said little during that first tenday, though he would occasionally compliment the barbarian about a good parry or counter, or more generally on the improvement Wulfgar was showing in such a short time. Wulfgar found himself eagerly anticipating the drow's remarks whenever he executed an especially difficult maneuver, and dreading the inevitable slap whenever he foolishly left himself vulnerable.

The young barbarian's respect for Drizzt continued to grow. Something about the drow, living without complaint in stoic solitude, touched Wulfgar's sense of honor. He couldn't yet guess why Drizzt had chosen such an existence, but he was certain from what he had already seen of the drow that it had something to do with principles.

By the middle of the second tenday, Wulfgar was in complete control of Aegis-fang, twisting its handle and head deftly to block the two whirring scimitars, and responding with cautiously measured thrusts of his own. Drizzt could see the subtle change taking place as the barbarian stopped reacting after the fact to the scimitars' deft cuts and thrusts and began recognizing his own vulnerable areas and anticipating the next attack.

When he became convinced that Wulfgar's defenses were sufficiently strengthened, Drizzt began the lessons of attack. The drow knew that his style of offense would not be the most effective mode for Wulfgar. The barbarian could use his unrivaled strength more effectively than deceptive feints and twists. Wulfgar's people were naturally aggressive fighters, and

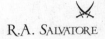

striking came more easily to them than parrying. The mighty barbarian could fell a giant with a single, well-placed blow.

All that he had left to learn was patience.

✗ ✗ ✗ ✗ ✗

Early one dark, moonless night, as he prepared himself for the evening's lesson, Wulfgar noticed the flare of a campfire far out on the plain. He watched, mesmerized, as several others sprang suddenly into sight, wondering if it might even be the fires of his own tribe.

Drizzt silently approached, unnoticed by the engrossed barbarian. The drow's keen eyes had noted the stirrings of the distant camp long before the firelight had grown strong enough for Wulfgar to see. "Your people have survived," he said to comfort the young man.

Wulfgar started at the sudden appearance of his teacher. "You know of them?" he asked.

Drizzt moved beside him and stared out over the tundra. "Their losses were great at the Battle of Bryn Shander," he said. "And the winter that followed bit hard at the many women and children who had no men to hunt for them. They fled west to find the reindeer, banding together with other tribes for strength. The peoples still hold to the names of the original tribes, but in truth there are only two remaining: the Tribe of the Elk and the Tribe of the Bear.

"You were of the Tribe of the Elk, I believe," Drizzt continued, drawing a nod from Wulfgar. "Your people have done well. They dominate the plain now, and though more years will have to pass before the people of the tundra regain the strength they held before the battle, the younger warriors are already coming into manhood."

Relief flooded through Wulfgar. He had feared that the Battle of Bryn Shander had decimated his people to a point from which they could never recover. The tundra was doubly harsh in the frozen winter, and Wulfgar often considered the possibility that the sudden loss of so many warriors— some of the tribes had lost every one of their menfolk—would doom the remaining people to slow death.

"You know much about my people," Wulfgar remarked.

"I have spent many days watching them," Drizzt explained, wondering what line of thought the barbarian was drawing, "learning their ways and tricks for prospering in such an unwelcoming land."

Wulfgar chuckled softly and shook his head, further impressed by the sincere reverence the drow showed whenever he spoke of the natives of Icewind Dale. He had known the drow less than two tendays, but already he understood the character of Drizzt Do'Urden well enough to know that his next observation about the drow was true to the mark.

"I'll wager you even felled deer silently in the darkness, to be found in the morning light by people too hungry to question their good fortune."

Drizzt neither answered the remark nor changed the set of his gaze, but Wulfgar was confident in his guess.

"Do you know of Heafstaag?" the barbarian asked after a few moments of silence. "He was king of my tribe, a man of many scars and great renown."

Drizzt remembered the one-eyed barbarian well. The mere mention of his name sent a dull ache into the drow's shoulder, where he had been wounded by the huge man's heavy axe. "He lives," Drizzt replied, somewhat shielding his contempt. "Heafstaag speaks for the whole of the north now. None of true enough blood remain to oppose him in combat or speak out against him to hold him in check."

"He is a mighty king," Wulfgar said, oblivious to the venom in the drow's voice.

"He is a savage fighter," Drizzt corrected. His lavender eyes bore into Wulfgar, catching the barbarian completely by surprise with their sudden flash of anger. Wulfgar saw the incredible character in those violet pools, an inner strength within the drow whose pure quality would make the most noble of kings envious.

"You have grown into a man in the shadow of a dwarf of indisputable character," Drizzt scolded. "Have you gained nothing for the experience?"

Wulfgar was dumbfounded and couldn't find the words to reply.

Drizzt decided that the time had come for him to lay bare the barbarian's principles and judge the wisdom and worth of teaching the young man. "A king is a man strong of character and conviction who leads by example

and truly cares for the sufferings of his people," he lectured. "Not a brute who rules simply because he is the strongest. I should think you would have learned to understand the distinction."

Drizzt noted the embarrassment on Wulfgar's face and knew that the years in the dwarven caves had shaken the very ground that the barbarian had grown on. He hoped that Bruenor's belief in Wulfgar's sense of conscience and principle proved true, for he, too, like Bruenor years before, had come to recognize the promise of the intelligent young man and found that he cared about Wulfgar's future. He turned suddenly and started away, leaving the barbarian to find the answers to his own questions.

"The lesson?" Wulfgar called after him, still confused and surprised.

"You have had your lesson for this night," Drizzt replied without turning or slowing. "Perhaps it was the most important that I will ever teach." The drow faded into the blackness of the night, though the distinct image of lavender eyes remained clearly imprinted in Wulfgar's thoughts.

The barbarian turned back to the distant campfire.

And wondered.

On the Wings of Doom

They came in under the cover of a violent squall line that swept down upon Ten-Towns from the open east. Ironically, they followed the same trail along the side of Kelvin's Cairn that Drizzt and Wulfgar had traveled just two tendays earlier. This band of verbeeg, though, headed south toward the settlements, rather than north to the open tundra. Though tall and thin—the smallest of the giants—they were still a formidable force.

A frost giant led the advance scouts of Akar Kessell's vast army. Unheard beneath the howling blasts of wind, they moved with all speed to a secret lair that had been discovered by orc scouts in a rocky spur on the southern side of the mountain. There was barely a score of the monsters, but each carried a huge bundle of weapons and supplies.

The leader pressed on toward its destination. Its name was Biggrin, a cunning and immensely strong giant whose upper lip had been torn away by the ripping maw of a huge wolf, leaving the grotesque caricature of a smile forever stamped upon its face. This disfigurement only added to the giant's stature, instilling the respect of fear in its normally unruly troops. Akar Kessell had hand-picked Biggrin as the leader of his forward scouts, though the wizard had been counseled to send a less conspicuous party, some of Heafstaag's people, for the delicate mission. But Kessell held Biggrin in high regard and was impressed with the enormous amount of supplies the small band of verbeeg could carry.

The troop settled into their new quarters before midnight and immediately went about fashioning sleeping areas, storage rooms, and a small kitchen. Then they waited, silently poised to strike the first lethal blows in Akar Kessell's glorious assault on Ten-Towns.

An orc runner came every couple of days to check on the band and deliver the latest instructions from the wizard, informing Biggrin of the progress of the next supply troop that was scheduled to arrive. Everything was proceeding according to Kessell's plan, but Biggrin noted with concern that many of his warriors grew more eager and anxious every time a new runner appeared, hoping that the time to march to war was finally upon them.

Always the instructions were the same, though: Stay hidden and wait.

In less than two tendays in the tense atmosphere of the stuffy cave, the camaraderie between the giants had disintegrated. Verbeeg were creatures of action, not contemplation, and boredom led them inescapably to frustration.

Arguments became the norm, often leading to vicious fights. Biggrin was never far away, and the imposing frost giant usually managed to break up the scuffles before any of the troops were seriously wounded. The giant knew beyond any doubt that it could not keep control of the battle-hungry band for much longer.

The fifth runner slipped into the cave on a particularly hot and uncomfortable night. As soon as the unfortunate orc entered the common room, it was surrounded by a score of grumbling verbeeg.

"What's the news, then?" one of them demanded impatiently.

Thinking that the backing of Akar Kessell was sufficient protection, the orc eyed the giant in open defiance. "Fetch your master, soldier," it ordered.

Suddenly a huge hand grabbed the orc by the scruff of the neck and shook the creature roughly. "Yous was asked a question, scum," said a second giant. "What's the news?"

The orc, now visibly unnerved, shot back an angry threat at its giant assailant. "The wizard will peel the skin from your hide while you watch!"

"I heared enough," growled the first giant, reaching down to clamp a huge hand around the orc's neck. It lifted the creature clear off the ground, using only one of its massive arms. The orc slapped and twisted pitifully, not bothering the verbeeg in the least.

"Aw, squeeze its filthy neck," came one call.

"Put its eyes out an' drop it in a dark hole!" said another.

Biggrin entered the room, quickly pushing through the ranks to discover the source of the commotion. The giant wasn't surprised to find the verbeeg tormenting an orc. In truth, the giant leader was amused by the spectacle, but it understood the danger of angering the volatile Akar Kessell. It had seen more than one unruly goblin put to a slow death for disobeying, or simply to appease the wizard's distorted taste for pleasure. "Put the miserable thing down," Biggrin ordered calmly.

Several groans and angry grumbles sprang up around the frost giant.

"Bash its 'ead in!" cried one.

"Bites its nose!" yelled another.

By now, the orc's face had grown puffy from lack of air, and it hardly struggled at all. The verbeeg holding it returned Biggrin's threatening stare for a few moments longer, then tossed its helpless victim at the frost giant's booted feet.

"Keep it then," the verbeeg snarled at Biggrin. "But if it wags its tongue at me agin, I'll eats it fer sure!"

"I've 'ad too much o' this hole," complained a giant, from the back of the ranks. "An' a whole dale o' filthy dwarfs fer the takin'!" The grumbling renewed with heightened intensity.

Biggrin looked around and studied the seething rage that had crept into all of the troops, threatening to bring down the whole lair in one sudden fit of irrepressible violence.

"Tomorrow night we starts goin' out t'see whats about us," Biggrin offered in response. It was a dangerous move, the frost giant knew, but the alternative was certain disaster. "Only three at a time, an' no one's to know!"

The orc had regained a measure of composure and heard Biggrin's proposal. It started to protest, but the giant leader silenced it immediately.

"Shut yer mouth, orc dog," Biggrin commanded, looking to the verbeeg that had threatened the runner and smiling wryly, "or I'll lets me friend eat!"

The giants howled their glee and exchanged shoulder claps with their companions, comrades again. Biggrin had given them back the promise of action, though the giant leader's doubts about its decision were far from dispelled by the lusty enthusiasm of the soldiers. Shouts of the various dwarven recipes the verbeegs had concocted—"Dwarf o' the Apple" and "Bearded, Basted, an' Baked" to name two—rang out to overwhelming hoots of approval.

Biggrin dreaded what might happen if any of the verbeeg came upon some of the short folk.

✕ ✕ ✕ ✕ ✕

Biggrin let the verbeeg out of the lair in groups of three, and only during the nighttime hours. The giant leader thought it unlikely that any dwarves would travel this far north up the valley, but knew that it was taking a huge gamble. A sigh of relief escaped from the giant's mouth whenever a patrol returned without incident.

Simply being allowed out of the cramped cave improved the verbeeg's morale tenfold. The tension inside the lair virtually disappeared as the troops regained their enthusiasm for the coming war. Up on the side of Kelvin's Cairn they often saw the lights of Caer-Konig and Caer-Dineval, Termalaine across the way to the west, and even Bryn Shander far to the south. Viewing the cities allowed them to fantasize about their upcoming victories, and the thoughts were enough to sustain them in their long wait.

Another tenday slipped by. Everything seemed to be going along well. Witnessing the improvement the small measure of freedom had brought to his troops, Biggrin gradually began to relax about the risky decision.

But then two dwarves, having been informed by Bruenor that there was some fine stone under the shadow of Kelvin's Cairn, made the trip to the north end of the valley to investigate its mining potential. They arrived on the southern slopes of the rocky mountain late one afternoon, and by dusk had made camp on a flat rock beside a swift stream.

This was their valley, and it had known no trouble in several years. They took few precautions.

So it happened that the first patrol of verbeeg to leave the lair that night soon spotted the flames of a campfire and heard the distinctive dialect of the hated dwarves.

⚔ ⚔ ⚔ ⚔ ⚔

On the other side of the mountain, Drizzt Do'Urden opened his eyes from his daytime slumber. Emerging from the cave into the growing gloom, he found Wulfgar in the customary spot, poised meditatively on a high stone, staring out over the plain.

"You long for your home?" the drow asked rhetorically.

Wulfgar shrugged his huge shoulders and answered absently, "Perhaps." The barbarian had come to ask many disturbing questions of himself about his people and their way of life since he had learned respect for Drizzt. The drow was an enigma to him, a confusing combination of fighting brilliance and absolute control. Drizzt seemed able to weigh every move he ever made in the scales of high adventure and indisputable morals.

Wulfgar turned a questioning gaze on the drow. "Why are you here?" he asked suddenly.

Now it was Drizzt who stared reflectively into the openness before them. The first stars of the evening had appeared, their reflections sparkling distinctively in the dark pools of the elf's eyes. But Drizzt was not seeing them; his mind was viewing long-past images of the lightless cities of the drow in their immense cavern complexes far beneath the ground.

"I remember," Drizzt recalled vividly, as terrible memories are often vivid, "the first time I ever viewed this surface world. I was a much younger elf then, a member of a large raiding party. We slipped out from a secret cave and descended upon a small elven village." The drow flinched at the images as they flashed again in his mind. "My companions slaughtered every member of the wood elf clan. Every female. Every child."

Wulfgar listened with growing horror. The raid that Drizzt was describing might well have been one perpetrated by the ferocious Tribe of the Elk.

"My people kill," Drizzt went on grimly. "They kill without mercy." He locked his stare onto Wulfgar to make sure that the barbarian heard him well.

"They kill without passion."

He paused for a moment to let the barbarian absorb the full weight of his words. The simple yet definitive description of the cold killers had confused Wulfgar. He had been raised and nurtured among passionate warriors, fighters whose entire purpose in life was the pursuit of battle glory—fighting in praise of Tempus. The young barbarian simply could not understand such emotionless cruelty. A subtle difference, though, Wulfgar had to admit. Drow or barbarian, the results of the raids were much the same.

"The demon goddess they serve leaves no room for the other races," Drizzt explained. "Particularly the other races of elves."

"But you will never come to be accepted in this world," said Wulfgar. "Surely you must know that the humans will ever shun you."

Drizzt nodded. "Most," he agreed. "I have few that I can call friends, yet I am content. You see, barbarian, I have my own respect, without guilt, without shame." He rose from his crouch and started away into the darkness. "Come," he instructed. "Let us fight well this night, for I am satisfied with the improvement of your skills, and this part of your lessons nears its end."

Wulfgar sat a moment longer in contemplation. The drow lived a hard and materially empty existence, yet he was richer than any man Wulfgar had ever known. Drizzt had clung to his principles against overwhelming circumstances, leaving the familiar world of his own people by choice to remain in a world where he would never be accepted or appreciated.

He looked at the departing elf, now a mere shadow in the gloom. "Perhaps we two are not so different," he mumbled under his breath.

⚔ ⚔ ⚔ ⚔ ⚔

"Spies!" whispered one of the verbeeg.

"Stupid fer spyin' with a fire," said another.

"Lets go squash 'em!" said the first, starting toward the orange light.

"The boss said no!" the third reminded the others. "We's to watch, but no squashin'!"

They started down the rocky path toward the small camp of the dwarves with as much stealth as they could muster, which made them about as quiet as a rolling boulder.

The two dwarves were well aware that someone or something was approaching. They drew their weapons as a precaution, but figured that Wulfgar and Drizzt, or perhaps some fishermen from Caer-Konig, had seen their light and were coming to share dinner with them.

When the camp came into sight just below, the verbeeg could see the dwarves standing firm, weapons in hand.

"They's seen us!" said one giant, ducking into the darkness.

"Aw, shut up," ordered the second.

The third giant, knowing as well as the second that the dwarves could not as yet know who they were, grasped the second's shoulder and winked evilly. "If they's seen us," it reasoned, "we's got no choice but to squash 'em!"

The second giant chuckled softly, poised its heavy club on its shoulder, and started for the camp.

The dwarves were completely stunned when the verbeeg came bounding around some boulders just a few yards from their camp and closed in on them. But a cornered dwarf is pound for pound as tough as anything in the world, and these were of the clan from Mithral Hall who had been waging battles on the merciless tundra for all of their lives. This fight would not be as easy as the verbeeg had expected.

The first dwarf ducked a lumbering swing from the lead verbeeg and countered by slamming his hammer onto the monster's toes. The giant instinctively lifted its injured foot and hopped on one leg, and the seasoned dwarf fighter promptly cut it down by bashing him in the knee.

The other dwarf had reacted quickly, launching his hammer with pinpoint accuracy. It caught another giant in the eye and spun the creature crashing into some rocks.

But the third verbeeg, the smartest of the three, had picked up a stone before it had charged and returned the dwarf's throw with tremendous force.

The stone deflected off the unfortunate dwarf's temple, snapping his neck violently to the side. His head lolled about uncontrollably on his shoulders as he fell dead to the ground.

The first dwarf would have soon finished off the giant he had felled, but the last of the monsters was upon him at once. The two combatants parried and countered, with the dwarf actually gaining a bit of an advantage. An advantage that lasted only until the giant who had been struck in the eye by the thrown hammer recovered enough to jump in.

The two verbeeg rained blow after heavy blow at the dwarf. He managed to dodge and deflect them for a short while, but then one landed squarely on his shoulder and dropped him to his back. He found his breath in a short time, for he was as tough as the stone he had landed on, but a heavy boot stomped on him and held him prone.

"Squish 'im!" begged the injured giant the dwarf had cut down. "Then we takes 'im to the cook!"

"We does not!" growled the giant above the dwarf. It ground its huge boot into the earth, slowly pressing the life from the unfortunate victim.

"Biggrin'll take us to the cook if 'e finds us out!" The other two grew genuinely afraid when they were reminded of the wrath of their brutal leader. They looked helplessly to their more cunning companion for a solution.

"We puts 'em an' their filthy things in a dark hole and says nothin' more o' this!"

⚔ ⚔ ⚔ ⚔ ⚔

Many miles to the east, in his solitary tower, Akar Kessell waited patiently. In the autumn, the last—and largest—of the trading caravans would roll back into Ten-Towns from Luskan, laden with riches and supplies for the long winter. His vast armies would be assembled and on the move by then, marching gloriously to destroy the pitiful fishermen. The mere thought of the fruits of his easy victory sent shivers of delight through the wizard.

He had no way of knowing that the first blows of the war had already been struck.

16
SHALLOW GRAVES

When Wulfgar awakened just before midday, rested from his long night's work, he was surprised to see Drizzt already up and about, busily preparing a pack for a long hike.

"Today we start a different type of lesson," Drizzt explained to the barbarian. "We'll set out right after you've had something to eat."

"To where?"

"First, the dwarven mines," replied Drizzt. "Bruenor will want to see you so he might measure your progress for himself." He smiled at the big man. "He shan't be disappointed!"

Wulfgar smiled, confident that his new-found prowess with the hammer would impress even the grumpy dwarf. "And then?"

"To Termalaine, on the banks of Maer Dualdon. I have a friend there. One of my few," he added quickly with a wink, drawing a smile from Wulfgar. "A man named Agorwal. I want you to meet some of the people of Ten-Towns so that you might better judge them."

"What have I to judge?" Wulfgar asked angrily. The drow's dark and knowing eyes bore into him. Wulfgar clearly understood what Drizzt had in mind. The dark elf was trying to personalize the people the barbarians had declared enemies, to show Wulfgar the everyday existence of the men, women, and children who might have been victims of his own heavy pole if the fight on the slopes had turned out differently. Fearless in any battle, Wulfgar was truly frightened of facing those people. Already the young barbarian had begun to question the virtues of his warlike people; the innocent faces he would encounter in the town his people had casually marked for burning could well complete the destruction of the foundations of his entire world.

The two companions set out a short time later, retracing their steps around the eastern trails of Kelvin's Cairn. A dusty wind was blowing in steadily from the east, assaulting them with fine grains of stinging sand as they crossed the exposed face of the mountain. Though the glaring sun was especially draining on Drizzt, he kept a strong pace and did not stop for rest.

In the late afternoon, when they finally rounded a southern spur, they were exhausted but in good spirits.

"In the shelter of the mines, I had forgotten how cruel the tundra wind could be!" laughed Wulfgar.

"We'll have some protection below the rim of the valley," said Drizzt. He patted the empty waterskin at his side. "Come, I know where we might refill these before we continue."

He led Wulfgar westward, below the southern slopes of the mountain. The drow knew of an icy stream a short distance away, its waters fed from the snow melt atop Kelvin's Cairn.

The brook sang merrily as it danced across the stones. Nearby birds cackled and cawed at the approach of the companions, and a lynx slipped silently away. Everything appeared as it should, but from the moment they arrived on the large, flat rock that was commonly used by travelers as a campsite, Drizzt sensed that something was terribly wrong. Moving in tentatively, he searched for some tangible sign that would confirm his growing suspicions.

Wulfgar, though, dived belly-down onto the stone and dunked his sweat- and dust-streaked face eagerly into the cold water. When he pulled it back out, the luster had returned to his eyes, as if the icy water had given him back his vitality.

But then the barbarian noticed crimson stains on the rock and followed their gory trail to the hairy piece of skin that had gotten caught on the sharp tip of a stone just above the rushing stream.

Both skilled trackers, the ranger and barbarian had little difficulty in ascertaining that a battle had recently been fought on this spot. They recognized the coarse hair on the patch of skin as a piece of beard, which of course led them to think of the dwarves. They found three sets of giant-size footprints nearby. Following a tangent line of tracks that stretched southward a short distance to a sandy patch of ground, they soon found the shallow graves.

"Not Bruenor," Drizzt said grimly, examining the two corpses. "Younger dwarves—Bundo, son of Fellhammer, and Dourgas, son of Argo Grimblade, I believe."

"We should make all haste to the mines," Wulfgar suggested.

"Soon," replied the drow. "We still have much to learn about what happened here, and tonight may be our only chance. Were these giants simply passing rogues, or are they lairing in the area? And are there more of the foul beasts?"

"Bruenor should be told," Wulfgar argued.

"And so he will," said Drizzt. "But if these three are still nearby, as I believe they are since they took the time to bury their kill, they might well return for some more sport when night falls." He directed Wulfgar's gaze to the west, where the sky had already begun to take on the pink shades of twilight. "Are you ready for a fight, barbarian?"

With a determined grunt, Wulfgar brought Aegis-fang down from his shoulder and slapped the adamantite handle across his free hand. "We shall see who finds sport this night."

They moved behind the secrecy of a rocky bluff south of the flat stone and waited as the sun passed below the horizon and the dark shadows deepened into evening.

It wasn't very long a wait, for the same verbeeg that had killed the dwarves the night before were again the first out of the lair, anxious to seek fresh victims. Soon the patrol came crashing over the mountain slopes and onto the flat rock beside the stream.

Wulfgar immediately moved to charge, but Drizzt stayed him before he gave their position away. The drow had every intention of killing these giants, but he wanted to see if he could learn anything about why they were here first.

"Drats an' dingers," grumbled one of the giants. "Not a dwarf to be found!"

"Rotten luck, it is," groaned another. "An' our last night out, too." The creature's companions looked at it curiously.

"The other group's comin' in tomorrow," the verbeeg explained. "Our numbers'll double, an' stinkin' ogres an' orcs to boot, an' the boss ain't to let us out 'til everthin's calmed again."

"A score more in that stinkin' hole," complained one of the others. "Rightly t'send us flippin'!"

"Let's be movin', then," said the third. "No huntin' 'ere an' no night fer wastin'."

The two adventurers behind the bluff tensed reflexively when the giants spoke of leaving.

"If we can get to that rock," Wulfgar reasoned, unknowingly pointing to the same boulder that the giants had used for their ambush the night before, "we'll have them before they even realize we're here!" He turned anxiously to Drizzt but backed off immediately when he saw the drow. The lavender eyes burned with a luster that Wulfgar had never witnessed before.

"There are only three of them," said Drizzt, his voice holding a fragile edge of calm that threatened to explode at any moment. "We need no surprise."

Wulfgar didn't quite know how to take this unexpected change in the dark elf. "You taught me to seek every advantage," he said cautiously.

"In battle, yes," answered Drizzt. "This is vengeance. Let the giants see us, let them feel the terror of impending doom!" The scimitars suddenly appeared in his slender hands as he walked out around the bluff, his steady stride unnervingly holding the unswerving promise of death.

One of the giants yelled out in surprise, and they all froze in their tracks when they saw the drow step out before them. Apprehensive and confused, they formed a defensive line across the flat rock. The verbeeg had heard legends of the drow, even some where the dark elves had joined forces with giants, but the sudden appearance of Drizzt caught them totally by surprise.

Drizzt enjoyed their nervous twitchings, and he held back to savor the moment.

"What are ye fer, then?" one of the giants asked cautiously.

"A friend of dwarves," Drizzt replied with a wicked laugh. Wulfgar leaped out beside him as the largest of the giants charged without hesitation. But Drizzt stopped him cold. The drow pointed one of his scimitars at the advancing giant and stated with deathly calm, "You are dead." At once, the verbeeg was limned by purplish flames. It yelled in terror and retreated a step, but Drizzt stalked it methodically.

An overwhelming impulse came over Wulfgar to throw the warhammer, as though Aegis-fang was exerting a will of its own. The weapon whistled through the night air and exploded into the giant standing in the middle, hurling its broken body into the swollen stream.

Wulfgar was truly awe-stricken with the power and deadliness of the throw, but he worried about how effectively he could fight off the third giant with a small dagger, the only weapon he had left. The giant recognized the advantage as well and charged wildly. Wulfgar went for the dagger.

But instead he found Aegis-fang magically returned to his grasp. He had no idea of this special power Bruenor had imbued upon the weapon, and he had no time now to pause and ponder.

Terrified, but having nowhere to run, the largest giant attacked Drizzt with abandon, giving the elf even more of an advantage. The monster lifted its heavy club high, the movement exaggerated by rage, and Drizzt quickly poked his pointed blades through the leather tunic and into the exposed belly. With only a slight hesitation, the giant continued its mighty swing, but the agile drow still had ample time to dodge the blow. And as the swing threw the lumbering giant off-balance, Drizzt jabbed two more tiny holes into its shoulder and neck.

"Are you watching, boy?" the drow called gaily to Wulfgar. "It fights like one of your kind."

Wulfgar was heavily engaged with the remaining giant, easily maneuvering Aegis-fang to deflect the monster's powerful blows, but he was able to catch glimpses of the battle to his side. The scene painted a grim reminder of the value of what Drizzt had taught him, for the drow was toying with the verbeeg, using its uncontrolled rage against it. Again and again, the monster reared for a killing blow, and each time Drizzt was quick to strike and dance away. Verbeeg blood flowed freely from a dozen wounds, and Wulfgar knew that Drizzt could finish the job at any time. But he was amazed that the dark elf was enjoying the tormenting game he played.

Wulfgar hadn't yet struck a solid blow on his opponent, biding his time, as Drizzt had taught him, until the enraged verbeeg wore itself out. Already the barbarian could see that the giant's blows were coming with less frequency and vigor. Finally, lathered in sweat and breathing heavily, the verbeeg slipped up and dropped its guard. Aegis-fang pounded home once, and then again, and the giant toppled in a lump.

The verbeeg fighting Drizzt was down on one knee now, the drow having deftly sliced out one of its hamstrings. When Drizzt saw the second giant fall before Wulfgar, he decided to end the game. The giant took one more futile swing, and Drizzt waded in behind the flow of the weapon, jabbing with one scimitar and this time following the cruel point with his full weight. The blade slipped through the giant's neck and upward into its brain.

⚔ ⚔ ⚔ ⚔

Later, one question pressed upon Drizzt as he and Wulfgar, resting on one knee, considered the results of their handiwork. "The hammer?" he asked simply.

Wulfgar looked down at Aegis-fang and shrugged. "I do not know," he answered honestly. "It returned to my hand by its own magic!"

Drizzt smiled to himself. He knew. How wondrous the crafting of Bruenor, he thought. And how deeply the dwarf must care for the boy to have given him such a gift!

"A score of verbeeg coming," groaned Wulfgar.

"And another twenty already here," added Drizzt. "Go straight away to Bruenor," he instructed. "These three just came from the lair; I shouldn't have much trouble backtracking and finding out where the rest of them are!"

Wulfgar nodded his assent, though he looked upon Drizzt with concern. The uncharacteristic smolder he had seen in the drow's eyes before they attacked the verbeeg had unnerved the barbarian. He wasn't quite sure just how daring the dark elf might be. "What do you mean to do when you find the lair?"

Drizzt said nothing but smiled wryly, adding to the barbarian's apprehension. Finally he eased his friend's worries. "Meet me back at this spot in the morning. I assure you that I shan't begin the fun without you!"

"I shall return before the first light of dawn," Wulfgar replied grimly. He spun on his heel and disappeared into the darkness, making his way as fast as he could under starlight.

Drizzt, too, started away, tracing the trail of the three giants westward across the face of Kelvin's Cairn. Eventually, he heard the baritone voices of giants, and shortly thereafter he saw the hastily constructed wooden doors that marked their lair, cunningly concealed behind some brush halfway up a rocky foothill.

Drizzt waited patiently and soon saw a second patrol of three giants emerge from the lair. And later on, when they returned, a third group came out. The drow was trying to discern if any alarms had gone up due to the absence of the first patrol. But verbeeg were almost always unruly and undependable, and Drizzt was reassured from the small snatches of conversation he was able to hear that the giants assumed their missing companions had either gotten lost or simply deserted. When the drow slipped away a few hours later to set his next plans, he was confident that he still had the element of surprise working for him.

⚔ ⚔ ⚔ ⚔ ⚔

Wulfgar ran all through the night. He delivered his message to Bruenor and started back to the north without waiting for the clan to be roused. His great strides took him to the flat rock more than an hour before the first light, even before Drizzt had returned from the lair. He went back behind the bluff to wait, his concern for the drow growing with every passing second.

Finally, able to stand the suspense no longer, he sought out the trail of the verbeeg and started tracking it toward the lair, determined to discover what was happening. He hadn't gone twenty feet when a hand cuffed him on the back of the head. Reflexively he spun to meet his attacker, but his astonishment turned to joy when he saw Drizzt standing before him.

Drizzt had returned to the rock shortly after Wulfgar but had remained hidden, watching the barbarian to see if the impulsive young warrior would trust in their pact or decide to take matters into his own hands. "Never doubt an appointed rendezvous until its hour has passed," the drow scolded sternly, touched as he was by the barbarian's concern for his well-being.

Any response that might have been coming from Wulfgar was cut short, for suddenly the two companions heard a gruff shout from a familiar voice. "Get me a pig-squealin' giant to kill!" Bruenor called from the flat stone by the stream behind them. Enraged dwarves can roll along at an incredible speed. In less than an hour, Bruenor's clan had assembled and started after the barbarian, nearly matching his frantic pace.

"Well met," Drizzt called as he moved to join the dwarf. He found Bruenor eyeing the three dead verbeeg with grim satisfaction. Fifty iron-visaged, battle-ready dwarves, more than half the clan, stood around their leader.

"Elf," Bruenor greeted with his customary consideration. "A lair, is it?"

Drizzt nodded. "A mile to the west, but let that be not your first concern. The giants there are not going anywhere, but they are expecting guests this very day."

"The boy told me," said Bruenor. "A score of reinforcements!' He swung his axe casually. "Somehow I get the feelin' they're not goin' t' make the lair! Any notion o' where they're to be comin' in?"

"North and east is the only way," Drizzt reasoned. "Somewhere down Icewind Pass, around the north of Lac Dinneshere. Your people will greet them, then?"

"Of course," replied Bruenor. "They'll be passin' Daledrop for certain!" A twinkle edged his eye. "What do ye mean to do?" he asked Drizzt. "An what o' the boy?"

"The boy remains with me," Drizzt insisted. "He needs rest. We'll watch over the lair."

The eager gleam in Drizzt's eye gave Bruenor the impression that the drow had more in mind than watching. "Crazy elf," he said under his breath. "Probably'll take on the whole lot of 'em by himself!" He looked around curiously again at the dead giants. "And win!" Then Bruenor studied the two adventurers, trying to match their weapons with the types of wounds on the verbeeg.

"The boy felled two," Drizzt replied to the dwarf's unspoken question.

A hint of a rare smile found its way onto Bruenor's face. "Two to yer one, eh? Yer slippin', elf."

"Nonsense," Drizzt retorted. "I recognized that he needed the practice!"

Bruenor shook his head, surprised by the extent of the pride he felt toward Wulfgar, though of course he wasn't about to tell the boy and swell his head. "Yer slippin'!" he called again as he moved up to the head of the clan. The dwarves took up a rhythmic chanting, an ancient tune that had once echoed off the silvery halls of their lost homeland.

Bruenor looked back at his two adventurous friends and honestly wondered what would be left of the giant lair by the time he and his fellow dwarves returned.

17

VENGEANCE

Tirelessly, the heavily laden dwarves marched on. They had come prepared for war, some carrying heavy packs and others shouldering the great weight of large wooden beams.

The drow's guess about which direction the reinforcements would be coming from seemed the only possible way, and Bruenor knew exactly where to meet them. There was only one pass that afforded easy access down into the rocky valley: Daledrop, up on the level of the tundra yet below the southern slopes of the mountain.

Though they had marched without rest throughout half of the night and most of the morning, the dwarves set right to work. They had no idea what time the giants would be coming in, though it probably wouldn't happen under the light of day; they wanted to make certain that everything was ready. Bruenor was determined to take out this war party quickly and with minimal losses to his people. Scouts were posted on the high spots of the mountainside, and others were sent out onto the plain. Under Bruenor's direction, the remainder of the clan prepared the area for an ambush. One group set to digging a trip-trench and another began reassembling the wooden beams into two ballistae. Heavy crossbowmen sought out the best vantage points among the boulders on the nearby mountainside from which to launch their assault.

In a short time, all was ready. But the dwarves still did not stop to rest. They continued canvassing every inch of the area, searching for any possible advantage they could gain over the verbeeg.

Late in the day, the sun already dipping its lowest edges below the horizon, one of the lookouts on the mountain announced that he had sighted a dust cloud growing in the distant east. Soon after, a scout came in from the plain to report that a troop of twenty verbeeg, a few ogres, and at least a dozen orcs was making speed toward Daledrop. Bruenor signaled the crossbowmen into their concealed positions. The ballista crews inspected the camouflage on the great bows and added perfecting touches. Then the strongest fighters of the clan, with Bruenor himself among them, dug themselves into small holes along the worn path of Daledrop, carefully cutting the tufts of thick grass so that they could roll it back over them.

They would strike the first blows.

⚔ ⚔ ⚔ ⚔ ⚔

Drizzt and Wulfgar had taken up a position among the boulders of Kelvin's Cairn above the giants' lair. They had slept in shifts throughout the day. The drow's only concern for Bruenor and his clan was that some of the giants would leave the lair to meet the incoming reinforcements and spoil the dwarves' advantage of surprise.

After several uneventful hours, Drizzt's worries proved true. The drow was resting in the shadow of a ledge while Wulfgar kept watch over the lair. The barbarian could hardly see the wooden doors concealed behind the brush, but he clearly heard the creak of a hinge when one of them opened. He waited for a few moments before moving to rouse the drow to make sure that some of the giants were actually coming out of the hole.

Then he heard giants talking within the blackness of the open door, and suddenly, a half dozen verbeeg emerged into the sunlight. He turned to Drizzt but found the ever-alert drow already standing behind him, his large eyes squinting as he watched the giants in the bright light.

"I do not know what they are about," Wulfgar told Drizzt.

"They're seeking their missing companions," Drizzt replied. He'd heard, more clearly with his keen ears than his friend, distinct pieces of the conversation that had taken place before the giants emerged. These verbeeg had been instructed to exercise all possible caution, but they were to find the long overdue patrol, or at least determine where the missing giants had gone off to. They were expected to return that same night, with or without the others.

"We must warn Bruenor," said Wulfgar.

"This group will have found their dead companions and alerted the lair long before we could return," replied Drizzt. "Besides, I believe that Bruenor has enough giants to deal with already."

"What, then?" asked Wulfgar. "Surely the lair will be tenfold more difficult to defeat if they expect trouble." The barbarian noticed that the simmering flame had returned to the drow's eye.

"The lair will be none the wiser if these giants never return," Drizzt said matter-of-factly, as though the task of stopping six hunting verbeeg was a minor obstacle. Wulfgar listened in disbelief, though he had already guessed what Drizzt had in mind.

The drow noted Wulfgar's apprehension and smiled broadly. "Come, boy," he instructed, using the condescending title to stir up the barbarian's pride. "You have trained hard for many tendays in preparation for a moment such as this." He sprang lightly across a small chasm on the stone ledge and turned back on Wulfgar, his eyes sparkling wildly as they caught the afternoon sun.

"Come," the drow repeated, beckoning with one hand. "There are only six of them!"

Wulfgar shook his head resignedly and sighed. During the tendays of training, he had come to know Drizzt as a controlled and deadly swordsman who weighed every feint and strike with calm precision. But in the last two days, Wulfgar had seen an overly daring—even reckless—side of the drow. Drizzt's unwavering confidence was the only thing that convinced Wulfgar that the elf wasn't suicidal, and the only thing that compelled Wulfgar to follow him against his own better judgment. He wondered if there was any limit to how far he would trust the drow.

He knew then and there that Drizzt would someday lead him into a situation from which there was no escape.

⚔ ⚔ ⚔ ⚔

The giant patrol traveled southward for a short while, Drizzt and Wulfgar secretly in tow. The verbeeg found no immediate trace of the missing giants and feared that they were getting too close to the dwarven mines, so they turned sharply back to the northeast, in the general direction of the flat rock where the skirmish had taken place.

"We must move on them soon," Drizzt told his companion. "Let us close in on our prey."

Wulfgar nodded. A short time later, they approached a broken area of jagged stones, where the narrow path twisted and turned suddenly. The ground was sloping upward slightly, and the companions recognized that the path they traveled would move out to the rim of a small chasm. The daylight had faded enough to provide some cover. Drizzt and Wulfgar exchanged knowing glances; the time had come for action.

Drizzt, by far the more battle-seasoned of the two, quickly discerned the mode of attack that offered the best chance of success. He motioned silently for Wulfgar to pause. "We have to strike and move away," he whispered, "and then strike again."

"Not an easy task against a wary foe," Wulfgar said.

"I have something that may aid us." The drow pulled his pack from his back and took out the small figurine and called his shadow. When the wondrous feline abruptly appeared, the barbarian gasped in horror and leaped away.

"What demon have you conjured?" he cried as loudly as he dared, his knuckles whitening under the pressure of his clutch on Aegis-fang.

"Guenhwyvar is no demon," Drizzt reassured his large companion. "She is a friend and a valuable ally." The cat growled, as if it understood, and Wulfgar took another step away.

"No natural beast," the barbarian retorted. "I shall not fight beside a demon conjured with sorcery!" The barbarians of Icewind Dale feared neither man nor beast, but the black arts were absolutely foreign to them, and their ignorance left them vulnerable.

"If the verbeeg learn the truth of the missing patrol, Bruenor and his kin will be in danger," Drizzt said darkly. "The cat will help us to stop this group. Will you allow your own fears to hinder the rescue of the dwarves?"

Wulfgar straightened and recaptured a measure of his composure. Drizzt's play on his pride and on the very real threat to the dwarves was pressuring him to temporarily put aside his revulsion for the black arts. "Send the beast away, we need no assistance."

"With the cat, we're certain to get them all. I will not risk the life of the dwarf because of your discomfort." Drizzt knew that it would take many hours for Wulfgar to accept Guenhwyvar as an ally, if it ever happened at all, but for now, all that he needed was Wulfgar's cooperation in the attack.

The giants had been marching for several hours. Drizzt watched patiently as their formation began to loosen, with one or two of the monsters occasionally lagging behind the others. Things were falling into place exactly as the drow had hoped.

The path took one last twist between two gigantic boulders, then widened considerably and sloped more steeply up the final expanse to the chasm rim. It turned sharply then, and continued along the ledge, a solid rock wall on one side, and a rocky drop on the other. Drizzt motioned to Wulfgar to stand ready, then sent the great cat into action.

⚔ ⚔ ⚔ ⚔ ⚔

The war party, a score of verbeeg with three ogres and a dozen orcs beside them, moved at an easy pace, reaching Daledrop well after the night had fallen. There were more monsters than the dwarves had originally expected, but they weren't overly concerned by the orcs and knew how to deal with ogres. The giants were the key to this battle.

The long wait did nothing to temper the raw edge of the dwarves' nerves. None of the clan had slept in nearly a day, and they remained tense and eager to avenge their kin.

The first of the verbeeg tramped onto the sloping field without incident, but when the last of the invading party reached the limits of the ambush zone, the dwarves of Mithral Hall attacked. Bruenor's group struck first, springing from their holes, often right beside a giant or orc and hacking at the nearest target. They aimed their blows to cripple, using the basic tenet of dwarven giant-fighting philosophy: the sharp edge of an axe cuts the tendon and muscles on the back of a knee, the flat head of a hammer crushes the kneecap in the front.

Bruenor felled a giant with one swing, then turned to flee, but he found himself facing the readied sword of an orc. Having no time to trade blows, Bruenor tossed his weapon into the air, shouting, "Catch!" The orc's eyes stupidly followed the axe's diversionary flight. Bruenor decked the creature by slamming his helmeted forehead on its chin, caught his axe as it fell, and scampered off into the night, pausing only for a second to kick the orc as he passed.

The monsters had been taken absolutely by surprise, and many of them already lay screaming on the ground. Then the ballistae opened up. Spear-size missiles blasted into the front ranks, knocking giants aside and into each other. The crossbowmen sprang from their concealment and launched a deadly barrage, then dropped their bows and charged down the mountainside. Bruenor's group, now in their fighting **V** formation, rushed back into the fray.

The monsters never had the chance to regroup, and by the time they were even able to raise their weapons in response, their ranks had been decimated.

The Battle of Daledrop was over in three minutes.

Not a dwarf was even seriously injured, and of the invading monsters, only the orc that Bruenor had knocked out remained alive.

⚔ ⚔ ⚔ ⚔

Guenhwyvar understood its master's wishes and leaped silently among the broken stones to the side of the trail, circling up ahead of the verbeeg and settling onto the rock wall above the path. It crouched low, no more than another of the deepening shadows. The first of the giants passed under, but the cat waited obediently, still as death, for the appropriate time. Drizzt and Wulfgar crept in closer, stealthily moving within clear sight of the back of the patrol's line.

The last of the giants, an extraordinarily fat verbeeg, paused for a moment to catch its breath.

Guenhwyvar struck quickly.

The lithe panther sprang from the wall and raked its long claws into the giant's face, then continued its bound over the monster, using the huge shoulder as a springboard, and returned to another spot on the wall. The giant howled in agony, clutching its torn face.

Aegis-fang took the creature in the back of the head, dropping it into the small gorge.

The giant in back of the remaining group heard the cry of pain and immediately charged back down the path, rounding the last bend just in time to see its unfortunate companion tumble down the rocky drop. The great cat didn't hesitate, dropping down upon its second victim, its sharp claws catching a firm hold on the giant's chest. Blood spurted wildly as the two-inch fangs sank deeply into the fleshy neck. Taking no chances, Guenhwyvar raked with all four of its mighty paws to deflect any counter, but the stunned giant was barely able to raise its arms in response before the deepest blackness closed over it.

With the rest of the patrol now coming fast, Guenhwyvar sprang away, leaving the gasping giant to drown in its own blood. Drizzt and Wulfgar took up positions behind the boulders on either side of the trail, the drow drawing his scimitars and the barbarian clutching the hammer that had returned to his hands.

The cat did not falter. It had played this scenario with its master many times before and understood well the advantage of surprise. It hesitated for a moment until the rest of the giants spotted it, then sprinted down the trail, darting between the rocks that hid its master and Wulfgar.

"Blimey!" cried one of the verbeeg, unconcerned with its dying companion. "A great huge cat, it is! An' black as me cook's kettles!"

"Be after it!" hollered another. "A new coat 'e'll make fer the one whats catches 'im!" They hopped over the fallen giant, never giving it a second thought, and charged down the trail after the panther.

Drizzt was the closest to the charging giants. He let the first two pass, concentrating on the remaining two. They crossed by the boulder side by side, and he jumped onto the path before them, jabbing the scimitar in his left hand deep into one giant's chest and blinding the other with a right-handed slash across the eyes. Using the scimitar that was planted into the first giant as a pivot, the drow wheeled behind his reeling foe and drove the other blade into the monster's back. He managed to free both blades with a subtle twist, dancing away as the mortally wounded giant toppled to the ground.

Wulfgar, too, let the lead giant go by. The second had pulled up nearly even with the barbarian when Drizzt attacked the back two. The giant stopped short and whirled, intending to help the others, but from his place behind the boulder, Wulfgar swung Aegis-fang in a sweeping arc and landed the heavy hammer squarely onto the verbeeg's chest. The monster dropped on its back, the air literally blasted from its lungs. Wulfgar reversed his swing quickly and launched Aegis-fang in the opposite direction. The lead giant spun about just in time to catch it in the face.

Without hesitation, Wulfgar pounced on the closest giant he had felled, wrapping his powerful arms around the monster's massive neck. The giant recovered quickly and put the barbarian in a bear hug, and though it was still sitting, it had little trouble lifting its smaller foe completely off the ground. But the years swinging a hammer and chopping stone in the dwarven mines had imbued the barbarian with the strength of iron. He tightened his grasp on the giant and slowly rotated his knotted arms. With a loud snap, the verbeeg's head lolled to the side.

The giant that Drizzt had blinded flailed about wildly with its huge club. The drow kept in constant motion, dancing around to each flank as the opportunity allowed, driving home thrust after thrust into the helpless monster. Drizzt aimed for any vital area he could safely reach, hoping to efficiently finish off his opponent.

Aegis-fang now securely back in his bands, Wulfgar walked over to the verbeeg he had struck in the face to make sure that it was dead. He kept an eye cautiously focused down the trail for any sign of the returning Guenhwyvar. Having seen the powerful cat at work, he had no desire to engage it personally.

When the last giant lay dead, Drizzt moved down the path to join his friend. "You have not yet come to understand your own prowess in battle!" he laughed, slapping the big man on the back. "Six giants are not beyond our ability!"

"Now do we go to find Bruenor?" Wulfgar asked, though he saw the fire still flickering dangerously in the drow's lavender eyes. He realized that they weren't leaving yet.

"No need," Drizzt replied. "I am confident that the dwarves have their situation well in hand.

"But we do have a problem," he continued. "We were able to kill the first group of giants and still retain the element of surprise. Very soon, though, with six more missing, the lair will become alert to any hint of danger."

"The dwarves should return in the morning," said Wulfgar. "We can attack the lair before midday."

"Too late," Drizzt said, pretending disappointment. "I fear that you and I may have to strike at them tonight, without delay."

Wulfgar wasn't surprised; he didn't even argue. He feared that he and the drow were taking on too much, that the drow's plan was too outrageous, but he was starting to accept one indisputable fact: he would follow Drizzt into any adventure, no matter how improbable their chances of surviving.

And he was beginning to admit to himself that he enjoyed gambling alongside the dark elf.

18

BIGGRIN'S HOUSE

Drizzt and Wulfgar were pleasantly surprised when they found the back entrance to the verbeeg lair. It sat high up on the steep incline on the western side of the rocky outcropping. Piles of garbage and bones lay strewn about the ground at the bottom of the rocks, and a thin but steady stream of smoke wafted out of the open cave, scented with the flavors of roasting mutton.

The two companions crouched in the brush below the entrance for a short while, noting the degree of activity. The moon had come up, bright and clear, and the night had lightened considerably. "I wonder if we'll be in time for dinner," remarked the drow, still smirking wryly. Wulfgar shook his head and laughed at the dark elf's uncanny composure.

Although the two often heard sounds from the shadows just beyond the opening, pots clanging and occasional voices, no giant showed itself outside the cave until shortly before moonset. A fat verbeeg, presumably the lair's cook from its dress, shuffled out onto the doorstep and dumped a load of garbage from a large iron pot down the slope.

"He's mine," said Drizzt, suddenly serious. "Can you provide a distraction?"

"The cat will do," Wulfgar answered, though he wasn't keen on being alone with Guenhwyvar.

Drizzt crept up the rocky slope, trying to stay in the dark shadows as he went. He knew that he would remain vulnerable in the moonlight until he got above the entrance, but the climb proved rougher than he had expected and the going was slow. When he was almost to the opening, he heard the giant chef stirring by the entrance, apparently lifting a second pot of garbage for dumping.

But the drow had nowhere to go. A call from within the cave diverted the cook's attention. Realizing how little time he had to get to safety, Drizzt sprinted the last few feet to the door level and peered around the corner into the torchlit kitchen.

The room was roughly square with a large stone oven on the wall across from the cave entrance. Next to the oven was a wooden door slightly ajar, and behind this Drizzt heard several giant voices. The cook was nowhere in sight, but a pot of garbage sat on the floor just inside the entrance.

"He'll be back soon," the drow muttered to himself as he picked his handholds and crept noiselessly up the wall and above the cave entrance. At the base of the slope, a nervous Wulfgar sat absolutely motionless as Guenhwyvar stalked back and forth before him.

A few minutes later the giant chef came out with the pot. As the verbeeg dumped the garbage, Guenhwyvar moved into view. One great leap took the cat to the base of the slope. Tilting its head up at the cook, the black panther growled.

"Ah, git outta here, ye mangy puss," snapped the giant, apparently unimpressed and unsurprised by the sudden appearance of the panther, "afore I squash yer head an' drop ye into a stewin' pot!"

The verbeeg's threat was an idle one. Even as it stood shaking an oversized fist, its attention fully on the cat, the dark shape that was Drizzt Do'Urden sprang from the wall onto its back. His scimitars already in hand the drow wasted no time in cutting an ear-to-ear smile into the giant's throat. Without uttering a cry the verbeeg tumbled down the rocks to settle in with the rest of the garbage. Abruptly Drizzt dropped to the cave step and spun around, praying that no other giants had entered the kitchen.

He was safe for the moment. The room was empty. As Guenhwyvar and then Wulfgar crested the ledge, he signaled to them silently to follow him in.

The kitchen was small (for giants) and sparsely stocked. There was one table on the right wall which held several pans. Next to it was a large chopping block with a garish cleaver, rusty and jagged and apparently unwashed for tendays, buried into it. Over to Drizzt's left were shelves holding spices and herbs and other supplies. The drow went to investigate these as Wulfgar moved to peer into the adjoining—and occupied—room.

Also square, this second area was a bit larger than the kitchen. A long table divided the room in half, and beyond it, directly across from where he stood, Wulfgar saw a second door. Three giants sat at the side of the table closest to Wulfgar, a fourth stood between them and the door, and two more sat on the opposite side. The group feasted on mutton and slurped thick stew, all the while cursing and taunting each other—a typical dinner gathering of verbeeg. Wulfgar noted with more than a passing interest that the monsters tore the meat from the bones with their bare bands. There weren't any weapons in the room.

Drizzt, holding a bag he had found on the shelves, drew one of his scimitars again and moved with Guenhwyvar to join Wulfgar. "Six," Wulfgar whispered, pointing to the room. The big barbarian hoisted Aegis-fang and nodded eagerly. Drizzt peeked through the door and quickly formulated an attack plan.

He pointed to Wulfgar, then to the door. "Right," he whispered. Then he indicated himself. "Behind you, left."

Wulfgar understood him perfectly, but wondered why he hadn't included Guenhwyvar. The barbarian pointed to the cat.

Drizzt merely shrugged and smiled, and Wulfgar understood. Even the skeptical barbarian was confident that Guenhwyvar would figure out where it best fit in.

Wulfgar shook the nervous tingles out of his muscles and clenched Aegis-fang tightly. With a quick wink to his companion, he burst through the door and pounced at the nearest target. The giant, the only one of the group standing at the time, managed to turn and face his attacker, but that was all. Aegis-fang swung in a low sweep and rose with deadly accuracy, smashing into its belly. Driving upward, it crushed the giant's lower chest. With his incredible strength, Wulfgar actually lifted the huge monster several feet off the ground. It fell, broken and breathless, beside the barbarian, but he paid it no more heed; he was already planning his second strike.

Drizzt, Guenhwyvar close on his heels, rushed past his friend toward the two stunned giants seated farthest to the left at the table. He jerked open the bag he held and twirled as he reached his targets, blinding them in a puff of flour. The drow never slowed as he passed, gouging his scimitar into the throat of one of the powdered verbeeg and then rolling backward over the top of the wooden table. Guenhwyvar sprang on the other giant, his powerful jaws tearing out the monster's groin.

The two verbeeg on the far side of the table were the first of their group to truly react. One leaped to stand ready to meet Drizzt's whirling charge, while the second, unwittingly singling itself out as Wulfgar's next target, bolted for the back door.

Wulfgar marked the escaping giant quickly and launched Aegis-fang without hesitation. If Drizzt, at that time in midroll across the table, had realized just how close his form had come to intercepting the twirling warhammer, he might have had a few choice words for his friend. But the hammer found its mark, bashing into the verbeeg's shoulder and knocking the monster into the wall with enough force to break its neck.

The giant Drizzt had gored lay squirming on the floor, clutching its throat in a futile attempt to quell the flow of its lifeblood. And Guenhwyvar was having little trouble dispatching the other. Only two verbeeg remained to fight.

Drizzt finished his roll and landed on his feet on the far side of the table, nimbly dodging the grasp of the waiting verbeeg. He darted around, putting himself between his opponent and the door. The giant, its huge hands outstretched, spun around and charged. But the drow's second scimitar was out with the first, interweaving in a mesmerizing dance of death. As each blade flashed out, it sent another of the giant's gnarled fingers spinning to the floor. Soon the verbeeg had nothing more than two bloodied stumps where its hands had once been. Enraged beyond sanity, it swung its clublike arms wildly. Drizzt's scimitar quickly slipped under the side of its skull, ending the creature's madness.

Meanwhile, the last giant had rushed the unarmed barbarian. It wrapped its huge arms around Wulfgar and lifted him into the air, trying to squeeze the life out of him. Wulfgar tightened his muscles in a desperate attempt to prevent his larger foe from snapping the bones in his back.

The barbarian had trouble finding his breath. Enraged, he slammed his fist into the giant's chin and raised his hand for a second blow.

But then, following the dweomer that Bruenor had cast upon it, the magical warhammer was back in his grasp. With a howl of glee, Wulfgar drove home the butt end of Aegis-fang and put out the giant's eye. The giant loosened its grip, reeling backward in agony. The world had become such a blur of pain to the monster that it didn't even see Aegis-fang arcing over Wulfgar's head and speeding toward its skull. It felt a hot explosion as the heavy hammer split open its head, bouncing the lifeless body into the table and knocking stew and mutton all over the floor.

"Don't spill the food!" cried Drizzt in mock anger as he rushed to retrieve a particularly juicy-looking chop.

Suddenly they heard heavy-booted footsteps and shouts coming down the corridor behind the second door. "Back outside!" yelled Wulfgar as he turned toward the kitchen.

"Hold!" shouted Drizzt. "The fun is just beginning!" He pointed to a dim, torchlit tunnel that ran off the left wall of the room. "Down there! Quickly!"

Wulfgar knew that they were pushing their luck, but once again he found himself listening to the elf.

And once again the barbarian was smiling.

Wulfgar passed the heavy wooden supports at the beginning of the tunnel and raced off into the dimness. He had gone about thirty feet, Guenhwyvar loping uncomfortably close at his side, when he realized that Drizzt wasn't following. He turned around just in time to see the drow stroll casually out of the room and past the wooden beams. Drizzt had sheathed his scimitars. Instead, he held a long dagger, its wicked tip planted firmly into a piece of mutton.

"The giants?" asked Wulfgar from the darkness.

Drizzt stepped to the side, behind one of the massive wooden beams.

"Right behind me," he explained calmly as he tore another bite off of his meal. Wulfgar's jaw dropped open when a pack of frothing verbeeg charged into the tunnel, never noticing the concealed drow.

"Prayne de crabug ahm keike rinedere be-yogt iglo kes gron!" Wulfgar shouted as he spun on his heel and sprinted off down the corridor, hoping that it didn't lead to a dead end.

Drizzt pulled the mutton off the end of his blade and accidentally dropped it to the ground, cursing silently at the waste of good food. Licking the dagger clean, he waited patiently. As the last verbeeg rambled past, he darted from his concealment, whipped the dagger into the back of the trailing giant's knee, and scooted around the other side of the beam. The wounded giant howled in pain, but by the time it or its companions had turned back around, the drow was nowhere to be seen.

Wulfgar rounded a bend and slipped against the wall, easily guessing what had stopped the pursuit. The pack had turned back when they found that there was another intruder nearer the exit.

A giant leaped through the supports and stood with its legs wide apart and its club ready, its eyes going from door to door as it tried to figure out which route the unseen assailant had taken. Behind it and off to the side, Drizzt pulled a small knife out of each of his boots and wondered how the giants could be stupid enough to fall for the same trick twice in a span of ten seconds. Not about to argue with good fortune, the elf scrambled out behind his next victim and before its companions still in the tunnel could shout a call of warning, drove one of the knives deep into the giant's thigh, severing the hamstring. The giant lurched over to the side and Drizzt, hopping by, marveled at how wonderful a target the thick veins in a verbeeg's neck make when the monster's jaw is clenched in pain.

But the drow had no time to pause and ponder the fortunes of battle. The rest of the pack—five angry giants—had already thrown aside their wounded companion in the tunnel and were only a few strides behind. He put the second knife deep into the verbeeg's neck and headed for the door leading deeper into the lair. He would have made it, except that the first giant coming back into the room happened to be carrying a stone. As a rule, verbeeg are quite adept at rock throwing, and this one was better than most. The drow's unhelmeted head was its target, and its throw was true.

Wulfgar's throw was on target, too. Aegis-fang shattered the backbone of the trailing giant as it passed its wounded companion in the tunnel. The injured verbeeg, working to get Drizzt's dagger out of its knee, stared in disbelief at its suddenly dead companion and at the berserk death charge of the ferocious barbarian.

Out of the corner of his eye, Drizzt saw the stone coming. He managed to duck enough to avoid getting his head caved in, but the heavy missile caught him in the shoulder and sent him flying to the floor. The world spun around him as though he was its axis. He fought to reorient himself, for in the back of his mind he understood that the giant was coming to finish him off. But everything seemed a blur. Then something lying close to his face managed to hold his attention. He fixed his eyes on it, straining to find a focus and force everything else to stop spinning.

A verbeeg finger.

The drow was back. Quickly, he reached for his weapon.

He knew that he was too late when he saw the giant, club raised for a death blow, towering above him.

The wounded giant stepped into the middle of the tunnel to meet the barbarian's charge. The monster's leg had gone numb, and it could not plant its feet firmly. Wulfgar, Aegis-fang comfortably back in his hands, swatted it aside and continued into the room. Two of the giants were waiting for him.

Guenhwyvar wove between a giant's legs as it turned and launched itself as high and far as its sleek muscles could take it. Just as the verbeeg standing over Drizzt started to swing its club at the prone elf, Drizzt saw a shade of black cross in front of its face. A jagged tear lined the giant's cheek. Drizzt understood what had happened when he heard Guenhwyvar's padded paws set down on the table and propel the cat further across the room. Though a second giant now joined the first and both had their clubs poised to strike, Drizzt had gained all the time that he needed. In a lightning movement, he slid one of the scimitars from its sheath and thrust it into the first giant's groin. The monster doubled over in agony, a shield for Drizzt, and caught the blow from its comrade on the back of its head. The drow mumbled "Thank you," as he rolled over the corpse, landing on his feet and again thrusting upward, this time lifting his body to follow the blade.

Hesitation had cost another giant its life. For as the stunned verbeeg stared dumbfoundedly at its friend's brains splattered all over its club, the drow's curved blade sliced under its rib cage, tearing through lungs and finding its mark in the monster's heart.

Time moved slowly for the mortally wounded giant. The club it had dropped seemed to take minutes to reach the floor. With the barely perceptible motion of a falling tree, the verbeeg slid back from the scimitar. It knew that it was falling, but the floor never came up to meet it. Never came up . . .

Wulfgar hoped that he had hit the wounded giant in the tunnel hard enough to keep it out of the fray for a while—he would be in a tight spot indeed if it came up behind him then. He had all that he could handle parrying and counterthrusting with the two giants he now faced. He needn't have worried about his backside, though, for the wounded verbeeg slumped against the wall in the tunnel, oblivious to its surroundings. And in the opposite direction, Drizzt had just finished off the other two giants. Wulfgar laughed aloud when he saw his friend wiping the blood from his blade and walking back across the room. One of the verbeeg noticed the dark elf, too, and it jumped out of its fight with the barbarian to engage this new foe.

"Ay, ye little runt, ye think ye can face me even up an' live to talk about it?" bellowed the giant.

Feigning desperation, Drizzt glanced all about him. As usual, he found an easy way to win this fight. Using a stalking belly-crawl, Guenhwyvar had slithered behind the giant bodies, trying to get into a favorable position. Drizzt took a small step backward, goading the giant into the great cat's path.

The giant's club crashed into Wulfgar's ribs and pushed him up against the wooden beam. The barbarian was made of tougher stuff than wood, though, and he took the blow stoically, returning it two-fold with Aegis-fang. Again the verbeeg struck, and again Wulfgar countered. The barbarian had been fighting with hardly a break for over ten minutes, but adrenaline coursed through his veins, and he barely felt winded. He began to appreciate the endless hours toiling for Bruenor in the mines, and the miles and miles of running Drizzt had led him through during their sessions as his blows started to fall with increasing frequency on his tiring opponent.

The giant advanced on Drizzt. "Arg, hold yer ground, ye miserable rat!" it growled. "An' none o' yer sneaky tricks! We wants to see how ye does in a fair fight."

Just as the two came together, Guenhwyvar darted the remaining few feet and sank his fangs deep into the back of the verbeeg's ankle. Reflexively, the giant shot a glance at the rear attacker, but it recovered quickly and shot its eyes back to the elf . . .

. . . Just in time to see the scimitar entering its chest.

Drizzt answered the monster's puzzled expression with a question. "Where in the nine hells did you ever find the notion that I would fight fair?"

The verbeeg lurched away. The blade hadn't found its heart, but it knew that the wound would soon prove fatal if untended. Blood poured freely down the monster's leather tunic, and it labored visibly as it tried to breath.

Drizzt alternated his attacks with Guenhwyvar, striking and ducking away from the lumbering counter while his partner rushed in on the monster's other side. They knew, and the giant did, too, that this fight would soon be over.

The giant fighting Wulfgar could no longer sustain a defensive posture with its heavy club. Wulfgar was beginning to tire as well, so he started to sing an old tundra war song, the Song of Tempus, its rousing notes inspiring him into one final barrage. He waited for the verbeeg's club to inch inevitably downward and then launched Aegis-fang once, twice, and then a third time. Wulfgar nearly collapsed in exhaustion after the third swing, but the giant lay crumpled on the floor. The barbarian leaned wearily on his weapon and watched his two friends nip and scratch their verbeeg to pieces.

"Well done!" Wulfgar laughed when the last giant fell. Drizzt walked over to the barbarian, his left arm hanging limply at his side. His jacket and shirt were torn where the stone had struck, and the exposed skin of his shoulder was swollen and bruised.

Wulfgar eyed the wound with genuine concern, but Drizzt answered his unspoken question by raising the arm above him, though he grimaced in pain with the effort. "It'll be quick to mend," he assured Wulfgar. "Just a nasty bump, and I find that a small cost to weigh against the bodies of thirteen verbeeg!"

A low groan issued from the tunnel.

"Twelve as yet," Wulfgar corrected. "Apparently one is not quite done kicking." With a deep breath, Wulfgar lifted Aegis-fang and turned to finish the task.

"A moment, first," insisted Drizzt, a thought pressing on his mind. "When the giants charged you in the tunnel, you yelled something in your home tongue, I believe. What was it you said?"

Wulfgar laughed heartily. "An old Elk tribe battle cry," he explained. "Strength to my friends, and death to my foes!"

Drizzt eyed the barbarian suspiciously and wondered just how deep ran Wulfgar's ability to fabricate a lie on demand.

⚔ ⚔ ⚔ ⚔ ⚔

The injured verbeeg was still propped against the tunnel wall when the two companions and Guenhwyvar came upon it. The drow's dagger remained deeply buried in the giant's knee, its blade caught fast between two bones. The giant eyed the men with hate-filled yet strangely calm eyes as they approached.

"Ye'll pay fer all o' this," it spat at Drizzt. "Biggrin'll play with ye afore killin' ye, be sure o' that!"

"So it has a tongue," Drizzt said to Wulfgar. And then to the giant, "Biggrin?"

"Laird o' the cave," answered the giant. "Biggrin'll be wantin' to meet ye."

"And we'll be wanting to meet Biggrin!" stormed Wulfgar. "We have a debt to repay—a little matter concerning two dwarves!" As soon as Wulfgar mentioned the dwarves, the giant spat again. Drizzt's scimitar flashed and poised an inch from the monster's throat.

"Kill me then an' have done," laughed the giant, genuinely un-caring. The monster's ease unnerved Drizzt. "I serve the master!" proclaimed the giant. "Glory is to die for Akar Kessell!"

Wulfgar and Drizzt looked at each other uneasily. They had never seen or heard of this kind of fanatical dedication in a verbeeg, and the sight disturbed them. The primary fault of the verbeeg which had always kept them from gaining dominance over the smaller races was their unwillingness to devote themselves wholeheartedly to any cause and their inability to follow one leader.

"Who is Akar Kessell?" demanded Wulfgar.

The giant laughed evilly. "If friends o' the towns ye be, ye'll know soon enough!"

"I thought you said that Biggrin was laird of this cave," said Drizzt.

"The cave," answered the giant. "And once a tribe. But Biggrin follows the master now!"

"We've got trouble," Drizzt mumbled to Wulfgar. "Have you ever heard of a verbeeg chieftain giving up its dominance to another without a fight?"

"I fear for the dwarves," said Wulfgar.

Drizzt turned back to the giant and decided to change the subject so that he could extract some information more immediate to their situation. "What is at the end of this tunnel?"

"Nothin'," said the verbeeg, too quickly. "Er, just a place for us t' sleep, is all."

Loyal, but stupid, noted Drizzt. He turned to Wulfgar again. "We have to take out Biggrin and any others in the cave who might be able to get back to warn this Akar Kessell."

"What about this one?" asked Wulfgar. But the giant answered the question for Drizzt. Delusions of glory pushed it to seek death in the wizard's service. It tightened its muscles, ignoring the pain in its knee, and lunged at the companions.

Aegis-fang smashed the verbeeg's collarbone and neck at the same time Drizzt's scimitar was slipping through its ribs and Guenhwyvar was locking onto its gut.

But the giant's death mask was a smile.

✕ ✕ ✕ ✕ ✕

The corridor behind the back door of the dining room was unlit, and the companions had to pull a torch from its sconce in the other corridor to take with them. As they wound their way down the long tunnel, moving deeper and deeper into the hill, they passed many small chambers, most empty, but some holding crated stores of various sorts: foodstuffs, skins, and extra clubs and spears. Drizzt surmised that Akar Kessell planned to use this cave as a home base for his army.

The blackness was absolute for some distance and Wulfgar, lacking the darkvision of his elven companion, grew nervous as the torch began to burn low. But then they came into a wide chamber, by far the largest they had seen, and beyond its reaches, the tunnel spilled out into the open night.

"We have come to the front door," said Wulfgar. "And it's ajar. Do you believe that Biggrin has left?"

"Sssh," hushed Drizzt. The drow thought that he had heard something in the darkness on the far right. He motioned for Wulfgar to stay in the middle of the room with the torch as he crept away into the shadows.

Drizzt stopped short when he heard gruff giant voices ahead, though he couldn't figure out why he couldn't see their bulky silhouettes. When he came upon a large hearth, he understood. The voices were echoing through the chimney.

"Biggrin?" asked Wulfgar when he came up.

"Must be," reasoned Drizzt. "Think you can fit through the chimney?"

The barbarian nodded. He hoisted Drizzt up first—the drow's left arm still wasn't of much use to him—and followed, leaving Guenhwyvar to keep watch.

The chimney snaked up a few yards, then came to an intersection. One way led down to a room from which the voices were coming, and the other thinned as it rose to the surface. The conversation was loud and heated now, and Drizzt moved down to investigate. Wulfgar held the drow's feet to help him inch down the final descent, as the slope became nearly vertical. Hanging upside down, Drizzt peeked under the rim of the hearth in another room. He saw three giants: one by a door at the far end of the room, looking as though it wanted to leave, and a second with its back to the hearth, being scolded by the third, an immensely wide and tall frost giant. Drizzt knew by the twisted, lipless smile that he looked upon Biggrin.

"To tell Biggrin!" pleaded the smaller giant.

"Ye ran from a fight," scowled Biggrin. "Ye left yer friends t' die!"

"No . . ." protested the giant, but Biggrin had heard enough. With one swipe of its huge axe, it lopped the smaller giant's head off.

⚔ ⚔ ⚔ ⚔

The men found Guenhwyvar diligently on watch when they came out of the chimney. The big cat turned and growled in recognition when it saw its companions, and Wulfgar, not understanding the throaty purr to be a friendly sound, took a cautious step away.

"There has to be a side tunnel off the main corridor further down," Drizzt reasoned, having no time to be amused by his friend's nervousness.

"Let's get this over with, then," said Wulfgar.

They found the passage as the drow had predicted and soon came to a door they figured would lead to the room with the remaining giants. They clapped each other on the shoulder for luck and Drizzt patted Guenhwyvar, though Wulfgar declined the drow's invitation to do likewise. Then they burst in.

The room was empty. A door previously invisible to Drizzt from his vantage point at the hearth stood ajar.

⚔ ⚔ ⚔ ⚔

Biggrin sent its lone remaining soldier out the secret side door with a message for Akar Kessell. The big giant had been disgraced, and it knew that the wizard wouldn't readily accept the loss of so many valuable troops. Biggrin's only chance was to take care of the two intruding warriors and hope that their heads would appease its unmerciful boss. The giant pressed its ear to the door and waited for its victims to enter the adjoining room.

× × × × ×

Wulfgar and Drizzt passed through the second door and came into a lavish chamber, its floor adorned with plush furs and large, puffy pillows. Two other doors led out of the room. One was slightly open, a darkened corridor beyond, and the other was closed.

Suddenly Wulfgar stopped Drizzt with an outstretched hand and motioned for the drow to be quiet. The intangible quality of a true warrior, the sixth sense that allows him to sense unseen danger, had come into play. Slowly the barbarian turned to the closed door and lifted Aegis-fang above his head. He paused for a moment and cocked his head, straining to hear a confirming sound. None came, but Wulfgar trusted his instincts. He roared to Tempus and launched the hammer. It split the door asunder with a thunderous snap and dropped the planks—and Biggrin—to the floor.

Drizzt noticed the swing of the open secret door across the room beyond the giant chieftain and realized that the last of the giants must have slipped away. Quickly the drow set Guenhwyvar into motion. The panther understood, too, for it bolted away, clearing the writhing form of Biggrin with one great bound, and charged out of the cave to give chase to the escaping verbeeg.

Blood streamed down the side of the big giant's head, but the thick bone of its skull had rejected the hammer. Drizzt and Wulfgar looked on in disbelief as the huge frost giant shook its jowls and rose to meet them.

"It can't do that," protested Wulfgar.

"This giant's a stubborn one," Drizzt shrugged.

The barbarian waited for Aegis-fang to return to his grasp, then moved with the drow to face Biggrin.

The giant stayed in the doorway to prevent either of its foes from flanking it as Wulfgar and Drizzt confidently moved in. The three exchanged ominous stares and a few easy swings as they felt each other out.

"You must be Biggrin," Drizzt said, bowing.

"That I am," proclaimed the giant. "Biggrin! The last foe yer eyes'll see!"

"Confident as well as stubborn," Wulfgar remarked.

"Little human," the giant retorted, "I've squashed a hunnerd o' yer puny kin!"

"More reason for us to kill you," Drizzt stated calmly.

With sudden speed and ferocity that surprised its two opponents, Biggrin took a wide sweep with its huge axe. Wulfgar stepped back out of its deadly range, and Drizzt managed to duck under the blow, but the drow shuddered when he saw the axe blade take a fair-sized chunk out of the stone wall.

Wulfgar jumped right back at the monster as the axe passed him, pounding on Biggrin's broad chest with Aegis-fang. The giant flinched but took the blow.

"Ye'll have t' hit me harder 'an that, puny man!" it bellowed as it launched a mighty backswing with the flat head of the axe.

Again Drizzt slipped below the swing. Wulfgar, however, battle-weary as he was, did not move quickly enough to back out of range. The barbarian managed to get Aegis-fang up in front of him, but the sheer force of Biggrin's heavy weapon smashed him into the wall. He crumpled to the floor.

Drizzt knew that they were in trouble. His left arm remained useless, his reflexes were slowing with exhaustion, and this giant was simply too powerful for him to parry any blows. He managed to slip in one short thrust with his scimitar as the giant recovered for its next swing, and then he fled toward the main corridor.

"Run, ye dark dog!" roared the giant. "I'll after ye, an' I'll have ye!" Biggrin charged after Drizzt, smelling the kill.

The drow sheathed his scimitar as he reached the main passage and looked for a spot to ambush the monster. Nothing presented itself, so he went halfway to the exit and waited.

"Where can ye hide?" Biggrin taunted as its huge bulk entered the corridor. Poised in the shadows, the drow threw his two knives. Both hit home, but Biggrin hardly slowed.

Drizzt moved outside the cave. He knew that if Biggrin didn't follow him, he would have to go back in; he certainly couldn't leave Wulfgar to die. The first rays of dawn had found their way onto the mountain, and Drizzt worried that the growing light would spoil any chance he had for ambush. Scrambling up one of the small trees that concealed the exit, he pulled out his dagger.

Biggrin charged out into the sunlight and looked around for signs of the fleeing drow. "Yer about, ye miserable dog! Ye've no place to run!"

Suddenly Drizzt was on top of the monster, gouging its face and neck in a barrage of stabs and slices. The giant howled in rage and jerked its massive body backward violently, sending Drizzt, who could not gain a firm hold with his weakened arm, flying back into the tunnel. The drow landed heavily on his injured shoulder and nearly swooned in agony. He squirmed and twisted for a moment, trying to regain his feet, but he bumped into a heavy boot. He knew that Biggrin couldn't have gotten to him so quickly. He turned slowly onto his back, wondering where this new giant had come from.

But the drow's outlook changed dramatically when he saw that Wulfgar stood over him, Aegis-fang firmly in his hand and a grim look stamped upon his face. Wulfgar never took his eyes off of the giant as it entered the tunnel.

"He's mine," the barbarian said grimly.

Biggrin looked hideous indeed. The side of its head where the hammer had struck was caked with dark, dried blood, while the other, and several spots on its face and neck, ran bright with blood from new wounds. The two knives Drizzt had thrown were still sticking in the giant's chest like morbid medals of honor.

"Can you take it again?" Wulfgar challenged as he sent Aegis-fang on a second flight toward the giant.

In answer, Biggrin stuck out his chest defiantly to block the blow. "I can take whatere' ye have t'give!" it boasted.

Aegis-fang slammed home, and Biggrin staggered back a step. The hammer had cracked a rib or two, but the giant could handle that.

More deadly, though, and unknown to Biggrin, Aegis-fang had driven one of Drizzt's knives through the lining of its heart.

"I can run, now," Drizzt whispered to Wulfgar when he saw the giant advancing again.

"I stay," the barbarian insisted without the slightest tremor of fear in his voice.

Drizzt pulled his scimitar. "Well spoken, brave friend. Let us fell this foul beast—there's food to be eaten!"

"Ye'll find that more a task than ye talk!" Biggrin retorted. It felt a sudden stinging in its chest, but it grunted away the pain. "I've felt the best that ye can hit, an' still I come at ye! Ye can no' hope t' win!"

Both Drizzt and Wulfgar feared that there was more truth to the giant's boasts than either of them would admit. They were on their last legs, wounded and winded, yet determined to stay and finish the task.

But the complete confidence of the great giant as it steadily approached was more than a little unnerving.

Biggrin realized that something was terribly wrong when it got within a few steps of the two companions. Wulfgar and Drizzt knew, too, for the giant's stride suddenly slowed visibly.

The giant looked at them in outrage as though it had been deceived. "Dogs!" it gasped, a gout of blood bursting from its mouth. "What trick . . ."

Biggrin fell dead without another word.

⚔ ⚔ ⚔ ⚔ ⚔

"Should we go after the cat?" Wulfgar asked when they got back to the secret door.

Drizzt was wrapping a torch out of some rags he had found. "Faith in the shadow," he answered. "Guenhwyvar will not let the verbeeg escape. Besides, I have a good meal waiting for me back in the cave."

"You go," Wulfgar told him. "I shall stay here and watch for the cat's return."

Drizzt clasped the big man's shoulder as he started to leave. They had been through a lot in the short time they had been together, and Drizzt suspected that the excitement was just beginning. The drow sang a feasting song as he started to the main passage, but only as a dodge to Wulfgar, for the dinner table wouldn't be his first stop. The giant they had spoken with earlier had been evasive when asked about what lay down the one tunnel they had yet to explore. And with everything else they had found, Drizzt believed that could only mean one thing—treasure.

ꗞ ꗞ ꗞ ꗞ ꗞ

The great panther loped along over the broken stones, easily gaining on the heavy-footed giant. Soon Guenhwyvar could hear the verbeeg's labored breathing as the creature struggled with every leap and climb. The giant was making for Daledrop and the open tundra beyond. But so frenzied was its flight that it didn't move off the face of Kelvin's Cairn to the easier ground of the valley. It sought a straighter route, believing it to be the quicker path to safety.

Guenhwyvar knew the areas of the mountain as well as its master, knew where every creature on the mountain laired. The cat had already discerned where it wanted the giant to go. Like a shepherd's dog, it closed the remaining distance and scratched at the giant's flanks, veering it into the direction of a deep mountain pool. The terrified verbeeg, certain that the deadly warhammer or darting scimitar weren't far behind, didn't dare stop and engage the panther. It surged blindly along the path Guenhwyvar had chosen.

A short time later, Guenhwyvar broke away from the giant and raced ahead. When the cat reached the edge of the cold water, it tilted its head and concentrated its keen senses, hoping to spy something that could help it complete the task. Then Guenhwyvar noticed a tiny shimmer of movement under the sparkles of the first light on the water. Its sharp eyes sorted out the long shape lying deathly still. Satisfied that the trap was set, Guenhwyvar moved back behind a nearby ledge to wait.

The giant lumbered up to the pool, breathing heavily. It leaned against a boulder for a moment, despite its terror. Things seemed safe enough for the moment. As soon as it had caught its breath, the giant looked around quickly for signs of pursuit, then started forward again.

There was only one path across the pool, a fallen log that spanned the

---

center, and all the alternative routes around the pool, though the water wasn't very wide, weaved around sheer drops and jutting rock faces and promised to be slow going.

The verbeeg tested the log. It seemed sturdy, so the monster cautiously started across. The cat waited for the giant to get close to the center of the pool, then charged from its hiding place and launched itself into the air at the verbeeg. The cat landed heavily into the surprised giant, planting its paws in the monster's chest and rebounding back toward the safety of the shore. Guenhwyvar splashed into the icy pool but scrambled quickly out of the perilous water. The giant, though, swung its arms wildly for a moment, trying to hold its precarious balance, then toppled in with a splash. The water rushed up to suck it down. Desperately, the giant lunged for a nearby floating log, the shape that Guenhwyvar had recognized earlier.

But as the verbeeg's hands came down, the form it had thought to be a log exploded into movement as the fifty-foot water constrictor threw itself around its prey with dizzying speed. The unrelenting coils quickly pinned the giant's arms to its side and began their merciless squeeze.

Guenhwyvar shook the freezing water from its glistening black coat and looked back to the pool. As yet another length of the monstrous snake locked under the verbeeg's chin and pulled the helpless monster under the surface, the panther was satisfied that the mission was complete. With a long, loud roar proclaiming victory, Guenhwyvar bounded off toward the lair.

19
GRIM TIÐINGS

Drizzt padded through the tunnels and past the bodies of the dead giants, slowing only to grab another hunk of mutton from the large table. He crossed through the support beams and started down the dim hallway, tempering his eagerness with common sense. If the giants had hidden their treasure down here, the chamber holding it might be behind a concealed door, or there might even be some beast, though not likely another giant, since it would have joined in the fighting.

The tunnel was quite long, running straight northward, and Drizzt figured that he was now moving underneath the mass of Kelvin's Cairn. He had passed the last torch, but he was glad for the darkness. He had lived the majority of his life traveling tunnels in the lightless subterranean world of his people, and his large eyes guided him in absolute darkness more accurately than in areas of light.

The hallway ended abruptly at a barred, iron-bound door, its metal holding bar locked into place by a large chain and padlock. Drizzt felt a pang of guilt for leaving Wulfgar behind. The drow had two weaknesses: foremost was the thrill of battle, but a close second was the tingle of uncovering the booty of his vanquished foes. It wasn't the gold or gems that lured Drizzt; he didn't care for wealth and rarely even kept any of the treasures he had won. It was simply the thrill of viewing them for the first time, the excitement of sifting through them and perhaps, discovering some incredible artifact that had been lost to knowledge in ages past, or maybe the spellbook of an ancient and powerful mage.

His guilt flew away as he pulled a small lockpick from his beltpouch. He had never been formally trained in the thieving arts, but he was as agile and coordinated as any master burglar. With his sensitive fingers and acute hearing, he wasn't particularly challenged by the clumsy lock; in a matter of seconds, it fell open. Drizzt listened carefully for any sounds behind the door. Hearing none, he gently lifted the large bar and set it aside. Listening one last time, he drew one of his scimitars, held his breath in anticipation, and pushed in the door.

His breath came back out with a disappointed sigh. The room beyond glowed with the waning light of two torches. It was small and empty, except for a large, metal-rimmed mirror standing in its center. Drizzt dodged out of the mirror's path, well aware of some of the strange magical properties these items had been known to exhibit, and moved in to examine it more closely.

It was about half the height of a man but propped up to eye level by an intricately worked iron stand. That it was lined in silver and in such an out-of-the-way chamber led Drizzt to believe that there was something more here than an ordinary mirror. Yet his scrutinizing inspection revealed no arcane runes or markings of any kind that hinted at its properties.

Able to discover nothing unusual about the piece, Drizzt carelessly stepped in front of the glass. Suddenly a pinkish mist began to swirl within the mirror, giving the appearance of a three-dimensional space trapped within the flatness of the glass. Drizzt jumped to the side, more curious than afraid, and watched the growing spectacle.

The mist thickened and puffed as though fed by some hidden fire. Then its center mushroomed out and opened into a clear image of a man's face, a gaunt, hollowed visage painted in the tradition of some of the southern cities.

"Why do you bother me?" the face asked at the empty room before the mirror. Drizzt took another step to the side, further away from the apparition's line of sight. He considered confronting the mysterious mage, but figured that his friends had too much at stake for him to take such a reckless chance.

"Stand before me, Biggrin!" commanded the image. It waited for several seconds, sneering impatiently, and growing increasingly tense. "When I discover which of you idiots inadvertently summoned me, I shall turn you into a coney and put you in a pit of wolves!" the image screamed wildly. The mirror flashed suddenly and returned to normal.

Drizzt scratched his chin and wondered if there was anything more he could do or discover here. He decided that the risks were simply too great at this time.

✕ ✕ ✕ ✕ ✕

When Drizzt returned through the lair, he found Wulfgar sitting with Guenhwyvar in the main passage just a few yards from the closed and barred front doors. The barbarian stroked the cat's muscled shoulders and neck.

"I see that Guenhwyvar has won your friendship," Drizzt said as he approached.

Wulfgar smiled. "A fine ally," he said, giving the animal a playful shake. "And a true warrior!" He started to rise but was thrown violently back to the floor.

An explosion rocked the lair as a ballista bolt slammed into the heavy doors, splintering their wooden bar and blasting them in. One of the doors broke cleanly in half and the other's top hinge tore away, leaving the door hanging awkwardly by its twisted bottom hinge.

Drizzt drew his scimitar and stood protectively over Wulfgar as the barbarian tried to regain his balance.

Abruptly, a bearded fighter leaped onto the hanging door, a circular shield, its standard a mug of foaming ale, slung over one arm and a notched and bloodstained battle-axe poised in the other. "Come out and play, giants!" Bruenor called, banging his shield with his axe—as if his clan hadn't already made enough noise to rouse the lair!

"Rest easy, wild dwarf," Drizzt-laughed. "The verbeeg are all dead."

Bruenor spotted his friends and hopped down into the tunnel, soon followed by the rest of the rowdy clan. "All dead!" the dwarf cried. "Damn ye, elf, I knew ye'd keep all the play to yerself!"

"What about the reinforcements?" Wulfgar asked.

Bruenor chuckled wickedly. "Some faith, will ye, boy? They're lumped in a common hole, though buryin's too good for 'em, I say! Only one's alive, a miserable orc who'll breath only as long as 'e wags 'is stinkin' tongue!"

After the episode with the mirror, Drizzt was more than a little interested in interrogating the orc. "Have you questioned him?" he asked Bruenor.

"Ah, he's mum for now," the dwarf replied. "But I've a few things should make 'im squeal!"

Drizzt knew better. Orcs were not loyal creatures, but under the enchantment of a mage, torturing techniques weren't usually much good. They needed something to counteract the magic, and Drizzt had a notion of what might work. "Go for Regis." he instructed Bruenor. "The halfling can make the orc tell us everything we want to know."

"Torturin'd be more fun," lamented Bruenor, but he, too, understood the wisdom of the drow's suggestion. He was more than a bit curious— and worried—about so many giants working together. And now with orcs beside them. . . .

⚔ ⚔ ⚔ ⚔ ⚔

Drizzt and Wulfgar sat in the far corner of the small chamber, as far from Bruenor and the other two dwarves as they could get. One of Bruenor's troops had returned from Lonelywood with Regis that same night, and though they were all exhausted from marching and fighting, they were too anxious about the impending information to sleep. Regis and the captive orc had moved into the adjoining room for a private conversation as soon as the halfling had gotten the prisoner firmly under his control with his ruby pendant.

Bruenor busied himself preparing a new recipe—giantbrain stew— boiling the wretched, foul-smelling ingredients right in a hollowed-out verbeeg skull. "Use yer heads!" he had argued in response to Drizzt and Wulfgar's expressions of horror and disgust. "A barnyard goose tastes better 'an a wild one cause it don't use its muscles. The same oughta hold true for a giant's brains!"

Drizzt and Wulfgar hadn't seen things quite the same way. They didn't want to leave the area and miss anything that Regis might have to say, though, so they huddled in the farthest corner of the room, carrying on a private conversation.

Bruenor strained to hear them, for they were talking of something that he had more than a passing interest in.

"Half for the last one in the kitchen," Wulfgar insisted, "and half for the cat."

"And you only get half for the one at the chasm," Drizzt retorted.

"Agreed," said Wulfgar. "And we split the one in the hall and Biggrin down the middle?"

Drizzt nodded. "Then with all halves and shared kills added up, it's ten and one-half for me and ten and one-half for you."

"And four for the cat," added Wulfgar.

"Four for the cat," Drizzt echoed. "Well fought, friend. You've held your own up to now, but I've a feeling that we have a lot more fighting before us, and my greater experience will win out in the end!"

"You grow old, good elf," Wulfgar teased, leaning back against the wall, the whiteness of a confident grin showing through his blond beard. "We shall see. We shall see."

Bruenor, too, was smiling, both at the good-natured competition between his friends and at his continued pride in the young barbarian. Wulfgar was doing well to keep pace with a skilled veteran like Drizzt Do'Urden.

Regis emerged from the room, and the gray pall upon his usually jovial face deadened the lighthearted atmosphere. "We are in trouble," the halfling said grimly.

"Where's the orc?" Bruenor demanded as he pulled his axe from his belt, misunderstanding the halfling's meaning.

"In there. He's all right," Regis replied. The orc had been happy to tell its newfound friend everything about Akar Kessell's plans to invade Ten-Towns and the size of the gathering forces. Regis visibly trembled as he told his friends the news.

"All of the orc and goblin tribes and verbeeg clans of this region of the Spine of the World are banding together under a sorcerer named Akar Kessell," the halfling began. Drizzt and Wulfgar looked at each other, recognizing Kessell's name. The barbarian had thought Akar Kessell to be a huge frost giant when the verbeeg had spoken of him, but Drizzt had suspected differently, especially after the incident at the mirror.

"They plan to attack Ten-Towns," Regis continued. "And even the barbarians, led by some mighty, one-eyed leader, have joined their ranks!"

Wulfgar's face reddened in anger and embarrassment. His people fighting beside orcs! He knew the leader that Regis spoke of, for Wulfgar was of the Tribe of the Elk and had even once carried the tribe's standard as Heafstaag's herald. Drizzt painfully recalled the one-eyed king, too. He put a comforting hand on Wulfgar's shoulder.

"Go to Bryn Shander," the drow told Bruenor and Regis. "The people must prepare!"

Regis winced at the futility. If the orc's estimation of the assembling army had been correct, all of Ten-Towns joined together could not withstand the assault. The halfling dropped his head and mouthed silently, not wanting to alarm his friends any more than was necessary, "We have to leave!"

⚔ ⚔ ⚔ ⚔ ⚔

Though Bruenor and Regis were able to convince Cassius of the urgency and importance of their news, it took several days to round up the other spokesmen for council. It was the height of knucklehead season, late summer, and the last push was on to land a big catch for the final trading caravan to Luskan. The spokesmen of the nine fishing villages understood their responsibilities to their community, but they were reluctant to leave the lakes even for a single day.

And so, with the exceptions of Cassius of Bryn Shander, Muldoon, the new spokesman from Lonelywood, who looked up to Regis as the hero of his town, Glensather of Easthaven, the community ever-willing to join in for the good of Ten-Towns, and Agorwal of Termalaine who held fierce loyalty to Bruenor, the mood of the council was not very receptive.

Kemp, still bearing a grudge against Bruenor for the incident over Drizzt after the Battle of Bryn Shander, was especially disruptive. Before Cassius even had the opportunity to present the Formalities of Order, the gruff spokesman from Targos leaped up from his seat and slammed his fists down on the table. "Damn the formal readings and be on with it!" Kemp growled. "By what right do you order us in from the lakes, Cassius? Even as we sit around this table, the merchants in Luskan are preparing for their journey!"

"We have news of an invasion, Spokesman Kemp," Cassius answered calmly, understanding the fisherman's anger. "I would not have summoned you, any of you, at this time of the season if it were not urgent."

"Then the rumors are true," Kemp sneered. "An invasion, you say? Bah! I see beyond this sham of a council!"

He turned on Agorwal. The fighting between Targos and Termalaine had escalated in the past few tendays, despite Cassius's efforts to diffuse it and bring the principals of the warring towns to the bargaining table. Agorwal had agreed to a meeting, but Kemp was steadfastly against it. And so, with suspicions running high, the timing of this urgent council could not have been worse.

"This is a pitiful attempt indeed!" Kemp roared. He looked around at his fellow spokesmen. "A pitiful effort by Agorwal and his scheming supporters to bring about a favorable settlement for Termalaine in their dispute with Targos!"

Incited by the aura of suspicion that Kemp had infused, Schermont, the new spokesman from Caer-Konig, pointed an accusing finger at Jensin Brent of Caer-Dineval. "What part have you played in this treachery?" he spat at his bitter rival. Schermont had come into his position after the first spokesman from Caer-Konig had been killed on the waters of Lac Dinneshere in a battle with a Dineval boat. Dorim Lugar had been Schermont's friend and leader, and the new spokesman's policies toward hated Caer-Dineval were even more iron-handed than those of his predecessor.

Regis and Bruenor sat back quietly in helpless dismay through all of the initial bickering. Finally Cassius slammed his gavel down, snapping its handle in two and quieting the others long enough to make a point. "A few moments of silence!" he commanded. "Hold your venomous words and listen to the messenger of grim tidings!" The others fell back to their seats and remained silent, but Cassius feared that the damage had already been done.

He turned the floor over to Regis.

Honestly terrified by what he had learned from the captive orc, Regis passionately told of the battle his friends had won over the verbeeg lair and on the grass of Daledrop. "And Bruenor has captured one of the orcs that was escorting the giants," he said emphatically. Some of the spokesmen sucked in their breath at the notion of such creatures banding together, but Kemp and some of the others, ever suspicious of the more immediate threats of their rivals, and already decided on the true purpose of the meeting, remained unconvinced.

"The orc told us," Regis continued grimly, "of the coming of a powerful wizard, Akar Kessell, and his vast host of goblins and giants! They mean to conquer Ten-Towns!" He thought that his dramatics would prove effective.

But Kemp was outraged. "On the word of an orc, Cassius? You summoned us in from the lakes at this critical time on the threat of a stinking orc?"

"The halfling's tale is not an uncommon one," Schermont added. "All of us have heard a captured goblin wag its tongue in any direction it could think of to save its worthless head."

"Or perhaps you had other motives," Kemp hissed, again eyeing Agorwal.

Cassius, though he truly believed the grim tidings, sat back in his chair and said nothing. With tensions on the lakes as high as they were, and the final trading fair of a particularly fruitless fishing season fast approaching, he had suspected that this would occur. He looked resignedly at Bruenor and Regis and shrugged as once again the council degenerated into a shouting match.

Amidst the ensuing commotion, Regis slipped the ruby pendant out from under his waistcoat and nudged Bruenor. They looked at it and each other in disappointment; they had hoped that the magical gem wouldn't be needed.

Regis pounded his gavel in a call for the floor and was granted it by Cassius. Then, as he had done five years previous, he hopped up on the table and walked toward his chief antagonist.

But this time the result wasn't what Regis had expected. Kemp had spent many hours over the last five years reflecting on that council before the barbarian invasion. The spokesman was glad of the final outcome of that whole situation, and in truth, realized that he and all of Ten-Towns were indebted to the halfling for making them heed his warning. Yet it bothered Kemp more than a little that his initial stance had been so easily swayed. He was a brawling type whose first love, even above fishing, was battle, but his mind was keen and always alert to danger. He had observed Regis several times over the last few years and had listened intently to tales of the halfling's prowess in the art of persuasion. As Regis approached, the burly spokesman averted his eyes.

"Be gone trickster!" he growled, shoving his chair defensively back from the table. "You seem to have a strange way of convincing people of your point of view, but I'll not fall under your spell this time!" He addressed the other spokesmen. "Ware the halfling! He has some magic about him, be sure!"

Kemp understood that he would have no way of proving his claims, but he also realized that he wouldn't have to. Regis looked about, flustered and unable to even answer the spokesman's accusations. Even Agorwal, though the spokesman from Termalaine tactfully tried to hide the fact, would no longer look Regis straight in the eye.

"Sit down, trickster!" Kemp taunted. "Your magic's no good once we're on to you!"

Bruenor, silent up to now, suddenly leaped up, his face contorted with rage. "Is this, too, a trick, dog of Targos?" the dwarf challenged. He pulled a sack from his belt and rolled its contents, a severed verbeeg head, down the table toward Kemp. Several of the spokesmen jumped back in horror, but Kemp remained unshaken.

"We have dealt with rogue giants many times before," the spokesman replied coolly.

"Rogues?" Bruenor echoed incredulously. "Two score o' the beasts we cut down, orcs and ogres besides!"

"A passing band," Kemp explained evenly, stubbornly. "And all dead, so you have said. Why, then, does this become a matter for the council? If it is accolades you desire, mighty dwarf, then you shall have them!" His voice dripped with venom, and he watched Bruenor's reddening face with deep pleasure. "Perhaps Cassius could make a speech in your honor before all of the people of Ten-Towns."

Bruenor slammed his fists onto the table, eyeing all of the men about him in an open threat to anyone who would continue Kemp's insults. "We have come before ye to help ye save yer homes an' yer kin!" he roared. "Might be that ye believe us and ye'll do something to survive. Or might be that ye'll hear the word's o' the dog o' Targos and ye'll do nothin'. Either way, I've had enough o' ye! Do as ye will, and may yer gods show ye favor!" He turned and stalked out of the room.

Bruenor's grim tone brought many of the spokesmen to realize that the threat was simply too grave to be passed off as the deception of a desperate captive, or even as a more insidious plan by Cassius and some conspirators. Yet Kemp, proud and arrogant, and certain that Agorwal and his non-human friends, the halfling and the dwarf, were using the facade of an invasion to gain some advantage over the superior city of Targos, would not budge. Second only to Cassius in all of Ten-Towns, Kemp's opinion carried great weight, especially to the people of Caer-Konig and Caer-Dineval, who, in light of Bryn Shander's unshakable neutrality in their struggle, sought the favor of Targos.

Enough spokesmen remained suspicious of their rivals and were willing to accept Kemp's explanation to prevent Cassius from bringing the council to decisive action. The lines were soon clearly drawn.

Regis watched the spectacle as the opposing sides volleyed back and forth, but the halfling's own credibility had been destroyed, and he had no impact on the rest of the meeting. In the end, little was decided. The most that Agorwal, Glensather, and Muldoon could squeeze out of Cassius was a public declaration that, "A general warning should go out to every household in Ten-Towns. Let the people know of our grim tidings, and let

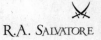

them be assured that I shall make room within the walls of Bryn Shander for every person who so desires our protection."

Regis eyed the divided spokesmen. Without unity, the halfling wondered how much protection even the high walls of Bryn Shander could offer.

20

A Slave to No Man

No arguin'," Bruenor snarled, though none of his four friends standing beside him on the rocky slopes of the climb had any intention of speaking against the decision. In their foolish pettiness and pride, the majority of the spokesmen had doomed their communities to almost certain destruction and neither Drizzt, Wulfgar, Catti-brie, nor Regis expected the dwarves to join in such a hopeless cause.

"When will you block the mines?" Drizzt asked. The drow hadn't yet decided if he would join the dwarves in the self-imposed prison of their caves, but he had planned to act as scout to Bryn Shander at least until Akar Kessell's army moved into the region.

"The preparin'll begin tonight," said Bruenor. "But once they're in place, we've no rush. We'll let the stinkin' orcs come right down our throats afore we drop the tunnels, an' take 'em in the fall. Are ye to stay with us, then?"

Drizzt shrugged his shoulders. Though he was still shunned by most of the people of Ten-Towns, the drow felt a strong sense of loyalty and wasn't sure that he could turn his back on his chosen home, even under suicidal circumstances. And Drizzt had little desire to return to the lightless underworld, even in the hospitable caverns of the dwarven town.

"And what's yer decision?" Bruenor asked Regis.

The halfling, too, was torn between his instincts for survival and his loyalty to Ten-Towns. With the help of the ruby, he had lived well during the last years on Maer Dualdon. But now his cover had been stripped away. After the rumors flowing out of the council, everyone in Bryn Shander whispered about the halfling's magical influence. It wouldn't be long before all of the communities heard about Kemp's accusations and avoided, if not openly shunned, him. Either way, Regis knew that his days of easy living in Lonelywood were nearing an end.

"Thank you for the invitation," he said to Bruenor. "I'll come in before Kessell arrives."

"Good," replied the dwarf. "Ye'll get a room near the boy, so none o' the dwarves has to hear yer bellyachin'!" He flashed Drizzt a good-natured wink.

"Nay," said Wulfgar. Bruenor looked at him curiously, misunderstanding the barbarian's intentions and wondering why he objected to having Regis beside him.

"Watch yerself, boy," the dwarf teased. "If ye're thinkin' ye're to be stayin' beside the girl, then be thinkin' about duckin' yer head from the swing o' me axe!"

Catti-brie chuckled softly, embarrassed yet truly touched.

"Your mines are not the place for me," Wulfgar said suddenly. "My life is on the plain."

"Ye forget that yer life is mine for choosin'!" Bruenor retorted. In truth, his yelling was more the short temper of a father than the outrage of a master.

Wulfgar rose before the dwarf, proud and stern. Drizzt understood and was pleased. Now Bruenor also had an idea of what the barbarian was getting at, and though he hated the thought of separation, he felt more pride in the boy at that moment than ever before.

"My time of indenture is not ended," Wulfgar began, "yet I have repaid my debt to you, my friend, and to your people many times over.

"I am Wulfgar!" he proudly proclaimed, his jaw firm and his muscles tightened with tension. "No more a boy but a man! A free man!"

Bruenor felt the moisture rimming his eyes. For the first time he did nothing to conceal it. He walked out before the huge barbarian and returned Wulfgar's unyielding stare with a look of sincere admiration.

"So ye are," Bruenor observed. "Then might I ask ye, on yer choice, if ye'll stay and fight beside me?"

Wulfgar shook his head. "My debt to you is paid, in truth. And forever I shall name you as my friend . . . dear friend. But I have another debt yet to pay." He looked out to Kelvin's Cairn and beyond. The countless stars shone clearly over the tundra, making the open plain seem even more vast and empty. "Out there, in another world!"

Catti-brie sighed and shuffled uncomfortably. She alone fully understood the vague picture that Wulfgar was painting. And she wasn't pleased with his choice.

Bruenor nodded, respecting the barbarian's decision. "Go then, and live well," he said, straining to hold his breaking voice even as he moved to the rocky trail. He paused for one last moment and looked back at the tall, young barbarian. "Yer a man, there's none to argue that," he said over his shoulder. "But don't ye never forget that ever ye'll be me boy!"

"I shan't," Wulfgar whispered softly as Bruenor disappeared into the tunnel. He felt Drizzt's hand on his shoulder.

"When do you leave?" the drow asked.

"Tonight," Wulfgar replied. "These grim days offer no leisure."

"And where do you go?" Catti-brie asked, already knowing the truth, and also the vague answer that Wulfgar would give.

The barbarian turned his misty gaze back out to the plain. "Home."

He started back down the trail, Regis following. But Catti-brie waited behind and motioned for Drizzt to do likewise.

"Say your farewells to Wulfgar this night," she told the drow. "I do not believe that he shall ever return."

"Home is a place for him to choose," Drizzt replied, guessing that the news about Heafstaag joining Kessell had played a part in Wulfgar's decision. He watched the departing barbarian with respect. "He has some private matters to attend to."

"More than you know," Catti-brie said. Drizzt looked at her curiously. "Wulfgar has an adventure in mind," she explained. She hadn't meant to break her trust with Wulfgar, but figured that Drizzt Do'Urden, above anyone else, might be able to find a way to help. "One that I believe has been put upon him before he is ready."

"Matters of the tribe are his own business," Drizzt said, guessing what the girl was suggesting. "The barbarians have their own ways and do not welcome outsiders."

"Of the tribes, I agree," said Catti-brie. "Yet Wulfgar's path, unless I am mistaken, does not lead directly home. He has something else ahead of him, an adventure that he has often hinted at but never fully explained. I only know that it involves great danger and a vow that even he fears is above his ability to fulfill alone."

Drizzt looked over the starry plain and considered the girl's words. He knew Catti-brie to be shrewd and observant beyond her years. He did not doubt her guesses.

The stars twinkled above the cool night, the celestial dome engulfing the flat rim of the horizon. A horizon as yet unmarked by the fires of an advancing army, Drizzt noted.

Perhaps he had time.

⚔ ⚔ ⚔ ⚔ ⚔

Although Cassius's proclamation reached even the most remote of the towns within two days, few groups of refugees came down the roads to Bryn Shander. Cassius had fully expected this, or he never would have made the bold offer of sheltering all who would come. Bryn Shander was a fair-sized city, and her present population was not as large as it had once been. There were many vacant buildings within the walls, and an entire section of the city, reserved for visiting merchant caravans, lay empty at the present time. However, if even half of the people of the other nine communities sought refuge, Cassius would be hard-pressed to honor his pledge.

The spokesman wasn't worried. The people of Ten-Towns were a hardy folk and lived under the threat of a goblin invasion every day. Cassius knew that it would take more than an abstract warning to make them leave their homes. And with the allegiance between the towns at such a low point, few of the town leaders would take any action at all to convince their people to flee.

As it turned out, Glensather and Agorwal were the only spokesmen to arrive at the gates of Bryn Shander. Nearly all of Easthaven stood behind their leader, but Agorwal had less than half of the people of Termalaine behind him. The rumors from the arrogant city of Targos, itself nearly as well-defended as Bryn Shander, made it clear that none of its people would leave. Many of Termalaine's fishermen, fearing the economic advantage that Targos would gain over them, had refused to give up the most lucrative month of the fishing season.

Such was also the case with Caer-Konig and Caer-Dineval. Neither of the bitter enemies dared give any edge to the other, and not a single person from either city fled to Bryn Shander. To the people of these embattled communities, the orcs were but a distant threat that would have to be dealt with if it ever materialized, but the fighting with their immediate neighbors was brutally real and evident in all their daily routines.

On the western outskirts, the town of Bremen remained fiercely independent of the other communities, viewing Cassius's offer as a feeble attempt by Bryn Shander to reaffirm its position of leadership. Good Mead and Dougan's Hole in the south had no intention of hiding in the walled city or of sending any troops to aid in the fighting. These two towns on Redwaters, smallest of the lakes and poorest in terms of knuckleheads, could not afford any time away from the boats. They had heeded the call for unity five years previous under the threat of a barbarian invasion, and though they had suffered the worst losses of all the towns in the battle, they had gained the least.

Several groups filtered in from Lonelywood, but many of the folk of the northernmost town preferred to stay out of the way. Their hero had lost face, and even Muldoon now viewed the halfling in a different light and passed the warning of invasion off as a misunderstanding, or perhaps even a calculated hoax.

The greater good of the region had fallen beneath the lesser personal gains of stubborn pride, with most of the people of Ten-Towns confusing unity with dependence.

⚔ ⚔ ⚔ ⚔ ⚔

Regis returned to Bryn Shander to make some personal arrangements on the morning after Wulfgar departed. He had a friend coming from Lonelywood with his prized belongings, so he remained in the city, watching in dismay as the days drifted by without any real preparations being made to meet the coming army. Even after the council, the halfling had held out some hope that the people would realize the impending doom and band together, but now he came to believe that the dwarves' decision to abandon Ten-Towns and lock themselves into their mines was the only option they had if they wished to survive.

Regis partially blamed himself for the coming tragedy, convinced that he had gotten careless. When he and Drizzt had concocted plans to use political situations and the power of the ruby to force the towns into unity against the barbarians, they had spent many hours predicting the initial responses of the spokesmen and weighing the worth of each town's alliance. This time, though, Regis had placed more faith in the people of Ten-Towns and in the stone, figuring that he could simply employ its power to sway any of the few remaining doubters of the severity of the situation.

Yet Regis could not sustain his own guilt as he heard the arrogant and mistrusting responses coming in from the towns. Why should he have to trick the people into defending themselves? If they were stupid enough to let their own pride bring about their destruction, then what responsibility, or even what right, did he have to rescue them?

"You get what you deserve!" the halfling said aloud, smiling in spite of himself when he realized that he was beginning to sound as cynical as Bruenor.

But callousness was his only protection against such a helpless situation. He hoped that his friend from Lonelywood would arrive soon.

His sanctuary lay underground.

⚔ ⚔ ⚔ ⚔ ⚔

Akar Kessell sat on the crystal throne in the Hall of Scrying, the third level of Cryshal-Tirith, his fingers tapping nervously on the arm of the great chair as he stared intently at the dark mirror before him. Biggrin was long overdue with the report on the reinforcement caravan. The last summons the wizard had received from the lair had been suspicious, with no one on the end to greet his reply. Now the mirror in the lair revealed only blackness, resisting all of the wizard's attempts to scry out the room.

If the mirror had been broken, Kessell would have been able to sense the shift in his visions. But this was more mysterious, for something he could not understand was blocking his distance sight. The dilemma unnerved him, made him think that he had been deceived or discovered. His fingers continued to rap nervously.

"Perhaps it is time to make a decision," Errtu, in its customary place at the side of the wizard's throne, suggested.

"We have not yet reached our fullest strength.'" Kessell retorted. "Many goblin tribes and a large clan of giants have not come in. And the barbarians are not yet ready."

"The troops thirst for battle," Errtu pointed out. "They fight with each other—you may find that your army will soon fall apart around you!"

Kessell agreed that holding so many goblin tribes together for long was a risky and dangerous proposition. Perhaps it would be better if they marched at once. But still, the wizard wanted to be certain. He wanted his forces at their strongest.

"Where is Biggrin?" Kessell wailed. "Why hasn't he answered my summons?"

"What preparations are the humans now making?" Errtu asked abruptly.

But Kessell was not listening. He rubbed the sweat from his face. Maybe the shard and the demon had been right about sending the less-conspicuous barbarians to the lair. What must the fishermen be thinking if they found such an unusual combination of monsters lairing in their area? How much had they guessed?

Errtu noted Kessell's discomfort with grim satisfaction.

The demon and the shard had been pushing Kessell to strike much earlier, as soon as Biggrin's messages had stopped coming in. But the cowardly wizard, needing more assurance that his numbers were over-whelming, had continued to delay.

"Shall I go to the troops?" Errtu asked, confident that Kessell's resistance was gone.

"Send runners to the barbarians and to the tribes that have not yet joined us," Kessell instructed. "Tell them that to fight beside us is to join in the feast of victory! But those who do not fight beside us shall fall before us! Tomorrow we march!"

Errtu rushed from the tower without delay, and soon cheers for the onset of war echoed throughout the huge encampment. Goblins and giants raced excitedly about, breaking down tents and packing supplies. They had anticipated this moment for long tendays, and now they wasted no time in making the final preparations.

That same night, the vast army of Akar Kessell pulled up its camp and began its long march toward Ten-Towns.

Back in the routed verbeeg lair, the scrying mirror sat unmoved and unbroken, securely covered by the heavy blanket that Drizzt Do'Urden had thrown over it.

EPILOGUE

He ran under the bright sun of day, he ran under the dim stars of the night, ever with the east wind in his face. His long legs and great strides carried him tirelessly, a mere speck of movement in the empty plain. For days Wulfgar pushed himself to the absolute limits of his endurance, even hunting and eating on the run, stopping only when exhaustion felled him in his tracks.

Far to the south of him, rolling out of the Spine of the World like a toxic cloud of foul-smelling vapors, came the goblin and giant forces of Akar Kessell. With minds warped by the willpower of the Crystal Shard, they wanted only to kill, only to destroy. Only to please Akar Kessell.

Three days out from the dwarven valley, the barbarian came across the jumbled tracks of many warriors all leading toward a common destination. He was glad that he was able to find his people so easily, but the presence of so many tracks told him that the tribes were gathering, a fact that only emphasized the urgency of his mission. Spurred by necessity, he charged onward.

It wasn't fatigue but solitude that was Wulfgar's greatest enemy. He fought hard to keep his thoughts on the past during the long hours, recalling his vow to his dead father and contemplating the possibilities of his victories. He avoided any thought of his present path, though, understanding well that the sheer desperation of his plan might well destroy his resolve.

Yet this was his only chance. He was not of noble blood, and he had no Rights of Challenge against Heafstaag. Even if he defeated the chosen king, none of his people would recognize him as their leader. The only way that one such as he could legitimatize a claim to tribal kingship was through an act of heroic proportions.

He bounded on, toward the same goal that had lured many would-be kings before him to their deaths. And in the shadows behind him, cruising with the graceful ease that marked his race, came Drizzt Do'Urden.

Ever eastward, toward the Reghed Glacier and a place called Evermelt.

Toward the lair of Ingeloakastimizilian, the white dragon the barbarians simply called "Icingdeath."

PART THREE

What does Wulfgar see when he looks out over the tundra—when his crystal blue eyes stare across the dark plain to the points of light that mark the fires of his people's encampment?

Does he view the past, perhaps, with a longing to return to that place and those ways? Does he view the present, comparing that which he has learned with me and Bruenor with those harsh lessons of life among his nomadic tribesmen?

CRYSHAL-TIRITH

Or does Wulfgar see the future, the potential for change, for bringing new and better ways to his people?

A bit of all three, I would guess. That is the turmoil within Wulfgar, I suspect, the simmering fire behind those blue eyes. He fights with such passion! Some of that comes from his upbringing among the fierce tribesmen, the wargames of the barbarian boys, often bloody, sometimes even fatal. Part of that passion for battle stems from Wulfgar's inner turmoil, the frustration he must feel when he contrasts his lessons at my hands and at Bruenor's hands with those gained in his years among his own people.

Wulfgar's people invaded Ten-Towns, entered with merciless rage ready to slaughter anyone who stood in their path without regard. How does Wulfgar reconcile that truth with the fact that Bruenor Battlehammer did not let him die on the field, that the dwarf saved him, though he tried to kill Bruenor in battle (though the foolish young lad made the mistake of swatting Bruenor on the head!)? How does Wulfgar reconcile the love Bruenor has shown him against his previous notions of dwarves as hateful, merciless enemies? For that is how the barbarians of Icewind Dale surely view dwarves, a lie that they perpetuate among themselves so they may justify their murderous raiding ways. It is not so different than the lies that the drow tell themselves to justify their hatred of anyone who is not drow.

But now Wulfgar has been faced with the truth of Bruenor and the dwarves. Irrevocably. He must weigh that personal revelation against every "truth" he spent his years of childhood learning. He must come to accept that what his parents and all the elders of the tribe told to him were lies. I know from personal experience that this is no easy thing to reconcile. For to do so is to admit that a great part of your own life was no more than a lie, that a great part of that which makes you who you are is wrong. I recognized the ills of Menzoberranzan early on, because its teachings went against logic and went against that which was in my heart. Yet even though those wrongs were painfully obvious, those first steps that carried me out of my homeland were not easy ones.

The errors of the barbarians of Icewind Dale pale compared to those of the drow, and so the steps that Wulfgar must take emotionally away from his people will be even more difficult, I fear. There is far more truth in the ways of the barbarians, more justification for their actions, warlike though they may be, yet it falls upon Wulfgar's strong, but painfully young, shoulders to differentiate between the ways of his people and those of his new friends, to accept compassion and acceptance above the solid walls of prejudice that have so encapsulated his entire youth.

I do not envy him the task before him, the confusion, the frustration.

It is good that he fights every day—I only pray that in a blind fit while playing out that frustration, my sparring companion does not tear the head from my shoulders.

—Drizzt Do'Urden

21
THE ICY TOMB

At the base of the great glacier, hidden off in a small dell where one of the ice spurs wound through broken rifts and boulders, was a place the barbarians called Evermelt. A hot spring fed a small pool, the warmed waters waging a relentless battle against ice floes and freezing temperatures. Tribesmen stranded inland by early snows, who could not find their way to the sea with the reindeer herd, often sought refuge at Evermelt, for even in the coldest months of winter, unfrozen, sustaining water could be found here. And the warming vapors of the pool made the temperatures of the immediate area bearable, if not comfortable. Yet the warmth and drinking water were only a part of Evermelt's worth.

Beneath the opaque surface of the misty water lay a hoard of gems and jewels, gold and silver, that rivaled the treasure of any king in this entire region of the world. Every barbarian had heard of the legend of the white dragon, but most considered it to be just a fanciful tale recounted by self-important old men for the amusement of children. For the dragon hadn't emerged from its hidden lair in many, many years.

Wulfgar knew better, though. In his youth his father had accidentally stumbled upon the entrance to the secret cave. When Beornegar later learned the legend of the dragon, he understood the potential value of his discovery and had spent years collecting all of the information he could find concerning dragons, especially white dragons, and Ingeloakastimizilian in particular.

Beornegar had been killed in a battle between tribes before he could make his attempt at the treasure, but living in a land where death was a common visitor, he had foreseen that grim possibility and had imparted his knowledge to his son. The secret did not die with him.

⚔ ⚔ ⚔ ⚔ ⚔

Wulfgar felled a deer with a throw of Aegis-fang and carried the beast the last few miles to Evermelt. He had been to this place twice before, but when he came upon it now, as always, its strange beauty stole his breath. The air above the pool was veiled in steam, and chunks of floating ice drifted through the misty waters like meandering ghost ships. The huge boulders surrounding the area were especially colorful, with varying hues of red and orange, and they were encapsulated in a thin layer of ice that caught the fire of the sun and reflected brilliant bursts of sparkling colors in startling contrast to the dull gray of the misted glacier ice. This was a silent place, sheltered from the mournful cry of the wind by walls of ice and rock, free of any distractions.

After his father was killed, Wulfgar had vowed, in tribute to the man, to make this journey and fulfill his father's dream. Now he approached the pool reverently, and though other matters pressed in on him, he paused for reflection. Warriors of every tribe on the tundra had come to Evermelt with the same hopes as he. None had ever returned.

The young barbarian resolved to change that. He firmed his proud jaw and set to work skinning the deer. The first barrier that he had to overcome was the pool itself. Beneath its surface the waters were deceptively warm and comfortable, but anyone who emerged from the pool into the air would be frozen dead in minutes.

Wulfgar peeled away the hide of the animal and began scraping away the underlying layer of fat. He melted this over a small fire until it attained the consistency of thick paint, then smeared it over every inch of his body. Taking a deep breath to steady himself and focus his thoughts on the task at hand he took hold of Aegis-fang and waded into Evermelt.

Under the deadening veil of mist, the waters appeared serene, but as soon as he moved away from the edges of the pool, Wulfgar could feel the strong, swirling currents of the hot stream.

Using a jutting rock overhang as a guidepost, he approximated the exact center of the pool. Once there, he took a final breath and confident of his father's instructions, opened himself to the currents and let himself sink into the water. He descended for a moment, then was suddenly swept away by the main flow of the stream toward the north end of the pool. Even beneath the mist the water was cloudy, forcing Wulfgar to trust blindly that he would break free of the water before his breath ran out.

He was within a few feet of the ice wall at the pool's edge before he could see the danger. He braced himself for the collision, but the current suddenly swirled, sending him deeper. The dimness darkened to blackness as he entered a hidden opening under the ice, barely wide enough for him to slip through, though the unceasing flow of the stream gave him no choice.

His lungs cried for air. He bit down on his lip to keep his mouth from bursting open and robbing him of the last wisps of precious oxygen.

Then he broke into a wider tunnel where the water flattened out and dropped below the level of his head. He hungrily gasped in air, but he was still sliding along helplessly in the rushing water.

One danger was past.

The slide twisted and turned, and the roar of a waterfall clearly sounded up ahead. Wulfgar tried to slow his ride, but couldn't find a handhold or any kind of a brace, for the floor and walls were of ice smoothed under centuries of the flowing stream. The barbarian tossed wildly, Aegis-fang flying from his hands as he futilely tried to drive them into the solid ice. Then he came into a wide and deep cavern and saw the drop before him.

A few feet beyond the crest of the fall were several huge icicles that stretched from the domed ceiling down below Wulfgar's line of sight. He saw his only chance. When he approached the lip of the drop, he sprang outward, wrapping his arms around an icicle. He dropped quickly as it tapered, but saw that it widened again as it neared the floor, as though a second icicle had grown up from the floor to meet this one.

Safe for a moment, he gazed around the strange cavern in awe. The waterfall captured his imagination. Steam rose from the chasm, adding surrealistic flavor to the spectacle. The stream poured over the drop, most of it continuing on its way through a small chasm, barely a crack in the floor thirty feet below at the base of the fall. The droplets that cleared the chasm, though, solidified as they separated from the main flow of the stream and bounced away in all directions as they hit the cavern's ice floor. Not yet completely hardened, the cubes stuck fast where they landed, and all about the base of the waterfall were strangely sculpted piles of broken ice.

Aegis-fang flew over the drop, easily clearing the small chasm to smash into one such sculpture, scattering shards of ice. Though his arms were numbed from the icicle slide, Wulfgar quickly rushed over to the hammer, already freezing fast where it had landed, and heaved it free of the ice's hardening grip.

Under the glassy floor where the hammer had cracked away the top layers, the barbarian noticed a dark shadow. He examined it more closely, then backed away from the grizzly sight. Perfectly preserved, one of his predecessors had apparently gone over the long drop, dying in the deepening ice where he had landed. How many others, Wulfgar wondered, had met this same fate?

He didn't have time to contemplate it further. One of his other concerns had been dispelled, for much of the cavern's roof was only a few feet below the daylit surface and the sun found its way in through those parts that were purely ice. Even the smallest glow coming from the ceiling was reflected a thousand times on the glassy floors and walls, and the whole cavern virtually exploded in sparkling bursts of light.

Wulfgar felt the cold acutely, but the melted fat had protected him sufficiently. He would survive the first dangers of this adventure.

But the spectre of the dragon loomed somewhere up ahead.

Several twisting tunnels led off of the main chamber, carved by the stream in long-past days when its waters ran high. Only one of these was large enough for a dragon, though. Wulfgar contemplated searching out the others first, to see if he might possibly find a less obvious way into the lair. But the glare and distortions of light and the countless icicles hanging from the ceiling like a predator's teeth dizzied him, and he knew that if he got lost or wasted too much time, the night would fall over him, stealing his light and dropping the temperature below even his considerable tolerance.

So he banged Aegis-fang on the floor to clear away any remaining ice that clung to it and started straight ahead down the tunnel he believed would lead him to the lair of Ingeloakastimizilian.

⚔ ⚔ ⚔ ⚔ ⚔

The dragon slept soundly beside its treasure in the largest chamber of the ice caves, confident after many years of solitude that it would not be disturbed. Ingeloakastimizilian, more commonly known as Icingdeath, had made the same mistake that many of its kin, with their lairs in similar caves of ice, had made. The flowing stream that offered entrance to and escape from the caves had diminished over the years, leaving the dragon trapped in a crystalline tomb.

Icingdeath had enjoyed its years of hunting deer and humans. In the short time the beast had been active, it had earned quite a respectable reputation for havoc and terror. Yet dragons, especially white ones who are rarely active in their cold environments, can live many centuries without meat. Their selfish love of their treasure can sustain them indefinitely, and Icingdeath's hoard, though small compared to the vast mounds of gold collected by the huge reds and blues that lived in more populated areas, was the largest of any of the tundra-dwelling dragons.

If the dragon had truly desired freedom, it could probably have broken through the cavern's ice ceiling. But Icingdeath considered the risk too great, and so it slept, counting its coins and gems in dreams that dragons considered quite pleasant.

The slumbering worm didn't fully realize, though, just how careless it had become. In its unbroken snooze, Icingdeath hadn't moved in decades. A cold blanket of ice had crept over the long form, gradually thickening until the only clear spot was a hole in front of the great nostrils, where the rhythmic blasts of exhaled snores had kept the frost away.

And so Wulfgar, cautiously stalking the source of the resounding snores, came upon the beast.

Viewing Icingdeath's splendor, enhanced by the crystalline ice blanket, Wulfgar looked upon the dragon with profound awe. Piles of gems and gold lay all about the cavern under similar blankets, but Wulfgar could not pull his eyes away. Never had he viewed such magnificence, such strength.

Confident that the beast was helplessly pinned, he dropped the hammer's head down by his side. "Greetings, Ingeloakastimizilian," he called, respectfully using the beast's full name.

The pale blue orbs snapped open; their seething flames immediately apparent even under their icy veil. Wulfgar stopped short at their piercing glare.

After the initial shock, he regained his confidence. "Fear not, mighty worm," he said boldly. "I am a warrior of honor and shall not kill you under these unfair circumstances." He smiled wryly. "My lust shall be appeased by simply taking your treasure!"

But the barbarian had made a critical mistake.

A more experienced fighter, even a knight of honor, would have looked beyond his chivalrous code, accepted his good fortune as a blessing, and slain the worm as it slept. Few adventurers, even whole parties of adventurers, had ever given an evil dragon of any color such a chance and lived to boast of it.

Even Icingdeath, in the initial shock of its predicament, had thought itself helpless when it had first awakened to face the barbarian. The great muscles, atrophied from inactivity, could not resist the weight and grip of the ice prison. But when Wulfgar mentioned the treasure, a new surge of energy blew away the dragon's lethargy.

Icingdeath found strength in anger, and with an explosion of power beyond anything the barbarian had ever imagined, the dragon flexed its cordlike muscles, sending great chunks of ice flying away. The entire cavern complex trembled violently, and Wulfgar, standing on the slippery floor, was thrown down on his back. He rolled aside at the very last moment to dodge the spearlike tip of a falling icicle dislodged by the tremor.

Wulfgar regained his feet quickly, but when he turned, he found himself facing a horned white head, leveled to meet his eyes. The dragon's great wings stretched outward, shaking off the last remnants of its blanket, and the blue eyes bore into Wulfgar.

The barbarian desperately looked around for an escape. He pondered throwing Aegis-fang, but knew that he couldn't possibly kill the monster with a single strike. And inevitably, the killing breath would come.

Icingdeath considered its foe for a moment. If it breathed, it would have to settle for frozen flesh. It was a dragon, after all, a terrible worm, and it believed, probably rightly so, that no single human could ever defeat it. This huge man, however, and particularly the magical hammer, for the dragon could sense its might, disturbed the worm. Caution had kept Icingdeath alive through many centuries. It would not close to melee with this man.

The cold air gathered in its lungs.

Wulfgar heard the intake of air and reflexively dived to the side. He couldn't fully escape the blast that followed, a frosting cone of unspeakable cold, but his agility, combined with the deer fat, kept him alive. He landed behind a block of ice, his legs actually burned by the cold and his lungs aching. He needed a moment to recover, but he saw the white head lifting slowly into the air, taking away the angle of the meager barrier.

The barbarian could not survive a second breath.

Suddenly, a globe of darkness engulfed the dragon's head and a black-shafted arrow, and then another, whirred by the barbarian and thudded unseen behind the blackness.

"Attack boy! Now!" cried Drizzt Do'Urden from the entrance to the chamber.

The disciplined barbarian instinctively obeyed his teacher. Grimacing through the pain, he moved around the ice block and closed in on the thrashing worm.

Icingdeath swung its great head to and fro, trying to shake free of the dark elf's spell. Hate consumed the beast as yet another stinging arrow found its mark. The dragon's only desire was to kill. Even blinded, its senses were superior; it marked out the drow's direction easily and breathed again.

But Drizzt was well-versed in dragon lore. He had gauged his distance from Icingdeath perfectly, and the strength of the deadly frost fell short. The barbarian charged in on the distracted dragon's side and slammed Aegis-fang with all of his great might against the white scales. The dragon winced in agony. The scales held under the blow, but the dragon had never felt such strength from a human and didn't care to test its hide against a second strike. It turned to release a third blast of breath on the exposed barbarian.

But another arrow cracked home.

Wulfgar saw a great gob of dragon blood splatter on the floor beside him, and he watched the globe of darkness lurch away. The dragon roared in anger. Aegis-fang struck again, and a third time. One of the scales cracked and flaked away, and the sight of exposed flesh renewed Wulfgar's hopes of victory.

Icingdeath had lived through many battles, though, and was far from finished. The dragon knew how vulnerable it was to the powerful hammer and kept its concentration focused enough to retaliate. The long tail circled over the scaly back and cracked into Wulfgar just as the barbarian had begun another swing. Instead of the satisfaction of feeling Aegis-fang crushing through dragon flesh, Wulfgar found himself slammed against a frozen mound of gold coins twenty feet away.

The cavern spun all about him, his watering eyes heightening the starred reflections of light and his consciousness slipping away. But he saw Drizzt, scimitars drawn, advancing boldly toward Icingdeath. He saw the dragon poised to breath again.

He saw, with crystalline clarity, the immense icicle hanging from the ceiling above the dragon.

Drizzt walked forward. He had no strategy against such a formidable foe; he hoped that he would spot some weakness before the dragon killed him. He thought that Wulfgar was out of the battle, and probably dead, after the mighty slash of the tail, and was surprised when he saw sudden movement off to the side.

Icingdeath sensed the barbarian's move as well and sent its long tail to squelch any further threat to its flank.

But Wulfgar had already played his hand. With the last burst of strength he could muster, he snapped up from the mound and launched Aegis-fang high into the air.

The dragon's tail struck home and Wulfgar didn't know if his desperate attempt was successful. He thought that he saw a lighter spot appear on the ceiling before he was thrown into blackness.

Drizzt bore witness to their victory. Mesmerized, the drow watched the silent descent of the huge icicle.

Icingdeath, blinded to the danger by the globe of darkness and thinking that the hammer had flown wildly, waved its wings. The clawed forelegs had just begun to lift up when the ice spear smashed into the dragon's back, driving it back to the floor.

With the ball of darkness planted on its head, Drizzt couldn't see the dragon's dying expression.

But he heard the killing "crack" as the whiplike neck, launched by the sudden reversal of momentum, rolled upward and snapped.

22

By Blood or by Deed

The heat of a small fire brought Wulfgar back to consciousness. He came to his senses groggily and at first, could not comprehend his surroundings as he wriggled out of a blanket that he did not remember bringing. Then he recognized Icingdeath, lying dead just a few yards away, the huge icicle rooted firmly in the dragon's back. The globe of darkness had dissipated, and Wulfgar gawked at how accurate the drow's approximated bowshots had been. One arrow protruded from the dragon's left eye, and the black shafts of two others stuck out from the mouth.

Wulfgar reached down to grasp the security of Aegis-fang's familiar handle. But the hammer was nowhere near him. Fighting the pervading numbness in his legs, the barbarian managed to stand up, searching around frantically for his weapon. And where, he wondered, was the drow?

Then he heard the tapping coming from a side chamber. Stiff-legged, he moved cautiously around a bend. There was Drizzt, standing atop a hill of coins, breaking away its icy covering with Wulfgar's warhammer.

Drizzt noticed Wulfgar approaching and bowed low in greeting. "Well met, Dragon's Bane!" he called.

"And to you, friend elf," Wulfgar responded, thoroughly pleased to see the drow again. "You have followed me a long way."

"Not too far," Drizzt replied, chopping another chunk of ice off the treasure. "There was little excitement to be found in Ten-Towns, and I could not let you forge ahead in our competition of kills! Ten and one-half to ten and one-half," he declared, smiling broadly, "and a dragon to split between us. I claim half the kill!"

"Yours and well earned," Wulfgar agreed. "And claim to half the booty."

Drizzt revealed a small pouch hanging on a fine silver chain around his neck. "A few baubles," he explained. "I need no riches and doubt that I would be able to carry much out of here, anyway! A few baubles will suffice."

He sifted through the portion of the pile he had just freed from the ice, uncovering a gem-encrusted sword pommel, its black adamantite hilt masterfully sculpted into the likeness of the toothed maw of a hunting cat. The lure of the intricate workmanship pulled at Drizzt, and with trembling fingers he slid the rest of the weapon out from under the gold.

A scimitar. Its curving blade was of silver, and diamond-edged. Drizzt raised it before him, marveling at its lightness and perfect balance.

"A few baubles . . . and this," he corrected.

⚔ ⚔ ⚔ ⚔ ⚔

Even before he had encountered the dragon, Wulfgar wondered how he would escape the underground caverns. "The current of the water is too strong and the ledge of the waterdrop too high to go back through Evermelt," he said to Drizzt, though he knew that the drow would have surmised the same thing. "Even if we somehow find our way through those barriers, I have no more deer blubber to protect us from the cold when we leave the water."

"I also have no mind to pass through the waters of Evermelt again," Drizzt assured the barbarian. "Yet I rely on my considerable experience to bring me into such situations prepared! Thus the wood for the fire and the blanket that I put upon you, both wrapped in sealskin. And also this." He produced a three-pronged grapple and some light but strong cord from his belt. He had already discovered an escape route.

Drizzt pointed up to a small hole in the roof above them. The icicle that had been dislodged by Aegis-fang had taken part of the chamber's ceiling with it. "I cannot hope to throw the hook so high, but your mighty arms should find the toss a minor challenge."

"In better times, perhaps," relied Wulfgar. "But I have no strength to make the attempt." The barbarian had come closer to death than he realized when the dragon's breath had descended upon him, and with the adrenaline of the fight now used up, he felt the pervading cold keenly. "I fear that my unfeeling hands could not even close upon the hook!"

"Then run!" yelled the drow. "Let your chilled body warm itself."

Wulfgar was off at once, jogging around the wide chamber, forcing his blood to circulate through his numbed legs and fingers. In a short while, he began to feel the inner warmth of his own body returning.

It took him only two throws to put the grapple through the hole and get it to catch fast on some ice. Drizzt was the first to go, the agile elf veritably running up the cord.

Wulfgar finished his business in the cavern, collecting a bag of riches and some other items he knew he would need. He had much more difficulty than Drizzt in ascending the cord, but with the drow's assistance from above, he managed to scramble onto the ice before the westering sun dipped below the horizon.

They camped beside Evermelt, feasting on venison and enjoying a much-needed and well-deserved rest in the comfort of the warming vapors.

Then they were off again before dawn, running west. They ran side by side for two days, matching the frenzied pace that had brought them so far east. When they came upon the trails of the gathering barbarian tribes, both of them knew that the time had come for them to part.

"Farewell, good friend," said Wulfgar as he bent low to inspect the trails. "I shall never forget what you have done for me."

"And to you, Wulfgar," Drizzt replied somberly. "May your mighty warhammer terrorize your enemies for years to come!" He sped off, not looking back, but wondering if he would ever see his large companion alive again.

⚔ ⚔ ⚔ ⚔

Wulfgar put aside the urgency of his mission to pause and ponder his emotions when he first viewed the large encampment of the assembled tribes. Five years before, proudly carrying the standard of the Tribe of the Elk, the younger Wulfgar had marched to a similar gathering, singing the Song of Tempus and sharing strong mead with men who would fight, and possibly die, beside him. He had viewed battle differently then, as a glorious test of a warrior. "Innocent savagery," he mumbled, listening to the contradiction of the words as he recalled his ignorance in those days so long ago. But his perceptions had undergone a considerable change. Bruenor and Drizzt, by becoming his friends and teaching him the intricacies of their world, had personalized the people he had previously looked upon merely as enemies, forcing him to face the brutal consequences of his actions.

A bitter bile welled in Wulfgar's throat at the thought of the tribes launching another raid against Ten-Towns. Even more repulsive, his proud people were marching to war alongside goblins and giants.

As he neared the perimeter, he saw that there was no Hengorot, no ceremonial Mead Hall, in all the camp. A series of small tents, each bearing the respective standards of the tribal kings, comprised the center of the assembly, surrounded by the open campfires of common soldiers. By reviewing the banners, Wulfgar could see that nearly all of the tribes were present, but their combined strength was little more than half the size of the assembly five years previous. Drizzt's observations that the barbarians hadn't yet recovered from the massacre on Bryn Shander's slopes rang painfully true.

Two guardsmen came out to meet Wulfgar. He had made no attempt to conceal his approach, and now he placed Aegis-fang at his feet and raised his hands to show that his intentions were honorable.

"Who are you that comes unescorted and uninvited to the council of Heafstaag?" asked one of the guards. He sized up the stranger, greatly impressed by Wulfgar's obvious strength and by the mighty weapon lying at his feet. "Surely you are no beggar, noble warrior, yet you are unknown to us."

"I am known to you, Revjak, son of Jorn the Red," Wulfgar replied, recognizing the man as a fellow tribesman. "I am Wulfgar, son of

Beornegar, warrior of the Tribe of the Elk. I was lost to you five years ago, when we marched upon Ten-Towns," he explained, carefully choosing his phrases to avoid the subject of their defeat. Barbarians did not talk of such unpleasant memories.

Revjak studied the young man closely. He had been friends with Beornegar, and he remembered the boy, Wulfgar. He counted the years, comparing the boy's age when he last saw him against the apparent age of this young man. He was soon satisfied that the similarities were more than coincidental. "Welcome home, young warrior!" he said warmly. "You have fared well!"

"I have indeed," replied Wulfgar. "I have seen great and wondrous things and learned much wisdom. Many are the tales that I shall tell, but in truth, I have not the time to idly converse. I have come to see Heafstaag."

Revjak nodded and immediately began leading Wulfgar through the rows of firepits. "Heafstaag will be glad of your return."

Too quietly to be heard Wulfgar replied, "Not so glad."

× × × × ×

A curious crowd gathered around the impressive young warrior as he neared the central tent of the encampment. Revjak went inside to announce Wulfgar to Heafstaag and returned immediately with the king's permission for Wulfgar to enter.

Wulfgar hoisted Aegis-fang upon his shoulder, but did not move toward the flap that Revjak held open. "What I have to say shall be spoken openly and before all the people," he said loudly enough for Heafstaag to hear. "Let Heafstaag come to me!"

Confused murmurs sprouted up all about him at these words of challenge, for the rumors that had been running throughout the crowd did not speak of Wulfgar, the son of Beornegar, as a descendant of royal bloodlines.

Heafstaag rushed out of the tent. He moved to within a few feet of the challenger, his chest puffed out and his one good eye glaring at Wulfgar. The crowd hushed, expecting the ruthless king to slay the impertinent youth at once.

But Wulfgar matched Heafstaag's dangerous stare and did not back away an inch. "I am Wulfgar," he proclaimed proudly, "son of Beornegar, son of Beorne before him; warrior of the Tribe of the Elk, who fought at the Battle of Bryn Shander; wielder of Aegis-fang, the Giant Foe;" he held the great hammer high before him, "friend to dwarven craftsmen and student to a ranger of Gwaeron Windstrom, giant-killer and lair-invader, slayer of the frost giant chieftain, Biggrin." He paused for a moment, his eyes squinted by a spreading smile, heightening the anticipation of his next proclamation. When he was satisfied that he held the crowd's fullest attention, he continued, "I am Wulfgar, Dragon's bane!"

Heafstaag flinched. No living man on all the tundra had claim to such a lofty title.

"I claim the Right of Challenge," Wulfgar growled in a low, threatening tone.

"I shall kill you," Heafstaag replied with as much calm as he could muster. He feared no man, but was wary of Wulfgar's huge shoulders and corded muscles. The king had no intention of risking his position at this time, on the brink of an apparent victory over the fishermen of Ten-Towns. If he could discredit the young warrior, then the people would never allow such a fight. They would force Wulfgar to relinquish his claim, or they would kill him at once. "By what birthright do you make such a claim?"

"You would lead our people at the beckon of a wizard," Wulfgar retorted. He listened closely to the sounds of the crowd to measure their approval or disapproval of his accusation. "You would have them raise their swords in a common cause with goblins and orcs!" No one dared protest aloud, but Wulfgar could sense that many of the other warriors were secretly enraged about the coming battle. That would explain the absence of the Mead Hall, as well, for Heafstaag was wise enough to realize that simmering anger often exploded in the high emotions of such a celebration.

Revjak interposed before Heafstaag could reply with words or with weapon. "Son of Beornegar," Revjak said firmly, "you have as yet earned no right to question the orders of the king. You have declared an open challenge; the rules of tradition demand that you justify, by blood or by deed, your right to such a fight."

Excitement revealed itself in Revjak's words, and Wulfgar knew immediately that his father's old friend had intervened to prevent the start of an unrecognized, and therefore unofficial, brawl. The older man obviously had faith that the impressive young warrior could comply with the demands. And Wulfgar further sensed that Revjak, and perhaps many others, hoped the challenge would be successfully carried through.

Wulfgar straightened his shoulders and grinned confidently at his opponent, gaining strength in the continuing proof that his people were following Heafstaag's ignoble course simply because they were bound to the one-eyed king and could produce no suitable challengers to defeat him.

"By deed," he said evenly. Without releasing Heafstaag from his stare, Wulfgar unstrapped the rolled blanket he carried on his back and produced two spearlike objects. He tossed them casually to the ground before the king. Those in the crowd who could clearly see the spectacle gasped in unison, and even unshakable Heafstaag paled and rocked back a step.

"The challenge cannot be denied!" cried Revjak.

The horns of Icingdeath.

⚔ ⚔ ⚔ ⚔ ⚔

The cold sweat on Heafstaag's face revealed his tension as he buffed the last burrs from the head of his huge axe. "Dragon's bane!" he huffed unconvincingly to his standard bearer, who had just entered the tent. "More likely that he stumbled upon a sleeping worm!"

"Your pardon, mighty king," the young man said. "Revjak has sent me to tell you that the appointed time is upon us."

"Good!" sneered Heafstaag, running his thumb across the shining edge of the axe. "I shall teach the son of Beornegar to respect his king!"

The warriors from the Tribe of the Elk formed a circle around the combatants. Though this was a private event for Heafstaag's people, the other tribes watched with interest from a respectable distance. The winner would hold no formal authority over them, but he would be the king of the most powerful and dominant tribe on the tundra.

Revjak stepped within the circle and moved between the two opponents.

"I proclaim Heafstaag!" he cried. "King of the Tribe of the Elk!" He went on to read the one-eyed king's long list of heroic deeds.

Heafstaag's confidence seemed to return during the reciting, though he was a bit confused and angry that Revjak had chosen to proclaim him first. He placed his hands on his wide hips and glared around threateningly at the closest onlookers, smiling as they backed away from him, one by one. He did the same to his opponent, but again his bullying tactics failed to intimidate Wulfgar.

"And I proclaim Wulfgar," Revjak continued, "son of Beornegar and challenger to the throne of the Tribe of the Elk!" The reciting of Wulfgar's list took much less time than Heafstaag's, of course. But the final deed that Revjak proclaimed brought a degree of parity to the two.

"Dragon's bane!" Revjak cried, and the crowd, respectfully silent up to this point, excitedly began recounting the numerous rumors that had begun concerning Wulfgar's slaying of Icingdeath.

Revjak looked to the two combatants and stepped out of the circle.

The moment of honor was upon them.

They waded around the circle of battle, cautiously stalking and measuring each other for hints of weakness. Wulfgar noted the impatience on Heafstaag's face, a common flaw among barbarian warriors. He would have been much the same were it not for the blunt lessons of Drizzt Do'Urden. A thousand humiliating slaps from the drow's scimitars had taught Wulfgar that the first blow was not nearly as important as the last.

Finally, Heafstaag snorted and roared in. Wulfgar also growled aloud, moving as if he would meet the charge head on. But then he sidestepped at the last moment and Heafstaag, pulled by the momentum of his heavy weapon, stumbled past his foe and into the first rank of onlookers.

The one-eyed king recovered quickly and charged back out, doubly enraged, or so Wulfgar believed. Heafstaag had been king for many years and had fought in countless battles. If he had never learned to adjust his fighting technique, he would have long ago been slain. He came at Wulfgar again, by all appearances more out of control than the first time. But when Wulfgar moved out of the path, he found Heafstaag's great axe waiting for him. The one-eyed-king, anticipating the dodge, swung his weapon sideways, gashing Wulfgar's arm from shoulder to elbow.

Wulfgar reacted quickly, thrusting Aegis-fang out defensively to deter any follow-up attacks. He had little weight behind his swing, but its aim was true and the powerful hammer knocked Heafstaag back a step. Wulfgar took a moment to examine the blood on his arm.

He could continue the fight.

"You parry well," Heafstaag growled as he squared off just a few steps from his challenger. "You would have served our people well in the ranks. A loss it is that I must kill you!" Again the axe arced in, raining blow after blow in a furious assault meant to end the fight quickly.

But compared to the whirring blades of Drizzt Do'Urden, Heafstaag's axe seemed to move sluggishly. Wulfgar had no trouble deflecting the attacks, even countering now and then with a measured jab that thudded into Heafstaag's broad chest.

Blood of frustration and weariness reddened the one-eyed king's face. "A tiring opponent will often move with all of his strength at once," Drizzt had explained to Wulfgar during the tendays of training. "But rarely will he move in the apparent direction, the direction that he thinks you think he is moving in."

Wulfgar watched intently for the expected feint.

Resigned that he could not break through the skilled defenses of his younger and faster foe, the sweating king brought the great axe up over his head and lunged forward, yelling wildly to emphasize the attack.

But Wulfgar's reflexes were honed to their finest fighting edge, and the over-emphasis that Heafstaag placed upon the attack told him to expect a change in direction. He raised Aegis-fang as if to block the feigned blow, but reversed his grip even as the axe dropped down off of Heafstaag's shoulder and came in deceptively low in a sidelong swipe.

Trusting fully in his dwarven-crafted weapon, Wulfgar shifted his front foot back, turning to meet the oncoming blade with a similarly angled cut from Aegis-fang.

The heads of the two weapons slammed together with incredible force. Heafstaag's axe shattered in his hands, and the violent vibrations knocked him backward to the ground.

Aegis-fang was unharmed. Wulfgar could have easily walked over and finished Heafstaag with a single blow.

Revjak clenched his fist in anticipation of Wulfgar's imminent victory.

"Never confuse honor with stupidity!" Drizzt had scolded Wulfgar after his dangerous inaction with the dragon. But Wulfgar wanted more from this battle than to simply win the leadership of his tribe; he wanted to leave a lasting impression on all of the witnesses. He dropped Aegis-fang to the ground and approached Heafstaag on even terms.

The barbarian king didn't question his good fortune. He sprang at Wulfgar, wrapping his arms about the younger man in an attempt to drive him backward to the ground.

Wulfgar leaned forward to meet the attack, planting his mighty legs firmly, and stopped the heavier man in his tracks.

They grappled viciously, exchanging heavy blows before managing to lock each other close enough to render punches ineffective. Both combatants' eyes were blue and puffy, bruises and cuts welled on face and chest alike.

Heafstaag was the wearier, though, his barrel chest heaving with each labored breath. He wrapped his arms around Wulfgar's waist and tried again to twist his relentless opponent to the ground.

Then Wulfgar's long fingers locked onto the sides of Heafstaag's head. The younger man's knuckles whitened, the huge muscles in his forearms and shoulders tightened. He began to squeeze.

Heafstaag knew at once that he was in trouble, for Wulfgar's grip was mightier than a white bear's. The king struggled wildly, his huge fists slugging into Wulfgar's exposed ribs, hoping only to break Wulfgar's deadly concentration.

This time one of Bruenor's lessons spurred him on: "Think o' the weasel, boy, take the minor hits, but never, never let 'em go once yer on!" His neck and shoulder muscles bulged as he drove the one-eyed king to his knees.

Horrified at the power of the grip, Heafstaag pulled at the younger man's iron-hard forearms, trying vainly to relieve the growing pressure.

Wulfgar realized that he was about to kill one of his own tribe. "Yield!" he shouted at Heafstaag, seeking some more acceptable alternative.

The proud king answered with a final punch.

Wulfgar turned his eyes to the sky. "I am not like him!" he yelled helplessly, vindicating himself to any who would listen. But there was only one path left open to him.

The young barbarian's huge shoulders reddened as the blood surged through them. He saw the terror in Heafstaag's eye transcend into incomprehension. He heard the crack of bone, he felt the skull squash beneath his mighty hands.

Revjak should have then stepped into the circle and heralded the new King of the Tribe of the Elk.

But like the other witnesses around him, he stood unblinking, his jaw hanging open.

 ⚔ ⚔ ⚔ ⚔ ⚔

Helped by the gusts of the cold wind at his back, Drizzt sped across the last miles to Ten-Towns. On the same night that he had split from Wulfgar, the snow-capped tip of Kelvin's Cairn came into view. The sight of his home drove the drow onward even faster, yet a nagging hint on the edge of his senses told him that something was out of the ordinary. A human eye could never have caught it, but the keen night vision of the drow finally sorted it out, a growing pillar of blackness blotting out the horizon's lowest stars south of the mountain. And a second, smaller column, south of the first.

Drizzt stopped short. He squinted his eyes to be sure of his guess. Then he started again, slowly, needing the time to sort through an alternate route that he could take.

Caer-Konig and Caer-Dineval were burning.

23
BESIEGED

Caer-Dineval's fleet trolled the southernmost waters of Lac Dinneshere, taking advantage of the areas left open when the people of Easthaven fled to Bryn Shander.

Caer-Konig's ships were fishing their familiar grounds by the lake's northern banks. They were the first to see the coming doom.

Like an angry swarm of bees, Kessell's foul army swept right around the northern bend of Lac Dinneshere and roared down Icewind Pass.

"Up anchor!" cried Schermont and many other ship's captains as soon as they had recovered from the initial shock. But they knew even then that they could not get back in time.

The leading arm of the goblin army tore into Caer-Konig.

The men on the boats saw the flames leap up as buildings were put to the torch. They heard the blood-crazed hoots of the vile invaders.

They heard the dying screams of their kin.

The women, children, and old men who were in Caer-Konig had no thoughts of resistance. They ran. For their lives, they ran. And the goblins chased them and cut them down.

Giants and ogres rushed down to the docks, squashing the pitiful humans who beckoned helplessly to the returning fleet, or forcing them into the cold death of the lake's waters.

The giants carried huge sacks, and as the brave fishermen rushed into port, their vessels were pummeled and crippled by hurled boulders.

Goblins continued to flow into the doomed city, yet the bulk of the vast army's trailing edge flowed past and continued on toward the second town, Caer-Dineval. By this time, the people in Caer-Dineval had seen the smoke and heard the screams and were already in full flight to Bryn Shander, or out on the docks begging their sailors to come home.

But Caer-Dineval's fleet, though they caught the strength of the east wind in their rush back across the lake, had miles of water before them. The fishermen saw the pillars of smoke growing over Caer-Konig, and many suspected what was happening and understood that their flight, even with their sails so full of wind, would be in vain. Still, groans of shock and disbelief could be heard on every deck when the black cloud began its ominous climb from the northernmost sections of Caer-Dineval.

Then Schermont made a gallant decision. Accepting that his own town was doomed, he offered his help to his neighbors. "We cannot get in!" he cried to a captain of a nearby ship. "Pass the word: away south! Dineval's docks are yet clear!"

⚔ ⚔ ⚔ ⚔ ⚔

From a parapet on Bryn Shander's wall, Regis, Cassius, Agorwal, and Glensather watched in horror as the wicked force flowed down the stretch away from the two sacked cities, gaining on the fleeing people of Caer-Dineval.

"Open the gates, Cassius!" Agorwal cried. "We must go out to them! They have no chance of gaining the city unless we slow the pursuit!"

"Nay," replied Cassius somberly, painfully aware of his greater responsibilities. "Every man is needed to defend the city. To go out onto the open plain against such overwhelming numbers would be futile. The towns on Lac Dinneshere are doomed!"

"They are helpless!" Agorwal shot back. "Who are we if we cannot defend our kinfolk? What right do we have to stand watching from behind this wall while our people are slaughtered?"

Cassius shook his head, resolute in his decision to protect Bryn Shander.

But then other refugees came running down the second pass, Bremen's Run, fleeing the open town of Termalaine in their hysteria when they saw the cities across the way put to the torch. More than a thousand refugees were now within sight of Bryn Shander. Judging their speed and the distance remaining, Cassius estimated that they would converge on the wide field just below the principal city's northern gates.

Where the goblins would catch them.

"Go," he told Agorwal. Bryn Shander couldn't spare the men, but the field would soon run red with the blood of women and children.

Agorwal led his valiant men down the northeastern road in search of a defensible position where they could dig in. They chose a small ridge, actually more like a crest where the road dipped slightly. Entrenched and ready to fight and die, they waited as the last of the refugees ran past, terrified, screaming because they believed they had no chance of reaching the safety of the city before the goblins descended upon them.

Smelling human blood, the fastest runners of the invading army were right behind the trailing people, mostly mothers clutching their babies. Intent on their easy victims, the lead monsters never even noticed Agorwal's force until the waiting warriors were upon them.

By then it was too late.

The brave men of Termalaine caught the goblins in a crossfire of arrows and then followed Agorwal into a fierce sword rush. They fought fearlessly, as men who had accepted what fate had dealt them. Dozens of monsters lay dead in their tracks and more fell with each passing minute as the enraged warriors pressed into their ranks.

But the line seemed endless. As one goblin fell, two replaced it. The men of Termalaine were soon engulfed in a sea of goblins.

Agorwal gained a high point and looked back toward the city. The fleeing women were a good distance across the field, but moving slowly. If his men broke their ranks and fled, they would overtake the refugees before the slopes of Bryn Shander. And the monsters would be right behind.

"We must go out and support Agorwal!" Glensather yelled at Cassius. But this time the spokesman from Bryn Shander remained resolute.

"Agorwal has accomplished his mission," Cassius responded. "The refugees will make the wall. I'll not send more men out to die! Even if the combined strength of all of Ten-Towns were on the field, it would not be able to defeat the foe before us!" Already the wise spokesman understood that they could not fight Kessell on even terms.

The kindly Glensather looked crestfallen. "Take some troops down the hill," Cassius conceded. "Help the exhausted refugees up the final climb."

Agorwal's men were hard-pressed now. The spokesman from Termalaine looked back again and was appeased; the women and children were safe. He scanned up to the high wall, aware that Regis, Cassius, and the others could see him, a solitary figure on the small rise, though he could not pick them out among the throng of spectators that lined Bryn Shander's parapets.

More goblins poured into the fray, now joined by ogres and verbeeg. Agorwal saluted his friends in the city. His contented smile was sincere as he spun around and charged back down the grade to join his victorious troops in their finest moment.

Then Regis and Cassius watched the black tide roll over every one of the brave men of Termalaine.

Below them, the heavy gates slammed shut. The last of the refugees were in.

⚔ ⚔ ⚔ ⚔

While Agorwal's men had won a victory of honor, the only force that actually battled Kessell's army that day and survived were the dwarves. The clan from Mithral Hall had spent days in industrious preparation for this invasion, yet it nearly passed them by altogether. Held by the wizard's compelling will into discipline unheard of among goblins, especially varied and rival tribes, Kessell's army had definite and direct plans for what they had to accomplish in the initial surge. As of this point, the dwarves were not included.

But Bruenor's boys had other plans. They weren't about to bury themselves in their mines without getting to lop off at least a few goblin heads, or without crushing the kneecaps of a giant or two.

Several of the bearded folk climbed to the southern tip of their valley. When the trailing edge of the evil army flowed past, the dwarves began to taunt them, shouting challenges and curses against their mothers. The insults weren't even necessary. Orcs and goblins despise dwarves more than anything else alive, and Kessell's straightforward plan flew from their minds at the mere sight of Bruenor and his kin. Ever hungry for dwarven blood, a substantial force broke away from the main army.

The dwarves let them close in, goading them with taunts until the monsters were nearly upon them. Then Bruenor and his kin slipped back over the rocky ledge and down the steep drop.

"Come an' play, stupid dogs," Bruenor chuckled wickedly as he disappeared from sight. He pulled a rope off of his back. There was one little trick he had thought up that he was anxious to try out.

The goblins charged into the rocky vale, outnumbering the dwarves four to one. And they were backed by a score of raging ogres.

The monsters didn't have a chance.

The dwarves continued to coax them on, down the steepest part of the valley, to the narrow, sloping ledges on the cliff face that crossed in front of the numerous entrances to the dwarven caves. An obvious place for an ambush, but the stupid goblins, frenzied at the sight of their most-hated enemies, came on anyway, heedless of the danger.

When the majority of the monsters were on the ledges and the rest were making the initial descent into the vale, the first trap was sprung. Catti-brie, heavily armed but positioned in the back of the inner tunnels, pulled a lever, dropping a post on the vale's upper crest. Tons of rocks and gravel tumbled down upon the tail of the monster's line, and those who managed to keep their precarious balance and escape the brunt of the avalanche found the trails behind them buried and closed to any escape.

Crossbows twanged from concealed nooks, and a group of dwarves rushed out to meet the lead goblins.

Bruenor wasn't with them. He had hidden himself further back on the trail and watched as the goblins, intent on the challenge up ahead, passed him by. He could have struck then, but he was after larger prey, waiting for the ogres to come into range. The rope had already been carefully measured and tied off. He slipped one of its looped ends around his waist and the other securely over a rock, then pulled two throwing axes from his belt.

It was a risky ploy, perhaps the most dangerous the dwarf had ever tried, but the sheer thrill of it became obvious in the form of a wide grin across Bruenor's face when he heard the lumbering ogres approaching. He could hardly contain his laughter when two of them crossed before him on the narrow trail.

Leaping from his concealment, Bruenor charged at the surprised ogres and threw the axes at their heads. The ogres twisted and managed to deflect the half-hearted throws, but the hurled weapons were merely a diversion.

Bruenor's body was the true weapon in this attack.

Surprised, and dodging from the axes, the two ogres were put off-balance. The plan was falling into place perfectly; the ogres could hardly find their footing. Twitching the powerful muscles in his stubby legs, Bruenor launched himself into the air, crashing into the closest monster. It fell with him onto the other.

And they tumbled, all three, over the edge.

One of the ogres managed to lock its huge hand onto the dwarf's face, but Bruenor promptly bit it, and the monster recoiled. For a moment, they were a falling jumble of flailing legs and arms, but then Bruenor's rope reached its length and sorted them out.

"'ave a nice landing, boys," Bruenor called as he broke free of the fall. "Give the rocks a big kiss for me!"

The backswing on the rope dropped Bruenor into the entrance of a mine-shaft on the next lowest ledge as his helpless victims dropped to their deaths. Several goblins in line behind the ogres had watched the spectacle in blank amazement. Now they recognized the opportunity of using the hanging cord as a shortcut to one of the caves, and one by one they climbed onto the rope and started down.

But Bruenor had anticipated this as well. The descending goblins couldn't understand why the rope felt so slick in their hands.

When Bruenor appeared on the lower ledge, the end of the rope in one hand and a lighted torch in the other, they figured it out.

Flames leaped up the oiled twine. The topmost goblin managed to scramble back on the ledge; the rest took the same route as the unfortunate ogres before them. One nearly escaped the fatal fall, landing heavily on the lower ledge. Before he could even regain his feet, though, Bruenor kicked him over.

The dwarf nodded approvingly as he admired the successful results of his handiwork. That was one trick he intended to remember. He slapped his hands together and darted back down the shaft. It sloped upward farther back to join the higher tunnels.

On the upper ledge, the dwarves were fighting a retreating action. Their plan was not to clash in a death fight outside, but to lure the monsters into the entrances of the tunnels. With the desire to kill blotting out any semblance of reason, the dimwitted invaders readily complied, assuming that their greater numbers were pushing the dwarves back into a corner.

Several tunnels soon rang out with the clash of sword on sword. The dwarves continued to back away, leading the monsters completely into the final trap. Then, from somewhere deeper in the caves, a horn sounded. On cue, the dwarves broke away from the melee and fled down the tunnels.

The goblins and ogres, thinking that they had routed their enemies, paused only to whoop out victory cries, then surged after the dwarves.

But deeper in the tunnels several levers were pulled. The final trap was sprung, and all of the tunnel entrances simply collapsed. The ground shook violently under the weight of the rock drop; the entire face of the cliff came crashing down.

The only monsters that survived were the ones at the very front of the lines. And disoriented, battered by the force of the drop and dizzied by the blast of dust, they were immediately cut down by the waiting dwarves.

Even the people as far away as Bryn Shander were shaken by the tremendous avalanche. They flocked to the north wall to watch the rising cloud of dust, dismayed, for they believed that the dwarves had been destroyed.

Regis knew better. The halfling envied the dwarves, safely entombed in their long tunnels. He had realized the moment he saw the fires rising from Caer-Konig that his delay in the city, waiting for his friend from Lonelywood, had cost him his chance to escape.

Now he watched helplessly and hopelessly as the black mass advanced toward Bryn Shander.

✕ ✕ ✕ ✕ ✕

The fleets on Maer Dualdon and Redwaters had put back to their home ports as soon as they realized what was happening. They found their families safe for the present time, except for the fishermen of Termalaine who sailed into a deserted town. All that the men of Termalaine could do as they reluctantly put back out to sea was hope that their kin had made it to Bryn Shander or some other sanctuary, for they saw the northern flank of Kessell's army swarming across the field toward their doomed city.

Targos, the second strongest city and the only one other than Bryn Shander with any hope of holding out for any length of time against the vast army, extended an invitation for Termalaine's ships to tie up at her docks. And the men of Termalaine, soon to be numbered among the homeless themselves, accepted the hospitality of their bitter enemies to the south. Their disputes with Kemp's people seemed petty indeed against the weight of the disaster that had befallen the towns.

✕ ✕ ✕ ✕ ✕

Back in the main battle, the goblin generals that led Kessell's army were confident they could overrun Bryn Shander before nightfall. They obeyed their leader's plan to the letter. The main body of the army veered away from Bryn Shander and moved down the swath of open ground between the principal city and Targos, thus cutting any possibility of the two powerful cities linking their forces.

Several of the goblin tribes had broken away from the main group and were bearing down on Termalaine, intent on sacking their third city of the day. But when they found the place deserted, they abstained from burning the buildings. Part of Kessell's army now had a ready-made camp where they could wait out the coming siege in comfort.

Like two great arms, thousands of monsters raced south from the main force. So vast was Kessell's army that it filled the miles of field between Bryn Shander and Termalaine and still had enough numbers to encircle the hill of the principal city with thick ranks of troops.

Everything had happened so quickly that when the goblins finally stalled their frenzied charge, the change seemed overly dramatic. After a few minutes of breath-catching calm, Regis felt the tension growing once again.

"Why don't they just get it over with?" he asked the two spokesmen standing beside him.

Cassius and Glensather, more knowledgeable in the ways of warfare, understood exactly what was happening.

"They are in no hurry, little friend," Cassius explained. "Time favors them."

Then Regis understood. During his many years in the more populated southlands, he had heard many vivid tales describing the terrible horrors of a siege.

The image of Agorwal's final salute out in the distance came back to him then, the contented look on the spokesman's face and his willingness to die valiantly. Regis had no desire to die in any way, but he could imagine what lay before him and the cornered people of Bryn Shander.

He found himself envying Agorwal.

24
CRYSHAL-TIRITH

Drizzt soon came upon the battered ground where the army had crossed. The tracks came as no surprise to the drow, for the smoke pillars had already told him much of what had transpired. His only remaining question was whether or not any of the towns had held out, and he trotted on toward the mountain wondering if he had a home to return to.

Then he sensed a presence, an otherworldly aura that strangely reminded him of the days of his youth. He bent to check the ground again. Some of the marks were fresh troll tracks, and a scarring on the ground that could not have been caused by any mortal being. Drizzt looked around nervously, but the only sound was the mourn of the wind and the only silhouettes on the horizons were the peaks of Kelvin's Cairn before him and the Spine of the World far to the south. Drizzt paused to consider the presence for a few moments, trying to bring the familiarity he felt into better focus.

He moved on tentatively. He understood the source of his recollections now, though their exact details remained elusive. He knew what he was following.

A demon had come to Icewind Dale.

Kelvin's Cairn loomed much larger before Drizzt caught up to the band. His sensitivity to creatures of the lower planes, brought about by centuries of associating with them in Menzoberranzan, told him that he was nearing the demon before it came into sight.

And then he saw the distant forms, a half-dozen trolls marching in a tight rank, and in their midst, towering over them, was a huge monster of the Abyss. No minor mane or midge, Drizzt knew at once, but a major demon. Kessell must be mighty indeed if he held this formidable monster under his control!

Drizzt followed them at a cautious distance. The band was intent on their destination, though, and his caution was unnecessary. But Drizzt wasn't about to take any chances at all, for he had many times witnessed the wrath of such demons. They were commonplace in the cities of the drow, further proof to Drizzt Do'Urden that the ways of his people were not for him.

He moved in closer, for something else had grabbed his attention. The demon was holding a small object which radiated such powerful magic that the drow, even at this distance, could sense it clearly. It was too masked by the demon's own emanations for Drizzt to get any clear perspectives on it, so he backed off cautiously once again.

The lights of thousands of campfires came into view as the party, and Drizzt, approached the mountain. The goblins had set scouts in this very area, and Drizzt realized that he had gone as far south as he could. He broke off his pursuit and headed for the better vantage points up the mountain.

The time best suited to the drow's underworld vision was the lightening hours just before sunrise, and though he was tired, Drizzt was determined to be in position by then. He quickly climbed up the rocks, gradually working his way around to the southern face of the mountain.

Then he saw the campfires encircling Bryn Shander. Further to the east, embers glowed in the rubble that had been Caer-Konig and Caer-Dineval. Wild shouts rang out from Termalaine, and Drizzt knew that the city on Maer Dualdon was in the hands of the enemy.

And then predawn blued the night sky, and much more became apparent. Drizzt first looked to the south end of the dwarven valley and was comforted that the wall opposite him had collapsed. Bruenor's people were safe at least, and Regis with them, the drow supposed.

But the sight of Bryn Shander was less comforting. Drizzt had heard the boasts of the captured orc and had seen the tracks of the army and their campfires, but he could never have imagined the vast assemblage that opened up before him when the light increased.

The sight staggered him.

"How many goblin tribes have you collected, Akar Kessell?" he gasped. "And how many of the giants call you master?"

He knew that the people in Bryn Shander would survive only as long as Kessell let them. They could not hope to hold out against this force.

Dismayed, he turned to seek out a hole where he could get some rest. He could be of no immediate help here, and exhaustion was heightening his hopelessness, preventing him from thinking constructively.

As he started away from the mountain face, sudden activity on the distant field caught his attention. He couldn't make out individuals at this great distance, the army seemed just a black mass, but he knew that the demon had come forth. He saw the blacker spot of its evil presence wade out to a cleared area only a few hundred yards below the gates of Bryn Shander. And he felt the supernatural aura of the powerful magic he had earlier sensed, like the living heart of some unknown life form, pulsating in the demon's clawed hands.

Goblins gathered around to watch the spectacle, keeping a respectable distance between them and Kessell's dangerously unpredictable captain.

"What is that?" asked Regis, crushed in among the watching throng on Bryn Shander's wall.

"A demon," Cassius answered. "A big one."

"It mocks our meager defenses!" Glensather cried. "How can we hope to stand against such a foe?"

The demon bent low, involved in the ritual to call out the dweomer of the crystalline object. It stood the Crystal Shard upright on the grass and stepped back, bellowing forth the obscure words of an ancient spell, rising to a crescendo as the sky began to brighten with the sun's imminent appearance.

"A glass dagger?" Regis asked, puzzled by the pulsating object.

Then the first ray of dawn broke the horizon. The crystal sparkled and summoned the light, bending the sunbeam's path and absorbing its energy.

The shard flared again. The pulsations intensified as more of the sun crept into the eastern sky, only to have its light sucked into the hungry image of Crenshinibon.

The spectators on the wall gaped in horror, wondering if Akar Kessell held power over the sun itself. Only Cassius had the presence of mind to connect the power of the shard with the light of the sun.

Then the crystal began to grow. It swelled as each pulse attained its peak, then shrank back a bit while the next throb grew. Everything around it remained in shadow, for it greedily consumed all the sunlight. Slowly, but inevitably, its girth widened and its tip rose high into the air. The people on the wall and the monsters on the field had to avert their eyes from the brightened power of Cryshal-Tirith. Only the drow from his distant vantage point and the demon who was immune to such sights witnessed another image of Crenshinibon being raised. The third Cryshal-Tirith grew to life. The tower released its hold on the sun as the ritual was completed, and all the region was bathed in morning sunlight.

The demon roared at its successful spellcasting and strode proudly into the new tower's mirrored doorway, followed by the trolls, the wizard's personal guard.

The besieged inhabitants of Bryn Shander and Targos looked upon the incredible structure with a confused mixture of awe, appreciation, and terror. They could not resist the unearthly beauty of Cryshal-Tirith, but they knew the consequences of the tower's appearance. Akar Kessell, master of goblins and giants, had come.

⚔ ⚔ ⚔ ⚔

Goblins and orcs fell to their knees, and all the vast army took up the chant of "Kessell! Kessell!" paying homage to the wizard with a fanatical devotion that brought shivers to the human witnesses to the spectacle.

Drizzt, too, was unnerved by the extent of the influence and devotion the wizard exerted over the normally independent goblin tribes. The drow determined at that moment that the only chance for survival for the people of Ten-Towns lay in the death of Akar Kessell. He knew even before he had considered any of the possible options that he would try to get to the wizard. For now, though, he needed to rest. He found a shadowed hole just back from the face of Kelvin's Cairn and let his exhaustion overtake him.

Cassius was also tired. The spokesman had stayed on the wall throughout the cold night, examining the campsites to determine how much of the natural enmity between the unruly tribes remained. He had seen some minor discord and name-calling, but nothing extreme enough to give him hope that the army would fall apart early into the siege. He couldn't understand how the wizard had achieved such a dramatic unification of the arch foes. The appearance of the demon and the raising of Cryshal-Tirith had shown him the incredible power that Kessell commanded. He had soon drawn the same conclusions as the drow.

Unlike Drizzt, though, the spokesman from Bryn Shander did not retire when the field calmed again, despite the protests of Regis and Glensather, concerned for his health. On his shoulders, Cassius carried the responsibility for the several thousand terrified people that lay huddled within his city's walls and there would be no rest for him. He needed information; he needed to find a weak link in the wizard's seemingly impregnable armor.

And so the spokesman watched diligently and patiently throughout the first long, uneventful day of the siege, noting the boundaries that the goblin tribes staked out as their own, and the order of hierarchy that determined the distance of each group from the center spot of Cryshal-Tirith.

✕ ✕ ✕ ✕ ✕

Away to the east, the fleets of Caer-Konig and Caer-Dineval moored alongside the docks of the deserted city of Easthaven. Several crews had gone ashore to gather supplies, but most of the people had remained on the boats, unsure of how far east Kessell's black arm extended.

Jensin Brent and his counterpart from Caer-Konig had taken full control of their immediate situation from the decks of the *Mist Seeker*, the flagship of Caer-Dineval. All disputes between the two cities had been called off, temporarily at least—though promises of continued friendship were heard on the decks of every ship on Lac Dinneshere. Both spokesmen were agreed that they would not yet leave the waters of the lake and flee, for they realized that they had nowhere to go. All of the ten towns were threatened by Kessell, and Luskan was fully four hundred miles away and across the path of Kessell's army. The ill-equipped refugees couldn't hope to reach it before the first of winter's snows caught up with them.

The sailors that had disembarked soon returned to the docks with the welcomed news that Easthaven had not yet been touched by the darkness. More crews were ordered ashore to collect extra food and blankets, but Jensin Brent played it cautiously, thinking it wise to keep most of the refugees out on the water beyond Kessell's reach.

More promising news came a short time later.

"Signals from Redwaters, Spokesman Brent!" the watchman atop the *Mist Seeker*'s crow's nest called out. "The people of Good Mead and Dougan's Hole are unharmed!" He held up his newsbearer, a small glasspiece crafted in Termalaine and designed to focus the light of the sun for signaling across the lakes, using intricate though limited signaling codes. "My calls have been answered!"

"Where are they, then?" Brent asked excitedly.

"On the eastern banks," the watchman replied. "They sailed out of their villages, thinking them undefendable. None of the monsters have yet approached, but the spokesmen felt that the far side of the lake would be safer until the invaders have departed."

"Keep the communication open," Brent ordered. "Let me know when you have more news."

"Until the invaders have departed?" Schermont echoed incredulously as he moved to Jensin Brent's side.

"A foolishly hopeful assessment of the situation, I agree," said Brent. "But I am relieved that our cousins to the south yet live!"

"Do we go to them? Join our forces?"

"Not yet," answered Brent. "I fear that we would be too vulnerable on the open ground between the lakes. We need more information before we can take any effective action. Let us keep the communications flowing between the two lakes. Gather volunteers to carry messages to Redwaters."

"They shall be sent off immediately," agreed Schermont as he headed away.

Brent nodded and looked back across the lake at the dying plume of smoke above his home. "More information," he muttered to himself.

Other volunteers headed out later that day into the more treacherous west to scout out the situation in the principal city.

Brent and Schermont had done a masterful job in quelling the panic, but even with the substantial gains in organization, the initial shock of the sudden and deadly invasion had left most of the survivors of Caer-Konig and Caer-Dineval in a state of utter despair. Jensin Brent was the glowing exception. The spokesman from Caer-Dineval was a courageous fighter who steadfastly refused to yield until the last breath had left his body. He sailed his proud flagship around the moorings of the others, rallying the people with his cries of promised revenge against Akar Kessell.

Now he watched and waited on the *Mist Seeker* for the critical news from the west. In mid-afternoon, he heard the call he had prayed for.

"She stands!" the watcher on the crow's nest cried out ecstatically when the newsbearer's signal flashed in. "Bryn Shander stands!"

Suddenly, Brent's optimism took on credibility. The miserable band of homeless victims assumed an angry posture bent on vengeance. More messengers were dispatched at once to carry the news to Redwaters that Kessell hadn't yet achieved complete victory.

On both lakes, the task of separating the warriors from the civilians soon began in earnest, with the women and children moving to the heaviest and least seaworthy boats, and the fighting men boarding the fastest vessels. The designated warships were then moved to the outbound moorings, where they could put out quickly across the lakes. Their sails were checked and tightened in preparation for the wild run that would carry their brave crews to war.

Or, by Jensin Brent's furious decree, "The run that would carry their brave crews to victory!"

⚔ ⚔ ⚔ ⚔ ⚔

Regis had rejoined Cassius on the wall when the newsbearer's signal had been spotted on the southwestern banks of Lac Dinneshere. The halfling had slept for most of the night and day, figuring that he might as well die doing the thing he loved to do best. He was surprised when he awakened, expecting his slumber to last into eternity.

Cassius was beginning to view things a bit differently, though. He had compiled a long list of potential breakdowns in Akar Kessell's unruly army: orcs bullying goblins and giants in turn bullying both. If he could only find a way for them to hold out long enough for the obvious hatred between the goblin races to take its toll on Kessell's force. . . .

And then, the signal from Lac Dinneshere and subsequent reports of similar flashes on the far side of Redwaters had given the spokesman sincere hope that the siege might well disintegrate and Ten-Towns survive.

But then the wizard made his dramatic appearance and Cassius's hopes were dashed.

It began as a pulse of red light circling within the glassy wall at the base of Cryshal-Tirith. Then a second pulse, this one blue, started up the tower, rotating in the opposite direction. Slowly they circled the diameter of the tower, blending into green as they converged, then separating and continuing on their way. All who could see the tantalizing show stared apprehensively, unsure of what would happen next, but convinced that a display of tremendous power was forthcoming.

The circling lights speeded up, their intensity increasing with their velocity. Soon the entire base of the tower was ringed in a green blur, so bright that the onlookers had to avert their eyes. And out of the blur stepped two hideous trolls, each bearing an ornate mirror.

The lights slowed and stopped altogether.

The mere sight of the disgusting trolls filled the people of Bryn Shander with revulsion, but intrigued, none would turn away. The monsters walked right to the base of the city's sloping hill and stood facing each other, aiming their mirrors diagonally toward each other, but still catching the reflection of Cryshal-Tirith.

Twin beams of light shot down from the tower, each striking one of the mirrors and converging with the other halfway between the trolls. A sudden pulse from the tower, like the flash of a lightning stroke, left the area between the monsters veiled in smoke, and when it cleared, instead of the converging beams of light, stood a thin, crooked shell of a man in a red, satiny robe.

Goblins fell to their knees again and hid their faces in the ground. Akar Kessell had come.

He looked up in the direction of Cassius on the wall, a cocky smile stretched across his thin lips. "Greetings spokesman of Bryn Shander!" he cackled. "Welcome to my fair city!" He laughed wryly.

Cassius had no doubt that the wizard had picked him out, though he had no recollection of ever seeing the man and didn't understand how he had been recognized. He looked to Regis and Glensather for an explanation, but they both shrugged their shoulders.

"Yes, I know you, Cassius," Kessell said. "And to you, good Spokesman Glensather, my greetings. I should have guessed that you would be here; ever were the people of Easthaven willing to join in a cause, no matter how hopeless!"

Now it was Glensather's turn to stare dumbfounded at his companions. But again, there were no explanations forthcoming.

"You know of us," Cassius replied to the apparition, "yet you are unknown to us. It seems that you hold an unfair advantage."

"Unfair?" protested the wizard. "I hold every advantage, foolish man!" Again the laugh. "You know of me—at least Glensather does."

The spokesman from Easthaven shrugged his shoulders again in reply to Cassius's inquiring glance. The gesture seemed to anger Kessell.

"I spent several months living in Easthaven," the wizard snapped. "In the guise of a wizard's apprentice from Luskan! Clever, don't you agree?"

"Do you remember him?" Cassius asked Glensather softly. "It could be of great import."

"It is possible that he stayed in Easthaven," Glensather replied in the same whispered tones, "though no group from the Hosttower has come into my city for several years. Yet we are an open city, and many foreigners arrive with every passing trading caravan. I tell you the truth, Cassius, I have no recollection of the man."

Kessell was outraged. He stamped his foot impatiently, and the smile on his face was replaced by a pouting pucker.

"Perhaps my return to Ten-Towns will prove more memorable, fools!" he snapped. He held his arms outstretched in self-important proclamation. "Behold Akar Kessell, the Tyrant of Icewind Dale!" he cried. "People of Ten-Towns, your master has come!"

"Your words are a bit premature—" Cassius began, but Kessell cut him short with a frenzied scream.

"Never interrupt me!" the wizard shouted, the veins in his neck taut and bulging and his face turning as red as blood.

Then, as Cassius quieted in disbelief, Kessell seemed to regain a measure of his composure. "You shall learn better, proud Cassius," he threatened. "You shall learn!"

He turned back to Cryshal-Tirith and uttered a simple word of command. The tower went black for a moment, as though it refused to release the reflections of the sun's light. Then it began to glow, far within its depths, with a light that seemed more its own than a reflection of the day. With each passing second, the hue shifted and the light began to climb and circle the strange walls.

"Behold Akar Kessell!" the wizard proclaimed, still frowning. "Look upon the splendor of Crenshinibon and surrender all hope!"

More lights began flashing within the tower's walls, climbing and dropping randomly and spinning about the structure in a frenzied dance that cried out for release. Gradually they were working their way up to the pointed pinnacle, and it began to flare as if on fire, shifting through the colors of the spectrum until its white flame rivaled the brightness of the sun itself.

Kessell cried out as a man in ecstasy.

The fire was released.

It shot out in a thin, searing line northward toward the unfortunate city of Targos. Many spectators lined Targos's high wall, though the tower was much farther away from them than it was from Bryn Shander, and it appeared as no more than a flashing speck on the distant plain. They had little idea of what was happening beneath the principal city, though they did see the ray of fire coming toward them.

But by then it was too late.

The wrath of Akar Kessell roared into the proud city, cutting a swath of instant devastation. Fires sprouted all along its killing line. People caught in the direct path never even had a chance to cry out before they were simply vaporized. But those who survived the initial assault, women and children and tundra-toughened men alike, who had faced death a thousand times and more, did scream. And their wails carried out across the still lake to Lonelywood and Bremen, to the cheering goblins in Termalaine, and down the plain to the horrified witnesses in Bryn Shander.

Kessell waved his hand and slightly altered the angle of the release, thus arcing the destruction throughout Targos. Every major structure within the city was soon burning, and hundreds of people lay dead or dying, pitifully rolling about on the ground to extinguish the flames that engulfed their bodies or gasping helplessly in a desperate search for air in the heavy smoke.

Kessell reveled in the moment.

But then he felt an involuntary shudder wrack his spine. And the tower, too, seemed to quiver. The wizard clutched at the relic, still tucked under the folds of his robe. He understood that he had pushed the limits of Crenshinibon's strength too far.

Back in the Spine of the World, the first tower that Kessell had raised crumbled into rubble. And far out on the open tundra, the second did likewise. The shard pulled in its borders, destroying the tower images that sapped away its strength.

Kessell, too, had been wearied by the effort, and the lights of the remaining Cryshal-Tirith began to calm and then to wane. The ray fluttered and died.

But it had finished its business.

When the invasion had first come, Kemp and the other proud leaders of Targos had promised their people that they would hold the city until the last man had fallen, but even the stubborn spokesman realized that they had no choice but to flee. Luckily, the city proper, which had taken the brunt of Kessell's attack, was on high ground overlooking the sheltered bay area. The fleets remained unharmed. And the homeless fishermen of Termalaine were already on the docks, having stayed with their boats after they had docked in Targos. As soon as they had realized the unbelievable extent of the destruction that was occurring in the city proper, they began preparing for the imminent influx of the war's latest refugees. Most of the boats of both cities sailed out within minutes of the attack, desperate to get their vulnerable sails safely away from the windblown sparks and debris. A few vessels remained behind, braving the growing hazards to rescue any later arrivals on the docks.

The people on Bryn Shander's dock wept at the continued screams of the dying. Cassius, though, consumed by his quest to seek out and understand the apparent weakness that Kessell had just revealed, had no time for tears. In truth, the cries affected him as deeply as anyone, but unwilling to let the lunatic Kessell view any hints of weakness from him, he transformed his visage from sorrow to an iron grimace of rage.

Kessell laughed at him. "Do not pout, poor Cassius," the wizard taunted, "it is unbecoming."

"You are a dog," Glensather retorted. "And unruly dogs should be beaten!"

Cassius stayed his fellow spokesman with an outstretched hand. "Be calm, my friend," he whispered. "Kessell will feed off of our panic. Let him talk— he reveals more to us than he believes."

"Poor Cassius," Kessell repeated sarcastically. Then suddenly, the wizard's face twisted in outrage. Cassius noted the abrupt swing keenly, filing it away with the other information he had collected.

"Mark well what you have witnessed here, people of Bryn Shander!" Kessell sneered. "Bow to your master, or the same fate shall befall you! And there is no water behind you! You have nowhere to run!"

He laughed wildly again and looked all about the city's hill, as though he was searching for something. "What are you to do?" he cackled. "You have no lake!

"I have spoken, Cassius. Hear me well. You will deliver an emissary unto me tomorrow, an emissary to bear the news of your unconditional surrender! And if your pride prevents such an act, remember the cries of dying Targos! Look to the city on the banks of Maer Dualdon for guidance, pitiful Cassius. The fires shall not have died when the morrow dawns!"

Just then a courier raced up to the spokesman. "Many ships have been spotted moving out from under the blanket of smoke in Targos. Newsbearer signals have already begun coming in from the refugees."

"And what of Kemp?" Cassius asked anxiously.

"He lives," the courier answered. "And he has vowed revenge."

Cassius breathed a sigh of relief. He wasn't overly fond of his peer from Targos, but he knew that the battle-seasoned spokesman would prove a valuable asset to Ten-Towns' cause before all was through.

Kessell heard the conversation and growled in disdain. "And where shall they run?" he asked Cassius.

The spokesman, intent on studying this unpredictable and unbalanced adversary, did not reply, but Kessell answered the question for him.

"To Bremen? But they cannot!" He snapped his fingers, beginning the chain of a prearranged message to his westernmost forces. At once, a large group of goblins broke rank and started out to the west.

Toward Bremen.

"You see? Bremen falls before the night is through, and yet another fleet will scurry out onto their precious lake. The scene shall be repeated in the town in the wood with predictable results. But what protection will the lakes offer these people when the merciless winter begins to fall?" he shouted. "How fast shall their ships sail away from me when the waters are frozen around them?"

He laughed again, but this time more seriously, more dangerously. "What protection do any of you have against Akar Kessell?"

Cassius and the wizard held each other in unyielding glares. The wizard barely mouthed the words, but Cassius heard him clearly. "What protection?"

✕ ✕ ✕ ✕ ✕

Out on Maer Dualdon, Kemp bit back his frustrated rage as he watched his city tumble in flames. Soot-blackened faces stared back to the burning ruins in horrified disbelief, shouting impossible denials and openly crying for their lost friends and kin.

But like Cassius, Kemp converted his despair into constructive anger. As soon as he learned of the goblin force departing for Bremen, he dispatched his fastest ship to warn the people of that distant city and to inform them of the happenings across the lake. Then he sent a second ship toward Lonelywood to beg for food and bandages, and perhaps an invitation to dock.

Despite their obvious differences, the spokesmen of the ten towns were in many ways alike. Like Agorwal, who had been happy to sacrifice everything for the good of the people, and Jensin Brent, who refused to yield to despair, Kemp of Targos set about rallying his people for a retaliatory strike. He didn't yet know how he would accomplish the feat, but he knew that he had not had his final say in the wizard's war.

And poised upon the wall of Bryn Shander, Cassius knew it, too.

25

ERRTU

Drizzt crawled out of his hidden chamber as the last lights of the setting sun began fading away. He scanned the southern horizon and was again dismayed. He had needed to rest, but he couldn't help feeling pangs of guilt when he saw the city of Targos burning, as though he had neglected his duty to bear witness to the suffering of Kessell's helpless victims.

Yet the drow had not been idle even during the hours of the meditative trance the elves called sleep. He had journeyed back into the underworld of his distant memories in search of a particular sensation, the aura of a powerful presence he had once known. Though he had not gotten close enough for a good look at the demon he had followed the previous night, something about the creature had struck a familiar chord in his oldest recollections.

A pervading, unnatural emanation surrounded creatures from the lower planes when they walked on the material world, an aura that the dark elves, moreso than any other race, had come to understand and recognize. Not only this type of demon, but this particular creature itself, was known to Drizzt. It had served his people in Menzoberranzan for many years.

"Errtu," he whispered as he sorted through his dreams.

Drizzt knew the demon's true name. It would come to his call.

⚔ ⚔ ⚔ ⚔ ⚔

The search to find an appropriate spot from which he could call the demon took Drizzt over an hour, and he spent several more preparing the area. His goal was to take away as many of Errtu's advantages—size and flight in particular—as he could, though he sincerely hoped that their meeting would not involve combat. People who knew the drow considered him daring, sometimes even reckless, but that was against mortal enemies who would recoil from the stinging pain of his whirring blades. Demons, especially one of Errtu's size and strength, were a different story altogether. Many times during his youth Drizzt had witnessed the wrath of such a monster. He had seen buildings thrown down, solid stone torn by the great clawed hands. He had seen mighty human warriors strike the monster with blows that would fell an ogre, only to find, in their dying horror, that their weapons were useless against such a powerful being from the lower planes.

His own people usually fared better against demons, actually receiving a measure of respect from them. Demons often allied with drow on even terms, or even served the dark elves outright, for they were wary of the powerful weapons and magic the drow possessed. But that was back in the underworld, where the strange emanations from the unique stone formations blessed the metals used by the drow craftsmen with mysterious and magical properties. Drizzt had none of the weapons from his homeland for their strange magic could not withstand the light of day; though he had been careful to keep them protected from the sun, they became useless shortly after he moved to the surface. He doubted that the weapons he now carried would be able to harm Errtu at all. And even if they did, demons of Errtu's stature could not be truly destroyed away from their native planes. If it came to blows, the most that Drizzt could hope to do was banish the creature from the Material Plane for one hundred years.

He had no intentions of fighting.

Yet he had to try something against the wizard who threatened the towns. His goal now was to gain some knowledge that might reveal a weakness in the wizard, and his method was deception and disguise, hoping that Errtu remembered enough about the dark elves to make his story credible, yet not too much to strip away the flimsy lies that would hold it together.

The place he had chosen for the meeting was a sheltered dell a few yards from the mountain's cliff face. A pinnacled roof formed by converging walls covered half of the area—the other half was open to the sky—but the entire place was set back into the mountainside behind high walls, safely out of view of Cryshal-Tirith. Now Drizzt worked with a dagger, scraping runes of warding on the walls and floor in front of where he would sit. His mental image of these magical symbols had fuzzied over the many years, and he knew that their design was far from perfect. Yet he realized that he would need any possible protection that they might offer if Errtu turned on him.

When he was finished, he sat crosslegged under the roofed section, behind the protected area, and tossed out the small statuette that he carried in his pack. Guenhwyvar would be a good test for his warding inscriptions.

The great cat answered the summons. It appeared in the other side of the cubby, its keen eyes scanning the area for any potential danger that threatened its master. Then, sensing nothing, it turned a curious glance on Drizzt.

"Come to me," Drizzt called, beckoning with his hand. The cat strode toward him, then stopped abruptly, as though it had walked into a wall. Drizzt sighed in relief when he saw that his runes held some measure of strength. His confidence was bolstered considerably, though he realized that Errtu would push the power of the runes to their absolute limits—and probably beyond.

Guenhwyvar lolled its huge head in an effort to understand what had deterred it. The resistance hadn't really been very strong, but the mixed signals from its master, calling for it yet warding it away, had confused the cat. It considered gathering its strength and walking right through the feeble barrier, but its master seemed pleased that it had stopped. So the cat sat where it was and waited.

Drizzt was busy studying the area, searching out the optimum place for Guenhwyvar to spring from and surprise the demon. A deep ledge on one of the high walls just beyond the portion that converged into a roof seemed to offer the best concealment. He motioned the cat into position and instructed it not to attack until his signal. Then he sat back and tried to relax, intent on his final mental preparations before he called the demon.

⚔ ⚔ ⚔ ⚔ ⚔

Across the valley in the magical tower, Errtu crouched in a shadowy corner of Kessell's harem room keeping its ever-vigilant guard over the evil wizard at play with his mindless girls. A seething fire of hatred burned in Errtu's eyes as it looked upon the foolish Kessell. The wizard had nearly ruined everything with his show of power that afternoon and his refusal to tear down the vacated towers behind him, further draining Crenshinibon's strength.

Errtu had been grimly satisfied when Kessell had come back into the Cryshal-Tirith and confirmed, through the use of scrying mirrors, that the other two towers had fallen to pieces. Errtu had warned Kessell against raising a third tower, but the wizard, frail of ego, had grown more stubborn with each passing day of the campaign, envisioning the demon's, or even Crenshinibon's, advice as a ploy to undermine his absolute control.

And so Errtu was quite receptive, even relieved, when it heard Drizzt's call floating down the valley. At first it denied the possibility of such a summons, but the inflections of its true name being spoken aloud sent involuntary shudders running along the demon's spine. More intrigued than angered at the impertinence of some mortal daring to utter its name, Errtu slipped away from the distracted wizard and moved outside Cryshal-Tirith.

Then the call came again, cutting through the harmony of the wind's endless song like a whitecapped wave on a still pond.

Errtu spread its great wings and soared northward over the plain, speeding toward the summoner. Terrified goblins fled from the darkness of the demon's passing shadow, for even in the faint glimmer of a thin moon, the creature of the Abyss left a wake of blackness that made the night seem bright in comparison.

Drizzt sucked in a tense breath. He sensed the unerring approach of the demon as it veered away from Bremen's Run and swept upward over the lower slopes of Kelvin's Cairn. Guenhwyvar lifted its head off its paws and growled, also sensing the approach of the evil monster. The cat ducked to the very back of the deep ledge and lay flat and still, awaiting its master's command confident that its heightened abilities of stealth could protect it even against the highly tuned senses of a demon.

Errtu's leathery wings folded up tight as it alighted on the ledge. It immediately pinpointed the exact location of the summoner and though it had to tuck its broad shoulders to pass through the narrow entrance to the dell, it charged straight in, intent on appeasing its curiosity and then killing the blasphemous fool that dared utter its name aloud.

Drizzt fought to hold his edge of control when the huge demon pushed in, its bulk filling the small area beyond his tiny sanctuary, blocking out the starlight before him. There could be no turning back from his dangerous course. He had no place to run.

The demon stopped suddenly in amazement. It had been centuries since Errtu had looked upon a drow, and it certainly never expected to find one on the surface, in the frozen wastelands of the farthest north.

Somehow Drizzt found his voice. "Greetings, master of chaos," he said calmly, bowing low. "I am Drizzt Do'Urden, of the house of Daermon N'a'shezbaernon, ninth family to the throne of Menzoberranzan. Welcome to my humble camp."

"You are a long way from home, drow," the demon said with obvious suspicion.

"As are thee, great demon of the Abyss," Drizzt replied coolly. "And lured to this high corner of the world for similar reasons, unless I miss my guess."

"I know why I am here," answered Errtu. "The business of the drow has ever been outside my understanding—or caring."

Drizzt stroked his slender chin and chuckled in feigned confidence. His stomach was tied in knots, and he felt the beginnings of a cold sweat coming on. He chuckled again and fought against the fear. If the demon sensed his unease, his credibility would be greatly diminished. "Ah, but this time, for the first time in many years, it seems that the roads of our business have crossed, mighty purveyor of destruction. My people have a curiosity, perhaps even a vested interest, in the wizard that you apparently serve!"

Errtu squared its shoulders, the first flickers of a dangerous flame evident in its red eyes. "Serve?" it echoed incredulously, the even tone of its voice quivering, as though it bordered on the edge of an uncontrollable rage.

Drizzt was quick to qualify his observation. "By all appearances, guardian of chaotic intentions, the wizard holds some power over you. Surely you work alongside Akar Kessell!"

"I serve no human!" Errtu roared, shaking the cave's very foundation with an emphatic stamp of its foot.

Drizzt wondered if the fight that he could not hope to win was about to begin. He considered calling out Guenhwyvar so that they could at least land the first blows.

But the demon suddenly calmed again. Convinced that it had half-guessed the reason for the unexpected presence of the drow, Errtu turned a scrutinizing eye on Drizzt. "Serve the wizard?" it laughed. "Akar Kessell is puny even by the low standards of humans! But you know this, drow, and do not dare to deny it. You are here, as I am here, for Crenshinibon, and Kessell be damned!"

The confused look on Drizzt's face was genuine enough to throw Errtu off balance. The demon still believed that it had guessed correctly, but it couldn't understand why the drow didn't comprehend the name. "Crenshinibon," it explained, sweeping its clawed hand to the south. "An ancient bastion of unspeakable power."

"The tower?" Drizzt asked.

Errtu's uncertainty bubbled up in the form of explosive fury. "Play no games of ignorance with me!" the demon bellowed. "The drow lords know well the power of Akar Kessell's artifact, or else they would not have come to the surface to seek it out!"

"Very well, you've guessed at the truth," Drizzt conceded. "Yet I had to be certain that the tower on the plain was indeed the ancient artifact that I seek. My masters show little mercy to careless spies."

Errtu smiled wickedly as it remembered the unholy torture chambers of Menzoberranzan. Those years it had spent among the dark elves had been enjoyable indeed!

Drizzt quickly pressed the conversation in a direction that might reveal some weaknesses of Kessell or his tower. "One thing has kept me puzzled, awesome spectre of unbridled evil," he began, careful to continue his string of unduplicated compliments. "By what right does this wizard possess Crenshinibon?"

"None at all," Errtu said. "Wizard, bah! Measured against your own people, he is barely an apprentice. His tongue twitches uneasily when he utters even the simplest of spells. But fate often plays such games. And more to the enjoyment, I say! Let Akar Kessell have his brief moment of triumph. Humans do not live a very long time!"

Drizzt knew that he was pursuing a dangerous line of questions, but he accepted the risk. Even with a major demon standing barely ten feet away, Drizzt figured that his chances for survival at this moment were better than those of his friends in Bryn Shander. "Still, my masters are concerned that the tower may be harmed in the coming battle with the humans," he bluffed.

Errtu took another moment to consider Drizzt. The appearance of the dark elves complicated the demon's simple plan to inherit Crenshinibon from Kessell. If the mighty drow lords of the huge city of Menzoberranzan truly had designs upon the relic, the demon knew that they would get it. Certainly Kessell, even with the power of the shard behind him, could not withstand them. The mere presence of this drow changed the demon's perceptions of its relationship with Crenshinibon. How Errtu wished that it could simply devour Kessell and flee with the relic before the dark elves were too involved!

Yet Errtu had never considered the drow as enemies, and the demon had come to despise the bumbling wizard. Perhaps an alliance with the dark elves could prove beneficial to both sides.

"Tell me, unequaled champion of darkness," Drizzt pressed, "is Crenshinibon in peril?"

"Bah!" snorted Errtu. "Even the tower that is merely a reflection of Crenshinibon is impervious. It absorbs all attacks directed against its mirrored walls and reflects them back on their source! Only the pulsating crystal of strength, the very heart of Cryshal-Tirith, is vulnerable, and that is safely hidden away."

"Inside?"

"Of course."

"But if someone were to get into the tower," Drizzt reasoned, "how well protected would he then find the heart?"

"An impossible task," the demon replied. "Unless the simple fishermen of Ten-Towns have some spirit at their service. Or perhaps a high priest, or an archmage to weave spells of unveiling. Surely your masters know that Cryshal-Tirith's door is invisible and undetectable to any beings inherent to the present plane the tower rests upon. No creature of this material world, your race included, could find its way in!"

"But—" Drizzt pressed anxiously.

Errtu cut him short. "Even if someone stumbled into the structure," he growled, impatient with the relentless stream of impossible suppositions, "he would have to pass by me. And the limit of Kessell's power within the tower is considerable indeed, for the wizard has become an extension of Crenshinibon itself, a living outlet for the Crystal Shard's unfathomable strength! The heart lies beyond the very focal point of Kessell's interaction with the tower, and up to the very tip . . ." The demon stopped, suddenly suspicious of Drizzt's line of questioning. If the lore-wise drow lords were truly intent upon Crenshinibon, why weren't they more aware of its strengths and weaknesses?

Errtu understood its mistake then. It examined Drizzt once again, but with a different focus. When it had first encountered the drow, stunned by the mere presence of a dark elf in this region, it had searched for deception in the physical attributes of Drizzt himself to determine if his drow features were an illusion, a clever yet simple shape-alteration trick within the power of even a minor mage.

When Errtu was convinced that a true drow and no illusion stood before it, it had accepted the credibility of Drizzt's story as consistent with the characteristics of the dark elves' style.

Now, though, the demon scoured the peripheral clues beyond Drizzt's black skin, noting the items he carried and the area he had staked out for their meeting. Nothing that Drizzt had upon his person, not even the weapons sheathed on his hips, emanated the distinct magical properties of the underworld. Perhaps the drow masters had outfitted their spies more appropriately for the surface world, Errtu reasoned. From what it had learned of the dark elves during its many years of service in Menzoberranzan, this drow's presence was certainly not outrageous.

But creatures of chaos survived by trusting no one.

Errtu continued his scan for a clue of Drizzt's authenticity. The only item the demon had spotted that reflected on Drizzt's heritage was a thin silver chain strung around his slender neck, a piece of jewelry common among the dark elves for holding a small pouch of wealth. Concentrating upon this, Errtu discovered a second chain, finer than the first, weaving in and out of the other. The demon followed the almost imperceptible crease in Drizzt's jerkin created by the long chain.

Unusual, it noted, and possibly revealing. Errtu pointed at the chain, spoke a command word, and raised its outstretched finger into the air.

Drizzt tensed when he felt the emblem slipping up from under his leather jerkin. It passed up over the neckline of the garment and dropped to the extent of the chain, hanging openly upon his chest.

Errtu's evil grin widened along with its squinting eyes. "Unusual choice for a drow," it hissed sarcastically. "I would have expected the symbol of Lolth, demon queen of your people. She would not be pleased!" From nowhere, it seemed, a many-thonged whip appeared in one of the demon's hands and a jagged, cruelly notched blade in the other.

At first, Drizzt's mind whirled down a hundred avenues, exploring the most feasible lies he could spin to get him out of this fix. But then he shook his head resolutely and pushed the lies away. He would not dishonor his deity.

At the end of the silver chain hung a gift from Regis, a carving the halfling had done from the bone of one of the few knuckleheads he had ever hooked. Drizzt had been deeply touched when Regis presented it to him, and he considered it the halfling's finest work. It twirled around on the long chain, its gentle grades and shading giving it the depth of a true work of art.

It was a white unicorn head, the symbol of the goddess Mielikki.

"Who are you, drow?" Errtu demanded. The demon had already decided that it would have to kill Drizzt, but it was intrigued by such an unusual meeting. A dark elf that followed the Lady of the Forest? And a surface dweller as well! Errtu had known many drow over the centuries, but had never even heard of one that had abandoned the drow's wicked ways. Cold-hearted killers, one and all, that had taught even the great demon of chaos a trick or two concerning the methods of excruciating torture.

"I am Drizzt Do'Urden, that much is true," Drizzt replied evenly. "He who forsook the House of Daermon N'a'shezbaernon." All fear had flown from Drizzt when he accepted beyond any hope that he would have to battle the demon. Now he assumed the calm readiness of a seasoned fighter, prepared to seize any advantage that might fall his way. "A ranger humbly serving Gwaeron Windstrom, hero of the goddess Mielikki." He bowed low in accordance with a proper introduction.

As he straightened, he drew his scimitars. "I must defeat you, scar of vileness," he declared, "and send you back to the swirling clouds of the bottomless Abyss. There is no place in the sunlit world for one of your kind!"

"You are confused, elf," the demon said. "You have lost the way of your heritage, and now you dare to presume that you might defeat me!" Flames sprang to life from the stone all around Errtu. "I would have killed you mercifully, with one clean stroke, out of respect for your kin. But your pride distresses me; I shall teach you to desire death! Come, feel the sting of my fire!"

Drizzt was already nearly overwhelmed by the heat of Errtu's demon fire, and the brightness of the flames stung his sensitive eyes so that the bulk of the demon seemed only the dulled blur of a shadow. He saw the darkness extend to the demon's right and knew that Errtu had raised its terrible sword. He moved to defend, but suddenly the demon lurched to the side and roared in surprise and outrage.

Guenhwyvar had latched firmly onto its upraised arm.

The huge demon held the panther at arm's length, trying to pin the cat between its forearm and the rock wall to keep the tearing claws and teeth away from a vital area. Guenhwyvar gnawed and raked the massive arm, tearing demon flesh and muscle.

Errtu winced away the vicious attack and determined to deal with the cat later. The demon's main concern remained the drow, for it respected the potential power of any of the dark elves. Errtu had seen too many foes fall beneath one of the dark elves' countless tricks.

The many-thonged whip lashed out at Drizzt's legs, too quickly for the drow, still reeling from the sudden burst of brightness of the flames, to deflect the blow or dodge aside. Errtu jerked the handle as the thongs tangled about the slender legs and ankles, the demon's great strength easily dropping Drizzt to his back.

Drizzt felt the stinging pain all through his legs, and he heard the rush of air pressed out of his lungs when he landed on the hard stone. He knew that he must react without delay, but the glare of the fire and Errtu's sudden strike had left him disoriented. He felt himself being dragged along the stone, felt the intensity of the heat increasing. He managed to lift his head just in time to view his tangled feet entering the demon fire.

"And so I die," he stated flatly.

But his legs did not burn.

Drooling to hear the agonized screams of its helpless victim, Errtu gave a stronger tug on the whip and pulled Drizzt completely into the flames. Though he was totally immolated, the drow barely felt warmed by the fire.

And then, with a final hiss of protest, the hot flames suddenly died away.

Neither of the opponents understood what had happened, both assuming that the other had been responsible.

Errtu struck quickly again. Bringing a heavy foot down upon Drizzt's chest, it began grinding him into the stone. The drow flailed out in desperation with one weapon, but it had no effect on the otherworldly monster.

Then Drizzt swung his other scimitar, the blade he had taken from the dragon's hoard.

Hissing like water on fire, it entered Errtu's knee joint. The hilt of the weapon heated up when the blade tore into the demon's flesh, nearly burning Drizzt's hand. Then it grew icy cold, as though dousing Errtu's hot life force with a cold strength of its own. Drizzt understood then what had extinguished the fires.

The demon gaped in blank horror, then screamed in agony. Never had it felt such a sting! It leaped back and tossed about wildly, trying to escape the weapon's terrible bite, dragging Drizzt, who could not let go of the hilt. Guenhwyvar was thrown in the violence of the demon's rage, flying from the monster's arm to crash heavily into a wall.

Drizzt eyed the wound incredulously as the demon backed away. Steam poured from the hole in Errtu's knee; and the edges of the cut were iced over!

But Drizzt, too, had been weakened by the strike. In its struggle with the mighty demon, the scimitar had drawn upon its wielder's life force, pulling Drizzt into the battle with the fiery monster.

Now the drow felt as though he hadn't even the strength left to stand. But he found himself lunging forward, blade fully extended before him, as if pulled by the scimitar's hunger.

The cubby entrance was too narrow. Errtu could neither dodge nor spring away.

The scimitar found the demon's belly.

The explosive surge as the blade touched the core of Errtu's life force drained away Drizzt's strength, tossing him backward. He cracked against the stone wall and crumpled, but managed to keep himself alert enough to witness the titanic struggle still raging.

Errtu got out onto the ledge. The demon was staggering now, trying to spread its wings. But they drooped weakly. The scimitar glowed white with power as it continued its assault. The demon could not bear to grasp it and tear it free, though the embedded blade, its magic quelching the fires it had been wrought to destroy, was surely winning the conflict.

Errtu knew that it had been careless, overconfident in its ability to destroy any mortal in single combat. The demon hadn't considered the possibility of such a wicked blade; it had never even heard of a weapon with such a sting.

Steam poured from Errtu's exposed entrails and enveloped the combatants. "And so you have banished me, treacherous drow!" it spat.

Dazed, Drizzt watched in amazement as the white glow intensified and the black shadow diminished.

"A hundred years; drow!" Errtu howled. "Not such a long time for the likes of you or me!" The vapor thickened as the shadow seemed to melt away.

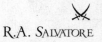

"A century, Drizzt Do'Urden!" came Errtu's fading cry from somewhere far away. "Look over your shoulder then! Errtu shall not be far behind!"

The vapor wafted up into the air and was gone.

The last sound Drizzt heard was the clang of the metal scimitar falling to the stone ledge.

26
RIGHTS OF VICTORY

Wulfgar leaned back in his chair at the head of the main table in the hastily constructed Mead Hall, his foot tapping nervously at the long delays necessitated by the demands of proper tradition. He felt that his people should already be on the move, but it was the restoration of the traditional ceremonies and celebrations that had immediately separated, and placed him above, the tyrant Heafstaag in the eyes of the skeptical and ever-suspicious barbarians.

Wulfgar, after all, had walked into their midst after a five-year absence and challenged their long-standing king. One day later, he had won the crown, and the day after that, he had been coronated King Wulfgar of the Tribe of the Elk.

And he was determined that his reign, short though he intended it to be, would not be marked by the threats and bullying tactics of his predecessor's. He would ask the warriors of the assembled tribes to follow him into battle, not command them, for he knew that a barbarian warrior was a man driven almost exclusively by fierce pride. Stripped of their dignity, as Heafstaag had done by refusing to honor the sovereignty of each individual king, the tribesmen were no better in battle than ordinary men. Wulfgar knew that they would need to regain their proud edge if they were to have any chance at all against the wizard's overwhelming numbers.

Thus Hengorot, the Mead Hall, had been raised and the Challenge of the Song initiated for the first time in nearly five years. It was a short, happy time of good-natured competition between tribes who had been suffocated under Heafstaag's unrelenting domination.

The decision to raise the deerskin hall had been difficult for Wulfgar. Assuming that he still had time before Kessell's army struck, he had weighed the benefits of regaining tradition against the pressing need of haste. He only hoped that in the frenzy of pre-battle preparations, Kessell would overlook the absence of the barbarian king, Heafstaag. If the wizard was at all sharp, it wasn't likely.

Now he waited quietly and patiently, watching the fires return to the eyes of the tribesmen.

"Like old times?" Revjak asked, sitting next to him.

"Good times," Wulfgar responded.

Satisfied, Revjak leaned back against the tent's deerskin wall, granting the new chief the solitude he obviously desired. And Wulfgar resumed his wait, seeking the best moment to unveil his proposition.

At the far end of the hall, an axe-throwing competition was beginning. Similar to the tactics Heafstaag and Beorg had used to seal a pact between the tribes at the last Hengorot, the challenge was to hurl an axe from as great a distance as possible and sink it deeply enough into a keg of mead to open a hole. The number of mugs that could be filled from the effort within a specified count determined the success of the throw.

Wulfgar saw his chance. He leaped from his stool and demanded, by rights of being the host, the first throw. The man who had been selected to judge the challenge acknowledged Wulfgar's right and invited him to come down to the first selected distance.

"From here," Wulfgar said, hoisting Aegis-fang to his shoulder.

Murmurs of disbelief and excitement arose from all corners of the hall. The use of a warhammer in such a challenge was unprecedented, but none complained or cited rules. Every man who had heard the tales, but not witnessed firsthand the splitting of Heafstaag's great axe, was anxious to see the weapon in action. A keg of mead was placed upon a stool at the back end of the hall.

"Another behind it!" Wulfgar demanded. "And another behind that!" His concentration narrowed on the task at hand and he didn't take the time to sort out the whispers he heard all around him.

The kegs were readied, and the crowd backed out of the young king's line of sight. Wulfgar grasped Aegis-fang tightly in his hands and sucked in a great breath, holding it in to keep himself steady. The unbelieving onlookers watched in amazement as the new king exploded into movement, hurling the mighty hammer with a fluid motion and strength unmatched among their ranks.

Aegis-fang tumbled, head over handle, the length of the long hall, blasting through the first keg, and then the second and beyond, taking out not only the three targets and their stools, but continuing on to tear a hole in the back of the Mead Hall. The closest warriors hurried to the opening to watch the remainder of its flight, but the hammer had disappeared into the night. They started out to retrieve it.

But Wulfgar stopped them. He sprang onto the table, lifting his arms before him. "Hear me, warriors of the northern plains!" he cried. Their mouths already agape at the unprecedented feat, some fell to their knees when Aegis-fang suddenly reappeared in the young king's hands.

"I am Wulfgar, son of Beornegar and King of the Tribe of the Elk! Yet I speak to you now not as your king but as a kindred warrior, horrified at the dishonor Heafstaag tried to place upon us all!" Spurred on by the knowledge that he had gained their attention and respect, and by the confirmation that his assumptions of their true desires had not been in error, Wulfgar seized the moment. These people had cried out for deliverance from the tyrannical reign of the one-eyed king and beaten almost to extinction in their last campaign and now about to fight beside goblins and giants, they longed for a hero to gain them back their lost pride.

"I am the dragonslayer!" he continued. "And by right of victory I possess the treasures of Icingdeath!"

Again the private conversations interrupted him, for the now unguarded treasure had become a subject for debate. Wulfgar let them continue their gossip for a long moment to heighten their interest in the dragon's gold.

When they finally quieted, he went on. "The tribes of the tundra do not fight in a common cause with goblins and giants!" he decreed to rousing shouts of approval. "We fight against them!"

The crowd suddenly hushed. A guard rushed into the tent, but did not dare interrupt the new king.

"I leave with the dawn for Ten-Towns," Wulfgar stated. "I shall battle against the wizard Kessell and the foul horde he has pulled from the holes of The Spine of the World!"

The crowd did not respond. They accepted the notion of battle against Kessell eagerly, but the thought of returning to Ten-Towns to help the people who had nearly destroyed them five years before had never occurred to them.

But the guard now intervened. "I fear that your quest shall be in vain, young king," he said. Wulfgar turned a distressed eye upon the man, guessing the news he bore. "The smoke clouds from great fires are even now rising above the southern plain."

Wulfgar considered the distressing news. He had thought that he would have more time. "Then I shall leave tonight!" he roared at the stunned assembly. "Come with me, my friends, my fellow warriors of the north! I shall show you the path to the lost glories of our past!"

The crowd seemed torn and uncertain. Wulfgar played his final card.

"To any man who will go with me, or to his surviving kin if he should fall, I offer an equal share of the dragon's treasure!"

He had swept in like a mighty squall off the Sea of Moving Ice. He had captured the imagination and heart of every barbarian warrior and had promised them a return to the wealth and glory of their brightest days.

That very night, Wulfgar's mercenary army charged out of their encampment and thundered across the open plain.

Not a single man remained behind.

27
THE CLOCK OF DOOM

Bremen was torched at dawn.

The people of the small, unwalled village had known better than to stand and fight when the wave of monsters rolled across the Shaengarne River. They put up token resistance at the ford, firing a few bursts of arrows at the lead goblins just to slow the ranks long enough for the heaviest and slowest ships to clear the harbor and reach the safety of Maer Dualdon. The archers then fled back to the docks and followed their fellow townsmen.

When the goblins finally entered the city, they found it completely deserted. They watched angrily as the sailing ships moved back toward the east to join the flotilla of Targos and Termalaine. Bremen was too far out of the way to be of any use to Akar Kessell, so, unlike the city of Termalaine which had been converted into a camp, this city was burned to the ground.

The people on the lake, the newest in the long line of homeless victims of Kessell's wanton destruction, watched helplessly as their homes fell in smoldering splinters.

From the wall of Bryn Shander, Cassius and Regis watched, too.

"He has made yet another mistake," Cassius told the halfling.

"How so?"

"Kessell has backed the people of Targos and Termalaine, Caer-Konig and Caer-Dineval, and now Bremen into a corner," Cassius explained. "They have nowhere to go now; their only hope lies in victory."

"Not much of a hope," Regis remarked. "You have seen what the tower can do. And even without it, Kessell's army could destroy us all! As he said, he holds every advantage."

"Perhaps," Cassius conceded. "The wizard believes that he is invincible, that much is certain. And that is his mistake, my friend. The meekest of animals will fight bravely when it is backed against a wall, for it has nothing left to lose. A poor man is more deadly than a rich man because he puts less value on his own life. And a man stranded homeless on the frozen steppes with the first winds of winter already beginning to blow is a formidable enemy indeed!

"Fear not, little friend," Cassius continued. "At our council this morning, we shall find a way to exploit the wizard's weaknesses."

Regis nodded, unable to dispute the spokesman's simple logic and unwilling to refute his optimism. Still, as he scanned the deep ranks of goblins and orcs that surrounded the city, the halfling held out little hope.

He looked northward, where the dust had finally settled on the dwarven valley. Bruenor's Climb was no more, having toppled with the rest of the cliff face when the dwarves closed up their caverns.

"Open a door for me, Bruenor," Regis whispered absently. "Please let me in."

⚔ ⚔ ⚔ ⚔ ⚔

Coincidentally, Bruenor and his clan were, at that very moment, discussing the feasibility of opening a door in their tunnels. But not to let anyone in. Soon after their smashing success against the ogres and goblins on the ledges outside their mines, the fighting longbeards had realized that they could not sit idly by while orcs and goblins and even worse monsters destroyed the world around them. They were eager to take a second shot at Kessell. In their underground womb, they had no idea if Bryn Shander was still standing, or if Kessell's army had already rolled over all of Ten-Towns, but they could hear the sounds of an encampment above the southernmost sections of their huge complex.

Bruenor was the one who had proposed the idea of a second battle, mainly because of his own anger at the imminent loss of his closest non-dwarven friends. Shortly after the goblins that had escaped the tunnel collapse had been cut down, the leader of the clan from Mithral Hall gathered the whole of his people around him.

"Send someone to the farthest ends o' the tunnels," he instructed. "Find out where the dogs'll do their sleepin'."

That night, the sounds of the marching monsters became obvious far in the south, under the field surrounding Bryn Shander. The industrious dwarves immediately set about reconditioning the little-used tunnels that ran in that direction. And when they had gotten under the army, they dug ten separate upward shafts, stopping just shy of the surface.

A special gleam had returned to their eyes: the sparkle of a dwarf who knows that he's about to chop off a few goblin heads. Bruenor's devious plan had endless potential for revenge with minimal risk. With five minutes' notice, they could complete their new exits. Less than a minute beyond that, their entire force would be up in the middle of Kessell's sleeping army.

⚔ ⚔ ⚔ ⚔ ⚔

The meeting that Cassius had labeled a council was truly more of a forum where the spokesman from Bryn Shander could unveil his first retaliatory strategies. Yet none of the gathered leaders, even Glensather, the only other spokesman in attendance, protested in the least. Cassius had studied every aspect of the entrenched goblin army and the wizard with meticulous attention to detail. The spokesman had outlined a layout of the entire force, detailing the most potentially explosive rivalries among the goblin and orc ranks and his best estimates about the length of time it would take for the inner fighting to sufficiently weaken the army.

Everyone in attendance was agreed, though, that the cornerstone holding the siege together was Cryshal-Tirith. The awesome power of the crystalline structure would cow even the most disruptive orcs into unquestioning obedience. Yet the limits of that power, as Cassius saw it, were the real issue.

"Why was Kessell so insistent on an immediate surrender?" the spokesman reasoned. "He could let us sit under the stress of a siege for a few days to soften our resistance!"

The others agreed with the logic of Cassius's line of thinking but had no answers for him.

"Perhaps Kessell does not command as strong a hold over his charges as we believe," Cassius himself proposed. "Might it be that the wizard fears his army will disintegrate around him if stalled for any length of time?"

"It might," replied Glensather of Easthaven. "Or maybe Akar Kessell simply perceives the strength of his advantage and knows that we have no choice but to comply. Do you, perhaps, confuse confidence with concern?"

Cassius paused for a moment to reflect on the question. "A point well taken," he said at length. "Yet immaterial to our plans." Glensather and several others cocked a curious eye at the spokesman.

"We must assume the latter," Cassius explained. "If the wizard is truly in absolute control of the gathered army, then anything we might attempt shall prove futile in any case. Therefore, we must act on the assumption that Kessell's impatience reveals well-founded concern.

"I do not perceive the wizard as an exceptional strategist. He has embarked on a path of destruction that he assumed would cow us into submission, yet which, in reality, has actually strengthened the resolve of many of our people to fight to the last. Long-standing rivalries between several of the towns, bitterness that a wise leader of an invading force would surely have twisted into an excellent advantage, have been mended by Kessell's blatant disregard of finesse and his displays of outrageous brutality."

Cassius knew by the attentive looks he was receiving that he was gaining support from every corner. He was trying to accomplish two things in this meeting: to convince the others to go along with the gamble he was about to unveil, and to lift their outlook and give them back some shred of hope.

"Our people are out there," he said, sweeping his arm in a wide arc. "On Maer Dualdon and Lac Dinneshere, the fleets have gathered, awaiting some sign from Bryn Shander that we shall support them. The people of Good Mead and Dougan's Hole do likewise on the southern lake, fully armed and knowing full well that in this struggle there is nothing left at all for any survivors if we are not victorious!" He leaned forward over the table, alternately catching and holding the gaze of each man seated before him and concluded grimly, "No homes. No hope for our wives. No hope for our children. Nowhere left to run."

Cassius continued to rally the others around him and was soon backed by Glensather, who had guessed at the spokesman's goal of increasing morale and recognized the value of it. Cassius searched for the most opportune moment. When the majority of the assembled leaders had replaced their frowns of despair with the determined grimace of survival, he put forth his daring plan.

"Kessell has demanded an emissary," he said, "and so we must deliver one."

"You or I would seem the most obvious choice," Glensather intervened. "Which shall it be?"

A wry smile spread across Cassius's face. "Neither," he replied. "One of us would be the obvious choice if we intended to go along with Kessell's demands. But we have one other option." He turned his gaze squarely upon Regis. The halfling squirmed uncomfortably, half-guessing what the spokesman had in mind. "There is one among us who has attained an almost legendary reputation for his considerable abilities of persuasion. Perhaps his charismatic appeal shall win us some valuable time in our dealings with the wizard."

Regis felt ill. He had often wondered when the ruby pendant was going to get him into trouble too deep to climb out of.

Several other people eyed Regis now, apparently intrigued by the potential of Cassius's suggestion. The stories of the halfling's charm and persuasive ability, and the accusation that Kemp had made at the council a few tendays earlier, had been told and retold a thousand times in every one of the towns, each storyteller typically enhancing and exaggerating the tales to increase his own importance. Though Regis hadn't been thrilled with losing the power of his secret—people seldom looked him straight in the eye anymore—he had come to enjoy a certain degree of fame. He hadn't considered the possible negative side effects of having so many people looking up to him.

"Let the halfling, the former spokesman from Lonelywood, represent us in Akar Kessell's court," Cassius declared to the nearly unanimous approval of the assembly. "Perhaps our small friend will be able to convince the wizard of the error of his evil ways!"

"You are mistaken!" Regis protested. "They are only rumors . . ."

"Humility," Cassius interrupted, "is a fine trait, good halfling. And all gathered here appreciate the sincerity of your self-doubts and appreciate even moreso your willingness to pit your talents against Kessell in the face of those self-doubts!"

Regis closed his eyes and did not reply, knowing that the motion would surely pass whether he approved or not.

It did, without a single dissenting vote. The cornered people were quite willing to grab at any sliver of hope they could find.

Cassius moved quickly to wrap up the council, for he believed that all other matters—problems of overcrowding and food hoarding—were of little importance at a time like this. If Regis failed, every other inconvenience would become immaterial.

Regis remained silent. He had only attended the council to lend support to his spokesmen friends. When he took his seat at the table, he had no intentions of even actively participating in the discussions, let alone becoming the focal point of the defense plan.

And so the meeting adjourned. Cassius and Glensather exchanged knowing winks of success, for everyone left the room feeling a bit more optimistic.

Cassius held Regis back when he moved to leave with the others. The spokesman from Bryn Shander shut the door behind the last of them, desiring a private briefing with the principal character of the first stages of his plan.

"You could have spoken to me about all of this first!" Regis grumbled at the spokesman's back as soon as the door was closed. "It seems only right that I should have been given the opportunity to make a decision in this matter!"

Cassius wore a grim visage as he turned to face the halfling. "What choice do any of us have?" he asked. "At least this way we have given them all some hope."

"You overestimate me," Regis protested.

"Perhaps you underestimate yourself," Cassius said. Though the halfling realized that Cassius would not back away from the plan that he had set in motion, the spokesman's confidence relayed an altruistic spirit to Regis that was genuinely comforting.

"Let us pray, for both our sakes, that the latter is the truth," Cassius continued, moving to his seat at the table. "But I truly believe this to be the case. I have faith in you, even if you do not. I remember well what you did to Spokesman Kemp at the council five years ago, though it took his own declaration that he had been tricked to make me realize the truth of the situation. A masterful job of persuasion, Regis of Lonelywood, and moreso because it held its secret for so long!"

Regis blushed and conceded the point.

"And if you can deal with the stubborn likes of Kemp of Targos, you should find Akar Kessell easy prey!"

"I agree with your perceptions of Kessell as something less than a man of inner strength," said Regis, "but wizards have a way of uncovering wizardlike tricks. And you forget the demon. I would not even attempt to deceive one of its kind!"

"Let us hope that you shall not have to deal with that one," Cassius agreed with a visible shudder. "Yet I feel that you must go to the tower and try to dissuade the wizard. If we cannot somehow hold the gathered army at bay until its own inner turmoil becomes our ally, then we are surely doomed. Believe me, as I am your friend, that I would not ask you to journey into such peril if I saw any other possible path." A pained look of helpless empathy had clearly worn through the spokesman's earlier facade of rousing optimism. His concern touched Regis, as would a starving man crying out for food.

Even beyond his feelings for the overly pressured spokesman, Regis was forced to admit the logic of the plan and the absence of other avenues to explore. Kessell hadn't given them much time to regroup after the initial attack. In the razing of Targos, the wizard had demonstrated his ability to likewise destroy Bryn Shander, and the halfling had little doubt that Kessell would carry out his vile threat.

So Regis came to accept his role as their only option. The halfling wasn't easily spurred to action, but when he made up his mind to do something, he usually tried to do it properly.

"First of all," he began, "I must tell you in the strictest of confidence that I do indeed have magical aid." A glimmer of hope returned to Cassius's eyes. He leaned forward, anxious to hear more, but Regis calmed him with an outstretched palm.

"You must understand however," the halfling explained, "that I do not, as some tales claim, have the power to pervert what is in a person's heart. I could not convince Kessell to abandon his evil path any more than I could convince Spokesman Kemp to make peace with Termalaine." He rose from his cushioned chair and paced around the table, his hands clasped behind his back. Cassius watched him in uncertain anticipation, unable to figure out exactly what he was leading up to with his admission and then disclaimer of power.

"Sometimes, though, I do have a way of making someone view his surroundings from a different perspective," Regis admitted. "Like the incident you have referred to, when I convinced Kemp that embarking upon a certain preferable course of action would actually help him to achieve his own aspirations.

"So tell me again, Cassius, all that you have learned about the wizard and his army. Let us see if we might discover a way to make Kessell doubt the very things that he has come to rely upon!"

The halfling's eloquence stunned the spokesman. Even though he hadn't looked Regis in the eye, he could see the promise of truth in the tales he had always presumed to be exaggerated.

"We know from the newsbearer that Kemp has taken command of the remaining forces of the four towns on Maer Dualdon," Cassius explained. "Likewise, Jensin Brent and Schermont are poised upon Lac Dinneshere, and combined with the fleets on Redwaters, they should prove a powerful force indeed!

"Kemp has already vowed revenge, and I doubt if any of the other refugees entertain thoughts of surrender or fleeing."

"Where could they go?" Regis muttered. He looked pitifully at Cassius, who had no words of comfort. Cassius had put on a show of confidence and hope for the others at the council and for the people in the town, but he could not look at Regis now and make hollow promises.

Glensather suddenly burst back into the room. "The wizard is back on the field!" he cried. "He has demanded our emissary—the lights on the tower have started again!"

The three rushed from the building, Cassius reiterating as much of the pertinent information as he could.

Regis silenced him. "I am prepared," he assured Cassius. "I don't know if this outrageous scheme of yours has any chance of working, but you have my vow that I'll work hard to carry out the deception."

Then they were at the gate. "It must work," Cassius said, clapping Regis on the shoulder. "We have no other hope." He started to turn away, but Regis had one final question that he needed answered.

"If I find that Kessell is beyond my power?" he asked grimly. "What am I to do if the deception fails?"

Cassius looked around at the thousands of women and children huddled against the chill wind in the city's common grounds. "If it fails," he began slowly, "if Kessell cannot be dissuaded from using the power of the tower against Bryn Shander," he paused again, if only to delay having to hear himself utter the words, "you are then under my personal orders to surrender the city."

Cassius turned away and headed for the parapets to witness the critical confrontation. Regis didn't hesitate any longer, for he knew that any pause at this frightening juncture would probably cause him to change his mind and run to find a hiding place in some dark hole in the city. Before he even had the chance to reconsider, he was through the gate and boldly marching down the hill toward the waiting specter of Akar Kessell.

Kessell had again appeared between two mirrors borne by trolls, standing with arms crossed and one foot tapping impatiently. The evil scowl on his face gave Regis the distinct impression that the wizard, in a fit of uncontrollable rage, would strike him dead before he even reached the bottom of the hill. Yet the halfling had to keep his eyes focused on Kessell to even continue his approach. The wretched trolls disgusted and revulsed him beyond anything he had ever encountered, and it took all of his willpower to move anywhere near them. Even from the gate, he could smell the foul odor of their rotting stench.

But somehow he made it to the mirrors and stood facing the evil wizard.

Kessell studied the emissary for quite a while. He certainly hadn't expected a halfling to represent the city and wondered why Cassius hadn't come personally to such an important meeting. "Do you come before me as the official representative of Bryn Shander and all who now reside within her walls?"

Regis nodded. "I am Regis of Lonelywood," he answered, "a friend to Cassius and former member of the Council of Ten. I have been appointed to speak for the people within the city."

Kessell's eyes narrowed in anticipation of his victory. "And do you bear their message of unconditional surrender?"

Regis shuffled uneasily, purposely shifting so that the ruby pendant would start into motion on his chest. "I desire private council with thee, mighty wizard, that we might discuss the terms of the agreement."

Kessell's eyes widened. He looked at Cassius upon the wall. "I said unconditional!" he shrieked. Behind him, the lights of Cryshal-Tirith began to swirl and grow. "Now you shall witness the folly of your insolence!"

"Wait!" pleaded Regis, jumping around to regain the wizard's attention. "There are some things that you should be aware of before all is decided!"

Kessell paid little attention to the halfling's rambling, but the ruby pendant suddenly caught his attention. Even through the protection offered by the distance between his physical body and the window of his image projection, he found the gem fascinating.

Regis couldn't resist the urge to smile, though only slightly, when he realized that the eyes of the wizard no longer blinked. "I have some information that I am sure you will find valuable," the halfling said quietly.

Kessell signaled for him to continue.

"Not here," Regis whispered. "There are too many curious ears about. Not all of the gathered goblins would be pleased to hear what I have to say!"

Kessell considered the halfling's words for a moment. He felt curiously subdued for some reason that he couldn't yet understand. "Very well, halfling," he agreed. "I shall hear your words." With a flash and a puff of smoke, the wizard was gone.

Regis looked back over his shoulder at the people on the wall and nodded.

Under telepathic command from within the tower, the trolls shifted the mirrors to catch Regis's reflection. A second flash and puff of smoke, and Regis, too, was gone.

On the wall, Cassius returned the halfling's nod, though Regis had already disappeared. The spokesman breathed a bit easier, comforted by the last look Regis had thrown him and by the fact that the sun was setting and Bryn Shander still stood. If his guess, based on the timing of the wizard's actions, was correct, Cryshal-Tirith drew most of its energy from the light of the sun.

It appeared that his plan had bought them at least one more night.

⚔ ⚔ ⚔ ⚔

Even through his bleary eyes, Drizzt recognized the dark shape that hovered over him. The drow had banged his head when he had been thrown from the scimitar's hilt and Guenhwyvar, his loyal companion, had kept a silent vigil throughout the long hours the drow had remained unconscious, even though the cat had also been battered in the fight with Errtu.

Drizzt rolled into a sitting position and tried to reorient himself to his surroundings. At first he thought that dawn had come, but then he realized that the dim sunlight was coming from the west. He had been out for the better part of a day, drained completely, for the scimitar had sapped his vital energy in its battle with the demon.

Guenhwyvar looked even more haggard. The cat's shoulder hung limp from its collision with the stone wall, and Errtu had torn a deep cut into one of its forelegs.

More than injuries, though, fatigue was wearing on the magical beast. It had overstayed the normal limits of its visit to the material plane by many hours. The cord between its home plane and the drow's was only kept intact by the cat's own magical energy, and each passing minute that it remained in this world drew away a bit of its strength.

Drizzt stroked the muscled neck tenderly. He understood the sacrifice Guenhwyvar had made for his sake, and he wished that he could comply with the cat's needs and send it back to its own world.

But he could not. If the cat returned to its own plane, it would be hours before it would regain the strength required to reestablish a link back to this world. And he needed the cat now.

"A bit longer," he begged. The faithful beast lay down beside him without any hint of protest. Drizzt looked upon it with pity and petted the neck once again. How he longed to release the cat from his service! Yet he could not.

From what Errtu had told him, the door to Cryshal-Tirith was invisible only to beings of the Material Plane.

Drizzt needed the cat's eyes.

28

A LIE WITHIN A LIE

Regis rubbed the after-image of the blinding flash out of his eyes and found himself again facing the wizard. Kessell lounged on a crystal throne, leaning back against one of its arms with his legs casually thrown over the other. They were in a squared room of crystal, giving a slick visual impression, but feeling as solid as stone. Regis knew immediately that he was inside the tower. The room was filled with dozens of ornate and strangely shaped mirrors. One of these in particular, the largest and most decorative, caught the halfling's eye, for a fire was ablaze within its depths. At first Regis looked opposite the mirror, expecting to see the source of the image, but then he realized that the flames were not a reflection but an actual event occurring within the dimensions of the mirror itself.

"Welcome to my home," the wizard laughed. "You should consider yourself fortunate to witness its splendor!" But Regis fixed his gaze upon Kessell, studying the wizard closely, for the tone of his voice did not resemble the characteristic slur of others he had entranced with the ruby.

"You'll forgive my surprise when first we met," Kessell continued. "I did not expect the sturdy men of Ten-Towns to send a halfling to do their work!" He laughed again, and Regis knew that something had disrupted the charm he had cast upon the wizard when they were outside.

The halfling could guess what had happened. He could feel the throbbing power of this room; it was evident that Kessell fed off of it. With his psyche outside, the wizard had been vulnerable to the magic of the gemstone, but in here his strength was quite beyond the ruby's influence.

"You said that you had information to tell me," Kessell de-manded suddenly. "Speak now, the whole of it, or I shall make your death an unpleasant one!"

Regis stuttered, trying to improvise an alternative tale. The insidious lies he had planned to weave would have little value on the unaffected wizard. In fact, in their obvious weaknesses they might reveal much of the truth about Cassius's strategies.

Kessell straightened on his throne and leaned over the halfling, imposing his gaze upon his counterpart. "Speak!" he commanded evenly.

Regis felt an iron will insinuating itself into all of his thoughts, compelling him to obey Kessell's every command. He sensed that the dominating force wasn't emanating from the wizard, though. Rather it seemed to be coming from some external source, perhaps the unseen object that the wizard occasionally clutched in a pocket of his robes.

Those of halfling stock possessed a strong natural resistance to such magic, however, and a countering force—the gemstone—helped Regis fight back against the insinuating will and gradually push it away. A sudden idea came over Regis. He had certainly seen enough individuals fall under his own charms to be able to imitate their revealing posture. He slouched a bit, as though he had suddenly been put completely at ease, and focused his blank stare on an image in the corner of the room beyond Kessell's shoulder. He felt his eyes drying out, but he resisted the temptation to blink.

"What information do you desire?" he responded mechanically.

Kessell slumped back again confidently. "Address me as Master Kessell," he ordered.

"What information do you desire, Master Kessell?"

"Good," the wizard smirked to himself. "Admit the truth, halfling, the story you were sent to tell me was a deception."

Why not? Regis thought. A lie flavored with the sprinklings of truth becomes that much stronger. "Yes," he answered. "To make you think that your truest allies plotted against you."

"And what was the purpose?" Kessell pressed, quite pleased with himself. "Surely the people of Bryn Shander know that I could easily crush them even without any allies at all. It seems a feeble plan to me."

"Cassius had no intentions of trying to defeat you, Master Kessell," Regis said.

"Then why are you here? And why didn't Cassius simply surrender the city as I demanded?"

"I was sent to plant some doubts," replied Regis, blindly improvising to keep Kessell intrigued and occupied. Behind the facade of his words, he was trying to put together some kind of an alternate plan. "To give Cassius more time to lay out his true course of action."

Kessell leaned forward. "And what might that course of action be?"

Regis paused, searching for an answer.

"You cannot resist me!" Kessell roared. "My will is too great! Answer or I shall tear the truth from your mind!"

"To escape," Regis blurted, and after he had said it, several possibilities opened up before him.

Kessell reclined again. "Impossible," he replied casually. "My army is too strong at every point for the humans to break through."

"Perhaps not as strong as you believe, Master Kessell," Regis baited. His path now lay clear before him. A lie within another lie. He liked the formula.

"Explain," Kessell demanded, a shadow of worry clouding his cocky visage.

"Cassius has allies within your ranks."

The wizard leaped from his chair, trembling in rage. Regis marveled at how effectively his simple imitation was working. He wondered for an instant if any of his own victims had likewise reversed the dupe on him. He put the disturbing thought away for future contemplation.

"Orcs have lived among the people of Ten-Towns for many months now," Regis went on. "One tribe actually opened up a trading relationship with the fishermen. They, too, answered your summons to arms, but they still hold loyalties, if any of their kind ever truly hold loyalties, to Cassius.

Even as your army was entrenching in the field around Bryn Shander, the first communications were exchanged between the orc chieftain and orc messengers that slipped out of Bryn Shander."

Kessell smoothed his hair back and rubbed his hand nervously across his face. Was it possible that his seemingly invincible army had a secret weakness?

No, none would dare oppose Akar Kessell!

But still, if some of them were plotting against him—if all of them were plotting against him—would he know? And where was Errtu? Could the demon be behind this?

"Which tribe?" he asked Regis softly, his tone revealing that the halfling's news had humbled him.

Regis drew the wizard fully into the deception. "The group that you sent to sack the city of Bremen, the Orcs of the Severed Tongue," he said, watching the wizard's widening eyes with complete satisfaction. "My job was merely to prevent you from taking any action against Bryn Shander before the fall of night, for the orcs shall return before dawn, presumably to regroup in their assigned position on the field, but in actuality, to open a gap in your western flank. Cassius will lead the people down the western slope to the open tundra. They only hope to keep you disorganized long enough to give them a solid lead. Then you shall be forced to pursue them all the way to Luskan!"

Many weak points were apparent in the plan, but it seemed a reasonable gamble for people in such a desperate situation to attempt. Kessell slammed his fist down on the arm of the throne. "The fools!" he growled.

Regis breathed a bit easier. Kessell was convinced.

"Errtu!" he screamed suddenly, unaware that the demon had been banished from the world.

There was no reply. "Oh, damn you, demon!" Kessell cursed. "You are never about when I most need you!" He spun on Regis. "You wait here. I shall have many more questions for you later!" The roaring fires of his anger simmered wickedly. "But first I must speak with some of my generals. I shall teach the Orcs of the Severed Tongue to oppose me!"

In truth, the observations Cassius had made had labeled the Orcs of the

Severed Tongue as Kessell's strongest and most fanatical supporters.

A lie within a lie.

× × × ×

Out on the waters of Maer Dualdon later that evening, the assembled fleet of the four towns watched suspiciously as a second group of monsters flowed out from the main force and headed in the direction of Bremen.

"Curious," Kemp remarked to Muldoon of Lonelywood and the spokesman from the burned city of Bremen, who were standing on the deck of Targos' flagship beside him. All of Bremen's populace was out on the lake. Certainly the first group of orcs, after the initial bowshots, had met no further resistance in the city. And Bryn Shander stood intact. Why, then, was the wizard further extending his line of power?

"Akar Kessell confuses me," said Muldoon. "Either his genius is simply beyond me or he truly makes glaring tactical errors!"

"Assume the second possibility," Kemp instructed hopefully, "for anything that we might try shall be in vain if the first is the truth!"

So they continued repositioning their warriors for an opportune strike, moving their children and womenfolk in the remaining boats to the as yet unassailed moorings of Lonelywood, similar to the strategies of the refugee forces on the other two lakes.

On the wall of Bryn Shander, Cassius and Glensather watched the division of Kessell's forces with deeper understanding.

"Masterfully done, halfling," Cassius whispered into the night wind.

Smiling, Glensather put a steadying hand on his fellow spokesman's shoulder. "I shall go and inform our field commanders," he said. "If the time for us to attack comes, we shall be ready!"

Cassius clasped Glensather's hand and nodded his approval. As the spokesman from Easthaven sped away, Cassius leaned upon the ridge of the wall, glaring determinedly at the now darkened walls of Cryshal-Tirith. Through gritted teeth, he declared openly, "The time shall come!"

× × × ×

From the high vantage point of Kelvin's Cairn, Drizzt Do'Urden had also witnessed the abrupt shift of the monster army. He had just completed the final preparations for his courageous assault on Cryshal-Tirith when the distant flickers of a large mass of torches suddenly flowed away to the west. He and Guenhwyvar sat quietly and studied the situation for a short while, trying to find some clue as to what had prompted such action.

Nothing became apparent, but the night was growing long and he had to make haste. He wasn't sure if the activity would prove helpful, by thinning out the camp's ranks, or disruptive, by heightening the remaining monsters' state of readiness. Yet he knew that the people of Bryn Shander could not afford any delays. He started down the mountain trail, the great panther trailing along silently behind him.

He made the open ground in good time and started his hasty trot down the length of Bremen's Run. If he had paused to study his surroundings or put one of his sensitive ears to the ground, he might have heard the distant rumble from the open tundra to the north of yet another approaching army.

But the drow's focus was on the south, his vision narrowed upon the waiting darkness of Cryshal-Tirith as he made haste. He was traveling light, carrying only items he believed essential to the task. He had his five weapons: the two scimitars sheathed in their leather scabbards on his hips, a dagger tucked in his belt at the middle of his back, and the two knives hidden in his boots. His holy symbol and pouch of wealth was around his neck and a small sack of flour, left over from the raid on the giant's lair, still hung on his belt—a sentimental choice, a comforting reminder of the daring adventures he had shared with Wulfgar. All of his other supplies, backpack, rope, waterskins, and other basic items of everyday survival on the harsh tundra, he had left in the small cubby.

He heard the shouts of goblin merrymaking when he crossed by the eastern outskirts of Termalaine. "Strike now, sailors of Maer Dualdon," the drow said quietly. But when he thought about it, he was glad that the boats remained out on the lake. Even if they could slip in and strike quickly at the monsters in the city, they could not afford the losses they would suffer. Termalaine could wait; there was a more important battle yet to be fought.

Drizzt and Guenhwyvar approached the outer perimeter of Kessell's main encampment. The drow was comforted by signs that the commotion within the camp had quieted. A solitary orc guard leaned wearily on its spear, half-heartedly watching the empty blackness of the northern horizon. Even had it been wary, it would not have noticed the stealthy approach of the two shapes, blacker than the darkness of night.

"Call in!" came a command from somewhere in the distance.

"Clear!" replied the guard.

Drizzt listened as the check was called in from various distant spots. He signaled for Guenhwyvar to hold back, then crept up within throwing range of the guard.

The tired orc never even heard the whistle of the approaching dagger.

And then Drizzt was beside it, silently breaking its fall into the darkness. The drow pulled his dagger from the orc's throat and laid his victim softly on the ground. He and Guenhwyvar, unnoticed shadows of death, moved on.

They had broken through the only line of guards that had been set on the northern perimeter and now easily picked their way among the sleeping camp. Drizzt could have killed dozens of orcs and goblins, even a verbeeg, though the cessation of its thundering snores might have drawn attention, but he couldn't afford to slow his pace. Each passing minute continued to drain Guenhwyvar, and now the first hints of a second enemy, the revealing dawn, were becoming apparent in the eastern sky.

The drow's hopes had risen considerably with the progress he had made, but he was dismayed when he came upon Cryshal-Tirith. A group of battle-ready ogre guards ringed the tower, blocking his way.

He crouched beside the cat, undecided on what they should do. To escape the breadth of the huge camp before the dawn exposed them, they would have to flee back the way they came. Drizzt doubted that Guenhwyvar, in its pitiful state, could even attempt that route. Yet to go on meant a hopeless fight with a group of ogres. There seemed no answer to the dilemma.

Then something happened back in the northeast section of the encampment, opening a path for the stealthy companions. Sudden shouts of alarm sprang up, drawing the ogres a few long strides away from their posts.

Drizzt thought at first that the murdered orc guard had been discovered, but the cries were too far to the east.

Soon the clang of steel on steel rang out in the predawn air. A battle had been joined. Rival tribes, Drizzt supposed, though he could not spot the combatants from this distance.

His curiosity wasn't overwhelming, however. The undisciplined ogres had moved even farther away from their appointed positions. And Guenhwyvar had spotted the tower door. The two didn't hesitate for a second.

The ogres never even noticed the two shadows enter the tower behind them.

⚔ ⚔ ⚔ ⚔ ⚔

A strange sensation, a buzzing vibration, came over Drizzt as he passed through Cryshal-Tirith's entryway, as though he had moved into the bowels of a living entity. He continued on, though, through the darkened hallway that led to the tower's first level, marveling at the strange crystalline material that comprised the walls and floors of the structure.

He found himself in a squared hall, the bottom chamber of the four-roomed structure. This was the hall where Kessell often met with his field generals, the wizard's primary audience hall for all but his top-ranking commanders.

Drizzt peered around at the dark forms in the room and the deeper shadows that they created. Though he sighted no movement, he sensed that he was not alone. He knew that Guenhwyvar had the same uneasy feelings, for the fur on the scruff of the black-coated neck was ruffled and the cat let out a low growl.

Kessell considered this room a buffer zone between himself and the rabble of the outside world. It was the one chamber in the tower that he rarely visited. This was the place where Akar Kessell housed his trolls.

29

OTHER OPTIONS

The dwarves of Mithral Hall completed the first of their secret exits shortly after sunset. Bruenor was the first to climb to the top of the ladder and peek out from under the cut sod at the settling monster army. So expert were the dwarven miners that they had been able to dig a shaft right up into the middle of a large group of goblins and ogres without even alerting the monsters in the least.

Bruenor was smiling when he came back down to rejoin his clansmen. "Finish th' other nine," he instructed as he moved down the tunnel, Catti-brie beside him. "Tonight's sleep'll be a sound one for some o' Kessell's boys!" he declared, patting the head of his belted axe.

"What role am I to play in the coming battle?" Catti-brie asked when they moved away from the other dwarves.

"Ye'll get to pull one o' the levers an' collapse the tunnels if any o' the swine come down," Bruenor replied.

"And if you are all killed on the field?" Catti-brie reasoned. "Being buried alone in these tunnels does not hold much promise for me."

Bruenor stroked his red beard. He hadn't considered that consequence, figuring only that if he and his clan were cut down on the field, Catti-brie would be safe enough behind the collapsed tunnels. But how could she live down here alone? What price would she pay for survival?

"Do ye want to come up an' fight then? Ye're fair enough with a sword, an' I'll be right beside ye!"

Catti-brie considered the proposition for a moment. "I'll stay with the lever," she decided. "You'll have enough to look after your own head up there. And someone has to be here to drop the tunnels; we cannot let goblins claim our halls as their home!

"Besides," she added with a smile, "it was stupid of me to worry. I know that you will come back to me, Bruenor. Never have you, nor any of your clan, failed me!" She kissed the dwarf on the forehead and skipped away.

Bruenor smiled after her. "Suren yer a brave girl, my Catti-brie," he muttered.

The work on the tunnels was finished a few hours later. The shafts had been dug and the entire tunnel complex around them had been rigged to collapse to cover any retreating action or squash any goblin advance. The entire clan, their faces purposely blackened with soot and their heavy armor and weapons muffled under layers of dark cloth, lined up at the base of the ten shafts. Bruenor went up first to investigate. He peeked out and smiled grimly. All around him ogres and goblins had bedded down for the night.

He was about to give the signal for his kinsmen to move when a commotion suddenly started up in the camp. Bruenor remained at the top of the shaft, though he kept his head beneath the sod layer (which got him stepped on by a passing goblin), and tried to figure out what had alerted the monsters. He heard shouts of command and a clatter like a large force assembling.

More shouts followed, calls for the death of the Severed Tongue. Though he had never heard that name before, the dwarf easily guessed that it described an orc tribe. "So, they're fightin' amongst themselves, are they?" he muttered softly, chuckling. Realizing that the dwarves' assault would have to wait, he climbed back down the ladder.

But the clan, disappointed in the delay, did not disperse. They were determined that this night's work would indeed be done. So they waited.

The night passed its mid-point and still the sounds of movement came from the camp above. Yet the wait wasn't dulling the edge of the dwarves' determination. Conversely, the delay was sharpening their intensity, heightening their hunger for goblin blood. These fighters were also blacksmiths, craftsmen who spent long hours adding a single scale to a dragon statue. They knew patience.

Finally, when all was again quiet, Bruenor went back up the ladder. Before he had even poked his head through the turf, he heard the comforting sounds of rhythmic breathing and loud snores.

Without further delay, the clan slipped out of the holes and methodically set about their murderous work. They did not revel in their roles as assassins, preferring to fight sword against sword, but they understood the necessity of this type of raid, and they placed no value whatsoever on the lives of goblin scum.

The area gradually quieted as more and more of the monsters entered the silent sleep of death. The dwarves concentrated on the ogres first, in case their attack was discovered before they were able to do much damage. But their strategy was unnecessary. Many minutes passed without retaliation.

By the time one of the guards noticed what was happening and managed to shout out a cry of alarm, the blood of more than a thousand of Kessell's charges wetted the field.

Cries went up all about them, but Bruenor did not call for a retreat. "Form up!" he commanded. "Tight around the tunnels!" He knew that the mad rush of the first wave of counterattackers would be disorganized and unprepared.

The dwarves formed into a tight defensive posture and had little trouble cutting the goblins down. Bruenor's axe was marked with many more notches before any goblin had even taken a swing at him.

Gradually, though, Kessell's charges became more organized. They came at the dwarves in formations of their own, and their growing numbers, as more and more of the camp was roused and alerted, began to press heavily on the raiders. And then a group of ogres, Kessell's elite tower guard, came charging across the field.

The first of the dwarves to retreat, the tunnel experts who were to make the final check on the preparations for the collapse, put their booted feet on the top rungs of the shaft ladders. The escape into the tunnels would be a delicate operation, and efficient haste would be the deciding factor in its success or failure.

But Bruenor unexpectedly ordered the tunnel experts to come back out of the shafts and the dwarves to hold their line.

He had heard the first notes of an ancient song, a song that, just a few years before, would have filled him with dread. Now, though, it lifted his heart with hope.

He recognized the voice that led the stirring words.

✕ ✕ ✕ ✕

A severed arm of rotted flesh splatted on the floor, yet another victim of the whirring scimitars of Drizzt Do'Urden.

But the fearless trolls crowded in. Normally, Drizzt would have known of their presence as soon as he entered the square chamber. Their terrible stench made it hard for them to hide. These ones, though, hadn't actually been in the chamber when the drow entered. As Drizzt had moved deeper into the room, he tripped a magical alarm that bathed the area in wizard's light and cued the guardians. They stepped in through the magical mirrors that Kessell had planted as watchposts throughout the room.

Drizzt had already dropped one of the wretched beasts, but now he was more concerned with running than fighting. Five others replaced the first and were more than a match for any fighter. Drizzt shook his head in disbelief when the body of the troll he had beheaded suddenly rose again and began flailing blindly.

And then, a clawed hand caught hold of his ankle. He knew without looking that it was the limb he had just cut free.

Horrified, he kicked the grotesque arm away from him and turned and sprinted to the spiraling stairway that ran up to the tower's second level from the back of the chamber. At his earlier command Guenhwyvar had already limped weakly up the stairs and now waited on the platform at the top.

Drizzt distinctly heard the sucking footsteps of his sickening pursuers and the scratching of the severed hand's filthy nails as it also took up the chase. The drow bounded up the stairway without looking back, hoping that his speed and agility would give him enough of a lead to find some way of escaping.

For there was no door on the platform.

The landing at the top of the stairs was rectangular and about ten feet across at its widest length. Two sides were open to the room; a third caught the lip of the cresting stairwell, and the fourth was a flat sheet of mirror, extending the exact length of the platform and secured between it and the chamber's ceiling. Drizzt hoped that he would be able to understand the nuances of this unusual door, if that was what the mirror actually was, when he examined it from the platform's level.

It wouldn't be that easy.

Though the mirror was filled with the reflection of an ornate tapestry hanging on the wall of the chamber directly opposite it, its surface appeared perfectly smooth and unbroken by any cracks or handles that might indicate a concealed opening. Drizzt sheathed his weapons and ran his hands across the surface to see if there was a handle hidden from his sharp eyes, but the even glide of the glass only confirmed his observation.

The trolls were on the stairway.

Drizzt tried to push his way through the glass, speaking all of the command words of opening he had ever learned, searching for an extra-dimensional portal similar to the ones that had held Kessell's hideous guards. The wall remained a tangible barrier.

The lead troll reached the halfway point on the stairs.

"There must be a clue somewhere!" the drow groaned. "Wizards love a challenge, and there is no sport to this!" The only possible answer lay in the intricate designs and images of the tapestry. Drizzt stared at it, trying to sort through the thousands of interwoven images for some special hint that would show him the way to safety.

The stench flowed up to him. He could hear the slobbering of the ever-hungry monsters.

But he had to control his revulsion and concentrate on the myriad images.

One thing in the tapestry caught his eye: the lines of a poem that wove through all of the other images along the top border. In contrast to the dulling colors of the rest of the ancient artwork, the calligraphed letters of the poem held the contrasting brightness of a newer addition. Something Kessell had added?

> *Come if ye will*
> *To the orgy within,*
> *But first ye must find the latch!*
> *Seen and not seen,*
> *Been yet not been*
> *And a handle that flesh cannot catch.*

One line in particular stood out in the drow's mind. He had heard the phrase "Been yet not been" in his childhood days in Menzoberranzan. They referred to Urgutha Forka, a vicious demon that had ravaged the planet with a particularly virulent plague in the ancient times when Drizzt's ancestors had walked on the surface. The surface elves had always denied the existence of Urgutha Forka, blaming the plague on the drow, but the dark elves knew better. Something in their physical make-up had kept them immune to the demon, and after they realized how deadly it was to their enemies, they had worked to fulfill the suspicions of the light elves by enlisting Urgutha as an ally.

Thus the reference "Been yet not been" was a derogatory line in a longer drow tale, a secret joke on their hated cousins who had lost thousands to a creature they denied even existed.

The riddle would have been impossible to anyone unaware of the tale of Urgutha Forka. The drow had found a valuable advantage. He scanned the reflection of the tapestry for some image that had a connection to the demon. And he found it on the far edge of the mirror at belt height: a portrayal of Urgutha itself, revealed in all of its horrible splendor. The demon was depicted smashing the skull of an elf with a black rod, its symbol. Drizzt had seen this same portrayal before. Nothing seemed out of place or hinted at anything unusual.

The trolls had turned the final corner of their ascent. Drizzt was nearly out of time.

He turned and searched the source of the image for some discrepancy. It struck him at once. In the original tapestry Urgutha was striking the elf with its fist; there was no rod!

"Seen and not seen."

Drizzt spun back on the mirror, grasping at the demon's illusory weapon. But all he felt was smooth glass. He nearly cried out in frustration.

His experience had taught him discipline, and he quickly regained his composure. He moved his hand back away from the mirror, attempting to position his own reflection at the same depth he judged the rod to be at. He slowly closed his fingers, watching his hand's image close around the rod with the excitement of anticipated success.

He shifted his hand slightly.

A thin crack appeared in the mirror.

The leading troll reached the top of the stairs, but Drizzt and Guenhwyvar were gone.

The drow slid the strange door back into its closed position, leaned back, and sighed with relief. A dimly lit stairway led up before him, ending with a platform that opened into the tower's second level. No door blocked the way, just hanging strands of beads, sparkling orange in the torchlight of the room beyond. Drizzt heard giggling,

Silently, he and the cat crept up the stairs and peeked over the rim of the landing. They had come to Kessell's harem room.

It was softly lit with torches glowing under screening shades. Most of the floor was covered with overstuffed pillows, and sections of the room were curtained off. The harem girls, Kessell's mindless playthings, sat in a circle in the center of the floor, giggling with the uninhibited enthusiasm of children at play. Drizzt doubted that they would notice him, but even if they did, he wasn't overly concerned. He understood right away that these pitiful, broken creatures were incapable of initiating any action against him.

He kept alert, though, especially of the curtained boudoirs. He doubted that Kessell would have put guards here, certainly none as unpredictably vicious as trolls, but he couldn't afford to make any mistakes.

With Guenhwyvar close at his side, he slipped silently from shadow to shadow, and when the two companions had ascended the stairs and were on the landing before the door to the third level, Drizzt was more relaxed.

But then the buzzing sound that Drizzt had heard when he first entered the tower returned. It gathered strength as it continued, as though its song came from the vibrations of the very walls of the tower. Drizzt looked all around for a possible source.

Chimes hanging from the room's ceiling began to tinkle eerily. The fires of the torches on the walls danced wildly.

Then Drizzt understood.

The structure was awakening with a life of its own. The field outside remained under the shadow of night, but the first fingers of dawn brightened the tower's high pinnacle.

The door suddenly swung open into the third level, Kessell's throne room.

"Well done!" cried the wizard. He was standing beyond the crystal throne across the room from Drizzt, holding an unlit candle and facing the open door. Regis stood obediently at his side, wearing a blank expression on his face.

"Please enter," Kessell said with false courtesy. "Fear not for my trolls that you injured, they will surely heal!" He threw his head back and laughed.

Drizzt felt a fool; to think that all of his caution and stealth had served no better purpose than to amuse the wizard! He rested his hands on the hilts of his sheathed scimitars and stepped through the doorway.

Guenhwyvar remained crouched in the shadows of the stairway, partly because the wizard had said nothing to indicate that he knew of the cat, and partly because the weakened cat didn't want to expend the energy of walking.

Drizzt halted before the throne and bowed low. The sight of Regis standing beside the wizard disturbed him more than a little, but he managed to hide that he recognized the halfling. Regis likewise had shown no familiarity when he had first seen the drow, though Drizzt couldn't be sure if that was a conscious effort or if the halfling was under the influence of some type of enchantment.

"Greetings, Akar Kessell," Drizzt stammered in the broken accent of denizens of the underworld, as though the common tongue of the surface was foreign to him. He figured that he might as well try the same tactics he had used against the demon. "I am sent from my people in good faith to parley with you on matters concerning our common interests."

Kessell laughed aloud. "Are you indeed!" A wide smile spread across his face, replaced abruptly with a scowl. His eyes narrowed evilly. "I know you, dark elf. Any man who has ever lived in Ten-Towns has heard the name of Drizzt Do'Urden in tale or in jest! So keep your lies unspoken!"

"Your pardon, mighty wizard," Drizzt said calmly, changing tactics. "In many ways, it seems, you are wiser than your demon."

The self-assured look disappeared from Kessell's face. He had been wondering what had prevented Errtu from answering his summons. He looked at the drow with more respect. Had this solitary warrior slain a major demon?

"Allow me to begin again," Drizzt said. "Greetings, Akar Kessell." He bowed low. "I am Drizzt Do'Urden, ranger of Gwaeron Windstrom, guardian of Icewind Dale. I have come to kill you."

The scimitars leaped out of their sheaths.

But Kessell moved, too. The candle he held suddenly flickered to life. Its flame was caught in the maze of prisms and mirrors that cluttered the entire chamber, focused and sharpened at each reflecting spot. Instantaneously with the lighting of the candle, three concentrated beams of light enclosed the drow in a triangular prison. None of the beams had touched him, but he sensed their power and dared not cross their path.

Drizzt clearly heard the tower humming as daylight filtered down its length. The room brightened considerably as several of the wall panels which had appeared mirrorlike in the torchlight showed themselves to be windows.

"Did you believe that you could walk right in here and simply dispose of me?" Kessell asked incredulously. "I am Akar Kessell, you fool! The Tyrant of Icewind Dale! I command the greatest army that has ever marched on the frozen steppes of this forsaken land!

"Behold my army!" He waved his hand and one of the scrying mirrors came to life, revealing part of the vast encampment that surrounded the tower, complete with the shouts of the awakening camp.

Then a death cry sounded from somewhere in the unseen reaches of the field. Instinctively, both the drow and the wizard tuned their ears on the distant clamor and heard the continuing ring of battle. Drizzt looked curiously at Kessell, wondering if the wizard knew what was happening in the northern section of his camp.

Kessell answered the drow's unspoken question with a wave of his hand. The image in the mirror clouded over with an inner fog for a moment, then shifted to the other side of the field. The shouts and clanging of the battle rang out loudly from within the depths of the scrying instrument. Then, as the mist cleared, the image of Bruenor's clansmen, fighting back to back in the midst of a sea of goblins, came clear. The field all around the dwarves was littered with the corpses of goblins and ogres.

"You see how foolish it is to oppose me?" Kessell squealed.

"It appears to me that the dwarves have done well."

"Nonsense!" Kessell screamed. He waved his hand again, and the fog returned to the mirror. Abruptly, the Song of Tempus resounded from within its depths. Drizzt leaned forward and strained to catch a glimpse of an image through the veil, anxious to see the leader of the song.

"Even as the stupid dwarves cut down a few of my lesser fighters, more warriors swarm to join the ranks of my army! Doom is upon you all, Drizzt Do'Urden! Akar Kessell is come!"

The fog cleared.

With a thousand fervent warriors behind him, Wulfgar approached the unsuspecting monsters. The goblins and orcs who were closest to the charging barbarians, holding unbending faith in the words of their master, cheered at the coming of their promised allies.

Then they died.

The barbarian horde drove through their ranks, singing and killing with wild abandonment. Even through the clatter of weapons, the sound of the dwarves joining in the Song of Tempus could be heard.

Wide-eyed, jaw hanging open, trembling with rage, Kessell waved the shocking image away and swung back on Drizzt. "It does not matter!" he said, fighting to keep his tone steady. "I shall deal with them mercilessly! And then Bryn Shander shall topple in flames!"

"But first, you, traitorous drow," the wizard hissed. "Killer of your own kin, what gods have you left to pray to?" He puffed on the candle, causing its flame to dance on its side.

The angle of reflection shifted and one of the beams landed on Drizzt, boring a hole completely through the hilt of his old scimitar and then drove deeper, cutting through the black skin of his hand. Drizzt grimaced in agony and clutched at his wound as the scimitar fell to the floor and the beam returned to its original path.

"You see how easy it is?" Kessell taunted. "Your feeble mind cannot begin to imagine the power of Crenshinibon! Feel blessed that I allowed you to feel a sample of that power before you died!"

Drizzt held his jaw firm, and there was no sign of pleading in his eyes as he glared at the wizard. He had long ago accepted the possibility of death as an acceptable risk of his trade, and he was determined to die with dignity.

Kessell tried to goad the sweat out of him. The wizard swayed the deadly candle tantalizingly about, causing the rays to shift back and forth. When he finally realized that he would not hear any whimpering or begging out of the proud ranger, Kessell grew tired of the game. "Farewell, fool," he growled and puckered his lips to puff on the flame.

Regis blew out the candle.

Everything seemed to come to a complete halt for several seconds. The wizard looked down at the halfling, whom he thought to be his slave, in horrified amazement. Regis merely shrugged his shoulders, as if he was as surprised by his uncharacteristically brave act as Kessell.

Relying on instinct, the wizard threw the silver plate that held the candle through the glass of the mirror and ran screaming toward the back corner of the room to a small ladder hidden in the shadows. Drizzt had just taken his first steps when the fires within the mirror roared. Four evil red eyes stared out, catching the drow's attention, and two hellhounds bounded through the broken glass.

Guenhwyvar intercepted one, leaping past its master and crashing headlong into the demon hound. The two beasts tumbled back toward the rear of the room, a black and tawny-red blur of fangs and claws, knocking Regis aside.

The second dog unleashed its fire breath at Drizzt, but again, as with the demon, the fire didn't bother the drow. Then it was his turn to strike. The fire-hating scimitar rang in ecstasy, cleaving the charging beast in half as Drizzt brought it down. Amazed at the power of the blade but not having time even to gawk at his mutilated victim, Drizzt resumed his chase.

He reached the bottom of the ladder. Up above, through the open trap door to the tower's highest floor, came the rhythmic flashing of a throbbing light. Drizzt felt the intensity of the vibrations increasing with each pulse. The heart of Cryshal-Tirith was beating stronger with the rising sun. Drizzt understood the danger that he was heading into, but he didn't have the time to stop and ponder the odds.

And then he was once again facing Kessell, this time in the smallest room of the structure. Between them, hanging eerily in midair, was the pulsating hunk of crystal—Cryshal-Tirith's heart. It was four-sided and tapered like an icicle. Drizzt recognized it as a miniature replica of the tower he stood in, though it was barely a foot long.

An exact image of Crenshinibon.

A wall of light emanated from it, cutting the chamber in half, with the drow on one side and the wizard on the other. Drizzt knew from the wizard's snicker that it was a barrier as tangible as one of stone. Unlike the cluttered scrying room below, only one mirror, appearing more like a window in the tower's wall, adorned this room, just to the side of the wizard.

"Strike the heart, drow," Kessell laughed. "Fool! The heart of Cryshal-Tirith is mightier than any weapon in the world! Nothing that you could ever do, magical or otherwise, could even put the slightest scratch upon its pure surface! Strike it; let your foolish impertinence be revealed!"

Drizzt had other plans, though. He was flexible and cunning enough to realize that some foes could not be defeated with force alone. There were always other options.

He sheathed his remaining weapon, the magical scimitar, and began untying the rope that secured the sack to his belt. Kessell looked on curiously, disturbed by the drow's calm, even when his death seemed inevitable. "What are you doing?" the wizard demanded.

Drizzt didn't reply. His actions were methodical and unshaken. He loosened the drawstring on the sack and pulled it open.

"I asked you what you were doing!" Kessell scowled as Drizzt began walking toward the heart. Suddenly the replica seemed vulnerable to the wizard. He had the uncomfortable feeling that perhaps this dark elf was more dangerous than he had originally estimated.

Crenshinibon sensed it, too. The Crystal Shard telepathically instructed Kessell to unleash a killing bolt and be done with the drow.

But Kessell was afraid.

Drizzt neared the crystal. He tried to put his hand over it, but the light wall repulsed him. He nodded, expecting as much, and pulled back the sack's opening as wide as it would go. His concentration was solely on the tower itself; he never looked at the wizard or acknowledged his ranting.

Then he emptied the bag of flour over the gemstone.

The tower seemed to groan in protest. It darkened.

The wall of light that separated the drow from the wizard disappeared.

But still Drizzt concentrated on the tower. He knew that the layer of suffocating flour could only block the gemstone's powerful radiations for a short time.

Long enough, though, for him to slip the now-empty bag over it and pull the drawstring tight. Kessell wailed and lurched forward, but halted before the drawn scimitar.

"No!" the wizard cried in helpless protest. "Do you realize the consequences of what you have done?" As if in answer, the tower trembled. It calmed quickly, but both the drow and the wizard sensed the approaching danger. Somewhere in the bowels of Cryshal-Tirith, the decay had already begun.

"I understand completely," replied Drizzt. "I have defeated you, Akar Kessell. Your short reign as self-proclaimed ruler of Ten-Towns is ended."

"You have killed yourself, drow!" Kessell retorted as Cryshal-Tirith shuddered again, this time even more violently. "You cannot hope to escape before the tower crumbles upon you!"

The quake came again. And again.

Drizzt shrugged, unconcerned. "So be it," he said. "My purpose is fulfilled, for you, too, shall perish."

A sudden, crazy cackle exploded from the wizard's lips. He spun away from Drizzt and dived at the mirror embedded in the tower wall. Instead of crashing through the glass and falling to the field below, as Drizzt expected, Kessell slipped into the mirror and was gone.

The tower shook again, and this time the trembling did not relent. Drizzt started for the trap door but could barely keep his footing. Cracks appeared along the walls.

"Regis!" he yelled, but there was no answer. Part of the wall in the room below had already collapsed, Drizzt could see the rubble at the base of the ladder. Praying that his friends had already escaped, he took the only route left open to him.

He dived through the magic mirror after Kessell.

30

THE BATTLE OF ICEWIND DALE

The people of Bryn Shander heard the fighting out on the field, but it wasn't until the lightening of full dawn that they could see what was happening. They cheered the dwarves wildly and were amazed when the barbarians crashed into Kessell's ranks, hacking down goblins with gleeful abandon.

Cassius and Glensather, in their customary positions upon the wall, pondered the unexpected turn of events, undecided as to whether or not they should release their forces into the fray.

"Barbarians?" gawked Glensather. "Are they our friends or foes?"

"They kill orcs," Cassius answered. "They are friends!"

Out on Maer Dualdon, Kemp and the others also heard the clang of battle, though they couldn't see who was involved. Even more confusing, a second fight had begun, this one to the southwest, in the town of Bremen. Had the men of Bryn Shander come out and attacked? Or was Akar Kessell's force destroying itself around him?

Then Cryshal-Tirith suddenly fell dark, its once glassy and vibrant sides taking on an opaque, deathly stillness.

"Regis," muttered Cassius, sensing the tower's loss of power. "If ever a hero we had!"

The tower shuddered and shook. Great cracks appeared over the length of its walls. Then it broke apart.

The monster army looked on in horrified disbelief as the bastion of the wizard they had come to worship as a god came crashing down.

The horns in Bryn Shander began to blow. Kemp's people cheered wildly and rushed for the oars. Jensin Brent's forward scouts signaled back the startling news to the fleet on Lac Dinneshere, who in turn relayed the message to Redwaters. Throughout the temporary sanctuaries that hid the routed people of Ten-Towns came the same command.

"Charge!"

The army assembled inside the great gates of Bryn Shander's wall poured out of the courtyard and onto the field. The fleets of Caer-Konig and Caer-Dineval on Lac Dinneshere and Good Mead and Dougan's Hole in the south lifted their sails to catch the east wind and raced across the lakes. The four fleets assembled on Maer Dualdon rowed hard, bucking that same wind in their haste to get revenge.

In a whirlwind rush of chaos and surprise, the final Battle of Icewind Dale had begun.

⚔ ⚔ ⚔ ⚔

Regis rolled out of the way as the embattled creatures tumbled past again, claws and fangs tearing and ripping in a desperate struggle. Normally, Guenhwyvar would have had little trouble dispatching the helldog, but in its weakened state the cat found itself fighting for its life. The hound's hot breath seared black fur; its great fangs bit into muscled neck.

Regis wanted to help the cat, but he couldn't even get close enough to kick at its foe. Why had Drizzt run off so abruptly?

Guenhwyvar felt its neck being crushed by the powerful maw. The cat rolled, its greater weight taking the dog over with it, but the hold of the canine jaws was not broken. Dizziness swept over the cat from lack of air. It began to send its mind back across the planes, to its true home, though it lamented having failed its master in his time of need.

Then the tower went dark. The startled hellhound relaxed its grip slightly, and Guenhwyvar was quick to seize the opportunity. The cat planted its paws against the dog's ribs and shoved free of the grasp, rolling away into the blackness.

The helldog scanned for its foe, but the panther's powers of stealth were beyond even the considerable awareness of its keen senses. Then the dog saw a second quarry. A single bound took it to Regis.

Guenhwyvar was playing a game that it knew better, now. The panther was a creature of the night, a predator that struck from the blackness and killed before its prey even sensed its presence. The helldog crouched for a strike at Regis, then dropped as the panther landed heavily upon its back, claws raking deeply into the rust-colored hide.

The dog yelped only once before the killing fangs found its neck.

Mirrors cracked and shattered. A sudden hole in the floor swallowed Kessell's throne. Blocks of crystalline rubble began falling all about as the tower shuddered in its death throes. Screams from the harem chamber below told Regis that a similar scene of destruction was common throughout the structure. He was gladdened when he saw Guenhwyvar dispatch the helldog, but he understood the futility of the cat's heroics. They had nowhere to run, no escape from the death of Cryshal-Tirith.

Regis called Guenhwyvar to his side. He couldn't see the cat's body in the blackness, but he saw the eyes, intent upon him and circling around, as though the cat was stalking him. "What?" the halfling balked in astonishment, wondering if the stress and the wounds the dog had inflicted upon Guenhwyvar had driven the cat into madness.

A chunk of wall crashed right beside him, sending him sprawling to the floor. He saw the cat's eyes rise high into the air; Guenhwyvar had sprung.

Dust choked him, and he felt the final collapse of the crystal tower begin. Then came a deeper darkness as the black cat engulfed him.

✕ ✕ ✕ ✕ ✕

Drizzt felt himself falling.

The light was too bright; he couldn't see. He heard nothing, not even the sound of air rushing by. Yet he knew for certain that he was falling.

And then the light dimmed in a gray mist, as though he were passing through a cloud. It all seemed so dreamlike, so completely unreal. He couldn't recall how he had gotten into this position. He couldn't recall his own name.

Then he dropped into a deep pile of snow and knew that he was not dreaming. He heard the howl of the wind and felt its freezing bite. He tried to stand and get a better idea of his surroundings.

And then he heard, far away and below, the screams of the raging battle. He remembered Cryshal-Tirith, remembered where he had been. There could only be one answer.

He was on top of Kelvin's Cairn.

✕ ✕ ✕ ✕

The soldiers of Bryn Shander and Easthaven, fighting arm in arm with Cassius and Glensather at their head, charged down the sloping hill and drove hard into the confused ranks of goblins. The two spokesmen had a particular goal in mind: they wanted to cut through the ranks of monsters and link up with Bruenor's charges. On the wall a few moments before, they had seen the barbarians attempting the same strategy, and they figured that if all three armies could be brought together in flanking support, their slim chances would be greatly improved.

The goblins gave way to the assault. In their absolute dismay and surprise at the sudden turn of events, the monsters were unable to organize any semblance of a defensive line.

When the four fleets on Maer Dualdon landed just north of the ruins of Targos, they encountered the same disorganized and disoriented resistance. Kemp and the other leaders had figured that they could easily gain a foothold on the land but their main concern was that the large goblin forces occupying Termalaine would sweep down behind them if they pushed in from the beach and cut off their only escape route.

They needn't have worried, though. In the first stages of the battle, the goblins in Termalaine had indeed rushed out with every intention of supporting their wizard. But then Cryshal-Tirith had tumbled down. The goblins were already skeptical, having heard rumors throughout the night that Kessell had dispatched a large force to wipe out the Orcs of the Severed Tongue in the conquered city of Bremen. And when they saw the tower, the pinnacle of Kessell's strength, crash down in ruins, they had reconsidered their alternatives, weighing the consequences of the choices before them. They fled back to the north and the safety of the open plain.

⚔ ⚔ ⚔ ⚔ ⚔

Blowing snow added to the heavy veil atop the mountain. Drizzt kept his eyes down, but he could hardly see his own feet as he determinedly placed one in front of the other. He still held the magical scimitar, and it glowed a pale light, as though it approved of the frigid temperatures.

The drow's numbing body begged him to start down the mountain, and yet he was moving farther along the high face, to one of the adjacent peaks. The wind carried a disturbing sound to his ears—the cackle of insane laughter.

And then he saw the blurred form of the wizard, leaning out over the southern precipice, trying to catch a glimpse of what was happening on the battlefield below.

"Kessell!'" Drizzt shouted. He saw the form shift abruptly and knew that the wizard had heard him, even through the howl of the wind. "In the name of the people of Ten-Towns, I demand that you surrender to me! Quickly, now, lest this unrelenting breath of winter freeze us where we stand!"

Kessell sneered. "You still do not understand what it is you face, do you?" he asked in amazement. "Do you truly believe that you have won this battle?"

"How the people below fare I do not yet know," Drizzt answered. "But you are defeated! Your tower is destroyed, Kessell, and without it you are but a minor trickster!" He continued moving while they talked and was now only a few feet from the wizard, though his opponent was still a mere black blur in a gray field.

Do you wish to know how they fare, drow?" Kessell asked. "Then look! Witness the fall of Ten-Towns!" He reached under his cloak and pulled out a shining object—a crystal shard. The clouds seemed to recoil from it. The wind halted within the wide radius of its influence. Drizzt could see its incredible power. The drow felt the blood returning to his numbed hands in the light of the crystal. Then the gray veil was burned away, and the sky before them was clear.

"The tower destroyed?" Kessell mocked. "You have broken just one of Crenshinibon's countless images! A sack of flour? To defeat the most powerful relic in the world? Look down upon the foolish men who dare to oppose me!"

The battlefield was spread wide before the drow. He could see the white, wind-filled sails of the boats of Caer-Dineval and Caer-Konig as they neared the western banks of Lac Dinneshere.

In the south, the fleets of Good Mead and Dougan's Hole had already docked. The sailors met no initial resistance, and even now were forming up for an inland strike. The goblins and orcs that had formed the southern half of Kessell's ring had not witnessed the fall of Cryshal-Tirith. Though they sensed the loss of power and guidance, and as many of them remained where they were or deserted their comrades and fled as rushed around Bryn Shander's hill to join in the battle.

Kemp's troops were also ashore, shoving off cautiously from the beaches with a wary eye to the north. This group had landed into the thickest concentration of Kessell's forces, but also into the area that was under the shadow of the tower, where the fall of Cryshal-Tirith had been the most disheartening. The fishermen found more goblins interested in running away than ones intent on a fight.

In the center of the field, where the heaviest fighting was taking place, the men of Ten-Towns and their allies also seemed to be faring well. The barbarians had nearly joined with the dwarves. Spurred by the might of Wulfgar's hammer and the unrivaled courage of Bruenor, the two forces were tearing apart all that stood between them. And they would soon become even more formidable, for Cassius and Glensather were close by and moving in at a steady pace.

"By the tale my eyes tell me, your army does not fare well," Drizzt retorted. "The 'foolish' men of Ten-Towns are not defeated yet!"

Kessell raised the Crystal Shard high above him, its light flaring to an even greater level of power. Down on the battlefield, even at the great distance, the combatants understood at once the resurgence of the powerful presence they had known as Cryshal-Tirith. Human, dwarf, and goblin alike, even those locked in mortal combat, paused for a second to look at the beacon on the mountain. The monsters, sensing the return of their god, cheered wildly and abandoned their heretofore defensive posture. Encouraged by the glorious reappearance of Kessell, they pressed the attack with savage fury.

"You see how my mere presence incites them!" Kessell boasted proudly.

But Drizzt wasn't paying attention to the wizard or the battle below. He was standing in puddles of water now from snow melting under the warmth of the shining relic. He was intent on a noise that his keen ears had caught among the clatter of the distant fighting. A rumble of protest from the frozen peaks of Kelvin's Cairn.

"Behold the glory of Akar Kessell!" the wizard cried, his voice magnified to deafening proportions by the power of the relic he held. "How easy it shall be for me to destroy the boats on the lake below!"

Drizzt realized that Kessell, in his arrogant disregard for the dangers growing around him, was making a flagrant mistake. All that he had to do was delay the wizard from taking any decisive actions for the next few moments. Reflexively, he grabbed the dagger at the back of his belt and flung it at Kessell, though he knew that Kessell was joined in some perverted symbiosis with Crenshinibon and that the small weapon had no chance of hitting its mark. The drow was hoping to distract and anger the wizard to divert his fury away from the battlefield.

The dagger sped through the air. Drizzt turned and ran.

A thin beam shot out from Crenshinibon and melted the weapon before it found its mark, but Kessell was outraged. "You should bow down before me!" he screamed at Drizzt. "Blasphemous dog, you have earned the distinction of being my first victim of the day!" He swung the shard away from the ledge to point it at the fleeing drow. But as he spun he sank, suddenly up to his knees in the melting snow.

Then he, too, heard the angry rumbles of the mountain.

Drizzt broke free of the relic's sphere of influence and without hesitating to look back, he ran, putting as much distance between himself and the southern face of Kelvin's Cairn as he could.

Immersed up to his chest now, Kessell struggled to get free of the watery snow. He called upon the power of Crenshinibon again, but his concentration wavered under the intense stress of impending doom.

Akar Kessell felt weak again for the first time in years. Not the Tyrant of Icewind Dale, but the bumbling apprentice who had murdered his teacher.

As if the Crystal Shard had rejected him.

Then the entire side of the mountain's snow cap fell. The rumble shook the land for many miles around. Men and orcs, goblins and even ogres, were thrown to the ground.

Kessell clutched the shard close to him when he began to fall. But Crenshinibon burned his hands, pushed him away. Kessell had failed too many times. The relic would no longer accept him as its wielder.

Kessell screamed when he felt the shard slipping through his fingers. His shriek, though, was drowned out by the thunder of the avalanche. The cold darkness of snow closed around him, falling, tumbling with him on the descent. Kessell desperately believed that if he still held the Crystal Shard, he could survive even this. Small comfort when he settled onto a lower peak of Kelvin's Cairn.

And half of the mountain's cap landed on top of him.

⚔ ⚔ ⚔ ⚔ ⚔

The monster army had seen their god fall again. The thread that had incited their momentum quickly began to unravel. But in the time that Kessell had reappeared, some measure of coordinating activity had taken place. Two frost giants, the only remaining true giants in the wizard's entire army, had taken command. They called the elite ogre guard to their side and then called for the orc and goblin tribes to gather around them and follow their lead.

Still, the dismay of the army was obvious. Tribal rivalries that had been buried under the iron-fisted domination of Akar Kessell resurfaced in the form of blatant mistrust. Only fear of their enemies kept them fighting, and only fear of the giants held them in line beside the other tribes.

"Well met, Bruenor!" Wulfgar sang out, splattering another goblin head, as the barbarian horde finally broke through to the dwarves.

"An' to yerself, boy!" the dwarf replied, burying his axe into the chest of his own opponent. "Time's almost passed that ye got back! I thought that I'd have to kill yer share o' the scum, too!"

Wulfgar's attention was elsewhere, though. He had discovered the two giants commanding the force. "Frost giants," he told Bruenor, directing the dwarf's gaze to the ring of ogres. "They are all that hold the tribes together!"

"Better sport!" Bruenor laughed. "Lead on!"

And so, with his principal attendants and Bruenor beside him, the young king started smashing a path through the goblin ranks.

The ogres crowded in front of their newfound commanders to block the barbarian's path.

Wulfgar was close enough by then.

Aegis-fang whistled past the ogre ranks and took one of the giants in the head, dropping it lifeless to the ground. The other, gawking in disbelief that a human had been able to deliver such a deadly blow against one of its kind from such a distance, hesitated for only a brief moment before it fled the battle.

Undaunted, the vicious ogres charged in on Wulfgar's group, pushing them back. But Wulfgar was satisfied, and he willingly gave ground before the press, anxious to rejoin the bulk of the human and dwarven army.

Bruenor wasn't so willing, though. This was the type of chaotic fighting that he most enjoyed. He disappeared under the long legs of the leading line of ogres and moved, unseen in the dust and confusion, among their ranks.

From the corner of his eye, Wulfgar saw the dwarf's odd departure. "Where are you off to?" he shouted after him, but battle-hungry Bruenor couldn't hear the call and wouldn't have heeded it anyway.

Wulfgar couldn't view the flight of the wild dwarf, but he could approximate Bruenor's position, or at least where the dwarf had just been, as ogre after ogre doubled over in surprised agony, clutching a knee, hamstring, or groin.

Above all of the commotion, those orcs and goblins who weren't engaged in direct combat kept a watchful eye on Kelvin's Cairn, awaiting the second resurgence.

But settled now on the lower slopes of the mountain, there was only snow.

⚔ ⚔ ⚔ ⚔

Lusting for revenge, the fighting men of Caer-Konig and Caer-Dineval brought their ships in under full sail, sliding them up recklessly onto the sands of the shallows to avoid the delays of mooring in deeper waters. They leaped from the boats and splashed ashore, rushing into the battle with a fearless frenzy that drove their opponents away.

Once they had established themselves on the land Jensin Brent brought them together in a tight formation and turned them south. The spokesman heard the fighting far off in that direction and knew that the men of Good Mead and Dougan's Hole were cutting a swath north to join up with his men. His plan was to meet them on the Eastway and then drive westward toward Bryn Shander with his reinforced numbers.

Many of the goblins on this side of the city had long since fled, and many more had gone northwest to the ruins of Cryshal-Tirith and the main fighting. The army of Lac Dinneshere made good speed toward their goal. They reached the road with few losses and dug in to wait for the southerners.

⚔ ⚔ ⚔ ⚔

Kemp watched anxiously for the signal from the lone ship sailing on the waters of Maer Dualdon. The spokesman from Targos, appointed commander of the forces of the four cities of the lake, had moved cautiously thus far for fear of a heavy assault from the north. He held his men in check, allowing them to fight only the monsters that came to them, though this conservative stance, with the sounds of raging battle howling across the field, was tearing at his adventurous heart.

As the minutes had dragged along with no sign of goblin reinforcements, the spokesman had sent a small schooner to run up the coastline and find out what was delaying the occupying force in Termalaine.

Then he spied the white sails gliding into view. Riding high upon the small ship's bow was the signal flag that Kemp had most desired but least expected: the red banner of the catch, though in this instance, it signaled that Termalaine was clear and the goblins were fleeing northward.

Kemp ran to the highest spot he could find, his face flushed with a vengeful desire. "Break the line, boys!" he shouted to his men. "Cut me a swath to the city on the hill! Let Cassius come back and find us sitting on the doorstep of his town!"

They shouted wildly with every step, men who had lost homes and kin and seen their cities burned out from under them. Many of them had nothing left to lose. All that they could hope to gain was a small taste of bitter satisfaction.

⚔ ⚔ ⚔ ⚔

The battle raged for the remainder of the morning, man and monster alike lifting swords and spears that seemed to have doubled their weight. Yet exhaustion, though it slowed their reflexes, did nothing to temper the anger that burned in the blood of every combatant.

The battlelines grew indistinguishable as the fighting wore on, with troops getting hopelessly separated from their commanders. In many places, goblins and orcs fought against each other, unable, even with a common foe so readily available, to sublimate their long-standing hatred for the rival tribes. A thick cloud of dust enveloped the heaviest concentrations of fighting; the dizzying clamor of steel grating on steel, swords banging against shields, and the expanding screams of death, agony, and victory degenerated the structured clash into an all-out brawl.

The sole exception was the group of battle-seasoned dwarves. Their ranks did not waver or disintegrate in the least, though Bruenor had not yet returned to them after his strange exit.

The dwarves provided a solid platform for the barbarians to strike from and for Wulfgar and his small group to mark for their return. The young king was back among the ranks of his men just as Cassius and his force linked up. The spokesman and Wulfgar exchanged intent stares, neither certain of where he stood with the other. Both were wise enough to trust fully in their alliance for the present, though. Both understood that intelligent foes put aside their differences in the face of a greater enemy.

Supporting each other would be the only advantage that the newly banded allies enjoyed. Together, they outnumbered and could overwhelm any individual orc or goblin tribe they faced. And since the goblin tribes would not work in unison, each group had no external support on its flanks. Wulfgar and Cassius, following and supporting each other's movements, sent out defensive spurs of warriors to hold off perimeter groups, while the main force of the combined army blasted through one tribe at a time.

Though his troops had cut down better than ten goblins for every man they had lost, Cassius was truly concerned. Thousands of the monsters had not even come in contact with the humans or raised a weapon yet, and his men were nearly dropping with fatigue. He had to get them back to the city. He let the dwarves lead the way.

Wulfgar, also apprehensive about his warriors' ability to maintain their pace, and knowing that there was no other escape route, instructed his men to follow Cassius and the dwarves. This was a gamble, for the barbarian king wasn't even certain that the people of Bryn Shander would let his warriors into the city.

Kemp's force had made impressive initial headway in their charge to the slopes of the principle city, but as they neared their goal, they ran up against heavier and more desperate concentrations of humanoids. Barely a hundred yards from the hill, they were bogged down and fighting on all sides.

The armies rolling in from the east had done better. Their rush down the Eastway had met with little resistance, and they were the first to reach the hill. They had sailed madly across the breadth of the lakes and ran and fought all the way across the plain, yet Jensin Brent, the lone surviving spokesman of the original four, for Schermont and the two from the southern cities had fallen on the Eastway, would not let them rest. He clearly heard the heated battle and knew that the brave men in the northern fields, facing the mass of Kessell's army, needed any support they could get.

Yet when the spokesman led his troops around the final bend to the city's north gate, they froze in their tracks and looked upon the spectacle of the most brutal battle they had ever seen or even heard of in exaggerated tales. Combatants battled atop the hacked bodies of the fallen, fighters who had somehow lost their weapons bit and scratched at their opponents.

Brent surmised at once that Cassius and his large force would be able to make it back to the city on their own. The armies of Maer Dualdon, though, were in a tight spot.

"To the west!" he cried to his men as he charged toward the trapped force. A new surge of adrenaline sent the weary army in full flight to the rescue of their comrades. On orders from Brent, they came down off of the slopes in a long, side-by-side line, but when they reached the battlefield, only the middle group continued forward. The groups at the ends of the formation collapsed into the middle, and the whole force had soon formed a wedge, its tip breaking all the way through the monsters to reach Kemp's embattled armies.

Kemp's men eagerly accepted the lifeline, and the united force was soon able to retreat to the northern face of the hill. The last stragglers stumbled in at the same time as the army of Cassius, Wulfgar's barbarians, and the dwarves broke free of the closest ranks of goblins and climbed the open ground of the hill. Now, with the humans and dwarves joined as one force, the goblins moved in tentatively. Their losses had been staggering. No giants or ogres remained, and several entire tribes of goblins and orcs lay dead. Cryshal-Tirith was a pile of blackened rubble, and Akar Kessell was buried in a frozen grave.

The men on Bryn Shander's hill were battered and wobbly with exhaustion, yet the grim set of their jaws told the remaining monsters unequivocally that they would fight on to their last breath. They had backed into the final corner, there would be no further retreat.

Doubts crept into the mind of every goblin and orc that remained to carry on the war. Though their numbers were still probably sufficient to complete the task, many more of them would yet fall before the fierce men of Ten-Towns and their deadly allies would be put down. Even then, which of the surviving tribes would claim victory? Without the guidance of the wizard, the survivors of the battle would certainly be hard-pressed to fairly divide the spoils without further fighting.

The Battle of Icewind Dale had not followed the course that Akar Kessell had promised.

31

VICTORY?

The men of Ten-Towns, along with their dwarven and barbarian allies, had fought their way from all sides of the wide field and now stood unified before the northern gate of Bryn Shander. And while their army had achieved a singular fighting stance, with all of the once-separate groups banded together toward the common goal of survival, Kessell's army had gone down the opposite road. When the goblins had first charged into Icewind Pass, their common purpose was victory for the glory of Akar Kessell. But Kessell was gone and Cryshal-Tirith destroyed, and the cord that had held together the long-standing, bitter enemies, the rival orc and goblin tribes, had begun to unravel.

The humans and dwarves looked upon the mass of invaders with returning hope, for on all the outer fringes of the vast force dark shapes continued to break away and flee from the battlefield and back to the tundra.

Still, the defenders of Ten-Towns were surrounded on three sides with their backs to Bryn Shander's wall. At this point the monsters made no move to press the attack, but thousands of goblins held their positions all around the northern fields of the city.

Earlier in the battle, when the initial attacks had caught the invaders by surprise, the leaders of the engaged defending forces would have considered such a lull in the fighting disastrous, stealing their momentum and allowing their stunned enemies to regroup into more favorable formations.

Now, though, the break came as a two-fold blessing: It gave the soldiers a desperately needed rest and let the goblins and orcs fully absorb the beating they had taken. The field on this side of the city was littered with corpses, many more goblin than human, and the crumbled pile that was Cryshal-Tirith only heightened the monsters' perceptions of their staggering losses. No giants or ogres remained to bolster their thinning lines, and each passing second saw more of their allies desert the cause.

Cassius had time to call all the surviving spokesmen to his side for a brief council.

A short distance away, Wulfgar and Revjak were meeting with Fender Mallot, the appointed leader of the dwarven forces in light of Bruenor's disturbing absence.

"Glad we are o' yer return, mighty Wulfgar," Fender said. "Bruenor knew ye'd be back."

Wulfgar looked out over the field, searching for some sign that Bruenor was still out there swinging. "Have you any news of Bruenor at all?"

"Ye, yerself, were the last to see 'im," Fender replied grimly.

And then they were silent, scanning the field.

"Let me hear again the ring of your axe," Wulfgar whispered.

But Bruenor could not hear him.

⚔ ⚔ ⚔ ⚔ ⚔

"Jensin," Cassius asked the spokesman from Caer-Dineval, "where are your womenfolk and children? Are they safe?"

"Safe in Easthaven," Jensin Brent replied. "Joined, by now, by the people of Good Mead and Dougan's Hole. They are well provisioned and watched. If Kessell's wretches make for the town, the people shall know of the danger with ample time left for them to put back out onto Lac Dinneshere."

"But how long could they survive on the water?" Cassius asked. Jensin Brent shrugged noncommittally. "Until the winter falls, I should guess.

They shall always have a place to land though, for the remaining goblins and orcs could not possibly encompass even half of the lake's shoreline."

Cassius seemed satisfied. He turned to Kemp.

"Lonelywood," Kemp answered to his unspoken question. "And I'll wager that they're better off than we are! They've enough boats in dock there to found a city in the middle of Maer Dualdon."

"That is good," Cassius told them. "It leaves yet another option open to us. We could, perhaps, hold our ground here for a while, then retreat back within the walls of the city. The goblins and orcs, even with their greater numbers, couldn't hope to conquer us there!"

The idea seemed to appeal to Jensin Brent, but Kemp scowled. "So our folk may be safe enough," he said, "but what of the barbarians?"

"Their women are sturdy and capable of surviving without them," Cassius replied.

"I care not the least for their foul-smelling women," Kemp blustered, purposely raising his voice so that Wulfgar and Revjak, holding their own council not far away, could hear him. "I speak of these wild dogs, themselves! Surely you're not going to open your door wide in invitation to them!"

Proud Wulfgar started toward the spokesmen.

Cassius turned angrily on Kemp. "Stubborn ass!" he whispered harshly. "Our only hope lies in unity!"

"Our only hope lies in attacking!" Kemp retorted. "We have them terrified, and you ask us to run and hide!"

The huge barbarian king stepped up before the two spokesmen, towering above them. "Greetings, Cassius of Bryn Shander," he said politely. "I am Wulfgar, son of Beornegar, and leader of the tribes who have come to join in your noble cause."

"What could your kind possibly know of nobility?" Kemp interrupted. Wulfgar ignored him.

"I have overheard much of your discussion," he continued, unshaken. "It is my judgment that your ill-mannered and ungrateful advisor," he paused for control, "has proposed the only solution."

Cassius, still expecting Wulfgar to be enraged at Kemp's insults, was at first confused.

"Attack," Wulfgar explained. "The goblins are uncertain now of what gains they can hope to make. They wonder why they ever followed the evil wizard to this place of doom. If they are allowed to find their battle-lust again, they will prove a more formidable foe."

"I thank you for your words, barbarian king," Cassius replied. "Yet it is my guess that this rabble will not be able to support a siege. They will leave the fields before a tenday has passed!"

"Perhaps," said Wulfgar. "Yet even then your people shall pay dearly. The goblins leaving of their own choice will not return to their caves empty-handed. There are still several unprotected cities that they could strike at on their way out of Icewind Dale.

"And worse yet, they shall not leave with fear in their eyes. Your retreat shall save the lives of some of your men, Cassius, but it will not prevent the future return of your enemies!"

"Then you agree that we should attack?" Cassius asked.

"Our enemies have come to fear us. They look about and see the ruin we have brought down upon them. Fear is a powerful tool, especially against cowardly goblins. Let us complete the rout, as your people did to mine five years ago . . ." Cassius recognized the pain in Wulfgar's eyes as he recalled the incident, ". . . and send these foul beasts scurrying back to their mountain homes! Many years shall pass before they venture out to strike at your towns again."

Cassius looked upon the young barbarian with profound respect, and also deep curiosity. He could hardly believe that these proud tundra warriors, who vividly remembered the slaughter they had suffered at the hands of Ten-Townsmen, had come to the aid of the fishing communities. "My people did indeed rout yours, noble king. Brutally. Why, then, have you come?"

"That is a matter we shall discuss after we have completed our task," Wulfgar answered. "Now, let us sing! Let us strike terror into the hearts of our enemies and break them!"

He turned to Revjak and some of his other leaders. "Sing, proud warriors!" he commanded. "Let the Song of Tempus foretell the death of the goblins!" A rousing cheer went up throughout the barbarian ranks, and they lifted their voices proudly to their god of war.

Cassius noted the immediate effect the song had on the closest monsters. They backed away a step and clutched their weapons tightly.

A smile crossed the spokesman's face. He still couldn't understood the barbarians' presence, but explanations would have to wait. "Join our barbarian allies!" he shouted to his soldiers. "Today is a day of victory!"

The dwarves had taken up the grim war chant of their ancient homeland. The fishermen of Ten-Towns followed the words of the Song of Tempus, tentatively at first, until the foreign inflections and phrases easily rolled from their lips. And then they joined in fully, proclaiming the glory of their individual towns as the barbarians did of their tribes. The tempo increased, the volume moved toward a powerful crescendo. The goblins trembled at the growing frenzy of their deadly enemies. The stream of deserters flowing away from the edges of the main gathering grew thicker and thicker.

And then, as one killing wave, the human and dwarven allies charged down the hill.

✕ ✕ ✕ ✕

Drizzt had been able to scramble far enough away from the southern face to escape the fury of the avalanche, but he still found himself in a dangerous predicament. Kelvin's Cairn wasn't a high mountain, but the top third was perpetually covered with deep snow and brutally exposed to the icy wind that gave this land its name.

Even worse for the drow, his feet had gotten wet in the melt caused by Crenshinibon, and now, as the moisture hardened around his skin to ice, movement through the snow was painful.

He resolved to plod on, making for the western face which offered the best protection against the wind. His motions were violent and exaggerated, expending all of the energy that he could to keep the circulation flowing through his veins. When he reached the lip of the mountain's peak and started down, he had to move more tentatively, fearing that any sudden jolts would deliver him into the same grim fate that had befallen Akar Kessell.

His legs were completely numb now, but he kept them moving, almost having to force his automatic reflexes.

But then he slipped.

✕ ✕ ✕ ✕ ✕

Wulfgar's fierce warriors were the first to crash into the goblin line, hacking and pushing back the first rank of monsters. Neither goblin nor orc dared stand before the mighty king, but in the crowded confusion of the fighting few could find their way out of his path. One after another they fell to the ground.

Fear had all but paralyzed the goblins, and their slight hesitation had spelled doom for the first groups to encounter the savage barbarians.

Yet the downfall of the army ultimately came from further back in the ranks. The tribes who had not even been involved in the fighting began to ponder the wisdom of continuing this campaign, for they recognized that they had gained enough of an advantage over their homeland rivals, weakened by heavy losses, to expand their territories back in the Spine of the World. Shortly after the second outburst of fighting had begun, the dust cloud of stamping feet once again rose above Icewind Pass as dozens of orc and goblin tribes headed home.

And the effect of the mass desertions on those goblins who could not easily flee was devastating. Even the most dim-witted goblin understood its people's chance for victory against the stubborn defenders of Ten-Towns lay in the overwhelming weight of their numbers.

Aegis-fang thudded repeatedly as Wulfgar, charging in alone, swept a path of devastation before him. Even the men of Ten-Towns shied away from him, unnerved by his savage strength. But his own people looked upon him with awe and tried their best to follow his glorious lead.

Wulfgar waded in on a group of orcs. Aegis-fang slammed home on one, killing it and knocking those behind it to the ground. Wulfgar's backswing with the hammer produced the same results on his other flank. In one burst, more than half of the group of orcs were killed or lying stunned.

Those remaining had no desire to move in on the mighty human.

Glensather of Easthaven also waded in on a group of goblins, hoping to incite his people with the same fury as his barbarian counterpart. But Glensather wasn't an imposing giant like Wulfgar, and he didn't wield a weapon as mighty as Aegis-fang. His sword cut down the first goblin he encountered, then spun back deftly and felled a second. The spokesman had done well, but one element was missing from his attack—the critical factor that elevated Wulfgar above other men. Glensather had killed two goblins, but he had not caused the chaos in their ranks that he needed to continue. Instead of fleeing, as they did before Wulfgar, the remaining goblins pressed in behind him.

Glensather had just come up beside the barbarian king when the cruel tip of a spear dived into his back and tore through, driving out the front of his chest.

Witnessing the gruesome spectacle, Wulfgar brought Aegis-fang over the spokesman, driving the head of the spear-wielding goblin down into its chest. Glensather heard the hammer connect behind him and even managed to smile his thanks before he fell dead to the grass.

The dwarves worked differently than their allies. Once again formed into their tight, supportive formation, they mowed down rows of goblins simultaneously. And the fishermen, fighting for the lives of their women and children, fought, and died, without fear.

In less than an hour, every group of goblins had been smashed, and half an hour after that, the last of the monsters fell dead to the blood-stained field.

⚔ ⚔ ⚔ ⚔ ⚔

Drizzt rode the white wave of falling snow down the side of the mountain. He tumbled helplessly, trying to brace himself whenever he saw the jutting tip of a boulder in his path. As he neared the base of the snowcap, he was thrown clear of the slide and sent bouncing through the gray rocks and boulders, as though the mountain's proud, unconquerable peaks had spit him out like an uninvited guest.

His agility—and a strong dose of pure luck—saved him. When he at last was able to stop his momentum and find a perch, he discovered that his numerous injuries were superficial, a scrape on his knee, a bloodied nose, and a sprained wrist being the worst of them. In retrospect, Drizzt had to consider the small avalanche a blessing, for he had made swift progress down the mountain, and he wasn't even certain that he could have otherwise escaped Kessell's frosty fate without it.

The battle in the south had begun again by this time. Hearing the sounds of the fighting, Drizzt watched curiously as thousands of goblins passed by on the other side of the dwarven valley, running up Icewind Pass on the first legs of their long journey home. The drow couldn't be sure of what was happening, though he was familiar with the cowardly reputation of goblins.

He didn't give it too much thought, though, for the battle was no longer his first concern. His vision followed a narrow path, to the mound of broken black stonework that had been Cryshal-Tirith. He finished his descent from Kelvin's Cairn and headed down Bremen's Run toward the rubble.

He had to find out if Regis or Guenhwyvar had escaped.

⚔ ⚔ ⚔ ⚔ ⚔

Victory.

It seemed a small comfort to Cassius, Kemp, and Jensin Brent as they looked around at the carnage on the scarred field. They were the only three spokesmen to have survived the struggle; seven others had been cut down. "We have won," Cassius declared grimly. He watched helplessly as more soldiers fell dead, men who had suffered mortal wounds earlier in the battle but had refused to fall down and die until they had seen it through. More than half of all the men of Ten-Towns lay dead, and many more would later die, for nearly half of those still alive had been grievously wounded. Four towns had been burned to the ground and another one looted and torn apart by occupying goblins.

They had paid a terrible price for their victory.

The barbarians, too, had been decimated. Mostly young and inexperienced, they had fought with the tenacity of their breeding and died accepting their fate as a glorious ending to their life's tale.

Only the dwarves, disciplined by many battles, had come through relatively unscathed. Several had been slain, a few others wounded, but most were all too ready to take up the fight again if only they could have found more goblins to bash! Their one great lament, though, was that Bruenor was missing.

"Go to your people," Cassius told his fellow spokesmen. "Then return this evening to council. Kemp shall speak for all the people of the four towns of Maer Dualdon, Jensin Brent for the people of the other lakes."

"We have much to decide and little time to do it," Jensin Brent said. "Winter is fast approaching."

"We shall survive!" Kemp declared with his characteristic defiance. But then he was aware of the sullen looks his peers had cast upon him, and he conceded a bit to their realism. "Though it will be a bitter struggle."

"So it shall be for my people," said another voice. The three spokesmen turned to see the giant Wulfgar striding out from the dusty, surrealistic scene of carnage. The barbarian was caked in dirt and spattered with the blood of his enemies, but he looked every bit the noble king. "I request an invitation to your council, Cassius. There is much that our people can offer to each other in this harsh time."

Kemp growled. "If we need beasts of burden, we'll buy oxen."

Cassius shot Kemp a dangerous look and addressed his unexpected ally. "You may indeed join the council, Wulfgar, son of Beornegar. For your aid this day, my people owe yours much. Again I ask you, why did you come?"

For the second time that day, Wulfgar ignored Kemp's insults. "To repay a debt," he replied to Cassius. "And perhaps to better the lives of both our peoples."

"By killing goblins?" Jensin Brent asked, suspecting that the barbarian had more in mind.

"A beginning," Wulfgar answered. "Yet there is much more that we may accomplish. My people know the tundra better than even the yetis. We understand its ways and know how to survive. Your people would benefit from our friendship, especially in the hard times that lay ahead for you."

"Bah!" Kemp snorted, but Cassius silenced him. The spokesman from Bryn Shander was intrigued by the possibilities.

"And what would your people gain from such a union?"

"A connection," Wulfgar answered. "A link to a world of luxuries that we have never known. The tribes hold a dragon's treasure in their hands, but gold and jewels do not provide warmth on a winter night, nor food when game is scarce.

"Your people have much rebuilding to do. My people have the wealth to assist in that task. In return, Ten-Towns will deliver my people into a better life!" Cassius and Jensin Brent nodded approvingly as Wulfgar laid out his plan.

"Finally, and perhaps most important," the barbarian concluded, "is the fact that we need each other, for the present at least. Both of our peoples have been weakened and are vulnerable to the dangers of this land. Together, our remaining strength would see us through the winter."

"You intrigue and surprise me," Cassius said. "Attend the council, then, with my personal welcome, and let us put in motion a plan that will benefit all who have survived the struggle against Akar Kessell!"

As Cassius turned, Wulfgar grabbed Kemp's shirt with one of his huge hands and easily hoisted the spokesman from Targos off the ground. Kemp swatted at the muscled forearm, but realized that he had no chance of breaking the barbarian's iron grip.

Wulfgar glared at him dangerously. "For now," he said, "I am responsible for all my people. Thus have I disregarded your insults. But when the day comes that I am no longer king, you would do well to cross my path no more!" With a flick of his wrist, he tossed the spokesman to the ground.

Kemp, too intimidated for the present to be angry or embarrassed, sat where he landed and did not respond. Cassius and Brent nudged each other and shared a low chuckle.

It lasted only until they saw the girl approaching, her arm in a bloody sling and her face and auburn hair caked with layers of dust. Wulfgar saw her, too, and the sight of her wounds pained him more than his own ever could.

"Catti-brie!" he cried, rushing to her. She calmed him with an outstretched palm.

"I am not badly injured," she assured Wulfgar stoically, though it was obvious to the barbarian that she had been sorely injured. "Though I dare not think of what would have befallen me if Bruenor had not arrived!"

"You have seen Bruenor?"

"In the tunnels," Catti-brie explained. "Some orcs found their way in—perhaps I should have collapsed the tunnel. Yet there weren't many, and I could hear that the dwarves were doing well on the field above.

"Bruenor came down then, but there were more orcs at his back. A support beam collapsed; I think Bruenor cut it out, and there was too much dust and confusion."

"And Bruenor?" Wulfgar asked anxiously.

Catti-brie looked back across the field. "Out there. He has asked for you."

✕ ✕ ✕ ✕

By the time Drizzt reached the rubble that had been Cryshal-Tirith, the battle was over. The sights and sounds of the horrible aftermath pressed in all about him, but his goal remained unchanged. He started up the side of the broken stones.

In truth, the drow thought himself a fool for following such a hopeless cause. Even if Regis and Guenhwyvar hadn't gotten out of the tower, how could he possibly hope to find them?

He pressed on stubbornly, refusing to give in to the inescapable logic that scolded him. This was where he differed from his people, this was what had driven him, finally, from the unbroken darkness of their vast cities. Drizzt Do'Urden allowed himself to feel compassion.

He moved up the side of the rubble and began digging around the debris with his bare hands. Larger blocks prevented him from going very deep into the pile, yet he did not yield, even squeezing into precariously tight and unstable crevices. He used his burned left hand little, and soon his right was bleeding from scraping. But he continued on, moving first around the pile, then scaling higher.

He was rewarded for his persistence, for his emotions. When he reached the top of the ruins, he felt a familiar aura of magical power. It guided him to a small crevice between two stones. He reached in tentatively, hoping to find the object intact, and pulled out the small feline figurine. His fingers trembled as he examined it for damage. But he found none—the magic within the object had resisted the weight of the rubble.

The drow's feelings at the find were mixed, however. Though he was relieved that Guenhwyvar had apparently survived, the presence of the figurine told him that Regis had probably not escaped to the field. His heart sank. And sank even farther when a sparkle within the same crevice caught his eye. He reached in and pulled out the golden chain with the ruby pendent, and his fears were confirmed.

"A fitting tomb for you, brave little friend," he said somberly, and he decided at that moment to name the pile Regis's Cairn. He could not understand though, what had happened to separate the halfling from his necklace, for there was no blood or anything else on the chain to indicate that Regis had been wearing it when he died.

"Guenhwyvar," he called. "Come to me, my shadow." He felt the familiar sensations in the figurine as he placed it on the ground before him. Then the black mist appeared and formed into the great cat, unharmed and somewhat restored by the few hours it had spent back on its own plane.

Drizzt moved quickly toward his feline companion, but then he stopped as a second mist appeared a short distance away and began to solidify.

Regis.

The halfling sat with eyes closed and his mouth opened wide, as though he was about to take an enjoyable and enormous bite out of some unseen delicacy. One of his hands was clenched to the side of his eager jowls, and the other open before him.

As his mouth snapped shut on empty air, his eyes snapped open in surprise. "Drizzt!" he groaned. "Really, you should ask before you steal me away! This perfectly marvelous cat had caught me the juiciest meal!"

Drizzt shook his head and smiled with a mixture of relief and disbelief.

"Oh, splendid," Regis cried. "You have found my gemstone. I thought that I had lost it; for some reason it didn't make the journey with the cat and me."

Drizzt handed the ruby back to him. The cat could take someone along on its travels through the planes? Drizzt resolved to explore this facet of Guenhwyvar's power later.

He stroked the cat's neck, then released it back to its own world where it could further recuperate. "Come, Regis," he said grimly. "Let us see where we might be of assistance!"

Regis shrugged resignedly and stood to follow the drow. When they crested the top of the ruins and saw the carnage spread out below them, the halfling realized the enormity of the destruction. His legs nearly faltered under him, but he managed, with some help from his agile friend, to make the descent.

"We won?" he asked Drizzt when they neared the level of the field, unsure if the people of Ten-Towns had labeled what he saw before him victory or defeat.

"We survived," Drizzt corrected.

A shout went up suddenly as a group of fishermen, seeing the two companions, rushed toward them, yelling with abandon. "Wizard-slayer and tower-breaker!" they cried.

Drizzt, ever humble, lowered his eyes.

"Hail Regis," the men continued, "the hero of Ten-Towns!"

Drizzt turned a surprised but amused eye on his friend. Regis merely shrugged helplessly, acting as much the victim of the error as Drizzt.

The men caught hold of the halfling and hoisted him to their shoulders. "We shall carry you in glory to the council taking place within the city!" one proclaimed. "You, above all others, should have a say in the decisions that will be made!" Almost as an afterthought, the man said to Drizzt. "You can come too, drow."

Drizzt declined. "All hail Regis," he said, a smile splayed across his face. "Ah, little friend, ever you have the fortune to find gold in the mud where others wallow!" He clapped the halfling on the back and stood aside as the procession began.

Regis looked back over his shoulder and rolled his eyes as though he were merely going along for the ride.

But Drizzt knew better.

⚔ ⚔ ⚔ ⚔

The drow's amusement was short-lived.

Before he had even moved away from the spot, two dwarves hailed him.

"It is good that we have found ye, friend elf," said one. The drow knew at once that they bore grim news.

"Bruenor?" he asked.

The dwarves nodded. "He lies near death, even now he might be gone. He has asked for ye."

Without another word, the dwarves led Drizzt across the field to a small tent they had set up near their tunnel exits and escorted him in.

Inside, candles flickered softly. Beyond the single cot, against the wall opposite the entrance, stood Wulfgar and Catti-brie, their heads bent reverently.

Bruenor lay on the cot, his head and chest wrapped in bloodstained bandages. His breathing was raspy and shallow, as though each breath would be his last. Drizzt moved solemnly to his side, stoically determined to hold back the uncharacteristic tears that welled in his lavender eyes. Bruenor would prefer strength.

"Is it . . . the elf?" Bruenor gasped when he saw the dark form over him.

"I have come, dearest of friends," Drizzt replied.

"To see . . . me on me way?"

Drizzt couldn't honestly answer so blunt a question. "On your way?" He forced a laugh from his constricting throat. "You have suffered worse! I'll hear no talk of dying—who then would find Mithral Hall?"

"Ah, my home. . . ." Bruenor settled back at the name and seemed to relax, almost as if he felt that his dreams would carry him through the dark journey before him. "Ye're to come with me, then?"

"Of course," Drizzt agreed. He looked to Wulfgar and Catti-brie for support, but lost in their own grief, they kept their eyes averted.

"But not now, no, no," Bruenor explained. "Wouldn't do with the winter so close!" He coughed. "In the spring. Yes, in the spring!" His voice trailed away and his eyes closed.

"Yes, my friend," Drizzt agreed. "In the spring. I shall see you to your home in the spring!"

Bruenor's eyes cracked open again, their deathly glaze washed away by a hint of the old sparkle. A contented smile widened across the dwarf's face, and Drizzt was happy that he had been able to comfort his dying friend.

The drow looked back to Wulfgar and Catti-brie and they, too, were smiling.

At each other, Drizzt noted curiously.

Suddenly, to Drizzt's surprise and horror, Bruenor sat up and tore away the bandages.

"There!" he roared to the amusement of the others in the tent. "Ye've said it, and I have witnesses to the fact!"

Drizzt, after nearly falling over with the initial shock, scowled at Wulfgar. The barbarian and Catti-brie fought hard to subdue their laughter.

Wulfgar shrugged, and a chuckle escaped. "Bruenor said that he would cut me down to the height of a dwarf if I said a word!"

"And so he would have!" Catti-brie added. The two of them made a hasty exit. "A council in Bryn Shander," Wulfgar explained hastily. Outside the tent, their laughter erupted unheeded.

"Damn you, Bruenor Battlehammer!" the drow scowled. Then unable to stop himself, he threw his arms around the barrel-shaped dwarf and hugged him.

"Get it over with," Bruenor groaned, accepting the embrace. "But be quick. We've a lot o' work to do through the winter! Spring'll be here sooner than ye think, and on the first warm day we leave for Mithral Hall!"

"Wherever that might be," Drizzt laughed, too relieved to be angered by the trick.

"We'll make it, drow!" Bruenor cried. "We always do!"

EPILOGUE

The people of Ten-Towns and their barbarian allies found the winter following the battle a difficult one, but by pooling their talents and resources, they managed to survive. Many councils were held throughout those long months with Cassius, Jensin Brent, and Kemp representing the people of Ten-Towns, and Wulfgar and Revjak speaking for the barbarian tribes. The first order of business was to officially recognize and condone the alliance of the two peoples, though many on both sides were strongly opposed.

Those cities left untouched by Akar Kessell's army were packed full of refugees during the brutal winter. Reconstruction began with the first signs of spring. When the region was well on its way to recovery, and after the barbarian expedition following Wulfgar's directions returned with the dragon's treasure, councils were held to divide the towns among the surviving people. Relations between the two peoples almost broke down several times and were held together only by the commanding presence of Wulfgar and the continued calm of Cassius.

When all was finally settled, the barbarians were given the cities of Bremen and Caer-Konig to rebuild, the homeless of Caer-Konig were moved into the reconstructed city of Caer-Dineval, and the refugees of Bremen who did not wish to live among the tribesmen were offered homes in the newly built city of Targos.

It was a difficult situation, where traditional enemies were forced to put aside their differences and live in close quarters. Though victorious in the battle, the people of the towns could not call themselves winners. Everyone had suffered tragic losses; no one had come out better for the fight.

Except Regis.

The opportunistic halfling was awarded the title of First Citizen and the finest house in all of Ten-Towns for his part in the battle. Cassius readily surrendered his palace to the "tower-breaker." Regis accepted the spokesman's offer and all of the other numerous gifts that rolled in from every city, for though he hadn't truly earned the accolades awarded him, he justified his good fortune by considering himself a partner of the unassuming drow. And since Drizzt Do'Urden wasn't about to come to Bryn Shander and collect the rewards, Regis figured that it was his duty to do so.

This was the pampered lifestyle that the halfling had always desired. He truly enjoyed the excessive wealth and luxuries, though he would later learn that there was indeed a hefty price to be paid for fame.

⚔ ⚔ ⚔ ⚔

Drizzt and Bruenor had spent the winter in preparation for their search for Mithral Hall. The drow intended to honor his word, though he had been tricked, because life hadn't changed much for him after the battle. Although he was in truth the hero of the fight, he still found himself barely tolerated among the people of Ten-Towns. And the barbarians, other than Wulfgar and Revjak, openly avoided him, mumbling warding prayers to their gods whenever they inadvertently crossed his path.

But the drow accepted the shunning with his characteristic stoicism.

⚔ ⚔ ⚔ ⚔

"The whispers in town say that you have given your voice at council to Revjak," Catti-brie said to Wulfgar on one of her many visits to Bryn Shander.

Wulfgar nodded. "He is older and wiser in many ways."

Catti-brie drew Wulfgar under the uncomfortable scrutiny of her dark eyes. She knew that there were other reasons for Wulfgar stepping down as king. "You mean to go with them," she stated flatly.

"I owe it to the drow," was Wulfgar's only explanation as he turned away, in no mood to argue with the fiery girl.

"Again you parry the question," Catti-brie laughed. "You go to pay no debt! You go because you choose the road!"

"What could you know of the road?" Wulfgar growled, pulled in by the girl's painfully accurate observation. "What could you know of adventure?"

Catti-brie's eyes sparkled disarmingly. "I know," she stated flatly. "Every day in every place is an adventure. This you have not yet learned. And so you chase down the distant roads, hoping to satisfy the hunger for excitement that burns in your heart. So go, Wulfgar of Icewind Dale. Follow your heart's trail and be happy!

"Perhaps when you return you will understand the excitement of simply being alive." She kissed him on the cheek and skipped to the door.

Wulfgar called after her, pleasantly surprised by her kiss. "Perhaps then our discussions will be more agreeable!"

"But not as interesting!" was her parting response.

⨯ ⨯ ⨯ ⨯ ⨯

One fine morning in early spring, the time finally came for Drizzt and Bruenor to leave. Catti-brie helped them pack their overstuffed sacks.

"When we've cleared the place, I'll take ye there!" Bruenor told the girl one more time. "Sure yer eyes'll shine when ye see the rivers runnin' silver in Mithral Hall!"

Catti-brie smiled indulgently.

"Ye're sure ye'll be all right, then?" Bruenor asked more seriously. He knew that she would, but his heart flooded with fatherly concern.

Catti-brie's smile widened. They had been through this discussion a hundred times over the winter. Catti-brie was glad that the dwarf was going, though she knew that she would miss him dearly, for it was clear that Bruenor would never truly be contented until he had at least tried to find his ancestral home.

And she knew, better than anyone, that the dwarf would be in fine company.

Bruenor was satisfied. The time had come to go.

The companions said their goodbyes to the dwarves and started off for Bryn Shander to bid farewell to their two closest friends.

They arrived at Regis's house later in the morning, and found Wulfgar sitting on the steps waiting for them, Aegis-fang and his pack by his side.

Drizzt eyed the barbarian's belongings suspiciously as they approached, half-guessing Wulfgar's intentions. "Well met, King Wulfgar," he said. "Are you off to Bremen, or perhaps Caer-Konig, to oversee the work of your people?"

Wulfgar shook his head. "I am no king," he replied. "Councils and speeches are better left to older men; I have had more of them than I can tolerate. Revjak speaks for the men of the tundra now."

"Then what o' yerself?" asked Bruenor.

"I go with you," Wulfgar replied. "To repay my last debt."

"Ye owe me nothin'!" Bruenor declared.

"To you I am paid," Wulfgar agreed. "And I have paid all that I owe to Ten-Towns, and to my own people as well. But there is one debt I am not yet free of." He turned to face Drizzt squarely. "To you, friend elf."

Drizzt didn't know how to reply. He clapped the huge man on the shoulder and smiled warmly.

⚔ ⚔ ⚔ ⚔

"Come with us, Rumblebelly," Bruenor said after they had finished an excellent lunch in the palace. "Four adventurers, out on the open plain. It'll do ye some good an' take a bit o' that belly o' yers away!"

Regis grasped his ample stomach in both hands and jiggled it. "I like my belly and intend to keep it, thank you. I may even add some more to it!

"I cannot begin to understand why you all insist on going on this quest, anyway," he said more seriously. He had spent many hours during the winter trying to talk Bruenor and Drizzt out of their chosen path. "We have an easy life here; why would you want to leave?"

"There is more to living than fine food and soft pillows, little friend," said Wulfgar. "The lust of adventure burns our blood. With peace in the region, Ten-Towns cannot offer the thrill of danger or the satisfaction of victory." Drizzt and Bruenor nodded their assent, though Regis shook his head.

"An' ye call this pitiful place wealth?" Bruenor chuckled, snapping his stubby fingers. "When I return from Mithral Hall, I'll build ye a home twice this size an' edged in gems like ye never seen afore!"

But Regis was determined that he had witnessed his last adventure. After the meal was finished, he accompanied his friends to the door. "If you make it back . . ."

"Your house shall be our first stop," Drizzt assured him.

They met Kemp of Targos when they walked outside. He was standing across the road from Regis's front step, apparently looking for them.

"He is waiting for me," Wulfgar explained, smiling at the notion that Kemp would go out of his way to be rid of him.

"Farewell, good spokesman," Wulfgar called, bowing low. "Prayne de crabug ahm rinedere be-yogt iglo kes gron."

Kemp flashed an obscene gesture at the barbarian and stalked away. Regis nearly doubled over with laughter.

Drizzt recognized the words, but was puzzled as to why Wulfgar had spoken them to Kemp. "You once told me that those words were an old tundra battle cry," he remarked to the barbarian. "Why would you offer them to the man you most despise?"

Wulfgar stammered over an explanation that would get him out of this jam, but Regis answered for him.

"Battle cry?" the halfling exclaimed. "That is an old barbarian house-mother's curse, usually reserved for adulterous old barbarian housefathers." The drow's lavender eyes narrowed on the barbarian as Regis continued. "It means: May the fleas of a thousand reindeer nest in your genitals."

Bruenor broke down into laughter, Wulfgar soon joining him. Drizzt couldn't help but go along.

"Come, the day is long," the drow said. "Let us begin this adventure—it should prove interesting!"

"Where will you go?" Regis asked somberly. A small part of the halfling actually envied his friends; he had to admit that he would miss them.

"To Bremen, first," replied Drizzt. "We shall complete our provisions there and strike out to the southwest."

"Luskan?"

"Perhaps, if the fates deem it."

"Good speed," Regis offered as the three companions started out without further delay.

Regis watched them disappear, wondering how he had ever picked such foolish friends. He shrugged it away and turned back to his palace—there was plenty of food left over from lunch.

He was stopped before he got through the door.

"First Citizen!" came a call from the street. The voice belonged to a warehouseman from the southern section of the city, where the merchant caravans loaded and unloaded. Regis waited for his approach.

"A man, First Citizen," the warehouseman said, bowing apologetically for disturbing so important a person. "Asking about you. He claims to be a representative from the Heroes Society in Luskan, sent to request your presence at their next meeting. He said that he would pay you well."

"His name?"

"He gave none, just this!" The warehouseman opened a small pouch of gold.

It was all that Regis needed to see. He left at once for the rendezvous with the man from Luskan.

Once again, sheer luck saved the halfling's life, for he saw the stranger before the stranger saw him. He recognized the man at once, though he hadn't seen him in years, by the emerald-encrusted dagger hilt protruding from the sheath on his hip. Regis had often contemplated stealing that beautiful weapon, but even he had a limit to his foolhardiness. The dagger belonged to Artemis Entreri.

Pasha Pook's prime assassin.

⚔ ⚔ ⚔ ⚔ ⚔

The three companions left Bremen before dawn the next day. Anxious to begin the adventure, they made good time and were far out into the tundra when the first rays of the sun peeked over the eastern horizon behind them.

Still, Bruenor was not surprised when he noticed Regis scrambling across the empty plain to catch up with them.

"Got 'imself into trouble again, or I'm a bearded gnome," the dwarf snickered to Wulfgar and Drizzt.

"Well met," said Drizzt. "But haven't we already said our farewells?"

"I decided that I could not let Bruenor run off into trouble without me being there to pull him out," Regis puffed, trying to catch his breath.

"Yer comin?" groaned Bruenor. "Ye've brought no supplies, fool halfling!"

"I don't eat much," Regis pleaded; an edge of desperation creeping into his voice.

"Bah! Ye eat more'n the three of us together! But no mind, we'll let ye tag along anyway."

The halfling's face brightened visibly, and Drizzt suspected that the dwarf's guess about trouble wasn't far off the mark.

"The four of us, then!" proclaimed Wulfgar. "One to represent each of the four common races: Bruenor for the dwarves, Regis for the halflings, Drizzt Do'Urden for the elves, and myself for the humans. A fitting troupe!"

"I hardly think the elves would choose a drow to represent them," Drizzt remarked.

Bruenor snorted. "Ye think the halflings'd choose Rumblebelly for their champion?"

"You're crazy, dwarf," retorted Regis.

Bruenor dropped his shield to the ground, leaped around Wulfgar, and squared off before Regis. His face contorted in mock rage as he grasped Regis by the shoulders and hoisted him into the air.

"That's right, Rumblebelly!" Bruenor cried wildly. "Crazy I am! An' never cross one what's crazier than yerself!"

Drizzt and Wulfgar looked at each other with knowing smiles.

It was indeed going to be an interesting adventure.

And with the rising sun at their back, their shadows standing long before them, they started off on their way.

To find Mithral Hall.

STREAMS OF SILVER

THE LEGEND OF DRIZZT BOOK V

On a dark throne in a dark place perched the dragon of shadow. Not a very large wyrm, but foulest of the foul, its mere presence, blackness; its talons, swords worn from a thousand thousand kills; its maw ever warm with the blood of victims; its black breath, despair.

A raven's coat was its tested scales, so rich in their blackness that they shimmered in colors, a scintillating facade of beauty for a soulless monster. Its minions named it Shimmergloom and paid it all honor.

PRELUDE

Gathering its strength over the course of centuries, as dragons do, Shimmergloom kept its wings folded back and moved not at all, except to swallow a sacrifice or to punish an insolent underling. It had done its part to secure this place, routing the bulk of the dwarven army that stood to face its allies.

How well the dragon had eaten that day! The hides of dwarves were tough and muscled, but a razor-toothed maw was well suited to such a meal.

And now the dragon's many slaves did all the work, bringing it food and heeding to its every desire. The day would come when they would need the power of the dragon again, and Shimmergloom would be ready. The huge mound of plundered treasures beneath it fueled the dragon's strength, and in this respect, Shimmergloom was surpassed by none of its kind, possessing a hoard beyond the imagination of the richest kings.

And a host of loyal minions, willing slaves to the dragon of darkness.

⋈ ⋈ ⋈ ⋈ ⋈

The chill wind that gave Icewind Dale its name whistled across their ears, its incessant groan eliminating the casual conversation the four friends usually enjoyed. They moved west across the barren tundra, and the wind, as always, came from the east, behind them, quickening their already strong pace.

Their posture and the determined drive of their strides reflected the eagerness of a newly begun quest, but the set of each adventurer's face revealed a different perspective of the journey.

The dwarf, Bruenor Battlehammer, leaned forward from his waist, his stocky legs pumping mightily beneath him, and his pointed nose, poking out above the shag of his wagging red beard, led the way. He seemed set in stone, apart from his legs and beard, with his many-notched axe held firmly before him in his gnarled hands, his shield, emblazoned with the standard of the foaming mug, strapped tightly on the back of his overstuffed pack, and his head, adorned in a many-dented horned helm, never turning to either side. Neither did his eyes deviate from the path and rarely did they blink. Bruenor had initiated this journey to find the ancient homeland of Clan Battlehammer, and though he fully realized that the silvery halls of his childhood were hundreds of miles away, he stomped along with the fervor of one whose long-awaited goal is clearly in sight.

Beside Bruenor, the huge barbarian, too, was anxious. Wulfgar loped along smoothly, the great strides of his long legs easily matching the dwarf's rolling pace. There was a sense of urgency about him, like a spirited horse on a short rein. Fires hungry for adventure burned in his pale eyes as clearly as in Bruenor's, but unlike the dwarf, Wulfgar's gaze was not fixed upon the straight road before them. He was a young man out to view the wide world for the first time and he continually looked about, soaking up every sight and sensation that the landscape had to offer.

He had come along to aid his friends on their adventure, but he had come, as well, to expand the horizons of his own world. The entirety of his young life had been spent within the isolating natural boundaries of Icewind Dale, limiting his experiences to the ancient ways of his fellow barbarian tribesmen and the frontier people of Ten-Towns.

There was more out there, Wulfgar knew, and he was determined to grasp as much of it as he possibly could.

Less interested was Drizzt Do'Urden, the cloaked figure trotting easily beside Wulfgar. His floating gait showed him to be of elf heritage, but the shadows of his low-pulled cowl suggested something else. Drizzt was a drow, a black elf, denizen of the lightless underworld. He had spent several years on the surface, denying his heritage, yet had found that he could not escape the aversion to the sun inherent in his people.

And so he sunk low within the shadow of his cowl, his stride nonchalant, even resigned, this trip being merely a continuation of his existence, another adventure in a life-long string of adventures. Forsaking his people in the dark city of Menzoberranzan, Drizzt Do'Urden had willingly embarked upon the road of the nomad. He knew that he would never be truly accepted anywhere on the surface; perceptions of his people were too vile (and rightly so) for even the most tolerant of communities to take him in. The road was his home now; he was always traveling to avoid the inevitable heartache of being forced from a place that he might have come to love.

Ten-Towns had been a temporary sanctuary. The forlorn wilderness settlement housed a large proportion of rogues and outcasts and though Drizzt wasn't openly welcomed, his hard-earned reputation as a guardian of the towns' borders had granted him a small measure of respect and tolerance from many of the settlers. Bruenor named him a true friend, though, and Drizzt had willingly set out beside the dwarf on the trek, despite his apprehension that once he moved out beyond the influence of his reputation, the treatment he received would be less than civil.

Every so often, Drizzt dropped back the dozen yards or so to check on the fourth member of the party. Huffing and puffing, Regis the halfling brought up the rear of the troupe (and not by choice) with a belly too round for the road and legs too short to match the pumping strides of the dwarf. Paying now for the months of luxury he had enjoyed in the palatial house in Bryn Shander, Regis cursed the turn of luck that had forced him to the road. His greatest love was comfort and he worked at perfecting the arts of eating and sleeping as diligently as a young lad with dreams of heroic deeds swung his first sword. His friends were truly surprised when he joined them on the road, but they were happy to have him along, and even Bruenor, so desperate to see his ancient homeland again, took care not to set the pace too far beyond Regis's ability to keep up.

Certainly Regis pushed himself to his physical limits, and without his customary complaining. Unlike his companions, though, whose eyes looked to the road up ahead, he kept glancing back over his shoulder, back toward Ten-Towns and the home he had so mysteriously abandoned to join in the journey.

Drizzt noted this with some concern.

Regis was running away from something.

⚔ ⚔ ⚔ ⚔ ⚔

The companions kept their westerly course for several days. To their south, the snow-capped peaks of the jagged mountains, the Spine of the World, paralleled their journey. This range marked the southern boundary to Icewind Dale and the companions kept an eye out for its end. When the westernmost peaks died away to flat ground, they would turn south, down the pass between the mountains and the sea, running out of the dale altogether and down the last hundred mile stretch to the coastal city of Luskan.

Out on the trail each morning before the sun rose at their backs, they continued running into the last pink lines of sunset, stopping to make camp at the very last opportunity before the chill wind took on its icy nighttime demeanor.

Then they were back on the trail again before dawn, each running within the solitude of his own perspectives and fears.

A silent journey, save the endless murmur of the eastern wind.

PART ONE

SEARCHES

I pray that the world never runs out of dragons. I say that in all sincerity, though I have played a part in the death of one great wyrm. For the dragon is the quintessential enemy, the greatest foe, the unconquerable epitome of devastation. The dragon, above all other creatures, even the demons and the devils, evokes images of dark grandeur, of the greatest beast curled asleep on the greatest treasure hoard. They are the ultimate test of the hero and the ultimate fright of the child. They are older than the elves and more akin to the earth than the dwarves. The great dragons are the preternatural beast, the basic element of the beast, that darkest part of our imagination.

The wizards cannot tell you of their origin, though they believe that a great wizard, a god of wizards, must have played some role in the first spawning of the beast. The elves, with their long fables explaining the creation of every aspect of the world, have many ancient tales concerning the origin of the dragons, but they admit, privately, that they really have no idea of how the dragons came to be.

My own belief is more simple, and yet, more complicated by far. I believe that dragons appeared in the world immediately after the spawning of the first reasoning race. I do not credit any god of wizards with their creation, but rather, the most basic imagination, wrought of unseen fears, of those first reasoning mortals.

We make the dragons as we make the gods, because we need them, because, somewhere deep in our hearts, we recognize that a world without them is a world not worth living in.

There are so many people in the land who want an answer, a definitive answer, for everything in life, and even for everything after life. They study and they test, and because those few find the answers for some simple questions, they assume that there are answers to be had for every question. What was the world like before there were people? Was there nothing but darkness before the sun and the stars? Was there anything at all? What were we, each of us, before we were born? And what, most importantly of all, shall we be after we die?

Out of compassion, I hope that those questioners never find that which they seek.

One self-proclaimed prophet came through Ten-Towns denying the possibility of an afterlife, claiming that those people who had died and were raised by priests, had, in fact, never died, and that their claims of experiences beyond the grave were an elaborate trick played on them by their own hearts, a ruse to ease the path to nothingness. For that is all there was, he said, an emptiness, a nothingness.

Never in my life have I ever heard one begging so desperately for someone to prove him wrong.

For what are we left with if there remains no mystery? What hope might we find if we know all of the answers?

What is it within us, then, that so desperately wants to deny magic and to unravel mystery? Fear, I presume, based on the many uncertainties of life and the greatest uncertainty of death. Put those fears aside, I say, and live free of them, for if we just step back and watch the truth of the world, we will find that there is indeed magic all about us, unexplainable by numbers and formulas. What is the passion evoked by the stirring speech of the commander before the desperate battle, if not magic? What is the peace that an infant might know in its mother's arms, if not magic? What is love, if not magic?

No, I would not want to live in a world without dragons, as I would not want to live in a world without magic, for that is a world without mystery, and that is a world without faith.

And that, I fear, for any reasoning, conscious being, would be the cruelest trick of all.

—Drizzt Do'Urden

I
A Dagger at Their Backs

He kept his cloak pulled tightly about him, though little light seeped in through the curtained windows, for this was his existence, secretive and alone. The way of the assassin.

While other people went about their lives basking in the pleasures of the sunlight and the welcomed visibility of their neighbors, Artemis Entreri kept to the shadows, the dilated orbs of his eyes focused on the narrow path he must take to accomplish his latest mission.

He truly was a professional, possibly the finest in the entire realms at his dark craft, and when he sniffed out the trail of his prey, the victim never escaped. So the assassin was unbothered by the empty house that he found in Bryn Shander, the principal city of the ten settlements in the wasteland of Icewind Dale. Entreri had suspected that the halfling had slipped out of Ten-Towns. But no matter; if this was indeed the same halfling that he had sought all the way from Calimport, a thousand miles and more to the south, he had made better progress than he ever could have hoped. His mark had no more than a two-tenday head start and the trail would be fresh indeed.

Entreri moved through the house silently and calmly, seeking hints of the halfling's life here that would give him the edge in their inevitable confrontation. Clutter greeted him in every room—the halfling had left in a hurry, probably aware that the assassin was closing in. Entreri considered this a good sign, further heightening his suspicions that this halfling, Regis, was the same Regis who had served the Pasha Pook those years ago in the distant southern city.

The assassin smiled evilly at the thought that the halfling knew he was being stalked, adding to the challenge of the hunt as Entreri pitted his stalking prowess against his intended victim's hiding ability. But the end result was predictable, Entreri knew, for a frightened person invariably made a fatal mistake.

The assassin found what he was looking for in a desk drawer in the master bedroom. Fleeing in haste, Regis had neglected to take precautions to conceal his true identity. Entreri held the small ring up before his gleaming eyes, studying the inscription that clearly identified Regis as a member of Pasha Pook's thieves' guild in Calimport. Entreri closed his fist about the signet, the evil smile widening across his face.

"I have found you, little thief," he laughed into the emptiness of the room. "Your fate is sealed. There is nowhere for you to run!"

His expression changed abruptly to one of alertness as the sound of a key in the palatial house's front door echoed up the hallway of the grand staircase. He dropped the ring into his bell pouch and slipped, as silent as death, to the shadows of the top posts of the stairway's heavy banister.

The large double doors swung open, and a man and a young woman stepped in from the porch ahead of two dwarves. Entreri knew the man, Cassius, the spokesman of Bryn Shander. This had been his home once, but he had relinquished it several months earlier to Regis, after the halfling's heroic actions in the town's battle against the evil wizard, Akar Kessell, and his goblin minions.

Entreri had seen the other human before, as well, though he hadn't yet discovered her connection to Regis. Beautiful women were a rarity in this remote setting, and this young woman was indeed the exception. Shiny auburn locks danced gaily about her shoulders, the intense sparkle of her dark blue eyes enough to bind any man hopelessly within their depths.

Her name, the assassin had learned, was Catti-brie. She lived with the dwarves in their valley north of the city, particularly with the leader of the dwarven clan, Bruenor, who had adopted her as his own a dozen years before when a goblin raid had left her orphaned.

This could prove a valuable meeting, Entreri mused. He cocked an ear through the banister poles to hear the discussion below.

"He's been gone but a tenday!" Catti-brie argued.

"A tenday with no word," snapped Cassius, obviously upset. "With my beautiful house empty and unguarded. Why, the front door was unlocked when I came by a few days ago!"

"Ye gave the house to Regis," Catti-brie reminded the man.

"Loaned!" Cassius roared, though in truth the house had indeed been a gift. The spokesman had quickly regretted turning over to Regis the key to this palace, the grandest house north of Mirabar. In retrospect, Cassius understood that he had been caught up in the fervor of that tremendous victory over the goblins, and he suspected that Regis had lifted his emotions even a step further by using the reputed hypnotic powers of the ruby pendant.

Like others who had been duped by the persuasive halfling, Cassius had come to a very different perspective on the events that had transpired, a perspective that painted Regis unfavorably.

"No matter the name ye call it," Catti-brie conceded, "ye should not be so hasty to decide that, Regis has forsaken the house."

The spokesman's face reddened in fury. "Everything out today!" he demanded. "You have my list. I want all of the halfling's belongings out of my house! Any that remain when I return tomorrow shall become my own by the rights of possession! And I warn you, I shall be compensated dearly if any of my property is missing or damaged!" He turned on his heel and stormed out the doors.

"He's got his hair up about this one," chuckled Fender Mallot, one of the dwarves. "Never have I seen one whose friends swing from loyalty to hatred more than Regis!"

Catti-brie nodded in agreement of Fender's observation. She knew that Regis played with magical charms, and she figured that his paradoxical relationships with those around him were an unfortunate side effect of his dabblings.

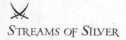

"Do ye suppose he's off with Drizzt and Bruenor?" Fender asked. Up the stairs, Entreri shifted anxiously.

"Not to doubt," Catti-brie answered. "All winter they've been asking him to join in the quest for Mithral Hall, an' to be sure, Wulfgar's joining added to the pressure."

"Then the little one's halfway to Luskan, or more," reasoned Fender. "And Cassius is right in wantin' his house back."

"Then let us get to packing," said Catti-brie. "Cassius has enough o' his own without adding to the hoard from Regis's goods."

Entreri leaned back against the banister. The name of Mithral Hall was unknown to him, but he knew the way to Luskan well enough. He grinned again, wondering if he might catch them before they ever reached the port city.

First, though, he knew that there still might be some valuable information to be garnered here. Catti-brie and the dwarves set about the task of collecting the halfling's belongings, and as they moved from room to room, the black shadow of Artemis Entreri, as silent as death, hovered about them. They never suspected his presence, never would have guessed that the gentle ripple in the drapes was anything more than a draft flowing in from the edges of the window, or that the shadow behind a chair was disproportionately long.

He managed to stay close enough to hear nearly all of their conversation, and Catti-brie and the dwarves spoke of little else than the four adventurers and their journey to Mithral Hall. But Entreri learned little for his efforts. He already knew of the halfling's famed companions—everyone in Ten-Towns spoke of them often: of Drizzt Do'Urden, the renegade drow elf, who had forsaken his darkskinned people in the bowels of the Realms and roamed the borders of Ten-Towns as a solitary guardian against the intrusions of the wilderness of Icewind Dale; of Bruenor Battlehammer, the rowdy leader of the dwarven clan that lived in the valley near Kelvin's Cairn; and most of all, of Wulfgar, the mighty barbarian, who was captured and raised to adulthood by Bruenor, returned with the savage tribes of the dale to defend Ten-Towns against the goblin army, then struck up a truce between all the peoples of Icewind Dale. A bargain that had salvaged, and promised to enrich, the lives of all involved.

"It seems that you have surrounded yourself with formidable allies, halfling," Entreri mused, leaning against the back of a large chair, as Catti-brie and the dwarves moved into an adjoining room. "Little help they will offer. You are mine!"

Catti-brie and the dwarves worked for about an hour, filling two large sacks, primarily with clothes. Catti-brie was astounded with the stock of possessions Regis had collected since his reputed heroics against Kessell and the goblins—mostly gifts from grateful citizens. Well aware of the halfling's love of comfort, she could not understand what had possessed him to run off down the road after the others. But what truly amazed her was that Regis hadn't hired porters to bring along at least a few of his belongings. And the more of his treasures that she discovered as she moved through the palace, the more this whole scenario of haste and impulse bothered her. It was too out of character for Regis. There had to be another factor, some missing element, that she hadn't yet weighed.

"Well, we got more'n we can carry, and most o' the stuff anyway!" declared Fender, hoisting a sack over his sturdy shoulder. "Leave the rest for Cassius to sort, I say!"

"I would no' give Cassius the pleasure of claiming any of the things," Catti-brie retorted. "There may yet be valued items to be found. Two of ye take the sacks back t' our rooms at the inn. I'll be finishing the work up here."

"Ah, yer too good to Cassius," Fender grumbled. "Bruenor had him marked right as a man taking too much pleasure in counting what he owns!"

"Be fair, Fender Mallot," Catti-brie retorted, though her agreeing smile belied any harshness in her tone. "Cassius served the towns well in the war and has been a fine leader for the people of Bryn Shander. Ye've seen as well as meself that Regis has a talent for putting up a cat's fur!"

Fender chuckled in agreement. "For all his ways of gettin' what he wants, the little one has left a row or two of ruffled victims!" He patted the other dwarf on the shoulder and they headed for the main door.

"Don't ye be late, girl," Fender called back to Catti-brie. "We're to the mines again. Tomorrow, no later!"

"Ye fret too much, Fender Mallot!" Catti-brie said, laughing.

Entreri considered the last exchange and again a smile widened across his face. He knew well the wake of magical charms. The "ruffled victims" that Fender had spoken of described exactly the people that Pasha Pook had duped back in Calimport. People charmed by the ruby pendant.

The double doors closed with a bang. Catti-brie was alone in the big house—or so she thought.

She was still pondering Regis's uncharacteristic disappearance. Her continued suspicions that something was wrong, that some piece of the puzzle was missing, began to foster within her the sense that something was wrong here in the house, as well.

Catti-brie suddenly became aware of every noise and shadow around her. The "click-click" of a pendulum clock. The rustle of papers on a desk in front of an open window. The swish of drapes. The scutterings of a mouse within the wooden walls.

Her eyes darted back to the drapes, still trembling slightly from their last movement. It could have been a draft through a crack in the window, but the alert woman suspected differently. Reflexively dropping to a crouch and reaching for the dagger on her hip, she started toward the open doorway a few feet to the side of the drapes.

Entreri had moved quickly. Suspecting that more could yet be learned from Catti-brie, and not willing to pass up the opportunity offered by the dwarves' departure, he had slipped into the most favorable position for an attack and now waited patiently atop the narrow perch of the open door, balanced as easily as a cat on a window sill. He listened for her approach, his dagger turning over casually in his hand.

Catti-brie sensed the danger as soon as she reached the doorway and saw the black form dropping to her side. But as quick as her reactions were, her own dagger was not halfway from its sheath before the thin fingers of a cool hand had clamped over her mouth, stifling a cry, and the razored edge of a jeweled dagger had creased a light line on her throat.

She was stunned and appalled. Never had she seen a man move so quickly, and the deadly precision of Entreri's strike unnerved her. A sudden tenseness in his muscles assured her that if she persisted in drawing her weapon, she would be dead long before she could use it. Releasing the hilt, she made no further move to resist.

The assassin's strength also surprised her as he easily lifted her to a chair. He was a small man, slender as an elf and barely as tall as she, but every muscle on his compact frame was toned to its finest fighting edge. His very presence exuded an aura of strength and an unshakable confidence. This, too, unnerved Catti-brie, because it wasn't the brash cockiness of an exuberant youngster, but the cool air of superiority of one who had seen a thousand fights and had never been bested.

Catti-brie's eyes never turned from Entreri's face as he quickly tied her to the chair. His angular features, striking cheekbones and a strong jaw line, were only sharpened by the straight cut of his raven black hair. The shadow of beard that darkened his face appeared as if no amount of shaving could ever lighten it. Far from unkempt, though, everything about the man spoke of control. Catti-brie might even have considered him handsome, except for his eyes.

Their gray showed no sparkle. Lifeless, devoid of any hint of compassion or humanity, they marked this man as an instrument of death and nothing more.

"What do ye want o' me?" Catti-brie asked when she mustered the nerve.

Entreri answered with a stinging slap across her face. "The ruby pendant!" he demanded suddenly. "Does the halfling still wear the ruby pendant?"

Catti-brie fought to stifle the tears welling in her eyes. She was disoriented and off guard and could not respond immediately to the man's question.

The jeweled dagger flashed before her eyes and slowly traced the circumference of her face.

"I have not much time," Entreri declared flatly. "You will tell me what I need to know. The longer it takes you to answer, the more pain you will feel."

His words were calm and spoken with honesty.

Catti-brie, toughened under Bruenor's own tutelage, found herself unnerved. She had faced and defeated goblins before, even a horrid troll once, but this collected killer terrified her. She tried to respond, but her trembling jaw would allow no words.

The dagger flashed again.

"Regis wears it!" Catti-brie shrieked, a tear tracing a solitary line down each of her cheeks.

Entreri nodded and smiled slightly. "He is with the dark elf, the dwarf, and the barbarian," he said matter-of-factly. "And they are on the road to Luskan. And from there, to a place called Mithral Hall. Tell me of Mithral Hall, dear girl." He scraped the blade on his own cheek, its fine edge poignantly clearing a small patch of beard. "Where does it lie?"

Catti-brie realized that her inability to answer would probably spell her end. "I-I know not," she stammered boldly, regaining a measure of the discipline that Bruenor had taught her, though her eyes never left the glint of the deadly blade.

"A pity," Entreri replied. "Such a pretty face . . ."

"Please," Catti-brie said as calmly as she could with the dagger moving toward her. "Not a one knows! Not even Bruenor! To find it is his quest."

The blade stopped suddenly and Entreri turned his head to the side, eyes narrowed and all of his muscles taut and alert.

Catti-brie hadn't heard the turn of the door handle, but the deep voice of Fender Mallot echoing down the hallway explained the assassin's actions.

"'Ere, where are ye, girl?"

Catti-brie tried to yell, "Run!" and her own life be damned, but Entreri's quick backhand dazed her and drove the word out as an indecipherable grunt.

Her head lolling to the side, she just managed to focus her vision as Fender and Grollo, battle-axes in hand, burst into the room. Entreri stood ready to meet them, jeweled dagger in one hand and a saber in the other.

For an instant, Catti-brie was filled with elation. The dwarves of Ten-Towns were an iron-fisted battalion of hardened warriors, with Fender's prowess in battle among the clan second only to Bruenor's.

Then she remembered who they faced, and despite their apparent advantage, her hopes were washed away by a wave of undeniable conclusions. She had witnessed the blur of the assassin's movements, the uncanny precision of his cuts.

Revulsion welling in her throat, she couldn't even gasp for the dwarves to flee.

Even had they known the depths of the horror in the man standing before them, Fender and Grollo would not have turned away. Outrage blinds a dwarven fighter from any regard for personal safety, and when these two saw their beloved Catti-brie bound to the chair, their charge at Entreri came by instinct.

Fueled by unbridled rage, their first attacks roared in with every ounce of strength they could call upon. Conversely, Entreri started slowly, finding a rhythm and allowing the sheer fluidity of his motions to build his momentum. At times he seemed barely able to parry or dodge the ferocious swipes. Some missed their mark by barely an inch, and the near hits spurred Fender and Grollo on even further.

But even with her friends pressing the attack, Catti-brie understood that they were in trouble. Entreri's hands seemed to talk to each other, so perfect was the complement of their movements as they positioned the jeweled dagger and saber. The synchronous shufflings of his feet kept him in complete balance throughout the melee. His was a dance of dodges, parries, and counterslashes.

His was a dance of death.

Catti-brie had seen this before, the telltale methods of the finest swordsman in all of Icewind Dale. The comparison to Drizzt Do'Urden was inescapable; their grace and movements were so alike, with every part of their bodies working in harmony.

But they remained strikingly different, a polarity of morals that subtly altered the aura of the dance.

The drow ranger in battle was an instrument of beauty to behold, a perfect athlete pursuing his chosen course of righteousness with unsurpassed fervor. But Entreri was merely horrifying, a passionless murderer callously disposing of obstacles in his path.

The initial momentum of the dwarves' attack began to diminish now, and both Fender and Grollo wore a look of amazement that the floor was not yet red with their opponent's blood. But while their attacks were slowing, Entreri's momentum continued to build. His blades were a blur, each thrust followed by two others that left the dwarves rocking back on their heels.

Effortless, his movements. Endless, his energy.

Fender and Grollo maintained a solely defensive posture, but even with all of their efforts devoted to blocking, everyone in the room knew that it was only a matter of time before a killing blade slipped through.

Catti-brie didn't see the fatal cut, but she saw vividly the bright line of blood that appeared across Grollo's throat. The dwarf continued fighting for a few moments, oblivious to the cause of his inability to find his breath. Then, startled, Grollo dropped to his knees, grasping his throat, and gurgled into the blackness of death.

Fury spurred Fender beyond his exhaustion. His axe chopped and cut wildly, screaming for revenge.

Entreri toyed with him, actually carrying the charade so far as to slap him on the side of the head with the flat of the saber.

Outraged, insulted, and fully aware that he was overmatched, Fender launched himself into a final, suicidal, charge, hoping to bring the assassin down with him.

Entreri sidestepped the desperate lunge with an amused laugh, and ended the fight, driving the jeweled dagger deep into Fender's chest, and following through with a skull-splitting slash of the saber as the dwarf stumbled by.

Too horrified to cry, too horrified to scream, Catti-brie watched blankly as Entreri retrieved the dagger from Fender's chest. Certain of her own impending death, she closed her eyes as the dagger came toward her, felt its metal, hot from the dwarf's blood, flat on her throat.

And then the teasing scrape of its edge against her soft, vulnerable skin as Entreri slowly turned the blade over in his hand.

Tantalizing. The promise, the dance of death.

Then it was gone. Catti-brie opened her eyes just as the small blade went back into its scabbard on the assassin's hip. He had taken a step back from her.

"You see," he offered in simple explanation of his mercy, "I kill only those who stand to oppose me. Perhaps, then, three of your friends on the road to Luskan shall escape the blade. I want only the halfling."

Catti-brie refused to yield to the terror he evoked. She held her voice steady and promised coldly, "You underestimate them. They will fight you."

With calm confidence, Entreri replied, "Then they, too, shall die."

Catti-brie couldn't win in a contest of nerves with the dispassionate killer. Her only answer to him was her defiance. She spat at him, unafraid of the consequences.

He retorted with a single stinging backhand, Her eyes blurred in pain and welling tears, and Catti-brie slumped into blackness. But as she fell unconscious, she heard a few seconds longer, the cruel, passionless laughter fading away as the assassin moved from the house.

Tantalizing. The promise of death.

2

CITY OF SAILS

"Well, there she is, lad, the City of Sails," Bruenor said to Wulfgar as the two looked down upon Luskan from a small knoll a few miles north of the city.

Wulfgar took in the view with a profound sigh of admiration. Luskan housed more than fifteen thousand small compared to the huge cities in the south and to its nearest neighbor, Waterdeep, a few hundred miles farther down the coast. But to the young barbarian, who had spent all of his eighteen years among nomadic tribes and the small villages of Ten-Towns, the fortified seaport seemed grand indeed. A wall encompassed Luskan, with guard towers strategically spaced at varying intervals. Even from this distance, Wulfgar could make out the dark forms of many soldiers pacing the parapets, their spear tips shining in the new light of the day.

"Not a promising invitation," Wulfgar noted.

"Luskan does not readily welcome visitors," said Drizzt, who had come up behind his two friends. "They may open their gates for merchants, but ordinary travelers are usually turned away."

"Our first contact is there," growled Bruenor. "And I mean to get in!"

Drizzt nodded and did not press the argument. He had given Luskan a wide berth on his original journey to Ten-Towns. The city's inhabitants, primarily human, looked upon other faces with disdain. Even surface elves and dwarves were often refused entry. Drizzt suspected that the guards would do more to a drow elf than simply put him out.

"Get the breakfast fire burning," Bruenor continued, his angry tones reflecting his determination that nothing would turn him from his course. "We're to break camp early, an' make the gates 'fore noon. Where's that blasted Rumblebelly?"

Drizzt looked back over his shoulder in the direction of the camp. "Asleep," he answered, though Bruenor's question was wholly rhetorical. Regis had been the first to bed and the last to awaken (and never without help) every day since the companions had set out from Ten-Towns.

"Well, give him a kick!" Bruenor ordered. He turned back to the camp, but Drizzt put a hand on his arm to stay him.

"Let the halfling sleep," the drow suggested. "Perhaps it would be better if we came to Luskan's gate in the less revealing light of dusk."

Drizzt's request confused Bruenor for just a moment—until he looked more closely at the drow's sullen visage and recognized the trepidation in his eyes. The two had become so close in their years of friendship that Bruenor often forgot that Drizzt was an outcast. The farther they traveled from Ten-Towns, where Drizzt was known, the more he would be judged by the color of his skin and the reputation of his people.

"Aye, let 'im sleep," Bruenor conceded. "Maybe I could use a bit more, meself!"

They broke camp late that morning and set a leisurely pace, only to discover later that they had misjudged the distance to the city. It was well past sunset and into the early hours of darkness when they finally arrived at the city's north gate.

The structure was as unwelcoming as Luskan's reputation: a single iron-bound door set into the stone wall between two short, squared towers was tightly shut before them. A dozen fur-capped heads poked out from the parapet above the gate and the companions sensed many more eyes, and probably bows, trained upon them from the darkness atop the towers.

"Who are you who come to the gates of Luskan?" came a voice from the wall.

"Travelers from the north," answered Bruenor. "A weary band come all the way from Ten-Towns in Icewind Dale!"

"The gate closed at sunset," replied the voice. "Go away!"

"Son of a hairless gnoll," grumbled Bruenor under his breath. He slapped his axe across his hands as though he meant to chop the door down.

Drizzt put a calming hand on the dwarf's shoulder, his own sensitive ears recognizing the clear, distinctive click of a crossbow crank.

Then Regis unexpectedly took control of the situation. He straightened his pants, which had dropped below the bulge of his belly, and hooked his thumbs in his belt, trying to appear somewhat important. Throwing his shoulders back he walked out in front of his companions.

"Your name, good sir?" he called to the soldier on the wall.

"I am the Nightkeeper of the North Gate. That is all you need to know!" came the gruff reply. "And who—"

"Regis, First Citizen of Bryn Shander. No doubt you have heard my name or seen my carvings."

The companions heard whispers up above, then a pause. "We have viewed the scrimshaw of a halfling from Ten-Towns. Are you he?"

"Hero of the goblin war and master scrimshander," Regis declared, bowing low. "The spokesmen of Ten-Towns will not be pleased to learn that I was turned into the night at the gate of our favored trading partner."

Again came the whispers, then a longer silence. Presently the four heard a grating sound behind the door, a portcullis being raised, knew Regis, and then the banging of the door's bolts being thrown. The halfling looked back over his shoulder at his surprised friends and smiled wryly.

"Diplomacy, my rough dwarven friend," he laughed.

The door opened just a crack and two men slipped out, unarmed but cautious. It was quite obvious that they were well protected from the wall. Grim-faced soldiers huddled along the parapets, monitoring every move the strangers made through the sights of crossbows.

"I am Jierdan," said the stockier of the two men, though it was difficult to judge his exact size because of the many layers of fur he wore.

"And I am the Nightkeeper," said the other. "Show me what you have brought to trade."

"Trade?" echoed Bruenor angrily. "Who said anything about trade?" He slapped his axe across his hands again, drawing nervous shufflings from above. "Does this look like the blade of a stinkin' merchant?"

Regis and Drizzt both moved to calm the dwarf, though Wulfgar, as tense as Bruenor, stayed off to the side, his huge arms crossed before him and his stern gaze boring into the impudent gatekeeper.

The two soldiers backed away defensively and the Nightkeeper spoke again, this time on the edge of fury. "First Citizen," he demanded of Regis, "why do you come to our door?"

Regis stepped in front of Bruenor and steadied himself squarely before the soldier. "Er . . . a preliminary scouting of the marketplace," he blurted out, trying to fabricate a story as he went along. "I have some especially fine carvings for market this season and I wanted to be certain that everything on this end, including the paying price for scrimshaw, shall be in place to handle the sale."

The two soldiers exchanged knowing smiles. "You have come a long way for such a purpose," the Nightkeeper whispered harshly. "Would you not have been better suited to simply come down with the caravan bearing the goods?"

Regis squirmed uncomfortably, realizing that these soldiers were far too experienced to fall for his ploy. Fighting his better judgement, he reached under his shirt for the ruby pendant, knowing that its hypnotic powers could convince the Nightkeeper to let them through, but dreading showing the stone at all and further opening the trail for the assassin that he knew wasn't far behind.

Jierdan started suddenly, however, as he noticed the figure standing beside Bruenor. Drizzt Do'Urden's cloak had shifted slightly, revealing the black skin of his face.

As if on cue, the Nightkeeper tensed as well and following his companion's lead, quickly discerned the cause of Jierdan's sudden reaction. Reluctantly, the four adventurers dropped their hands to their weapons, ready for a fight they didn't want.

But Jierdan ended the tension as quickly as he had begun it, by bringing his arm across the chest of the Nightkeeper and addressing the drow openly.

"Drizzt Do'Urden?" he asked calmly, seeking confirmation of the identity he had already guessed.

The drow nodded, surprised at the recognition.

"Your name, too, has come down to Luskan with the tales from Icewind Dale," Jierdan explained. "Pardon our surprise." He bowed low. "We do not see many of your race at our gates."

Drizzt nodded again, but did not answer, uncomfortable with this unusual attention, Never before had a gatekeeper bothered to ask him his name or his business. And the drow had quickly come to understand the advantage of avoiding gates altogether, silently slipping over a city's wall in the darkness and seeking the seedier side, where he might at least have a chance of standing unnoticed in the dark corners with the other rogues. Had his name and heroics brought him a measure of respect even this far from Ten-Towns?

Bruenor turned to Drizzt and winked, his own anger dissipated by the fact that his friend had finally been given his due from a stranger.

But Drizzt wasn't convinced. He didn't dare hope for such a thing—it left him too vulnerable to feelings that he had fought hard to hide. He preferred to keep his suspicions and his guard as close to him as the dark cowl of his cloak. He cocked a curious ear as the two soldiers backed away to hold a private conversation.

"I care not of his name," he heard the Nightkeeper whisper at Jierdan. "No drow elf shall pass my gate!"

"You err," Jierdan retorted. "These are the heroes of Ten-Towns. The halfling is truly First Citizen of Bryn Shander, the drow a ranger with a deadly, but undeniably honorable, reputation, and the dwarf—note the foaming mug standard on his shield—is Bruenor Battlehammer, leader of his clan in the dale."

"And what of the giant barbarian?" asked the Nightkeeper, using a sarcastic tone in an attempt to sound unimpressed, though he was obviously a bit nervous. "What rogue might he be?"

Jierdan shrugged. "His great size, his youth, and a measure of control beyond his years. It seems unlikely to me that he should be here, but he might be the young king of the tribes that the tale-tellers have spoken of.

We should not turn these travelers away; the consequences may be grave."

"What could Luskan possibly fear from the puny settlements in Icewind Dale?" the Nightkeeper balked.

"There are other trading ports," Jierdan retorted. "Not every battle is fought with a sword. The loss of Ten-Towns' scrimshaw would not be viewed favorably by our merchants, nor by the trading ships that put in each season."

The Nightkeeper scrutinized the four strangers again. He didn't trust them at all, despite his companion's grand claims, and he didn't want them in his city. But he knew, too, that if his suspicions were wrong and he did something to jeopardize the scrimshaw trade, his own future would be bleak. The soldiers of Luskan answered to the merchants, who were not quick to forgive errors that thinned their purses.

The Nightkeeper threw up his hands in defeat. "Go in, then," he told the companions. "Keep to the wall and make your way down to the docks. The last lane holds the Cutlass, and you'll be warm enough there!"

Drizzt studied the proud strides of his friends as they marched through the door, and he guessed that they had also overheard pieces of the conversation. Bruenor confirmed his suspicions when they had moved away from the guard towers, down the road along the wall.

"Here, elf," the dwarf snorted, nudging Drizzt and being obviously pleased. "So the word's gone beyond the dale and we're heared of even this far south. What have ye to say o' that?"

Drizzt shrugged again and Bruenor chuckled, assuming that his friend was merely embarrassed by the fame. Regis and Wulfgar, too, shared in Bruenor's mirth, the big man giving the drow a good-hearted slap on the back as he slipped to the lead of the troupe.

But Drizzt's discomfort stemmed from more than embarrassment. He had noted the grin on Jierdan's face as they had passed, a smile that went beyond admiration. And while he had no doubts that some tales of the battle with Akar Kessell's goblin army had reached the City of Sails, it struck Drizzt odd that a simple soldier knew so much about him and his friends, while the gatekeeper, solely responsible for determining who passed into the city, knew nothing.

Luskan's streets were tightly packed with two- and three-story buildings, a reflection of the desperation of the people there to huddle within the safety of the city's high wall, away from the ever-present dangers of the savage northland. An occasional tower, a guard post, perhaps, or a prominent citizen's or guild's way to show superiority, sprouted from the roofline. A wary city, Luskan survived, even flourished, in the dangerous frontier by holding fast to an attitude of alertness that often slipped over the line into paranoia. It was a city of shadows, and the four visitors this night keenly felt the curious and dangerous stares peeking out from every darkened hole as they made their way.

The docks harbored the roughest section of the city, where thieves, outlaws, and beggars abounded in their narrow alleys and shadowed crannies. A perpetual ground fog wafted in from the sea, blurring the already dim avenues into even more mysterious pathways.

Such was the lane the four friends found themselves turning down, the last lane before the piers themselves, a particularly decrepit run called Half-Moon Street. Regis, Drizzt, and Bruenor knew immediately that they had entered a collecting ground for vagabonds and ruffians, and each put a hand to his weapon. Wulfgar walked openly and without fear, though he, too, sensed the threatening atmosphere. Not understanding that the area was atypically foul, he was determined to approach his first experience with civilization with an open mind.

"There's the place," said Bruenor, indicating a small group, probably thieves, congregating before the doorway of a tavern. The weatherbeaten sign above the door named the place the Cutlass.

Regis swallowed hard, a frightening mixture of emotions welling within him. In his early days as a thief in Calimport, he had frequented many places like this, but his familiarity with the environment only added to his apprehension. The forbidden allure of business done in the shadows of a dangerous tavern, he knew, could be as deadly as the hidden knives of the rogues at every table. "You truly want to go in there?" he asked his friends squeamishly.

"No arguing from ye!" Bruenor snapped back. "Ye knew the road ahead when ye joined us in the dale. Don't ye be whining now!"

"You are well guarded," Drizzt put in to comfort Regis.

Overly proud in his inexperience, Wulfgar pressed the statement even further. "What cause would they have to do us harm? Surely we have done no wrong," he demanded. Then he proclaimed loudly to challenge the shadows, "Fear not, little friend. My hammer shall sweep aside any who stand against us!"

"The pride o' youth," Bruenor grumbled as he, Regis, and Drizzt exchanged incredulous looks.

⚔ ⚔ ⚔ ⚔

The atmosphere inside the Cutlass was in accord with the decay and rabble that marked the place outside. The tavern portion of the building was a single open room, with a long bar defensively positioned in the corner of the rear wall, directly across from the door. A staircase rose up from the side of the bar to the structure's second level, a staircase more often used by painted, over-perfumed women and their latest companions than by guests of the inn. Indeed, merchant sailors who put into Luskan usually came ashore only for brief periods of excitement and entertainment, returning to the safety of their vessels if they could manage it before the inevitable drunken sleep left them vulnerable.

More than anything else, though, the tavern at the Cutlass was a room of the senses, with myriad sounds and sights and smells. The aroma of alcohol, from strong ale and cheap wine to rarer and more powerful beverages, permeated every corner. A haze of smoke from exotic pipeweeds, like the mist outside, blurred the harsh reality of the images into softer, dreamlike sensations.

Drizzt led the way to an empty table tucked beside the door, while Bruenor approached the bar to make arrangements for their stay. Wulfgar started after the dwarf, but Drizzt stopped him. "To the table," he explained. "You are too excited for such business; Bruenor can take care of it."

Wulfgar started to protest, but was cut short.

"Come on," Regis offered. "Sit with Drizzt and me. No one will bother a tough old dwarf, but a tiny halfling and a skinny elf might look like good sport to the brutes in here. We need your size and strength to deter such unwanted attention."

Wulfgar's chin firmed up at the compliment and he strode boldly toward the table. Regis shot Drizzt a knowing wink and turned to follow.

"Many lessons you will learn on this journey, young friend," Drizzt mumbled to Wulfgar, too softly for the barbarian to hear. "So far from your home."

Bruenor came back from the bar bearing four flagons of mead and grumbling under his breath. "We're to get our business finished soon," he said to Drizzt, "and get back on the road. The cost of a room in this orc-hole is open thievery!"

"The rooms were not meant to be taken for a whole night," Regis snickered.

But Bruenor's scowl remained. "Drink up," he told the drow. "Rat Alley is but a short walk, by the tellin's of the barmaid, and it might be that we can make contact yet this night."

Drizzt nodded and sipped the mead, not really wanting any of it, but hoping that a shared drink might relax the dwarf. The drow, too, was anxious to be gone from Luskan, fearful that his own identity—he kept his cowl pulled even tighter in the tavern's flickering torchlight—might bring them more trouble. He worried further for Wulfgar, young and proud, and out of his element. The barbarians of Icewind Dale, though merciless in battle, were undeniably honorable, basing their society's structure entirely on strict and unbending codes. Drizzt feared that Wulfgar would fall easy prey to the false images and treachery of the city. On the road in the wild lands Wulfgar's hammer would keep him safe enough, but here he was likely to find himself in deceptive situations involving disguised blades, where his mighty weapon and battle-prowess offered little help.

Wulfgar downed his flagon in a single gulp, wiped his lips with zeal, and stood. "Let us be going," he said to Bruenor. "Who is it that we seek?"

"Sit yerself back down and shut yer mouth, boy," Bruenor scolded, glancing around to see if any unwanted attention had fallen upon them. "This night's work is for me and the drow. No place for a too-big fighter like yerself! Ye stay here with Rumblebelly an' keep yer mouth shut and yer back to the wall!"

Wulfgar slumped back in humiliation, but Drizzt was glad that Bruenor seemed to have come to similar conclusions about the young warrior. Once again, Regis saved a measure of Wulfgar's pride.

"You are not leaving with them!" he snapped at the barbarian. "I have no desire to go, but I would not dare to remain here alone. Let Drizzt and Bruenor have their fun in some cold, smelly alley. We'll stay here and enjoy a well-deserved evening of high entertainment!"

Drizzt slapped Regis's knee under the table in thanks and rose to leave. Bruenor quaffed his flagon and leaped from his chair.

"Let's be going, then," he said to the drow. And then to Wulfgar, "Keep care of the halfling, and beware the women! They're mean as starved rats, and the only thing they aim to bite at is your purse!"

Bruenor and Drizzt turned at the first empty alleyway beyond the Cutlass, the dwarf standing nervous guard at its entrance while Drizzt moved down a few steps into the darkness. Convinced that he was safely alone, Drizzt removed from his pouch a small onyx statuette, meticulously carved into the likeness of a hunting cat, and placed it on the ground before him.

"Guenhwyvar," he called softly. "Come, my shadow."

His beckon reached out across the planes, to the astral home of the entity of the panther. The great cat stirred from her sleep. Many months hid passed since her master had called, and the cat was anxious to serve.

Guenhwyvar leaped out across the fabric of the planes, following a flicker of light that could only be the calling of the drow. Then the cat was in the alley with Drizzt, alert at once in the unfamiliar surroundings.

"We walk into a dangerous web, I fear," Drizzt explained. "I need eyes where my own cannot go."

Without delay and without a sound, Guenhwyvar sprang to a pile of rubble, to a broken porch landing, and up to the rooftops. Satisfied, and feeling much more secure now, Drizzt slipped back to the street where Bruenor waited.

"Well, where's that blasted cat?" Bruenor asked, a hint of relief in his voice that Guenhwyvar was actually not with the drow. Most dwarves are suspicious of magic, other than the magical enchantments placed upon weapons, and Bruenor had no love for the panther.

"Where we need her most," was the drow's answer. He started off down Half-Moon Street. "Fear not, mighty Bruenor, Guenhwyvar's eyes are upon us, even if ours cannot return their protective gaze!"

The dwarf glanced all around nervously, beads of sweat visible at the base of his horned helm. He had known Drizzt for several years, but had never gotten comfortable around the magical cat.

Drizzt hid his smile under his cowl.

Each lane, filled with piles of rubble and refuse, appeared the same, as they made their way along the docks. Bruenor eyed each shadowed niche with alert suspicion. His eyes were not as keen in the night as those of the drow, and if he had seen into the darkness as clearly as Drizzt, he might have clutched his axe handle even more tightly.

But the dwarf and drow weren't overly concerned. They were far from typical of the drunkards that usually stumbled into these parts at night, and not easy prey for thieves. The many notches on Bruenor's axe and the sway of the two scimitars on the drow's belt would serve as ample deterrent to most ruffians.

In the maze of streets and alleyways, it took them a long while to find Rat Alley. Just off the piers, it ran parallel to the sea, seemingly impassable through the thick fog. Long, low warehouses lined both its sides, and broken crates and boxes cluttered the alley, reducing the already narrow passage in many places to single-file breadth.

"Nice place to be walkin' down on a gloomy night," Bruenor stated flatly.

"Are you certain that this is the lane?" Drizzt asked, equally unenthused about the area before them.

"By the words o' the merchant in Ten-Towns, if one's alive that can get me the map, the one be Whisper. An' the place to find Whisper is Rat Alley—always Rat Alley."

"Then on with it," said Drizzt. "Foul business is best finished quickly."

Bruenor slowly led the way into the alley. The two had barely gone ten feet when the dwarf thought he heard the click of a crossbow. He stopped short and looked back at Drizzt. "They're on us," he whispered.

"In the boarded window above and to the right of us," Drizzt explained, his exceptional night vision and hearing having already discerned the sound's source. "A precaution, I hope. Perhaps a good sign that your contact is close."

"Never called a crossbow aimed at me head a good sign!" argued the dwarf. "But on, then, and keep yerself at the ready. This place reeks of danger!" He started again through the rubble.

A shuffle to their left told them that eyes were upon them from that way as well. But still they continued, understanding that they couldn't have expected any different a scenario when they had started out from the Cutlass. Rounding a final mound of broken planks, they saw a slender figure leaning against one of the alleyway's walls, cloak pulled tightly against the chill of the evening mist.

Drizzt leaned over Bruenor's shoulder. "May that be the one?" he whispered.

The dwarf shrugged, and said, "Who else?" He took one more step forward, planted his feet firmly, wide apart, and addressed the figure. "I be looking for a man named Whisper," he called. "Might that be yerself?"

"Yes, and no," came the reply. The figure turned toward them, though the low-pulled cloak revealed little.

"What games do ye play?" Bruenor shot back.

"Whisper I am," replied the figure, letting the cloak slip back a little. "But for sure no man!"

They could see clearly now that the figure addressing them was indeed a woman, a dark and mysterious figure with long black hair and deeply set, darting eyes that showed experience and a profound understanding of survival on the street.

3

NIGHT LIFE

The Cutlass grew busier as the night wore on. Merchant sailors crowded in from their ships and the locals were quick into position to feed upon them. Regis and Wulfgar remained at the side table, the barbarian wide-eyed with curiosity at the sights around him, and the halfling intent on cautious observation.

Regis recognized trouble in the form of a woman sauntering toward them. Not a young woman, and with the haggard appearance all too familiar on the dockside, but her gown, quite revealing in every place that a lady's gown should not be, hid all her physical flaws behind a barrage of suggestions. The look on Wulfgar's face, his chin nearly level with the table, Regis thought, confirmed the halfling's fears.

"Well met, big man," the woman purred, slipping comfortably into the chair next to the barbarian.

Wulfgar looked at Regis and nearly laughed out loud in disbelief and embarrassment.

"You are not from Luskan," the woman went on. "Nor do you bear the appearance of any merchants now docked in port. Where are you from?"

"The north," Wulfgar stammered. "The dale . . . Icewind."

Regis hadn't seen such boldness in a woman since his years in Calimport, and he fell that he should intervene. There was something wicked about such women, a perversion of pleasure that was too extraordinary. Forbidden fruit made easy. Regis suddenly found himself homesick for Calimport. Wulfgar would be no match for the wiles of this creature.

"We are poor travelers," Regis explained, emphasizing the "poor" in an effort to protect his friend. "Not a coin left, but with many miles to go."

Wulfgar looked curiously at his companion, not quite understanding the motive behind the lie.

The woman scrutinized Wulfgar once again and smacked her lips. "A pity," she groaned, and then asked Regis, "Not a coin?"

Regis shrugged helplessly.

"A pity it is," the woman repeated, and she rose to leave.

Wulfgar's face blushed a deep red as he began to comprehend the true motives behind the meeting.

Something stirred in Regis, as well. A longing for the old days, running in Calimport's bowery, tugged at his heart beyond his strength to resist. As the woman started past him, he grabbed her elbow. "Not a coin," he explained to her inquiring face, "but this." He pulled the ruby pendant out from under his coat and set it dangling at the end of its chain. The sparkles caught the woman's greedy eye at once and the magical gemstone sucked her into its hypnotic entrancement. She sat down again, this time in the chair closest to Regis, her eyes never leaving the depths of the wondrous, spinning ruby.

Only confusion prevented Wulfgar from erupting in outrage at the betrayal, the blur of thoughts and emotions in his mind showing themselves as no more than a blank stare.

Regis caught the barbarian's look, but shrugged it away with his typical penchant for dismissing negative emotions, such as guilt. Let the morrow's dawn expose his ploy for what it was; the conclusion did not diminish his ability to enjoy this night. "Luskan's night bears a chill wind," he said to the woman.

She put a hand on his arm. "We'll find you a warm bed, have no fear."

The halfling's smile nearly took in his ears.

Wulfgar had to catch himself from falling off of his chair.

✕ ✕ ✕ ✕ ✕

Bruenor regained his composure quickly, not wanting to insult Whisper, or to let her know that his surprise in finding a woman gave her a bit of an advantage over him. She knew the truth, though, and her smile left Bruenor even more flustered. Selling information in a setting as dangerous as Luskan's dockside meant a constant dealing with murderers and thieves, and even within the structure of an intricate support network it was a job that demanded a hardened hide. Few who sought Whisper's services could hide their obvious surprise at finding a young and alluring woman practising such a trade.

Bruenor's respect for the informant did not diminish, though, despite his surprise, for the reputation Whisper had earned had come to him across hundreds of miles. She was still alive, and that fact alone told the dwarf that she was formidable.

Drizzt was considerably less taken aback by the discovery. In the dark cities of the drow elves, females normally held higher stations than males, and were often more deadly. Drizzt understood the advantage Whisper carried over male clients who tended to underestimate her in the male-dominated societies of the dangerous northland.

Anxious to get this business finished and get back on the road, the dwarf came straight to the purpose of the meeting. "I be needing a map," he said, "and been told that yerself was the one to get it."

"I possess many maps," the woman replied coolly.

"One of the north," Bruenor explained. "From the sea to the desert, and rightly naming the places in the ways o' what races live there!"

Whisper nodded. "The price shall be high, good dwarf," she said, her eyes glinting at the mere notion of gold.

Bruenor tossed her a small pouch of gems. "This should pay for yer trouble," he growled, never pleased to be relieved of coin.

Whisper emptied the contents into her hand and scrutinized the rough stones. She nodded as she slipped them back into the pouch, aware of their considerable value.

"Hold!" Bruenor squawked as she began to tie the pouch to her belt. "Ye'll be taking none o' me stones till I be seeing the map!"

"Of course," the woman replied with a disarming smile. "Wait here. I shall return in a short while with the map you desire." She tossed the pouch back to Bruenor and spun about suddenly, her cloak snapping up and carrying a gust of the fog with it. In the flurry, there came a sudden flash, and the woman was gone.

Bruenor jumped back and grabbed at his axe handle. "What sorcerous treachery is this?" he cried.

Drizzt, unimpressed, put a hand on the dwarf's shoulder. "Calm, mighty dwarf," he said. "A minor trick and no more, masking her escape in the fog and the flash." He pointed toward a small pile of boards. "Into that sewer drain."

Bruenor followed the line of the drow's arm and relaxed. The lip of an open hole was barely visible, its grate leaning against the warehouse wall a few feet farther down the alley.

"Ye know these kind better than meself, elf," the dwarf stated, flustered at his lack of experience in handling the rogues of a city street. "Does she mean to bargain fair, or do we sit here, set up for her thievin' dogs to plunder?"

"No to both," answered Drizzt. "Whisper would not be alive if she collared clients for thieves. But I would hardly expect any arrangement she might strike with us to be a fair bargain."

Bruenor took note that Drizzt had slipped one of his scimitars free of its sheath as he spoke. "Not a trap, eh?" the dwarf asked again, indicating the readied weapon.

"By her people, no," Drizzt replied. "But the shadows conceal many other eyes."

✕ ✕ ✕ ✕

More eyes than just Wulfgar's had fallen upon the halfling and the woman.

The hardy rogues of Luskan's dockside often took great sport in tormenting creatures of less physical stature, and halflings were among their favorite targets. This particular evening, a huge, overstuffed man with furry eyebrows and beard bristles that caught the foam from his ever-full mug dominated the conversation at the bar, boasting of impossible feats of strength and threatening everybody around him with a beating if the flow of ale slowed in the least.

All of the men gathered around him at the bar, men who knew him, or of him, nodded their heads in enthusiastic agreement with his every word, propping him up on a pedestal of compliments to dispel their own fears of him. But the fat man's ego needed further sport, a new victim to cow, and as his gaze floated around the perimeter of the tavern, it naturally fell upon Regis and his large but obviously young friend. The spectacle of a halfling wooing the highest priced lady at the Cutlass presented an opportunity too tempting for the fat man to ignore.

"Here now, pretty lady," he slobbered, ale spouting with every word. "Think the likes of a half-a-man'll make the night for ye?" The crowd around the bar, anxious to keep in the fat man's high regard, exploded into over-zealous laughter.

The woman had dealt with this man before and she had seen others fall painfully before him. She tossed him a concerned look, but remained firmly tied to the pull of the ruby pendant. Regis, though, immediately looked away from the fat man, turning his attention to where he suspected the trouble most likely would begin—to the other side of the table and Wulfgar.

He found his worries justified. The proud barbarian's knuckles whitened from the grasp he had on the table, and the seething look in his eye told Regis that he was on the verge of exploding.

"Let the taunts pass!" Regis insisted. "This is not worth a moment of your time!"

Wulfgar didn't relax a bit, his glare never releasing his adversary. He could brush away the fat man's insults, even those cutting at Regis and the woman. But Wulfgar understood the motivation behind those insults. Through exploitation of his less able friends, Wulfgar was being challenged by the bully. How many others had fallen victim to this hulking slob? he wondered. Perhaps it was time for the fat man to learn some humility.

Recognizing some potential for excitement, the grotesque bully came a few steps closer.

"There, move a bit, half-a-man," he demanded, waving Regis aside.

Regis took a quick inventory of the tavern's patrons. Surely there were many in here who might jump in for his cause against the fat man and his obnoxious cronies. There was even a member of the official city guard, a group held in high respect in every section of Luskan.

Regis interrupted his scan for a moment and looked at the soldier. How out of place the man seemed in a dog-infested spittoon like the Cutlass. More curious still, Regis knew the man as Jierdan, the soldier at the gate who had recognized Drizzt and had arranged for them to pass into the city just a couple of hours earlier.

The fat man came a step closer, and Regis didn't have time to ponder the implications.

Hands on hips, the huge blob stared down at him. Regis felt his heart pumping, the blood coursing through his veins, as it always did in this type of on-the-edge confrontation that had marked his days in Calimport. And now, like then, he had every intention of finding a way to run away.

But his confidence dissipated when he remembered his companion.

Less experienced, and Regis would be quick to say, "less wise!" Wulfgar would not let the challenge go unanswered. One spring of his long legs easily carried him over the table and placed him squarely between the fat man and Regis. He returned the fat man's ominous glare with equal intensity.

The fat man glanced to his friends at the bar, fully aware that his proud young opponent's distorted sense of honor would prevent a first strike. "Well, look ye here," he laughed, his lips turned back in drooling anticipation, "seems the young one has a thing to say."

He started slowly to turn back on Wulfgar, then lunged suddenly for the barbarian's throat, expecting that his change in tempo would catch Wulfgar by surprise.

But though he was inexperienced in the ways of taverns, Wulfgar understood battle. He had trained with Drizzt Do'Urden, an ever-alert warrior, and had toned his muscles to their sharpest fighting edge. Before the fat man's hands ever came near his throat, Wulfgar had snapped one of his own huge paws over his opponent's face and had driven the other into the fat man's groin.

His stunned opponent found himself rising into the air.

For a moment, onlookers were too amazed to react at all, except for Regis, who slapped a hand across his own disbelieving face and inconspicuously slid under the table.

The fat man outweighed three average men, but the barbarian brought him up easily over the top of his seven-foot frame, and even higher, to the full extension of his arms.

Howling in helpless rage, the fat man ordered his supporters to attack. Wulfgar watched patiently for the first move against him.

The whole crowd seemed to jump at once. Keeping his calm, the trained warrior searched out the tightest concentration, three men, and launched the human missile, noting their horrified expressions just before the waves of blubber rolled over them, blasting them backward. Then their combined momentum smashed an entire section of the bar from its supports, knocking the unfortunate innkeeper away and sending him crashing into the racks holding his finest wines.

Wulfgar's amusement was short-lived, for other ruffians were quickly upon him. He dug his heels in where he was, determined to keep his footing, and lashed out with his great fists, swatting his enemies aside, one by one, and sending them sprawling into the far corners of the room.

Fighting erupted all around the tavern. Men who could not have been spurred to action if a murder had been committed at their feet sprang upon each other with unbridled rage at the horrifying sight of spilled booze and a broken bar.

Few of the fat man's supporters were deterred by the general row, though. They rolled in on Wulfgar, wave after wave. He held his ground well, for none could delay him long enough for their reinforcements to get in. Still, the barbarian was being hit as often as he was connecting with his own blows. He took the punches stoically, blocking out the pain through sheer pride and his fighting tenacity that simply would not allow him to lose.

From his new seat under the table, Regis watched the action and sipped his drink. Even the barmaids were into it now, riding around on some unfortunate combatants' backs, using their nails to etch intricate designs into the men's faces. In fact, Regis soon discerned that the only other person in the tavern who wasn't in the fight, other than those who were already unconscious, was Jierdan. The soldier sat quietly in his chair, unconcerned with the brawling beside him and interested only, it seemed, in watching and measuring Wulfgar's prowess.

This, too, disturbed the halfling, but once again he found that he didn't have time to contemplate the soldier's unusual actions. Regis had known from the start that he would have to pull his giant friend out of this, and now his alert eyes had caught the expected flash of steel. A rogue in the line directly behind Wulfgar's latest opponents had drawn a blade.

"Damn!" Regis muttered, setting down his drink and pulling his mace from a fold in his cloak. Such business always left a foul taste in his mouth.

Wulfgar threw his two opponents aside, opening a path for the man with the knife. He charged forward, his eyes up and staring into those of the tall barbarian. He didn't even notice Regis dart out from between Wulfgar's long legs, the little mace poised to strike. It slammed into the man's knee, shattering the kneecap, and sent him sprawling forward, blade exposed, toward Wulfgar.

Wulfgar side-stepped the lunge at the last moment and clasped his hand over the hand of his assailant. Rolling with the momentum, the barbarian knocked aside the table and slammed into the wall. One squeeze crushed the assailant's fingers on the knife hilt, while at the same time Wulfgar engulfed the man's face with his free hand and hoisted him from the ground. Crying out to Tempus, the god of battle, the barbarian, enraged at the appearance of a weapon, slammed the man's head through the wooden planks of the wall and left him dangling, his feet fully a foot from the floor.

An impressive move, but it cost Wulfgar time. When he turned back toward the bar, he was buried under a flurry of fists and kicks from several attackers.

✕ ✕ ✕ ✕ ✕

"Here she comes," Bruenor whispered to Drizzt when he saw Whisper returning, though the drow's heightened senses had told him of her coming long before the dwarf was aware of it. Whisper had only been gone a half-hour or so, but it seemed much longer to the two friends in the alley, dangerously open to the sights of the crossbowmen and other thugs they knew were nearby.

Whisper sauntered confidently up to them. "Here is the map you desire," she said to Bruenor, holding up a rolled parchment.

"A look, then," the dwarf demanded, starting forward.

The woman recoiled and dropped the parchment to her side. "The price is higher," she stated flatly. "Ten times what you have already offered."

Bruenor's dangerous glare did not deter her. "No choice is left to you," she hissed. "You shall find no other who can deliver this unto you. Pay the price and be done with it!"

"A moment," Bruenor said with sudden calm. "Me friend has a say in this." He and Drizzt moved a step away.

"She has discovered who we are," the drow explained, though Bruenor had already come to the same conclusion. "And how much we can pay."

"Be it the map?" Bruenor asked.

Drizzt nodded. "She would have no reason to believe that she is in any danger, not down here. Have you the coin?"

"Aye," said the dwarf, "but our road is long yet, and I fear we'll be needing what I've got and more."

"It is settled then," Drizzt replied. Bruenor recognized the fiery gleam that flared up in the drow's lavender eyes. "When first we met this woman, we struck a fair deal," he went on. "A deal we shall honor."

Bruenor understood and approved. He felt the tingle of anticipation start in his blood. He turned back on the woman and noticed at once that she now held a dagger at her side instead of the parchment. Apparently she understood the nature of the two adventurers she was dealing with.

Drizzt, also noticing the metallic glint, stepped back from Bruenor, trying to appear unmenacing to Whisper, though in reality, he wanted to get a better angle on some suspicious cracks that he had noticed in the wall—cracks that might be the edgings of a secret door.

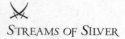
Bruenor approached the woman with his empty arms outstretched. "If that be the price," he grumbled, "then we have no choice but to pay. But I'll be seein' the map first!"

Confident that she could put her dagger into the dwarf's eye before either of his hands could get back to his belt for a weapon, Whisper relaxed and moved her empty hand to the parchment under her cloak.

But she underestimated her opponent.

Bruenor's stubby legs twitched, launching him up high enough to slam his helmet into the woman's face, splattering her nose and knocking her head into the wall. He went for the map, dropping the original purse of gems onto Whisper's limp form and muttering, "As we agreed."

Drizzt, too, had sprung into motion. As soon as the dwarf flinched, he had called upon the innate magic of his heritage to conjure a globe of darkness in front of the window harboring the crossbowmen. No bolts came through, but the angered shouts of the two archers echoed throughout the alley.

Then the cracks in the wall split open, as Drizzt had anticipated, and Whisper's second line of defense came rushing through. The drow was prepared, scimitars already in his hands. The blades flashed, blunt sides only, but with enough precision to disarm the burly rogue that stepped out. Then they came in again, slapping the man's face, and in the same fluidity of motion, Drizzt reversed the angle, slamming one pommel, and then the other, into the man's temples. By the time Bruenor had turned around with the map, the way was clear before them.

Bruenor examined the drow's handiwork with true admiration.

Then a crossbow quarrel ticked into the wall just an inch from his head.

"Time to go," Drizzt observed.

"The end'll be blocked, or I'm a bearded gnome," Bruenor said as they neared the exit to the alley. A growling roar in the building beside them, followed by terrified screams, brought them some comfort.

"Guenhwyvar," Drizzt stated as two cloaked men burst out into the street before them and fled without looking back.

"Sure that I'd forgotten all about that cat!" cried Bruenor.

"Be glad that Guenhwyvar's memory is greater than your own," laughed Drizzt, and Bruenor, despite his feelings for the cat, laughed with him.

They halted at the end of the alley and scouted the street. There were no signs of any trouble, though the heavy fog provided good cover for a possible ambush.

"Take it slow," Bruenor offered. "We'll draw less attention."

Drizzt would have agreed, but then a second quarrel, launched from somewhere down the alley, knocked into a wooden beam between them.

"Time to go!" Drizzt stated more decisively, though Bruenor needed no further encouragement, his little legs already pumping wildly as he sped off into the fog.

They made their way through the twists and turns of Luskan's rat maze, Drizzt gracefully gliding over any rubble barriers and Bruenor simply crashing through them. Presently, they grew confident that there was no pursuit, and they changed their pace to an easy glide.

The white of a smile showed through the dwarf's red beard as he kept a satisfied eye cocked over his shoulder. But when he turned back to view the road before him, he suddenly dived down to the side, scrambling to find his axe.

He had come face up with the magical cat.

Drizzt couldn't contain his laughter.

"Put the thing away!" Bruenor demanded.

"Manners, good dwarf," the drow shot back. "Remember that Guenhwyvar cleared our escape trail."

"Put her away!" Bruenor declared again, his axe swinging at the ready.

Drizzt stroked the powerful cat's muscled neck. "Do not heed his words, friend," he said to the cat. "He is a dwarf, and cannot appreciate the finer magics!"

"Bah!" Bruenor snarled, though he breathed a bit easier as Drizzt dismissed the cat and replaced the onyx statue in his pouch.

The two came upon Half-Moon Street a short while later, stopping in a final alley to look for any signs of ambush. They knew at once that there had been trouble, for several injured men stumbled, or were carried, past the alley's entrance.

Then they saw the Cutlass, and two familiar forms sitting on the street out in front.

"What're ye doin' out here?" Bruenor asked as they approached.

"Seems our big friend answers insults with punches," said Regis, who hadn't been touched in the fray. Wulfgar's face, though, was puffy and bruised, and he could barely open one eye. Dried blood, some of it his own, caked his fists and clothes.

Drizzt and Bruenor looked at each other, not too surprised.

"And our rooms?" Bruenor grumbled.

Regis shook his head. "I doubt it."

"And my coins?"

Again the halfling shook his bead.

"Bah!" snorted Bruenor, and he stamped off toward the door of the Cutlass.

"I wouldn't . . ." Regis started, but then he shrugged and decided to let Bruenor find out for himself.

Bruenor's shock was complete when he opened the tavern door. Tables, glass, and unconscious patrons lay broken all about the floor. The innkeeper slumped over one part of the shattered bar, a barmaid wrapping his bloodied head in bandages. The man Wulfgar had implanted into the wall still hung limply by the back of his head, groaning softly, and Bruenor couldn't help but chuckle at the handiwork of the mighty barbarian. Every now and then, one of the barmaids, passing by the man as she cleaned, gave him a little push, taking amusement at his swaying.

"Good coins wasted," Bruenor surmised, and he walked back out the door before the innkeeper noticed him and set the barmaids upon him.

"Hell of a row!" he told Drizzt when he returned to his companions. "Everyone in on it?"

"All but one," Regis answered. "A soldier."

"A soldier of Luskan, down here?" asked Drizzt, surprised by the obvious inconsistency.

Regis nodded. "And even more curious," he continued, "it was the same guard, Jierdan, that let us into the city."

Drizzt and Bruenor exchanged concerned looks.

"We've killers at our backs, a busted inn before us, and a soldier paying us more mind than he should," said Bruenor.

"Time to go," Drizzt responded for the third time. Wulfgar looked at him incredulously. "How many men did you down tonight?" Drizzt asked him, putting the logical assumption of danger right out before him. "And how many of them would drool at the opportunity to put a blade in your back?"

"Besides," added Regis before Wulfgar could answer, "I've no desire to share a bed in an alley with a host of rats!"

"Then to the gate," said Bruenor.

Drizzt shook his head. "Not with a guard so interested in us. Over the wall, and let none know of our passing."

An hour later, they were trotting easily across the open grass, feeling the wind again beyond the break of Luskan's wall.

Regis summed up their thoughts, saying, "Our first night in our first city, and we've betrayed killers, fought down a host of ruffians, and caught the attention of the city guard. An auspicious beginning to our journey!"

"Aye, but we've got this!" cried Bruenor, fairly bursting with anticipation of finding his homeland now that the first obstacle, the map, had been overcome.

Little did he or his friends know, however, that the map he clutched so clearly detailed several deadly regions, one in particular that would test the four friends to their limits—and beyond.

4

THE CONJURING

A landmark of wonder marked the very center of the City of Sails, a strange building that emanated a powerful aura of magic. Unlike any other structure in all Faerûn, the Hosttower of the Arcane seemed literally a tree of stone, boasting five tall spires, the largest being the central, and the other four, equally high, growing out of the main trunk with the graceful curving arc of an oak. Nowhere could any sign of the mason be seen; it was obvious to any knowledgeable viewer that magic, not physical labor, had produced this artwork.

The Archmage, undisputed Master of the Hosttower, resided in the central tower, while the other four housed the wizards closest in the line of succession. Each of these lesser towers, representing the four compass directions, dominated a different side of the trunk, and its respective wizard held responsibility for watching over and influencing the events in the direction he overlooked. Thus, the wizard west of the trunk spent his days looking out to sea, and to the merchant ships and pirates riding out on Luskan's harbor.

A conversation in the north spire would have interested the companions from Ten-Towns this day.

"You have done well, Jierdan," said Sydney, a younger, and lesser, mage in the Hosttower, though displaying enough potential to have gained an apprenticeship with one of the mightiest wizards in the guild. Not a pretty woman, Sydney cared little for physical appearances, instead devoting her energies to her unrelenting pursuit of power. She had spent most of her twenty-five years working toward one goal—the title of Wizard—and her determination and poise gave most around her little doubt about her ability to attain it.

Jierdan accepted the praise with a knowing nod, understanding the condescending manner in which it was offered. "I only performed as I was instructed," he replied under a facade of humility, tossing a glance to the frail-looking man in brown mottled robes who stood staring out of the room's sole window.

"Why would they come here?" the wizard whispered to himself. He turned to the others, and they recoiled instinctively from his gaze. He was Dendybar the Mottled, Master of the North Spire, and though he appeared weak from a distance, closer scrutiny revealed a power in the man mightier than bulging muscles. And his well-earned reputation for valuing life far less than the pursuit of knowledge intimidated most who came before him. "Did the travelers give any reason for coming here?"

"None that I would believe," Jierdan replied quietly. "The halfling spoke of scouting out the marketplace, but I—"

"Not likely," interrupted Dendybar, speaking more to himself than to the others. "Those four weigh more into their actions than simply a merchant expedition."

Sydney pressed Jierdan, seeking to keep her high favor with the Master of the North Spire. "Where are they now?" she demanded.

Jierdan didn't dare fight back against her in front of Dendybar. "On the docks . . . somewhere," he said, then shrugged.

"You do not know?" hissed the young mage.

"They were to stay at the Cutlass," Jierdan retorted. "But the fight put them out on the street."

"And you should have followed them!" Sydney scolded, dogging the soldier relentlessly.

"Even a soldier of the city would be a fool to travel alone about the piers at night," Jierdan shot back. "It does not matter where they are right now.

I have the gates and the piers watched. They cannot leave Luskan without my knowledge!"

"I want them found!" Sydney ordered, but then Dendybar silenced her.

"Leave the watch as it is," he told Jierdan. "They must not depart without my knowledge. You are dismissed. Come before me again when you have something to report."

Jierdan snapped to attention and turned to leave, casting one final glare at his competitor for the mottled wizard's favor as he passed. He was only a soldier, not a budding mage like Sydney, but in Luskan, where the Hosttower of the Arcane was the true, secretive force behind all of the power structures in the city, a soldier did well to find the favor of a wizard. Captains of the guard only attained their positions and privileges with the prior consent of the Hosttower.

"We cannot allow them to roam freely," argued Sydney when the door had closed behind the departing soldier.

"They shall bring no harm for now," replied Dendybar. "Even if the drow carries the artifact with him, it will take him years to understand its potential. Patience, my friend, I have ways of learning what we need to know. The pieces of this puzzle will fit together nicely before much longer."

"It pains me to think that such power is so close to our grasp," sighed the eager young mage. "And in the possession of a novice!"

"Patience," repeated the Master of the North Spire.

Sydney finished lighting the ring of candles that marked the perimeter of the special chamber and moved slowly toward the solitary brazier that stood on its iron tripod just outside the magic circle inscribed upon the floor. It disappointed her to know that once the brazier was also burning, she would be instructed to depart. Savoring every moment in this rarely opened room, considered by many to be the finest conjuring chamber in all the northland, Sydney had many times begged to remain in attendance.

But Dendybar never let her stay, explaining that her inevitable inquiries would prove too much of a distraction. And when dealing with the nether worlds, distractions usually proved fatal.

Dendybar sat cross-legged within the magic circle, chanting himself into a deep meditative trance and not even aware of Sydney's actions as she completed the preparations. All of his senses looked inward, searching his own being to ensure that he was fully prepared for such a task. He had left only one window in his mind open to the outside, a fraction of his awareness hinging on a single cue: the bolt of the heavy door being snapped back into place after Sydney had departed.

His heavy eyelids cracked open, their narrow line of vision solely fixed upon the fires of the brazier. These flames would be the life of the summoned spirit, giving it a tangible form for the period Dendybar kept it locked to the material plane.

"Ey vesus venerais dimin dou," the wizard began, chanting slowly at first, then building into a solid rhythm. Swept away by the insistent pull of the casting, as though the spell, once given a flicker of life, drove itself to the completion of its dweomer, Dendybar rolled on through the various inflections and arcane syllables with ease, the sweat on his face reflecting eagerness more than nerves.

The mottled wizard reveled in summoning, dominating the will of beings beyond the mortal world through the sheer insistence of his considerable mental strength. This room represented the pinnacle of his studies, the indisputable evidence of the vast boundaries of his powers.

This time he was targeting his favorite informant, a spirit that truly despised him, but could not refuse his call. Dendybar came to the climactic point in the casting, the naming. "Morkai," he called softly.

The brazier's flame brightened for just an instant.

"Morkai!" Dendybar shouted, tearing the spirit from its hold on the other world. The brazier puffed into a small fireball, then died into blackness, its flames transmuted into the image of a man standing before Dendybar.

The wizard's thin lips curled upward. How ironic, he thought, that the man he had arranged to murder would prove to be his most valuable source of information.

The specter of Morkai the Red stood resolute and proud, a fitting image of the mighty wizard he had once been. He had created this very room back in the days when he served the Hosttower in the role of Master of the North Spire. But then Dendybar and his cronies had conspired against him, using his trusted apprentice to drive a dagger into his heart, and thus opening the trail of succession for Dendybar himself to reach the coveted position in the spire.

That same act had set a second, perhaps more significant, chain of events into motion, for it was that same apprentice, Akar Kessell, who had eventually come to possess the Crystal Shard, the mighty artifact that Dendybar now believed in Drizzt Do'Urden's hands. The tales that had filtered down from Ten-Towns of Akar Kessell's final battle had named the dark elf as the warrior who had brought him down.

Dendybar could not know that the Crystal Shard now lay buried beneath a hundred tons of ice and rock on the mountain in Icewind Dale known as Kelvin's Cairn, lost in the avalanche that had killed Kessell. All that he knew of the tale was that Kessell, the puny apprentice, had nearly conquered all of Icewind Dale with the Crystal Shard and that Drizzt Do'Urden was the last to see Kessell alive.

Dendybar wrung his hands eagerly whenever he thought of the power that the relic would bring to a more learned wizard.

"Greetings, Morkai the Red," Dendybar laughed. "How polite of you to accept my invitation."

"I accept every opportunity to gaze upon you, Dendybar the Assassin," replied the specter. "I shall know you well when you ride Death's barge into the darkened realm. Then we shall be on even terms again . . ."

"Silence!" Dendybar commanded. Though he would not admit the truth to himself, the mottled wizard greatly feared the day when he would have to face the mighty Morkai again. "I have brought you here for a purpose," he told the specter. "I have no time for your empty threats."

"Then tell me the service I am to perform," hissed the specter, "and let me be gone. Your presence offends me."

Dendybar fumed, but did not continue the argument. Time worked against a wizard in a spell of summoning, for it drained him to hold a spirit on the material plane, and each second that passed weakened him a little bit more. The greatest danger in this type of spell was that the conjuror would attempt to hold control for too long, until he found himself too weak to control the entity he had summoned.

"A simple answer is all that I require from you this day, Morkai,"

Dendybar said, carefully selecting each word as he went. Morkai noted the caution and suspected that Dendybar was hiding something.

"Then what is the question?" the specter pressed.

Dendybar held to his cautious pace, considering every word before he spoke it. He did not want Morkai to get any hint of his motives in seeking the drow, for the specter would surely pass the information across the planes. Many powerful beings, perhaps even the spirit of Morkai himself, would go after such a powerful relic if they had any idea of the shard's whereabouts.

"Four travelers, one a drow elf, came to Luskan from Icewind Dale this day," the mottled wizard explained. "What business do they have in the city? Why are they here?"

Morkai scrutinized his nemesis, trying to find the reason for the question. "That is a query better asked of your city guard," he replied. "Surely the guests stated their business upon entering the gate."

"But I have asked you!" Dendybar screamed, exploding suddenly in rage. Morkai was stalling, and each passing second now took its toll on the mottled wizard. The essence of Morkai had lost little power in death, and he fought stubbornly against the spell's binding dweomer. Dendybar snapped open a parchment before him.

I have a dozen of these penned already," he warned.

Morkai recoiled. He understood the nature of the writing, a scroll that revealed the true name of his very being. And once read, stripping the veil of secrecy from the name and laying bare the privacy of his soul, Dendybar would invoke the true power of the scroll, using off-key inflections of tone to distort Morkai's name and disrupt the harmony of his spirit, thus racking him to the core of his being.

"How long shall I search for your answers?" Morkai asked.

Dendybar smiled at his victory, though the drain on him continued to heighten. "Two hours," he replied without delay, having carefully decided the length of the search before the summoning, choosing a time limit that would give Morkai enough opportunity to find some answers, but not long enough to allow the spirit to learn more than he should.

Morkai smiled, guessing the motives behind the decision. He snapped backward suddenly and was gone in a puff of smoke, the flames that had sustained his form relegated back to their brazier to await his return.

Dendybar's relief was immediate. Though he still had to concentrate to keep the gate to the planes in place, the pull against his will and the drain on his power lessened considerably when the spirit had gone. Morkai's will power had nearly broken him during their encounter, and Dendybar shook his head in disbelief that the old master could reach out from the grave so mightily. A shudder ran up his spine as he pondered his wisdom in plotting against one so powerful. Every time he summoned Morkai, he was reminded that his own day of reckoning would surely come.

Morkai had little trouble in learning about the four adventurers. In fact, the specter already knew much about them. He had taken a great interest in Ten-Towns during his reign as Master of the North Spire, and his curiosity had not died with his body. Even now, he often looked in on the doings in Icewind Dale, and anyone who concerned himself with Ten-Towns in recent months knew something of the four heroes.

Morkai's continued interest in the world he had left behind was not an uncommon trait in the spirit world. Death altered the ambitions of the soul, replacing the love of material or social gains with an eternal hunger for knowledge. Some spirits had looked down upon the Realms for centuries untold, simply collecting information and watching the living go about their lives. Perhaps it was envy for the physical sensations they could no longer feel. But whatever the reason, the wealth of knowledge in a single spirit often outweighed the collected works in all of the libraries in the Realms combined.

Morkai learned much in the two hours Dendybar had allotted him. His turn now came to choose his words carefully. He was compelled to satisfy the summoner's request, but he intended to answer in as cryptic and ambiguous a manner as he possibly could.

Dendybar's eyes glinted when he saw the brazier's flames begin their tell-tale dance once again. Had it been two hours already? he wondered, for his rest seemed much shorter, and he felt that he had not fully recovered from his first encounter with the specter. He could not refute the dance of the flames, though. He straightened himself and tucked his ankles in closer, tightening and securing his cross-legged, meditative position.

The ball of fire puffed in its climactic throes and Morkai appeared before him. The specter stood back obediently, not offering any information until Dendybar specifically asked for it. The complete story behind the visit of the four friends to Luskan remained sketchy to Morkai, but he had learned much of their quest, and more than he wanted Dendybar to find out about. He still hadn't discerned the true intentions behind the mottled wizard's inquiries, but felt certain that Dendybar was up to no good, whatever his goals.

"What is the purpose of the visit?" Dendybar demanded, angry at Morkai's stalling tactics.

"You yourself have summoned me," Morkai responded slyly. "I am compelled to appear."

"No games!" growled the mottled wizard. He glared at the specter, fingering the scroll of torment in open threat. Notorious for answering literally, beings from other planes often flustered their conjurors by distorting the connotative meaning of a question's exact wording.

Dendybar smiled in concession to the specter's simple logic and clarified the question. "What is the purpose of the visit to Luskan by the four travelers from Icewind Dale?"

"Varied reasons," Morkai replied. "One has come in search of the homeland of his father, and his father before him."

"The drow?" Dendybar asked, trying to find some way to link his suspicions that Drizzt planned to return to the underworld of his birth with the Crystal Shard. Perhaps an uprising by the dark elves, using the power of the shard? "Is it the drow who seeks his homeland?"

"Nay," replied the specter, pleased that Dendybar had fallen off on atangent, delaying the more specific, and more dangerous line of questioning. The passing minutes would soon begin to dissipate Dendybar's hold upon the specter, and Morkai hoped that he could find a way to get free of the mottled wizard before revealing too much about Bruenor's company. "Drizzt Do'Urden has forsaken his homeland altogether. He shall never return to the bowels of the world, and certainly not with his dearest friends in tow!"

"Then who?"

"Another of the four flees from danger at his back," Morkai offered, twisting the line of inquiry.

"Who seeks his homeland?" Dendybar demanded more emphatically.

"The dwarf, Bruenor Battlehammer," replied Morkai, compelled to obey. "He seeks his birthplace, Mithral Hall, and his friends have joined in his quest. Why does this interest you? The companions have no connection to Luskan, and pose no threat to the Hosttower."

I did not summon you here to answer your questions!" Dendybar scolded. "Now tell me who is running from danger. And what is the danger?"

"Behold," the specter instructed. With a wave of his hand, Morkai imparted an image upon the mind of the mottled wizard, a picture of a black-cloaked rider wildly charging across the tundra. The horse's bridle was white with lather, but the rider pressed the beast onward relentlessly.

"The halfling flees from this man," Morkai explained, "though the rider's purpose remains a mystery to me." Telling Dendybar even this much angered the specter, but Morkai could not yet resist the commands of his nemesis. He felt the bonds of the wizard's will loosening, though, and suspected that the summoning neared its end.

Dendybar paused to consider the information.

Nothing of what Morkai had told him gave any direct link to the Crystal Shard, but he had learned, at least, that the four friends did not mean to stay in Luskan for very long. And he had discovered a potential ally, a further source of information. The black-cloaked rider must be mighty indeed to have set the halfling's formidable troupe fleeing down the road.

Dendybar was beginning to formulate his next moves, when a sudden insistent pull of Morkai's stubborn resistance broke his concentration. Enraged, he shot a threatening glare back at the specter and began unrolling the parchment. "Impudent!" he growled, and though he could have stretched out his hold on the specter a bit longer if he had put his energies into a battle of wills, he started reciting the scroll.

Morkai recoiled, though he had consciously provoked Dendybar to this point. The specter could accept the racking, for it signaled the end of the inquisition. And Morkai was glad that Dendybar hadn't forced him to reveal the events even farther from Luskan, back in the dale just beyond the borders of Ten-Towns.

As Dendybar's recitations twanged discordantly on the harmony of his soul, Morkai removed the focal point of his concentration across hundreds of miles, back to the image of the merchant caravan now one day out from Bremen, the closest of the Ten-Towns, and to the image of the brave young woman who had joined up with the traders. The specter took comfort in the knowledge that she had, for a while at least, escaped the probings of the mottled wizard.

Not that Morkai was altruistic; he had never been accused of an abundance of that trait. He simply took great satisfaction in hindering in any way he could the knave who had arranged his murder.

⚔ ⚔ ⚔ ⚔ ⚔

Catti-brie's red-brown locks tossed about her shoulders. She sat high up on the lead wagon of the merchant caravan that had set out from Ten-Towns on the previous day, bound for Luskan. Unbothered by the chill breeze, she kept her eyes on the road ahead, searching for some sign that the assassin had passed that way. She had relayed information about Entreri to Cassius, and he would pass it along to the dwarves. Catti-brie wondered now if she had been justified in sneaking away with the merchant caravan before Clan Battlehammer could organize its own chase.

But only she had seen the assassin at work. She knew well that if the dwarves went after him in a frontal assault, their caution wiped away in their lust of revenge for Fender and Grollo, many more of the clan would die.

Selfishly, perhaps, Catti-brie had determined that the assassin was her own business. He had unnerved her, had stripped away years of training and discipline and reduced her to the quivering semblance of a frightened child. But she was a young woman now, no more a girl. She had to personally respond to that emotional humiliation, or the scars from it would haunt her to her grave, forever paralyzing her along her path to discover her true potential in life.

She would find her friends in Luskan and warn them of the danger at their backs, and then together they would take care of Artemis Entreri.

"We make a strong pace," the lead driver assured her, sympathetic to her desire for haste.

Catti-brie did not look at him; her eyes rooted on the flat horizon before her. "Me heart tells me 'tisn't strong enough," she lamented.

The driver looked at her curiously, but had learned better than to press her on the point. She had made it clear to them from the start that her business was private. And being the adopted daughter of Bruenor Battlehammer, and reputedly a fine fighter in her own right, the merchants had counted themselves lucky to have her along and had respected her desire for privacy. Besides, as one of the drivers had so eloquently argued during their informal meeting before the journey, "The notion of staring at an ox's ass for near to three-hunnerd miles makes the thought o' having that girl along for company sit well with me!"

They had even moved up their departure date to accommodate her.

"Do not worry, Catti-brie," the driver assured her, "we'll get you there!"

Catti-brie shook her blowing hair out of her face and looked into the sun as it set on the horizon before her. "But can it be in time?" she asked softly and rhetorically, knowing that her whisper would break apart in the wind as soon as it passed her lips.

5

THE CRAGS

Drizzt took the lead as the four companions jogged along the banks of the river Mirar, putting as much ground between themselves and Luskan as possible. Though they hadn't slept in many hours, their encounters in the City of Sails had sent a burst of adrenaline through their veins and none of them was weary.

Something magical hung in the air that night, a crispy tingling that would have made the most exhausted traveler lament closing his eyes to it. The river, rushing swiftly and high from the spring melt, sparkled in the evening glow, its whitecaps catching the starlight and throwing it back into the air in a spray of bejeweled droplets.

Normally cautious, the friends could not help but let their guard down. They felt no danger lurking near, felt nothing but the sharp, refreshing chill of the spring night and the mysterious pull of the heavens. Bruenor lost himself in dreams of Mithral Hall; Regis in memories of Calimport; even Wulfgar, so despondent about his ill-fated encounter with civilization, felt his spirits soar. He thought of similar nights on the open tundra, when he had dreamed of what lay beyond the horizons of his world. Now, out beyond those horizons, Wulfgar found only one element missing. To his surprise, and against the adventuring instincts that denied such comfortable thoughts, he wished that Catti-brie, the woman he had grown to cherish, was with him now to share the beauty of this night.

If the others had not been so preoccupied with their own enjoyment of the evening, they would have noticed an extra bounce in Drizzt Do'Urden's graceful step as well. To the drow, these magical nights, when the heavenly dome reached down below the horizon, bolstered his confidence in the most important and difficult decision he had ever made, the choice to forsake his people and his homeland. No stars sparkled above Menzoberranzan, the dark city of the black elves. No unexplainable allure tugged at the heart-strings from the cold stone of the immense cavern's lightless ceiling.

"How much my people have lost by walking in darkness," Drizzt whispered into the night. The pull of the mysteries of the endless sky carried the joy of his spirit beyond its normal boundaries and opened his mind to the unanswerable questions of the multiverse. He was an elf, and though his skin was black, there remained in his soul a semblance of the harmonic joy of his surface cousins. He wondered how general these feelings truly ran among his people. Did they remain in the hearts of all drow? Or had eons of sublimation extinguished the spiritual flames? To Drizzt's reckoning, perhaps the greatest loss that his people had suffered when they retreated to the depths of the world was the loss of the ability to ponder the spirituality of existence simply for the sake of thought.

The crystalline sheen of the Mirar gradually dulled as the lightening dawn dimmed the stars. It came as an unspoken disappointment to the friends as they set their camp in a sheltered spot near the banks of the river.

"Be knowin' that nights like that are few," Bruenor observed as the first ray of light crept over the eastern horizon. A glimmer edged his eye, a hint of the wondrous fantasizing that the normally practical dwarf rarely enjoyed.

Drizzt noted the dwarf's dreamy glow and thought of the nights that he and Bruenor had spent on Bruenor's Climb, their special meeting place, back in the dwarf's valley in Ten-Towns. "Too few," he agreed.

With a resigned sigh, they set to work, Drizzt and Wulfgar starting breakfast while Bruenor and Regis examined the map they had obtained in Luskan.

For all of his grumbling and teasing about the halfling, Bruenor had pressured him to come along for a very definite reason, aside from their friendship, and though the dwarf had masked his emotions well, he was truly overjoyed when Regis had come up huffing and puffing on the road out of Ten-Towns in a last-minute plea to join the quest.

Regis knew the land south of the Spine of the World better than any of them. Bruenor himself hadn't been out of Icewind Dale in nearly two centuries, and then he had been just an unbearded dwarf-child. Wulfgar had never left the dale, and Drizzt's only trek across the world's surface had been a nighttime adventure, skipping from shadow to shadow and avoiding many of the places the companions would need to search out, if they were ever to find Mithral Hall.

Regis ran his fingers across the map, excitedly recalling to Bruenor his experiences in each of the places listed, particularly Mirabar, the mining city of great wealth to the north, and Waterdeep, true to its name as the City of Splendors, down the coast to the south.

Bruenor slipped his finger across the map, studying the physical features of the terrain. "Mirabar'd be more to me liking," he said at length, tapping the mark of the city tucked within the southern slopes of the Spine of the World. "Mithral Hall's in mountains, that much I know, and not aside the sea."

Regis considered the dwarf's observations for just a moment, then plunked his finger down on yet another spot, by the scale of the map a hundred miles and more inland from Luskan. "Longsaddle," he said. "Halfway to Silverymoon, and halfway between Mirabar and Waterdeep. A good place to search out our course."

"A city?" Bruenor asked, for the mark on the map was no more than a small black dot.

"A village," Regis corrected. "There are not many people there, but a family of wizards, the Harpells, have lived there for many years and know the northland as well as any. They would be happy to help us."

Bruenor scratched his chin and nodded. "A fair hike. What might we be seeing along the way?"

"The crags," Regis admitted, a bit disheartened as he remembered the place. "Wild and orc-filled. I wish we had another road, but Longsaddle still seems the best choice."

"All roads in the north hold danger," Bruenor reminded him.

They continued their scrutiny of the map, Regis recalling more and more as they went. A series of unusual and unidentified markings—three in particular, running in an almost straight line due east of Luskan to the river network south of Lurkwood—caught Bruenor's eye.

"Ancestral mounds," Regis explained. "Holy places of the Uthgardt."

"Uthgardt?"

"Barbarians," answered Regis grimly. "Like those in the dale. More wise to the ways of civilization, perhaps, but no less fierce. Their separate tribes are all about the northland, wandering the wilds."

Bruenor groaned in understanding of the halfling's dismay, all too familiar himself with the savage ways and fighting prowess of barbarians. Orcs would prove much less formidable foes.

By the time the two had finished their discussion, Drizzt was stretching out in the cool shade of a tree overhanging the river and Wulfgar was halfway through his third helping of breakfast.

"Yer jaw still dances for food, I see!" Bruenor called as he noted the meager portions left on the skillet.

"A night filled with adventure," Wulfgar replied gaily, and his friends were glad to observe that the brawl had apparently left no scars upon his attitude. "A fine meal and a fine sleep, and I shall be ready for the road once more!"

"Well don't ye get too comfortable yet!" Bruenor ordered. "Ye've a third of a watch to keep this day!"

Regis looked about, perplexed, always quick to recognize an increase in his workload. "A third?" he asked. "Why not a fourth?"

"The elf's eyes are for the night," Bruenor explained. "Let him be ready to find our way when the day's flown."

"And where is our way?" Drizzt asked from his mossy bed. "Have you come to a decision for our next destination?"

"Longsaddle," Regis replied. "Two hundred miles east and south, around Neverwinter Wood and across the crags."

"The name is unknown to me," Drizzt replied.

"Home of the Harpells," Regis explained. "A family of wizards reknowned for their good-natured hospitality. I spent some time there on my way to Ten-Towns."

Wulfgar balked at the idea. The barbarians of Icewind Dale despised wizards, considering the black arts a power employed only by cowards. "I have no desire to view this place," he stated flatly.

"Who asked ye?" growled Bruenor, and Wulfgar found himself backing down from his resolve, like a son refusing to hold a stubborn argument in the face of a scolding by his father.

"You will enjoy Longsaddle," Regis assured him. "The Harpells have truly earned their hospitable reputation, and the wonders of Longsaddle will show you a side of magic you never expected. They will even accept . . ." He found his hand involuntarily pointing to Drizzt, and he cut short the statement in embarrassment.

But the stoic drow just smiled. "Fear not, my friend," he consoled Regis. "Your words ring of truth, and I have come to accept my station in your world." He paused and looked individually into each uncomfortable stare that was upon him. "I know my friends, and I dismiss my enemies," he stated with a finality that dismissed their worries.

"With a blade, ye do," Bruenor added with a soft chuckle, though Drizzt's keen ears caught the whisper.

"If I must," the drow agreed, smiling. Then he rolled over to get some sleep, fully trusting in his friends' abilities to keep him safe.

They passed a lazy day in the shade beside the river. Late in the afternoon, Drizzt and Bruenor ate a meal and discussed their course, leaving Wulfgar and Regis soundly asleep, at least until they had eaten their own fill.

"We'll stay with the river for a night more," Bruenor said. "Then southeast across the open ground. That'd clear us of the wood and lay open a straight path 'fore us."

"Perhaps it would be better if we traveled only by night for a few days," Drizzt suggested. "We know not what eyes follow us out of the City of Sails."

"Agreed," replied Bruenor. "Let's be off, then. A long road before us, and a longer one after that!"

"Too long," murmured Regis, opening a lazy eye.

Bruenor shot him a dangerous glare. He was nervous about this trek and about bringing his friends on a dangerous road, and in an emotional defense, he took all complaints about the adventure personally.

"To walk, I mean," Regis quickly explained. "There are farmhouses in this area, so there must be some horses about."

"Horses'd bring too a high price in these parts," replied Bruenor.

"Maybe . . ." said the halfling slyly, and his friends could easily guess what he was thinking. Their frowns reflected a general disapproval.

"The crags stand before us!" Regis argued. "Horses might outrun orcs, but without them, we shall surely fight for every mile of our hike! Besides, it would only be a loan. We could return the beasts when we were through with them."

Drizzt and Bruenor did not approve of the halfling's proposed trickery, but could not refute his logic. Horses would certainly aid them at this point of the journey.

"Wake the boy," Bruenor growled.

"And about my plan?" asked Regis.

"We'll make the choice when we find the opportunity!"

Regis was contented, confident that his friends would opt for the horses. He ate his fill, then scraped together the supper's meager remnants and went to wake Wulfgar.

They were on the trail again soon after, and a short time after that, they saw the lights of a small settlement in the distance.

"Take us there," Bruenor told Drizzt. "Mighten be that Rumblebelly's plan's worth a try."

Wulfgar, having missed the conversation at the camp, didn't understand, but offered no argument, or even questioned the dwarf. After the disaster at the Cutlass, he had resigned himself to a more passive role on the trip, letting the other three decide which trails they were to take. He would follow without complaint, keeping his hammer ready for when it became needed.

They moved inland away from the river for a few miles, then came upon several farms clustered together inside a stout wooden fence.

"There are dogs about," Drizzt noted, sensing them with his exceptional hearing.

"Then Rumblebelly goes in alone," said Bruenor.

Wulfgar's face twisted in confusion, especially since the halfling's look indicated that he wasn't thrilled with the idea. "That I cannot allow," the barbarian spouted. "If any among us needs protection, it is the little one. I'll not hide here in the dark while he walks alone into danger!"

"He goes in alone," Bruenor said again. "We're here for no fight, boy. Rumblebelly's to get us some horses."

Regis smiled helplessly, caught fully in the trap that Bruenor had clearly set for him. Bruenor would allow him to appropriate the horses, as Regis had insisted, but with the grudging permission came a measure of responsibility and bravery on his part. It was the dwarf's way of absolving himself of involvement in the trickery.

Wulfgar remained steadfast in his determination to stand by the halfling, but Regis knew that the young warrior might inadvertently cause him problems in such delicate negotiations. "You stay with the others," he explained to the barbarian. "I can handle this deal alone."

Mustering up his nerve, he pulled his belt over the hang of his belly and strode off toward the small settlement.

The threatening snarls of several dogs greeted him as he approached the fence's gate. He considered turning back—the ruby pendant probably wouldn't do him much good against vicious dogs—but then he saw the silhouette of a man leave one of the farmhouses and start his way.

"What do you want?" the farmer demanded, standing defiantly on the other side of the gate and clutching an antique pole arm, probably passed down through his family's generations.

"I am but a weary traveler," Regis started to explain, trying to appear as pitiful as he could. It was a tale the farmer had heard far too often.

"Go away!" he ordered.

"But—"

"Get you gone!"

Over a ridge some distance away, the three companions watched the confrontation, though only Drizzt viewed the scene in the dim light well enough to understand what was happening. The drow could see the tenseness in the farmer by the way he gripped the halberd, and could judge the deep resolve in the man's demands by the unbending scowl upon his face.

But then Regis pulled something out from under his jacket, and the farmer relaxed his grip upon the weapon almost immediately. A moment later, the gate swung open and Regis walked in.

The friends waited anxiously for several grueling hours with no further sign of Regis. They considered confronting the farmers themselves, worried that some foul treachery had befallen the halfling. Then finally, with the moon well past its peak, Regis emerged from the gate, leading two horses and two ponies. The farmers and their families waved good-bye to him as he left, making him promise to stop and visit if he ever passed their way again.

"Amazing," laughed Drizzt. Bruenor and Wulfgar just shook their heads in disbelief.

For the first time since he had entered the settlement, Regis pondered that his delay might have caused his friends some distress. The farmer had insisted that he join in for supper before they sat down to discuss whatever business he had come about, and since Regis had to be polite (and since he had only eaten one supper that day) he agreed, though he kept the meal as short as possible and politely declined when offered his fourth helping. Getting the horses proved easy enough after that. All he had to do was promise to leave them with the wizards in Longsaddle when he and his friends moved on from there.

Regis felt certain that his friends could not stay mad at him for very long. He had kept them waiting and worrying for half the night, but his endeavor would save them many days on a dangerous road. After an hour or two of feeling the wind rushing past them as they rode, they would forget any anger they held for him, he knew. Even if they didn't so easily forgive, a good meal was always worth a little inconvenience to Regis.

Drizzt purposely kept the party moving more to the east than the southeast. He found no landmarks on Bruenor's map that would let him approximate the straight course to Longsaddle. If he tried the direct route and missed the mark, no matter how slightly, they would come upon the main road from the northern city of Mirabar not knowing whether to turn north or south. By going directly east, the drow was assured that they would hit the road to the north of Longsaddle. His path would add a few miles, but perhaps save them several days of backtracking.

Their ride was clear and easy for the next day and night, and after that, Bruenor decided that they were far enough from Luskan to assume a more normal traveling schedule. "We can go by day, now," he announced early in the afternoon of their second day with the horses.

"I prefer the night," Drizzt said. He had just awakened and was brushing down his slender, well-muscled black stallion.

"Not me," argued Regis. "Nights are for sleeping, and the horses are all but blind to holes and rocks that could lame them up."

"The best for both then," offered Wulfgar, stretching the last sleep out of his bones. "We can leave after the sun peaks, keeping it behind us for Drizzt, and ride long into the night."

"Good thinking, lad," laughed Bruenor. "Seems to be after noon now, in fact. On the horses, then! Time's for going!"

"You might have held your thoughts to yourself until after supper!" Regis grumbled at Wulfgar, reluctantly hoisting the saddle onto the back of the little white pony.

Wulfgar moved to help his struggling friend. "But we would have lost half a day's ride," he replied.

"A pity that would have been," Regis retorted.

That day, the fourth since they had left Luskan, the companions came upon the crags, a narrow stretch of broken mounds and rolling hills. A rough, untamed beauty defined the place, an overpowering sense of wilderness that gave every traveler here a feeling of conquest, that he might be the first to gaze upon any particular spot. And as was always the case in the wilds, with the adventurous excitement came a degree of danger. They had barely entered the first dell in the up-and-down terrain when Drizzt spotted tracks that he knew well: the trampling march of an orc band.

"Less than a day old," he told his concerned companions.

"How many?" asked Bruenor.

Drizzt shrugged. "A dozen at least, maybe twice that number."

"We'll keep to our path," the dwarf suggested. "They're in front of us, and that's better'n behind."

When sunset came, marking the halfway point of that day's journey, the companions took a short break, letting the horses graze in a small meadow.

The orc trail was still before them, but Wulfgar, taking up the rear of the troupe had his sights trained behind.

"We are being followed," he said to his friends' inquiring faces.

"Orcs?" Regis asked.

The barbarian shook his head. "None like I have ever seen. By my reckoning, our pursuit is cunning and cautious."

"Might be that the orcs here are more wise to the ways of goodly folk than be the orcs of the dale," said Bruenor, but he suspected something other than orcs, and he didn't have to look at Regis to know that the halfling shared his concerns. The first map marking that Regis had identified as an ancestral mound could not be far from their present position.

"Back to the horses," Drizzt suggested. "A hard ride might do much to improve our position."

"Go till after moonset," Bruenor agreed. "And stop when ye've found a place we can hold against attack. I've a feeling we're to see some fighting 'fore the dawn finds us!"

They encountered no tangible signs during the ride, which took them nearly across the span of the crags. Even the orc trail faded off to the north, leaving the path before them apparently clear. Wulfgar was certain, though, that he caught several sounds behind them, and movements along the periphery of his vision.

Drizzt would have liked to continue until the crags were fully behind them, but in the harsh terrain, the horses had reached the limit of their endurance. He pulled up into a small copse of fir trees set on top of a small rise, fully suspecting, like the others, that unfriendly eyes were watching them from more than one direction.

Drizzt was up one of the trees before the others had even dismounted. They tethered the horses close together and set themselves around the beasts. Even Regis would find no sleep, for, though he trusted Drizzt's night vision, his blood had already begun pumping in anticipation of what was to come.

Bruenor, a veteran of a hundred fights, felt secure enough in his battle prowess. He propped himself calmly against a tree, his many-notched axe across his chest, one hand firmly in place upon its handle.

Wulfgar, though, made other preparations. He began by gathering together broken sticks and branches and sharpening their points. Seeking every advantage, he set them in strategic positions around the area to provide the best layout for his stand, using their deadly points to cut down the routes of approach for his attackers. Other sticks he cunningly concealed in angles that would trip up and stick the orcs before they ever reached him.

Regis, the most nervous of all, watched it all and noted the differences in his friends' tactics. He felt that there was little he could do to prepare himself for such a fight, and he sought only to keep himself far enough out of the way so as not to hinder the efforts of his friends. Perhaps the opportunity would arise for him to make a surprise strike, but he didn't even consider such possibilities at this point. Bravery came to the halfling spontaneously. It was certainly nothing he ever planned.

With all of their diversions and preparations deflecting their nervous anticipation, it came as almost a relief when, barely an hour later, their anxiety became reality. Drizzt whispered down to them that there was movement on the fields below the copse.

"How many?" Bruenor called back.

"Four to one against us, and maybe more," Drizzt replied.

The dwarf turned to Wulfgar "Ye ready, boy?"

Wulfgar slapped his hammer out before him. "Four against one?" he laughed. Bruenor liked the young warrior's confidence, though the dwarf realized that the odds might actually prove more lopsided, since Regis wouldn't likely be out in the open fighting.

"Let 'em in, or hit them out in the field?" Bruenor asked Drizzt.

"Let them in," the drow replied. "Their stealthy approach shows me that they believe surprise is with them."

"And a turned surprise is better'n a first blow from afar," Bruenor finished. "Do what ye can with yer bow when it's started, elf. We'll be waitin' fer ye!"

Wulfgar imagined the fire seething in the drow's lavender eyes, a deadly gleam that always belied Drizzt's outward calm before a battle. The barbarian took comfort, for the drow's lust for battle outweighed even his own, and he had never seen the whirring scimitars outdone by any foe. He slapped his hammer again and crouched in a hole beside the roots of one of the trees.

Bruenor slipped between the bulky bodies of two of the horses, pulling his feet up into a stirrup on each, and Regis, after he had stuffed the bedrolls to give the appearance of sleeping bodies, scooted under the low-hanging boughs of one of the trees.

The orcs approached the camp in a ring, obviously looking for an easy strike. Drizzt smiled in hope as he noted the gaps in their ring, open flanks that would prevent quick support to any isolated group. The whole band would hit the perimeter of the copse together, and Wulfgar, closest to the edge, would most likely launch the first strike.

The orcs crept in, one group slipping toward the horses, another toward the bedrolls. Four of them passed Wulfgar, but he waited a second longer, allowing the others to get close enough to the horses for Bruenor to strike.

Then the time for hiding had ended.

Wulfgar sprang from his concealment, Aegis-fang, his magical warhammer, already in motion. "Tempus!" he cried to his god of battle, and his first blow crashed in, swatting two of the orcs to the ground.

The other group rushed to get the horses free and out of the camp, hoping to cut off any escape route.

But were greeted by the snarling dwarf and his ringing axe!

As the surprised orcs leaped into the saddles, Bruenor clove one down the middle, and took a second one's head clean from its shoulders before the remaining two even knew that they had been attacked.

Drizzt picked as targets the orcs closest to the groups under attack, delaying the support against his friends for as long as possible. His bowstring twanged, once, twice, and a third time, and a like number of orcs fell to the earth, their eyes closed and their hands helplessly clenched upon the shafts of the killing arrows.

The surprise strikes had cut deeply into the ranks of their enemies, and now the drow pulled his scimitars and dropped from his perch, confident that he and his companions could finish the rest off quickly. His smile was short-lived, though, for as he descended, he noticed more movement in the field.

Drizzt had come down in the middle of three creatures, his blades in motion before his feet had even touched the ground. The orcs were not totally surprised—one had seen the drow dropping—but Drizzt had them off balance and swinging around to bring their weapons to bear.

With the drow's lightninglike strikes, any delay at all meant certain death, and Drizzt was the only one in the jumble of bodies under control. His scimitars slashed and thrust into orcan flesh with killing precision.

Wulfgar's fortunes were equally bright. He faced two of the creatures, and though they were vicious fighters, they could not match the giant barbarian's power. One got its crude weapon up in time to block Wulfgar's swing, but Aegis-fang blasted through the defense, shattering the weapon and then the unfortunate orc's skull without even slowing for the effort.

Bruenor fell into trouble first. His initial attacks went off perfectly, leaving him with only two standing opponents—odds that the dwarf liked. But in the excitement, the horses reared and bolted, tearing their tethers free from the branches. Bruenor tumbled to the ground, and before he could recover, was clipped in the head by the hoof of his own pony. One of the orcs was similarly thrown down, but the last one landed free of the commotion and rushed to finish off the stunned dwarf as the horses cleared the area.

Luckily, one of those spontaneous moments of bravery came over Regis at that moment. He slipped out from under the tree, falling in silently behind the orc. It was tall for an orc, and even on the tips of his toes, Regis did not like the angle of a strike at its head. Shrugging resignedly, the halfling reversed his strategy.

Before the orc could even begin to strike at Bruenor, the halfling's mace came up between its knees and higher, driving into its groin and lifting it clear off the ground. The howling victim grasped at its injury, its eyes lolling about aimlessly, and dropped to the ground with no further ambitions for battle.

It had all happened in an instant, but victory was not yet won. Another six orcs poured into the fray, two cutting off Drizzt's attempt to get to Regis and Bruenor, three more going to the aid of their lone companion facing the giant barbarian. And one, creeping along the same line Regis had taken, closed on the unsuspecting halfling.

At the same moment Regis made out the drow's warning call, a club slammed between his shoulder blades, blasting the wind from his lungs and tossing him to the ground.

Wulfgar was pressed on all four sides, and despite his boasts before the battle, he found that he didn't care for the situation. He concentrated on parrying, hoping that the drow could get to him before his defenses broke down.

He was too badly outnumbered.

An orcan blade cut into a rib, another clipped his arm.

Drizzt knew that he could defeat the two he now faced, but doubted that it would be in time for him to help his barbarian friend or the halfling. And there were still reinforcements on the field.

Regis rolled onto his back to lay right beside Bruenor, and the dwarf's groaning told him that the fight was over for both of them. Then the orc was above him, its club raised above its head, and an evil smile spread wide upon its ugly face. Regis closed his eyes, having no desire to watch the descent of the blow that would kill him.

Then he heard the sound of impact . . . above him.

Startled, he opened his eyes. A hatchet was embedded into his attacker's chest. The orc looked down at it, stunned. The club dropped harmlessly behind the orc, and it, too, fell backward, quite dead.

Regis didn't understand. "Wulfgar?" he asked into the air.

A huge form, nearly as large as Wulfgar's, sprang over him and pounced upon the orc, savagely tearing the hatchet free. He was human, and wearing the furs of a barbarian, but unlike the tribes of Icewind Dale, this man's hair was black.

"Oh, no," Regis groaned, remembering his own warnings to Bruenor about the Uthgardt barbarians. The man had saved his life, but knowing the savage reputation, Regis doubted that a friendship would grow out of the encounter. He started to sit up, wanting to express his sincere thanks

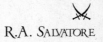

R.A. Salvatore

and dispel any unfriendly notions the barbarian might have about him. He even considered using the ruby pendant to evoke some friendly feelings.

But the big man, noting the movement, spun suddenly and kicked him in the face.

And Regis fell backward into blackness.

429

6

SKY PONIES

Black-haired barbarians, screaming in the frenzy of battle, burst into the copse. Drizzt realized at once that these burly warriors were the forms he had seen moving behind the orcan ranks on the field, but he wasn't yet certain of their allegiance.

Whatever their ties, their arrival struck terror into the remaining orcs. The two fighting Drizzt lost all heart for the battle, a sudden shift in their posture revealing their desire to break off the confrontation and flee. Drizzt obliged, assured that they wouldn't get far anyway, and sensing that he, too, would be wise to slip from sight.

The orcs fled, but their pursuers soon caught them in another battle just beyond the trees. Less obvious in his flight, Drizzt slipped unnoticed back up the tree where he had left his bow.

Wulfgar could not so easily sublimate his battle lust. With two of his friends down, his thirst for orcan blood was insatiable, and the new group of men that had joined the fight cried out to Tempus, his own god of battle, with a fervor that the young warrior could not ignore. Distracted by the sudden developments, the ring of orcs around Wulfgar let up for just a moment, and he struck hard.

One orc looked away, and Aegis-fang tore its face off before its eyes returned to the fight at hand. Wulfgar bore through the gap in the ring, jostling a second orc as he passed. As it stumbled in its attempt to turn and realign its defense, the mighty barbarian chopped it down. The two remaining turned and fled, but Wulfgar was right behind. He launched his hammer, blasting one from life, and sprang upon the other, bearing it to the ground beneath him and then crushing the life from it with his bare hands.

When he was finished, when he had heard the final crack of neckbone, Wulfgar remembered his predicament and his friends. He sprang up and backed away, his back against the trees.

The black-haired barbarians kept their distance, respectful of his prowess, and Wulfgar could not be sure of their intentions. He scanned around for his friends. Regis and Bruenor lay side by side near where the horses had been tethered; he could not tell if they were alive or dead. There was no sign of Drizzt, but a fight continued beyond the other edge of the trees.

The warriors fanned out in a wide semi-circle around him, cutting off any routes of escape. But they stopped their positioning suddenly, for Aegis-fang had magically returned to Wulfgar's grasp.

He could not win against so many, but the thought did not dismay him. He would die fighting, as a true warrior, and his death would be remembered. If the black-haired barbarians came at him, many, he knew, would not return to their families. He dug his heels in and clasped the warhammer tightly. "Let us be done with it," he growled into the night.

"Hold!" came a soft, but imperative whisper from above. Wulfgar recognized Drizzt's voice at once and relaxed his grip. "Keep to your honor, but know that more lives are at stake than your own!"

Wulfgar understood then that Regis and Bruenor were probably still alive. He dropped Aegis-fang to the ground and called out to the warriors, "Well met."

They did not reply, but one of them, nearly as tall and heavily muscled as Wulfgar, broke rank and closed in to stand before him. The stranger wore a single braid in his long hair, running down the side of his face and over his shoulder. His cheeks were painted white in the image of wings. The hardness of his frame and disciplined set of his face reflected a life in the harsh wilderness, and were it not for the raven color of his hair, Wulfgar would have thought him to be of one of the tribes of Icewind Dale.

The dark-haired man similarly recognized Wulfgar, but better versed in the overall structures of the societies in the northland, was not so perplexed by their similarities. "You are of the dale," he said in a broken form of the common tongue. "Beyond the mountains, where the cold wind blows."

Wulfgar nodded. "I am Wulfgar, son of Beornegar, of the Tribe of the Elk. We share gods, for I, too, call to Tempus for strength and courage."

The dark-haired man looked around at the fallen orcs. "The god answers your call, warrior of the dale."

Wulfgar's jaw lifted in pride. "We share hatred for the orcs, as well," he continued, "but I know nothing of you or your people."

"You shall learn," the dark-haired man replied. He held out his hand and indicated the warhammer. Wulfgar straightened firmly, having no intentions of surrendering, no matter the odds. The dark-haired man looked to the side, drawing Wulfgar's eyes with his own. Two warriors had picked up Bruenor and Regis and slung them over their backs, while others had recaptured the horses and were leading them in.

"The weapon," the dark-haired man demanded. "You are in our land without our say, Wulfgar, son of Beornegar. The price of that crime is death. Shall you watch our judgement over your small friends?"

The younger Wulfgar would have struck then, damning them all in a blaze of glorious fury. But Wulfgar had learned much from his new friends, Drizzt in particular. He knew that Aegis-fang would return to his call, and he knew, too, that Drizzt would not abandon them. This was not the time to fight.

He even let them bind his hands, an act of dishonor that no warrior of the Tribe of the Elk would ever allow. But Wulfgar had faith in Drizzt. His hands would be freed again. Then he would have the last word.

By the time they reached the barbarian camp, both Regis and Bruenor had regained consciousness and were bound and walking beside their barbarian friend. Dried blood crusted Bruenor's hair and he had lost his helm, but his dwarven toughness had carried him through another encounter that should have finished him.

They crested a rise and came upon the perimeter of a ring of tents and blazing campfires. Whooping their war cries to Tempus, the returning war party roused the camp, tossing severed orc heads into the ring to announce their glorious arrival. The fervor inside the camp soon matched the level of the entering war party, and the three prisoners were pushed in first, to be greeted by a score of howling barbarians.

"What do they eat?" Bruenor asked, more in sarcasm than concern.

"Whatever it is, feed them quickly," Regis replied, drawing a clap on the back of his head and a warning to be silent from the guard behind him.

The prisoners and horses were herded into the center of the camp and the tribe encircled them in a victory dance, kicking orc heads around in the dust and singing out, in a language unknown to the companions, their praise to Tempus and to Uthgar, their ancestral hero, for the success this night.

It went on for nearly an hour, and then, all at once, it ended and every face in the ring turned to the closed flap of a large and decorated tent.

The silence held for a long moment before the flap swung open. Out jumped an ancient man, as slender as a tent pole, but showing more energy than his obvious years would indicate. His face painted in the same markings as the warriors, though more elaborately, he wore a patch with a huge green gemstone sewn upon it over one eye. His robe was the purest white, its sleeves showing as feathered wings whenever he flapped his arms out to the side. He danced and twirled through the ranks of the warriors, and each held his breath, recoiling until he had passed.

"Chief?" Bruenor whispered.

"Shaman," corrected Wulfgar, more knowledgeable in the ways of tribal life. The respect the warriors showed this man came from a fear beyond what a mortal enemy, even a chieftain, could impart.

The shaman spun and leaped, landing right before the three prisoners. He looked at Bruenor and Regis for just a moment, then turned his full attention upon Wulfgar.

"I am Valric High Eye," he screeched suddenly. "Priest of the followers of the Sky Ponies! The children of Uthgar!"

"Uthgar!" echoed the warriors, clapping their hatchets against their wooden shields.

Wulfgar waited for the commotion to die away, then presented himself. "I am Wulfgar, son of Beornegar, of the Tribe of the Elk."

"And I'm Bruenor—" began the dwarf.

"Silence!" Valric shouted at him, trembling with rage. "I care nothing for you!"

Bruenor closed his mouth and entertained dreams concerning his axe and Valric's head.

"We meant no harm, nor trespass," Wulfgar began, but Valric put his hand up, cutting him short.

"Your purpose does not interest me," he explained calmly, but his excitement resurged at once. "Tempus has delivered you unto us, that is all! A worthy warrior?" He looked around at his own men and their response showed eagerness for the coming challenge.

"How many did you claim?" he asked Wulfgar.

"Seven fell before me," the young barbarian replied proudly.

Valric nodded in approval. "Tall and strong," he commented. "Let us discover if Tempus is with you. Let us judge if you are worthy to run with the Sky Ponies!"

Shouts started at once and two warriors rushed over to unbind Wulfgar. A third, the leader of the war party who had spoken to Wulfgar at the copse of trees, tossed down his hatchet and shield and stormed into the ring.

⚔ ⚔ ⚔ ⚔

Drizzt waited in his tree until the last of the war party had given up the search for the rider of the fourth horse and departed. Then the drow moved quickly, gathering together some of the dropped items: the dwarf's axe and Regis's mace. He had to pause and steady himself when he found Bruenor's helm, though, blood-stained and newly dented, and with one of its horns broken away. Had his friend survived?

He shoved the broken helm into his sack and slipped out after the troupe, keeping a cautious distance.

Relief flooded through him when he came upon the camp and spotted his three friends, Bruenor standing calmly between Wulfgar and Regis.

Satisfied, Drizzt put aside his emotions and all thoughts of the previous encounter, narrowing his vision to the situation before him, formulating a plan of attack that would free his friends.

✕ ✕ ✕ ✕ ✕

The dark-haired man held his open hands out to Wulfgar, inviting his blond counterpart to clasp them. Wulfgar had never seen this particular challenge before, but it was not so different from the tests of strength that his own people practised.

"Your feet do not move!" instructed Valric. "This is the challenge of strength! Let Tempus show us your worth!"

Wulfgar's firm visage didn't reveal a hint of his confidence that he could defeat any man at such a test. He brought his hands up level with those of his opponent.

The man grabbed at them angrily, snarling at the large foreigner. Almost immediately, before Wulfgar had even straightened his grip or set his feet, the shaman screamed out to begin, and the dark-haired man drove his hands forward, bending Wulfgar's back over his wrists. Shouting erupted from every corner of the encampment; the dark-haired man roared and pushed with all his strength, but as soon as the moment of surprise had passed, Wulfgar fought back.

The iron-corded muscles in Wulfgar's neck and shoulders snapped taut and his huge arms reddened with the forced surge of blood into their veins. Tempus had blessed him truly; even his mighty opponent could only gape in amazement at the spectacle of his power. Wulfgar looked him straight in the eye and matched the snarl with a determined glare that foretold the inevitable victory. Then the son of Beornegar drove forward, stopping the dark-haired man's initial momentum and forcing his own hands back into a more normal angle with his wrists. Once he had regained parity, Wulfgar realized that one sudden push would put his opponent into the same disadvantage that he had just escaped. From there, the dark-haired man would have little chance of holding on.

But Wulfgar wasn't anxious to end this contest. He didn't want to humiliate his opponent—that would breed only an enemy—and even more importantly, he knew that Drizzt was about. The longer he could keep the contest going, and the eyes of every member of the tribe fixed upon him, the longer Drizzt would have to put some plan into motion.

The two men held there for many seconds, and Wulfgar couldn't help but smile when he noticed a dark shape slip in among the horses, behind the enthralled guards at the other end of the camp. Whether it was his imagination, he could not tell, but he thought that he saw two points of lavender flame staring out at him from the darkness. A few seconds more, he decided, though he knew that he was taking a chance by not finishing the challenge. The shaman could declare a draw if they held for too long.

But then it was over. The veins and sinews in Wulfgar's arms bulged and his shoulders lifted even higher. "Tempus!" he growled, praising the god for yet another victory, and then with a sudden, ferocious explosion of power, he drove the dark-haired man to his knees. All around, the camp went silent, even the shaman being stricken speechless by the display.

Two guards moved tentatively to Wulfgar's side.

The beaten warrior pulled himself to his feet and stood facing Wulfgar. No hints of anger marred his face, just honest admiration, for the Sky Ponies were an honorable people.

"We would welcome you," Valric said. "You have defeated Torlin, son of Jerek Wolf-slayer, Chieftain of the Sky Ponies. Never before has Torlin been bested!"

"What of my friends?" Wulfgar asked.

"I care nothing for them!" Valric snapped back. "The dwarf will be set free on a trail leading from our land. We have no quarrel with him or his kind, nor do we desire any dealings with them!"

The shaman eyed Wulfgar slyly. "The other is a weakling," he stated. "He shall serve as your passage to the tribe, your sacrifice to the winged horse."

Wulfgar did not immediately respond. They had tested his strength, and now were testing his loyalties. The Sky Ponies had paid him their highest honor in offering him a place in their tribe, but only on condition that he show his allegiance beyond any doubt. Wulfgar thought of his own people, and the way they had lived for so many centuries on the tundra.

Even in this day, many of the barbarians of Icewind Dale would have accepted the terms and killed Regis, considering the life of a halfling a small price for such an honor. This was the disillusionment of Wulfgar's existence with his people, the facet of their moral code that had proved unacceptable to his personal standards.

"No," he replied to Valric without blinking.

"He is a weakling!" Valric reasoned. "Only the strong deserve life!"

"His fate is not mine to decide," Wulfgar replied. "Nor yours."

Valric motioned to the two guards and they immediately rebound Wulfgar's hands.

"A loss for our people," Torlin said to Wulfgar. "You would have received a place of honor among us."

Wulfgar didn't answer, holding Torlin's stare for a long moment, sharing respect and also the mutual understanding that their codes were too different for such a joining. In a shared fantasy that could not be, both imagined fighting beside the other, felling orcs by the score and inspiring the bards to a new legend.

It was time for Drizzt to strike. The drow had paused by the horses to view the outcome of the contest and also to better measure his enemies. He planned his attack for effect more than for damage, wanting to put on a grand show to cow a tribe of fearless warriors long enough for his friends to break free of the ring.

No doubt, the barbarians had heard of the dark elves. And no doubt, the tales they had heard were terrifying.

Silently, Drizzt tied the two ponies behind the horses, then mounted the horses, a foot in one stirrup on each. Rising between them, he stood tall and threw back the cowl of his cloak. The dangerous glow in his lavender eyes sparkling wildly, he bolted the mounts into the ring, scattering the stunned barbarians closest to him.

Howls of rage rose up from the surprised tribesmen, the tone of the shouts shifting to one of terror when they viewed the black skin. Torlin and Valric turned to face the oncoming menace, though even they did not know how to deal with a legend personified.

And Drizzt had a trick ready for them. With a wave of his black hand, purple flames spouted from Torlin and Valric's skin, not burning, but casting both the superstitious tribesmen into a horrified frenzy. Torlin dropped to his knees, clasping his arms in disbelief, while the high-strung shaman dived to the ground and began rolling in the dirt.

Wulfgar took his cue. Another surge of power through his arms snapped the leather bonds at his wrists. He continued the momentum of his hands, swinging them upward, catching both of the guards beside him squarely in the face and dropping them to their backs.

Bruenor also understood his part. He stomped heavily onto the instep of the lone barbarian standing between him and Regis, and when the man crouched to grasp his pained foot, Bruenor butted him in the head. The man tumbled as easily as Whisper had back in Rat Alley in Luskan.

"Huh, works as well without the helmet!" Bruenor marveled.

"Only for a dwarf's head!" Regis remarked as Wulfgar grabbed both of them by the back of their collars and hoisted them easily onto the ponies.

He was up then, too, beside Drizzt, and they charged through the other side of the camp. It had all happened too quickly for any of the barbarians to ready a weapon or form any kind of defense.

Drizzt wheeled his horse behind the ponies to protect the rear. "Ride!" he yelled to his friends, slapping their mounts on the rump with the flat of his scimitars. The other three shouted in victory as though their escape was complete, but Drizzt knew that this had been the easy part. The dawn was fast approaching, and in this up-and-down, unfamiliar terrain, the native barbarians could easily catch them.

The companions charged into the silence of pre-dawn, picking the straightest and easiest path to gain as much ground as possible. Drizzt still kept an eye behind them, expecting the tribesmen to be fast on their trail. But the commotion in the camp had died away almost immediately after the escape, and the drow saw no signs of pursuit.

Now only a single call could be heard, the rhythmic singing of Valric in a tongue that none of the travelers understood. The look of dread on Wulfgar's face made all of them pause. "The powers of a shaman," the barbarian explained.

Back in the camp, Valric stood alone with Torlin inside the ring of his people, chanting and dancing through the ultimate ritual of his station, summoning the power of his tribe's Spiritual Beast. The appearance of the drow elf had completely unnerved the shaman. He stopped any pursuit before it had even begun and ran to his tent for the sacred leather satchel needed for the ritual, deciding that the spirit of the winged horse, the Pegasus, should deal with these intruders.

Valric targeted Torlin as the recipient of the spirit's form, and the son of Jerek awaited the possession with stoic dignity, hating the act, for it stripped him of his identity, but resigned to absolute obedience to his shaman.

From the moment it began, however, Valric knew that in his excitement, he had overstepped the urgency of the summoning.

Torlin shrieked and dropped to the ground, writhing in agony. A gray cloud surrounded him, its swirling vapors molding with his form, reshaping his features. His face puffed and twisted, and suddenly spurted outward into the semblance of a horse's head. His torso, as well, transmuted into something not human. Valric had meant only to impart some of the strengths of the spirit of the Pegasus in Torlin, but the entity itself had come, possessing the man wholly and bending his body into its own likeness.

Torlin was consumed.

In his place loomed the ghostly form of the winged horse. All in the tribe fell to their knees before it, even Valric, who could not face the image of the Spiritual Beast. But the Pegasus knew the shaman's thoughts and understood its children's needs. Smoke fumed from the spirit's nostrils and it rose into the air in pursuit of the escaping intruders.

The friends had settled their mounts into a more comfortable, though still swift, pace. Free of their bonds, with the dawn breaking before them and no apparent pursuit behind them, they had eased up a bit. Bruenor fiddled with his helmet, trying to push the latest dent out far enough for him to get the thing back on his head. Even Wulfgar, so shaken a short time before when he had heard the chanting of the shaman, began to relax.

Only Drizzt, ever wary, was not so easily convinced of their escape. And it was the drow who first sensed the approach of danger.

In the dark cities, the black elves often dealt with otherworldly beings, and over the many centuries they had bred into their race a sensitivity for the magical emanations of such creatures. Drizzt stopped his horse suddenly and wheeled about.

"What do ye hear?" Bruenor asked him.

"I hear nothing," Drizzt answered, his eyes darting about for some sign. "But something is there."

Before they could respond, the gray cloud rushed down from the sky and was upon them. Their horses bucked and reared in uncontrollable terror and in the confusion none of the friends could sort out what was happening. The Pegasus then formed right in front of Regis and the halfling fell a deathly chill penetrate his bones. He screamed and dropped from his mount.

Bruenor, riding beside Regis, charged the ghostly form fearlessly. But his descending axe found only a cloud of smoke where the apparition had been. Then, just as suddenly, the ghost was back, and Bruenor, too, felt the icy cold of its touch. Tougher than the halfling, he managed to hold to his pony.

"What?" he cried out vainly to Drizzt and Wulfgar.

Aegis-fang whistled past him and continued on at the target. But the Pegasus was only smoke again and the magical warhammer passed unhindered through the swirling cloud.

In an instant, the spirit was back, swooping down upon Bruenor. The dwarf's pony spun down to the ground in a frantic effort to scramble away from the thing.

"You cannot hit it!" Drizzt called after Wulfgar, who went rushing to the dwarf's aid. "It does not exist fully on this plane!"

Wulfgar's mighty legs locked his terrified horse straight and he struck as soon as Aegis-fang returned to his hands.

But again he found only smoke before his blow.

"Then how?" he yelled to Drizzt, his eyes darting around to spot the first signs of the reforming spirit.

Drizzt searched his mind for answers. Regis was still down, lying pale and unmoving on the field, and Bruenor, though he had not been too badly injured in his pony's fall, appeared dazed and shivering from the chill of unearthly cold. Drizzt grasped at a desperate plan. He pulled the onyx statue of the panther from his pouch and called for Guenhwyvar.

The ghost returned, attacking with renewed fury. It descended upon Bruenor first, mantling the dwarf with its cold wings. "Damn ye back to the Abyss!" Bruenor roared in brave defiance.

Rushing in, Wulfgar lost all sight of the dwarf, except for the head of his axe bursting harmlessly through the smoke.

Then the barbarian's mount halted in its tracks, refusing, against all efforts, to move any closer to the unnatural beast. Wulfgar leaped from his saddle and charged in, crashing right through the cloud before the ghost could reform, his momentum carrying both him and Bruenor out the other side of the smoky mantle. They rolled away and looked back, only to find that the ghost had disappeared altogether again.

Bruenor's eyelids drooped heavily and his skin held a ghastly hue of blue, and for the first time in his life, his indomitable spirit had no gumption for the fight. Wulfgar, too, had suffered the icy touch in his pass through the ghost, but he was still more than ready for another round with the thing.

"We can't fight it!" Bruenor gasped through his chattering teeth. "Here for a strike, it is, but gone when we hit back!"

Wulfgar shook his head defiantly. "There is a way!" he demanded, though he had to concede the dwarf's point. "But my hammer cannot destroy clouds!"

Guenhwyvar appeared beside her master and crouched low, seeking the nemesis that threatened the drow.

Drizzt understood the cat's intentions. "No!" he commanded. "Not here." The drow had recalled something that Guenhwyvar had done several months earlier. To save Regis from the falling stone of a crumbling tower, Guenhwyvar had taken the halfling on a journey through the planes of existence. Drizzt grabbed onto the panther's thick coat.

"Take me to the land of the ghost," he instructed. "To its own plane, where my weapons will bite deeply into its substantial being."

The ghost appeared again as Drizzt and the cat faded into their own cloud.

"Keep swinging!" Bruenor told his companion. "Keep it as smoke so's it can't get at ye!"

"Drizzt and the cat have gone!" Wulfgar cried.

"To the land of the ghost," Bruenor explained.

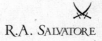
⚔ ⚔ ⚔ ⚔

It took Drizzt a long moment to set his bearings. He had come into a place of different realities, a dimension where everything, even his own skin, assumed the same hue of gray, objects being distinguishable only by a thin waver of black that outlined them. His depth perception was useless, for there were no shadings, and no discernible light sources to use as a guide. And he found no footing, nothing tangible beneath him, nor could he even know which way was up or down. Such concepts didn't seem to fit here.

He did make out the shifting outlines of the Pegasus as it jumped between planes, never fully in one place or the other. He tried to approach it and found propulsion to be an act of the mind, his body automatically following the instructions of his will. He stopped before the shifting lines, his magical scimitar poised to strike when the target fully appeared.

Then the outline of the Pegasus was complete and Drizzt plunged his blade into the black waver that marked its form. The line shifted and bent, and the outline of the scimitar shivered as well, for here even the properties of the steel blade took on a different composition. But the steel proved the stronger and the scimitar resumed its curved edge and punctured the line of the ghost. There came a sudden tingling in the grayness, as though Drizzt's cut had disturbed the equilibrium of the plane, and the ghost's line trembled in a shiver of agony.

Wulfgar saw the smoke cloud puff suddenly, almost reforming into the ghost shape. "Drizzt!" he called out to Bruenor. "He has met the ghost on even terms!"

"Get ye ready, then!" Bruenor replied anxiously, though he knew that his own part in the fight had ended. "The drow might bring it back to ye long enough for a hit!" Bruenor clutched at his sides, trying to hug the deathly cold out of his bones, and stumbled over to the halfling's unmoving form.

The ghost turned on Drizzt, but the scimitar struck again. And Guenhwyvar jumped into the fray, the cat's great claws tearing into the black outline of her enemy. The Pegasus reeled away from them, understanding that it held no advantage against foes on its own plane. Its only recourse was a retreat back to the material plane.

Where Wulfgar waited.

As soon as the cloud resumed its shape, Aegis-fang hammered into it. Wulfgar felt a solid strike for just a moment, and knew that he had hit his mark. Then the smoke blew away before him.

The ghost was back with Drizzt and Guenhwyvar, again facing their relentless stabs and rakes. It shifted back again, and Wulfgar struck quickly. Trapped with no retreat, the ghost took hits from both planes. Every time it materialized before Drizzt, the drow noted that its outline came thinner and less resistant to his thrusts. And every time the cloud reformed before Wulfgar, its density had diminished. The friends had won, and Drizzt watched in satisfaction as the essence of the Pegasus slipped free of the material form and floated away through the grayness.

"Take me home," the weary drow instructed Guenhwyvar. A moment later, he was back on the field beside Bruenor and Regis.

"He'll live," Bruenor stated flatly at Drizzt's inquiring look. "More to faintin' than to dying'd be me guess."

A short distance away, Wulfgar, too, was hunched over a form, broken and twisted and caught in a transformation somewhere between man and beast. "Torlin, son of Jerek," Wulfgar explained. He lifted his gaze back toward the barbarian camp. "Valric has done this. The blood of Torlin soils his hands!"

"Torlin's own choice, perhaps?" Drizzt offered.

"Never!" Wulfgar insisted. "When we met in challenge, my eyes looked upon honor. He was a warrior. He would never have allowed this!" He stepped away from the corpse, letting its mutilated remains emphasize the horror of the possession. In the frozen pose of death, Torlin's face had retained half the features of a man, and half of the equine ghost.

"He was the son of their chieftain," Wulfgar explained. "He could not refuse the demands of the shaman."

"He was brave to accept such a fate," Drizzt remarked.

"Son of their chieftain?" snorted Bruenor. "Seems we've put even more enemies on the road behind us! They'll be looking to settle this score."

"As will I!" Wulfgar proclaimed. "His blood is yours to carry, Valric High Eye!" he shouted into the distance, his calls echoing around the mounds of the crags. Wulfgar looked back to his friends, rage seething in his features, as he declared grimly, "I shall avenge Torlin's dishonor."

Bruenor nodded his approval at the barbarian's dedication to his principles.

"An honorable task," Drizzt agreed, holding his blade out to the east, toward Longsaddle, the next stop along their journey. "But one for another day."

7
DAGGER AND STAFF

Entreri stood on a hill a few miles outside the City of Sails, his campfire burning low behind him. Regis and friends had used this same spot for their last stop before they entered Luskan and in fact, the assassin's fire burned in the very same pit. This was no coincidence, though. Entreri had mimicked every move the halfling's party had made since he had picked up their trail just south of the Spine of the World. He would move as they moved, shadowing their marches in an effort to better understand their actions.

Now, unlike the party before him, Entreri's eyes were not on the city wall, nor toward Luskan at all. Several campfires had sprung up in the night to the north, on the road back to Ten-Towns. It wasn't the first time those lights had appeared behind him, and the assassin sensed that he, too, was being followed. He had slowed his frantic pace, figuring that he could easily make up the ground while the companions went about their business in Luskan. He wanted to secure his own back from any danger before concentrating on snaring the halfling. Entreri had even left telltale signs of his passing, baiting his pursuers in closer.

He kicked the embers of the fire low and climbed back into the saddle, deciding it better to meet a sword face to face than to take a dagger in the back.

Into the night he rode, confident in the darkness. This was his time, where every shadow added to the advantage of one who lived in shadows.

He tethered his mount before midnight, close enough to the campfires to finish the trek on foot. He realized now that this was a merchant caravan; not an uncommon thing on the road to Luskan at this time of year. But his sense of danger nagged at him. Many years of experience had honed his instinct for survival and he knew better than to ignore it.

He crept in, seeking the easiest way into the circle of wagons. Merchants always lined many sentries around the perimeter of their camps, and even the pull-horses presented a problem, for the merchants kept them tied close beside their harnesses.

Still, the assassin would not waste his ride. He had come this far and meant to find out the purpose of those who followed him. Slithering on his belly, he made his way to the perimeter and began circling the camp underneath the defensive ring. Too silently for even wary ears to hear, he passed two guards playing at bones. Then he went under and between the horses, the beasts lowering their ears in fear, but remaining quiet.

Halfway around the circle, he was nearly convinced that this was an ordinary merchant caravan, and was just about to slip back into the night when he heard a familiar female voice.

"Ye said ye saw a spot o' light in the distance."

Entreri stopped, for he knew the speaker.

"Yeah, over there," a man replied.

Entreri slipped up between the next two wagons and peeked over the side. The speakers stood a short distance from him, behind the next wagon, peering into the night in the direction of his camp. Both were dressed for battle, the woman wearing her sword comfortably.

"I have underestimated you," Entreri whispered to himself as he viewed Catti-brie. His jeweled dagger was already in his hand. "A mistake I shan't repeat," he added, then crouched low and searched for a path to his target.

"Ye been good to me, for bringing me so fast," Catti-brie said. "I'm owing to ye, as Regis and the others'll be."

"Then tell me," the man urged. "What causes such urgency?"

Catti-brie struggled with the memories of the assassin. She hadn't yet come to terms with her terror that day in the halfling's house, and knew that she wouldn't until she had avenged the deaths of the two dwarven friends and resolved her own humiliation. Her lips tightened and she did not reply.

"As you wish," the man conceded. "Your reasons justify the run, we do not doubt. If we seem to pry, it only shows our desire to help you however we may."

Catti-brie turned to him, a smile of sincere appreciation on her face. Enough had been said, and the two stood and stared at the empty horizon in silence.

Silent, too, was the approach of death.

Entreri slipped out from under the wagon and rose suddenly between them, one hand outstretched to each. He grasped Catti-brie's neck tightly enough to prevent her scream, and he silenced the man forever with his blade.

Looking across the breadth of Entreri's shoulders, Catti-brie saw the horrific expression locked onto her companion's face, but she couldn't understand why he hadn't cried out, for his mouth was not covered.

Entreri shifted back a bit and she knew. Only the jeweled dagger's hilt was visible, its crosspiece flat against the underside of the man's chin. The slender blade had found the man's brain before he ever realized the danger. Entreri used the weapon's handle to guide his victim quietly to the ground, then jerked it free.

Again the woman found herself paralyzed before the horror of Entreri. She felt that she should wrench away and shout out to the camp, even though he would surely kill her. Or draw her sword and at least try to fight back. But she watched helplessly as Entreri slipped her own dagger from her belt and pulling her low with him, replaced it in the man's fatal wound.

Then he took her sword and pushed her down under the wagon and out beyond the camp's perimeter.

Why can't I call out? she asked herself again and again, for the assassin, confident of the level of terror, didn't even hold her as they slipped deeper into the night. He knew, and she had to admit to herself, that she would not give up her life so easily.

Finally, when they were a safe distance from the camp, he spun her around to face him—and the dagger. "Follow me?" he asked, laughing at her. "What could you hope to gain?"

She did not answer, but found some of her strength returning.

Entreri sensed it, too. "If you call out, I shall kill you," he declared flatly. "And then, by my word, I shall return to the merchants and kill them all as well!"

She believed him.

"I often travel with the merchants," she lied, holding the quiver in her voice. "It is one of the duties of my rank as a soldier of Ten-Towns."

Entreri laughed at her again. Then he looked into the distance, his features assuming an introspective tilt. "Perhaps this will play to my advantage," he said rhetorically, the beginnings of a plan formulating in his mind.

Catti-brie studied him, worried that he had found some way to turn her excursion into harm for her friends.

"I'll not kill you—not yet," he said to her. "When we find the halfling, his friends will not defend him. Because of you."

"I'll do nothing to aid ye!" Catti-brie spat. "Nothing!"

"Precisely," Entreri hissed. "You shall do nothing. Not with a blade at your neck—" he brought the weapon up to her throat in a morbid tease— "scratching at your smooth skin. When I am done with my business, brave girl, I shall move on, and you shall be left with your shame and your guilt. And your answers to the merchants who believe you murdered their companion!" In truth, Entreri didn't believe for a moment that his simple trick with Catti-brie's dagger would fool the merchants. It was merely a psychological weapon aimed at the young woman, designed to instill yet another doubt and worry into her jumble of emotions

Catti-brie did not reply to the assassin's statements with any sign of emotion. No, she told herself, it won't be like that!

But deep inside, she wondered if her determination only masked her fear, her own belief that she would be held again by the horror of Entreri's presence, and that the scene would unfold exactly as he had predicted.

Jierdan found the campsite with little difficulty. Dendybar had used his magic to track the mysterious rider all the way from the mountains and had pointed the soldier in the right direction.

Tensed and his sword drawn, Jierdan moved in. The place was deserted, but it had not been that way for long. Even from a few feet away, the soldier from Luskan could feel the dying warmth of the campfire. Crouching low to mask his silhouette against the line of the horizon, he crept toward a pack and blanket off to the side of the fire.

Entreri rode his mount back into camp slowly, expecting that what he had left might have drawn some visitors. Catti-brie sat in front of him, securely bound and gagged, though she fully believed, to her own disgust, that her own terror made the bonds unnecessary.

The wary assassin realized that someone had entered the camp, before he had ever gotten near the place. He slid from his saddle, taking his prisoner with him. "A nervous steed," he explained to Catti-brie, taking obvious pleasure in the grim warning as he tied her to the horse's rear legs, "If you struggle, he will kick the life from you."

Then Entreri was gone, blending into the night as though he were an extension of its darkness.

Jierdan dropped the pack back to the ground, frustrated, for its contents were merely standard traveling gear and revealed nothing about the owner. The soldier was a veteran of many campaigns and had bested man and orc alike a hundred times, but he was nervous now, sensing something unusual, and deadly, about the rider. A man with the courage to ride alone on the brutal course from Icewind Dale to Luskan was no novice to the ways of battle.

Jierdan was startled, then, but not too surprised, when the tip of a blade came to rest suddenly in the vulnerable hollow on the back of his neck, just below the base of his skull. He neither moved nor spoke, hoping that the rider would ask for some explanation before driving the weapon home.

Entreri could see that his pack had been searched, but he recognized the furred uniform and knew that this man was no thief. "We are beyond the borders of your city," he said, holding his knife steady. "What business have you in my camp, soldier of Luskan?"

"I am Jierdan of the north gate," he replied. "I have come to meet a rider from Icewind Dale."

"What rider?"

"You."

Entreri was perplexed and uncomfortable with the soldier's response. Who had sent this man, and how had he known where to look? The assassin's first thoughts centered on Regis's party. Perhaps the halfling had arranged for some help from the city guard. Entreri slipped his knife back into its sheath, certain that he could retrieve it in time to foil any attack.

Jierdan understood the calm confidence of the act as well, and any thoughts that he might have had for striking at this man flew from him. "My master desires your audience," he said, thinking it wise to explain himself more completely. "A meeting to your mutual benefit."

"Your master?" asked Entreri.

"A citizen of high standing," Jierdan explained. "He has heard of your coming and believes that he may help with your quest."

"What does he know of my business?" Entreri snapped, angered that someone had dared to spy on him. But he was relieved, too, for the involvement of some other power structure within the city explained much, and possibly eliminated the logical assumption that the halfling was behind this meeting.

Jierdan shrugged. "I am merely his courier. But I, too, can be of assistance to you. At the gate."

"Damn the gate," Entreri snarled. "I'll take the wall easily enough. It is a more direct route to the places I seek."

"Even so, I know of those places, and of the people who control them."

The knife leaped back out, cutting in and stopping just before Jierdan's throat. "You know much, but you explain little. You play dangerous games, soldier of Luskan."

Jierdan didn't blink. "Four heroes from Ten-Towns came into Luskan five days ago: a dwarf, a halfling, a barbarian, and a black elf." Even Artemis Entreri couldn't hide a hint of excitement at the confirmation of his suspicions, and Jierdan noted the signs. "Their exact location escapes me, but I know the area where they are hiding. Are you interested?"

The knife returned again to its sheath. "Wait here," Entreri instructed. "I have a companion who shall travel with us."

"My master said that you rode alone," Jierdan queried.

Entreri's vile grin sent a shiver through the soldier's spine. "I acquired her," he explained. "She is mine and that is all that you ever need to know."

Jierdan didn't press the point. His sigh of relief was audible when Entreri had disappeared from sight.

Catti-brie rode to Luskan untied and ungagged, but Entreri's hold upon her was no less binding. His warning to her when he had retrieved her in the field had been succinct and undeniable. "A foolish move," he had said, "and you die. And you die with the knowledge that the dwarf, Bruenor, shall suffer for your insolence."

The assassin had told Jierdan no more about her, and the soldier didn't ask, though the woman intrigued him more than a little. Dendybar would get the answers, Jierdan knew.

They moved into the city later that morning, under the suspicious eye of the Daykeeper of the North Gate. It had cost Jierdan a tenday's pay to bribe them through, and the soldier knew he would owe even more when he returned that night, for the original deal with the Daykeeper allowed the passage of one outsider; nothing had been said about the woman. But if Jierdan's actions brought him Dendybar's favor, then they would be well worth the price.

According to the city code, the three gave up their horses at the stable just inside the wall, and Merdan led Entreri and Catti-brie through the streets of the City of Sails, past the sleepy-eyed merchants and vendors who had been out since before dawn and into the very heart of the city.

The assassin was not surprised an hour later when they came upon a long grove of thick pine trees. He had suspected that Jierdan was somehow connected to this place. They passed through a break in the line and stood before the tallest structure in the city, the Hosttower of the Arcane.

"Who is your master?" Entreri asked bluntly.

Jierdan chuckled, his nerve bolstered by the sight of Dendybar's tower. "You shall meet him soon enough."

"I shall know now," Entreri growled. "Or our meeting is ended. I am in the city, soldier, and I do not require your assistance any longer."

"I could have the guards expel you," Jierdan shot back. "Or worse!"

But Entreri had the last word. "They would never find the remains of your body," he promised, the cold certainty of his tone draining the blood from Jierdan's face.

Catti-brie noted the exchange with more than a passing concern for the soldier, wondering if the time might soon come when she could exploit the untrusting nature of her captors to her own advantage.

"I serve Dendybar the Mottled, Master of the North Spire," Jierdan declared, drawing further strength from the mention of his powerful mentor's name.

Entreri had heard the name before. The Hosttower was a common topic of the whisperings all around Luskan and the surrounding countryside, and the name of Dendybar the Mottled came up often in conversation, describing the wizard as an ambitious power seeker in the tower, and hinting at a dark and sinister side of the man that allowed him to get what he wanted. He was dangerous, but potentially a powerful ally. Entreri was pleased. "Take me to him now," he told Jierdan. "Let us discover if we have business or no."

Sydney was waiting to escort them from the entry room of the Hosttower. Offering no introduction, and asking for none, she led them through the twisting passages and secret doors to the audience hall of Dendybar the Mottled. The wizard waited there in grand style, wearing his finest robes and with a fabulous luncheon set before him.

"Greetings, rider," Dendybar said after the necessary, yet uncomfortable, moments of silence when each of the parties sized up the other. "I am Dendybar the Mottled, as you are already aware. Will you and your lovely companion partake of my table?"

His raspy voice grated on Catti-brie's nerves, and though she hadn't eaten since the supper the day before, she had no appetite for this man's hospitality.

Entreri shoved her forward. "Eat," he commanded.

She knew that Entreri was testing both her and the wizards. But it was time for her to test Entreri as well. "No," she answered, looking him straight in the eye.

His backhand knocked her to the floor. Jierdan and Sydney started reflexively, but seeing no help forthcoming from Dendybar, quickly stopped and settled back to watch. Catti-brie moved away from the killer and remained in a defensive crouch.

Dendybar smiled at the assassin. "You have answered some of my questions about the girl," he said with an amused smile. "What purpose does she serve?"

I have my reasons," was all that Entreri replied.

"Of course. And might I learn your name?"

Entreri's expression did not change.

"You seek the four companions from Ten-Towns, I know," Dendybar continued, having no desire to bandy the issue. "I seek them, as well, but for different reasons, I am sure."

"You know nothing of my reasons," Entreri replied.

"Nor do I care," laughed the wizard. "We can help each other to our separate goals. That is all that interests me."

"I ask for no help."

Dendybar laughed again. "They are a mighty force, rider. You underestimate them."

"Perhaps," replied Entreri. "But you have asked my purpose, yet have not offered your own. What business does the Hosttower have with travelers from Ten-Towns?"

"Fairly asked," answered Dendybar. "But I should wait until we have formalized an agreement before rendering an answer."

"Then I shan't sleep well for worry," Entreri spat.

Again the wizard laughed. "You may change your mind before this is finished," he said. "For now I offer a sign of good faith. The companions are in the city. Dockside. They were to stay in the Cutlass. Do you know it?"

Entreri nodded, now very interested in the, wizard's words.

"But we have lost them in the alleyways of the western city," Dendybar explained, shooting a glare at Jierdan that made the soldier shift uneasily.

"And what is the price of this information?" Entreri asked.

"None," replied the wizard. "Telling you helps my own cause. You will get what you want; what I desire will remain for me."

Entreri smiled, understanding that Dendybar intended to use him as a hound to sniff out the prey.

"My apprentice will show you out," Dendybar said, motioning to Sydney.

Entreri turned to leave, pausing to meet the gaze of Jierdan. "Ware my path, soldier," the assassin warned. "Vultures eat after the cat has feasted!"

"When he has shown me to the drow, I'll have his head," Jierdan growled when they had gone.

"You shall keep clear of that one," Dendybar instructed.

Jierdan looked at him, puzzled. "Surely you want him watched."

"Surely," agreed Dendybar. "But by Sydney, not you. Keep your anger," Dendybar said to him, noting the outraged scowl. "I preserve your life. Your pride is great, indeed, and you have earned the right. But this one is beyond your prowess, my friend. His blade would have you before you ever knew he was there."

Outside, Entreri led Catti-brie away from the Hosttower without a word, silently replaying and reviewing the meeting, for he knew that he had not seen the last of Dendybar and his cohorts.

Catti-brie was glad of the silence, too, engulfed in her own contemplations. Why would a wizard of the Hosttower be looking for Bruenor and the others? Revenge for Akar Kessell, the mad wizard that her friends had helped defeat before the last winter? She looked back to the treelike structure, and to the killer at her side, amazed and horrified at the attention her friends had brought upon themselves.

Then she looked into her own heart, reviving her spirit and her courage. Drizzt, Bruenor, Wulfgar, and Regis were going to need her help before this was all over. She must not fail them.

PART TWO

He wants to go home. He wants to find a
world he once knew. I know not if it is the
promise of riches or of simplicity that now drives
Bruenor. He wants to go and find Mithral Hall,
to clear it of whatever monsters
might now inhabit the place, to ALLIES
reclaim it for Clan Battlehammer.

On the surface that desire seems a reasonable,
even noble, thing. We all quest for adventure,
and for those whose families have lived in
noble tradition, the desire to avenge a wrong
and restore family name and position cannot
be underestimated.

Our road to Mithral Hall will not likely
be an easy one. Many dangerous, uncivilized
lands lay between Icewind Dale and the region
far to the east of Luskan, and certainly that
road promises to become even darker if we do
find the entrance to those lost dwarven mines.
But I am surrounded by capable and powerful

friends, and so I fear no monsters—none that we can fight with sword, at least. No, my one fear concerning this journey we undertake is a fear for Bruenor Battlehammer. He wants to go home, and there are many good reasons why he should. There remains one good reason why he should not, and if that reason, nostalgia, is the source of his desire, then I fear he will be bitterly disappointed.

Nostalgia is possibly the greatest of the lies that we all tell ourselves. It is the glossing of the past to fit the sensibilities of the present. For some, it brings a measure of comfort, a sense of self and of source, but others, I fear, take these altered memories too far, and because of that, paralyze themselves to the realities about them.

How many people long for that "past, simpler, and better world," I wonder, without ever recognizing the truth that perhaps it was they who were simpler and better, and not the world about them?

As a drow elf, I expect to live several centuries, but those first few decades of life for a drow, and for a surface elf, are not so different in terms of emotional development from those of a human, or a halfling or a dwarf. I, too, remember that idealism and energy of my more youthful days, when the world seemed an uncomplicated place, when right and wrong were plainly written on the path before my every stride. Perhaps, in a strange sort of way, because of the fact that my early years were so full of terrible experiences, were so full of an environment and an experience that I simply could not tolerate, I am better off now. For unlike so many of those I have met on the surface, my existence has steadily improved.

Has that contributed to my optimism, for my own existence and for all the world around me?

So many people, particularly humans who have passed the middle of their expected lives, continue to look back for their paradise, continue to claim that the world was a far better place when they were young.

I cannot believe that. There may be specific instances where that is true—a tyrant king replaces a compassionate ruler, an era of health engulfs the land after a plague—but I believe, I must believe, that the people of the world are an improving lot, that the natural evolution of civilizations, though not necessarily a straight-line progression, moves toward the betterment of the world. For every time a better way is found, the people will naturally gravitate in that direction while failed experiments will be abandoned. I have listened to Wulfgar's renderings of the history of his people, the barbarian tribes of Icewind Dale, for example, and I am amazed and horrified by the brutality of their past, the constant fighting of tribe against tribe, the wholesale rape of captured women and the torture of captured men. The tribesmen of Icewind Dale are still a brutal lot, no doubt, but not, if the oral traditions are to be believed, on a par with their predecessors. And that makes perfect sense to me, and thus, I have hopes that the trend will continue. Perhaps one day, a great barbarian leader will emerge who truly finds love with a woman, who finds a wife who forces from him a measure of respect practically unknown among the barbarians. Will that leader somewhat elevate the status of women among the tribes?

If that happens, the barbarians tribes of Icewind Dale will find a strength that they simply do not understand within half of their population. If that happens, if the barbarian women find an elevation of status, then the tribesmen will never, ever, force them back into their current roles that can only be described as slavery.

And all of them, man and woman, will be better for the change.

Because for change to be lasting among reasoning creatures, that change must be for the better. And so civilizations, peoples, evolve to a better understanding and a better place.

For the Matron Mothers of Menzoberranzan, as with many generations of tyrant families, as with many rich landowners, change can be seen as a definite threat to their power base, and so their resistance to it seems logical, even expected. How, then, can we find explanation in the fact that so many, many people, even people who live in squalor, as did their parents and their parents' parents, and back for generation after generation, view any change with an equal fear and revulsion? Why would not the lowliest peasant desire evolution of civilization if that evolution might lead to a better life for his children?

That would seem logical, but I have seen that it is not the case, for many if not most of the short-lived humans who have passed their strongest and healthiest years, who have put their own better days behind them, accepting any change seems no easy thing. No, so many of them clutch at the past, when the world was "simpler and better." They rue change on a personal level, as if any improvements those coming behind them might make will shine a bright and revealing light on their own failings.

Perhaps that is it. Perhaps it is one of our most basic fears, and one wrought of foolish pride, that our children will know better than we do. At the same time that so many people tout the virtues of their children, is there some deep fear within them that those children will see the errors of their parents?

I have no answers to this seeming paradox, but for Bruenor's sake, I pray that he seeks Mithral Hall for the right reasons, for the adventure and the challenge, for the sake of his heritage and the restoration of his family name, and not for any desire he might have to make the world as it once was.

Nostalgia is a necessary thing, I believe, and a way for all of us to find peace in that which we have accomplished, or even failed to accomplish. At the same time, if nostalgia precipitates actions to return to that fabled, rosy-painted time, particularly in one who believes his life to be a failure, then it is an empty thing, doomed to produce nothing but frustration and an even greater sense of failure. Even worse, if nostalgia throws barriers in the path toward evolution, then it is a limiting thing indeed.

—Drizzt Do'Urden

8
To the Peril Of Low-Flying Birds

The companions broke out of the twists and dips of the crags later in the afternoon, to their absolute relief. It had taken them some time to round up their mounts after the encounter with the Pegasus, particularly the halfling's pony, which had bolted early in the fight when Regis had gone down. In truth, the pony would not be ridden again, anyway; it was too skittish and Regis was in no condition to ride. But Drizzt had insisted that both horses and both ponies be found, reminding his companions of their responsibility to the farmers, especially considering the way they had appropriated the beasts.

Regis now sat before Wulfgar on the barbarian's stallion, leading the way with his pony tied behind and Drizzt and Bruenor a short distance back, guarding the rear. Wulfgar kept his great arms close around the halfling, his protective hold secure enough to allow Regis some much-needed sleep.

"Keep the setting sun at our backs," Drizzt instructed the barbarian.

Wulfgar called out his acknowledgement and looked back to confirm his bearings.

"Rumblebelly couldn't find a safer place in all the Realms," Bruenor remarked to the drow.

Drizzt smiled. "Wulfgar has done well."

"Aye," the dwarf agreed, obviously pleased. "Though I be wondering how much longer I can keep to callin' him a boy! Ye should have seen the Cutlass, elf," the dwarf chuckled, "A boatload of pirates who'd been seeing naught but the sea for a year and a day couldn't've done more wrecking!"

"When we left the dale, I worried if Wulfgar was ready for the many societies of this wide world," replied Drizzt. "Now I worry that the world may not be ready for him. You should be proud."

"Ye've had as much a hand in him as meself," said Bruenor. "He's me boy, elf, surer'n if I'd sired him meself. Not a thought to his own fears on the field back there. Ne'er have I viewed such courage in a human as when ye'd gone to the other plane. He waited—he hoped, I tell ye!—for the wretched beast to come back so he could get a good swing in to avenge the hurt to meself and the halfling."

Drizzt enjoyed this rare moment of vulnerability from the dwarf. A few times before, he had seen Bruenor drop his callous facade, back on the climb in Icewind Dale when the dwarf thought of Mithral Hall and the wondrous memories of his childhood.

"Aye, I'm proud," Bruenor continued. "And I'm finding meself willing to follow his lead and trust in his choices."

Drizzt could only agree, having come to the same conclusions many months before, when Wulfgar had united the peoples of Icewind Dale, barbarian and Ten-Towner alike, in a common defense against the harsh tundra winter. He still worried about bringing the young warrior into situations like the dockside of Luskan, for he knew that many of the finest persons in the Realms had paid dearly for their first encounters with the guilds and underground power structures of a city, and that Wulfgar's deep compassion and unwavering code of honor could be manipulated against him.

But on the road, in the wild, Drizzt knew that he would never find a more valuable companion.

They encountered no further problems that day or night, and the next morning came upon the main road, the trading route from Waterdeep to Mirabar and passing Longsaddle on the way. No landmarks stood out to guide them, as Drizzt had anticipated, but because of his plan in keeping more to the east than the straight line southeast, their direction from here was clearly south.

Regis seemed much better this day and was anxious to see Longsaddle. He alone of the group had been to the home of the magic-using Harpell family and he looked forward to viewing the strange, and often outrageous, place again.

His excited chatting only heightened Wulfgar's trepidations, though, for the barbarian's distrust of the dark arts ran deep. Among Wulfgar's people, wizards were viewed as cowards and evil tricksters.

"How long must we remain in this place?" he asked Bruenor and Drizzt, who, with the crags safely behind them, had come up to ride beside him on the wide road.

"Until we get some answers," Bruenor answered. "Or until we figure a better place to go." Wulfgar had to be satisfied with the answer.

Soon they passed some of the outlying farms, drawing curious stares from the men in the fields who leaned on their hoes and rakes to study the party. Shortly after the first of these encounters, they were met on the road by five armed men called Longriders, representing the outer watch of the town.

"Greetings, travelers," said one politely. "Might we ask your intentions in these parts?"

"Ye might . . ." started Bruenor, but Drizzt stopped his sarcastic remark with an outstretched hand.

"We have come to see the Harpells," Regis replied. "Our business does not concern your town, though we seek the wise counsel of the family in the mansion."

"Well met, then," answered the Longrider. "The hill of the Ivy Mansion is just a few miles farther down the road, before Longsaddle proper." He stopped suddenly, noticing the drow. "We could escort you if you desire," he offered, clearing his throat in an effort to politely hide his gawking at the black elf.

"It is not necessary," said Drizzt. "I assure you that we can find the way, and that we mean no ill toward any of the people of Longsaddle."

"Very well." The Longrider stepped his mount aside and the companions continued on.

"Keep to the road, though," he called after them. "Some of the farmers get anxious about people near the boundaries of their land."

"They are kindly folk," Regis explained to his companions as they moved down the road, "and they trust in their wizards."

"Kindly, but wary," Drizzt retorted, motioning to a distant field where the silhouette of a mounted man was barely visible on the far tree line. "We are being watched."

"But not bothered," said Bruenor. "And that's more than we can say about anywhere we've been yet!"

The hill of the Ivy Mansion comprised a small hillock sporting three buildings, two that resembled the low, wooden design of farmhouses. The third, though, was unlike anything the four companions had ever seen. Its walls turned at sharp angles every few feet, creating niches within niches, and dozens and dozens of spires sprouted from its many-angled roof, no two alike. A thousand windows were visible from this direction alone, some huge, others no bigger than an arrow slit.

No one design, no overall architectural plan or style, could be found here. The Harpells' mansion was a collage of independent ideas and experiments in magical creation. But there was truly a beauty within the chaos, a sense of freedom that defied the term "structure" and carried with it a feeling of welcome.

A rail fence surrounded the hillock and the four friends approached curiously, if not excitedly. There was no gate, just an opening and the road continuing through. Seated on a stool inside the fence, staring blankly at the sky, was a fat, bearded man in a carmine robe.

He noticed their arrival with a start. "Who are you and what do you want?" he demanded bluntly, angered at the interruption of his meditation.

"Weary travelers," replied Regis, "come to seek the wisdom of the reknowned Harpells."

The man seemed unimpressed. "And?" he prompted.

Regis turned helplessly to Drizzt and Bruenor, but they could only answer him with shrugs of their own, not understanding what more was required of them. Bruenor started to move his pony out in front to reiterate the group's intentions when another robed man came shuffling out of the mansion to join the first.

He had a few quiet words with the fat mage, then turned to the road. "Greetings," he offered the companions. "Excuse poor Regweld, here—" he patted the fat mage's shoulder—"for he has had an incredible run of bad luck with some experimenting—not that things will not turn out, mind you. They just might take some time."

"Regweld is really a fine wizard," he continued, patting the shoulder again. "And his ideas for crossbreeding a horse and a frog are not without merit; never mind the explosion! Alchemy shops can be replaced!"

The friends sat atop their mounts, biting back their amazement at the rambling discourse. "Why, think of the advantages for crossing rivers!" the robed man cried. "But enough of that. I am Harkle. How might I assist you?"

"Harkle Harpell?" Regis snickered. The man bowed.

"Bruenor of Icewind Dale, I be," Bruenor proclaimed when he had found his voice. "Me friends and meself have come hundreds of miles seeking the words of the wizards of Longsaddle. . . ."

He noticed that Harkle, distracted by the drow, wasn't paying any attention to him. Drizzt had let his cowl slip back purposely to judge the reaction of the reputedly learned men of Longsaddle. The Longrider back on the road had been surprised, but not outraged, and Drizzt had to learn if the town in general would be more tolerant of his heritage.

"Fantastic," muttered Harkle. "Simply unbelievable!" Regweld, too, had now noticed the black elf and seemed interested for the first time since the party had arrived.

"Are we to be allowed passage?" Drizzt asked.

"Oh, yes, please do come in," replied Harkle, trying unsuccessfully to mask his excitement for the sake of etiquette.

Striding his horse out in front, Wulfgar started them up the road.

"Not that way," said Harkle. "Not the road; of course, it is not really a road. Or it is, but you cannot get through."

Wulfgar stopped his mount. "Be done with your foolery, wizard!" he demanded angrily, his years of distrust for practitioners of the magic arts boiling over in his frustration. "May we enter, or not?"

"There is no foolery, I assure you," said Harkle, hoping to keep the meeting amiable. But Regweld cut in.

"One of those," the fat mage said accusingly, rising from his stool.

Wulfgar glared at him curiously.

"A barbarian," Regweld explained. "A warrior trained to hate that which he cannot comprehend. Go ahead, warrior, take that big hammer off of your back."

Wulfgar hesitated, seeing his own unreasonable anger, and looked to his friends for support. He didn't want to spoil Bruenor's plans for the sake of his own pettiness.

"Go ahead," Regweld insisted, moving to the center of the road. "Take up your hammer and throw it at me. Satisfy your heartfelt desire to expose the foolery of a wizard! And strike one down in the process! A bargain if ever I heard one!" He pointed to his chin. "Right here," he chided.

"Regweld," sighed Harkle, shaking his head. "Please oblige him, warrior. Bring a smile to his downcast face."

Wulfgar looked once more to his friends, but again they had no answers. Regweld settled it for him.

"Bastard son of a caribou."

Aegis-fang was out and twirling through the air before the fat mage had finished the insult, bearing straight in on its mark. Regweld didn't flinch, and just before Aegis-fang would have crossed over the fence line, it smacked into something invisible, but as tangible as stone. Resounding like a ceremonial gong, the transparent wall shuddered and waves rolled out along it, visible to the astounded onlookers as mere distortions of the images behind the wall. The friends noticed for the first time that the rail fencing was not real, rather a painting on the surface of the transparent wall.

Aegis-fang dropped to the dust, as though all power had been drained from it, taking a long moment to reappear in Wulfgar's grasp.

Regweld's laughter was more of victory than of humor, but Harkle shook his head. "Always at the expense of others," he scolded. "You had no right to do that."

"He's better for the lesson," Regweld retorted. "Humility is also a valuable commodity for a fighter."

Regis had bitten his lip for as long as he could. He had known about the invisible wall all along, and now his laughter burst out. Drizzt and Bruenor could not help but follow the halfling's lead, and even Wulfgar, after he had recovered from the shock, smirked at his own "foolery."

Of course, Harkle had no choice but to stop his scolding and join in. "Do come in," he begged the friends. "The third post is real; you can find the gate there. But first, dismount and unsaddle your horses."

Wulfgar's suspicions came back suddenly, his scowl burying the smile. "Explain," he requested of Harkle.

"Do it!" Regis ordered, "or you shall find a bigger surprise than the last one."

Drizzt and Bruenor had already slipped from their saddles, intrigued, but not the least bit fearful of the hospitable Harkle Harpell. Wulfgar threw his arms out helplessly and followed, pulling the gear from the roan and leading the beast, and Regis's pony, after the others.

Regis found the entrance easily and swung it open for his friends. They came in without fear, but were suddenly assailed by blinding flashes of light.

When their eyes cleared again, they found that the horses and ponies had been reduced to the size of cats!

"What?" blurted Bruenor, but Regis was laughing again and Harkle acted as though nothing unusual had happened.

"Pick them up and come along," he instructed. "It is nearly time to sup, and the meal at The Fuzzy Quarterstaff is particularly delicious this night!"

He led them around the side of the weird mansion to a bridge crossing the center of the hillock. Bruenor and Wulfgar felt ridiculous carrying their mounts, but Drizzt accepted it with a smile and Regis thoroughly enjoyed the whole outrageous spectacle, having learned on his first visit that Longsaddle was a place to be taken lightly, appreciating the idiosyncrasies and unique ways of the Harpells purely for the sake of amusement.

The high-arcing bridge before them, Regis knew, would serve as yet another example. Though its span across the small stream was not great, it was apparently unsupported, and its narrow planks were completely unadorned, even without handrails.

Another robed Harpell, this one incredibly old, sat on a stool, his chin in his hand, mumbling to himself and seemingly taking no notice of the strangers whatsoever.

When Wulfgar, in the front beside Harkle, neared the bank of the stream, he jumped back, gasping and stuttering. Regis snickered, knowing what the big man had seen, and Drizzt and Bruenor soon understood.

The stream flowed UP the side of the hill, then vanished just before the top, though the companions could hear that water was indeed rushing along before them. Then the stream reappeared over the hill's crest, flowing down the other side.

The old man sprang up suddenly and rushed over to Wulfgar. "What can it mean?" he cried desperately. "How can it be?" He banged on the barbarian's massive chest in frustration.

Wulfgar looked around for an escape, not wanting to even grab the old man in restraint for fear of breaking his frail form. Just as abruptly as he had come, the old man dashed back to the stool and resumed his silent pose.

"Alas, poor Chardin," Harkle said somberly. "He was mighty in his day. It was he who turned the stream up the hill. But near a score of years now he has been obsessed with finding the secret of the invisibility under the bridge."

"Why is the stream so different from the wall?" wondered Drizzt. "Certainly this dweomer is not unknown among the wizard community."

"Ah, but there is a difference," Harkle was quick to reply, excited at finding someone outside the Ivy Mansion apparently interested in their works. "An invisible object is not so rare, but a field of invisibility . . ." He swept his hand to the stream. "Anything that enters the river there takes on the property," he explained. "But only for as long as it remains in the field. And to a person in the enchanted area—I know because I have done this test myself—everything beyond the field is unseen, though the water and fish within appear normal. It defies our knowledge of the properties of invisibility and may actually reflect a tear into the fabric of a wholly unknown plane of existence!" He saw that his excitement had gone beyond the comprehension or interest of the drow's companions some time ago, so he calmed himself and politely changed the subject.

"The housing for your horses is in that building," he said, pointing to one of the low, wooden structures. "The underbridge will get you there. I must attend to another matter now. Perhaps we can meet later in the tavern."

Wulfgar, not completely understanding Harkle's directions, stepped lightly onto the first wooden planks of the bridge, and was promptly thrown backward by some unseen force.

"I said the *under*bridge," cried Harkle, pointing under the bridge. "You cannot cross the river this way by the overbridge; that is used for the way back! Stops any arguments in crossing," he explained.

Wulfgar had his doubts about a bridge he could not see, but he didn't want to appear cowardly before his friends and the wizard. He moved beside the bridge's ascending arc and gingerly moved his foot out under the wooden structure, feeling for the invisible crossing. There was only the air, and the unseen rush of water just below his foot, and he hesitated.

"Go on," coaxed Harkle.

Wulfgar plunged ahead, setting himself for a fall into the water. But to his absolute surprise, he did not fall down.

He fell up!

"Whoa!" the barbarian cried out as he thunked into the bottom of the bridge, headfirst. He lay there for a long moment, unable to get his bearings, flat on his back against the bottom of the bridge, looking down instead of up.

"You see!" screeched the wizard. "The *underbridge!*"

Drizzt moved next, leaping, into the enchanted area with an easy tumble, and landing lightly on his feet beside his friend.

"Are you all right?" he asked.

"The road, my friend," groaned Wulfgar. "I long for the road, and the orcs. It is safer."

Drizzt helped him struggle to his feet, for the barbarian's mind argued every inch of the way against standing upside-down under a bridge, with an invisible stream rushing above his head.

Bruenor, too, had his reservations, but a taunt from the halfling moved him along, and soon the companions rolled back onto the grass of the natural world on the other bank of the stream. Two buildings stood before them, and they moved to the smaller, the one Harkle had indicated.

A blue-robed woman met them at the door. "Four?" she asked rhetorically. "You really should have sent word ahead."

"Harkle sent us," Regis explained. "We are not from these lands. Forgive our ignorance of your customs."

"Very well, then," huffed the woman. "Come along in. We are actually unusually unbusy for this time of the year. I am sure that I have room for your horses." She led them into the structure's main room, a square chamber. All four walls were lined, floor to ceiling, with small cages, just big enough for a cat-sized horse to stretch its legs. Many were occupied, their nameplates indicating that they were reserved for particular members of the Harpell clan, but the woman found four empty ones all together and put the companions' horses inside.

"You may get them whenever you desire," she explained, handing each of them a key to the cage of his particular mount. She paused when she got to Drizzt, studying his handsome features. "Who have we here?" she asked, not losing her calm monotone. "I had not heard of your arrival, but I am sure that many will desire an audience with you before you go! We have never seen one of your kind."

Drizzt nodded and did not reply, growing increasingly uncomfortable with this new type of attention. Somehow it seemed to degrade him even more than the threats of ignorant peasants. He understood the curiosity, though, and figured that he owed the wizards a few hours of conversation, at least.

The Fuzzy Quarterstaff, on the back side of the Ivy Mansion, filled a circular chamber. The bar sat in the middle, like the hub of a wheel, and inside its wide perimeter was another room, an enclosed kitchen area. A hairy man with huge arms and a bald head wiped his rag endlessly along the shiny surface of the bar, more to pass the time than to clean any spills.

Off to the rear, on a raised stage, musical instruments played themselves, guided by the jerking gyrations of a white-haired, wand-wielding wizard in black pants and a black waistcoat. Whenever the instruments hit a crescendo, the wizard pointed his wand and snapped the fingers of his free hand, and a burst of colored sparks erupted from each of the four corners of the stage.

The companions took a table within sight of the entertaining wizard. They had their pick of location, for as far as they could tell, they were the only patrons in the room. The tables, too, were circular, made of fine wood and sporting a many-faceted, huge green gemstone on a silver pedestal as a centerpiece.

"A stranger place I never heared of," grumbled Bruenor, uncomfortable since the underbridge, but resigned to the necessity of speaking with the Harpells.

"Nor I," said the barbarian. "And may we leave it soon."

"You are both stuck in the small chambers of your minds," Regis scolded. "This is a place to enjoy—and you know that no danger lurks here." He winked as his gaze fell upon Wulfgar. "Nothing serious, anyway."

"Longsaddle offers us a much needed rest," Drizzt added. "Here, we can lay the course of our next trek in safety and take back to the road refreshed. It was two tendays from the dale to Luskan, and nearly another to here, without reprieve. Weariness draws away the edge and takes the advantage from a skilled warrior." He looked particularly at Wulfgar as he finished the thought. "A tired man will make mistakes. And mistakes in the wild are, more often than not, fatal."

"So let us relax and enjoy the hospitality of the Harpells," said Regis.

"Agreed," said Bruenor, glancing around, "but just a short rest. And where in the nine hells might the barmaid be, or do ye have to get to it yerself for food and drink?"

"If you want something, then just ask," came a voice from the center of the table. Wulfgar and Bruenor both leaped to their feet, on guard. Drizzt noted the flare of light within the green gem and studied the object, immediately guessing the setup. He looked back over his shoulder at the barkeep, who stood beside a similar gemstone.

"A scrying device," the drow explained to his friends, though they, by now, had come to the same understanding and felt very foolish standing in the middle of an empty tavern with their weapons in their hands.

Regis had his head down, his shoulders rolling with his sobs of laughter.

"Bah! Ye knew all along!" Bruenor growled at him. "Ye've been takin' a bit of fun at our cost, Rumblebelly," the dwarf warned. "For meself, I'm wondering how much longer our road holds room for ye."

Regis looked up at the glare of his dwarven friend, matching it suddenly with a firm stare of his own. "We have walked and ridden more than four hundred miles together!" he retorted. "Through cold winds and orc raids, brawls and battles with ghosts. Allow me my pleasure for a short while, good dwarf. If you and Wulfgar would loosen the straps of your packs and see this place for what it is, you might find an equal share of laughter yourself!"

Wulfgar did smile. Then, all at once, he jerked back his head and roared, throwing away all of his anger and prejudice, so that he might take the halfling's advice and view Longsaddle with an open mind. Even the musical wizard stopped his playing to observe the spectacle of the barbarian's soul-cleansing scream.

And when he had finished, Wulfgar laughed. Not an amused chuckle, but a thunderous roll of laughter that flowed up from his belly and exploded out his wide-thrown mouth.

"Ale!" Bruenor called into the gemstone. Almost immediately, a floating disk of blue light slipped over the bar, bearing to them enough strong ale to last the night. A few minutes later, all traces of the tensions of the road had flown, and they toasted and quaffed their mugs with enthusiasm.

Only Drizzt kept his reserve, sipping his drink and staying alert to his surroundings. He felt no direct danger here, but he wanted to keep control against the wizards' inevitable probing.

Shortly, the Harpells and their friends began to make a steady stream into The Fuzzy Quarterstaff. The companions were the only newcomers in town this night, and all of the diners pulled their tables close by, trading stories of the road and toasts of lasting friendship over fine meals, and later, beside a warm hearth. Many, led by Harkle, concerned themselves with Drizzt and their interest in the dark cities of his people, and he had few reservations about answering their questions.

Then came the probing about the journey that had brought the companions so far. Bruenor actually initiated it, jumping up onto his table and proclaiming, "Mithral Hall, home of me fathers, ye shall be mine again!"

Drizzt grew concerned. Judging by the inquisitive reaction of the gathering, the name of Bruenor's ancient homeland was known here, at least in legend. The drow didn't fear any malicious actions by the Harpells, but he simply did not want the purpose of the adventure following, and possibly even preceding, him and his friends on the next leg of the journey. Others might well be interested in learning the location of an ancient dwarven stronghold, a place referred to in tales as, "the mines where silver rivers run."

Drizzt took Harkle aside. "The night grows long. Are there rooms available in the village beyond?"

"Nonsense," huffed Harkle. "You are my guests and shall remain here. The rooms have already been prepared."

"And the price for all of this?"

Harkle pushed Drizzt's purse away. "The price in the Ivy Mansion is a good tale or two, and bringing some interest into our existence. You and your friends have paid for a year and more!"

"Our thanks," replied Drizzt. "I think that it is time for my companions to rest. We have had a long ride, with much more before us."

"Concerning the road before you," said Harkle. "I have arranged for a meeting with DelRoy, the eldest of the Harpells now in Longsaddle. He, more than any of us, might be able to help steer your way."

"Very good," said Regis, leaning over to hear the conversation.

"This meeting holds a small price," Harkle told Drizzt. "DelRoy desires a private audience with you. He has sought knowledge of the drow for many years, but little is available to us."

"Agreed," replied Drizzt. "Now, it is time for us to find our beds."

"I shall show you the way."

"What time are we to meet with DelRoy?" asked Regis.

"Morning," replied Harkle.

Regis laughed, then leaned over to the other side of the table where Bruenor sat holding a mug motionless in his gnarled hands, his eyes unblinking. Regis gave the dwarf a little shove and Bruenor toppled, thudding into the floor without even a groan of protest. "Evening would be better," the halfling remarked, pointing across the room to another table.

Wulfgar was underneath it.

Harkle looked at Drizzt. "Evening," he agreed. "I shall speak to DelRoy."

The four friends spent the next day recuperating and enjoying the endless marvels of the Ivy Mansion. Drizzt was called away early for a meeting with DelRoy, while the others were guided by Harkle on a tour through the great house, passing through a dozen alchemy shops, scrying rooms, meditation chambers, and several secured rooms specifically designed for conjuring otherworldly beings. A statue of one Matherly Harpell was of particular interest, since the statue was actually the wizard himself. An unsuccessful mix of potions had left him stoned, literally.

Then there was Bidderdoo, the family dog, who had once been Harkle's second cousin—again, a bad potion mix.

Harkle kept no secrets from his guests, recounting the history of his clan, its achievements, and its often disastrous failures. And he told them of the lands around Longsaddle, of the Uthgardt barbarians, the Sky Ponies, they had encountered, and of other tribes they might yet meet along their way.

Bruenor was glad that their relaxation carried a measure of valuable information. His goal pressed in on him every minute of every day, and when he spent any time without making any gains toward Mithral Hall, even if he simply needed to rest, he felt pangs of guilt. "Ye have to want it with all yer heart," he often scolded himself.

But Harkle had provided him with an important orientation to this land that would no doubt aid his cause in the days ahead, and he was satisfied when he sat down for supper at The Fuzzy Quarterstaff. Drizzt rejoined them there, sullen and quiet, and he wouldn't say much when questioned about his discussion with DelRoy.

"Think to the meeting ahead," was the drow's answer to Bruenor's probing. "DelRoy is very old and learned. He may prove to be our best hope of ever finding the road to Mithral Hall."

Bruenor was indeed thinking to the meeting ahead.

And Drizzt sat back quietly throughout the meal, considering the tales and the images of his homeland that he had imparted to DelRoy, remembering the unique beauty of Menzoberranzan.

And the malicious hearts that had despoiled it.

A short time later, Harkle took Drizzt, Bruenor, and Wulfgar to see the old mage—Regis had begged out of the meeting in lieu of another party at the tavern. They met DelRoy in a small, torchlit, and shadowy chamber, the flickerings of light heightening the mystery in the aged wizard's face. Bruenor and Wulfgar came at once to agree with Drizzt's observations of DelRoy, for decades of experience and untold adventures were etched visibly into the features of his leathery brown skin. His body was failing him now, they could see, but the sheen of his pale eyes told of inner life and left little doubt about the sharp edge of his mind.

Bruenor spread his map out on the room's circular table, beside the books and scrolls that DelRoy had brought. The old mage studied it carefully for a few seconds, tracing the line that had brought the companions to Longsaddle. "What do you recall of the ancient halls, dwarf?" he asked. "Landmarks or neighboring peoples?"

Bruenor shook his head. "The pictures in me head show the deep halls and workplaces, the ringing sound of iron on the anvil. The flight of me clan started in mountains; that's all I know."

"The northland is a wide country," Harkle remarked. "Many long ranges could harbor such a stronghold."

"That is why Mithral Hall, for all of its reputed wealth, has never been found," replied DelRoy.

"And thus our dilemma," said Drizzt. "Deciding where to even begin to look!"

"Ah, but you have already begun," answered DelRoy. "You have chosen well to come inland; most of the legends of Mithral Hall stem from the lands east of here, even farther from the coast. It seems likely that your goal lies between Longsaddle and the great desert, though north or south, I cannot guess. You have done well."

Drizzt nodded and broke off the conversation as the old mage fell back into his silent examination of Bruenor's map, marking strategic points and referring often to the stack of books he had piled beside the table. Bruenor hovered beside DelRoy, anxious for any advice or revelations that might be forthcoming. Dwarves were patient folk, though, a trait that allowed their crafting to outshine the work of the other races, and Bruenor kept his calm as best he could, not wanting to press the wizard.

Some time later, when DelRoy was satisfied that his sorting of all the pertinent information was complete, he spoke again. "Where would you go next," he asked Bruenor, "if no advice were offered here?"

The dwarf looked back to his map, Drizzt peering over his shoulder, and traced a line east with his stubby finger. He looked to Drizzt for consent when he had reached a certain point that they had discussed earlier on the road. The drow nodded. "Citadel Adbar," Bruenor declared, tapping his finger on the map.

"The dwarven stronghold," said DelRoy, not too surprised. "A fine choice. King Harbromm and his dwarves may be able to aid you greatly. They have been there, in the Mithral Mountains, for centuries uncounted. Certainly Adbar was old even in the days when the hammers of Mithral Hall rang out in dwarven song."

"Is Citadel Adbar your advice to us, then?" Drizzt asked.

"It is your own choice, but as good a destination as I can offer," replied DelRoy. "But the way is long, five tendays at the least if all goes well. And on the east road beyond Sundabar, that is unlikely, Still, you may get there before the first colds of winter, though I doubt that you would be able to take Harbromm's information and resume your journey before the next spring!"

"Then the choice seems clear," declared Bruenor. "To Adbar!"

"There is more you should know," said DelRoy. "And this is the true advice that I shall give to you: Do not be blinded to the possibilities along the road by the hopeful vision at the road's end. Your course so far has followed straight runs, first from Icewind Dale to Luskan, then from Luskan to here. There is little, other than monsters, along either of those roads to give a rider cause to turn aside. But on the journey to Adbar, you shall pass Silverymoon, city of wisdom and legacy, and the Lady Alustriel, and the Vault of Sages, as fine a library as exists in all the northland. Many in that fair city may be able to offer more aid to your quest than I, or even than King Harbromm.

"And beyond Silverymoon you shall find Sundabar, itself an ancient dwarven stronghold, where Helm, reknowned dwarf-friend, rules. His ties to your race run deep, Bruenor, tracing back many generations. Ties, perhaps, even to your own people."

"Possibilities!" beamed Harkle.

"We shall heed your wise advice, DelRoy," said Drizzt.

"Aye," agreed the dwarf, his spirits high. "When we left the dale, I had no idea beyond Luskan. Me hopes were to follow a road of guesses, expectin' half and more to be nothing of value. The halfling was wise in guiding us to this spot, for we've found a trail of clues! And clues to lead to more clues!" He looked around at the excited group, Drizzt, Harkle, and DelRoy, and then noticed Wulfgar, still sitting quietly in his chair, his huge arms crossed on his chest, watching without any apparent emotion. "What of yerself, boy?" Bruenor demanded. "Have ye a notion to share?"

Wulfgar leaned forward, resting his elbows on the table. "Neither my quest, nor my land," he explained. "I follow you, confident in any path you choose.

"And I am glad of your mirth and excitement," he added quietly.

Bruenor took the explanation as complete, and turned back to DelRoy and Harkle for some specific information on the road ahead. Drizzt, though, unconvinced of the sincerity of Wulfgar's last statement, let his gaze linger on the young barbarian, noting the expression in his eyes as he watched Bruenor.

Sorrow?

They spent two more restful days in the Ivy Mansion, though Drizzt was hounded constantly by curious Harpells who wanted more information about his rarely seen race. He took the questions politely, understanding their good intentions, and answered as best he could. When Harkle came to escort them out on the fifth morning, they were refreshed and ready to get on with their business. Harkle promised to arrange for the return of the horses to their rightful owners, saying that it was the least he could do for the strangers who had brought so much interest to the town.

But in truth, the friends had benefited more for the stay. DelRoy and Harkle had given them valuable information and perhaps even more importantly, had restored their hope in the quest. Bruenor was up and about before dawn that last morning, his adrenaline pumping at the thought of returning to the road now that he had somewhere to go.

They moved out from the mansion throwing many good-byes and lamenting looks over their shoulders, even from Wulfgar, who had come in so steadfast in his antipathy toward wizards.

They crossed the overbridge, saying farewell to Chardin, who was too lost in his meditations of the stream to even notice, and soon discovered that the structure beside the miniature stable was an experimental farm. "It will change the face of the world!" Harkle assured them as he veered them toward the building for a closer look. Drizzt guessed his meaning even before they entered, as soon as he heard the high-pitched bleating and cricketlike chirping. Like the stable, the farm was one room, though part of it had no roof and was actually a field within walls. Cat-sized cows and sheep mulled about, while chickens the size of field mice dodged around the animals' tiny feet.

"Of course, this is the first season and we have not seen results yet,"explained Harkle, "but we expect a high yield considering the small amount of resources involved."

"Efficiency," laughed Regis. "Less feed, less space, and you can blow them back up when you want to eat them!"

"Precisely!" said Harkle.

They next went to the stable, where Harkle picked out fine mounts for them, two horses and two ponies. These were gifts, Harkle explained, only to be returned at the companions' leisure. "It's the least we could do to aid such a noble quest," Harkle said with a low bow to stop any protests from Bruenor and Drizzt.

The road meandered, continuing on down the back of the hill. Harkle stood for a moment scratching his chin, a puzzled expression on his face. "The sixth post," he told himself, "but to the left or the right?"

A man working on a ladder (another amusing curiosity-to see a ladder rise up above the phony rails of the fence and come to rest in mid-air against the top of the invisible wall) came to their aid. "Forgot again?" he chuckled at Harkle. "He pointed to the railing off to one side. "Sixth post to your left!"

Harkle shrugged away his embarrassment and moved on.

The companions watched the workman curiously as they passed from the hill, their mounts still tucked under their arms. He had a bucket and some rags and was rubbing several reddish-brown spots from the invisible wall.

"Low-flying birds," Harkle explained apologetically. "But have no fear, Regweld is working on the problem even as we speak.

"Now we have come to the end of our meeting, though many years shall pass before you are forgotten in the Ivy Mansion! The road takes you right through the village of Longsaddle. You can restock your supplies there—it has all been arranged."

"Me deepest regards to yerself and yer kin," said Bruenor, bowing low. "Suren Longsaddle has been a bright spot on a bleary road!" The others were quick to agree.

"Farewell then, Companions of the Hall," sighed Harkle. "The Harpells expect to see a small token when you at last find Mithral Hall and start the ancient forges burning again!"

"A king's treasure!" Bruenor assured him as they moved away.

⚔ ⚔ ⚔ ⚔ ⚔

They were back on the road beyond Longsaddle's borders before noon, their mounts trotting along easily with fully stuffed packs.

"Well, which do ye prefer, elf," Bruenor asked later that day, "the jabs of a mad soldier's spear, or the pokings of a wonderin' wizard's nose?"

Drizzt chuckled defensively as he thought about the question. Longsaddle had been so different from anywhere he had ever been, and yet, so much the same. In either case, his color singled him out as an oddity, and it wasn't so much the hostility of his usual treatment that bothered him, as the embarrassing reminders that he would ever be different.

Only Wulfgar, riding beside him, caught his mumbled reply.

"The road."

9

THERE IS NO HONOR

Why do you approach the city before the light of dawn?" the Nightkeeper of the North Gate asked the emissary for the merchant caravan that had pulled up outside Luskan's wall. Jierdan, in his post beside the Nightkeeper, watched with special interest, certain that this troupe had come from Ten-Towns.

"We would not impose upon the regulations of the city if our business were not urgent," answered the spokesman. "We have not rested for two days." Another man emerged from the cluster of wagons, a body limp across his shoulders.

"Murdered on the road," explained the spokesman. "And another of the party taken. Catti-brie, daughter of Bruenor Battlehammer himself!"

"A dwarf-maid?" Jierdan blurted out, suspecting otherwise, but masking his excitement for fear that it might implicate him.

"Nay, no dwarf. A woman," lamented the spokesman. "Fairest in all the dale, maybe in all the north. The dwarf took her in as an orphaned child and claimed her as his own."

"Orcs?" asked the Nightkeeper, more concerned with potential hazards on the road than with the fate of a single woman.

"This was not the work of orcs," replied the spokesman. "Stealth and cunning took Catti-brie from us and killed the driver. We did not even discover the foul deed until the next morn."

Jierdan needed no further information, not even a more complete description of Catti-brie, to put the pieces together. Her connection to Bruenor explained Entreri's interest in her. Jierdan looked to the eastern horizon and the first rays of the coming dawn, anxious to be cleared of his duties on the wall so that he could go report his findings to Dendybar. This little piece of news should help to alleviate the mottled wizard's anger at him for losing the drow's trail on the docks.

⚔ ⚔ ⚔ ⚔

"He has not found them?" Dendybar hissed at Sydney.

"He has found nothing but a cold trail," the younger mage replied. "If they are on the docks yet, they are well disguised."

Dendybar paused to consider his apprentice's report. Something was out of place with this scenario. Four distinctive characters simply could not have vanished. "Have you learned anything of the assassin, then, or of his companion?"

"The vagabonds in the alleys fear him. Even the ruffians give him a respectfully wide berth."

"So our friend is known among the bowel-dwellers," Dendybar mused.

"A hired killer, I would guess," reasoned Sydney. "Probably from the south—Waterdeep, perhaps, though we should have heard more of him if that were the case. Perhaps even farther south, from the lands beyond our vision."

"Interesting," replied Dendybar, trying to formulate some theory to satisfy all the variables. "And the girl?"

Sydney shrugged, "I do not believe that she follows him willingly, though she has made no move to be free of him. And when you saw him in Morkai's vision, he was riding alone."

"He acquired her," came an unexpected reply from the doorway. Jierdan entered the room.

"What? Unannounced?" sneered Dendybar.

"I have news—it could not wait," Jierdan replied boldly.

"Have they left the city?" Sydney prompted, voicing her suspicions to heighten the anger she read on the mottled wizard's pallid face. Sydney well understood the dangers and the difficulties of the docks, and almost pitied Jierdan for incurring the wrath of the merciless Dendybar in a situation beyond his control. But Jierdan remained her competition for the mottled wizard's favor, and she wouldn't let sympathy stand in the way of her ambitions.

"No," Jierdan snapped at her. "My news does not concern the drow's party." He looked back to Dendybar. "A caravan arrived in Luskan today—in search of the woman."

"Who is she?" asked Dendybar, suddenly very interested and forgetting his anger at the intrusion.

"The adopted daughter of Bruenor Battlehammer," Jierdan replied. "Cat—"

"Catti-brie! Of course!" hissed Dendybar, himself familiar with most of the prominent people in Ten-Towns. "I should have guessed!" He turned to Sydney. "My respect for our mysterious rider grows each day. Find him and bring him back to me!"

Sydney nodded, though she feared that Dendybar's request would prove more difficult than the mottled wizard believed, probably even beyond her skills altogether.

⚔ ⚔ ⚔ ⚔ ⚔

She spent that night, until the early hours of the following morning, searching the alleyways and meeting places of the dockside area. But even using her contacts on the docks and all the magical tricks at her disposal, she found no sign of Entreri and Catti-brie, and no one willing or able to pass along any information that might help her in her search.

Tired and frustrated, she returned to the Hosttower the next day, passing the corridor to Dendybar's room, even though he had ordered her to report to him directly upon her return. Sydney was in no mood to listen to the mottled wizard's ranting about her failure.

She entered her small room, just off the main trunk of the Hosttower on the northern branch, below the rooms of the Master of the North Spire, and bolted the doors, further sealing them against unwelcomed intrusion with a magical spell.

She had barely fallen into her bed when the surface of her coveted scrying mirror began to swirl and glow. "Damn you, Dendybar," she growled, assuming that the disturbance was her master's doing. Dragging her weary body to the mirror, she stared deeply into it, attuning her mind to the swirl to bring the image clearer. It was not Dendybar that she faced, to her relief, but a wizard from a distant town, a would-be suitor that the passionless Sydney kept dangling by a thread of hope so that she could manipulate him as she needed.

"Greetings, fair Sydney," the mage said. "I pray I did not disturb your sleep, but I have exciting news!"

Normally, Sydney would have tactfully listened to the mage, feigned interest in the story, and politely excused herself from the encounter. But now, with Dendybar's pressing demands lying squarely across her shoulders, she had no patience for distractions. "This is not the time!" she snapped.

The mage, so caught up in his own news, seemed not to notice her definitive tone. "The most marvelous thing has happened in our town," he rambled.

"Harkle!" Sydney cried to break his babbling momentum.

The mage halted, crestfallen. "But, Sydney," he said.

"Another time," she insisted.

"But how often in this day does one actually see and speak with a drow elf?" Harkle persisted.

"I cannot—" Sydney stopped short, digesting Harkle's last words. "A drow elf?" she stammered.

"Yes," Harkle beamed proudly, thrilled that his news had apparently impressed his beloved Sydney. "Drizzt Do'Urden, by name. He left Longsaddle just two days ago. I would have told you earlier, but the mansion has just been astir about the whole thing!"

"Tell me more, dear Harkle," Sydney purred enticingly. "Do tell me everything."

✕ ✕ ✕ ✕

"I am in need of information."

Whisper froze at the sound of the unexpected voice, guessing the speaker immediately. She knew that he was in town, and knew, too, that he was the only one who could have slipped through her defenses to get into her secret chambers.

"Information," Entreri said again, moving out from the shadows behind a dressing screen.

Whisper slid the jar of healing unguent into her pocket and took a good measure of the man. Rumors spoke of him as the deadliest of assassins, and she, all too familiar with killers, knew at once that the rumors rang with truth. She sensed Entreri's power, and the easy coordination of his movements. "Men do not come to my room uninvited," she warned bravely.

Entreri moved to a better vantage point to study the bold woman. He had heard of her as well, a survivor of the rough streets, beautiful and deadly. But apparently Whisper had lost an encounter. Her nose was broken and disjointed, splayed across her cheek.

Whisper understood the scrutiny. She squared her shoulders and threw her head back proudly. "An unfortunate accident," she hissed.

"It is not my concern," Entreri came back. "I have come for information."

Whisper turned away to go about her routine, trying to appear unbothered. "My price is high," she said coolly.

She turned back to Entreri, the intense but frighteningly calm look on his face telling her beyond doubt that her life would be the only reward for cooperation.

"I seek four companions," said Entreri. "A dwarf, a drow, a young man, and a halfling."

Whisper was unused to such situations. No crossbows supported her now, no bodyguards waited for her signal behind a nearby secret door. She tried to remain calm, but Entreri knew the depth of her fear. She chuckled and pointed to her broken nose. "I have met your dwarf, and your drow, Artemis Entreri." She emphasized his name as she spoke it, hoping that her recognition would put him back on the defensive.

"Where are they?" Entreri asked, still in control. "And what did they request of you?"

Whisper shrugged. "If they remain in Luskan, I do not know where. Most probably they are gone; the dwarf has a map of the northland."

Entreri considered the words. "Your reputation speaks more highly of you," he said sarcastically. "You accept such a wound and let them slip through your grasp?"

Whisper's eyes narrowed in anger. "I choose my fights carefully," she hissed. "The four are too dangerous for actions of frivolous vengeance. Let them go where they will. I want no business with them again,"

Entreri's calm visage sagged a bit. He had already been to the Cutlass and heard of Wulfgar's exploits. And now this. A woman like Whisper was not easily cowed. Perhaps he should indeed reevaluate the strength of his opponents.

"Fearless is the dwarf," Whisper offered, sensing his dismay and taking pleasure in furthering his discomfort. "And ware the drow, Artemis Entreri," she hissed pointedly, attempting to relegate him to a similar level of respect for the companions with the grimness of her tone. "He walks in shadows that we cannot see, and strikes from the darkness. He conjures a demon in the form of a great cat and—"

Entreri turned and started away, having no intention of allowing Whisper to gain any more of an advantage.

Reveling in her victory, Whisper couldn't resist the temptation to throw one final dart. "Men do not come to my room uninvited," she said again. Entreri passed into an adjoining room and Whisper heard the door to the alley close.

"I choose my fights carefully," she whispered to the emptiness of the room, regaining a measure of her pride with the threat.

She turned back to a small dressing table and took out the jar of unguent, quite pleased with herself. She examined her wound in the table's mirror. Not too bad. The salve would erase it as it had erased so many scars from the trials of her profession.

She understood her stupidity when she saw the shadow slip past her reflection in the mirror, and felt the brush of air at her back. Her business allowed no tolerance for errors, and offered no second chance. For the first and last time in her life, Whisper had let her pride rise above her judgment.

A final groan escaped her as the jeweled dagger sunk deeply into her back.

"I, too, choose my fights with care," Entreri whispered into her ear.

The next morning found Entreri outside a place he did not want to enter: the Hosttower of the Arcane. He knew that he was running out of options. Convinced now that the companions had long since left Luskan, the assassin needed some magical assistance to heat up the trail again. It had taken him nearly two years to sniff out the halfling in Ten-Towns, and his patience was wearing thin.

Catti-brie reluctantly but obediently at his side, he approached the structure, and was promptly escorted to Dendybar's audience hall, where the mottled wizard and Sydney waited to greet him.

"They have left the city," Entreri said bluntly, before any exchange of greetings.

Dendybar smiled to show Entreri that he had the upper hand this time. "As long as a tenday ago," he replied calmly.

"And you know where they are," Entreri reasoned.

Dendybar nodded, the smile still curling into his hollow cheeks.

The assassin didn't enjoy the game. He spent a long moment measuring his counterpart, searching for some hint of the wizard's intentions. Dendybar did likewise, still very much interested in an alliance with the formidable killer—but only on favorable terms.

"The price of the information?" Entreri asked.

"I do not even know your name," was Dendybar's reply.

Fair enough, the assassin thought. He bowed low. "Artemis Entreri," he said, confident enough to speak truthfully.

"And why do you seek the companions, carrying the dwarf's daughter in tow?" Dendybar pressed, playing his hand out to give the cocky assassin something to worry about.

"That is my own care," hissed Entreri, the narrowing of his eyes the only indication that Dendybar's knowledge had perturbed him.

"It is mine, as well, if we are to be allies in this!" shouted Dendybar, rising to stand tall and ominous and intimidate Entreri.

The assassin, though, cared little for the wizard's continuing antics, too engrossed in assessing the value of such an alliance. "I ask nothing of your business with them," Entreri replied at length. "Tell me only which one of the four it concerns."

It was Dendybar's turn to ponder. He wanted Entreri in his court, if for no other reason than he feared having the assassin working against him. And he liked the notion that he would not have to disclose anything about the artifact that he sought to this very dangerous man.

"The drow has something of mine, or knowledge of where I can find it," he said. "I want it back."

"And the halfling is mine," Entreri demanded. "Where are they?"

Dendybar motioned to Sydney. "They have passed through Longsaddle," she said. "And are headed to Silverymoon, more than two tendays, to the east."

The names were unknown to Catti-brie, but she was glad that her friends had a good lead. She needed time to sort out a plan, though she wondered how effective she could be surrounded by such powerful captors.

"And what do you propose?" Entreri asked.

"An alliance," replied Dendybar.

"But I have the information I need," Entreri laughed. "What do I gain in an alliance with you?"

"My powers can get you to them, and can aid in defeating them. They are not a weak force. Consider it of mutual benefit."

"You and I on the road? You seem more fitted to a book and a desk, wizard."

Dendybar locked an unblinking glare on the arrogant assassin. "I assure you that I can get wherever I desire more effectively than you ever could imagine," he growled. He let go of his anger quickly, though, being more interested in completing business. "But I shall remain here. Sydney will go in my stead, and Jierdan, the soldier, will be her escort."

Entreri did not like the idea of traveling with Jierdan, but he decided not to press the point. It might be interesting, and helpful, in sharing the hunt with the Hosttower of the Arcane. He agreed to the terms.

"And what of her?" Sydney asked, pointing to Catti-brie.

"She goes with me," Entreri was quick to answer.

"Of course," agreed Dendybar. "No purpose in wasting such a valuable hostage."

"We are three against five," Sydney reasoned. "If things do not work out as easily as the two of you seem to expect, the girl may prove to be our downfall."

"She goes!" demanded Entreri.

Dendybar had the solution already worked out. He turned a wry smile at Sydney. "Take Bok," he chuckled.

Sydney's face drooped at the suggestion, as though Dendybar's command had stolen her desire for the hunt.

Entreri wasn't sure if he liked this new development or not.

Sensing the assassin's discomfort, Dendybar motioned Sydney to a curtained closet at the side of the room. "Bok," she called softly when she got there, the hint of a tremble in her voice.

It stepped through the curtain. Fully eight feet tall and three wide at the shoulders, the monster strode stiffly to the woman's side. A huge man, it seemed, and indeed the wizard had used pieces of human bodies for many of its parts. Bok was bigger and more square than any man living, nearly the size of a giant, and had been magically empowered with strength beyond the measures, of the natural world.

"A golem," Dendybar proudly explained. "My own creation. Bok could kill us all right now. Even your fell blade would be of little use against it, Artemis Entreri."

The assassin wasn't so convinced, but he could not completely mask his intimidation. Dendybar had obviously tipped the scales of their partnership in his own favor, but Entreri knew that if he backed away from the bargain now he would be aligning the mottled wizard and his minions against him, and in direct competition with him for the dwarf's party. Furthermore, it would take him tendays, perhaps even months, to catch the travelers by normal means and he did not doubt that Dendybar could get there faster.

Catti-brie shared the same uncomfortable thoughts. She had no desire to travel with the gruesome monster, but she wondered what carnage she would find when she finally caught up to Bruenor and the others if Entreri decided to break away from the alliance.

"Fear not," Dendybar comforted. "Bok is harmless, incapable of any independent thought, for you see, Bok has no mind. The golem answers to my commands, or to Sydney's, and would walk into a fire to be consumed if we merely asked it to do so!"

"I have business to finish in the city," Entreri said, not doubting Dendybar's words and having little desire to hear any more about the golem. "When do we depart?"

"Night would be best," reasoned Dendybar. "Come back to the green outside the Hosttower when the sun is down. We shall meet there and get you on your way."

Alone in his chamber, save for Bok, Dendybar stroked the golem's muscled shoulders with deep affection. Bok was his hidden trump, his protection against the resistance of the companions, or the treachery of Artemis Entreri. But Dendybar did not part with the monster easily, for it played a powerful role, as well, in protecting him from would-be successors in the Hosttower. Dendybar had subtly but definitely passed along the warning to other wizards that any of them striking against him would have to deal with Bok, even if Dendybar were dead.

But the road ahead might be long, and the Master of the North Spire could not forsake his duties and expect to hold his title. Especially not with the Archmage just looking for any excuse to be rid of him, understanding the dangers of Dendybar's outspoken aspirations to the central tower.

"Nothing can stop you, my pet," Dendybar told the monster. In truth, he was simply reaffirming his own fears about his choice to send the inexperienced mage in his stead. He didn't doubt her loyalty, nor Jierdan's, but Entreri and the heroes from Icewind Dale were not to be taken lightly.

"I have given you the hunting power," Dendybar explained, as he tossed the scroll tube and the now useless parchment to the floor. "The drow is your purpose and you can now sense his presence from any distance. Find him! Do not return to me without Drizzt Do'Urden!"

A guttural roar issued from Bok's blue lips, the only sound the unthinking instrument was capable of uttering.

Entreri and Catti-brie found the wizard's party already assembled when they arrived at the Hosttower later that night.

Jierdan stood alone, off to the side, apparently none too thrilled about partaking in the adventure, but having little choice. The soldier feared the golem, and had no love, or trust, for Entreri. He feared Dendybar more, though, and his uneasiness about the potential dangers on the road did not measure up against the certain dangers he would face at the hands of the mottled wizard if he refused to go.

Sydney broke away from Bok and Dendybar and walked across the way to meet her companions. "Greetings," she offered, more interested in appeasement now than competition with her formidable partner. "Dendybar prepares our mounts. The ride to Silverymoon shall be swift indeed!"

Entreri and Catti-brie looked to the mottled wizard. Bok stood beside him, holding an unrolled parchment out in view while Dendybar poured a smoky liquid from a beaker over a white feather and chanted the runes of the spell.

A mist grew at the wizard's feet, swirling and thickening into something with a definite shape. Dendybar left it to its transformation and moved to repeat the ritual a short way off. By the time the first magical horse had appeared, the wizard was creating the fourth and final one.

Entreri raised his brow. "Four?" he asked Sydney. "We are now five."

"Bok could not ride," she replied, amused at the notion. "It will run." She turned and headed back toward Dendybar, leaving Entreri with the thought.

"Of course," Entreri muttered to himself, somehow less thrilled than ever about the presence of the unnatural thing.

But Catti-brie had begun to view things a bit differently. Dendybar had obviously sent Bok along more to gain an advantage over Entreri than to ensure victory over her friends. Entreri must have known it, too.

Without realizing it, the wizard had set up just the type of nervous environment that Catti-brie hoped for, a tense situation that she might find a way to exploit.

10

BONDS OF REPUTATION

The sun beamed brightly on the morning of the first day out from Long-saddle. The companions, refreshed by their visit with the Harpells, rode at a strong pace, but still managed to enjoy the clear weather and the clear road. The land was flat and unmarked, not a tree or hill anywhere near.

"Three days to Nesmé, maybe four," Regis told them.

"More to three if the weather holds," said Wulfgar.

Drizzt shifted under his cowl. However pleasant the morning might seem to them, he knew they were still in the wilds. Three days could prove to be a long ride indeed.

"What do ye know of this place, Nesmé?" Bruenor asked Regis.

"Just what Harkle told us," Regis replied. "A fair-sized city, trading folk. But a careful place. I have never been there, but tales of the brave people living on the edge of the Evermoors reach far across the northland."

"I am intrigued by the Evermoors," said Wulfgar. "Harkle would say little of the place, just shake his head and shiver whenever I asked of it."

"Not to doubt, a place with a name beyond truth," Bruenor said, laughing, unimpressed by reputations. "Could it be worse than the dale?"

Regis shrugged, not fully convinced by the dwarf's argument. "The tales of the Trollmoors, for that is the name given to those lands, may be exaggerated, but they are always foreboding. Every city in the north salutes the bravery of the people of Nesmé for keeping the trading route along the Surbrin open in the face of such trials."

Bruenor laughed again. "Might it be that the tales be coming from Nesmé, to paint them stronger than what they are?"

Regis did not argue.

By the time they broke for lunch, a high haze veiled the sunshine. Away to the north, a black line of clouds had appeared, rushing their way. Drizzt had expected as much. In the wild, even the weather proved an enemy.

That afternoon the squall line rolled over them, carrying sheets of rain and hailstones that clinked off of Bruenor's dented helm. Sudden cuts of lightning sliced the darkened sky and the thunder nearly knocked them from their mounts. But they plodded on through the deepening mud.

"This is the true test of the road!" Drizzt yelled to them through the howling wind. "Many more travelers are defeated by storms than by orcs, because they do not anticipate the dangers when they begin their journey!"

"Bah! A summer rain is all!" Bruenor snorted defiantly.

As if in prideful reply, a lightning bolt exploded just a few yards to the side of the riders. The horses jumped and kicked. Bruenor's pony went down, stumbling split-legged into the mud and nearly crushing the stunned dwarf in its scramble.

His own mount out of control, Regis managed to dive from the saddle and roll away.

Bruenor got to his knees and wiped the mud from his eyes, cursing all the while. "Damn!" he spat, studying the pony's movements. "The thing's lame!"

Wulfgar steadied his own horse and tried to start after Regis's bolting pony, but the hailstones, driven by the wind, pelted him, blinded him, and stung his horse, and again he found himself fighting to hold his seat.

Another lightning bolt thundered in. And another.

Drizzt, whispering softly and covering his horse's head with his cloak to calm it, moved slowly beside the dwarf.

"Lame!" Bruenor shouted again, though Drizzt could barely hear him.

Drizzt only shook his head helplessly and pointed to Bruenor's axe.

More lightning came, and another blast of wind. Drizzt rolled to the side of his mount to shield himself, aware that he could not keep the beast calm much longer.

The hailstones began to come larger, striking with the force of slung bullets.

Drizzt's terrified horse jerked him to the ground and bucked away, trying to flee beyond the reach of the punishing storm.

Drizzt was up quickly beside Bruenor, but any emergency plans the two might have had were immediately deterred, for then Wulfgar stumbled back toward them.

He was walking—barely—leaning against the wind's push, using it to hold him upright. His eyes seemed droopy, his jaw twitched, and blood mixed with the rain on his cheek. He looked at his friends blankly, as if he had no comprehension of what had happened to him.

Then he fell, face down, into the mud at their feet.

A shrill whistle cut through the blunt wall of wind, a singular point of hope against the storm's mounting power. Drizzt's keen ears caught it as he and Bruenor hoisted their young friend's face from the muck. So far away the whistle seemed, but Drizzt understood how storms could distort one's perceptions.

"What?" Bruenor asked of the noise, noticing the drow's sudden reaction, for Bruenor had not heard the call.

"Regis!" Drizzt answered. He started dragging Wulfgar in the direction of the whistle, Bruenor following his lead. They didn't have time to discern if the young man was even alive.

The quick-thinking halfling saved them that day. Fully aware of the killing potential of squalls rolling down from the Spine of the World, Regis had crawled around in search of some shelter in the empty land. He stumbled across a hole in the side of a small ridge, an old wolf den perhaps, empty now.

Following the beacon of his whistles, Drizzt and Bruenor soon found him.

"It'll fill with the rain and we'll be drowned!" Bruenor yelled, but he helped Drizzt drag Wulfgar inside and prop him up against the rear wall of the cave, then took his place beside his friends as they worked to build a barrier of dirt and their remaining packs against the feared flood.

A groan from Wulfgar sent Regis scurrying to his side. "He's alive!" the halfling proclaimed. "And his wounds don't seem too bad!"

"Tougher'n a badger in a corner," Bruenor remarked.

Soon they had their den tolerable, if not comfortable, and even Bruenor stopped his complaining.

"The true test of the road," Drizzt said again to Regis, trying to cheer up his thoroughly miserable friend as they sat in the mud and rode out the night, the incessant booming of the thunder and pounding of the hail a constant reminder of the small margin of safety.

In reply, Regis poured a stream of water out of his boot.

"How many miles do ye reckon we made?" Bruenor grumbled at Drizzt.

"Ten, perhaps," the drow answered.

"Two tendays to Nesmé, at this rate!" Bruenor muttered, folding his arms across his chest.

"The storm will pass," Drizzt offered hopefully, but the dwarf was no longer listening.

✕ ✕ ✕ ✕ ✕

The next day began without rain, though thick gray clouds hung low in the sky. Wulfgar was fine by morning, but he still did not understand what had happened to him. Bruenor insisted that they start out at once, though Regis would have preferred that they remain in their hole until they were certain the storm had passed.

"Most of the provisions are lost," Drizzt reminded the halfling. "You might not find another meal beyond a pittance of dried bread until we reach Nesmé."

Regis was the first one out of the hole.

Unbearable humidity and muddy ground kept the pace slow, and the friends soon found their knees aching from the constant twisting and sloshing. Their sodden clothes clung to them uncomfortably and weighed on their every step.

They came upon Wulfgar's horse, a burned and smoking form half-buried in the mud. "Lightning," Regis observed.

The three looked at their barbarian friend, amazed that he could have survived such a hit. Wulfgar, too, stared in shock, realizing what had dropped him from his mount in the night.

"Tougher'n a badger!" Bruenor hailed again to Drizzt.

Sunshine teasingly found a crack in the overcast now and then. The sunlight was nothing substantial, though, and by noon, the day had actually grown darker. Distant thunder foretold a dismal afternoon.

The storm had already spent its killing might, but that night they found no shelter beyond their wet clothes, and whenever the crackle of lightning lit up the sky, four hunched forms could be seen sitting in the mud, their heads downcast as they accepted their fate in helpless resignation.

For two more days they lumbered on through the rain and wind, having little choice and nowhere to go but forward. Wulfgar proved to be the savior of the party's morale at this low time. He scooped Regis up from the sodden ground, tossing the halfling easily onto his back, and explaining that he needed the extra weight for balance. By sparing the halfling's pride this way, the barbarian even managed to convince the surly dwarf to ride for a short time. And always, Wulfgar was indomitable. "A blessing, I tell you," he kept crying at the gray heavens. "The storm keeps the insects—and the orcs—out of our faces! And how many months shall it be before we want for water?"

He worked hard to keep their spirits high. At one point, he watched the lightning closely, timing the delay between the flash and the ensuing thunder. As they neared the blackened skeleton of a long-dead tree, the lightning flashed and Wulfgar pulled his trick. Yelling "Tempus!" he heaved his warhammer so that it smashed into, and leveled, the trunk at precisely the moment the thunder exploded around them. His amused friends looked back to him only to find him standing proud, arms and eyes uplifted to the gods as though they had personally answered his call.

Drizzt, accepting this whole ordeal with his customary stoicism, silently applauded his young friend and knew again, even more than before, that they had made a wise decision in bringing him along. The drow understood that his own duty in these rough times was to continue his role as sentry, keeping his diligent guard despite the barbarian's proclamation of safety.

Finally, the storm was blown away by the same brisk wind that had ushered it in. The bright sunshine and clear blue skies of the subsequent dawn lightened the companions' mood immeasurably and allowed them to think again of what lay ahead,

Especially Bruenor. The dwarf leaned forward in his pressing march, just as he had when they had first begun their journey back in Icewind Dale.

Red beard wagging with the intensity of his pumping stride, Bruenor found his narrow focus once again. He fell back into the dreams of his homeland, seeing the flickering shadows of the torchlight against the silver-streamed walls and the wondrous artifacts of his people's meticulous labors. His heightened concentration on Mithral Hall over the last few months had sparked clearer, and new, memories in him, and on the road now he remembered, for the first time in more than a century, the Hall of Dumathoin.

The dwarves of Mithral Hall had made a fine living in the trade of their crafted items, but they always kept their very finest pieces, and the most precious gifts bestowed upon them from outsiders, to themselves. In a large and decorated chamber that opened wide the eyes of every visitor, the legacy of Bruenor's ancestors sat in open display, serving as inspiration for the clan's future artists.

Bruenor chuckled softly at the memory of the wondrous hall and the marvelous pieces, mostly weapons and armor. He looked at Wulfgar striding beside him, and at the mighty warhammer he had crafted the year before. Aegis-fang might have hung in the Hall of Dumathoin if Bruenor's clan still ruled Mithral Hall, sealing Bruenor's immortality in the legacy of his people.

But watching Wulfgar handling the hammer, swinging it as easily as he would swing his own arm, Bruenor had no regrets.

The next day brought more good news. Shortly after they broke camp, the friends discovered that they had traveled farther than they had anticipated during the trials of the storm, for as they marched, the landscape around them went through subtle but definite transformations. Where before the ground had been sparsely overgrown with thin patches of scraggly weeds, a virtual sea of mud under the torrent of rain, they now found lush grasses and scattered copses of tall elms. Cresting a final ridge confirmed their suspicions, for before them lay the Dessarin Valley. A few miles ahead, swollen from the spring melt and the recent storm, and clearly visible from their high perch, the arm of the great river rolled steadily along its southbound trek.

The long winter dominated this land, but when they finally bloomed, the plants here made up for their short season with a vibrancy unmatched in all the world. Rich colors of spring surrounded the friends as they made their way down the slope to the river. The carpet of grass was so thick that they took off their boots and walked barefoot through the spongy softness. The vitality here was truly obvious, and contagious.

"Ye should see the halls," Bruenor remarked on sudden impulse. "Veins of purest mithral wider than yer hand! Streams of silver, they be, and bested in beauty only by what a dwarf's hand makes of 'em."

"The want of such a sight keeps our path running straight through the hardships," Drizzt replied.

"Bah!" Bruenor snorted good-heartedly. "Ye're here because I tricked ye into being here, elf. Ye had run outa reasons for holding back me adventure anymore!"

Wulfgar had to chuckle. He had been in on the deception that had duped Drizzt into agreeing to make this journey. After the great battle in Ten-Towns with Akar Kessell, Bruenor had feigned mortal injury, and on his apparent deathbed had begged the drow to journey with him to his ancient homeland. Thinking the dwarf about to expire, Drizzt could not refuse.

"And yerself!" Bruenor roared at Wulfgar. "I see why ye've come, even if ye're skull's too thick for ye to know!

"Pray tell me," Wulfgar replied with a smile.

"Ye're running! But ye can't get away!" the dwarf cried. Wulfgar's mirth shifted to confusion.

"The girl's spooked him, elf," Bruenor explained to Drizzt. "Catti-brie's caught him in a net his muscles canno' break!"

Wulfgar laughed along with Bruenor's blunt conclusions, taking no offense. But in the images triggered by Bruenor's allusions to Catti-brie, memories of a sunset view on the face of Kelvin's Cairn, or of hours spent talking on the rise of rocks called Bruenor's Climb, the young barbarian found a disturbing element of truth in the dwarf's observations.

"And what of Regis?" Drizzt asked Bruenor. "Have you discerned his motive for coming along? Might it be his love of ankle-deep mud that sucks his little legs in to the knees?"

Bruenor stopped laughing and studied the halfling's reaction to the drow's questions. "Nay, I have not," he replied seriously after a few unrevealing moments. "This alone I know: If Rumblebelly chooses the road, it means only that the mud and the orcs measure up better than what he's leaving behind." Bruenor kept his eyes upon his little friend, again seeking some revelations in the halfling's response.

Regis kept his head bowed, watching his furry feet, visible below the diminishing roll of his belly for the first times in many months, as they plowed through the thick waves of green. The assassin, Entreri, was a world away, he thought. And he had no intention of dwelling on a danger that had been avoided.

A few miles up the bank they came upon the first major fork in the river, where the Surbrin, from the northeast, emptied into the main flow of the northern arm of the great river network.

The friends looked for a way to cross the larger river, the Dessarin, and get into the small valley between it and the Surbrin. Nesmé, their next, and final stopover before Silverymoon, was farther up the Surbrin, and though the city was actually on the east bank of the river, the friends, taking the advice of Harkle Harpell, had decided to travel up the west bank and avoid the lurking dangers of the Evermoors.

They crossed the Dessarin without too much trouble, thanks to the incredible agility of the drow, who ran out over the river along an overhanging tree limb and leaped to a similar perch on the branch of a tree on the opposite bank. Soon after, they were all easily plodding along the Surbrin, enjoying the sunshine, the warm breeze, and the endless song of the river. Drizzt even managed to fell a deer with his bow, promising a fine supper of venison and restocked packs for the road ahead.

They camped right down by the water, under starshine for the first time in four nights, sitting around a fire and listening to Bruenor's tales of the silvery halls and the wonders they would find at the end of their road.

The serenity of the night did not carry over into the morning, though, for the friends were awakened by the sounds of battle. Wulfgar immediately scrambled up a nearby tree to learn who the combatants were.

"Riders!" he yelled, leaping and drawing out his warhammer even before he hit the ground. "Some are down! They do battle with monsters I do not know!" He was off and running to the north, Bruenor on his heels, and Drizzt circling to their flank down along the river. Less enthusiastic, Regis hung back, pulling out his small mace but hardly preparing for open battle.

Wulfgar was first on the scene. Seven riders were still up, trying vainly to maneuver their mounts into some form of a defensive line. The creatures they battled were quick and had no fear of running under stamping legs to trip up the horses. The monsters were only about three feet high, with arms twice that length. They resembled little trees, though undeniably animated, running about wildly, whacking with their clublike arms or, as another unfortunate rider discovered just as Wulfgar entered the fray, winding their pliable limbs around their foes to pull them from their mounts.

Wulfgar barreled between two creatures, knocking them aside, and bore down on the one that had just taken down the rider. The barbarian underestimated the monsters, though, for their rootlike toes found balance quickly and their long arms caught him from behind before he had gone two steps, grappling him on either side and stopping him in his tracks.

Bruenor charged in right behind. The dwarf's axe chopped through one of the monsters, splitting it down the middle like firewood, and then cut in wickedly on the other, sending a great chunk of its torso flying away.

Drizzt came up even with the battle, anxious but tempered, as always, by the overruling sensibility that had kept him alive through hundreds of encounters. He moved down to the side, below the drop of the bank, where he discovered a ramshackle bridge of logs spanning the Surbrin. The monsters had built it, Drizzt knew; apparently they weren't unthinking beasts.

Drizzt peered over the bank. The riders had rallied around the unexpected reinforcements, but one right before him had been wrapped by a monster and was being dragged from his horse. Seeing the treelike nature of their weird foes, Drizzt understood why the riders all wielded axes, and wondered how effective his slender scimitars would prove.

But he had to act. Springing from his concealment he thrust both his scimitars at the creature. They nicked into the mark, having no more effect than if Drizzt had stabbed a tree.

Even so, the drow's attempt had saved the rider. The monster clubbed its victim one last time to keep him dazed, then released its hold to face Drizzt. Thinking quickly, the drow went to an alternate attack, using his ineffective blades to parry the clubbing limbs. Then, as the creature rushed in on him, he dived at its feet, uprooting it, and rolled it back over him toward the riverbank. He poked his scimitars into the barklike skin and pushed off, sending the monster tumbling toward the Surbrin. It caught a hold before it went into the water, but Drizzt was on it again. A flurry of well-placed kicks put the monster into the flow and the river carried it away.

The rider, by this time, had regained his seat and his wits. He stepped his horse to the bank to thank his rescuer.

Then he saw the black skin.

"Drow!" he screamed, and his axeblade cut down.

Drizzt was caught off guard. His keen reflexes got one blade up enough to deflect the edge of the axe, but the flat of the weapon struck his head and sent him reeling. He dived with the momentum of the hit and rolled, trying to put as much ground between himself and the rider as he could, realizing that the man would kill him before he could recover.

"Wulfgar!" Regis screamed from his own concealment a short way back on the bank. The barbarian finished off one of the monsters with a thunderous smack that sent cracks all along its length, and turned just as the rider was bringing his horse about to get at Drizzt.

Wulfgar roared in rage and bolted from his own fight, grabbing the horse's bridle while it was still in its turn and heaving with all his strength. Horse and rider toppled to the ground. The horse was up again at once, shaking its head and nervously trotting about, but the rider stayed down, his leg crushed under his mount's weight in the fall.

The remaining five riders worked in unison now, charging into groups of monsters and scattering them. Bruenor's wicked axe cut away, the dwarf all the while singing a woodchopper's song that he had learned as a boy.

"Go split the wood for the fire, me son,
"Heat up the kettle and the meal's begun!" he sang out as he methodically cut down one monster after another.

Wulfgar defensively straddled Drizzt's form, his mighty hammer shattering, with a single strike, any of the monsters that ventured too near.

The rout was on, and in seconds the few surviving creatures scampered in terror across the bridge over the Surbrin.

Three riders were down and dead, a fourth leaned heavily against his horse, nearly overcome by his wounds, and the one Wulfgar had dropped had fainted away for his agony. But the five remaining astride did not go to their wounded. They formed a semi-circle around Wulfgar and Drizzt, who was just now getting back to his feet, and kept the two pinned against the riverbank with axes ready.

"This is how ye welcome yer rescuers?" Bruenor barked at them, slapping aside one horse so that he could join his friends. "Me bet's that the same folk don't come to yer aid twice!"

"Foul company you keep, dwarf!" one of the riders retorted.

"Your friend would be dead if it were not for that foul company!" Wulfgar replied, indicating the rider lying off to the side. "And he repays the drow with a blade!"

"We are the Riders of Nesmé," the rider explained. "Our lot is to die on the field, protecting our kin. We accept this fate willingly."

"Step yer horse one more foot and ye'll get yer wish," Bruenor warned.

"But you judge us unfairly," Wulfgar argued. "Nesmé is our destination. We come in peace and friendship."

"You'll not get in—not with him!" spat the rider. "The ways of the foul drow elves are known to all. You ask us to welcome him?"

"Bah, yer a fool and so's yer mother," Bruenor growled.

"Ware your words, dwarf," the rider warned. "We are five to three, and mounted."

"Try yer threat, then," Bruenor shot back. "The buzzards won't get much eatin' with those dancing trees." He ran his finger along the edge of his axe. "Let's give 'em something better to peck at."

Wulfgar swung Aegis-fang easily back and forth at the end of one arm. Drizzt made no move toward his weapons, and his steady calm was perhaps the most unnerving action of all to the riders.

Their speaker seemed less cocksure after the failure of his threat, but he held to a facade of advantage. "But we are not ungrateful for your assistance. We shall allow you to walk away. Be gone and never return to our lands."

"We go where we choose," snarled Burenor.

"And we choose not to fight," Drizzt added. "It is not our purpose, nor our desire, to lay injury to you or to your town, Riders of Nesmé. We shall pass, keeping our own business to ourselves and leaving yours to you."

"You shan't go anywhere near my town, black elf!" another rider cried. "You may cut us down on the field, but there are a hundred more behind us, and thrice that behind them! Now be gone!" His companions seemed to regain their courage at his bold words, their horses stepping nervously at the sudden tensing of the bridles.

"We have our course," Wulfgar insisted.

"Damn 'em!" Bruenor roared suddenly. "I've seen too much of this band already! Damn their town. May the river wash it away!" He turned to his friends. "They do us a favor. A day and more we'll save by going straight through to Silverymoon, instead of around with the river."

"Straight through?" questioned Drizzt. "The Evermoors?"

"Can it be worse than the dale?" Bruenor replied. He spun back on the riders. "Keep yer town, and yer heads, for now," he said. "We're to cross the bridge here and be rid of yerselves and all of Nesmé!"

"Fouler things than bog blokes roam the Trollmoors, foolish dwarf," the rider replied with a grin. "We have come to destroy this bridge. It will be burned behind you."

Bruenor nodded and returned the grin.

"Keep your course to the east," the rider warned. "Word will go out to all the riders. If you are sighted near Nesmé, you will be killed."

"Take your vile friend and be gone," another rider taunted, "before my axe bathes in the blood of a black elf! Though I would then have to throw the tainted weapon away!" All the riders joined in the ensuing laughter.

Drizzt hadn't even heard it. He was concentrating on a rider in the back of the group, a quiet one who could use his obscurity in the conversation to gain an unnoticed advantage. The rider had slipped a bow off of his shoulder and was inching his hand, ever so slowly, toward his quiver.

Bruenor was done talking. He and Wulfgar turned away from the riders and started to the bridge. "Come on, elf," he said to Drizzt as he passed. "Me sleep'll come better when we're far away from these orc-sired dogs."

But Drizzt had one more message to send before he would turn his back on the riders. In one blinding movement, he spun the bow from his back, pulled an arrow from his quiver, and sent it whistling through the air. It knocked into the would-be bowman's leather cap, parting his hair down the middle, and stuck in a tree immediately behind, its shaft quivering a clear warning.

"Your misguided insults, I accept, even expect," Drizzt explained to the horrified horsemen. "But I'll brook no attempts to injure my friends, and I will defend myself. Be warned, and only once warned: if you make another move against us, you will die." He turned abruptly and moved down to the bridge without looking back.

The stunned riders certainly had no intention of hindering the drow's party any further. The would-be bowman hadn't even looked for his cap.

Drizzt smiled at the irony of his inability to clear himself of the legends of his heritage. Though he was shunned and threatened on the one hand, the mysterious aura surrounding the black elves also gave him a bluff powerful enough to dissuade most potential enemies.

Regis joined them at the bridge, bouncing a small rock in his hand. "Had them lined up," he explained of his impromptu weapon. He flicked the stone into the river. "If it began, I would have had the first shot."

"If it began," Bruenor corrected, "ye'd have soiled the hole ye hid in!"

Wulfgar considered the rider's warning of their path. "Trollmoors," he echoed somberly, looking up the slope across the way to the blasted land before them. Harkle had told them of the place. The burned-out land and bottomless bogs. The trolls and even worse horrors that had no names.

"Save us a day and more!" Bruenor repeated stubbornly.

Wulfgar wasn't convinced.

⚔ ⚔ ⚔ ⚔ ⚔

"You are dismissed," Dendybar told the specter.

As the flames reformed in the brazier, stripping him of his material form, Morkai considered this second meeting. How often would Dendybar be calling upon him? he wondered. The mottled wizard had not yet fully recovered from their last encounter, but had dared to summon him again so soon. Dendybar's business with the dwarf's party must be urgent indeed! That assumption only made Morkai despise his role as the mottled wizard's spy even more.

Alone in the room again, Dendybar stretched out from his meditative position and grinned wickedly as he considered the image Morkai had shown him. The companions had lost their mounts and were marching into the foulest area in all the North. Another day or so would put his own party, flying on the hooves of his magical steeds, even with them, though thirty miles to the north.

Sydney would get to Silverymoon long before the drow.

II

SILVERYMOON

The ride from Luskan was swift indeed. Entreri and his cohorts appeared to any curious onlookers as no more than a shimmering blur in the night wind. The magical mounts left no trail of their passing, and no living creature could have overtaken them. The golem, as always, lumbered tirelessly behind with great stiff-legged strides.

So smooth and easy were the seats atop Dendybar's conjured steeds that the party was able to keep up its run past the dawn and throughout the entire next day with only short rests for food. Thus, when they set their camp after the sunset of the first full day on the road, they had already put the crags behind them.

Catti-brie fought an inner battle that first day. She had no doubt that Entreri and the new alliance would overtake Bruenor. As the situation stood now, Catti-brie would be only a detriment to her friends, a pawn for Entreri to play at his convenience.

She could do little to remedy the problem, unless she found some way to diminish, if not overcome, the grip of terror that the assassin held on her. That first day she spent in concentration, blocking out her surroundings as much as she could and searching her inner spirit for the strength and courage she would need.

Bruenor had given her many tools over the years to wage such a battle, skills of discipline and self-confidence that had seen her through many difficult situations. On the second day of the ride, then, more confident and comfortable with her situation, Catti-brie was able to focus on her captors. Most interesting were the glares that Jierdan and Entreri shot each other. The proud soldier had obviously not forgotten the humiliation he had suffered the night of their first meeting on the field outside of Luskan. Entreri, keenly aware of the grudge, even fueling it in his willingness to bring the issue to confrontation, kept an untrusting eye on the man.

This growing rivalry may prove to be her most promising—perhaps her only—hope of escaping, Catti-brie thought. She conceded that Bok was an indestructible, mindless destroying machine, beyond any manipulation she might try to lay upon it, and she learned quickly that Sydney offered nothing.

Catti-brie had tried to engage the young mage in conversation that second day, but Sydney's focus was too narrow for any diversions. She would be neither side-tracked nor persuaded from her obsession in any way. She didn't even acknowledge Catti-brie's greeting when they sat down for their midday meal. And when Catti-brie pestered her further, Sydney instructed Entreri to "keep the whore away."

Even in the failed attempt, though, the aloof mage had aided Catti-brie in a way that neither of them could foresee. Sydney's open contempt and insults came as a slap in Catti-brie's face and instilled in her another tool that would help to overcome the paralysis of her terror: anger.

They passed the halfway point of their journey on the second day, the landscape rolling surrealistically by them as they sped along, and camped in the small hills northeast of Nesmé, with the city of Luskan now fully two hundred miles behind them.

Campfires twinkled in the distance, a patrol from Nesmé, Sydney theorized.

"We should go there and learn what we may," Entreri suggested, anxious for news of his target.

"You and I," Sydney agreed. "We can get there and back before half the night is through."

Entreri looked at Catti-brie. "What of her?" he asked the mage. "I would not leave her with Jierdan."

"You think that the soldier would take advantage of the girl?" Sydney replied. "I assure you that he is honorable."

"That is not my concern," Entreri smirked. "I fear not for the daughter of Bruenor Battlehammer. She would dispose of your honorable soldier and be gone into the night before we ever returned."

Catti-brie didn't welcome the compliment. She understood that Entreri's comment was more of an insult to Jierdan, who was off gathering firewood, than any recognition of her own prowess, but the assassin's unexpected respect for her would make her task doubly difficult. She didn't want Entreri thinking of her as dangerous, even resourceful, for that would keep him too alert for her to move.

Sydney looked to Bok. "I go," she told the golem, purposely loud enough for Catti-brie to easily hear. "If the prisoner tries to flee, run her down and kill her!" She shot Entreri an evil grin. "Are you content?"

He returned her smile and swung his arm out in the direction of the distant camp.

Jierdan returned then, and Sydney told him of their plans. The soldier didn't seem overjoyed to have Sydney and Entreri running off together, though he said nothing to dissuade the mage. Catti-brie watched him closely and knew the truth. Being left alone with her and the golem didn't bother him, she surmised, but he feared any budding friendship between his two road-mates. Catti-brie understood and even expected this, for Jierdan was in the weakest position of the three—subservient to Sydney and afraid of Entreri. An alliance between those two, perhaps even a pact excluding Dendybar and the Hosttower altogether, would at the least put him out, and more probably spell his end.

"Suren the nature of their dark business works against them," Catti-brie whispered as Sydney and Entreri left the camp, speaking the words aloud to reinforce her growing confidence.

"I could help ye with that," she offered to Jierdan as he worked to complete the campsite.

The soldier glared at her. "Help?" he scoffed. "I should make you do all of it by yourself."

"Yer anger is known to me," Catti-brie countered sympathetically. "I meself have suffered at Entreri's foul hands."

Her pity enraged the proud soldier. He rushed at her threateningly, but she held her composure and did not flinch. "This work is below yer station."

Jierdan stopped suddenly, his anger diffused by his intrigue at the compliment. An obvious ploy, but to Jierdan's wounded ego, the young woman's respect came as too welcome to be ignored.

"What could you know of my station?" he asked.

"I know ye are a soldier of Luskan," Catti-brie replied. "Of a group that's feared throughout all the northland. Ye should not do the grovel work while the mage and the shadow-chaser are off playing in the night."

"You're making trouble!" Jierdan growled, but he paused to consider the point. "You set the camp," he ordered at length, regaining a measure of his own self-respect by displaying his superiority over her. Catti-brie didn't mind, though. She went about the work at once, playing her subservient role without complaint. A plan began to take definite shape in her mind now, and this phase demanded that she make an ally among her enemies, or at least put herself in a position to plant the seeds of jealousy in Jierdan's mind.

She listened, satisfied, as the soldier moved away, muttering under his breath.

✠ ✠ ✠ ✠

Before Entreri and Sydney even got close enough for a good view of the encampment, ritualistic chanting told them that this was no caravan from Nesmé. They inched in more cautiously to confirm their suspicions.

Long-haired barbarians, dark and tall, and dressed in ceremonial feathered garb, danced a circle around a wooden griffon totem.

"Uthgardt," Sydney explained. "The Griffon tribe. We are near to Shining White, their ancestral mound." She edged away from the glow of the camp. "Come," she whispered. "We will learn nothing of value here."

Entreri followed her back toward their own campsite. "Should we ride now?" he asked when they were safely away. "Gain more distance from the barbarians?"

"Unnecessary," Sydney replied. "The Uthgardt will dance the night through. All the tribe partakes of the ritual; I doubt that they even have sentries posted."

"You know much about them," the assassin remarked in an accusing tone, a hint to his sudden suspicions that there might be some ulterior plot controlling the events around them.

"I prepared myself for this journey," Sydney countered. "The Uthgardt keep few secrets; their ways are generally known and documented. Travelers in the northland would do well to understand these people."

"I am fortunate to have such a learned road companion," Entreri said, bowing in sarcastic apology.

Sydney, her eyes straight ahead, did not respond.

But Entreri would not let the conversation die so easily. There was method in his leading line of suspicions. He had consciously chosen this time to play out his hand and reveal his distrust even before they had learned the nature of the encampment. For the first time the two were alone, without Catti-brie or Jierdan to complicate the confrontation, and Entreri meant to put an end to his concerns, or put an end to the mage.

"When am I to die?" he asked bluntly.

Sydney didn't miss a step. "When the fates decree it, as with us all."

"Let me ask the question a different way," Entreri continued, grabbing her by the arm and turning her to face him. "When are you instructed to try to kill me?

"Why else would Dendybar have sent the golem?" Entreri reasoned. "The wizard puts no store in pacts and honor. He does what he must to accomplish his goals in the most expedient way, and then eliminates those he no longer needs. When my value to you is ended, I am to be slain. A task you may find more difficult than you presume."

"You are perceptive," Sydney replied coolly. "You have judged Dendybar's character well. He would have killed you simply to avoid any possible complications. But you have not considered my own role in this. On my insistence, Dendybar put the decision of your fate into my hands." She paused a moment to let Entreri weigh her words. He could easily kill her right now, they both knew that, so the candor of her calm admission of a plot to murder him halted any immediate actions and forced him to hear her out.

"I am convinced that we seek different ends to our confrontation with the dwarf's party," Sydney explained, "and thus I have no intention of destroying a present, and potentially future, ally."

In spite of his ever-suspicious nature, Entreri fully understood the logic in her line of reasoning. He recognized many of his own characteristics in Sydney. Ruthless, she let nothing get in the way of her chosen path, but she did not stray from that path for any diversion, no matter how strong her feelings. He released her arm. "But the golem travels with us," he said absently, turning into the empty night. "Does Dendybar believe that we will need it to defeat the dwarf and his companions?"

"My master leaves little to chance," Sydney answered. "Bok was sent to seal Dendybar's claim on that which he desires. Protection against unexpected trouble from the companions. And against you."

Entreri carried her line of thinking a step farther. "The object the wizard desires must be powerful indeed," he reasoned.

Sydney nodded.

"Tempting for a younger mage, perhaps."

"What do you imply?" Sydney demanded, angry that Entreri would question her loyalty to Dendybar.

The assassin's assured smile made her squirm uncomfortably. "The golem's purpose is to protect Dendybar against unexpected trouble . . . from you!"

Sydney stammered but could not find the words to reply. She hadn't considered that possibility. She tried logically to dismiss Entreri's outlandish conclusion, but the assassin's next remark clouded her ability to think.

"Simply to avoid any possible complications," he said grimly, echoing her earlier words.

The logic of his assumptions slapped her in the face. How could she think herself above Dendybar's malicious plotting? The revelation sent shivers through her, but she had no intention of searching for the answer with Entreri standing next to her. "We must trust in each other," she said to him. "We must understand that we both benefit from the alliance, and that it costs neither of us anything."

"Send the golem away then, " Entreri replied.

An alarm went off in Sydney's mind. Was Entreri trying to instill doubt in her merely to gain an advantage in their relationship?

"We do not need the thing," he said. "We have the girl. And even if the companions refuse our demands, we have the strength to take what we want." He returned the mage's suspicious look. "You speak of trust?"

Sydney did not reply, and started again for their camp. Perhaps she should send Bok away. The act would satisfy Entreri's doubts about her, though it certainly would give him the upper hand against her if any trouble did come to pass. But dismissing the golem might also answer some of the even more disturbing questions that weighed upon her, the questions about Dendybar.

⚔ ⚔ ⚔ ⚔

The next day was the quietest, and the most productive, of the ride. Sydney fought with her turmoil about the reasons for the golem's presence. She had come to the conclusion that she should send Bok away, if for no better reason than to prove to herself her master's trust.

Entreri watched the telltale signs of her struggle with interest, knowing that he had weakened the bond between Sydney and Dendybar enough to strengthen his own position with the young mage. Now he simply had to wait and watch for his next chance to realign his companions.

Likewise, Catti-brie kept her eye out for more opportunities to cultivate the seeds she had planted in Jierdan's thoughts. The snarls that she saw the soldier hide from Entreri, and from Sydney, told her that her plan was off to a grand start.

They made Silverymoon shortly after noon on the following day. If Entreri had any doubts left about his decision to join the Hosttower's party, they were dismissed when he considered the enormity of their accomplishment. With the tireless magical steeds, they had covered nearly five hundred miles in four days. And in the effortless ride, the absolute ease in guiding their mounts, they were hardly worn when they arrived in the foothills of the mountains just west of the enchanted city.

"The river Rauvin," Jierdan, at the front of the party, called back to them. "And a guard post."

"Pass it by," Entreri replied.

"No," Sydney said. "These are the guides across the Moonbridge. They will let us pass, and their aid will make our journey into the city much easier."

Entreri looked back to Bok, lumbering up the trail behind them. "All of us?" he asked incredulously.

Sydney hadn't forgotten the golem. "Bok," she said when the golem had caught up to them, "you are no longer needed. Return to Dendybar and tell him that all goes well."

Catti-brie's eyes lit up at the thought of sending the monster back, and Jierdan, startled, looked back with growing anxiety. Watching him, Catti-brie saw another advantage to this unexpected turn. By dismissing the golem, Sydney gave more credence to the fears of an alliance between Sydney and Entreri that Catti-brie had planted upon the soldier.

The golem did not move.

"I said go!" Sydney demanded. She saw Entreri's unsurprised stare from the comer of her eye. "Damn you," she whispered to herself. Still, Bok did not move.

"You are indeed perceptive," she snarled at Entreri.

"Remain here, then," she hissed at the golem. "We shall stay in the city for several days." She slipped down from her seat and stomped away, humbled by the assassin's wry smile at her back.

"What of the mounts?" Jierdan asked.

"They were created to get us to Silverymoon, no more," Sydney replied, and even as the four walked away down the path, the shimmering lights that were the horses faded into a soft blue glow, then were gone altogether.

They had little trouble getting through the guard post, especially when Sydney identified herself as a representative of the Hosttower of the Arcane. Unlike most cities in the hostile northland, bordering on paranoia in their fears of outsiders, Silverymoon did not keep itself hemmed within foreboding walls and lines of wary soldiers. The people of this city looked upon visitors as an enhancement to their culture, not as a threat to their way of life.

One of the Knights of Silver, the guardsmen at the post on the Rauvin, led the four travelers to the entrance of the Moonbridge, an arcing, invisible structure that spanned the river before the main gate of the city. The strangers crossed tentatively, uncomfortable for the lack of visible material under their feet. But soon enough they found themselves strolling down the meandering roadways of the magical city. Their pace unconsciously slowed, caught under the infectious laziness, the relaxed, contemplative atmosphere that dissipated even Entreri's narrow-visioned intensity.

Tall, twisting towers and strangely shaped structures greeted them at every turn. No single architectural style dominated Silverymoon, unless it was the freedom of a builder to exercise his or her personal creativity without fear of judgement or scorn. The result was a city of endless splendors, not rich in counted treasures, as were Waterdeep and Mirabar, its two mightiest neighbors, but unrivaled in aesthetic beauty. A throwback to the earliest days of the Realms, when elves and dwarves and humans had enough room to roam under the sun and stars without fear of crossing some invisible borderline of a hostile kingdom, Silverymoon existed in open defiance of the conquerors and tyrants of the world, a place where no one held claim over another.

People of all the good races walked freely here and without fear, down every road and alleyway on the darkest of nights, and if the travelers passed by someone and were not greeted with a welcoming word, it was only because the person was too profoundly engaged in meditative contemplation.

"The dwarf's party is less than a tenday out of Longsaddle," Sydney mentioned as they moved through the city. "We may have several days of wait."

"Where do we go?" Entreri asked, feeling out of place. The values that obviously took precedence in Silverymoon were unlike those of any city he had ever encountered, and were completely foreign to his own perceptions of the greedy, lusting world.

"Countless inns line the streets," Sydney answered. "Guests are plentiful here, and are welcomed openly."

"Then our task in finding the companions, once they arrive, shall prove difficult indeed," Jierdan groaned.

"Not so," Sydney replied wryly. "The dwarf comes to Silverymoon in search of information. Soon after they arrive, Bruenor and his friends will make their way to the vault of Sages, the most reknowned library in all the north."

Entreri squinted his eyes, and said, "And we will be there to greet them."

12

THE TROLLMOORS

This was a land of blackened earth and misted bogs, where decay and an imposing sensation of peril overruled even the sunniest of skies. The landscape climbed and dropped continually, and the crest of each rise, mounted in hopes of an end to the place by any traveler here, brought only despair and more of the same unchanging scenes.

The brave Riders of Nesmé ventured into the moors each spring to set long lines of fires and drive the monsters of the hostile land far from the borders of their town. The season was late and several tendays had passed since the last burning, but even now the low dells lay heavy with smoke and the waves of heat from the great fires still shimmered in the air around the thickest of the charred piles of wood.

Bruenor had led his friends into the Trollmoors in stubborn defiance of the riders, and was determined to pound his way through to Silverymoon. But after only the first day's travel, even he began to doubt the decision. The place demanded a constant state of alertness, and each copse of burned-out trees they passed made them pause, the black, leafless stumps and fallen logs bearing an uncomfortable resemblance to bog blokes. More than once, the spongy ground beIneath their feet suddenly became a deep pit of mud, and only the quick reactions of a nearby companion kept them from finding out how deep any of the pits actually were.

A continual breeze blew across the moors, fueled by the contrasting patches of hot ground and cool bogs, and carrying an odor more foul than the smoke and soot of the fires, a sickly sweet smell disturbingly familiar to Drizzt Do'Urden—the stench of trolls.

This was their domain, and all the rumors about the Evermoors the companions had heard, and had laughed away in the comfort of The Fuzzy Quarterstaff, could not have prepared them for the reality that suddenly descended upon them when they entered the place.

Bruenor had estimated that their party could clear the moors in five days if they kept a strong pace. That first day, they actually covered the necessary distance, but the dwarf had not foreseen the continual backtracking they would have to do to avoid the bogs. While they had marched for more than twenty miles that day, they were less than ten from where they started into the moors.

Still, they encountered no trolls, nor any other kind of fiend, and they set their camp that night under a guise of quiet optimism.

"Ye'll keep to the guard?" Bruenor asked Drizzt, aware that the drow alone had the heightened senses they would need to survive the night.

Drizzt nodded. "The night through," he replied, and Bruenor didn't argue. The dwarf knew that none of them would get any sleep that night, whether on guard, or not.

Darkness came suddenly and completely. Bruenor, Regis, and Wulfgar couldn't see their own hands if they held them inches from their faces. With the blackness came the sounds of an awakening nightmare. Sucking, sloshing footsteps closed in all about them. Smoke mixed with the nighttime fog and rolled in around the trunks of the leafless trees. The wind did not increase, but the intensity of its foul stench did, and it carried now the groans of the tormented spirits of the moors' wretched dwellers.

"Gather your gear," Drizzt whispered to his friends.

"What do ye see, then?" Bruenor asked softly.

"Nothing directly," came the reply. "But I feel them about, as do you all. We cannot let them find us sitting. We must move among them to keep them from gathering about us."

"My legs ache," complained Regis. "And my feet have swelled. I don't even know if I can get my boots back on!"

"Help him, boy," Bruenor told Wulfgar. "The elf's right. We'll carry ye if we must, Rumblebelly, but we're not staying."

Drizzt took the lead, and at times he had to hold Bruenor's hand behind him, and so on down the line to Wulfgar in the rear, to keep his companions from stumbling from the path he had picked.

They could all sense the dark shapes moving around them, smell the foulness of the wretched trolls. Clearly viewing the host gathering about them, Drizzt alone understood just how precarious their position was, and he pulled his friends as fast as he could.

Luck was with them, for the moon came up then, transforming the fog into a ghostly silver blanket, and revealing to all the friends the pressing danger. Now with the movement visible on every side, the friends ran.

Lanky, lurching forms loomed up in the mist beside them, clawed fingers stretching out to snag at them as they rushed past. Wulfgar moved up to Drizzt's side, swatting the trolls aside with great sweeps of Aegis-fang, while the drow concentrated on keeping them going in the right direction.

For hours they ran, and still the trolls came on. Beyond all feelings of exhaustion, past the ache, and then the numbness in their limbs, the friends ran with the knowledge of the certain horrible death that would befall them if they faltered for even a second, their fear overruling their bodies' cries of defeat. Even Regis, too fat and soft, and with legs too short for the road, matched the pace and pushed those before him to greater speeds.

Drizzt understood the futility of their course. Wulfgar's hammer invariably slowed, and they all stumbled more and more with each minute that passed. The night had many hours more, and even the dawn did not guarantee an end to the pursuit. How many miles could they run? When would they turn down a path that ended in a bottomless bog, with a hundred trolls at their backs?

Drizzt changed his strategy. No longer seeking only to flee, he began looking for a defensible piece of ground. He spied a small mound, ten feet high perhaps, with a steep, almost sheer, grade on the three sides he could see from his angle. A solitary sapling grew up its face. He pointed the place out to Wulfgar, who understood the plan immediately and veered in. Two trolls loomed up to block their way, but Wulfgar, snarling in rage, charged to meet them. Aegis-fang slammed down in furious succession again and again, and the other three companions were able to slip behind the barbarian and make it to the mound.

Wulfgar spun away and rushed to join them, the stubborn trolls close in pursuit and now joined by a long line of their wretched kin.

Surprisingly nimble, even despite his belly, Regis scampered up the tree to the top of the mound. Bruenor, though, not built for such climbing, struggled for every inch.

"Help him!" Drizzt, his back to the tree and scimitars readied, cried to Wulfgar. "Then you get up! I shall hold them."

Wulfgar's breath came in labored gasps, and a line of bright blood was etched across his forehead. He stumbled into the tree and started up behind the dwarf. Roots pulled away under their combined weight, and they seemed to lose an inch for every one they gained. Finally, Regis was able to clasp Bruenor's hand and help him over the top, and Wulfgar, with the way clear before him, moved to join them. With their own immediate safety assured, they looked back in concern for their friend.

Drizzt battled three of the monsters, and more piled in behind. Wulfgar considered dropping back from his perch halfway up the tree and dying at the drow's side, but Drizzt, periodically looking back over his shoulder to check his friends' progress, noted the barbarian's hesitation and read his mind. "Go!" he shouted. "Your delay does not help!"

Wulfgar had to pause and consider the source of the command. His trust of, and respect for, Drizzt overcame his instinctive desire to rush back into the fray, and he grudgingly pulled himself up to join Regis and Bruenor on the small plateau.

Trolls moved to flank the drow, their filthy claws reaching out at him from every side. He heard his friends, all three, imploring him to break away and join them, but knew that the monsters had already slipped in behind to cut off his retreat.

A smile widened across his face. The light in his eyes flared.

He rushed into the main host of trolls, away from the unattainable mound and his horrified friends.

The three companions had little time to dwell on the drow's fortunes, however, for they soon found themselves assailed from every side as the trolls came relentlessly on, scratching to get at them.

Each friend stood to defend his own side. Luckily, the climb up the back of the mound proved even steeper, at some places inverted, and the trolls could not effectively get at them from behind.

Wulfgar was most deadly, knocking a troll from the mound's side with each smack of his mighty hammer. But before he could even catch his breath, another had taken its place.

Regis, slapping with his little mace, was less effective. He banged with all his strength on fingers, elbows, even heads as the trolls edged in closer, but he could not dislodge the clutching monsters from their perch. Invariably, as each one crested the mound, either Wulfgar or Bruenor had to twist away from his own fight and swat the beast away.

They knew that the first time they failed with a single stroke, they would find a troll up and ready beside them on the top of the mound.

Disaster struck after only a few minutes. Bruenor spun to aid Regis as yet another monster pulled its torso over the top. The dwarf's axe cut in cleanly.

Too cleanly. It sliced into the troll's neck and drove right through, beheading the beast. But though the head flew from the mound, the body kept coming. Regis fell back, too horrified to react.

"Wulfgar!" Bruenor cried out.

The barbarian spun, not slowing long enough to gape at the headless foe, and slammed Aegis-fang into the thing's chest, blasting it from the mound.

Two more hands grabbed at the lip. From Wulfgar's side, another troll had crawled more than halfway over the crest. And behind them, where Bruenor had been, a third was up and straddling the helpless halfling.

They didn't know where to start. The mound was lost. Wulfgar even considered leaping down into the throng below to die as a true warrior by killing as many of his enemies as he could, and also so that he would not have to watch as his two friends were torn to pieces.

But suddenly, the troll above the halfling struggled with its balance, as though something was pulling it from behind. One of its legs buckled and then it fell backward into the night.

Drizzt Do'Urden pulled his blade from the thing's calf as it went over him, then deftly rolled to the top of the mound, regaining his feet right beside the startled halfling. His cloak streamed in tatters, and lines of blood darkened his clothing in many places.

But he still wore his smile, and the fire in his lavender eyes told his friends that he was far from finished. He darted by the gaping dwarf and barbarian and hacked at the next troll, quickly dispatching it from the side.

"How?" Bruenor asked, gawking, though he knew as he rushed back to Regis that no answer would be forthcoming from the busy drow.

Drizzt's daring move down below had gained him an advantage over his enemies. Trolls were twice his size, and those behind the ones he fought had no idea that he was coming through. He knew that he had done little lasting damage to the beasts—the stab wounds lie drove in as he passed would quickly heal, and the limbs he severed would grow back—but the daring maneuver gained him the time he needed to clear the rushing horde and circle out into the darkness. Once free in the black night, he had picked his path back to the mound, cutting through the distracted trolls with the same blazing intensity. His agility alone had saved him when he got to the base, for he virtually ran up the mound's side, even over the back of a climbing troll, too quickly for the surprised monsters to grasp him.

The defense of the mound solidified now. With Bruenor's wicked axe, Wulfgar's pounding hammer, and Drizzt's whirring scimitars, each holding a side, the climbing trolls had no easy route to the top, Regis stayed in the middle of the small plateau, alternately darting in to help his friends whenever a troll got too close to gaining a hold.

Still the trolls came on, the throng below growing with every minute. The friends understood clearly the inevitable outcome of this encounter. The only chance lay in breaking the gathering of monsters below to give them a route of escape, but they were too engaged in simply beating back their latest opponents to search for the solution.

Except for Regis.

It happened almost by accident. A writhing arm, severed by one of Drizzt's blades, crawled into the center of their defenses. Regis, utterly revolted, whacked at the thing wildly with his mace. "It won't die!" he screamed as the thing kept wriggling and grabbing at the little weapon. "It won't die! Someone hit it! Someone cut it! Someone burn it!"

The other three were too busy to react to the halfling's desperate pleas, but Regis's last statement, cried out in dismay, brought an idea into his own head. He jumped upon the writhing limb, pinning it down for a moment while he fumbled in his pack for his tinderbox and flint.

His shaking hands could hardly strike the stone, but the tiniest spark did its killing work. The troll arm ignited and crackled into a crisp ball. Not about to miss the opportunity before him, Regis scooped up the fiery limb and ran over to Bruenor. He held back the dwarf's axe, telling Bruenor to let his latest opponent get above the line of the ridge.

When the troll hoisted itself up, Regis put the fire in its face. The head virtually exploded into flame and screaming in agony, the troll dropped from the mound, bringing the killing fire to its own companions.

Trolls did not fear the blade or the hammer. Wounds inflicted by these weapons healed quickly, and even a severed head would soon grow back. Such encounters actually helped propagate the wretched species, for a troll would regrow a severed arm, and a severed arm would regrow another troll! More than one hunting cat or wolf had feasted upon a troll carcass only to bring its own horrible demise when a new monster grew in its belly.

But even trolls were not completely without fear. Fire was their bane, and the trolls of Evermoor were more than familiar with it. Burns could not regenerate and a troll killed by flames was dead forever. Almost as if it were purposely in the gods' design, fire clung to a troll's dry skin as readily as to dry kindling.

The monsters on Bruenor's side of the mound fled away or fell in charred lumps. Bruenor patted the halfling on the back as he observed the welcomed spectacle, hope returning to his weary eyes.

"Wood," reasoned Regis. "We need wood."

Bruenor slipped his pack off his back. "Ye'll get yer wood, Rumblebelly," he laughed, pointing at the sapling running up the side of the mound before him. "And there's oil in me pouch!" He ran across to Wulfgar. "The tree, boy! Help the halfling," was the only explanation he gave as he moved in front of the barbarian.

As soon as Wulfgar turned around and saw Regis fumbling with a flask of oil, he understood his part in the plan. No trolls as yet had returned to that side of the mound, and the stench of the burned flesh at the base was nearly overwhelming. With a single heave, the muscled barbarian tore the sapling from its roots and brought it up to Regis. Then he went back and relieved the dwarf, allowing Bruenor to put his axe to use in slicing up the wood.

Soon flaming missiles lit the sky all about the mound and fell into the troll horde with killing sparks popping all about. Regis ran to the lip of the mound with another flask of oil and sprinkled it down on the closest trolls, sending them into a terrified frenzy. The rout was on, and between the stampede and the quick spread of flames, the area below the mound was cleared in minutes, and not another movement did the friends see for the few remaining hours of the night, save the pitiful writhing of the mass of limbs, and the twitchings of burned torsos. Fascinated, Drizzt wondered how long the things would survive with their cauterized wounds that would not regenerate.

As exhausted as they were, none of the companions managed any sleep that night. With the breaking of dawn, and no sign of trolls around them, though the filthy smoke hung heavily in the air, Drizzt insisted that they move along.

They left their fortress and walked, because they had no other choice, and because they refused to yield where others might have faltered. They encountered nothing immediately, but could sense the eyes of the moors upon them still, a hushed silence that foretold disaster.

Later that morning, as they plodded along on the mossy turf, Wulfgar stopped suddenly and heaved Aegis-fang into a small copse of blackened trees. The bog bloke, for that is what the barbarian's target truly was, crossed its arms defensively before it, but the magical warhammer hit with enough power to split the monster down the middle. Its frightened companions, nearly a dozen, fled their similar positions and disappeared into the moors.

"How could you know?" Regis asked, for he was certain that the barbarian had barely considered the clump of trees.

Wulfgar shook his head, honestly not knowing what had compelled him. Drizzt and Bruenor both understood, and approved. They were all operating on instinct now, their exhaustion rendering their minds long past the point of consistent, rational thought. Wulfgar's reflexes remained at their level of fine precision. He might have caught a flicker of movement out of the corner of his eye, so minuscule that his conscious mind hadn't even registered it. But his instinct for survival had reacted. The dwarf and the drow looked to each other for confirmation, not too surprised this time at the barbarian's continued show of maturity as a warrior.

The day became unbearably hot, adding to their discomfort. All they wanted to do was fall down and let their weariness overcome them.

But Drizzt pulled them onward, searching for another defensible spot, though he doubted that he could find one as well-designed as the last. Still, they had enough oil remaining to get them through another night if they could hold a small line long enough to put the flames to their best advantage. Any hillock, perhaps even a copse of trees, would suffice.

What they found instead was another bog, this one stretching as far as they could see in every direction, miles perhaps. "We could turn to the north," Drizzt suggested to Bruenor. "We may have come far enough east by now to break clear of the moors beyond the influence of Nesmé."

"The night'll catch us along the bank," Bruenor observed grimly.

"We could cross," Wulfgar suggested.

"Trolls take to water?" Bruenor asked Drizzt, intrigued by the possibilities. The drow shrugged.

"Worth a try, then!" Bruenor proclaimed.

"Gather some logs," instructed Drizzt. "Take no time to bind them together—we can do that out on the water, if we must."

Floating the logs as buoys by their sides, they slipped out into the cold, still waters of the huge bog.

Though they weren't thrilled with the sucking, muddy sensation that pulled at them with each step, Drizzt and Wulfgar found that they could walk in many places, propelling the makeshift raft steadily along. Regis and Bruenor, too short for the water, lay across the logs. Eventually they grew more comfortable with the eerie hush of the bog, and accepted the water route as a quiet rest.

The return to reality was rude indeed.

The water around them exploded, and three troll-like forms hit them in sudden ambush. Regis, nearly asleep across his log, was thrown off it and into the water. Wulfgar took a hit in the chest before he could ready Aegis-fang, but he was no halfling, and even the considerable strength of the monster could not move him backward. The one that rose before the ever-alert drow found two scimitars at work on its face before its head even cleared the water.

The battle proved as fast and furious as its abrupt beginning. Enraged by the continued demands of the relentless moors, the friends reacted to the assault with a counterattack of unmatched fury. The drow's troll was sliced apart before it even stood straight, and Bruenor had enough time to prepare himself to get at the monster that had dropped Regis.

Wulfgar's troll, though it landed a second blow behind the first, was hit with a savage flurry that it could not have expected. Not an intelligent creature, its limited reasoning and battle experience led it to believe that its foe should not have remained standing and ready to retaliate after it had squarely landed two heavy blows.

Its realization, though, served as little comfort as Aegis-fang pummeled the monster back under the surface.

Regis bobbed back to the surface then and slung an arm over the log. One side of his face was bright with a welt and a painful-looking scrape.

"What were they?" Wulfgar asked the drow.

"Some manner of troll," Drizzt reasoned, still stabbing at the unmoving form lying under the water before him.

Wulfgar and Bruenor understood the reason for his continued attacks. In sudden fright, they took up whacking at the forms lying beside them, hoping to mutilate the corpses enough so that they might be miles gone before the things rose to life once again.

✕ ✕ ✕ ✕

Beneath the bog's surface, in the swirlless solitude of the dark waters, the severe thumping of axe and hammer disturbed the slumber of other denizens. One in particular had slept away a decade and more, unbothered by any of the potential dangers that lurked nearby, safe in its knowledge of supremacy.

✕ ✕ ✕ ✕

Dazed and drained from the hit he had taken, as if the unexpected ambush had bent his spirit beyond its breaking point, Regis slumped helplessly over the log and wondered if he had any fight left in him. He didn't notice when the log began to drift slightly in the hot moors' breeze. It hooked around the exposed roots of a small line of trees and floated free into the lilypad-covered waters of a quiet lagoon.

Regis stretched out lazily, only half aware of the change in his surroundings. He could still hear the conversation of his friends faintly in the background.

He cursed his carelessness and struggled against the stubborn hold of his lethargy, though, when the water began to churn before him. A purplish, leathery form broke the surface, and then he saw the huge circular maw with its cruel rows of daggerlike teeth.

Regis, up now, did not cry out or react in any way, fascinated by the specter of his own death looming before him.

A giant worm.

✕ ✕ ✕ ✕

"I thought the water would offer us some protection from the foul things, at least," Wulfgar groaned, giving one final smack at the troll corpse that lay submerged beside him.

"At least the moving's easier," Bruenor put in. "Get the logs together, and let's move along. No figuring how many kin these three have stalking the area."

"I have no desire to stay and count," replied Wulfgar. He looked around, puzzled, and asked, "Where is Regis?"

It was the first time in the confusion of the fight that any of them noticed that the halfling had floated off. Bruenor started to call out, but Drizzt slapped a hand across his mouth.

"Listen," he said.

The dwarf and Wulfgar held very still and listened in the direction that the drow was now intently staring. After a moment of adjustment, they heard the halfling's quivering voice.

". . . really is a beautiful stone," they heard, and knew at once that Regis was using the pendant to get himself out of trouble.

The seriousness of the situation came clear immediately, for Drizzt had sorted out the blur of images that he saw through a line of trees, perhaps a hundred feet to the west. "Worm!" he whispered to his companions. "Huge beyond anything I have ever seem!" He indicated a tall tree to Wulfgar, then started on a flanking course around to the south, pulling the onyx statue out of his pack as he went, and calling for Guenhwyvar. They would need all the help they could get with this beast.

Dipping low in the water, Wulfgar eased his way up to the tree line and started shinning up a tree, the scene now clear before him. Bruenor followed him, but slipped between the trees, going even deeper into the bog, and came into position on the other side.

"There are more, too, " Regis bargained in a louder voice hoping that his friends would hear and rescue him. He kept the hypnotizing ruby spinning on its chain. He didn't think for a moment that the primitive monster understood him, but it seemed perplexed enough by the gem's sparkles to refrain from gobbling him up, at least for the present. In truth, the magic of the ruby did little against the creature. Giant worms had no minds to speak of, and charms had no effect on them at all. But the huge worm, not really hungry and mesmerized by the dance of the light, allowed Regis to play through his game.

Drizzt came into position farther down the tree line, his bow now in hand, while Guenhwyvar stealthily slipped even farther around to the monster's rear. Drizzt could see Wulfgar poised, high in the tree above Regis and ready to leap into action. The drow couldn't see Bruenor, but he knew that the crafty dwarf would find a way to be effective.

Finally the worm tired of its game with the halfling and his spinning gem. A sudden sucking of air sizzled with acidic drool.

Recognizing the danger, Drizzt acted first, conjuring a globe of darkness around the halfling's log. Regis, at first, thought the sudden blackness signified the end of his life, but when the cold water hit his face and then swallowed him up as he rolled limply from the log, he understood.

The globe confused the monster for a moment, but the beast spat a stream of its killing acid anyway, the wicked stuff sizzling as it hit the water and setting the log ablaze.

Wulfgar sprang from his high perch, launching himself through the air fearlessly and screaming, "Tempus!" his legs flung wide, but his arm cocked with the warhammer fully under control and ready to strike.

The worm lolled its head to the side to move away from the barbarian, but it didn't react quite fast enough. Aegis-fang crunched through the side of its face, tearing through the purplish hide and twisting the outer rim of its maw, snapping through teeth and bone. Wulfgar had given all that he possibly could in that one mighty blow, and he could not imagine the enormity of his success as he slapped belly-first into the cold water, beneath the drow's darkness.

Enraged by pain and suddenly more injured than it had ever been, the great worm issued a roar that split trees asunder and sent creatures of the moors scurrying for cover miles away. It rolled an arch along its fifty-foot length, up and down, in a continual splash that sent bursts of water high into the air.

Drizzt opened up, his fourth arrow nocked and ready before the first even reached its mark. The worm roared again in agony and spun on the drow, releasing a second stream of acid.

But the agile elf was gone long before the acid sizzled into the water where he had been standing. Bruenor, meanwhile, had completely gone under the water, blindly stumbling toward the beast. Nearly ground into the mud by the worm's frenzied gyrations, he came up just behind the curl of the monster. The breadth of its massive torso measured fully twice his height, but the dwarf didn't hesitate, smacking his axe against the tough hide.

Guenhwyvar then sprang upon the monster's back and ran up its length, finding a perch on its head. The cat's clawed paws dug into the worm's eyes before it even had time to react to the new attackers.

Drizzt plucked away, his quiver nearly empty and a dozen feathered shafts protruding from the worm's maw and head. The beast decided to concentrate on Bruenor next, his vicious axe inflicting the most severe wounds. But before it could roll over onto the dwarf, Wulfgar emerged from the darkness and heaved his warhammer. Aegis-fang thudded into the maw again and the weakened bone cracked apart. Acidic blobs of blood and bone hissed into the bog and the worm roared a third time in agony and protest.

The friends did not relent. The drow's arrows stung home in a continuous line. The cat's claws raked deeper and deeper into the flesh. The dwarf's axe chopped and hacked, sending pieces of hide floating away. And Wulfgar pounded away.

The giant worm reeled. It could not retaliate. In the wave of dizzying darkness that fast descended upon it, it was too busy merely holding to its stubborn balance. Its maw was broken wide open and one eye was out. The relentless beating of the dwarf and barbarian had blasted through its protective hide, and Bruenor growled in savage pleasure when his axe at last sank deep into exposed flesh.

A sudden spasm from the monster sent Guenhwyvar flying into the bog and knocked Bruenor and Wulfgar away. The friends didn't even try to get back, aware that their task was completed. The worm trembled and twitched in its last efforts of life.

Then it toppled into the bog in a sleep that would outlast any it had ever known—the endless sleep of death.

13
THE LAST RUN

The dissipating globe of darkness found Regis once again clinging to his log, which was now little more than a black cinder, and shaking his head. "We are beyond ourselves," he sighed. "We cannot make it through."

"Faith, Rumblebelly," Bruenor comforted, sloshing through the water to join the halfling. "Tales we be making, for telling to our children's children, and for others to tell when we're no more!"

"You mean today, then?" Regis snipped. "Or perhaps we'll live this day and be no more tomorrow."

Bruenor laughed and grabbed hold of the log. "Not yet, me friend," he assured Regis with an adventurous smile. "Not till me business is done!"

Drizzt, moving to retrieve his arrows, noted how heavily Wulfgar leaned upon the worm's body. From a distance, he thought that the young barbarian was simply exhausted, but when he drew near, he began to suspect something more serious. Wulfgar clearly favored one leg in his pose, as though it, or perhaps his lower back, had been injured.

When Wulfgar saw the drow's concerned took, he straightened stoically. "Let us move on," he suggested, moving away toward Bruenor and Regis and doing his best to hide a limp.

Drizzt didn't question him about it. The young man was made of stuff as hard as the tundra in midwinter, and too altruistic and proud to admit an injury when nothing could be gained by the admission. His friends couldn't stop to wait for him to heal, and they certainly couldn't carry him, so he would grimace away the pain and plod on.

But Wulfgar truly was injured. When he splashed into the water after his fall from the tree, he had wickedly twisted his back. In the heat of the battle, his adrenaline pumping, he hadn't felt the wrenching pain. But now each step came hard.

Drizzt saw it as clearly as he saw the despair upon Regis's normally cheerful face, and as clearly as the exhaustion that kept the dwarf's axe swinging low, despite Bruenor's optimistic boasting. He looked all about at the moors, which seemed to stretch forever in every direction, and wondered for the first time if he and his companions had indeed gone beyond themselves.

Guenhwyvar hadn't been injured in the battle, just a bit shaken up, but Drizzt, recognizing the cat's limited range of movement in the bog, sent her back to her own plane. He would have liked to keep the wary panther at their point. But the water was too deep for the cat, and the only way Guenhwyvar could have kept moving would have been by springing from tree to tree. Drizzt knew it wouldn't work; he and his friends would have to go on alone.

Reaching deep within themselves to reinforce their resolve, the companions kept to their work, the drow inspecting the worm's head to salvage any of the score of arrows that he had fired, knowing all too well that he would probably need them again before they saw the end of the moors, while the other three retrieved the rest of the logs and provisions.

Soon after, the friends drifted through the bog with as little physical effort as they could manage, fighting every minute to keep their minds alert to the dangerous surroundings. With the heat of the day, though—the hottest one yet—and the gentle rocking of the logs on the quiet water, all but Drizzt dropped off, one by one, to sleep.

The drow kept the makeshift raft moving, and remained vigilant; they couldn't afford any delay, or any lapses. Luckily, the water opened up beyond the lagoon, and there were few obstructions for Drizzt to deal with.

The bog became a great blur to him after a while, his tired eyes recording little detail, just general outlines and any sudden movements in the reeds.

He was a warrior, though, with lightning reflexes and uncanny discipline. The water trolls hit again, and the tiny flicker of consciousness that Drizzt Do'Urden had remaining summoned him back to reality in time to deny the monsters' advantage of surprise.

Wulfgar, and Bruenor, too, sprang from their slumber at the instant of his call, weapons in hand. Only two trolls rose to meet them this time and the three dispatched them in a few short seconds.

Regis slept through the whole affair.

The cool night came, mercifully dissipating the waves of heat. Bruenor made the decision to keep moving, two of them up and pushing at all times, and two of them at rest.

"Regis cannot push," Drizzt reasoned. "He is too short for the bog."

"Then let him sit and keep guard while I push," Wulfgar offered stoically. "I need no help."

"Then the two of ye take the first shift," said Bruenor. "Rumblebelly's slept the whole day away. He should be good for an hour or two!"

Drizzt climbed up on the logs for the first time that day and put his head down on his pack. He did not close his eyes, though. Bruenor's plan of working in turns sounded fair, but impractical. In the black night, only he could guide them and keep any kind of lookout for approaching danger. More than a few times while Wulfgar and Regis took their shift, the drow lifted his head and gave the halfling some insight about their surroundings and some advice about their best direction.

There would be no sleep for Drizzt again this night. He vowed to rest in the morning, but when dawn at last broke, he found the trees and reeds again hunched in around them. The anxiety of the moors itself closed upon them, as though it were a single, sentient being watching over them and plotting against their passage.

The wide water actually proved of benefit to the companions. The ride on its glassy surface was easier than hiking, and despite the crouching perils, they encountered nothing hostile after their second rout of the water trolls. When their path finally returned to blackened land after days and nights of gliding, they suspected that they might have covered most of the distance to the other side of the Evermoors. Sending Regis up the tallest tree they could find, for the halfling was the only one light enough to get to the highest branches (especially since the journey had all but dissipated the roundness of his belly), their hopes were confirmed. Far on the eastern horizon, but no more than a day or two away, Regis saw trees—not the small copses of birch or the moss-covered swamp trees of the moors, but a thick forest of oak and elm.

They moved forward with a renewed spring in their step, despite their exhaustion. They walked upon solid ground again, and knew that they would have to camp one more time with the hordes of wandering trolls lurking near, but they now also carried the knowledge that the ordeal of the Evermoors was almost at an end. They had no intention of letting its foul inhabitants defeat them on this last leg of the journey.

"We should end our trek this day," Drizzt suggested, though the sun was more than an hour from the western horizon. The drow had already sensed the gathering presence, as the trolls awakened from their daytime rest and caught the strange scents of the visitors to the moors. "We must pick our campsite carefully. The moors have not yet freed us of their grasp."

"We'll lose an hour and more," Bruenor stated, more to open up the negative side of the plan than to argue. The dwarf remembered the horrible battle at the mound all too well, and had no desire to repeat that colossal effort.

"We shall gain the time back tomorrow," reasoned Drizzt. "Our need at present is to stay alive."

Wulfgar wholly agreed. "The smell of the foul beasts grows stronger each step," he said, "from every side. We cannot run away from them. So let us fight."

"But on our own terms," Drizzt added.

"Over there," Regis suggested, pointing to a heavily overgrown ridge off to their left.

"Too open," said Bruenor. "Trolls'd climb it as easily as we, and too many at a time for us to stop them!"

"Not while it's burning," Regis countered with a sneaky smile, and his companions came to agree with the simple logic.

They spent the rest of the daylight preparing their defenses. Wulfgar and Bruenor carried in as much dead wood as they could find, placing it in strategic lines to lengthen the diameter of the targeted area, while Regis cleared a firebreak at the top of the ridge and Drizzt kept a cautious lookout. Their defense plan was simple: let the trolls come at them, then set the entire ridge outside their camp ablaze.

Drizzt alone recognized the weakness of the plan, though he had nothing better to offer. He had fought trolls before they had ever come to these moors, and he understood the stubbornness of the wretched beasts. When the flames of their ambush finally died away—long before the dawning of the new day—he and his friends would be wide open to the remaining trolls. They could only hope that the carnage of the fires would dissuade any further enemies.

Wulfgar and Bruenor would have liked to do more, the memories of the mound too vivid for them to be satisfied with any defenses constructed against the moors. But when dusk came, it brought hungry eyes upon them. They joined Regis and Drizzt at the camp on top of the ridge and crouched low in anxious wait.

An hour passed, seeming like ten to the friends, and the night deepened.

"Where are they?" Bruenor demanded, his axe slapping nervously against his hand, belying uncharacteristic impatience from the veteran fighter.

"Why don't they come on?" Regis agreed, his anxiety bordering on panic.

"Be patient and be glad," Drizzt offered. "The more of the night we put behind us before we do battle, the better our chance to see the dawn. They may not have yet found us."

"More like they be gathering to rush us all at once," Bruenor said grimly.

"That is good," said Wulfgar, comfortably crouched and peering into the gloom. "Let the fire taste as much of the foul blood as it may!"

Drizzt took note of the settling effect the big man's strength and resolve had upon Regis and Bruenor. The dwarf's axe stopped its nervous bounce and came to rest calmly at Bruenor's side, poised for the task ahead. Even Regis, the most reluctant warrior, took up his small mace with a snarl, his knuckles whitening under his grip.

Another long hour passed.

The delay did not at all ease the companions' guard. They knew that danger was very near now—they could smell the stench gathering in the mist and darkness beyond their view.

"Strike up the torches," Drizzt told Regis.

"We'll bring the beasts upon us from miles around!" Bruenor argued.

"They have found us already," answered Drizzt, pointing down the ridge, though the trolls he saw shuffling in the darkness were beyond the limited night vision of his friends. "The sight of the torches may keep them back and grant us more time."

As he spoke, however, the first troll ambled up the ridge. Bruenor and Wulfgar waited in their crouch until the monster was nearly upon them, then sprang out with sudden fury, axe and warhammer leading the way in a brutal flurry of well-placed blows. The monster went down at once.

Regis had one of the torches lit. He threw it to Wulfgar and the barbarian set the writhing body of the fallen troll ablaze. Two other trolls that had come to the bottom of the ridge rushed back into the mist at the sight of the hated flames.

"Ah, ye pulled the trick too soon!" Bruenor groaned. "We're naught to catch a one with the torches in plain sight!"

"If the torches keep them back, then the fires have served us well," Drizzt insisted, though he knew better than to hope for such an occurrence.

Suddenly, as if the very moors had spit their venom at them, a huge host of trolls lined the entire base of the ridge. They came on tentatively, not thrilled by the presence of fire. But they came on relentlessly, stalking up the hill with drooling desire.

"Patience," Drizzt told his companions, sensing their eagerness. "Keep them behind the firebreak, but let as many as will get within the rings of kindling."

Wulfgar rushed out to the edge of the ring, waving his torch menacingly.

Bruenor stood back up, his last two flasks of oil in his hands, oil-soaked rags hanging from their spouts, and a wild smile across his face. "Season's a bit green for burning," he said to Drizzt with a wink. "Might need a little help in getting the thing going!"

Trolls swarmed on the ridge all around them, the slavering horde coming on determinedly, their ranks swelling with each step.

Drizzt moved first. Torch in hand, he ran to the kindling and set it burning. Wulfgar and Regis joined in right behind, putting as many fires as they could between them and the advancing trolls. Bruenor threw his torch over the first ranks of the monsters, hoping to get them in the middle of two blazes, then heaved his oil flasks into the most heavily concentrated groups.

Flames leaped up into the night sky, lightening the immediate area, but deepening the blackness beyond their influence. Crowded in so tightly, the trolls could not easily turn and flee, and the fire, as if it understood this, descended upon them methodically,

When one began to burn, its frenzied dance spread the light even farther down the ridge line.

All across the vast moors, creatures stopped their nightly actions and took notice of the growing pillar of flame and the wind-carried shrieks of dying trolls.

Huddled close at the top of the ridge, the companions found themselves nearly overcome by the great heat. But the fire peaked quickly with its feast of volatile troll flesh, and started to diminish, leaving a revulsive stench in the air and yet another blackened sear of carnage on the Evermoors.

The companions readied more torches for their flight from the ridge. Many trolls stood to do battle, even after the fire, and the friends could not hope to hold their ground with the fuel of their fires consumed. At Drizzt's insistence, they awaited the first clear escape route down the eastern side of the ridge, and when it opened, they charged into the night, bursting through the initial groups of unsuspecting trolls with a sudden assault that scattered the monsters and left several burning.

Into the night they ran, blindly rushing through mud and bramble, hoping that luck alone would keep them from being sucked in by some bottomless bog. So complete was their surprise at the ridge that for many minutes they heard no signs of pursuit.

But it didn't take the moors long to respond. Groans and shrieks soon echoed all about them.

Drizzt took the lead. Relying on his instincts as much as his vision, he swerved his friends left and right, through the areas of least apparent resistance, while keeping their course generally east. Hoping to play upon the monsters' single fear, they torched anything that would burn as they passed.

They encountered nothing directly as the night wore on, but the groans and sucking footsteps just yards behind them did not relent. They soon began to suspect a collective intelligence working against them, for though they were obviously outdistancing the trolls that were behind them and to their sides, more were always waiting to take up the chase. Something evil permeated the land, as though the Evermoors themselves were the true enemies. Trolls were all about, and that was the immediate danger, but even if all the trolls and other denizens of the moors were slain or driven away, the friends suspected that this would remain a foul place.

Dawn broke, but it brought no relief. "We've angered the moors themselves!" Bruenor cried when he realized that the chase would not end as easily this time. "We be finding no rest until her foul borders are behind us!"

Onward they charged, seeing the lanky forms lurching out at them as they weaved their way, and those running parallel to them or right behind, grimly visible and just waiting for someone to trip up. Heavy fogs closed in on them, preventing them from holding their bearings, further evidence for their fears that the moors themselves had risen against them.

Past all thinking, past all hope, they kept on, pushing themselves beyond their physical and emotional limits for lack of any alternatives.

Barely conscious of his actions, Regis stumbled and went down. His torch rolled away, though he didn't notice—he couldn't even figure how to get back up, or that he was down at all! Hungry mouths descended toward him, a feast assured.

The ravenous monster was foiled, though, as Wulfgar came by and scooped the halfling into his great arms. The huge barbarian slammed into the troll, knocking it aside, but held his own footing and continued past.

Drizzt abandoned all tactics of finesse now, understanding the situation that was fast developing behind him. More than once he had to slow for Bruenor's stumbling and he doubted Wulfgar's ability to continue while carrying the halfling. The exhausted barbarian obviously couldn't hope to raise Aegis-fang to defend himself. Their only chance was straight flight to the border. A wide bog would defeat them, a box gully would entrap them, and even if no natural barriers blocked their way, they had little hope of keeping free of the trolls for much longer. Drizzt feared the difficult decision he saw forthcoming: flee to his own safety, for he alone seemed to have the possibility of escape, or stand beside his doomed friends in a battle they could not win.

They continued on, and made solid progress for another hour, but time itself began to affect them. Drizzt heard Bruenor mumbling behind him, lost in some delusion of his childhood days in Mithral Hall. Wulfgar, with the unconscious halfling, ambled along behind, reciting a prayer to one of his gods, using the rhythm of his chants to keep his feet steadily pumping.

Then Bruenor fell, smacked down by a troll that had veered in on them uncontested.

The fateful decision came easily to Drizzt. He swung back around, scimitars ready. He couldn't possibly carry the stout dwarf, nor could he defeat the horde of trolls that even now closed in. "And so our tale ends, Bruenor Battlehammer!" he cried out. "In battle, as it should!"

Wulfgar, dazed and gasping, did not consciously choose his next move. It was simply a reaction to the scene before him, a maneuver perpetrated by the stubborn instincts of a man who refused to surrender. He stumbled over to the fallen dwarf, who by this time had struggled back to his hands and knees, and scooped him up with his free arm. Two trolls had them trapped.

Drizzt Do'Urden was close by, and the young barbarian's heroic act inspired the drow. Seething flames danced again within his lavender eyes, and his blades whirred into their own dance of death.

The two trolls reached out to claw their helpless prey, but after a single lightning pass by Drizzt, the monsters had no arms left with which to grab.

"Run on!" Drizzt called, guarding the party's rear and spurring Wulfgar on with a constant stream of rousing words. All weariness flew from the drow in this final burst of battle lust. He leaped all about and shouted challenge to the trolls. Any that came too near found the sting of his blades.

Grunting with every painful step, his eyes burning from his sweat, Wulfgar charged blindly ahead. He didn't think about how long he could keep up the pace with his load. He didn't think about the certain, horrible death that shadowed him on every side, and had probably cut off his route as well. He didn't think about the wrenching pain in his injured back, or about the new sting that he keenly felt on the back of his knee. He concentrated only on putting one heavy boot in front of the other.

They crunched through some brambles, swung down one rise and around another. Their hearts both leaped and fell, for before them loomed the clean forest that Regis had spied, the end of the Evermoors. But between them and the wood waited a solid line of trolls, standing three deep.

The Evermoors' grasp was not so easily broken.

"Keep on," Drizzt said into Wulfgar's ear in a quiet whisper, as though he feared that the moors might be listening. "I have one more trick left to play."

Wulfgar saw the line before him, but even in his present state, his trust in Drizzt overruled any objections of his common sense. Heaving Bruenor and Regis into a more comfortable hold, he put his head low and roared at the beasts, crying out in frenzied rage.

When he had almost reached them, with Drizzt a few steps behind, and the trolls drooling and huddled to stop his momentum, the drow played his final card.

Magical flames sprouted from the barbarian. They had no power to burn, either Wulfgar or the trolls, but to the monsters, the specter of the huge, flame-enshrouded wild man bearing down upon them shot terror into their normally fearless hearts.

Drizzt timed the spell perfectly, allowing the trolls only a split second to react to their imposing foe. Like water before the prow of a high-riding ship they parted, and Wulfgar, nearly overbalancing for his expectations of impact, lumbered through, Drizzt dancing at his heels.

By the time the trolls regrouped to pursue, their prey was already climbing the last rise out of the Evermoors and into the forest—a wood under the protective eye of Lady Alustriel and the gallant Knights of Silver.

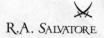

Drizzt turned under the boughs of the first tree to watch for signs of pursuit. Heavy fog swirled back down at the moors, as though the foul land had slammed its door behind them. No trolls came through.

The drow sank back against the tree, too drained to smile.

14

STAR LIGHT, STAR BRIGHT

Wulfgar set Regis and Bruenor down on a mossy bed in a small clearing deeper in the wood then toppled over in pain. Drizzt caught up to him a few minutes later.

"We must camp here," the drow was saying, "though I wish we could put more distance . . ." He stopped when he saw his young friend writhing on the ground and grasping at his injured leg, nearly overcome by the pain. Drizzt rushed over to examine the knee, his eyes widening in shock and disgust.

A troll's hand, probably from one of those he had hacked apart when Wulfgar rescued Bruenor, had latched on to the barbarian as he ran, finding a niche in the back of his knee. One clawed finger had already buried itself deep into the leg, and two others were even now boring in.

"Do not look," Drizzt advised Wulfgar. He reached into his pack for his tinderbox and set a small stick burning, then used it to prod the wretched hand. As soon as the thing began to smoke and wriggle about, Drizzt slid it from the leg and threw it to the ground. It tried to scurry away, but Drizzt sprang upon it, pinning it with one of his scimitars and lighting it fully with the burning stick.

He looked back to Wulfgar, amazed at the sheer determination that had allowed the barbarian to continue with so wicked a wound. But now their flight was ended, and Wulfgar had already succumbed to the pain and the exhaustion. He lay sprawled unconscious on the ground beside Bruenor and Regis.

"Sleep well," Drizzt said softly to the three of them. "You have earned the right." He moved to each of them to make sure they were not too badly hurt. Then, satisfied that they would all recover, he set to his vigilant watch.

Even the valiant drow, though, had overstepped the bounds of his stamina during the rush through the Ever-moors, and soon he too nodded his head and joined his friends in slumber.

Late the next morning Bruenor's grumbling roused them. "Ye forgot me axe!" the dwarf shouted angrily. "I can't be cutting stinkin' trolls without me axe!"

Drizzt stretched out comfortably, somewhat refreshed, but still far from recovered. "I told you to take the axe," he said to Wulfgar, who was similarly shaking off his sound slumber.

"I said it clearly," Drizzt scolded mockingly. "Take the axe and leave the ungrateful dwarf."

" 'Twas the nose that confused me," Wulfgar replied. "More akin to an axe-head than to any nose I have ever seen!"

Bruenor unconsciously looked down his long snout. "Bah!" he growled, "I'll find me a club!" and he tromped off into the forest.

"Some quiet, if you will!" Regis snapped as the last hint of his pleasant dreams flitted away. Disgusted at being awakened so early, he rolled back over and covered his head with his cloak.

They could have made Silverymoon that very day, but a single night's rest would not erase the weariness of the days they had spent in the Evermoors, and on a tough road before that. Wulfgar, for one, with his injured leg and back, had to use a walking stick, and the sleep that Drizzt had found the night before had been his first in nearly a tenday. Unlike the moors, this forest seemed quite wholesome. And though they knew that they were still in the wild lands, they felt safe enough to stretch out the road to the city and enjoy, for the first time since they had left Ten-Towns, a leisurely walk.

They broke out of the forest by noon of the next day and covered the last few miles to Silverymoon. Before sunset, they came over the final climb, and looked down upon the River Rauvin and the countless spires of the enchanted city.

They all felt the sensation of hope and relief when they glanced down upon that magnificent sight, but none felt it more keenly than Drizzt Do'Urden. The drow had hoped from the earliest planning of their adventure that its path would take him through Silverymoon, though he had done nothing to sway Bruenor's decision in choosing a course. Drizzt had heard of Silverymoon after his arrival in Ten-Towns, and were it not for the fact that he had found some measure of tolerance in the rugged frontier community, he would have set back at once for the place. Reknowned for their acceptance of all who came in search of knowledge, regardless of race, the people of Silverymoon offered the renegade black elf a true opportunity to find a home.

Many times he had considered traveling to the place, but something within him, perhaps the fear of false hope and unfulfilled expectations, kept him within the security of Icewind Dale. Thus, when the decision had been made in Longsaddle that Silverymoon would be their next destination, Drizzt had found himself squarely facing the fantasy he had never dared to dream. Looking down now on his one hope for true acceptance in the surface world, he courageously forced his apprehensions away.

"The Moonbridge," Bruenor remarked when a wagon below crossed the Rauvin, seemingly floating in mid-air. Bruenor had heard of the invisible structure as a boy, but had never seen it firsthand.

Wulfgar and Regis watched the spectacle of the flying wagon in blank amazement. The barbarian had overcome many of his fears of magic during his stay in Longsaddle, and he was truly looking forward to exploring this legendary city. Regis had been here once before, but his familiarity with the place did nothing to lessen his excitement.

They approached the guard post on the Rauvin eagerly, despite their weariness, the same post that Entreri's party had passed four days before, with the same guards who had allowed the evil group to enter the city.

"Greetings," Bruenor offered in a tone that could be considered jovial for the dour dwarf. "And know ye that the sight of yer fair city has bringed new life into me weary heart."

The guards hardly heard him, intent upon the drow, who had pulled back his cowl. They seemed curious, for they had never actually seen a black elf, but they didn't appear too surprised by Drizzt's arrival.

"May we be escorted to the Moonbridge now?" Regis asked after a period of silence that grew increasingly uncomfortable. "You cannot guess how anxious we are to view Silverymoon. So much we have heard!"

Drizzt suspected what was forthcoming. An angry lump welled in his throat.

"Go away," the guard said quietly. "You may not pass."

Bruenor's face reddened in rage, but Regis cut off his explosion. "Surely we have done nothing to cause such a harsh judgement," the halfling protested calmly. "We are simple travelers, seeking no trouble." His hand went to his jacket, and to the hypnotic ruby, but a scowl from Drizzt halted his plan.

"Your reputation seems to outweigh your actions," Wulfgar remarked to the guards.

"I am sorry," replied one, "but I have my duties, and I see them through."

"Us, or the drow?" Bruenor demanded.

"The drow," answered the guard. "The rest of you may go to the city, but the drow may not pass!"

Drizzt felt the walls of hope crumbling around him. His hands trembled at his sides. Never before had he experienced such pain, for never before had he come to a place without the expectation of rejection. Still, he managed to sublimate his immediate anger and remind himself that this was Bruenor's quest, not his own, for good or for ill.

"Ye dogs!" Bruenor cried. "Th' elf's worth a dozen of ye, and more! I owe him me life a hundred times, and ye think to say that he's not good enough for yer stinking city! How many trolls be layin' dead for the work of yer sword?"

"Be calm, my friend," Drizzt interrupted, fully in control of himself. "I expect as much. They cannot know Drizzt Do'Urden. Just the reputation of my people. And they cannot be blamed. You go in, then. I will await your return."

"No!" Bruenor declared in a tone that brooked no debate. "If ye can't go in, then none of us will!"

"Think of our goal, stubborn dwarf," Drizzt scolded. "The Vault of Sages is in the city. Perhaps our only hope."

"Bah!" Bruenor snorted. "To the Abyss with this cursed city and all who live here! Sundabar sits less than a tenday's walking. Helm, the dwarf-friend, will be more inviting, or I'm a bearded gnome!"

"You should enter," Wulfgar said. "Let not our anger defeat our purpose. But I remain with Drizzt. Where he cannot go, Wulfgar, son of Beornegar, refuses to go!"

But the determined stomps of Bruenor's stocky legs were already carrying him down the road back out from the city. Regis shrugged at the other two and started after, as loyal to the drow as any of them.

"Choose your camp as you wish, and without fear," the guard offered, almost apologetically. "The Knights of Silver will not disturb you, nor will they let any monsters near the borders of Silverymoon."

Drizzt nodded, for though the sting of the rejection had not diminished, he understood that the guard had been helpless to change the unfortunate situation. He started slowly away, the disturbing questions that he had avoided for so many years already beginning to press in upon him.

Wulfgar was not so forgiving. "You have wronged him," he said to the guard when Drizzt moved away. "Never has he raised sword against any who did not deserve it, and this world, yours and mine, is better off for having Drizzt Do'Urden about!"

The guard looked away, unable to answer the justifiable scolding.

"And I question the honor of one who heeds to unjust commands," Wulfgar declared.

The guard snapped an angry glare on the barbarian. "The Lady's reasons are not asked," he answered, hand on sword hilt. He sympathized with the anger of the travelers, but would accept no criticism of the Lady Alustriel, his beloved leader. "Her commands follow a righteous course, and are beyond the wisdom of me, or you!" he growled.

Wulfgar did not justify the threat with any show of concern. He turned away and started down the road after his friends.

Bruenor purposely positioned their camp just a few hundred yards down the Rauvin, in clear sight of the guard post. He had sensed the guard's discomfort at turning them away and he wanted to play upon that guilt as strongly as he could.

"Sundabar'll show us the way," he kept saying after they had supped, trying to convince himself as much as the others that their failure at Silverymoon would not hurt the quest. "And beyond that lies Citadel Adbar. If any in all the Realms know of Mithral Hall, it be Harbromm and the dwarves of Adbar!"

"A long way," Regis commented. "Summer may run out before we ever reach the fortress of King Harbromm."

"Sundabar," Bruenor reiterated stubbornly. "And Adbar if we must!"

The two went back and forth with the conversation for a while. Wulfgar didn't join in, too intent on the drow, who had moved a short distance away from the camp right after the meal—which Drizzt had hardly touched— and stood silently staring at the city up the Rauvin.

Presently, Bruenor and Regis settled themselves off to sleep, angry still, but secure enough in the safety of the camp to succumb to their weariness. Wulfgar moved to join the drow.

"We shall find Mithral Hall," he offered in comfort, though he knew that Drizzt's lament did not concern their current objective.

Drizzt nodded, but did not reply.

"Their rejection hurt you," Wulfgar observed. "I thought that you had accepted your fate willingly. Why is this time so different?"

Again the drow made no move to answer.

Wulfgar respected his privacy. "Take heart, Drizzt Do'Urden, noble ranger and trusted friend. Have faith that those who know you would die willingly for you or beside you." He put a hand on Drizzt's shoulder as he turned to leave. Drizzt said nothing, though he truly appreciated Wulfgar's concern. Their friendship had gone far beyond the need for spoken thanks, though, and Wulfgar only hoped that he had given his friend some comfort as he returned to the camp, leaving Drizzt to his thoughts.

The stars came out and found the drow still standing alone beside the Rauvin. Drizzt had made himself vulnerable for the first time since his initial days on the surface, and the disappointment he now felt triggered the same doubts that he had believed resolved years ago, before he had ever left Menzoberranzan, the city of the black elves. How could he ever hope to find any normalcy in the daylight world of the fair-skinned elves? In Ten-Towns, where murderers and thieves often rose to positions of respect and leadership, he was barely tolerated. In Longsaddle, where prejudice was secondary to the fanatical curiosity of the unsinkable Harpells, he had been placed on display like some mutated farm animal, mentally poked and prodded. And though the wizards meant him no harm, they lacked any compassion or respect for him as anything other than an oddity to be observed.

Now Silverymoon, a city founded and structured on tenets of individuality and fairness, where peoples of all races found welcome if they came in goodwill, had shunned him. All races, it seemed, except for the dark elves.

The inevitability of Drizzt's life as an outcast had never before been so clearly laid out before him. No other city, not even a remote village, in all the Realms could offer him a home, or an existence anywhere but on the fringes of its civilization. The severe limitations of his options, and even more so, of his future hopes for change, appalled him.

He stood now under the stars, looking up at them with the same profound level of love and awe as any of his surface cousins had ever felt, but sincerely reconsidering his decision to leave the underworld.

Had he gone against a divine plan, crossed the boundaries of some natural order? Perhaps he should have accepted his lot in life and remained in the dark city, among his own kind.

A twinkle in the night sky brought him out of his introspection. A star above him pulsed and grew, already beyond normal proportions. Its light bathed the area around Drizzt in a soft glow, and still the star pulsed.

Then the enchanting light was gone, and standing before Drizzt was a woman, her hair shining silver and her sparkling eyes holding years of experience and wisdom within the luster of eternal youth. She was tall, taller than Drizzt, and straight, wearing a gown of the finest silk and a high crown of gold and gems.

She looked upon him with sincere sympathy, as if she could read his every thought and understood completely the jumble of emotions that he himself had yet to sort through.

"Peace, Drizzt Do'Urden," she said in a voice that chimed like sweet music. "I am Alustriel, High Lady of Silverymoon."

Drizzt studied her more closely, though her manner and beauty left him no doubts as to her claim. "You know of me?" he asked.

"Many by now have heard of the Companions of the Hall, for that is the name Harkle Harpell has put upon your troupe. A dwarf in search of his ancient home is not so rare in the Realms, but a drow elf walking beside him certainly catches the notice of all those he passes."

She swallowed hard and looked deeply into his lavender eyes. "It was I who denied you passage into the city," she admitted.

"Then why come to me now?" Drizzt asked, more in curiosity than in anger, unable to reconcile that act of rejection with the person who now stood before him. Alustriel's fairness and tolerance were well known throughout the northland, though Drizzt had begun to wonder how exaggerated the stories must be after his encounter at the guard post. But now that he saw the high lady, wearing her honest compassion openly, he could not disbelieve the tales.

"I felt I must explain," she replied.

"You need not justify your decision."

"But I must," said Alustriel. "For myself and my home as much as for you. The rejection has hurt you more than you admit." She moved closer to him.

"It pained me as well," she said softly,

"Then why?" Drizzt demanded, his anger slipping through his calm facade. "If you know of me, then you know as well that I carry no threat to your people."

She ran her cool hand across his cheek. "Perceptions," she explained. "There are elements at work in the north that make perceptions vital at this time, sometimes even overruling what is just. A sacrifice has been forced upon you."

"A sacrifice that has become all too familiar to me."

"I know," Alustriel whispered. "We learned from Nesmé that you had been turned away, a scenario that you commonly face."

"I expect it," Drizzt said coldly.

"But not here," Alustriel retorted. "You did not expect it from Silverymoon, nor should you have."

Her sensitivity touched Drizzt. His anger died away as he awaited her explanation, certain now that the woman had good cause for her actions.

"There are many forces at work here that do not concern you, and should not," she began. "Threats of war and secret alliances; rumors and suspicions that have no basis in fact, nor would make any sense to reasonable people. I am no great friend to the merchants, though they freely pass through Silverymoon. They fear our ideas and ideals as a threat to their structures of power, as well they should. They are very powerful, and would see Silverymoon more akin to their own views.

"But enough of this talk. As I said, it does not concern you. All that I ask you to understand is that, as leader of my city, I am forced at times to act for the overall good, whatever the cost to an individual."

"You fear the lies and suspicions that might befall you if a black elf walks freely in Silverymoon?" Drizzt sighed incredulously. "Simply allowing a drow to walk among your people would implicate you in some devious alliance with the underworld?"

"You are not just any drow elf,'" Alustriel explained. "You are Drizzt Do'Urden, a name that is destined to be heard throughout the Realms. For now, though, you are a drow who is fast becoming visible to the northern rulers, and initially at least, they will not understand that you have forsaken your people.

"And this tale gets more complicated, it seems," Alustriel continued. "Know you that I have two sisters?"

Drizzt shook his head.

"Storm, a bard of reknown, and Dove Falconhand, a ranger. Both have taken an interest in the name of Drizzt Do'Urden—Storm as a growing legend in need of proper song, and Dove . . . I have yet to discern her motives. You have become a hero to her, I think, the epitome of those qualities that she, as a fellow ranger, strives to perfect. She came into the city just this morn, and knew of your impending arrival.

"Dove is many years younger than I," Alustriel went on. "And not so wise in the politics of the world."

"She might have sought me out," Drizzt reasoned, seeing the implications that Alustriel feared.

"She will, eventually," the lady answered. "But I cannot allow it now, not in Silverymoon." Alustriel stared at him intently, her gaze hinting at deeper and more personal emotions. "And more so, I myself would have sought audience with you, as I do now."

The implications of such a meeting within the city seemed obvious to Drizzt in light of the political struggles that Alustriel had hinted at. "Another time, another place perhaps," he queried. "Would it bother you so much?"

She replied with a smile. "Not at all."

Satisfaction and trepidation descended upon Drizzt all at once. He looked back to the stars, wondering if he would ever completely discover the truth about his decision to come to the surface world, or if his life would forever remain a tumult of dangled hope and shattered expectations.

They stood in silence for several moments before Alustriel spoke again.

"You came for the Vault of Sages," she said, "to discover if anything in there spoke of Mithral Hall."

"I urged the dwarf to go in," Drizzt answered. "But he is a stubborn one."

"I assumed as much," laughed Alustriel. "But I did not want my actions to interfere with your most noble quest. I have perused the vault myself. You cannot imagine its size! You would not have known where to begin your search of the thousands of volumes that line the walls. But I know the vault as well as anyone alive. I have learned things that would have taken you and your friends tendays to find. But truthfully, very little has been written about Mithral Hall, and nothing at all that gives more than a passing hint about the general area where it lies."

"Then perhaps we are the better for being turned away."

Alustriel blushed in embarrassment, though Drizzt meant no sarcasm in his observation. "My guards have informed me that you plan to move on to Sundabar," the lady said.

"True," answered Drizzt, "and from there to Citadel Adbar if need be."

"I advise you against this course," said Alustriel. "From everything that I could find in the vault, and from my own knowledge of the legends of the days when treasures flowed from Mithral Hall, my guess is that it lies in the west, not the east."

"We have come from the west, and our trail, seeking those with knowledge of the silvery halls, has led us continually eastward," Drizzt countered. "Beyond Silverymoon, the only hopes we have are Helm and Harbromm, both in the east."

"Helm may have something to tell you," Alustriel agreed. "But you will learn little from King Harbromm and the dwarves of Adbar. They themselves undertook the quest to find the ancient homeland of Bruenor's kin just a few years ago, and they passed through Silverymoon on their journey—heading west. But they never found the place, and returned home convinced that it was either destroyed and buried deep in some unmarked mountain, or that it had never existed and was simply the ruse of southern merchants dealing their goods in the northland."

"You do not offer much hope," Drizzt remarked.

"But I do," Alustriel countered "To the west of here, less than a day's march, along an unmarked path running north from the Rauvin, lies the Herald's Holdfast, an ancient bastion of accumulated knowledge. The herald, Old Night, can guide you, if anyone can in this day. I have informed him of your coming and he has agreed to sit with you, though he has not entertained visitors for decades, other than myself and a few select scholars."

"We are in your debt," said Drizzt, bowing low.

"Do not hope for too much," Alustriel warned. "Mithral Hall came and went in the knowledge of this world in the flash of an eye. Barely three generations of dwarves ever mined the place, though I grant you that a dwarven generation is a considerable amount of time, and they were not so open with their trade. Only rarely did they allow anyone to their mines, if the tales are true. They brought out their works in the dark of night and fed them through a secret and intricate chain of dwarven agents to be brought to market."

"They protected themselves well from the greed of the outside world," Drizzt observed.

"But their demise came from within the mines," said Alustriel. "An unknown danger that may lurk there still, you are aware."

Drizzt nodded.

"And still you choose to go?"

"I care not for the treasures, though if they are indeed as splendid as Bruenor describes, then I would wish to look upon them. But this is the dwarf's search, his great adventure, and I would be a sorry friend indeed if I did not help him to see it through."

"Hardly could that label be mantled upon your neck, Drizzt Do'Urden," Alustriel said. She pulled a small vial from a fold in her gown. "Take this with you," she instructed.

"What is it?"

"A potion of remembrance," Alustriel explained. "Give it to the dwarf when the answers to your search seem near at hand. But beware, its powers are strong! Bruenor will walk for a time in the memories of his distant past as well as the experiences of his present.

"And these," she said, producing a small pouch from the same fold and handing it to Drizzt, "are for all of you. Unguent to help wounds to heal, and biscuits that refresh a weary traveler."

"My thanks and the thanks of my friends," said Drizzt.

"In light of the terrible injustice that I have forced upon you, they are little recompense."

"But the concern of their giver was no small gift," Drizzt replied. He looked straight into her eyes, holding her with his intensity. "You have renewed my hope, Lady of Silverymoon. You have reminded me that there is indeed reward for those who follow the path of conscience, a treasure far greater than the material baubles that too often come to unjust men."

"There is, indeed," she agreed. "And your future will show you many more, proud ranger. But now the night is half gone and you must rest. Fear not, for you are watched this night. Farewell, Drizzt Do'Urden, and may the road before you be swift and clear."

With a wave of her hand, she faded into the starlight, leaving Drizzt to wonder if he had dreamed the whole encounter. But then her final words drifted down to him on the gentle breeze. "Farewell, and keep heart, Drizzt Do'Urden. Your honor and courage do not go unnoticed!"

Drizzt stood silently for a long while. He bent low and picked a wildflower from the riverbank, rolling it over between his fingers and wondering if he and the Lady of Silverymoon might indeed meet again on more accommodating terms. And where such a meeting might lead.

Then he tossed the flower into the Rauvin.

"Let events take their own course," he said resolutely, looking back to the camp and his closest friends. "I need no fantasies to belittle the great treasures that I already possess." He took a deep breath to blow away the remnants of his self-pity.

And with his faith restored, the stoic ranger went to sleep.

15
THE GOLEM'S EYES

Drizzt had little trouble convincing Bruenor to reverse their course and head back to the west. While the dwarf was anxious to get to Sundabar and find out what Helm might know, the possibility of valuable information less than a day away set him off and running.

As to how he had come by the information, Drizzt offered little explanation, saying only that he had met up with a lone traveler on the road to Silverymoon during the night. Though the story sounded contrived to them, his friends, respecting his privacy and trusting him fully, did not question him about it. When they ate breakfast, though, Regis hoped that more information would be forthcoming, for the biscuits that this traveler had given to Drizzt were truly delicious and incredibly refreshing. After only a few bites, the halfling felt as if he had spent a tenday at rest. And the magic salve immediately healed Wulfgar's injured leg and back, and he walked without a cane for the first time since they had left the Evermoors.

Wulfgar suspected that Drizzt's encounter had involved someone of great importance long before the drow revealed the marvelous gifts. For the drow's inner glow of optimism, the knowing sparkle in his eyes that reflected the indomitable spirit that had kept him going through trials that would have crushed most men, had returned, fully and dramatically. The barbarian didn't need to know the identity of the person; he was just glad that his friend had come through the depression.

When they moved out later that morning, they seemed more a party just beginning an adventure than a road-weary band. Whistling and talking, they followed the flow of the Rauvin on its westerly course. For all of the close calls, they had come through the brutal march relatively unscathed and it appeared, had made good progress toward their goal. The summer sun shone down upon them and all the pieces of the puzzle of Mithral Hall seemed to be within their grasp.

They could not have guessed that murderous eyes were upon them.

From the foothills north of the Rauvin, high above the travelers, the golem sensed the drow elf's passing. Following the tug of magic spells of seeking that Dendybar had bestowed upon it, Bok soon looked down upon the band as they moved across the trail. Without hesitation the monster obeyed its directives and started out to find Sydney.

Bok tossed aside a boulder that lay in its path, then climbed over another that was too big to move, not understanding the advantages of simply walking around the stones. Bok's path was clearly set and the monster refused to deviate from that course by an inch.

"He is a big one!" chuckled one of the guards at the post on the Rauvin when he saw Bok across the clearing. Even as the words left his mouth, though, the guard realized the impending danger—that this was no ordinary traveler!

Courageously, he rushed out to meet the golem head on, his sword drawn and his companion close behind.

Transfixed by his goal, Bok paid no heed to their warnings.

"Hold where you are!" the soldier commanded one final time as Bok covered the last few feet between them.

The golem did not know emotion, so it bore no anger toward the guards as they struck. They stood to block the way, though, and Bok swatted them aside without a second thought, the incredible force of its magically strong arms blasting through their parrying defenses and launching them through the air. Without even a pause, the golem continued on to the river and did not slow, disappearing under the rushing waters.

Alarms rang out in the city, for the soldiers at the gate across the river saw the spectacle at the guard post. The huge gates were drawn tight and secured as the Knights of Silver watched the Rauvin for the reappearance of the monster.

Bok kept its line straight across the bottom of the river, plowing through the silt and mud and easily holding its course against the mighty push of the currents. When the monster re-emerged directly across from the guard post, the knights lining the city gate gasped in disbelief but held their stations, grim-faced and weapons ready.

The gate was farther up the Rauvin from the angle of Bok's chosen path. The golem continued on to the city wall, but didn't alter its course to bring it to the gate.

It punched a hole in the wall and walked right through.

⚔ ⚔ ⚔ ⚔ ⚔

Entreri paced anxiously in his room at the Inn of the Wayward Sages, near the center of the city, "They should have come by now," he snapped at Sydney, sitting on the bed and tightening the bonds that held Catti-brie.

Before Sydney could respond, a ball of flame appeared in the center of the room, not a real fire, but the image of flames, illusionary, like something burning in that particular spot on another plane. The fires writhed and transformed into the apparition of a robed man.

"Morkai!" Sydney gasped.

"My greetings," replied the specter. "And the greetings of Dendybar the Mottled."

Entreri slipped back into the corner of the room, wary if the thing. Catti-brie, helpless in her bonds, sat very still.

Sydney, versed in the subtleties of conjuring, knew that the otherworldly being was under Dendybar's control, and she was not afraid. "Why has my master bid you to come here?" she asked boldly.

"I bear news," replied the specter. "The party you seek was turned into the Evermoors a tenday ago, to the south of Nesmé."

Sydney bit her lip in anticipation of the specter's next revelation, but Morkai fell silent and waited as well.

"And where are they now?" Sydney pressed impatiently.

Morkai smiled. "Twice I have been asked, but not yet compelled!" The flames puffed again and the specter was gone.

"The Evermoors," said Entreri. "That would explain their delay."

Sydney nodded her agreement absently, for she had other things on her mind. "Not yet compelled," she whispered to herself, echoing the specter's parting words. Disturbing questions nagged at her. Why had Dendybar waited a tenday to send Morkai with the news? And why couldn't the wizard have forced the specter to reveal more recent activity of the drow's party? Sydney knew the dangers and limitations of summoning, and understood the tremendous drain of the act on a wizard's power. Dendybar had conjured Morkai at least three times recently—once when the drow's party had first entered Luskan, and at least twice since she and her companions had set out in pursuit. Had Dendybar abandoned all caution in his obsession with the Crystal Shard? Sydney sensed that the mottled wizard's hold over Morkai had lessened greatly, and she hoped that Dendybar would be prudent with any future summonings, at least until he had fully rested.

"Tendays could pass before they arrive!" Entreri spat, considering the news. "If ever they do."

"You may be right," agreed Sydney. "They might have fallen in the moors."

"And if they have?"

"Then we go in after them," Sydney said without hesitation.

Entreri studied her for a few moments. "The prize you seek must be great indeed," he said.

"I have my duty, and I shall not fail my master," she replied sharply. "Bok will find them even if they lay at the bottom of the deepest bog!"

"We must decide our course soon," Entreri insisted. He turned his evil glare on Catti-brie. "I grow weary of watching this one."

"Nor do I trust her," Sydney agreed. "Though she shall prove useful when we meet with the dwarf. Three more days we will wait. After that we go back to Nesmé, and into the Evermoors if we must."

Entreri nodded his reluctant approval of the plan. "Did you hear?" he hissed at Catti-brie. "You have three more days to live, unless your friends arrive. If they are dead in the moors, we have no need of you."

Catti-brie showed no emotion throughout the entire conversation, determined not to let Entreri gain any advantage by learning of her weakness, or strength. She had faith that her friends were not dead. The likes of Bruenor Battlehammer and Drizzt Do'Urden were not destined to die in an unmarked grave in some desolate fen. And Catti-brie would never accept that Wulfgar was dead until the proof was irrefutable. Holding to her faith, her duty to her friends was to maintain a blank facade. She knew that she was winning her personal battle, that the paralyzing fear Entreri held over her lessened every day. She would be ready to act when the time came. She just had to make certain that Entreri and Sydney didn't realize it.

She had noted that the labors of the road, and his new companions, were affecting the assassin. Entreri revealed more emotion, more desperation, every day to get this job over and done. Was it possible that he might make a mistake?

"It has come!" echoed a cry from the hallway, and all three started reflexively, then recognized the voice as Jierdan's, who had been watching the Vault of Sages. A second later, the door burst in and the soldier scrambled into the room, his breathing ragged.

"The dwarf?" Sydney asked, grabbing Jierdan to steady him.

"No!" Jierdan cried. "The golem! Bok has entered Silverymoon! They have it trapped down by the west gate. A wizard was summoned."

"Damn!" Sydney spat and she started from the room. Entreri moved to follow her, grabbing Jierdan's arm and yanking him around, bringing them face to face.

"Stay with the girl," the assassin ordered.

Jierdan glared at him. "She is your problem."

Entreri easily could have killed the soldier right there, Catti-brie noted, hoping that Jierdan had read the assassin's deadly look as clearly as she.

"Do as you are told!" Sydney screamed at Jierdan, ending further argument.

She and Entreri left, the assassin slamming the door behind them.

"He would have killed you," Catti-brie told Jierdan when Entreri and Sydney had gone. "You know that."

"Silence," Jierdan growled. "I've had enough of your vile words!" He approached her threateningly, fists clenched at his sides.

"Strike me, then," Catti-brie challenged, knowing that even if he did, his code as a soldier would not allow him to continue such an assault on a helpless foe. "Though in truth I be yer only friend on this cursed road!"

Jierdan stopped his advance. "Friend?" he balked.

"As close as ye'll find out here," Catti-brie replied. "Ye're a prisoner here suren as I be." She recognized the vulnerability of this proud man, who had been reduced to servitude by the arrogance of Sydney and Entreri, and drove her point home hard. "They mean to kill ye, ye know that now, and even if ye escape the blade, ye'll have nowhere to go. Ye've abandoned yer fellows in Luskan, and the wizard in the tower'd put ye to a bad end if ye ever went back there, anyway!"

Jierdan tensed in frustrated rage, but did not lash out.

"Me friends are close by," Catti-brie continued despite the warning signs. "They be living still, I know, and we'll be meeting them any day. That'll be our time, soldier, to live or to die. For meself, I see a chance. Whether me friends win or I be bargained over, me life'll be me own. But for yerself, the road looks dark indeed! If me friends win, they'll cut ye down, and if yer mates win . . ." She let the grim possibilities hang unspoken for a few moments to let Jierdan weigh them fully.

"When they get what they seek, they'll need ye no more," she said grimly. She noted his trembling, not of fear, but of rage, and pushed him past the edge of control. "They may let ye live," she said, snidely. "Might that they be needin' a lackey!"

He did strike her then, just once, and recoiled.

Catti-brie accepted the blow without complaint, even smiling through the pain, though she was careful to hide her satisfaction. Jierdan's loss of self restraint proved to her that the continual disrespect Sydney, and especially Entreri, had shown for him had fueled the flames of discontent to the verge of explosion.

She knew, too, that when Entreri returned and saw the bruise Jierdan had given her, those fires would burn even brighter.

Sydney and Entreri rushed through the streets of Silverymoon, following the obvious sounds of commotion. When they reached the wall, they found Bok encapsulated in a sphere of glowing green lights. Riderless horses paced about to the groans of a dozen injured soldiers, and one old man, the wizard, stood before the globe of light, scratching his beard and studying the trapped golem. A Knight of Silver of considerable rank stood impatiently beside him, twitching nervously and clasping the pommel of his sheathed sword tightly.

"Destroy the thing and be done with it," Sydney heard the knight say to the wizard.

"Oh, no!" exclaimed the wizard. "But it is marvelous!"

"Do you mean to hold it here forever?" the knight snapped back. "Just look around—"

"Your pardon, good sirs," Sydney interrupted. "I am Sydney, of the Hosttower of the Arcane in Luskan. Perhaps I may be of some help."

"Well met," said the wizard. "I am Mizzen of the Second School of Knowledge. Know you the possessor of this magnificent creature?"

"Bok is mine," she admitted.

The knight stared at her, amazed that a woman, or anyone for that matter, controlled the monster that had knocked aside some of his finest warriors and taken down a section of the city wall. "The price shall be high, Sydney of Luskan," he snarled.

"The Hosttower shall make amends," she agreed. "Now would you release the golem to my control?" she asked the wizard. "Bok will obey me."

"Nay!" snapped the knight. "I'll not have the thing turned loose again."

"Calm, Gavin," Mizzen said to him. He turned to Sydney. "I should like to study the golem, if I may. Truly the finest construction I have ever witnessed, with strength beyond the expectations of the books of creation."

"I am sorry," Sydney answered, "but my time is short. I have many roads yet to travel. Name the price of the damage wrought by the golem and I shall relay it to my master, on my word as a member of the Hosttower."

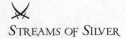

"You'll pay now," argued the guard.

Again Mizzen silenced him. "Excuse Gavin's anger," he said to Sydney. He surveyed the area. "Perhaps we might strike a bargain. None seem to have been seriously injured."

"Three men have been carried away!" Gavin rebutted. "And at least one horse is lame and will have to be destroyed!"

Mizzen waved his hand as if to belittle the claims. "They will heal," he said. "They will heal. And the wall needed repairs anyway." He looked at Sydney and scratched his beard again. "Here is my offer, and a fairer one you'll not hear! Give me the golem for one night, just one, and I shall amend the damage it has wreaked. Just one night."

"And you'll not disassemble Bok," Sydney stated.

"Not even the head?" Mizzen begged.

"Not even the head," Sydney insisted. "And I shall come for the golem at the first light of dawn."

Mizzen scratched his beard again. "A marvellous work," he mumbled, peering into the magical prison. "Agreed!"

"If that monster—" Gavin began angrily.

"Oh, where is your sense of adventure, Gavin?" Mizzen shot back before the knight could even finish his warning. "Remember the precepts of our town, man. We are here to learn. If you only understood the potential of such a creation!"

They started away from Sydney, paying her no more mind, the wizard still rambling into Gavin's ear. Entreri slipped from the shadows of a nearby building to Sydney's side.

"Why did the thing come?" he asked her.

She shook her head. "There can be only one answer."

'The drow?"

"Yes," she said. "Bok must have followed them into the city."

"Unlikely," reasoned Entreri, "though the golem might have seen them. If Bok came crashing through behind the drow and his valiant friends, they would have been down here at the battle, helping to fend it off."

"Then they might be out there still."

"Or perhaps they were leaving the city when Bok saw them," said Entreri.

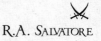

"I will make inquiries with the guards at the gate. Fear not, our prey is close at hand!"

⚔ ⚔ ⚔ ⚔

They arrived back at the room a couple of hours later. From the guards at the gate they had learned of the drow's party being turned away and now they were anxious to retrieve Bok and be on their way.

Sydney started a string of instructions to Jierdan concerning their departure in the morning, but what grabbed Entreri's immediate attention was Catti-brie's bruised eye. He moved over to check her bonds and satisfied that they were intact, spun on Jierdan with his dagger drawn.

Sydney, quickly surmising the situation, cut him off. "Not now!" she demanded. "Our rewards are at hand. We cannot afford this!"

Entreri chuckled evilly and slid the dagger away. "We will yet discuss this," he promised Jierdan with a snarl. "Do not touch the girl again."

Perfect, Catti-brie thought. From Jierdan's perspective, the assassin might as well have said outright that he meant to kill him.

More fuel for the flames.

⚔ ⚔ ⚔ ⚔

When she retrieved the golem from Mizzen the next morning, Sydney's suspicions that Bok had seen the drow's party were confirmed. They set out from Silverymoon at once, Bok leading them down the same trail Bruenor and his friends had taken the morning before

Like the previous party, they, too, were watched.

Alustriel brushed her flowing hair from her fair face, catching the morning sun in her green eyes as she looked down upon the band with growing curiosity. The lady had learned from the gatekeepers that someone had been inquiring about the dark elf.

She couldn't yet figure out what part this new group leaving Silverymoon played in the quest, but she suspected that they were up to no good. Alustriel had sated her own thirst for adventure many years before, but she wished now that she could somehow aid the drow and his friends on their noble mission. Affairs of state pressed in on her, though, and she had no time for such diversions. She considered for a moment dispatching a patrol to capture this second party, so that she could learn its intentions.

Then she turned back to her city, reminding herself that she was just a minor player in the search for Mithral Hall. She could only trust in the abilities of Drizzt Do'Urden and his friends.

In my travels on the surface, I once met a man who wore his religious beliefs like a badge of honor upon the sleeves of his tunic. "I am a Gondsman!" he proudly told me as we sat beside each other at a tavern bar, I sipping my wine, and he, I fear, partaking a bit too much of

Trails Anew

his more potent drink. He went on to explain the premise of his religion, his very reason for being, that all things were based in science, in mechanics, and in discovery. He even asked if he could take a piece of my flesh, that he might study it to determine why the skin of the drow elf is black. "What element is missing," he wondered, "that makes your race different from your surface kin?"

I think that the Gondsman honestly believed his claim that if he could merely find the various elements that comprised the drow skin, he might affect a change in that pigmentation to make the dark elves become more akin to their surface relatives. and given his devotion, almost fanaticism, it seemed to me as if he felt he could affect a change in more than physical appearance.

Because, in his view of the world, all things could be so explained and corrected.

How could I even begin to enlighten him to the complexity? How could I show him the variations between drow and surface elf in the very view of the world resulting from eons of walking widely disparate roads?

To a Gondsman fanatic, everything can be broken down, taken apart and put back together. Even a wizard's magic might be no more than a way of conveying universal energies—and that, too, might one day be replicated. My Gondsman companion promised me that he and his fellow inventor priests would one day replicate every spell in any wizard's repertoire, using natural elements in the proper combinations.

But there was no mention of the discipline any wizard must attain as he perfects his craft. There was no mention of the fact that powerful wizardly magic is not given to anyone, but rather, is earned, day by day, year by year, and decade by decade. It is a lifelong pursuit with a gradual increase in power, as mystical as it is secular.

So it is with the warrior. The Gondsman spoke of some weapon called an' arquebus, a tubular missile thrower with many times the power of the strongest crossbow.

Such a weapon strikes terror into the heart of the true warrior, and not because he fears that he will fall victim to it, or even that he fears that it will one day replace him. Such weapons offend because the true warrior understands that while one is learning how to use a sword, one should also be learning why and when to use a sword. To grant the power of a weapon master to anyone at all, without effort, without training and proof that the lessons have taken hold, is to deny the responsibility that comes with such power.

Of course, there are wizards and warriors who perfect their craft without learning the level of emotional discipline to accompany it, and certainly there are those who attain great prowess in either profession to the detriment of all the world—Artemis Entreri seems a perfect example—but these individuals are, thankfully, rare, and mostly because their emotional lacking will be revealed early in their careers, and it often brings about a fairly abrupt downfall. But if the Gondsman has his way, if his errant view of paradise should come to fruition, then all the years of training will mean little. Any fool could pick up an arquebus or some other powerful weapon and summarily destroy a skilled warrior. Or any child could utilize a Gondsman's magic machine and replicate a fireball, perhaps, and burn down half a city.

When I pointed out some of my fears to the Gondsman, he seemed shocked—not at the devastating possibilities, but rather, at my, as he put it, arrogance. "The inventions of the Priests of Gond will make all equal!" he declared. "We will lift up the lowly peasant."

Hardly. All that the Gondsman and his cronies would do is ensure death and destruction at a level heretofore unknown across the Realms.

There was nothing more to be said, for I knew that the man would never hear my words. He thought me, or, for that matter, anyone who achieved a level of skill in the fighting or magic arts, arrogant, because he could not appreciate the sacrifice and dedication necessary for such achievement.

Arrogant? If the Gondsman's so-called lowly peasant came to me with a desire to learn the fighting arts, I would gladly teach him. I would revel in his successes as much as in my own, but I would demand, always I would demand, a sense of humility, dedication and an understanding of this power I was teaching, an appreciation of the potential for destruction. I would teach no one who did not continue to display an appropriate level of compassion and community. To learn how to use a sword, one must first master when to use a sword.

There is one other error in the Gondsman's line of reasoning, I believe, on a purely emotional level. If machines replace achievement, then to what will people aspire? And who are we, truly, without such goals?

Beware the engineers of society, I say, who would make everyone in all the world equal. Opportunity should be equal, must be equal, but achievement must remain individual.

—Drizzt Do'Urden

16
DAYS OF OLD

A squat stone tower stood in a small dell against the facing of a steep hill.
Because it was ivy covered and overgrown, a casual passer-by would not
even have noticed the structure.

But the Companions of the Hall were not casual in their search. This was
the Herald's Holdfast, possibly the solution to their entire search.

"Are you certain that this is the place?" Regis asked Drizzt as they
peered over a small bluff. Truly the ancient tower appeared more a ruin.
Not a thing stirred anywhere nearby, not even animals, as though an eerie,
reverent hush surrounded the place.

"I am sure," Drizzt replied. "Feel the age of the tower. It has stood for
many centuries. Many centuries."

"And how long has it been empty?" Bruenor asked, thus far disappointed in
the place that had been described to him as the brightest promise to his goal.

"It is not empty," Drizzt replied. "Unless the information I received was
in err."

Bruenor jumped to his feet and stormed over the bluff. "Probably
right," he grumbled. "Some troll or scab yeti's inside the door watching us
right now, I'll wager, drooling for us to come in! Let's be on with it, then!
Sundabar's a day more away than when we left!"

The dwarf's three friends joined him on the remnants of the overgrown path that had once been a walkway to the tower's door. They approached the ancient stone door cautiously, with weapons drawn.

Moss-covered and worn to a smooth finish by the toll of time, apparently it hadn't been opened in many, many years.

"Use yer arms, boy," Bruenor told Wulfgar. "If any man can get this thing opened, it's yerself!"

Wulfgar leaned Aegis-fang against the wall and moved before the huge door. He set his feet as best he could and ran his hands across the stone in search of a good niche to push against.

But as soon as he applied the slightest pressure to the stone portal, it swung inward, silently and without effort.

A cool breeze wafted out of the still darkness within, carrying a blend of unfamiliar scents and an aura of great age. The friends sensed the place as otherworldly, belonging to a different time, perhaps, and it was not without a degree of trepidation that Drizzt led them in.

They stepped lightly, though their footfalls echoed in the quiet darkness. The daylight beyond the door offered little relief, as though some barrier remained between the inside of the tower and the world beyond.

"We should light a torch—" Regis began, but he stopped abruptly, frightened by the unintentional volume of his whisper.

"The door!" Wulfgar cried suddenly, noticing that the silent portal had begun to close behind them. He leaped to grab it before it shut completely, sinking them into absolute darkness, but even his great strength could not deny the magical force that moved it. It shut without a bang, just a hushed rush of air that resounded like a giant's sigh.

The lightless tomb they all envisioned as the huge door blocked out the final slit of sunlight did not come to pass, for as soon as the door closed, a blue glow lit up the room, the entrance hall to the Herald's Holdfast.

No words could they speak above the profound awe that enveloped them. They stood in view of the history of the race of Man within a bubble of time-lessness that denied their own perspectives of age and belonging. In the blink of an eye they had been propelled into the position of removed observers, their own existence suspended in a different time and place, looking in on the passing of the human race as might a god. Intricate tapestries, their once-vivid colors faded and their distinct lines now blurred, swept the friends into a fantastic collage of images that displayed the tales of the race, each one retelling a story again and again; the same tale, it seemed, but subtly altered each time, to present different principles and varied outcomes.

Weapons and armor from every age lined the walls, beneath the standards and crests of a thousand long forgotten kingdoms. Bas-relief images of heroes and sages, some familiar but most unknown to any but the most studious of scholars, stared down at them from the rafters, their captured visages precise enough to emote the very character of the men they portrayed.

A second door, this one of wood, hung directly across the cylindrical chamber from the first, apparently leading into the hill behind the tower. Only when it began to swing open did the companions manage to break free of the spell of the place.

None went for their weapons, though, understanding that whoever, or whatever, inhabited this tower would be beyond such earthly strength.

An ancient man stepped into the room, older than anyone they had ever seen before. His facehad retained its fullness, not hollowed with age, but his skin appeared almost wooden in texture, with lines that, seemed more like cracks and a rough edge that defied time as stubbornly as an ancient tree. His walk was more a flow of quiet movement, a floating passing that transcended the definition of steps. He came in close to the friends and waited, his arms, obviously thin even under the folds of his long, satiny robe, peacefully dropped to his sides.

"Are you the herald of the tower?" Drizzt asked.

"Old Night, I am," the man replied in a voice singing with serenity. "Welcome, Companions of the Hall. The Lady Alustriel informed me of your coming, and of your quest."

Even consumed in the solemn respect of his surroundings, Wulfgar did not miss the reference to Alustriel. He glanced over at Drizzt, meeting the drow's eyes with a knowing smile.

Drizzt turned away and smiled, too.

"This is the Chamber of Man," Old Night proclaimed. "The largest in the Holdfast, except for the library, of course."

He noticed Bruenor's disgruntled scowl. "The tradition of your race runs deep, good dwarf, and deeper yet does the elves'," he explained. "But crises in history are more often measured in generations than in centuries. The short-lived humans might have toppled a thousand kingdoms and built a thousand more in the few centuries that a single dwarven king would rule his people in peace."

"No patience!" Bruenor huffed, apparently appeased.

"Agreed," laughed Old Night. "But come now, let us dine. We have much to do this night."

He led them through the doorway and down a similarly lit hallway. Doors on either side of them identified the various chambers as they passed—one for each of the goodly races, and even a few for the history of orcs, goblins, and giantkind.

The friends and Old Night supped at a huge, round table, its ancient wood as hard as mountain stone. Runes were inscribed all around its edge, many in tongues long lost to the world, that even Old Night could not remember. The food, like everything else, gave the impression of a distant past. Far from stale, though, it was delicious, with a flavor somewhat different from anything the friends had ever eaten before. The drink, a crystalline wine, possessed a rich bouquet surpassing even the legendary elixirs of the elves.

Old Night entertained them as they ate, retelling grand tales of ancient heroes, and of events that had shaped the Realms into their present state. The companions were an attentive audience, though in all probability substantial clues about Mithral Hall loomed only a door or two away.

When the meal was finished, Old Night rose from his chair and looked around at them with a weird, curious intensity. "The day will come, a millennium from now, perhaps, when I shall entertain again. On that day, I am sure, one of the tales I tell will concern the Companions of the Hall and their glorious quest."

The friends could not reply to the honor that the ancient man had paid them. Even Drizzt, even-keeled and unshakable, sat unblinking for a long, long moment.

"Come," Old Night instructed, "let your road begin anew." He led them through another door, the door to the greatest library in all the North.

Volumes thick and thin covered the walls and lay about in high piles on the many tables positioned throughout the large room. Old Night indicated one particular table, a smaller one off to the side, with a solitary book opened upon it.

"I have done much of your research for you," Old Night explained. "And in all the volumes concerning dwarves, this was the only one I could find that held any reference to Mithral Hall."

Bruenor moved to the book, grasping its edges with trembling hands. It was written in High Dwarven, the language of Dumathoin, Keeper of Secrets Under the Mountain, a script nearly lost in the Realms. But Bruenor could read it. He surveyed the page quickly, then read aloud the passages of concern.

" 'King Elmor and his people profited mightily from the labors of Garumn and the kin of Clan Battlehammer, but the dwarves of the secret mines did not refute Elmor's gains. Settlestone proved a valuable and trustworthy ally whence Garumn could begin the secret trail to market of the mithral works.' " Bruenor looked up at his friends, a gleam of revelation in his eye.

"Settlestone," he whispered. "I know that name." He dived back into the book.

"You shall find little else," Old Night said. "For the words of Mithral Hall are lost to the ages. The book merely states that the flow of mithral soon ceased, to the ultimate demise of Settlestone."

Bruenor wasn't listening. He had to read it for himself, to devour every word penned about his lost heritage, no matter the significance.

"What of this Settlestone?" Wulfgar asked Old Night. "A clue?"

"Perhaps," the old herald replied. "Thus far I have found no reference to the place other than this book, but I am inclined to believe from the work that Settlestone was rather unusual for a dwarven town."

"Above the ground!" Bruenor suddenly cut in.

"Yes," agreed Old Night. "A dwarven community housed in structures above the ground. Rare these days and unheard of back in the time of Mithral Hall. Only two possibilities, to my knowledge."

Regis let out a cry of victory.

"Your enthusiasm may be premature," remarked Old Night. "Even if we discern where Settlestone once lay, the trail to Mithral Hall merely begins there."

Bruenor flipped through a few pages of the book, then replaced it on the table. "So close!" he growled, slamming his fist down on the petrified wood. "And I should know!"

Drizzt moved over to him and pulled a vial out from under his cloak. "A potion," he explained to Bruenor's puzzled look, "that will make you walk again in the days of Mithral Hall."

"A mighty spell," warned Old Night. "And not to be controlled. Consider its use carefully, good dwarf."

Bruenor was already moving, teetering on the verge of a discovery he had to find. He quaffed the liquid in one gulp, then steadied himself on the edge of the table against its potent kick. Sweat beaded on his wrinkled brow and he twitched involuntarily as the potion sent his mind drifting back across the centuries.

Regis and Wulfgar moved over to him, the big man clasping his shoulders and easing him into a seat.

Bruenor's eyes were wide open, but he saw nothing in the room before him. Sweat lathered him now, and the twitch had become a tremble.

"Bruenor," Drizzt called softly, wondering if he had done right in presenting the dwarf with such a tempting opportunity.

"No, me father!" Bruenor screamed. "Not here in the darkness! Come with me, then. What might I do without ye?"

"Bruenor," Drizzt called more emphatically.

"He is not here," Old Night explained, familiar with the potion, for it was often used by longlived races, particularly elves, when they sought memories of their distant past. Normally the imbibers returned to a more pleasant time, though. Old Night looked on with grave concern, for the potion had returned Bruenor to a wicked day in his past, a memory that his mind had blocked out, or at least blurred, to defend him against powerful emotions. Those emotions would now be laid bare, revealed to the dwarf's conscious mind in all their fury:

"Bring him to the Chamber of the Dwarves," Old Night instructed. "Let him bask in the images of his heroes. They will aid in remembering, and give him strength throughout his ordeal."

Wulfgar lifted Bruenor and bore him gently down the passage to the Chamber of the Dwarves, laying him in the center of the circular floor. The friends backed away, leaving the dwarf to his delusions.

Bruenor could only half-see the images around him now, caught between the worlds of the past and present. Images of Moradin, Dumathoin, and all his deities and heroes looked down upon him from their perches in the rafters, adding a small bit of comfort against the waves of tragedy. Dwarven-sized suits of armor and cunningly crafted axes and warhammers surrounded him, and he bathed in the presence of the highest glories of his proud race.

The images, though, could not dispell the horror he now knew again, the falling of his clan, of Mithral Hall, of his father.

"Daylight!" he cried, torn between relief and lament. "Alas for me father, and me father's father! But yea, our escape is at hand! Settlestone . . ." he faded from consciousness for a moment, overcome, ". . . shelter us. The loss, the loss! Shelter us!"

"The price is high," said Wulfgar, pained at the dwarf's torment.

"He is willing to pay," Drizzt replied.

"It will be a sorry payment if we learn nothing," said Regis. "There is no direction to his ramblings. Are we to sit by and hope against hope?"

"His memories have already brought him to Settlestone, with no mention of the trail behind him," Wulfgar observed.

Drizzt drew a scimitar and pulled the cowl of his cloak low over his face.

"What?" Regis started to ask, but the drow was already moving. He rushed to Bruenor's side and put his face close to the dwarf's sweat-lathered cheek.

"I am a friend," he whispered to Bruenor. "Come at the news of the falling of the hall! My allies await! Vengeance will be ours, mighty dwarf of Clan Battlehammer! Show us the way so that we might restore the glories of the hall!"

"Secret," Bruenor gasped, on the edge of consciousness.

Drizzt pressed harder. "Time is short! The darkness is falling!" he shouted. "The way, dwarf, we must know the way!"

Bruenor mumbled some inaudible sounds and all the friends gasped in the knowledge that the drow had broken through the final mental barrier that hindered Bruenor from finding the hall.

"Louder!" Drizzt insisted.

"Fourthpeak!" Bruenor screamed back. "Up the high run and into Keeper's Dale!"

Drizzt looked over to Old Night, who was nodding in recognition, then turned back to Bruenor. "Rest, mighty dwarf," he said comfortingly. "Your clan shall be avenged!"

"With the description the book gives of Settlestone, Fourthpeak can describe only one place," Old Night explained to Drizzt and Wulfgar when they got back to the library. Regis remained in the Chamber of the Dwarves to watch over Bruenor's fretful sleep.

The herald pulled a scroll tube down from a high shelf and unrolled the ancient parchment it held: a map of the central northland, between Silverymoon and Mirabar.

"The only dwarven settlement in the time of Mithral Hall above ground, and close enough to a mountain range to give a reference to a numbered peak, would be here," he said, marking the southernmost peak on the southernmost spur of the Spine of the World, just north of Nesmé and the Evermoors. "The deserted city of stone is simply called "the Ruins" now, and it was commonly known as Dwarvendarrows when the bearded race lived there. But the ramblings of your companion have convinced me that this is indeed the Settlestone that the book speaks of."

"Why, then, would the book not refer to it as Dwarvendarrow?" asked Wulfgar.

"Dwarves are a secretive race," Old Night explained with a knowing chuckle, "especially where treasure is concerned. Garumn of Mithral Hall was determined to keep the location of his trove hidden from the greed of the outside world. He and Elmor of Settlestone no doubt worked out an arrangement that included intricate codes and constructed names to reference their surroundings. Anything to throw prying mercenaries off the trail. Names that now appear in disjointed places throughout the tomes of dwarven history. Many scholars have probably even read of Mithral Hall, called by some other name that the readers assumed referred to another of the many ancient dwarven homelands now lost to the world."

The herald paused for a moment to digest everything that had occurred. "You should be away at once," he advised. "Carry the dwarf if you must, but get him to Settlestone before the effects of the potion wear away. Walking in his memories, Bruenor might be able to retrace his steps of two hundred years ago back up the mountains to Keeper's Dale, and to the gate of Mithral Hall."

Drizzt studied the map and the spot that Old Night had marked as the location of Settlestone. "Back to the west," he muttered, echoing Alustriel's suspicions. "Barely two days march from here."

Wulfgar moved in close to view the parchment and added, in a voice that held both anticipation and a measure of sadness, "Our road nears its end."

17
THE CHALLENGE

They left under stars and did not stop until stars filled the sky once again. Bruenor needed no support. Quite the opposite. It was the dwarf, recovered from his delirium and his eyes focused at last upon a tangible path to his long-sought goal, who drove them, setting the strongest pace since they had come out of Icewind Dale. Glassy-eyed and walking both in past and present, Bruenor's obsession consumed him. For nearly two hundred years he had dreamed of this return, and these last few days on the road seemed longer than the centuries that had come before.

The companions had apparently beaten their worst enemy: time. If their reckoning at the Holdfast was correct, Mithral Hall loomed just a few days away, while the short summer had barely passed its midpoint. With time no longer a pressing issue, Drizzt, Wulfgar, and Regis had anticipated a moderate pace as they prepared to leave the Holdfast. But Bruenor, when he awoke and learned of the discoveries, would hear no arguments about his rush. None were offered, though, for in the excitement, Bruenor's already surly disposition had grown even fouler.

"Keep yer feet moving!" he kept snapping at Regis, whose little legs could not match the dwarfs frantic pace. "Ye should've stayed in Ten-Towns with yer belly hanging over yer belt!" The dwarf would then sink into quiet grumbling, bending even lower over his pumping feet, and driving onward, his ears blocked to any remarks that Regis might shoot back or any comments forthcoming from Wulfgar or Drizzt concerning his behavior.

They angled their path back to the Rauvin, to use its waters as a guide. Drizzt did manage to convince Bruenor to veer back to the northwest as soon as the peaks of the mountain range came into view. The drow had no desire to meet any patrols from Nesmé again, certain that it was that city's warning cries that had forced Alustriel to keep him out of Silverymoon.

Bruenor found no relaxation at the camp that night, even though they had obviously covered far more than half the distance to the ruins of Settlestone. He stomped about the camp like a trapped animal, clenching and unclenching his gnarly fists and mumbling to himself about the fateful day when his people had been pushed out of Mithral Hall, and the revenge he would find when he at last returned.

"Is it the potion?" Wulfgar asked Drizzt later that evening as they stood to the side of the camp and watched the dwarf.

"Some of it, perhaps," Drizzt answered, equally concerned about his friend. "The potion has forced Bruenor to live again the most painful experience of his long life. And now, as the memories of that past find their way into his emotions, they keenly edge the vengeance that has festered within him all these years."

"He is afraid," Wulfgar noted.

Drizzt nodded. "This is the trial of his life. His vow to return to Mithral Hall holds within it all the value that he places upon his own existence."

"He pushes too hard," Wulfgar remarked, looking at Regis, who had collapsed, exhausted, right after they had supped. "The halfling cannot keep the pace."

"Less than a day stands before us," Drizzt replied. "Regis will survive this road, as shall we all." He patted the barbarian on the shoulder and Wulfgar, not fully satisfied, but resigned to the fact that he could not sway the dwarf, moved away to find some rest. Drizzt looked back to the pacing dwarf, and his dark face bore at look of deeper concern than he had revealed to the young barbarian.

Drizzt truly wasn't worried about Regis. The halfling always found a way to come through better off than he should. Bruenor, though, troubled the drow. He remembered when the dwarf had crafted Aegis-fang, the mighty warhammer. The weapon had been Bruenor's ultimate creation in a rich career as a craftsman, a weapon worthy of legend. Bruenor could not hope to outdo that accomplishment, nor even equal it. The dwarf had never put hammer to anvil again.

Now the journey to Mithral Hall, Bruenor's lifelong goal. As Aegis-fang had been Bruenor's finest crafting, this journey would be his highest climb. The focus of Drizzt's concern was more subtle, and yet more dangerous, than the success or failure of the search; the dangers of the road affected all of them equally, and they had accepted them willingly before starting out. Whether or not the ancient halls were reclaimed, Bruenor's mountain would be crested. The moment of his glory would be passed.

"Calm yourself, good friend," Drizzt said, moving beside the dwarf.

"It's me home, elf," Bruenor shot back, but he did seem to compose himself a bit.

"I understand," Drizzt offered. "It seems that we shall indeed look upon Mithral Hall, and that raises a question we must soon answer."

Bruenor looked at him curiously, though he knew well enough what Drizzt was getting at.

"So far we have concerned ourselves only with finding Mithral Hall, and little has been said of our plans beyond the entrance to the place."

"By all that is right, I am King of the Hall," Bruenor growled.

"Agreed," said the drow, "but what of the darkness that may remain? A force that drove your entire clan from the mines. Are we four to defeat it?"

"It may have gone on its own, elf," Bruenor replied in a surly tone, not wanting to face the possibilities. "For all our knowing, the halls may be clean."

"Perhaps. But what plans have you if the darkness remains?"

Bruenor paused for a moment of thought. "Word'll be sent to Icewind Dale," he answered. "Me kin'll be with us in the spring."

"Barely a hundred strong," Drizzt reminded him.

"Then I'll call to Adbar if more be needed!" Bruenor snapped. "Harbromm'll be glad to help, for a promise of treasure."

Drizzt knew that Bruenor wouldn't be so quick to make such a promise, but he decided to end the stream of disturbing but necessary questions. "Sleep well," he bid the dwarf. "You shall find your answers when you must."

☒ ☒ ☒ ☒

The pace was no less frantic the morning of the next day. Mountains soon towered above them as they ran along, and another change came over the dwarf. He stopped suddenly, dizzied and fighting for his balance. Wulfgar and Drizzt were right beside him, propping him up.

"What is it?" Drizzt asked.

"Dwarvendarrow," Bruenor answered in a voice that seemed far removed. He pointed to an outcropping of rock jutting from the base of the nearest mountain.

"You know the place?"

Bruenor didn't answer. He started off again, stumbling, but rejecting any offers of help. His friends shrugged helplessly and followed.

An hour later, the structures came into view. Like giant houses of cards, great slabs of stone had been cunningly laid together to form dwellings, and though they had been deserted for more than a hundred years, the seasons and the wind had not reclaimed them. Only dwarves could have imbued such strength into the rock, could have laid the stones so perfectly that they would last as the mountains themselves lasted, beyond the generations and the tales of the bards, so that some future race would look upon them in awe and marvel at their construction without the slightest idea of who had created them.

Bruenor remembered. He wandered into the village as he had those many decades ago, a tear rimming his gray eye and his body trembling against the memories of the darkness that had swarmed over his clan.

His friends let him go about for a while, not wanting to interrupt the solemn emotions that had found their way through his thick hide. Finally, as afternoon waned, Drizzt moved over to him.

"Do you know the way?" he asked.

Bruenor looked up at a pass that climbed along the side of the nearest mountain. "Half a day," he replied.

"Camp here?" Drizzt asked.

"It would do me good," said Bruenor. "I've much to think over, elf. I'll not forget the way, fear not." His eyes narrowed in tight focus at the trail he had fled on the day of darkness, and he whispered, "I'll never forget the way again."

⨯ ⨯ ⨯ ⨯

Bruenor's driven pace proved fortunate for the friends, for Bok had easily continued along the drow's trail outside of Silverymoon and had led its group with similar haste. Bypassing the Holdfast altogether—the tower's magical wards would not have let them near it in any case—the golem's party had made up considerable ground.

In a camp not far away, Entreri stood grinning his evil smile and staring at the dark horizon, and at the speck of light he knew to be the campfire of his victim.

Catti-brie saw it, too, and knew that the next day would bring her greatest challenge. She had spent most of her life with the battle-seasoned dwarves, under the tutelage of Bruenor himself. He had taught her both discipline and confidence. Not a facade of cockiness to hide deeper insecurities, but a true self-belief and measured evaluation of what she could and could not accomplish. Any trouble that she had finding sleep that night was more due to her eagerness to face this challenge than her fear of failure.

They broke camp early and arrived at the ruins just after dawn. No more anxious than Bruenor's party, though, they found only the remnants of the companions' campsite.

"An hour—perhaps two," Entreri observed, bending low to feel the heat of the embers.

"Bok has already found the new trail," said Sydney, pointing to the golem moving off toward the foothills of the closest mountain.

A smile filled Entreri's face as the thrill of the chase swept over him. Catti-brie paid little attention to the assassin, though, more concerned with the revelations painted on Jierdan's face.

The soldier seemed unsure of himself. He took up after them as soon as Sydney and Entreri started behind Bok, but with forced steps. He obviously wasn't looking forward to the pending confrontation, as were Sydney and Entreri.

Catti-brie was pleased.

They charged ahead through the morning, dodging sharp ravines and boulders, and picking their way up the side of the mountains. Then, for the first time since he had begun his search more than two years before, Entreri saw his prey.

The assassin had come over a boulder-strewn mound and was slowing his strides to accommodate a sharp dip into a small dell thick with trees, when Bruenor and his friends broke clear of some brush and made their way across the facing of a steep slope far ahead. Entreri dropped into a crouch and signaled for the others to slow behind him.

"Stop the golem," he called to Sydney, for Bok had already disappeared into the copse below him and would soon come crashing out of the other side and onto another barren mound of stone, in clear sight of the companions.

Sydney rushed up. "Bok, return to me!" she yelled as loudly as she dared, for while the companions were far in the distance, the echoes of noises on the mountainside seemed to carry forever.

Entreri pointed to the specks moving across the facing ahead of them, "We can catch them before they get around the side of the mountain," he told Sydney. He jumped back to meet Jierdan and Catti-brie, and roughly bound Catti-brie's hands behind her back. "If you cry out, you will watch your friends die," he assured her. "And then your own end will be most unpleasant."

Catti-brie painted her most frightened look across her face, all the while pleased that the assassin's latest threat seemed quite hollow to her. She had risen above the level of terror that Entreri had played against her when they had first met back in Ten-Towns. She had convinced herself, against her instinctive revulsion of the passionless killer, that he was, after all, only a man.

Entreri pointed to the steep valley below the facing and the companions. "I will go through the ravine," he explained to Sydney, "and make the first contact. You and the golem continue along the path and close in from behind."

"And what of me?" Jierdan protested.

"Stay with the girl!" Entreri commanded as absently as if he was speaking to a servant. He spun away and started off, refusing to hear any arguments.

Sydney did not even turn to look at Jierdan as she stood waiting for Bok's return. She had no time for such squabbles and figured that if Jierdan could not speak for himself, he wasn't worth her trouble.

"Act now," Catti-brie whispered to Jierdan, "for yerself and not for me!" He looked at her, more curious than angry, and vulnerable to any suggestions that might help him from this uncomfortable position.

"The mage has thrown all respect for ye, man," Catti-brie continued. "The assassin has replaced ye, and she'd be liken to stand by him above ye. This is yer chance to act, yer last one if me eyes be tellin' me right! Time to show the mage yer worth, Soldier of Luskan!"

Jierdan glanced about nervously. For all of the manipulations he expected from the woman, her words held enough truth to convince him that her assessment was correct.

His pride won over. He spun on Catti-brie and smacked her to the ground, then rushed past Sydney in pursuit of Entreri.

"Where are you going?" Sydney called after him, but Jierdan was no longer interested in pointless talk.

Surprised and confused, Sydney turned to check on the prisoner. Catti-brie had anticipated this and she groaned and rolled on the hard stone as though she had been knocked senseless, though in truth she had turned enough away from Jierdan's blow that he had merely glanced her. Fully conscious and coherent, her movements were calculated to position her where she could slip her tied hands down around her legs and bring them up in front of her.

Catti-brie's act satisfied Sydney enough so that the mage put her attention fully on the coming confrontation between her two comrades. Hearing Jierdan's approach, Entreri had spun on him, his dagger and saber drawn.

"You were told to stay with the girl!" he hissed.

"I did not come on this journey to play guard to your prisoner!" Jierdan retorted, his own sword out.

The characteristic grin made its way onto Entreri's face again. "Go back," he said one last time to Jierdan, though he knew, and was glad, that the proud soldier would not turn away.

Jierdan took another step forward.

Entreri struck.

Jierdan was a seasoned fighter, a veteran of many skirmishes, and if Entreri expected to dispatch him with a single thrust, he was mistaken. Jierdan's sword knocked the blow aside and he returned the thrust.

Recognizing the obvious contempt that Entreri showed to Jierdan, and knowing the level of the soldier's pride, Sydney had feared this confrontation since they had left the Hosttower. She didn't care if one of them died now—she suspected that it would be Jierdan—but she would not tolerate anything that put her mission in jeopardy. After the drow was safely in her hands, Entreri and Jierdan could settle their differences.

"Go to them!" she called to the advancing golem. "Stop this fight!" Bok turned at once and rushed toward the combatants, and Sydney, shaking her head in disgust, believed that the situation would soon be under control and they could resume their hunt.

What she didn't see was Catti-brie rising up behind her.

Catti-brie knew that she had only one chance. She crept up silently and brought her clasped hands down on the back of the mage's neck. Sydney dropped straight to the hard stone and Catti-brie ran by, down into the copse of trees, her blood coursing through her veins. She had to get close enough to her friends to yell a clear warning before her captors overtook her.

Just after Catti-brie slipped into the thick trees, she heard Sydney gasp, "Bok!"

The golem swung back at once, some distance behind Catti-brie, but gaining with each long stride.

Even if they had seen her flight, Jierdan and Entreri were too caught up in their own battle to be concerned with her.

"You shall insult me no more!" Jierdan cried above the clang of steel.

"But I shall!" Entreri hissed. "There are manyways to defile a corpse, fool, and know that I shall practice every one on your rotting bones." He pressed in harder, his concentration squarely on his foe, his blades gaining deadly momentum in their dance.

Jierdan countered gamely, but the skilled assassin had little trouble in meeting all of his thrusts with deft parries and subtle shifts. Soon the soldier had exhausted his repertoire of feints and strikes, and he hadn't even come close to hitting his mark. He would tire before Entreri—he saw that clearly even this early in the fight.

They exchanged several more blows, Entreri's cuts moving faster and faster, while Jierdan's double-handed swings slowed to a crawl. The soldier had hoped that Sydney would intervene by this point. His weakness of stamina had been clearly revealed to Entreri, and he couldn't understand why the mage had not said anything about the battle. He glanced about, his desperation growing. Then he saw Sydney, lying face down on the stone.

An honorable way out, he thought, still more concerned with himself. "The mage!" he cried to Entreri. "We must help her!" The words fell upon deaf ears.

"And the girl!" Jierdan yelled, hoping to catch the assassin's interest. He tried to break free of the combat, jumping back from Entreri and lowering his sword. "We shall continue this later," he declared in a threatening tone, though he had no intention of engaging the assassin in a fair fight again.

Entreri didn't answer, but lowered his blades accordingly. Jierdan, ever the honorable soldier, turned about to see to Sydney.

A jeweled dagger whistled into his back.

Catti-brie stumbled along, unable to hold her balance with her hands bound together. Loose stone slipped beneath her and more than once she tumbled to the ground. As agile as a cat, she was up quickly.

But Bok was the swifter.

Catti-brie fell again and rolled over a sharp crest of stone. She started down a dangerous slope of slippery rocks, heard the golem stomping behind her, and knew that she could not possibly outrun the thing. Yet she had no choice. Sweat burned a dozen scrapes and stung her eyes, and all hope had flown from her. Still she ran, her courage denying the obvious end.

Against her despair and terror, she found the strength to search for an option. The slope continued down another twenty feet, and right beside her was the slender and rotting stump of a long-dead tree. A plan came to her then, desperate, but with enough hope for her to try it. She stopped for a moment to survey the root structure of the rotting stump, and to estimate the effect that uprooting the thing might have on the stones.

She backed a few feet up the slope and waited, crouched for her impossible leap. Bok came over the crest and bore down on her, rocks bouncing away from the heavy plodding of its booted feet. It was right behind her, reaching out with horrid arms.

And Catti-brie leaped.

She hooked the rope that bound her hands over the stump as she flew past, throwing all of her weight against the hold of its roots.

Bok lumbered after her, oblivious to her intentions. Even as the stump toppled, and the network of dead roots pulled up from the ground, the golem couldn't understand the danger. As the loose stones shifted and began their descent, Bok kept its focus straight ahead on its prey.

Catti-brie bounced down ahead and to the side of the rockslide. She didn't try to rise, just kept rolling and scrambling in spite of the pain to gain every inch between herself and the crumbling slope. Her determination got her to the thick trunk of an oak, and she rolled around behind it and turned back to look at the slope.

Just in time to see the golem go down under a ton of bouncing stone.

18

THE SECRET OF KEEPER'S DALE

Keeper's Dale," Bruenor declared solemnly. The companions stood on a high ledge, looking down hundreds of feet to the broken floor of a deep and rocky gorge.

"How are we to get down there?" Regis gasped, for every side appeared absolutely sheer, as though the canyon had been purposely cut from the stone.

There was a way down, of course, and Bruenor, walking still with the memories of his youth, knew it well. He led his friends around to the eastern rim of the gorge and looked back to the west, to the peaks of the three nearest mountains. "Ye stand upon Fourthpeak," he explained, "named for its place beside th' other three.

"Three peaks to seem as one," the dwarf recited, an ancient line from a longer song that all the young dwarves of Mithral Hall were taught before they were even old enough to venture out of the mines.

"Three peaks to seem as one,
Behind ye the morning sun."

Bruenor shifted about to find the exact line of the three western mountains, then moved slowly to the very edge of the gorge and looked over. "We have come to the entrance of the dale," he stated calmly, though his heart was pounding at the discovery.

The other three moved up to join him. Just below the rim they saw a carved step, the first in a long line moving down the face of the cliff, and shaded perfectly by the coloration of the stone to make the entire construction virtually invisible from any other angle.

Regis swooned when he looked over, nearly overwhelmed by the thought of descending hundreds of feet on a narrow stair without even a handhold. "We'll surely fall to our deaths!" he squeaked and backed away.

But again Bruenor wasn't asking for opinions, or arguments. He started down, and Drizzt and Wulfgar moved to follow, leaving Regis with no choice but to go. Drizzt and Wulfgar sympathized with his distress, though, and they helped him as much as they could, Wulfgar even scooping him up in his arms when the wind began to gust.

The descent was tentative and slow, even with Bruenor in the lead, and it seemed like hours before the stone of the canyon floor had moved any closer to them.

"Five hundred to the left, then a hundred more," Bruenor sang when they finally got to the bottom. The dwarf moved along the wall to the south, counting his measured paces and leading the others past towering pillars of stone, great monoliths of another age that had seemed as mere piles of fallen rubble from the rim. Even Bruenor, whose kin had lived here for many centuries, did not know any tales that spoke of the monoliths' creation or purpose. But whatever the reason, they had stood a silent and imposing vigil upon the canyon floor for uncounted centuries, ancient before the dwarves even arrived, casting ominous shadows and belittling mere mortals who had ever walked here.

And the pillars bent the wind into an eerie and mournful cry and gave the entire floor the sensation of something beyond the natural, timeless like the Holdfast, and imposing a realization of mortality upon onlookers, as though the monoliths mocked the living with their ageless existence.

Bruenor, unbothered by the towers, finished his count.

> *"Five hundred to the left, then a hundred more,*
> *The hidden lines of the secret door."*

He studied the wall beside him for any marking that would indicate the entrance to the halls.

Drizzt, too, ran his sensitive hands across the smooth stone. "Are you certain?" he asked the dwarf after long minutes of searching, for he had felt no cracks at all.

"I am!" Bruenor declared. "Me people were cunning with their workings and I fear that the door is too well in hiding for an easy find."

Regis moved in to help, while Wulfgar, uncomfortable beneath the shadows of the monoliths, stood guard at their backs.

Just a few seconds later, the barbarian noticed movement from where they'd come, back over by the stone stair. He dipped into a defensive crouch, clutching Aegis-fang as tightly as ever before. "Visitors," he said to his friends, the hiss of his whisper echoing around as though the monoliths were laughing at his attempt at secrecy.

Drizzt sprang out to the nearest pillar and started making his way around, using Wulfgar's frozen squint as a guide. Angered at the interruption, Bruenor pulled a small hatchet from his belt and stood ready beside the barbarian, and Regis behind them.

Then they heard Drizzt call out, "Catti-brie!" and were too relieved and elated to pause and consider what might have possibly brought their friend all the way from Ten-Towns, or how she had ever found them.

Their smiles disappeared when they saw her, bruised and bloodied and stumbling toward them. They rushed to meet her, but the drow, suspecting that someone might be in pursuit, slipped along through the monoliths and took up a lookout.

"What bringed ye?" Bruenor cried, grabbing Catti-brie and hugging her close. "And who was it hurt ye? He'll feel me hands on his neck!"

"And my hammer!" Wulfgar added, enraged at the thought of someone striking Catti-brie.

Regis hung back now, beginning to suspect what had happened.

"Fender Mallot and Grollo are dead," Catti-brie told Bruenor.

"On the road with ye? But why?" asked the dwarf.

"No, back in Ten-Towns," Catti-brie answered. "A man, a killer, was there, looking for Regis. I chased after him, trying to get to ye to warn ye, but he caught me and dragged me along."

Bruenor spun a glare upon the halfling, who was even farther back now, and hanging his head.

"I knew ye'd found trouble when ye came running up on the road outside the towns!" He scowled. "'What is it, then? And no more of yer lying tales!'"

"His name is Entreri," Regis admitted. "Artemis Entreri. He came from Calimport, from Pasha Pook." Regis pulled out the ruby pendant. "For this."

"But he is not alone," Catti-brie added. "Wizards from Luskan search for Drizzt."

"For what reason?" Drizzt called from the shadows.

Catti-brie shrugged. "They been taking care not to tell, but me guess is that they seek some answers about Akar Kessell."

Drizzt understood at once. They sought the Crystal Shard, the powerful relic that had been buried beneath the avalanche on Kelvin's Cairn.

"How many?" asked Wulfgar. "And how far behind?"

"Three they were," Catti-brie answered. "The assassin, a mage, and a soldier from Luskan. A monster they had with them. A golem, they called it, but I've ne'er seen its likes before."

"Golem," Drizzt echoed softly. He had seen many such creations in the undercity of the dark elves. Monsters of great power and undying loyalty to their creators. These must be mighty foes indeed, to have one along

"But the thing is gone," Catti-brie continued. "It chased me on me flight, and would have had me, no doubting, but I pulled a trick on it and sent a mountain of rock on its head!"

Bruenor hugged her close again. "Well done, me girl," he whispered.

"And I left the soldier and the assassin in a terrible fight," Catti-brie went on. "One is dead, I guess, and the soldier seems most likely. A pity, it is, for he was a decent sort."

"He'd have found me blade for helping the dogs at all!" Bruenor retorted. "But enough of the tale; there'll be time for telling. Ye're at the hall, girl, do ye know? Ye're to see for yerself the splendors I been telling ye about all these years! So go and rest up." He turned around to tell Wulfgar to see to her, but noticed Regis instead. The halfling had problems of his own, hanging his head and wondering if he had pushed his friends too far this time.

"Fear not, my friend," said Wulfgar, also seeing Regis's distress. "You acted to survive. There is no shame in that. Though you should have told us the danger!"

"Ah, put yer head up, Rumblebelly!" Bruenor snapped. "We expect as much from ye, ye nogood trickster! Don't ye be thinkin' we're surprised!" Bruenor's rage, an angry possessor somehow growing of its own volition, suddenly mounted as he stood there chastising the halfling.

"How dare ye to put this on us?" he roared at Regis, moving Catti-brie aside and advancing a step. "And with me home right before me!"

Wulfgar was quick to block Bruenor's path to Regis, though he was truly amazed at the sudden shift in the dwarf. He had never seen Bruenor so consumed by emotion. Catti-brie, too, looked on, stunned.

" 'Twas not the halfling's fault," she said. "And the wizards would've come anyway!"

Drizzt returned to them then. "No one has made the stair yet," he said, but when he took a better notice of the situation, he realized that his words had not been heard.

A long and uncomfortable silence descended upon them, then Wulfgar took command. "We have come too far along this road to argue and fight among ourselves!" he scolded Bruenor.

Bruenor looked at him blankly, not knowing how to react to the uncharacteristic stand Wulfgar had taken against him. "Bah!" the dwarf said finally, throwing up his hands in frustration. "The fool halfling'll get us killed . . . but not to worry!" he grumbled sarcastically, moving back to the wall to search for the door.

Drizzt looked curiously at the surly dwarf, but was more concerned with Regis at this point. The halfling, thoroughly miserable, had dropped to a sitting position and seemed to have lost all desire to go on. "Take heart,"

Drizzt said to him. "Bruenor's anger will pass. The essence of his dreams stands before him."

"And about this assassin who seeks your head," Wulfgar said, moving to join the two. "He shall find a mighty welcome when he gets here, if ever he does." Wulfgar patted the head of his warhammer. "Perhaps we can change his mind about this hunt!"

"If we can get into the mines, our trail might be lost to them," Drizzt said to Bruenor, trying to further soothe the dwarf's anger.

"They'll not make the stair," said Catti-brie. "Even watching your climb down, I had trouble finding it!"

"I would rather stand against them now!" Wulfgar declared. "They have much to explain, and they'll not escape my punishment for the way they have treated Catti-brie!"

"Ware the assassin," Catti-brie warned him. "His blades mean death, and no mistaking!"

"And a wizard can be a terrible foe," added Drizzt. "We have a more important task before us—we do not need to take on fights that we can avoid."

"No delays!" said Bruenor, ending any rebuttals from the big barbarian. "Mithral Hall stands before me, and I'm meaning to go in! Let them follow, if they dare." He turned back to the wall to resume his search for the door, calling for Drizzt to join him. "Keep the watch, boy," he ordered Wulfgar. "And see to me girl."

"A word of opening, perhaps?" Drizzt asked when he stood alone again with Bruenor before the featureless wall.

"Aye," said Bruenor, "there be a word. But the magic that holds to it leaves it after a while, and a new word must be named. None were here to name it!"

"Try the old word, then."

"I have, elf, a dozen times when we first came here." He banged his fist on the stone. "Another way there be, I know," he growled in frustration.

"You will remember," Drizzt assured him. And they set back to inspecting the wall.

Even the stubborn determination of a dwarf does not always pay off, and the night fell and found the friends sitting outside the entrance in the darkness, not daring to light a fire for fear of alerting their pursuers. Of all their trials on the road, the waiting so very close to their goal was possibly the most trying. Bruenor began to second-guess himself, wondering if this was even the correct place for the door. He recited the song he had learned as a child in Mithral Hall over and over, searching for some clues he might have missed.

The others slept uneasily, especially Catti-brie, who knew that the silent death of an assassin's blade stalked them. They would not have slept at all, except that they knew that the keen, ever vigilant eyes of a drow elf watched over them.

⚔ ⚔ ⚔ ⚔

A few miles down the trail behind them, a similar camp had been set. Entreri stood quietly, peering to the trails of the eastern mountains for signs of a campfire, though he doubted that the friends would be so careless as to light one if Catti-brie had found and warned them. Behind him, Sydney lay wrapped in a blanket upon the cool stone, resting and recovering from the blow Catti-brie had struck her.

The assassin had considered leaving her—normally he would have without a second thought—but Entreri needed to take some time anyway to regroup his thoughts and figure out his best course of action.

Dawn came and found him standing there still, unmoving and contemplative. Behind him, the mage awoke.

"Jierdan?" she called, dazed. Entreri stepped back and crouched over her.

"Where is Jierdan?" she asked.

"Dead," Entreri answered, no hint of remorse in his voice. "As is the golem."

"Bok?" Sydney gasped.

"A mountain fell on him," Entreri replied.

"And the girl?"

"Gone." Entreri looked back to the east. "When I have seen to your needs, I will go," he said. "Our chase is ended."

"They are close," Sydney argued. "You will give up your hunt?"

Entreri grinned. "The halfling will be mine,'" he said evenly, and Sydney had no doubt that he spoke the truth. "But our party is disbanded. I will return to my own hunt, and you to yours, though I warn you, if you take what is mine, you will mark yourself as my next prey."

Sydney considered the words carefully. "Where did Bok fall?" she asked on a sudden thought.

Entreri looked along the trail to the east. "In a vale beyond the copse."

"Take me there," Sydney insisted. "There is something that must be done."

Entreri helped her to her feet and led her along the path, figuring that he would part with her when she had put her final business to rest. He had come to respect this young mage and her dedication to her duty, and he trusted that she would not cross him. Sydney was no wizard, and no match for him, and they both knew that his respect for her would not slow his blade if she got in his way.

Sydney surveyed the rocky slope for a moment, then turned on Entreri, a knowing smile upon her face. "You say that our quest together is ended, but you are wrong. We may prove of value to you still, assassin."

"We?"

Sydney turned to the slope. "Bok!" she called loudly and kept her gaze upon the slope.

A puzzled look crossed Entreri's face. He, too, studied the stones, but saw no sign of movement

"Bok!" Sydney called again, and this time there was indeed a stir. A rumble grew beneath the layer of boulders, and then one shifted and rose into the air, the golem standing beneath it, stretching into the air. Battered and twisted, but apparently feeling no pain, Bok tossed the huge stone aside and moved toward its master.

"A golem is not so easily destroyed," Sydney explained, drawing satisfaction from the amazed expression on Entreri's normally emotionless face. "Bok still has a road to travel, a road it will not so easily forsake."

"A road that will again lead us to the drow," Entreri laughed. "Come, my companion," he said to Sydney, "let us be on with the chase."

⚔ ⚔ ⚔ ⚔

The friends still had found no clues when dawn came. Bruenor stood before the wall, shouting a tirade of arcane chants, most of which had nothing to do with words of opening.

Wulfgar took a different approach. Reasoning that a hollow echo would help them ensure that they had come to the correct spot, he moved methodically along with his ear to the wall, tapping with Aegis-fang. The hammer chimed off the solid stone, singing in the perfection of its crafting.

But one blow did not reach its mark. Wulfgar brought the hammer's head in, but just as it reached the stone, it was stopped by a blanket of blue light. Wulfgar jumped back, startled. Creases appeared in the stone, the outline of a door. The rock continued to shift and slide inward, and soon it cleared the wall and slid aside, revealing the entry hall to the dwarven homeland. A gust of air, bottled up within for centuries and carrying the scents of ages past, rushed out upon them.

"A magic weapon!" cried Bruenor. "The only trade me people would accept at the mines!"

"When visitors came here, they entered by tapping the door with a magical weapon?" Drizzt asked.

The dwarf nodded, though his attention was now fixed squarely on the gloom beyond the wall. The chamber directly before them was unlit, except by the daylight shining through the open door, but down a corridor behind the entry hall, they could see the flicker of torches.

"Someone is here," said Regis.

"Not so," replied Bruenor, many of his long-forgotten images of Mithral Hall flooding back to him. "The torches ever burn, for the life of a dwarf and more." He stepped through the portal, kicking dust that had settled untouched for two hundred years.

His friends gave him a moment alone, then solemnly joined him. All around the chamber lay the remains of many dwarves. A battle had been fought here, the final battle of Bruenor's clan before they were expelled from their home.

"By me own eyes, the tales be true," the dwarf muttered. He turned to his friends to explain. "The rumors that came down to Settlestone after me and the younger dwarves arrived there told of a great battle at the entry hall. Some went back to see what truth the rumors held, but they never returned to us."

Bruenor broke off, and on his lead, the companions moved about to inspect the place. Dwarven-sized skeletons lay about in the same poses and places where they had fallen. Mithral armor, dulled by the dust but not rusted, and shining again with the brush of a hand, clearly marked the dead of Clan Battlehammer. Intertwined with those dead were other, similar skeletons in strangely crafted mail, as though the fighting had pitted dwarf against dwarf. It was a riddle beyond the surface dwellers' experience, but Drizzt Do'Urden understood. In the city of the dark elves, he had known the Duergar, the malicious gray dwarves, as allies. Duergar were the dwarven equivalent of the drow, and because their surface cousins sometimes delved deep into the earth, and into their claimed territory, the hatred between the dwarven races was even more intense than the clash between the races of elves. The Duergar skeletons explained much to Drizzt, and to Bruenor, who also recognized the strange armor, and who for the first time understood what had driven his kin out of Mithral Hall. If the gray ones were in the mines still, Drizzt knew, Bruenor would be hard-pressed to reclaim the place.

The magical door slid shut behind them, dimming the chamber even further. Catti-brie and Wulfgar moved close together for security, their eyes weak in the dimness, but Regis darted about, searching for the gems and other treasures that a dwarven skeleton might possess.

Bruenor had also seen something of interest. He moved over to two skeletons lying back to back. A pile of gray dwarves had fallen around them, and that alone told Bruenor who these two were, even before he saw the foaming mug crest upon their shields.

Drizzt moved behind him, but kept a respectable distance.

"Bangor, me father," Bruenor explained. "And Garumn, me father's father, King of Mithral Hall. Suren they took their toll before they fell!"

"As mighty as their next in line," Drizzt remarked.

Bruenor accepted the compliment silently and bent to dust the dirt from Garumn's helm. "Garumn wears still the armor and weapons of Bruenor, me namesake and the hero of me clan. Me guess is that they cursed this place as they died," he said, "for the gray ones did not return and loot."

Drizzt agreed with the explanation, aware of the power of the curse of a king when his homeland has fallen.

Reverently, Bruenor lifted Garumn's remains and bore them into a side chamber. Drizzt did not follow, allowing the dwarf his privacy in this moment. Drizzt returned to Catti-brie and Wulfgar to help them comprehend the importance of the scene around them.

They waited patiently for many minutes, imagining the course of the epic battle that had taken place and their minds hearing clearly the sounds of axe on shield, and the brave war cries of Clan Battlehammer.

Then Bruenor returned and even the mighty images the friends' minds had concocted fell short of the sight before them. Regis dropped the few baubles he had found in utter amazement, and in fear that a ghost from the past had returned to thwart him.

Cast aside was Bruenor's battered shield. The dented and one-horned helm was strapped on his backpack. He wore the armor of his namesake, shining mithral, the mug standard on the shield of solid gold, and the helm ringed with a thousand glittering gemstones. "By me own eyes, I proclaim the legends as true," he shouted boldly, lifting the mithral axe high above him. "Garumn is dead and me father, too. Thus I claim me title: Eighth King of Mithral Hall!"

19

SHADOWS

"Garumn's Gorge," Bruenor said, drawing a line across the rough map he had scratched on the floor. Even though the effects of Alustriel's potion had worn off, simply stepping inside the home of his youth had rekindled a host of memories in the dwarf. The exact location of each of the halls was not clear to him, but he had a general idea of the overall design of the place. The others huddled close to him, straining to see the etchings in the flickers of the torch that Wulfgar had retrieved from the corridor.

"We can get out on the far side," Bruenor continued. "There's a door, opening one way and for leaving only, beyond the bridge."

"Leaving?" Wulfgar asked.

"Our goal was to find Mithral Hall," Drizzt answered, playing the same argument he had used on Bruenor before this meeting. "If the forces that defeated Clan Battlehammer reside here still, we few would find reclaiming it an impossible task. We must take care that the knowledge of the hall's location does not die in here with us."

"I'm meaning to find out what we're to face," Bruenor added "We mighten be going back out the door we came in; it'd open easy from the inside. Me thinking is to cross the top level and see the place out. I'm needing to know how much is left afore I call on me kin in the dale, and others if I must." He shot Drizzt a sarcastic glance.

Drizzt suspected that Bruenor had more in mind than "seeing the place out," but he kept quiet, satisfied that he had gotten his concerns through to the dwarf, and that Catti-brie's unexpected presence would temper with caution all of Bruenor's decisions.

"You will come back, then," Wulfgar surmised.

"An army at me heels!" snorted Bruenor. He looked at Catti-brie and a measure of his eagerness left his dark eyes.

She read it at once, "Don't ye be holding back for me!" she scolded. "Fought beside ye before, I have, and held me own, too! I didn't want this road, but it found me and how I'm here with ye to the end!"

After the many years of training her, Bruenor could not now disagree with her decision to follow their chosen path. He looked around at the skeletons in the room. "Get yerself armed and armored then, and let's be off—if we're agreed."

"'Tis your road to choose," said Drizzt. "For 'tis your search. We walk beside you, but do not tell you which way to go."

Bruenor smiled at the irony of the statement. He noted a slight glimmer in the drow's eyes, a hint of their customary sparkle for excitement. Perhaps Drizzt's heart for the adventure was not completely gone.

"I will go," said Wulfgar. "I did not walk those many miles, to return when the door was found!"

Regis said nothing. He knew that he was caught up in the whirlpool of their excitement, whatever his own feelings might be. He patted the little pouch of newly acquired baubles on his belt and thought of the additions he might soon find if these halls were truly as splendid as Bruenor had always said. He honestly felt that he would rather walk the nine hells beside his formidable friends than go back outside and face Artemis Entreri alone.

As soon as Catti-brie was outfitted, Bruenor led them on. He marched proudly in his grandfather's shining armor, the mithral axe swinging beside him, and the crown of the king firmly upon his head. "To Garumn's Gorge!" he cried as they started from the entry chamber. "From there we'll decide to go out, or down. Oh, the glories that lay before us, me friends. Pray that I be taking ye to them this time through!"

Wulfgar marched beside him, Aegis-fang in one hand and the torch in the other. He wore the same grim but eager expression. Catti-brie and Regis followed, less eager and more tentative, but accepting the road as unavoidable and determined to make the best of it.

Drizzt moved along the side, sometimes ahead of them, sometimes behind, rarely seen and never heard, though the comforting knowledge of his presence made them all step easier down the corridor.

The hallways were not smooth and flat, as was usually the case with dwarven construction. Alcoves jutted out on either side every few feet, some ending inches back, others slipping away into the darkness to join up with other whole networks of corridors. The walls all along the way were chipped and flaked with jutting edges and hollowed depressions, designed to enhance the shadowy effect of the ever-burning torches. This was a place of mystery and secret, where dwarves could craft their finest works in an atmosphere of protective seclusion.

This level was a virtual maze, as well. No outsider could have navigated his way through the endless number of splitting forks, intersections, and multiple passageways. Even Bruenor, aided by scattered images of his childhood and an understanding of the logic that had guided the dwarven miners who had created the place, chose wrong more often than right, and spent as much time backtracking as going forward.

There was one thing that Bruenor did remember, though. "Ware yer step," he warned his friends. "The level ye walk upon is rigged for defending the halls, and a stoneworked trap'd be quick to send ye below!"

For the first stretch of their march that day, they came into wider chambers, mostly unadorned and roughly squared, and showing no signs of habitation. "Guard rooms and guest rooms," Bruenor explained. "Most for Elmor and his kin from Settlestone when they came to collect the works for market."

They moved deeper. A pressing stillness engulfed them, their footfalls and the occasional crackle of a torch the only sounds, and even these seemed stifled in the stagnant air. To Drizzt and Bruenor, the environment only enhanced their memories of their younger days spent under the surface, but for the other three, the closeness and the realization of tons of stone hanging over their heads was a completely foreign experience, and more than a little uncomfortable.

Drizzt slipped from alcove to alcove, taking extra care to test the floor before stepping in. In one shallow depression, he felt a sensation on his leg, and upon closer inspection found a slight draft flowing in through a crack at the base of the wall. He called his friends over.

Bruenor bent low and scratched his beard, knowing at once what the breeze meant, for the air was warm, not cool as an outside draft would be. He removed a glove and felt the stone. "The furnaces," he muttered, as much to himself as to his friends.

"Then someone is below," Drizzt reasoned.

Bruenor didn't answer. It was a subtle vibration in the floor, but to a dwarf, so attuned to the stone, its message came as clear as if the floor had spoken to him; the grating of sliding blocks far below, the machinery of the mines.

Bruenor looked away and tried to realign his thoughts, for he had nearly convinced himself, and had always hoped, that the mines would be empty of any organized group and easy for the taking. But if the furnaces were burning, those hopes were flown.

✕ ✕ ✕ ✕ ✕

"Go to them. Show them the stair," Dendybar commanded.

Morkai studied the wizard for a long moment. He knew that he could break free of Dendybar's weakening hold and disobey the command. Truly, Morkai was amazed that Dendybar had dared to summon him again so soon, for the wizard's strength had obviously not yet returned. The mottled wizard hadn't yet reached the point of exhaustion, upon which Morkai could strike at him, but Dendybar had indeed lost most of his power to compel the specter.

Morkai decided to obey this command. He wanted to keep this game with Dendybar going for as long as possible. Dendybar was obsessed with finding the drow, and would undoubtedly call upon Morkai another time soon. Perhaps then the mottled wizard would be weaker still.

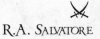
⚔ ⚔ ⚔ ⚔ ⚔

"And how are we to get down?" Entreri asked Sydney. Bok had led them to the rim of Keeper's Dale, but now they faced the sheer drop.

Sydney looked to Bok for the answer, and the golem promptly started over the edge. Had she not stopped it, it would have dropped off the cliff. The young mage looked at Entreri with a helpless shrug.

They then saw a shimmering blur of fire, and the specter, Morkai, stood before them once again. "Come," he said to them. "I am bid to show you the way."

Without another word, Morkai led them to the secret stair, then faded back into flames and was gone.

"Your master proves to be of much assistance," Entreri remarked as he took the first step down.

Sydney smiled, masking her fears. "Four times, at least," she whispered to herself, figuring the instances when Dendybar had summoned the specter. Each time Morkai had seemed more relaxed in carrying out his appointed mission. Each time Morkai had seemed more powerful. Sydney moved to the stair behind Entreri. She hoped that Dendybar would not call upon the specter again—for all their sakes.

When they had descended to the gorge's floor, Bok led them right to the wall and the secret door. As if realizing the barrier that it faced, it stood patiently out of the way, awaiting further instructions from the mage.

Entreri ran his fingers across the smooth rock, his face close against it as he tried to discern any substantial crack in it.

"You waste your time," Sydney remarked. "The door is dwarven crafted and will not be found by such inspection."

"If there is a door," replied the assassin.

"There is," Sydney assured him. "Bok followed the drow's trail to this spot, and knows that it continues through the wall. There is no way that they could have diverted the golem from the path."

"Then open your door," Entreri sneered. "They move farther from us with each moment!"

Sydney took a steadying breath and rubbed her hands together nervously. This was the first time since she had left the Hosttower that she had found opportunity to use her magical powers, and the extra spell energy tingled within her, seeking release.

She moved through a string of distinct and precise gestures, mumbled several lines of arcane words, then commanded, *"Bausin saumine!"* and threw her hands out in front of her, toward the door.

Entreri's belt immediately unhitched, dropping his saber and dagger to the ground.

"Well done," he remarked sarcastically, retrieving his weapons.

Sydney looked at the door, perplexed. "It resisted my spell," she said, observing the obvious. "Not unexpected from a door of dwarven crafting. The dwarves use little magic themselves, but their ability to resist the spell-castings of others is considerable."

"Where do we turn?" hissed Entreri, "There is another entrance, perhaps?"

"This is our door," Sydney insisted. She turned to Bok and snarled, "Break it down!" Entreri jumped far aside when the golem moved to the wall.

Its great hands pounding like battering rams, Bok slammed the wall, again and again, heedless of the damage to its own flesh. For many seconds, nothing happened, just the dull thud of the fists punching the stone.

Sydney was patient. She silenced Entreri's attempt to argue their course and watched the relentless golem at work. A crack appeared in the stone, and then another. Bok knew no weariness; its tempo did not slow.

More cracks showed, then the clear outline of the door. Entreri squinted his eyes in anticipation.

With one final punch, Bok drove its hand through the door, splitting it asunder and reducing it to a pile of rubble.

For the second time that day, the second time in nearly two hundred years, the entry chamber of Mithral Hall was bathed in daylight.

"What was that?" Regis whispered after the echoes of the banging had finally ended.

Drizzt could guess easily enough, though with the sound bouncing at them from the bare rock walls in every direction, it was impossible to discern the direction of its source.

Catti-brie had her suspicions, too, remembering well the broken wall in Silverymoon.

None of them said anything more about it. In their situation of ever-present danger, echoes of a potential threat in the distance did not spur them to action. They continued on as though they had heard nothing, except that they walked even more cautiously, and the drow kept himself more to the rear of the party.

Somewhere in the back of his mind, Bruenor sensed danger huddling in around them, watching them, poised to strike. He could not be certain if his fears were justified, or if they were merely a reaction to his knowledge that the mines were occupied and to his rekindled memories of the horrible day when his clan had been driven out.

He forged ahead, for this was his homeland, and he would not surrender it again.

At a jagged section of the passageway, the shadows lengthened into a deeper, shifting gloom.

One of them reached out and grabbed Wulfgar.

A sting of deathly chill shivered into the barbarian. Behind him, Regis screamed, and suddenly moving blots of darkness danced all around the four.

Wulfgar, too stunned to react, was hit again. Catti-brie charged to his side, striking into the blackness with the short sword she had picked up in the entry hall. She felt a slight bite as the blade knifed through the darkness, as though she had hit something that was somehow not completely there. She had no time to ponder the nature of her weird foe, and she kept flailing away.

Across the corridor, Bruenor's attacks were even more desperate. Several black arms stretched out to strike the dwarf at once, and his furious parries could not connect solidly enough to push them away. Again and again he felt the stinging coldness as the darkness grasped him.

Wulfgar's first instinct when he had recovered was to strike with Aegis-fang, but recognizing this, Catti-brie stopped him with a yell. "The torch!" she cried. "Put the light into the darkness!"

Wulfgar thrust the flame into the shadows' midst. Dark shapes recoiled at once, slipping away from the revealing brightness. Wulfgar moved to pursue and drive them even farther away, but he tripped over the halfling, who was huddled in fear, and fell to the stone.

Catti-brie scooped up the torch and waved it wildly to keep the monsters at bay.

Drizzt knew these monsters. Such things were commonplace in the realms of the drow, sometimes even allied with his people. Calling again on the powers of his heritage, he conjured magical flames to outline the dark shapes, then charged in to join the fight.

The monsters appeared humanoid, as the shadows of men might appear, though their boundaries constantly shifted and melded with the gloom about them. They outnumbered the companions, but their greatest ally, the concealment of darkness, had been stolen by the drow's flames. Without the disguise, the living shadows had little defense against the party's attacks and they quickly slipped away through nearby cracks in the stone.

The companions wasted no more time in the area either. Wulfgar hoisted Regis from the ground and followed Bruenor and Catti-brie as they sped down the passageway, Drizzt lingering behind to cover their retreat.

They had put many turns and halls behind them before Bruenor dared to slow the pace. Disturbing questions again hovered about the dwarf's thoughts, concerns about his entire fantasy of reclaiming Mithral Hall, and even about the wisdom in bringing his dearest friends into the place. He looked at every shadow with dread now, expecting a monster at each turn.

Even more subtle was the emotional shift that the dwarf had experienced. It had been festering within his subconscious since he had felt the vibrations on the floor, and now the fight with the monsters of darkness had pushed it to completion. Bruenor accepted the fact that he no longer felt as though he had returned home, despite his earlier boastings. His memories of the place, good memories of the prosperity of his people in the early days, seemed far removed from the dreadful aura that surrounded the fortress now. So much had been despoiled, not the least of which were the shadows of the ever-burning torches. Once representative of his god, Dumathoin, the Keeper of Secrets, the shadows now merely sheltered the denizens of darkness.

All of Bruenor's companions sensed the disappointment and frustration that he felt. Wulfgar and Drizzt, expecting as much before they had ever entered the place, understood better than the others and were now even more concerned. If, like the crafting of Aegis-fang, the return to Mithral Hall represented a pinnacle in Bruenor's life—and they had worried about his reaction assuming the success of their quest—how crushing would be the blow if the journey proved disastrous?

Bruenor pushed onward, his vision narrowed upon the path to Garumn's Gorge and the exit. On the road these long tendays, and when he had first entered the halls, the dwarf had every intention of staying until he had taken back all that was rightfully his, but now all of his senses cried to him to flee the place and not return.

He felt that he must at least cross the top level, out of respect for his long dead kin, and for his friends, who had risked so much in accompanying him this far. And he hoped that the revulsion he felt for his former home would pass, or at least that he might find some glimmer of light in the dark shroud that encompassed the halls. Feeling the axe and shield of his heroic namesake warm in his grasp, he steeled his bearded chin and moved on.

The passageway sloped down, with fewer halls and side corridors. Hot drafts rose up all through this section, a constant torment to the dwarf, reminding him of what lay below. The shadows were less imposing here, though, for the walls were carved smoother and squared. Around a sharp turn, they came to a great stone door, its singular slab blocking the entire corridor.

"A chamber?" Wulfgar asked, grasping the heavy pull ring.

Bruenor shook his head, not certain of what lay beyond. Wulfgar pulled the door open, revealing another empty stretch of corridor that ended in a similarly unmarked door.

"Ten doors," Bruenor remarked, remembering the place again. "Ten doors on the down slope," he explained. "Each with a locking bar behind it." He reached inside the portal and pulled down a heavy metal rod, hinged on one end so that it could be easily dropped across the locking latches on the door. "And beyond the ten, ten more going up, and each with a bar on th' other side."

"So if ye fled a foe, either way, ye'd lock the doors behind ye," reasoned Catti-brie. "Meeting in the middle with yer kin from the other side."

"And between the center doors, a passage to the lower levels," added Drizzt, seeing the simple but effective logic behind the defensive structure.

"The floor's holding a trap door," Bruenor confirmed.

"A place to rest, perhaps," said the drow.

Bruenor nodded and started on again. His recollections proved accurate, and a few minutes later, they passed through the tenth door and into a small, oval-shaped room, facing a door with the locking bar on their side. In the very center of the room was a trap door, closed for many years, it seemed, and also with a bar to lock it shut. All along the room's perimeter loomed the familiar darkened alcoves.

After a quick search to ensure that the room was safe, they secured the exits and began stripping away some of their heavy gear, for the heat had become oppressive and the stuffiness of the unmoving air weighed in upon them.

"We have come to the center of the top level," Bruenor said absently. "Tomorrow we're to be finding the gorge."

"Then where?" Wulfgar asked, the adventurous spirit within him still hoping for a deeper plunge into the mines.

"Out, or down," Drizzt answered, emphasizing the first choice enough to make the barbarian understand that the second was unlikely. "We shall know when we arrive."

Wulfgar studied his dark friend for some hint of the adventurous spirit he had come to know, but Drizzt seemed nearly as resigned to leaving as Bruenor. Something about this place had diffused the drow's normally unstoppable verve. Wulfgar could only guess that Drizzt, too, battled unpleasant memories of his past in a similarly dark place.

The perceptive young barbarian was correct. The drow's memories of his life in the underworld had indeed fostered his hopes that they might soon leave Mithral Hall, but not because of any emotional upheaval he was experiencing upon his return to his childhood realm. What Drizzt now remembered keenly about Menzoberranzan were the dark things that lived in dark holes under the earth. He felt their presence here in the ancient dwarven halls, horrors beyond the surface dwellers' imagination. He didn't worry for himself. With his drow heritage, he could face these monsters on their own terms. But his friends, except perhaps the experienced dwarf, would be at a sorry disadvantage in such fighting, ill-equipped to battle the monsters they would surely face if they remained in the mines.

And Drizzt knew that eyes were upon them.

⚔ ⚔ ⚔ ⚔

Entreri crept up and put his ear against the door, as he had nine times before. This time, the clang of a shield being dropped to the stone brought a smile to his face. He turned back to Sydney and Bok and nodded.

He had at last caught his prey.

⚔ ⚔ ⚔ ⚔

The door they had entered shuddered from the weight of an incredible blow. The companions, just settled in after their long march, looked back in amazement and horror just as the second blow fell and the heavy stone splintered and broke away. The golem crashed into the oval room, kicking Regis and Catti-brie aside before they could even reach for their weapons.

The monster could have squashed both of them right there, but its target, the goal that pulled at all of its senses, was Drizzt Do'Urden. It rushed by the two into the middle of the room to locate the drow.

Drizzt hadn't been so surprised, slipping into the shadows on the side of the room and now making his way toward the broken door to secure it against further entry. He couldn't hide from the magical detections that Dendybar had bestowed upon the golem, though, and Bok turned toward him almost immediately.

Wulfgar and Bruenor met the monster head on.

Entreri entered the chamber right after Bok, using the commotion caused by the golem to slip unnoticed through the door and off into the shadows in a manner strikingly similar to the drow. As they approached the midpoint of the oval room's wall, each was met by a shadow so akin to his own that he had to stop and take measure of it before he engaged.

"So at last I meet Drizzt Do'Urden," Entreri hissed.

"The advantage is yours," replied Drizzt, "for I know naught of you."

"Ah, but you will, black elf!" the assassin said, laughing. In a blur, they came together, Entreri's cruel saber and jeweled dagger matching the speed of Drizzt's whirring scimitars.

Wulfgar pounded his hammer into the golem with all his might, the monster, distracted by its pursuit of the drow, not even raising a pretense of defense. Aegis-fang knocked it back, but it seemed not to notice, and started again toward its prey. Bruenor and Wulfgar looked at each other in disbelief and drove in on it again, hammer and axe flailing.

Regis lay unmoving against the wall, stunned by the kick of Bok's heavy foot. Catti-brie, though, was back up on one knee, her sword in hand. The spectacle of grace and skill of the combatants along the wall held her in check for a moment.

Sydney, just outside the doorway, was likewise distracted, for the battle between the dark elf and Entreri was unlike anything she had ever seen, two master swordsmen weaving and parrying in absolute harmony.

Each anticipated the other's movements exactly, countering the other's counter, back and forth in a battle that seemed as though it could know no victor. One appeared the reflection of the other, and the only thing that kept the onlookers aware of the reality of the struggle was the constant clang of steel against steel as scimitar and saber came ringing together. They moved in and out of the shadows, seeking some small advantage in a fight of equals. Then they slipped into the darkness of one of the alcoves.

As soon as they disappeared from sight, Sydney remembered her part in the battle. Without further delay, she drew a thin wand from her belt and took aim on the barbarian and the dwarf. As much as she would have liked to see the battle between Entreri and the dark elf played out to its end, her duty told her to free up the golem and let it take the drow quickly.

Wulfgar and Bruenor dropped Bok to the stone, Bruenor ducking between the monster's legs while Wulfgar slammed his hammer home, toppling Bok over the dwarf.

Their advantage was short lived. Sydney's bolt of energy sliced into them, its force hurling Wulfgar backward into the air. He rolled to his feet near the opposite door, his leather jerkin scorched and smoking, and his entire body tingling in the aftermath of the jolt.

Bruenor was slammed straight down to the floor and he lay there for a long moment. He wasn't too hurt—dwarves are as tough as mountain-stone and especially resistant to magic—but a specific rumble that he heard while his ear was against the floor demanded his attention. He remembered that sound vaguely from his childhood, but couldn't pinpoint its exact source.

He did know, though, that it foretold doom.

The tremor grew around them, shaking the chamber, even as Bruenor lifted his head. The dwarf understood. He looked helplessly to Drizzt and yelled, "Ware elf!" the second before the trap sprang and part of the alcove's floor fell away.

Only dust emerged from where the drow and the assassin had been. Time seemed to freeze for Bruenor, who was fixated upon that one horrible moment. A heavy block dropped from the ceiling in the alcove, stealing the very last of the dwarf's futile hopes.

The execution of the stonework trap only multiplied the violent tremors in the chamber. Walls cracked apart, chunks of stone shook loose from the ceiling. From one doorway, Sydney cried for Bok, while at the other, Wulfgar threw the locking bar aside and yelled for his friends.

Catti-brie leaped to her feet and rushed to the fallen halfling. She dragged him by the ankles toward the far door, calling for Bruenor to help.

But the dwarf was lost in the moment, staring vacantly at the ruins of the alcove.

A wide crack split the floor of the chamber, threatening to cut off their escape. Catti-brie gritted her teeth in determination and charged ahead, making the safety of the hallway. Wulfgar screamed for the dwarf, and even started back for him.

Then Bruenor rose and moved toward them—slowly, his head down, almost hoping in his despair that a crack would open beneath him and drop him into a dark hole.

And put an end to his intolerable grief.

20
END OF A DREAM

When the last tremors of the cave-in had finally died away, the four remaining friends picked their way through the rubble and the veil of dust back to the oval chamber. Heedless of the piles of broken stone and the great cracks in the floor that threatened to swallow them up, Bruenor scrambled into the alcove, the others close on his heels.

No blood or any other sign of the two master swordsmen was anywhere to be found, just the mound of rubble covering the hole of the stonework trap. Bruenor could see the edgings of darkness beneath the pile, and he called out to Drizzt. His reason told him, against his heart and hopes, that the drow could not hear, that the trap had taken Drizzt from him.

The tear that rimmed his eye dropped to his cheek when he spotted the lone scimitar, the magical blade that Drizzt had plundered from a dragon's lair, resting against the ruins of the alcove. Solemnly, he picked it up and slid it into his belt.

"Alas for ye, elf," he cried into the destruction. "Ye deserved a better end." If the others had not been so caught up in their own reflections at that moment, they would have noticed the angry undertone to Bruenor's mourning. In the face of the loss of his dearest and most trusted friend, and already questioning the wisdom of continuing through the halls before the tragedy, Bruenor found his grief muddled with even stronger feelings of guilt. He could not escape the part he had played in bringing about the dark elf's fall. He remembered bitterly how he had tricked Drizzt into joining the quest, feigning his own death and promising an adventure the likes of which none of them had ever seen.

He stood now, quietly, and accepted his inner torment.

Wulfgar's grief was equally deep, and uncomplicated by other feelings. The barbarian had lost one of his mentors, the warrior who had transformed him from a savage, brutish warrior to a calculating and cunning fighter.

He had lost one of his truest friends. He would have followed Drizzt to the bowels of the Abyss in search of adventure. He firmly believed that the drow would one day get them into a predicament from which they could not escape, but when he was fighting beside Drizzt, or competing against his teacher, the master, he felt alive, existing on the very dangerous edge of his limits. Often Wulfgar had envisioned his own death beside the drow, a glorious finish that the bards would write and sing about long after the enemies who had slain the two friends had turned to dust in unmarked graves.

That was an end the young barbarian did not fear.

"Ye've found yer peace now, me friend," Catti-brie said softly, understanding the drow's tormented existence better than anyone. Catti-brie's perceptions of the world were more attuned to Drizzt's sensitive side, the private aspect of his character that his other friends could not see beneath his stoic features. It was the part of Drizzt Do'Urden that had demanded he leave Menzoberranzan and his evil race, and had forced him into a role as an outcast. Catti-brie knew the joy of the drow's spirit, and the unavoidable pain he had suffered at the snubbings of those who could not see that spirit for the color of his skin.

She realized, too, that both the causes of good and evil had lost a champion this day, for in Entreri Catti-brie saw the mirror-image of Drizzt. The world would be better for the loss of the assassin.

But the price was too high.

Any relief that Regis might have felt at the demise of Entreri was lost in the swirling mire of his anger and sorrow. A part of the halfling had died in that alcove. No longer would he have to run—Pasha Pook would pursue him no more—but for the first time in his entire life Regis had to accept some consequences for his actions, He had joined up with Bruenor's party knowing that Entreri would be close behind, and understanding the potential danger to his friends.

Ever the confident gambler, the thought of losing this challenge had never entered his head. Life was a game that he played hard and to the edge, and never before had he been expected to pay for his risks. If anything in the world could temper the halfling's obsession with chance, it was this, the loss of one of his few true friends because of a risk he had chosen to take.

"Farewell, my friend," he whispered into the rubble. Turning to Bruenor, he then said, "Where do we go? How do we get out of this terrible place?"

Regis hadn't meant the remark as an accusation, but forced into a defensive posture by the mire of his own guilt, Bruenor took it as such and struck back. "Ye did it yerself!" he snarled at Regis. "Ye bringed the killer after us!" Bruenor took a threatening step forward, his face contorted by mounting rage and his hands whitened by the intensity of their clench.

Wulfgar, confused by this sudden pulse of anger, moved a step closer to Regis. The halfling did not back away, but made no move to defend himself, still not believing that Bruenor's anger could be so consuming.

"Ye thief!" Bruenor roared. "Ye go along picking yer way with no concern for what yer leaving behind—and yer friends pay for it!" His anger swelled with each word, again almost a separate entity from the dwarf, gaining its own momentum and strength.

His next step would have brought him right up to Regis, and his motion showed them all clearly, that he meant to strike, but Wulfgar stepped between the two and halted Bruenor with an unmistakable glare.

Broken from his angry trance by the barbarian's stern posture, Bruenor realized then what he was about to do. More than a little embarrassed, he covered his anger beneath his concern for their immediate survival and turned away to survey the remains of the room. Few, if any, of their supplies had survived the destruction. "Leave the stuff; no time for wasting!" Bruenor told the others, clearing the choked growls from his throat. "We're to be putting this foul place far behind us!"

Wulfgar and Catti-brie scanned the rubble, searching for something that could be salvaged and not so ready to agree with Bruenor's demands that they press on without any supplies. They quickly came to the same conclusion as the dwarf, though, and with a final salute to the ruins of the alcove, they followed Bruenor back into the corridor.

"I'm meaning to make Garumn's Gorge afore the next rest," Bruenor exclaimed. "So ready yerselves for a long walk."

"And then where?" Wulfgar asked, guessing, but not liking, the answer.

"Out!" Bruenor roared. "Quick as we can!" He glared at the barbarian, daring him to argue.

"To return with the rest of your kin beside us?" Wulfgar pressed.

"Not to return," said Bruenor. "Never to return!"

"Then Drizzt has died in vain!" Wulfgar stated bluntly. "He sacrificed his life for a vision that will never be fulfilled."

Bruenor paused to steady himself in the face of Wulfgar's sharp perception. He hadn't looked at the tragedy in that cynical light, and he didn't like the implications. "Not for nothing!" he growled at the barbarian. "A warning it is to us all to be gone from the place. Evil's here, thick as orcs on mutton! Don't ye smell it, boy? Don't yer eyes and nose tell ye to be gone from here?"

"My eyes tell me of the danger," Wulfgar replied evenly. "As often they have before. But I am a warrior and pay little heed to such warnings!"

"Then ye're sure to be a dead warrior," Catti-brie put in.

Wulfgar glared at her. "Drizzt came to help take back Mithral Hall, and I shall see the deed done!"

"Ye'll die trying," muttered Bruenor, the anger off his voice now. "We came to find me home, boy, but this is not the place. Me people once lived, here, 'tis true, but the darkness that creeped into Mithral Hall has put an end to me claim on it. I've no wish to return once I'm clear of the stench of the place, know that in yer stubborn head. It's for the shadows now, and the gray ones, and may the whole stinkin' place fall in on their stinkin' heads!"

Bruenor had said enough. He turned abruptly on his heel and stamped off down the corridor, his heavy boots pounding into the stone with uncompromising determination.

Regis and Catti-brie followed closely, and Wulfgar, after a moment to consider the dwarf's resolve, trotted to catch up with them.

⨯ ⨯ ⨯ ⨯ ⨯

Sydney and Bok returned to the oval chamber as soon as the mage was certain the companions had left. Like the friends before her, she made her way to the ruined alcove and stood for a moment reflecting on the effect this sudden turn of events would have on her mission. She was amazed at the depth of her sorrow for the loss of Entreri, for though she didn't fully trust the assassin and suspected that he might actually be searching for the same powerful artifact she and Dendybar sought, she had come to respect him. Could there have been a better ally when the fighting started?

Sydney didn't have a lot of time to mourn for Entreri, for the loss of Drizzt Do'Urden conjured more immediate concerns for her own safety. Dendybar wasn't likely to take the news lightly, and the mottled wizard's talent at punishment was widely acknowledged in the Hosttower of the Arcane.

Bok waited for a moment, expecting some command from the mage, but when none was forthcoming, the golem stepped into the alcove and began removing the mound of rubble.

"Stop," Sydney ordered.

Bok kept on with its chore, driven by its directive to continue its pursuit of the drow.

"Stop!" Sydney said again, this time with more conviction. "The drow is dead, you stupid thing!" The blunt statement forced her own acceptance of the fact and set her thoughts into motion. Bok did stop and turn to her, and she waited a moment to sort out the best course of action.

"We will go after the others," she said offhandedly, as much trying to enlighten her own thoughts with the statement as to redirect the golem. "Yes, perhaps if we deliver the dwarf and the other companions to Dendybar he will forgive our stupidity in allowing the drow to die."

She looked to the golem, but of course its expression had not changed to offer any encouragement.

"It should have been you in the alcove," Sydney muttered, her sarcasm wasted on the thing. "Entreri could at least offer some suggestions. But no matter, I have decided. We shall follow the others and find the time when we might take them. They will tell us what we need to know about the Crystal Shard!"

Bok remained motionless, awaiting her signal. Even with its most basic of thought patterns, the golem understood that Sydney best knew how they could complete their mission.

⚔ ⚔ ⚔ ⚔ ⚔

The companions moved through huge caverns, more natural formations than dwarf-carved stone. High ceilings and walls stretched out into the blackness, beyond the glow of the torches, leaving the friends dreadfully aware of their vulnerability. They kept close together as they marched, imagining a host of gray dwarves watching them from the unlit reaches of the caverns, or expecting some horrid creature to swoop down upon them from the darkness above.

The ever-present sound of dripping water paced them with its rhythm, its "plip, plop" echoing through every hall, accentuating the emptiness of the place.

Bruenor remembered this section of the complex well, and found himself once again deluged by long-forgotten images of his past. These were the Halls of Gathering, where all of Clan Battlehammer would come together to hear the words of King Garumn, or to meet with important visitors. Battle plans were laid here, and strategies set for commerce with the outside world. Even the youngest dwarves were present at the meetings, and Bruenor recalled fondly the many times he had sat beside his father, Bangor, behind his grandfather, King Garumn, with Bangor pointing out the king's techniques for capturing the audience, and instructing the young Bruenor in the arts of leadership that he would one day need.

The day he became King of Mithral Hall.

The solitude of the caverns weighed heavily on the dwarf, who had heard them ring out in the common cheering and chanting of ten thousand dwarves. Even if he were to return with all of the remaining members of the clan, they would fill only a tiny corner of one chamber.

"Too many gone," Bruenor said into the emptiness, his soft whisper louder than he had intended in the echoing stillness. Catti-brie and Wulfgar, concerned for the dwarf and scrutinizing his every action, noted the remark and could easily enough guess the memories and emotions that had prompted it. They looked to each other and Catti-brie could see that the edge of Wulfgar's anger at the dwarf had dissipated in a rush of sympathy.

Hall after great hall loomed up with only short corridors connecting them. Turns and side exits broke off every few feet, but Bruenor felt confident that he knew the way to the gorge. He knew, too, that anyone below would have heard the crashing of the stonework trap and would be coming to investigate. This section of the upper level, unlike the areas they had left behind, had many connecting passages to the lower levels. Wulfgar doused the torch and Bruenor led them on under the protective dimness of the gloom.

Their caution soon proved prudent, for as they entered yet another immense cavern, Regis grabbed Bruenor by the shoulder, stopping him, and motioned for all of them to be silent. Bruenor almost burst out in rage, but saw at once the sincere look of dread on Regis's face.

His hearing sharpened by years of listening for the click of a lock's tumblers, the halfling had picked out a sound in the distance other than the dripping of water. A moment later, the others caught it, too, and soon they identified it as the marching steps of many booted feet. Bruenor took them into a dark recess where they watched and waited.

They never saw the passing host clearly enough to count its numbers or identify its members, but they could tell by the number of torches crossing the far end of the cavern that they were outnumbered by at least ten to one, and they could guess the nature of the marchers.

"Gray ones, or me mother's a friend of orcs," Bruenor grumbled. He looked at Wulfgar to see if the barbarian had any further complaints about his decision to leave Mithral Hall.

Wulfgar accepted the stare with a conceding nod. "How far to Garumn's Gorge?" he asked, fast becoming as resigned to leaving as the others. He still felt as though he was deserting Drizzt, but he understood the wisdom of Bruenor's choice. It grew obvious now that if they remained, Drizzt Do'Urden would not be the only one of them to die in Mithral Hall.

"An hour to the last passage," Bruenor answered. "Another hour, no more, from there."

The host of gray dwarves soon cleared the cavern and the companions started off again, using even more caution and dreading each shuffling footfall that thumped the floor harder than intended.

His memories coming clearer with each passing step, Bruenor knew exactly where they were, and made for the most direct path to the gorge, meaning to be out of the halls as quickly as possible. After many minutes of walking, though, he came across a side passage that he simply could not pass by. Every delay was a risk, he knew, but the temptation emanating from the room at the end of this short corridor was too great for him to ignore. He had to discover how far the despoilment of Mithral Hall had gone; he had to learn if the most treasured room of the upper level had survived.

The friends followed him without question and soon found themselves standing before a tall, ornate metal door inscribed with the hammer of Moradin, the greatest of the dwarven gods, and a series of runes beneath it. Bruenor's heavy breathing belied his calmness.

"Herein lie the gifts of our friends," Bruenor read solemnly, "and the craftings of our kin. Know ye as ye enter this hallowed hall that ye look upon the heritage of Clan Battlehammer. Friends be welcome, thieves beware!" Bruenor turned to his companions, beads of nervous sweat on his brow. "The Hall of Dumathoin," he explained.

"Two hundred years of your enemies in the halls," Wulfgar reasoned. "Surely it has been pillaged."

"Not so," said Bruenor. "The door is magicked and would not open for enemies of the clan. A hundred traps are inside to take the skin from a gray one who was to get through!" He glared at Regis, his gray eyes narrowed in a stern warning. "Watch to yer own hands, Rumblebelly. Mighten be that a trap won't know ye to be a friendly thief!"

The advice seemed sound enough for Regis to ignore the dwarf's biting sarcasm. Unconsciously admitting the truth of Bruenor's words, the halfling slipped his hands into his pockets.

"Fetch a torch from the wall," Bruenor told Wulfgar. "Me thoughts tell me that no lights burn within."

Before Wulfgar even returned to them, Bruenor began opening the huge door. It swung easily under the push of the hands of a friend, swinging wide into a short corridor that ended in a heavy black curtain. A pendulum blade hung ominously in the center of the passage, a pile of bones beneath it.

"Thieving dog," Bruenor chuckled with grim satisfaction. He stepped by the blade and moved to the curtain, waiting for all of his friends to join him before he entered the chamber.

Bruenor paused, mustering the courage to open the last barrier to the hall, sweat glistening on all the friends' faces now as the dwarf's anxiety swept through them.

With a determined grunt, Bruenor pulled the curtain aside. "Behold the Hall of Duma—" he began, but the words stuck in his throat as soon as he looked beyond the opening. Of all the destruction they had witnessed in the halls, none was more complete than this. Mounds of stone littered the floor. Pedestals that had once held the finest works of the clan lay broken apart, and others had been trampled into dust.

Bruenor stumbled in blindly, his hands shaking and a great scream of outrage lumped in his throat. He knew before he even looked upon the entirety of the chamber that the destruction was complete.

"How?" Bruenor gasped. Even as he asked, though, he saw the huge hole in the wall. Not a tunnel carved around the blocking door, but a gash in the stone, as though some incredible ram had blasted through.

"What power could have done such a thing?" Wulfgar asked, following the line of the dwarf's stare to the hole.

Bruenor moved over, searching for some clue, Catti-brie and Wulfgar with him. Regis headed the other way, just to see if anything of value remained.

Catti-brie caught a rainbowlike glitter on the floor and moved to what she thought was a puddle of some dark liquid. Bending close, though, she realized that it wasn't liquid at all, but a scale, blacker than the blackest night and nearly the size of a man. Wulfgar and Bruenor rushed to her side at the sound of her gasp.

"Dragon!" Wulfgar blurted, recognizing the distinctive shape. He grasped the thing by its edge and hoisted it upright to better inspect it. Then he and Catti-brie turned to Bruenor to see if he had any knowledge of such a monster.

The dwarf's wide-eyed, terror-stricken stare answered their question before it was asked.

"Blacker than the black," Bruenor whispered, speaking again the most common words of that fateful day those two hundred years ago. "Me father told me of the thing," he explained to Wulfgar and Catti-brie. "A demon-spawned dragon, he called it, a darkness blacker than the black. 'Twas not the gray ones that routed us—we would've fought them head on to the last. The dragon of darkness took our numbers and drove us from the halls. Not one in ten remained to stand against its foul hordes in the smaller halls at th' other end."

A hot draft of air from the hole reminded them that it probably connected to the lower halls, and the dragon's lair.

"Let's be leaving," Catti-brie suggested, "afore the beast gets a notion that we're here."

Regis then cried out from the other side of the chamber. The friends rushed to him, not knowing if he had stumbled upon treasure or danger.

They found him crouched beside a pile of stone, peering into a gap in the blocks.

He held up a silver-shafted arrow. "I found it in there," he explained. "And there's something more—a bow, I think."

Wulfgar moved the torch closer to the gap and they all saw clearly the curving arc that could only be the wood of a longbow, and the silvery shine of a bowstring. Wulfgar grasped the wood and tugged lightly, expecting it to break apart in his hands under the enormous weight of the stone.

But it held firmly, even against a pull of all his strength. He looked around at the stones, seeking the best course to free the weapon.

Regis, meanwhile, had found something more, a golden plaque wedged in another crack in the pile. He managed to slip it free and brought it into the torchlight to read its carved runes.

" 'Taulmaril the Heartseeker,' " he read. " 'Gift of—' "

"Anariel, Sister of Faerun," Bruenor finished without even looking at the plaque. He nodded in recognition to Catti-brie's questioning glance.

"Free the bow, boy," he told Wulfgar. "Suren it might be put to a better use than this."

Wulfgar had already discerned the structure of the pile and started lifting away specific blocks at once. Soon Catti-brie was able to wiggle the longbow free, but she saw something else beyond its nook in the pile and asked Wulfgar to keep digging.

While the muscled barbarian pushed aside more stones, the others marveled at the beauty of the bow. Its wood hadn't even been scratched by the stones and the deep finish of its polish returned with a single brush of the hand. Catti-brie strung it easily and held it up, feeling its solid and even draw.

"Test it," Regis offered, handing her the silver arrow.

Catti-brie couldn't resist. She fitted the arrow to the silvery string and drew it back, meaning only to try its fit and not intending to fire.

"A quiver!" Wulfgar called, lifting the last of the stones. "And more of the silver arrows."

Bruenor pointed into the blackness and nodded. Catti-brie didn't hesitate.

A streaking tail of silver followed the whistling missile as it soared into the darkness, ending its flight abruptly with a crack. They all rushed after it, sensing something beyond the ordinary. They found the arrow easily, for it was buried halfway to its fletches in the wall!

All about its point of entry, the stone had been scorched, and even tugging with all of his might, Wulfgar couldn't budge the arrow an inch.

"Not to fret," said Regis, counting the arrows in the quiver that Wulfgar held. "There are nineteen . . . twenty more!" He backed away, stunned. The others looked at him in confusion.

"Nineteen, there were," Regis explained. "My count was true."

Wulfgar, not understanding, quickly counted the arrows. "'Twenty," he said.

"Twenty now," Regis answered. "But nineteen when I first counted."

"So the quiver holds some magic, too," Catti-brie surmised. "A mighty gift, indeed, the Lady Anariel gave to the clan!"

"What more might we find in the ruins of this place?" Regis asked, rubbing his hands together.

"No more," Bruenor answered gruffly. "We're for leaving, and not a word of arguin' from ye!"

Regis knew with a look at the other two that he had no support against the dwarf, so he shrugged helplessly and followed them back through the curtain and into the corridor.

"The gorge!" Bruenor declared, starting them off again.

✕ ✕ ✕ ✕ ✕

"Hold, Bok," Sydney whispered when the companions' torchlight re-entered the corridor a short distance ahead of them.

"Not yet," she said, an anticipating smile widening across her dust-streaked face. "We shall find a better time!"

21

SILVER IN THE SHADOWS

S uddenly, he found a focus in the blur of gray haze, something tangible amid the swirl of nothingness. It hovered before him and turned over slowly.

Its edges doubled and rolled apart, then rushed together again. He fought the dull ache in his head, the inner blackness that had consumed him and now fought to keep him in its hold. Gradually, he became aware of his arms and legs, who he was, and how he had come to be here.

In his startled awareness, the image sharpened to a crystalline focus. The tip of a jeweled dagger.

Entreri loomed above him, a dark silhouette against the backdrop of a single torch set into the wall a few yards beyond, his blade poised to strike at the first sign of resistance. Drizzt could see that the assassin, too, had been hurt in the fall, though he had obviously been the quicker to recover.

"Can you walk?" Entreri asked, and Drizzt was smart enough to know what would happen if he could not.

He nodded and moved to rise, but the dagger shot in closer.

"Not yet," Entreri snarled. "We must first determine where we are, and where we are to go."

Drizzt turned his concentration away from the assassin then and studied their surroundings, confident that Entreri would have already killed him if that was the assassin's intent. They were in the mines, that much was apparent, for the walls were roughly carved stone supported by wooden columns every twenty feet or so.

"How far did we fall?" he asked the assassin, his senses telling him that they were much deeper than the room they had fought in.

Entreri shrugged. "I remember landing on hard stone after a short drop, and then sliding down a steep and twisting chute. It seemed like many moments before we finally dropped in here." He pointed to an opening at the corner of the ceiling, where they had fallen through. "But the flow of time is different for a man thinking he is about to die, and the whole thing may have been over much more quickly than I remember."

"Trust in your first reaction," Drizzt suggested, "for my own perceptions tell me that we have descended a long way indeed."

"How can we get out?"

Drizzt studied the slight grade in the floor and pointed to his right. "The slope is up to that direction," he said.

"Then on your feet," Entreri said, extending a hand to help the drow.

Drizzt accepted the assistance and rose cautiously and without giving any sign of a threat. He knew that Entreri's dagger would cut him open long before he could strike a blow of his own.

Entreri knew it, too, but didn't expect any trouble from Drizzt in their present predicament. They had shared more than an exchange of swordplay up in the alcove, and both looked upon tile other with grudging respect.

"I need your eyes," Entreri explained, though Drizzt had already figured as much. "I have found but one torch, and that will not last long enough to get me out of here. Your eyes, black elf, can find their way in the darkness. I will be close enough to feel your every move, close enough to kill you with a single thrust!" He turned the dagger over again to emphasize his point, but Drizzt understood him well enough without the visual aid.

When he got to his feet, Drizzt found that he wasn't as badly injured as he had feared. He had twisted his ankle and knee on one leg and knew as soon as he put any weight upon it that every step would be painful. He couldn't let on to Entreri, though. He wouldn't be much of an asset to the assassin if he couldn't keep up.

Entreri turned to retrieve the torch and Drizzt took a quick look at his equipment. He had seen one of his scimitars tucked into Entreri's belt, but the other, the magical blade, was nowhere around. He felt one of his daggers still tucked into a hidden sheath in his boot, though he wasn't sure how much it would help him against the saber and dagger of his skilled enemy. Facing Entreri with any kind of a disadvantage was a prospect reserved only for the most desperate situation.

Then, in sudden shock, Drizzt grabbed at his belt pouch, his fear intensifying when he saw that its ties were undone. Even before he had slipped his hand inside, he knew that Guenhwyvar was gone. He looked about frantically, and saw only the fallen rubble.

Noting his distress, Entreri smirked evilly under the cowl of his cloak. "We go," he told the drow.

Drizzt had no choice. He certainly couldn't tell Entreri of the magical statue and take the risk that Guenhwyvar would once again fall into the possession of an evil master. Drizzt had rescued the great panther from that fate once, and would rather that she remained forever buried under the tons of stone than return to an unworthy master's hands. A final mourning glance at the rubble, and he stoically accepted the loss, taking comfort that the cat lived, quite unharmed, on her own plane of existence.

The tunnel supports drifted past them with disturbing regularity, as though they were passing the same spot again and again. Drizzt sensed that the tunnel was arcing around in a wide circle as it slightly climbed. This made him even more nervous. He knew the prowess of dwarves in tunneling, especially where precious gems or metals were concerned, and he began to wonder how many miles they might have to walk before they even reached the next highest level.

Though he had less keen underground perception and was unfamiliar with dwarven ways, Entreri shared the same uneasy feelings. An hour became two and still the line of wooden supports stretched away into the blackness.

"The torch burns low," Entreri said, breaking the silence that had surrounded them since they had started. Even their footfalls, the practiced steps of stealthy warriors, died away in the closeness of the low passage.

"Perhaps the advantage will shift to you, black elf."

Drizzt knew better. Entreri was a creature of the night as much as he, with heightened reflexes and ample experience to more than compensate for his lack of vision in the blackness. Assassins did not work under the light of the midday sun.

Without answering, Drizzt turned back to the path ahead, but as he was looking around, a sudden reflection of the torch caught his eye. He moved to the corridor wall, ignoring Entreri's uneasy shuffle behind him, and started feeling the surface's texture, and peered intently at it in hopes of seeing another flash. It came for just a second as Entreri shifted behind him, a flicker of silver along the wall.

"Where silver rivers run," he muttered in disbelief.

"What?" demanded Entreri.

"Bring the torch," was Drizzt's only reply. He moved his hands eagerly over the wall now, seeking the evidence that would overcome his own stubborn logic and vindicate Bruenor from his suspicions that the dwarf had exaggerated the tales of Mithral Hall.

Entreri was soon beside him, curious. The torch showed it clearly: a stream of silver running along the wall, as thick as Drizzt's forearm and shining brightly in its purity.

"Mithral," Entreri said, gawking. "A king's hoard!"

"But of little use to us," Drizzt said to diffuse their excitement. He started again down the hall, as though the lode of mithral did not impress him. Somehow he felt that Entreri should not look upon this place, that the assassin's mere presence fouled the riches of Clan Battlehammer. Drizzt did not want to give the assassin any reason to seek these halls again. Entreri shrugged and followed.

The grade in the passageway became more apparent as they went along, and the silvery reflections of the mithral veins reappeared with enough regularity to make Drizzt wonder if Bruenor may have even understated the prosperity of his clan.

Entreri, always no more than a step behind the drow, was too intent upon watching his prisoner to take much notice of the precious metal, but he understood well the potential that surrounded him. He didn't care much for such ventures himself, but knew that the information would prove valuable and might serve him well in future bargaining.

Before long the torch died away, but the two found that they could still see, for a dim light source was somewhere up ahead, beyond the turns of the tunnel. Even so, the assassin closed the gap between he and Drizzt, putting the dagger tip against Drizzt's back and taking no chances of losing his only hope of escape if the light faded completely.

The glow only brightened, for its source was great indeed. The air grew warmer around them and soon they heard the grinding of distant machinery echoing down the tunnel. Entreri tightened his reins even further, grasping Drizzt's cloak and pulling himself closer. "You are as much an intruder here as I," he whispered. "Avoidance is ally to both of us."

"Could the miners prove worse than the fate you offer?" Drizzt asked with a sarcastic sigh.

Entreri released the cloak and backed away. "It seems I must offer you something more to ensure your agreement," he said.

Drizzt studied him closely, not knowing what to expect. "Every advantage is yours," he said.

"Not so," replied the assassin. Drizzt stood perplexed as Entreri slid his dagger back into its sheath. "I could kill you, I agree, but to what gain? I take no pleasure in killing."

"But murder does not displease you," Drizzt retorted.

"I do as I must," Entreri said, dismissing the biting comment under a veil of laughter.

Drizzt recognized this man all too well. Passionless and pragmatic, and undeniably skilled in the ways of dealing death. Looking at Entreri, Drizzt saw what he himself might have become if he had remained in Menzoberranzan among his similarly amoral people. Entreri epitomized the tenets of drow society, the selfish heartlessness that had driven Drizzt from the bowels of the world in outrage. He eyed the assassin squarely, detesting every inch of the man, but somehow unable to detach himself from the empathy he felt.

He had to make a stand for his principles now, he decided, just as he had those years ago in the dark city. "You do as you must," he spat in disgust, disregarding the possible consequences. "No matter the cost."

"No matter the cost," Entreri echoed evenly, his self-satisfying smile distorting the insult into a compliment. "Be glad that I am so practical, Drizzt Do'Urden, else you would never have awakened from your fall.

"But enough of this worthless arguing. I have a deal to offer you that might prove of great benefit to us both." Drizzt remained silent and gave no hints to the level of his interest.

"Do you know why I am here?" Entreri asked.

"You have come for the halfling."

"You are in error," replied Entreri. "Not for the halfling, but for the halfling's pendant. He stole it from my master, though I doubt that he would have admitted as much to you."

"I guess more than I am told," Drizzt said, ironically leading into his next suspicion. "Your master seeks vengeance as well, does he not?"

"Perhaps," said Entreri without a pause. "But the return of the pendant is paramount. So I offer this to you: We shall work together to find the road back to your friends. I offer my assistance on the journey and your life in exchange for the pendant. Once we are there, persuade the halfling to surrender it to me and I shall go on my way and not return. My master retrieves his treasure and your little friend lives out the rest of his life without looking over his shoulder."

"On your word?" Drizzt balked.

"On my actions," Entreri retorted. He pulled the scimitar from his belt and tossed it to Drizzt. "I have no intentions of dying in these forsaken mines, drow, nor do you, I would hope."

"How do you know I will go along with my part when we rejoin my companions?" asked Drizzt, holding the blade out before him in inspection, hardly believing the turn of events.

Entreri laughed again. "You are too honorable to put such doubts in my mind, dark elf. You will do as you agree, of that I am certain! A bargain, then?"

Drizzt had to admit the wisdom of Entreri's words. Together, they stood a fair chance of escaping from the lower levels. Drizzt wasn't about to pass up the opportunity to find his friends, not for the price of a pendant that usually got Regis into more trouble than it was worth. "Agreed," he said.

The passageway continued to brighten at each turn, not with flickering light, as with torches, but in a continuous glow. The noise of machinery increased proportionately and the two had to shout to each other to be understood.

Around a final bend, they came to the abrupt end of the mine, its last supports opening into a huge cavern. They moved tentatively through the supports and onto a small ledge that ran along the side of a wide gorge—the great undercity of Clan Battlehammer.

Luckily they were on the top level of the chasm, for both walls had been cut into huge steps right down to the floor, each one holding rows of the decorated doorways that had once marked the entrances to the houses of Bruenor's kin. The steps were mostly empty now, but Drizzt, with the countless tales Bruenor had told to him, could well imagine the past glory of the place. Ten thousand dwarves, untiring in their passion for their beloved work, hammering at the mithral and singing praises to their gods.

What a sight that must have been! Dwarves scrambling from level to level to show off their latest work, a mithral item of incredible beauty and value. And yet, judging from what Drizzt knew of the dwarves in Icewind Dale, even the slightest imperfection would send the artisans scurrying back to their anvils, begging their gods for forgiveness and the gift of skill sufficient to craft a finer piece. No race in all the Realms could claim such pride in their work as the dwarves, and the folk of Clan Battlehammer were particular even by the standards of the bearded people.

Now only the very floor of the chasm bustled in activity, for, hundreds of feet below them and stretching off in either direction, loomed the central forges of Mithral Hall, furnaces hot enough to melt the hard metal from the mined stone. Even at this height Drizzt and Entreri felt the searing heat, and the intensity of the light made them squint. Scores of squat workers darted about, pushing barrows of ore or fuel for the fires. Duergar, Drizzt assumed, though he couldn't see them clearly in the glare from this height.

Just a few feet to the right of the tunnel exit, a wide, gently arching ramp spiraled down to the next lower step. To the left, the ledge moved on along the wall, narrow and not designed for casual passage, but farther down its course, Drizzt could see,the black silhouette of a bridge arching across the chasm.

Entreri motioned him back into the tunnel. "The bridge seems our best route," the assassin said. "But I am wary of moving out across the ledge with so many about."

"We have little choice," Drizzt reasoned. "We could backtrack and search for some of the side corridors that we passed, but I believe them to be no more than extensions of the mine complex and I doubt that they would lead us back even this far."

"We must go on," Entreri agreed. "Perhaps the noise and glare will provide us ample cover." Without further delay, he slipped out onto the ledge and began making his way to the dark outline of the chasm bridge, Drizzt right behind.

Though the ledge was no more than two feet wide at any point and much narrower than that at most, the nimble fighters had no trouble navigating it. Soon they stood before the bridge, a narrow walk of stone arching over the bustle below.

Creeping low, they moved out easily. When they crossed the midpoint and began the descent down the back half of the arch, they saw a wider ledge running along the chasm's other wall. At the end of the bridge loomed a tunnel, torchlit like the ones they had left on the upper level. To the left of the entrance, several small shapes, Duergar, stood huddled in conversation, taking no notice of the area. Entreri looked back at Drizzt with a sneaky smile and pointed to the tunnel.

As silent as cats and invisible in the shadows, they crossed into the tunnel, the group of Duergar oblivious to their passing.

Wooden supports rolled past the two easily now as they took up a swift gait, leaving the undercity far behind. Roughhewn walls gave them plenty of shadowy protection in the torchlight, and as the noise of the workers behind them dimmed to a distant murmur they relaxed a bit and began looking ahead to the prospect of meeting back up with the others.

They turned a bend in the tunnel and nearly ran over a lone Duergar sentry.

"What're yer fer?" the sentry barked, mithral broadsword gleaming with each flicker of the torchlight. His armor, too, chain mail, helm, and shining shield, were of the precious metal, a king's treasure to outfit a single soldier!

Drizzt passed his companion and motioned for Entreri to hold back. He didn't want a trail of bodies to follow their escape route. The assassin understood that the black elf might have some luck in dealing with this other denizen of the underworld. Not wanting to let on that he was human, and possibly hinder the credibility of whatever story Drizzt had concocted, he hitched his cloak up over his face.

The sentry jumped back a step, his eyes wide in amazement when he recognized Drizzt as a drow. Drizzt scowled at him and did not reply.

"Er . . . what might ye be doin' in the mines?" the Duergar asked, rephrasing both his question and tone politely.

"Walking," Drizzt replied coldly, still, feigning anger at the gruff greeting he had initially received.

"And . . . uh . . . who might ye be?" stuttered the guard.

Entreri studied the gray dwarf's obvious terror of Drizzt. It appeared that the drow carried even more fearful respect among the races of the underworld than among the surface dwellers. The assassin made a mental note of this, determined to deal with Drizzt even more cautiously in the future.

"I am Drizzt Do'Urden, of the house of Daermon N'a'shezbaernon, ninth family of the throne to Menzoberranzan," Drizzt said, seeing no reason to lie.

"Greetings!" cried the sentry, overly anxious to gain the favor of the stranger. "Mucknuggle I be, of Clan Bukbukken." He bowed low, his gray beard sweeping the floor. "Not often do we greet guests in the mines. Be it someone ye seek? Or something that I could be helpin, ye with?"

Drizzt thought for a moment. If his friends had survived the cavein, and he had to go on his hopes that they had, they would be making for Garumn's Gorge. "My business here is complete," he told the Duergar. "I am satisfied."

Mucknuggle looked at him curiously. "Satisfied?"

"Your people have delved too deep," Drizzt explained. "You have disturbed one of our tunnels with your digging. Thus we have come to investigate this complex, to ensure that it is not again inhabited by enemies of the drow. I have seen your forges, gray one, you should be proud."

The sentry straightened his belt and sucked in his belly. Clan Bukbukken was indeed proud of its setup, though they had in truth stolen the entire operation from Clan Battlehammer. "And ye're satisfied, ye say. Then where might ye be headin' now, Drizzt Do'Urden? T'see the boss?"

"Who would I seek if I were?"

"Ain't ye not heared o' Shimmergloom?" answered Mucknuggle with a knowing chuckle. "The Drake o' Darkness, he be, black as black and fiercer than a pin-stuck demon! Don't know 'ow he'll take to drow elves in his mines, but we'll be seein'!"

"I think not," replied Drizzt. "I have learned all that I came to learn, and now my trail leads home. I shan't disturb Shimmergloom, nor any of your hospitable clan again."

"Me thinkin's that ye're goin' to the boss," said Mucknuggle, drawing more courage from Drizzt's politeness and from the mention of his mighty leader's name. He folded his gnarly arms across his chest, the mithral sword resting most visibly on the shining shield.

Drizzt resumed his scowl and poked a finger into the fabric under his cloak, pointing in the Duergar's direction. Mucknuggle noted the move, as did Entreri, and the assassin nearly fell back in confusion at the reaction of the Duergar. A noticeable ashen pall came over Mucknuggle's already gray features and he stood perfectly still, not even daring to draw breath.

"My trail leads home," Drizzt said again.

"Home, it do!" cried Mucknuggle. "Mighten I be of some help in findin' the way? The tunnels get rightly mixed up back that way."

Why not? Drizzt thought, figuring their chances would be better if they at least knew the quickest route. "A chasm," he told Mucknuggle. "In the time before Clan Bukbukken, we heard it named as Garumn's Gorge."

"Shimmergloom's Run it is now," Mucknuggle corrected. "The left tunnel at the next fork," he offered, pointing down the hallway. "And a straight run from there."

Drizzt didn't like the sound of the gorge's new name. He wondered what monster his friends might find waiting for them if they reached the gorge. Not wanting to waste any more time, he nodded to Mucknuggle and walked past. The Duergar was all too willing to let him by without further conversation, stepping as far aside as he could.

Entreri looked back at Mucknuggle as they passed and saw him wiping nervous sweat from his brow. "We should have killed him," he told Drizzt when they were safely away. "He will bring his kin after us."

"No faster than a dead body, or a missing sentry would have set off a general alarm," replied Drizzt. "Perhaps a few will come to confirm his tale, but at least we now know the way out. He would not have dared to lie to me, in fear that my inquiry was just a test of the truth of his words. My people have been known to kill for such lies."

"What did you do to him?" Entreri asked.

Drizzt couldn't help but chuckle at the ironic benefits of his people's sinister reputation. He poked the finger under the fabric of his cloak again. "Envision a crossbow small enough to fit into your pocket," he explained. "Would it not make such an impression when pointed at a target? The drow are well known for such crossbows."

"But how deadly could so small a bolt prove against a suit of mithral?" Entreri asked, still not understanding why the threat had been so effective.

"Ah, but the poison," Drizzt smirked, moving away down the corridor.

Entreri stopped and grinned at the obvious logic. How devious and merciless the drow must be to command so powerful a reaction to so simple a threat! It seemed that their deadly reputation was not an exaggeration.

Entreri found that he was beginning to admire these black elves.

The pursuit came faster than they had expected, despite their swift pace. The stamp of boots sounded loudly and then disappeared, only to reappear at the next turn even closer than before. Side-passages, Drizzt and Entreri both understood, cursing every turn in their own twisting tunnel. Finally, when their pursuers were nearly upon them, Drizzt stopped the assassin.

"Just a few," he said, picking out each individual footfall.

"The group from the ledge," Entreri surmised. "Let us make a stand. But be quick, there are more behind them, no doubt!" The excited light that came into the assassin's eyes seemed dreadfully familiar to Drizzt.

He didn't have time to ponder the unpleasant implications. He shook them from his head, regaining full concentration for the business at hand, then pulled the hidden dagger out of his boot—no time for secrets from

Entreri now—and found a shadowed recess on the tunnel wall. Entreri did likewise, positioning himself a few feet farther down from the drow and across the corridor.

Seconds passed slowly with only the faint shuffle of boots. Both companions held their breath and waited patiently, knowing that they had not been passed by.

Suddenly the sound multiplied as the Duergar came rushing out of a secret door and into the main tunnel.

"Can't be far now!" Drizzt and Entreri heard one of them say.

"The drake'll be feedin' us well fer this catch!" hooted another.

All clad in shining mail and wielding mithral weapons, they rounded the last bend and came into sight of the hidden companions.

Drizzt looked at the dull steel of his scimitar and considered how precise his strikes must be against armor of mithral. A resigned sigh escaped him as he wished that he now held his magical weapon.

Entreri saw the problem, too, and knew that they had to somehow balance the odds. Quickly he pulled a pouch of coins from his belt and hurled it farther down the corridor. It sailed through the gloom and clunked into the wall where the tunnel twisted again.

The Duergar band straightened as one. "Just ahead!" one of them cried, and they bent low to the stone and charged for the next bend. Between the waiting drow and assassin.

The shadows exploded into movement and fell over the stunned gray dwarves. Drizzt and Entreri struck together, seizing the moment of best advantage when the first of the band had reached the assassin and the last was passing Drizzt.

The Duergar shrieked in surprised horror. Daggers, saber, and scimitar danced all about them in a flurry of flashing death, poking at the seams of their armor, seeking an opening through the unyielding metal. When they found one, they drove the point home with merciless efficiency.

By the time the Duergar recovered from the initial shock of the attack, two lay dead at the drow's feet, a third at Entreri's, and yet another stumbled away, holding his belly in with a blood-soaked hand.

"Back to back!" Entreri shouted, and Drizzt, thinking the same strategy, had already begun quick-stepping his way through the disorganized dwarves. Entreri took another one down just as they came together, the unfortunate Duergar looking over its shoulder at the approaching drow just long enough for the jeweled dagger to slip through the seam at the base of its helmet.

Then they were together, back against back, twirling in the wake of each other's cloak and maneuvering their weapons in blurred movements so similar that the three remaining Duergar hesitated before their attack to sort out where one enemy ended and the other began.

With cries to Shimmergloom, their godlike ruler, they came on anyway.

Drizzt scored a series of hits at once that should have felled his opponent, but the armor was of tougher stuff than the steel scimitar and his thrusts were turned aside. Entreri, too, had trouble finding an opening to poke through against the mithral mail and shields.

Drizzt turned one shoulder in and let the other fall away from his companion. Entreri understood and followed the drow's lead, dipping around right behind him.

Gradually their circling gained momentum, as synchronous as practiced dancers, and the Duergar did not even try to keep up. Opponents changed continually, the drow and Entreri coming around to parry away the sword or axe that the other had blocked on the last swing. They let the rhythm hold for a few turns, allowed the Duergar to fall into the patterns of their dance, and then, Drizzt still leading, stuttered their steps, and even reversed the flow.

The three Duergar, evenly spaced about the pair, did not know which direction would bring the next attack.

Entreri, practically reading the drow's every thought by this point, saw the possibilities. As he moved away from one particularly confused dwarf, he feigned a reversed attack, freezing the Duergar just long enough for Drizzt, coming in from the other side, to find an opening.

"Take him!" the assassin cried in victory.

The scimitar did its work.

Now they were two against two. They stopped the dance and faced off evenly.

Drizzt swooped about his smaller foe with a sudden leap and shuffle along the wall. The Duergar, intent on the killing blades of the drow, hadn't noticed Drizzt's third weapon join the fray.

The gray dwarf's surprise was only surmounted by his anticipation of the coming fatal blow when Drizzt's trailing cloak floated in and fell over him, enshrouding him in a blackness that would only deepen into the void of death.

Contrary to Drizzt's graceful technique, Entreri worked with sudden fury, tying up his dwarf with undercuts and lightning-fast counters, always aimed at the weapon hand. The gray dwarf understood the tactic as his fingers began to numb under the nicks of several minor hits.

The Duergar overcompensated, turning his shield in to protect the vulnerable hand.

Exactly as Entreri had expected. He rolled around opposite the movement of his opponent, finding the back of the shield, and a seam in the mithral armor just beneath the shoulder. The assassin's dagger drove in furiously, taking a lunge and hurling the Duergar to the stone floor. The gray dwarf lay there, hunched up on one elbow, and gasped out his final breaths.

Drizzt approached the final dwarf, the one who had been wounded in the initial attack, leaning against the wall only a few yards away, torchlight reflecting grotesque red off the pool of blood below him. The dwarf still had fight in him. He raised his broadsword to meet the drow.

It was Mucknuggle, Drizzt saw, and a silent plea of mercy came into the drow's mind and took the fiery glow from his eyes.

A shiny object, glittering in the hues of a dozen distinct gemstones, spun by Drizzt and ended his internal debate.

Entreri's dagger buried deep into Mucknuggle's eye. The dwarf didn't even fall, so clean was the blow. He just held his position, leaning against the stone. But now the blood pool was fed from two wounds.

Drizzt stopped himself cold in rage and did not even flinch as the assassin walked coolly by to retrieve the weapon.

Entreri pulled the dagger out roughly then turned to face Drizzt as Mucknuggle tumbled down to splash in the blood.

"Four to four," the assassin growled. "You did not believe that I would let you get the upper count?"

Drizzt did not reply, nor blink.

Both felt the sweat in their palms as they clutched their weapons, a pull upon them to complete what they had started in the alcove above.

So alike, yet so dramatically different.

The rage at Mucknuggle's death did not play upon Drizzt at that moment, no more than to further confirm his feelings about his vile companion. The longing he held to kill Entreri went far deeper than the anger he might hold for any of the assassin's foul deeds. Killing Entreri would mean killing the darker side of himself, Drizzt believed, for he could have been as this man. This was the test of his worth, a confrontation against what he might have become. If he had remained among his kin, and often were the times that he considered his decision to leave their ways and their dark city a feeble attempt to distort the very order of nature, his own dagger would have found Mucknuggle's eye.

Entreri looked upon Drizzt with equal disdain. What potential he saw in the drow! But tempered by an intolerable weakness. Perhaps in his heart the assassin was actually envious for the capacity for love and compassion that he recognized in Drizzt. So much akin to him, Drizzt only accentuated the reality of his own emotional void.

Even if those feelings were truly within, they would never gain a perch high enough to influence Artemis Entreri. He had spent his life building himself into an instrument for killing, and no shred of light could ever cut through that callous barrier of darkness. He meant to prove, to himself and to the drow, that the true fighter has no place for weakness.

They were closer now, though neither of them knew which one had moved, as if unseen forces were acting upon them. Weapons twitched in anticipation, each waiting for the other to show his hand.

Each wanting the other to be the first to yield to their common desire, the ultimate challenge of the tenets of their existence.

The stamp of booted feet broke the spell.

22

THE DRAGON OF DARKNESS

At the heart of the lower levels, in an immense cavern of uneven and twisting walls pocketed with deep shadows, and a ceiling too high for the light of the brightest fire to find, rested the present ruler of Mithral Hall, perched upon a solid pedestal of the purest mithral that rose from a high and wide mound of coins and jewelry, goblets and weapons, and countless other items pounded from the rough blocks of mithral by the skilled hands of dwarven craftsmen.

Dark shapes surrounded the beast, huge dogs from its own world, obedient, long-lived, and hungry for the meat of human or elf, or anything else that would give them the pleasure of their gory sport before the kill.

Shimmergloom was not now amused. Rumblings from above foretold of intruders, and a band of Duergar spoke of murdered kin in the tunnels and whispered rumors that a drow elf had been seen.

The dragon was not of this world. It had come from the Plane of Shadows, a dark image of the lighted world, unknown to the dwellers here except in the less substantial stuff of their blackest nightmares. Shimmergloom had been of considerable standing there, old even then, and in high regard among its dragon kin that ruled the plane. But when the foolish and greedy dwarves that once inhabited these mines had delved into deep holes of sufficient darkness to open a gate to its plane, the dragon had been quick to come through. Now possessing a treasure tenfold beyond the greatest of its own plane, Shimmergloom had no intentions of returning.

It would deal with the intruders.

For the first time since the routing of Clan Battlehammer, the baying of the shadow hounds filled the tunnels, striking dread even into the hearts of their gray dwarf handlers. The dragon sent them west on their mission, up toward the tunnels around the entry hall in Keeper's Dale, where the companions had first entered the complex. With their powerful maws and incredible stealth, the hounds were indeed a deadly force, but their mission now was not to catch and kill—only to herd.

In the first fight for Mithral Hall, Shimmergloom alone had routed the miners in the lower caverns and in some of the huge chambers on the eastern end of the upper level. But final victory had escaped the dragon, for the end had come in the western corridors, too tight for its scaly bulk.

The beast would not miss the glory again. It set its minions in motion, to drive whoever or whatever had come into the halls toward the only entrance that it had to the upper levels: Garumn's Gorge.

Shimmergloom stretched to the limit of its height and unfolded its leathery wings for the first time in nearly two hundred years, blackness flowing out under them as they extended to the sides. Those Duergar who had remained in the throne room fell to their knees at the sight of their rising lord, partly in respect, but mostly in fear.

The dragon was gone, gliding down a secret tunnel at the back of the chamber, to where it had once known glory, the place its minions had named Shimmergloom's Run in praise of their lord.

A blur of indistinguishable darkness, it moved as silently as the cloud of blackness that followed.

⚔ ⚔ ⚔ ⚔ ⚔

Wulfgar worried just how low he would be crouching by the time they reached Garumn's Gorge, for the tunnels became dwarven sized as they neared the eastern end of the upper level. Bruenor knew this as a good sign, the only tunnels in the complex with ceilings below the six foot mark were those of the deepest mines and those crafted for defense of the gorge.

Faster than Bruenor had hoped, they came upon the secret door to a smaller tunnel breaking off to the left, a spot familiar to the dwarf even after his two-century absence. He ran his hand across the unremarkable wall beneath the torch and its telltale red sconce, searching for the brailed pattern that would lead his fingers to the precise spot. He found one triangle, then another, and followed their lines to the central point, the bottommost point in the valley between the peaks of the twin mountains that they signified, the symbol of Dumathoin, the Keeper of Secrets Under the Mountain. Bruenor pushed with a single finger, and the wall fell away, opening yet another low tunnel. No light came from this one, but a hollow sound, like the wind across a rock face, greeted them.

Bruenor winked at them knowingly and started right in, but slowed when he saw the runes and sculpted reliefs carved into the walls. All along the passage, on every surface, dwarven artisans had left their mark. Bruenor swelled with pride, despite his depression, when he saw the admiring expressions upon his friends' faces.

A few turns later they came upon a portcullis, lowered and rusted, and beyond it saw the wideness of another huge cavern.

"Garumn's Gorge," Bruenor proclaimed, moving up to the iron bars. " 'Tis said ye can throw a torch off the rim and it'll burn out afore ever it hits."

Four sets of eyes looked through the gate in wonder. If the journey through Mithral Hall had been a disappointment to them, for they had not yet seen the grander sights Bruenor had often told them of, the sight before them now made up for it. They had reached Garumn's Gorge, though it seemed more a full-sized canyon than a gorge, spanning hundreds of feet across and stretching beyond the limits of their sight. They were above the floor of the chamber, with a stairway running down to the right on the other side of the portcullis. Straining to poke as much of their heads as they could through the bars, they could see the light of another room at the base of the stairs, and hear clearly the ruckus of several Duergar.

To the left, the wall arced around to the edge, though the chasm continued on beyond the bordering wall of the cavern. A single bridge spanned the break, an ancient work of stone fitted so perfectly that its slight arch could still support an army of the hugest mountain giants.

Bruenor studied the bridge carefully, noting that something about its understructure did not seem quite right. He followed the line of a cable across the chasm, figuring it to continue under the stone flooring and connect to a large lever sticking up from a more recently constructed platform across the way. Two Duergar sentries milled about the lever, though their lax attitude spoke of countless days of boredom.

"They've rigged the thing to fall!" Bruenor snorted.

The others immediately understood what he was talking about. "Is there another way across, then?" Catti-brie asked.

"Aye," replied the dwarf. "A ledge to the south end of the gorge. But hours o' walking, and the only way to it is through this cavern!"

Wulfgar grasped the iron bars of the portcullis and tested them. They held fast, as he suspected. "We could not get through these bars, anyway," he put in "Unless you know where we might find their crank."

"Half a day's walking," Bruenor replied, as though the answer, perfectly logical to the mindset of a dwarf protecting his treasures, should have been obvious. "The other way."

"Fretful folk," Regis said under his breath.

Catching the remark, Bruenor growled and grabbed Regis by the collar, hoisting him from the ground and pressing their faces together. "Me people are a careful lot," he snarled, his own frustration and confusion boiling out again in his misdirected rage. "We like to keep what's our own to keep, especially from little thieves with little fingers and big mouths."

"Suren there's another way in," Catti-brie reasoned, quick to diffuse the confrontation.

Bruenor dropped the halfling to the floor. "We can get to that room," he replied, indicating the lighted area at the base of the stairs.

"Then let's be quick," Catti-brie demanded. "If the noise of the cave-in called out alarms, the word might not have reached this far."

Bruenor led them back down the small tunnel swiftly, and back to the corridor behind the secret door.

Around the next bend in the main corridor, its walls, too, showing the runes and sculpted reliefs of the dwarven craftsmen, Bruenor was again engulfed in the wonder of his heritage and quickly lost all thoughts of anger at Regis. He heard again in his mind the ringing of hammers in Garumn's day, and the singing of common gatherings. If the foulness that they had found here, and the loss of Drizzt, had tempered his fervent desire to reclaim Mithral Hall, the vivid recollections that assaulted him as he moved along this corridor worked to refuel those fires.

Perhaps he would return with his army, he thought. Perhaps the mithral would again ring out in the smithies of Clan Battlehammer.

Thoughts of regaining his people's glory suddenly rekindled, Bruenor looked around to his friends, tired, hungry, and grieving for the drow, and reminded himself that the mission before him now was to escape the complex and get them back to safety.

A more intense glow ahead signaled the end of the tunnel. Bruenor slowed their pace and crept along to the exit cautiously. Again the companions found themselves on a stone balcony, overlooking yet another corridor, a huge passageway, nearly a chamber in itself, with a high ceiling and decorated walls. Torches burned every few feet along both sides, running parallel below them.

A lump welled in Bruenor's throat when he looked upon the carvings lining the opposite wall across the way, great sculpted basreliefs of Garumn and Bangor, and of all the patriarchs of Clan Battlehammer. He wondered, and not for the first time, if his own bust would ever take its place alongside his ancestors'.

"Half-a-dozen to ten, I make them," Catti-brie whispered, more intent on the clamor rolling out of a partly opened door down to the left, the room they had seen from their perch in the chamber of the gorge. The companions were fully twenty feet above the floor of the larger corridor. To the right, a stairway descended to the floor, and beyond it the tunnel wound its way back into the great halls.

"Side rooms where others might be hiding?" Wulfgar asked Bruenor.

The dwarf shook his head. "One anteroom there be, and only one," he answered. "But more rooms lay within the cavern of Garumn's Gorge.

Whether they be filled with gray ones or no, we cannot know. But no mind to them; we're to get through this room, and through the door across its way to come to the gorge."

Wulfgar slapped his hammer into a fighting grip. "Then let us go," he growled, starting for the stair.

"What about the two in the cavern beyond?" asked Regis, staying the anxious warrior with his hand.

"They'll drop the bridge afore we ever make the gorge," added Catti-brie.

Bruenor scratched his beard, then looked to his daughter. "How well do ye shoot?" he asked her.

Catti-brie held the magical bow out before her. "Well enough to take the likes of two sentries!" she answered.

"Back to th' other tunnel with ye," said Bruenor. "At first sound of battle, take 'em out. And be fast, girl; the cowardly scum're likely to drop the bridge at the first signs of trouble!"

With a nod, she was gone. Wulfgar watched her disappear back down the corridor, not so determined to have this fight now, without knowing that Catti-brie would be safe behind him. "What if the gray ones have reinforcements near?" he asked Bruenor. "What of Catti-brie? She will be blocked from returning to us."

"No whinin', boy!" Bruenor snapped, also uncomfortable with his decision to separate. "Yer heart's for her is me guess, though ye aren't to admit it to yerself. Keep in yer head that Cat's a fighter, trained by meself. The other tunnel's safe enough, still secret from the gray ones by all the signs I could find. The girl's battle-smart to taking care of herself! So put yer thoughts to the fight before ye. The best ye can do for her is to finish these gray bearded dogs too quick for their kin to come!"

It took some effort, but Wulfgar tore his eyes away from the corridor and refocused his gaze on the open door below, readying himself for the task at hand.

Alone now, Catti-brie quietly trotted back the short distance down the corridor and disappeared through the secret door.

"Hold!" Sydney commanded Bok, and she, too, froze in her tracks, sensing that someone was just ahead. She crept forward, the golem on her heel, and peeked around the next turn in the tunnel, expecting that she had come up on the companions. There was only empty corridor in front of her.

The secret door had closed.

⚔ ⚔ ⚔ ⚔

Wulfgar took a deep breath and measured the odds. If Catti-brie's estimate was correct, he and Bruenor would be outnumbered several times when they burst through the door. He knew that they had no options open before them. With another breath to steady himself, he started again down the stairs, Bruenor moving on his cue and Regis following tentatively behind.

The barbarian never slowed his long strides, or turned from the straightest path to the door, yet the first sounds that they all heard were not the thumps of Aegis-fang or the barbarian's customary war cry to Tempus, but the battle song of Bruenor Battlehammer.

This was his homeland and his fight, and the dwarf placed the responsibility for the safety of his companions squarely upon his own shoulders. He dashed by Wulfgar when they reached the bottom of the stairs and crashed through the door, the mithral axe of his heroic namesake raised before him.

"This one's for me father!" he cried, splitting the shining helm of the closest Duergar with a single stroke. "This one's for me father's father!" he yelled, felling the second. "And this one's for me father's father's father!"

Bruenor's ancestral line was long indeed. The gray dwarves never had a chance.

Wulfgar had started his charge right after he realized Bruenor was rushing by him but by the time he got into the room, three Duergar lay dead and the furious Bruenor was about to drop the fourth. Six others scrambled around trying to recover from the savage assault, and mostly trying to get out the other door and into the cavern of the gorge where they could regroup. Wulfgar hurled Aegis-fang and took another, and Bruenor pounced upon his fifth victim before the gray dwarf got through the portal.

Across the gorge, the two sentries heard the start of battle at the same time as Catti-brie, but not understanding what was happening, they hesitated.

Catti-brie didn't.

A streak of silver flashed across the chasm, exploding into the chest of one of the sentries, its powerful magic blasting through his mithral armor and hurling him backward into death.

The second lunged immediately for the lever, but Catti-brie coolly completed her business. The second streaking arrow took him in the eye.

The routed dwarves in the room below poured out into the cavern below her, and others from rooms beyond the first charged out to join them. Wulfgar and Bruenor would come through soon, too, Catti-brie knew, right into the midst of a ready host!

Bruenor's evaluation of Catti-brie had been on target. A fighter she was, and as willing to stand against the odds as any warrior alive. She buried any fears that she might have had for her friends and positioned herself to be of greatest assistance to them. Eyes and jaw steeled in determination, she took up Taulmaril and launched a barrage of death at the assembling host that put them into chaos and sent many of them scrambling for cover.

Bruenor roared out, blood-spattered, his mithral axe red from kills, and still with a hundred great-great ancestors as yet unavenged. Wulfgar was right behind, consumed by the blood lust, singing to his war god, and swatting aside his smaller enemies as easily as he would part ferns on a forest path.

Catti-brie's barrage did not relent, arrow after streaking arrow finding its deadly mark. The warrior within her possessed her fully and her actions stayed on the edges of her conscious thoughts. Methodically, she called for another arrow, and the magical quiver of Anariel obliged. Taulmaril played its own song, and in the wake of its notes lay the scorched and blasted bodies of many Duergar.

Regis hung back throughout the fight, knowing that he would be more trouble than use to his friends in the main fray, just adding one more body for them to protect when they already had all they could handle in looking out for themselves. He saw that Bruenor and Wulfgar had gained enough of an early advantage to claim victory, even against the many enemies that had come into the cavern to face them, so Regis worked to make sure their fallen opponents in the room were truly down and would not come sneaking up behind.

Also, though, to make sure that any valuables these gray ones possessed were not wasted on corpses.

He heard the heavy thump of a boot behind him. He dived aside and rolled to the corner just as Bok crashed through the doorway, oblivious to his presence. When Regis recovered his voice, he moved to yell a warning to his friends.

But then Sydney entered the room.

⚔ ⚔ ⚔ ⚔

Two at a time fell before the sweeps of Wulfgar's warhammer. Spurred by the snatches that he caught of the enraged dwarf's battle cries, " . . . for me father's father's father's father's father's father's . . ." Wulfgar wore a grim smile as he moved through the Duergar's disorganized ranks. Arrows burned lines of silver right beside him as they sought their victims, but he trusted enough in Catti-brie not to fear a stray shot. His muscles flexed in another crushing blow, even the Duergar's shining armor offering no protection against his brute strength.

But then arms stronger than his own caught him from behind.

The few Duergar that remained before him did not recognize Bok as an ally. They fled in terror to the chasm bridge, hoping to cross and destroy the route of any pursuit behind them.

Catti-brie cut them down.

⚔ ⚔ ⚔ ⚔

Regis didn't make any sudden moves, knowing Sydney's power from the encounter back in the oval room. Her bolt of energy had flattened both Bruenor and Wulfgar; the halfling shuddered to think what it could do to him.

His only chance was the ruby pendant, he thought. If he could get Sydney caught in its hypnotizing spell, he might hold her long enough for his friends to return. Slowly, he moved his hand under his jacket, his eyes trained upon the mage, wary for the beginnings of any killing bolt.

Sydney's wand remained tucked into her belt. She had a trick of her own planned for the little one. She muttered a quick chant, then rolled her hand open to Regis and puffed gently, launching a filmy string in his direction.

Regis understood the spell's nature when the air around him was suddenly saturated with floating webs—sticky spiders' webs. They clung to every part of him, slowing his movements, and filled the area around him. He had his hand around the magical pendant, but the web had him fully within its own grip.

Pleased in the exercising of her power, Sydney turned to the door and the battle beyond. She preferred calling upon the powers within her, but understood the strength of these other enemies, and drew her wand.

⚔ ⚔ ⚔ ⚔ ⚔

Bruenor finished the last of the gray dwarves facing him. He had taken many hits, some serious, and much of the blood covering him was his own. The rage within him that he had built over the course of centuries, though, blinded him to the pain. His blood lust was sated now, but only until he turned back toward the anteroom and saw Bok lifting Wulfgar high into the air and crushing the life out of him.

Catti-brie saw it, too. Horrified, she tried to get a clear shot at the golem, but with Wulfgar's desperate struggling, the combatants stumbled about too often for her to dare. "Help him!" she begged to Bruenor under her breath, as all that she could do was watch.

Half of Wulfgar's body was numbed under the incredible force of Bok's magically strengthened arms. He did manage to squirm around and face his foe, though, and he put a hand in the golem's eye and pushed with all his strength, trying to divert some of the monster's energy from the attack.

Bok seemed not to notice.

Wulfgar slammed Aegis-fang into the monster's face with all the force he could muster under the tight circumstances, still a blow that would have felled a giant.

Again Bok seemed not to notice.

The arms closed relentlessly. A wave of dizziness swept through the barbarian. His fingers tingled with numbness. His hammer dropped to the ground.

Bruenor was almost there, axe poised and ready to begin chopping. But as the dwarf passed the open door to the anteroom, a blinding flash of energy shot out at him. It struck his shield, luckily, and deflected up to the cavern ceiling, but the sheer force of it hurled Bruenor from his feet. He shook his head in disbelief and struggled to a sitting position.

Catti-brie saw the bolt and remembered the similar blast that had dropped both Bruenor and Wulfgar back in the oval room. Instinctively, without the slightest hesitation or concern for her own safety, she was off, running back down the passageway, driven by the knowledge that if she couldn't get to the mage, her friends didn't have a chance.

Bruenor was more prepared for the second bolt. He saw Sydney inside the anteroom lift the wand at him. He dived on his belly and threw his shield above his head, facing the mage. It held again against the blast, deflecting the energy harmlessly away, but Bruenor felt it weaken under the impact and knew that it would not withstand another.

The stubborn survival instincts of the barbarian brought his drifting mind from the swoon and back into focus on the battle. He didn't call for his hammer, knowing it to be of little use against the golern and doubting that he could have clasped it anyway. He summoned his own strength, wrapping his huge arms around Bok's neck. His corded muscles tensed to their limits and ripped beyond as he struggled. No breath would come to him; Bruenor would not get there in time. He growled away the pain and the fear, grimaced through the sensations of numbness.

And twisted with all his might.

Regis at last managed to get his hand and the pendant out from under his jacket. "Wait, mage!" he cried at Sydney, not expecting her to listen, but only hoping to divert her attention long enough for her to glimpse the gemstone, and praying that Entreri had not informed her of its hypnotizing powers.

Again the mistrust and secrecy of the evil party worked against them. Oblivious to the dangers of the halfling's ruby, Sydney glanced at him out of the corner of her eye, more to ensure that her web still held him tightly than to listen to any words he might have to say.

A sparkle of red light caught her attention more fully than she had intended, and long moments passed before she would look away.

In the main passage, Catti-brie crouched low and sped along as swiftly as she could. Then she heard the baying.

The hunting shadow hounds filled the corridors with their excited cries, and filled Catti-brie with dread. The hounds were far behind, but her knees went weak as the unearthly sound descended upon her, echoing from wall to wall and encasing her in a dizzying jumble. She gritted her teeth against the assault and pressed on. Bruenor needed her, Wulfgar needed her. She would not fail them.

She made the balcony and sprinted down the stairs, finding the door to the anteroom closed. Cursing the luck, for she had hoped to get a shot at the mage from a distance, she slung Taulmaril over her shoulder, drew her sword, and boldly, blindly, charged through.

Locked in a killing embrace, Wulfgar and Bok stumbled around the cavern, sometimes dangerously close to the gorge. The barbarian matched his muscle against Dendybar's magical work; never before had he faced such a foe. Wildly, he jerked Bok's massive head back and forth, breaking the monster's ability to resist. Then he began turning it in one direction, driving on with every ounce of power that he had left to give. He couldn't remember the last time he had found a breath; he no longer knew who he was, or where he was.

His sheer stubbornness refused to yield.

He heard the snap of bone, and couldn't be sure if it had been his own spine or the golem's neck. Bok never flinched, nor loosened its vicelike grip. The head turned easily now, and Wulfgar, driven on by the final darkness that began its descent upon him, tugged and turned in a final flurry of defiance.

Skin ripped away. The blood-stuff of the wizard's creation poured onto Wulfgar's arms and chest, and the head tore free. Wulfgar, to his own amazement, thought that he had won.

Bok seemed not to notice.

The beginnings of the ruby pendant's hypnotizing spell shattered when the door crashed in, but Regis had played his part. By the time Sydney recognized the coming danger, Catti-brie was too close for her to cast her spells.

Sydney's gaze locked into a stunned, wide-eyed stare of confused protest. All of her dreams and future plans fell before her in that one instant. She tried to scream out a denial, certain that the gods of fate had a more important role planned for her in their scheme of the universe, convinced that they would not allow the shining star of her budding power to be extinguished before it ever came to its potential.

But a thin, wooden wand is of little use in parrying a metal blade.

Catti-brie saw nothing but her target, felt nothing in that instant but the necessity of her duty. Her sword snapped through the feeble wand and plunged home.

She looked at Sydney's face for the first time. Time itself seemed to halt.

Sydney's expression had not changed, her eyes and mouth still open in denial of this possibility.

Catti-brie watched in helpless horror as the last flickers of hope and ambition faded from Sydney's eyes. Warm blood gushed over Catti-brie's arm. Sydney's final gasp of breath seemed impossibly loud.

And Sydney slid, ever so slowly, from the blade and into the realm of death.

A single, vicious cut from the mithral axe severed one of Bok's arms, and Wulfgar fell free. He landed on one knee, barely on the edge of consciousness. His huge lungs reflexively sucked in a volume of revitalizing oxygen.

Sensing the dwarf's presence clearly, but without eyes to focus upon its target, the headless golem lunged confusedly at Bruenor and missed badly.

Bruenor had no understanding of the magical forces that guided the monster, or kept it alive, and he had little desire to test his fighting skills against it. He saw another way. "Come on, ye filthy mold of orc-dung," he teased, moving toward the gorge. In a more serious tone, he called to Wulfgar, "Get yer hammer ready, boy."

Bruenor had to repeat the request over and over, and by the time Wulfgar began to hear it, Bok had backed the dwarf right up to the ledge.

Only half aware of his actions, Wulfgar found the warhammer returned to his hand.

Bruenor stopped, his heels clear of the stone floor, a smile on his face that accepted death. The golem paused, too, somehow understanding that Bruenor had nowhere left to run.

Bruenor dropped to the floor as Bok lunged forward. Aegis-fang slammed into its back, pushing it over the dwarf. The monster fell silently, with no ears to hear the sound of the air rushing past.

Catti-brie was still standing motionless over the mage's body when Wulfgar and Bruenor entered the anteroom. Sydney's eyes and mouth remained open in silent denial, a futile attempt to belie the pool of blood that deepened around her body.

Lines of tears wetted Catti-brie's face. She had felled goblinoids and gray dwarves, once an ogre and a tundra yeti, but never before had she killed a human. Never before had she looked into eyes akin to her own and watched the light leave them. Never before had she understood the complexity of her victim, or even that the life she had taken existed outside the present field of battle.

Wulfgar moved to her and embraced her in full sympathy while Bruenor cut the halfling free of the remaining strands of webbing.

The dwarf had trained Catti-brie to fight and had reveled in her victories against orcs and the like, foul beasts that deserved death by all accounts. He had always hoped, though, that his beloved Catti-brie would be spared this experience.

Again Mithral Hall loomed as the source of his friends' suffering.

Distant howls echoed from beyond the open door behind them. Catti-brie slid the sword into its sheath, not even thinking to wipe the blood from it, and steadied herself. "The pursuit is not ended," she stated flatly. "It is past time we leave."

She led them from the room then, but left a part of herself, the pedestal of her innocence, behind.

23
THE BROKEN HELM

Air rolled across its black wings like the continuous rumble of distant thunder as the dragon swept out of the passageway and into Garumn's Gorge, using the same exit that Drizzt and Entreri had passed just a few moments before. The two, a few dozen yards higher on the wall, held perfectly still, not even daring to breathe. They knew that the dark lord of Mithral Hall had come.

The black cloud that was Shimmergloom rushed by them, unnoticing, and soared down the length of the chasm. Drizzt, in the lead, scrambled up the side of the gorge, clawing at the stone to find whatever holds he could and trusting to them fully in his desperation. He had heard the sounds of battle far above him when he first entered the chasm, and knew that even if his friends had been victorious thus far, they would soon be met by a foe mightier than anything they had ever faced.

Drizzt was determined to stand beside them.

Entreri matched the drow's pace, wanting to keep close to him, though he hadn't yet formulated his exact plan of action.

Wulfgar and Catti-brie supported each other as they walked. Regis kept beside Bruenor, concerned for the dwarf's wounds, even if the dwarf was not. "Keep ye worries for yer own hide, Rumblebelly," he kept snapping at the halfling, though Regis could see that the depth of Bruenor's gruffness had diminished. The dwarf seemed somewhat embarrassed for the way be had acted earlier. "Me wounds'll heal; don't ye be thinking ye've gotten rid of me so easy! There'll be time for looking to them once we've put this place behind us."

Regis had stopped walking, a puzzled expression on his face. Bruenor looked back at him, confused, too, and wondered if he had somehow offended the halfling again. Wulfgar and Catti-brie stopped behind Regis and waited for some indication of the trouble, not knowing what had been said between him and the dwarf.

"What's yer grief?" Bruenor demanded.

Regis was not bothered by anything Bruenor had said, nor with the dwarf at all at that moment. It was Shimmergloom that he had sensed, a sudden coldness that had entered the cavern, a foulness that insulted the companions' caring bond with its mere presence.

Bruenor was about to speak again, when he, too, felt the coming of the dragon of darkness. He looked to the gorge just as the tip of the black cloud broke the chasm's rim, far down to the left beyond the bridge, but speeding toward them.

Catti-brie steered Wulfgar to the side, then he was pulling her with all his speed. Regis scurried back toward the anteroom.

Bruenor remembered.

The dragon of darkness, the ultimately foul monster that had decimated his kin and sent them fleeing for the smaller corridors of the upper level. His mithral axe raised, his feet frozen to the stone below them, he waited.

The blackness dipped under the arch of the stone bridge, then rose to the ledge. Spearlike talons gripped the rim of the gorge, and Shimmergloom reared up before Bruenor in all its horrid splendor, the usurping worm facing the rightful King of Mithral Hall.

"Bruenor!" Regis cried, drawing his little mace and turning back to the cavern, knowing that the best he could do would be to die beside his doomed friend.

Wulfgar threw Catti-brie behind him and spun back on the dragon.

The worm, eyes locked with the dwarf's unyielding stare, did not even notice Aegis-fang spinning toward it, nor the fearless charge of the huge barbarian.

The mighty warhammer struck home against the raven black scales, but was harmlessly turned away. Infuriated that someone had interrupted the moment of its victory, Shimmergloom snapped its glare at Wulfgar.

And it breathed.

Absolute blackness enveloped Wulfgar and sapped the strength from his bones. He felt himself falling, forever falling, though there seemed to be no stone to catch him.

Catti-brie screamed and rushed to him, oblivious to her own danger as she plunged into the black cloud of Shimmergloom's breath.

Bruenor trembled in outrage, for his long-dead kin and for his friend. "Get yerself from me home!" he roared at Shimmergloom, then charged head-on and dived into the dragon, his axe flailing wildly, trying to drive the beast over the edge. The mithral weapon's razored edge had more effect on the scales than the warhammer, but the dragon fought back.

A heavy foot knocked Bruenor back to the ground, and before he could rise, the whiplike neck snapped down upon him and he was lifted in the dragon's maw.

Regis fell back again, shaking with fear. "Bruenor!" he cried again, this time his words coming out as no more than a whisper.

The black cloud dissipated around Catti-brie and Wulfgar, but the barbarian had taken the full force of Shimmergloom's insidious venom. He wanted to flee, even if the only route of escape meant plunging headlong over the side of the gorge. The shadow hounds' baying, though it was still many minutes behind them, closed in upon him. All of his wounds, the crushing of the golem, the nicks the gray dwarves had put into him, hurt him vividly, making him flinch with every step, though his adrenaline of battle had many times before dismissed far more serious and painful injuries.

The dragon seemed ten times mightier to Wulfgar, and he couldn't even have brought himself to raise a weapon against it, for he believed in his heart that Shimmergloom could not be defeated.

Despair had stopped him where fire and steel had not. He stumbled back with Catti-brie toward another room, having no strength to resist her pull.

Bruenor felt his breath blasted out, as the terrible maw crunched into him. He stubbornly held onto the axe, and even managed a swing or two.

Catti-brie pushed Wulfgar through the doorway and into the shelter of the small room, then turned back to the fight in the cavern. "Ye bastard son of a demon lizard!" she spat, as she set Taulmaril into motion. Silver-streaking arrows blasted holes into Shimmergloom's black armor. When Catti-brie understood the measure of the effectiveness of her weapon, she grasped at a desperate plan. Aiming her next shots at the monster's feet, she sought to drive it from the ledge.

Shimmergloom hopped in pain and confusion as the stinging bolts whistled in. The seething hatred of the dragon's narrowed eyes bore down upon the brave young woman. It spat Bruenor's broken form across the floor and roared, "Know fear, foolish girl! Taste of my breath and know you are doomed!" The black lungs expanded, perverting the intaken air into the foul cloud of despair.

Then the stone at the edge of the gorge broke away.

Little joy came to Regis when the dragon fell. He managed to drag Bruenor back into the anteroom, but had no idea of what to do next. Behind him, the relentless pursuit of the shadow hounds drew closer; he was separated from Wulfgar and Catti-brie, and he didn't dare cross the cavern without knowing if the dragon was truly gone. He looked down at the battered and blood-covered form of his oldest friend, having not the slightest notion of how he might begin to help him, or even if Bruenor was still alive.

Only surprise delayed Regis's immediate squeals of joy when Bruenor opened his gray eyes and winked.

⋊ ⋊ ⋊ ⋊ ⋊

Drizzt and Entreri flattened themselves against the wall as the rockslide from the broken ledge tumbled dangerously close. It was over in a moment and Drizzt started up at once, desperate to get to his friends.

He had to stop again, though, and wait nervously as the black form of the dragon dropped past him, then recovered quickly and moved back up toward the rim.

"How?" Regis asked, gawking at the dwarf.

Bruenor shifted uncomfortably and struggled to his feet. The mithral mail had held against the dragon's bite, though Bruenor had been squeezed terribly and bore rows of deep bruises, and probably a host of broken ribs, for the experience. The tough dwarf was still very much alive and alert, though, dismissing his considerable pain for the more important matter before him—the safety of his friends.

"Where's the boy, and Catti-brie?" he pressed immediately, the background howls of the shadow hounds accentuating the desperation of his tone.

"Another room," Regis answered, indicating the area to the right beyond the door to the cavern.

"Cat!" Bruenor shouted. "How do ye fare?"

After a stunned pause, for Catti-brie, too, had not expected to hear Bruenor's voice again, she called back, "Wulfgar's gone for the fight, I fear! A dragon's spell, for all I can make it! But for meself, I'm for leaving! The dogs'll be here sooner than I like!"

"Aye!" agreed Bruenor, clutching at a twinge of pain in his side when he yelled. "But have ye seen the worm?"

"No, nor heared the beast!" came the uncertain reply.

Bruenor looked to Regis.

"It fell, and has been gone since," the halfling answered the questioning stare, equally unconvinced that Shimmergloom had been defeated so easily.

"Not a choice to us, then!" Bruenor called out. "We're to make the bridge! Can ye bring the boy?"

"It's his heart for fightin' that's been bruised, no more!" replied Catti-brie. "We'll be along!"

Bruenor clasped Regis's shoulder, lending support to his nervous friend. "Let's be going, then!" he roared in his familiar voice of confidence.

Regis smiled in spite of his dread at the sight of the old Bruenor again. Without further coaxing, he walked beside the dwarf out of the room.

Even as they took the first step toward the gorge, the black cloud that was Shimmergloom again crested the rim.

"Ye see it?" cried Catti-brie.

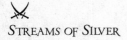

Bruenor fell back into the room, viewing the dragon all too clearly. Doom closed in all around him, insistent and inescapable. Despair denied his determination, not for himself, for he knew that he had followed the logical course of his fate in coming back to Mithral Hall—a destiny that had been engraved upon the fabric of his very being from the day his kin had been slaughtered—but his friends should not perish this way. Not the halfling, who always before could find an escape from every trap. Not the boy, with so many glorious adventures left before him upon his road.

And not his girl. Catti-brie, his own beloved daughter. The only light that had truly shone in the mines of Clan Battlehammer in Icewind Dale.

The fall of the drow alone, willing companion and dearest friend, had been too high a price for his selfish daring. The loss that faced him now was simply too much for him to bear.

His eyes darted around the small room. There had to be an option. If ever he had been faithful to the gods of the dwarves, he asked them now to grant him this one thing. Give him an option.

There was a small curtain against one of the room's walls. Bruenor looked curiously at Regis.

The halfling shrugged. "A storage area," he said. "Nothing of value. Not even a weapon."

Bruenor wouldn't accept the answer. He dashed through the curtain and started tearing through the crates and sacks that lay within. Dried food. Pieces of wood. An extra cloak. A skin of water.

A keg of oil.

⚔ ⚔ ⚔ ⚔

Shimmergloom swooped back and forth along the length of the gorge, waiting to meet the intruders on its own terms in the open cavern and confident that the shadow hounds would flush them out.

Drizzt had nearly reached the level of the dragon, pressing on in the face of peril with no other concerns than those he felt for his friends.

"Hold!" Entreri called to him from a short distance below. "Are you so determined to get yourself killed?"

"Damn the dragon!" Drizzt hissed back. "I'll not cower in the shadows and watch my friends be destroyed."

"There is value in dying with them?" came the sarcastic reply. "You are a fool, drow. Your worth outweighs that of all your pitiful friends!"

"Pitiful?" Drizzt echoed incredulously. "It is you that I pity, assassin."

The drow's disapproval stung Entreri more than he would have expected. "Then pity yourself!" he shot back angrily. "For you are more akin to me than you care to believe!"

"If I do not go to them, your words will hold the truth," Drizzt continued, more calmly now. "For then my life will be of no value, less even than your own! Beyond my embrace of the heartless emptiness that rules your world, my entire life would then be no more than a lie." He started up again, fully expecting to die, but secure in his realization that he was indeed very different from the murderer that followed him.

Secure, too, in the knowledge that he had escaped his own heritage.

✘ ✘ ✘ ✘ ✘

Bruenor came back through the curtain, a wild smirk upon his face, an oil-soaked cloak slung over his shoulder, and the keg tied to his back. Regis looked upon him in complete confusion, though he could guess enough of what the dwarf had in mind to be worried for his friend.

"What are ye lookin' at?" Bruenor said with at wink.

"You are crazy," Regis replied, Bruenor's plan coming into clearer focus the longer he studied the dwarf.

"Aye, we agreed on that afore our road e'er began!" snorted Bruenor. He calmed suddenly, the wild glimmer mellowing to a caring concern for his little friend. "Ye deserve better'n what I've given ye, Rumblebelly," he said, more comfortable than he had ever been in apology.

"Never have I known a more loyal friend than Bruenor Battlehammer," Regis replied.

Bruenor pulled the gem-studded helmet from his head and tossed it to the halfling, confusing Regis even more. He reached around to his back and loosened a strap fastened between his pack and his belt and took out his old helm. He ran a finger over the broken horn, smiling in remembrance of the wild adventures that had given this helm such a battering. Even the dent where Wulfgar had hit him, those years ago, when first they met as enemies.

Bruenor put the helm on, more comfortable with its fit, and Regis saw him in the light of old friend.

"Keep the helm safe," Bruenor told Regis, "It's the crown of the King of Mithral Hall!"

"Then it is yours," Regis argued, holding the crown back out to Bruenor.

"Nay, not by me right or me choice. Mithral Hall is no more, Rumble—Regis. Bruenor of Icewind Dale, I am, and have been for two hundred years, though me head's too thick to know it!

"Forgive me old bones," he said. "Suren me thoughts've been walking in me past and me future."

Regis nodded and said with genuine concern, "What are you going to do?"

"Mind to yer own part in this!" Bruenor snorted, suddenly the snarling leader once more. "Ye'll have enough gettin' yerself from these cursed halls when I'm through!" He growled threateningly at the halfling to keep him back, then moved swiftly, pulling a torch from the wall and dashing through the door to the cavern before Regis could even make a move to stop him.

The dragon's black form skimmed the rim of the gorge, dipping low beneath the bridge and returning to its patrolling level. Bruenor watched it for a few moments to get a feel for the rhythm of its course.

"Yer mine, worm!" he snarled under his breath, and then he charged. "Here's one from yer tricks, boy!" he cried at the room holding Wulfgar and Catti-brie. "But when me mind's to jumping on the back of a worm, I ain't about to miss!"

"Bruenor!" Catti-brie screamed when she saw him running out toward the gorge.

It was too late. Bruenor put the torch to the oil-soaked cloak and raised his mithral axe high before him. The dragon heard him coming and swerved in closer to the rim to investigate—and was as amazed as the dwarf's friends when Bruenor, his shoulder and back aflame, leaped from the edge and streaked down upon it.

Impossibly strong, as though all of the ghosts of Clan Battlehammer had joined their hands with Bruenor's upon the weapon handle and lent him their strength, the dwarf's initial blow drove the mithral axe deep into Shimmergloom's back. Bruenor crashed down behind, but held fast to the embedded weapon, even though the keg of oil broke apart with the impact and spewed flames all across the monster's back.

Shimmergloom shrieked in outrage and swerved wildly, even crashing into the stone wall of the gorge.

Bruenor would not be thrown. Savagely, he grasped the handle, waiting for the opportunity to tear the weapon free and drive it home again.

Catti-brie and Regis rushed to the edge of the gorge, helplessly calling out to their doomed friend. Wulfgar, too, managed to drag himself over, still fighting the black depths of despair.

When the barbarian looked upon Bruenor, sprawled amid the flames, he roared away the dragon's spell and without the slightest hesitation, launched Aegis-fang. The hammer caught Shimmergloom on the side of its head and the dragon swerved again in its surprise, clipping the other wall of the gorge.

"Are ye mad?" Catti-brie yelled at Wulfgar.

"Take up your bow," Wulfgar told her. "If a true friend of Bruenor's you be, then let him not fall in vain!" Aegis-fang returned to his grasp and he launched it again, scoring a second hit.

Catti-brie had to accept the reality. She could not save Bruenor from the fate he had chosen. Wulfgar was right—she could aid the dwarf in gaining his desired end. Blinking away the tears that came to her, she took Taulmaril in hand and sent the silver bolts at the dragon.

※ ※ ※ ※ ※

Both Drizzt and Entreri watched Bruenor's leap in utter amazement. Cursing his helpless position, Drizzt surged ahead, nearly to the rim. He shouted out for his remaining friends, but in the commotion, and with the roaring of the dragon, they could not hear.

Entreri was directly below him. The assassin knew that his last chance was upon him, though he risked losing the only challenge he had ever found in this life. As Drizzt scrambled for his next hold, Entreri grabbed his ankle and pulled him down.

Oil found its way in through the seams in Shimmergloom's scales, carrying the fire to the dragon flesh. The dragon cried out from a pain it never believed it could know.

The thud of the warhammer! The constant sting of those streaking lines of silver! And the dwarf! Relentless in his attacks, somehow oblivious to the fires.

Shimmergloom tore along the length of the gorge, dipping suddenly, then swooping back up and rolling over and about. Catti-brie's arrows found it at every turn. And Wulfgar, wiser with each of his strikes, sought the best opportunities to throw the warhammer, waiting for the dragon to cut by a rocky outcropping in the wall, then driving the monster into the stone with the force of his throw.

Flames, stone, and dust flew wildly with each thunderous impact.

Bruenor held on. Singing out to his father and his kin beyond that, the dwarf absolved himself of his guilt, content that he had satisfied the ghosts of his past and given his friends a chance for survival. He didn't feel the bite of the fire, nor the bump of stone. All he felt was the quivering of the dragon flesh below his blade, and the reverberations of Shimmergloom's agonized cries.

✕ ✕ ✕ ✕ ✕

Drizzt tumbled down the face of the gorge, desperately scrambling for some hold. He slammed onto a ledge twenty feet below the assassin and managed to stop his descent.

Entreri nodded his approval and his aim, for the drow had landed just where he had hoped. "Farewell, trusting fool!" he called down to Drizzt and he started up the wall.

Drizzt never had trusted in the assassin's honor, but he had believed in Entreri's pragmatism. This attack made no practical sense. "Why?" he called back to Entreri. "You could have had the pendant without recourse!"

"The gem is mine," Entreri replied.

"But not without a price!" Drizzt declared. "You know that I will come after you, assassin!"

Entreri looked down at him with an amused grin. "Do you not understand, Drizzt Do'Urden? That is exactly the purpose!"

The assassin quickly reached the rim, and peered above it. To his left, Wulfgar and Catti-brie continued their assault on the dragon. To his right, Regis stood enamored of the scene, completely unaware.

The halfling's surprise was complete, his face blanching in terror, when his worst nightmare rose up before him. Regis dropped the gem-studded helm and went limp with fear as Entreri silently picked him up and started for the bridge.

Exhausted, the dragon tried to find another method of defense. Its rage and pain had carried it too far into the battle, though. It had taken too many hits, and still the silver streaks bit into it again and again.

Still the tireless dwarf twisted and pounded the axe into its back.

One last time the dragon cut back in mid-flight, trying to snake its neck around so that it could at least take vengeance upon the cruel dwarf. It hung motionless for just a split second, and Aegis-fang took it in the eye.

The dragon rolled over in blinded rage, lost in a dizzying swirl of pain, headlong into a jutting portion of the wall.

The explosion rocked the very foundations of the cavern, nearly knocking Catti-brie from her feet and Drizzt from his precarious perch.

One final image came to Bruenor, a sight that made his heart leap one more time in victory: the piercing gaze of Drizzt Do'Urden's lavender eyes bidding him farewell from the darkness of the wall.

Broken and beaten, the flames consuming, it, the dragon of darkness glided and spun, descending into the deepest blackness it would ever know, a blackness from which there could be no return. The depths of Garumn's Gorge.

And bearing with it the rightful King of Mithral Hall.

24
EULOGY FOR MITHRAL HALL

The burning dragon drifted lower and lower, the light of the flames slowly diminishing to a mere speck at the bottom of Garumn's Gorge.

Drizzt scrambled up over the ledge and came up beside Catti-brie and Wulfgar, Catti-brie holding the gem-studded helm, and both of them staring helplessly across the chasm. The two of them nearly fell over in surprise when they turned to see their drow friend returned from the grave. Even the appearance of Artemis Entreri had not prepared Wulfgar and Catti-brie for the sight of Drizzt.

"How?" Wulfgar gasped, but Drizzt cut him short. The time for explanations would come later; they had more urgent business at hand.

Across the gorge, right next to the lever hooked to the bridge, stood Artemis Entreri, holding Regis by the throat before him and grinning wickedly. The ruby pendant now hung around the assassin's neck.

"Let him go," Drizzt said evenly. "As we agreed. You have the gem."

Entreri laughed and pulled the lever. The stone bridge shuddered, then broke apart, tumbling into the darkness below.

Drizzt had thought that he was beginning to understand the assassin's motivations for this treachery, reasoning now that Entreri had taken Regis to ensure pursuit, continuing his own personal challenge with Drizzt. But now with the bridge gone and no apparent escape open before Drizzt and his friends, and the incessant baying of the shadow hounds growing closer at their backs, the drow's theories didn't seem to hold up. Angered by his confusion, he reacted quickly. Having lost his own bow back in the alcove, Drizzt grabbed Taulmaril from Catti-brie and fitted an arrow.

Entreri moved just as fast. He rushed to the ledge, scooped Regis up by an ankle, and held him by one hand over the edge. Wulfgar and Catti-brie sensed the strange bond between Drizzt and the assassin and knew that Drizzt was better able to deal with this situation. They moved back a step and held each other close.

Drizzt kept the bow steady and cocked, his eyes unblinking as he searched for the one lapse in Entreri's defenses.

Entreri shook Regis dangerously and laughed again. "The road to Calimport is long indeed, drow. You shall have your chance to catch up with me."

"You have blocked our escape," Drizzt retorted.

"A necessary inconvenience," explained Entreri. "Surely you will find your way through this, even if your other friends do not. And I will be waiting!"

"I will come," Drizzt promised. "You do not need the halfling to make me want to hunt you down, foul assassin."

" 'Tis true," said Entreri. He reached into his pouch, pulled out a small item, and tossed it into the air. It twirled up above him then dropped. He caught it just before it passed beyond his reach and would have fallen into the gorge. He tossed it again. Something small, something black.

Entreri tossed it a third time, teasingly, the smile widening across his face as Drizzt lowered the bow.

Guenhwyvar.

"I do not need the halfling," Entreri stated flatly and he held Regis farther out over the chasm.

Drizzt dropped the magical bow behind him, but kept his glare locked upon the assassin.

Entreri pulled Regis back in to the ledge. "But my master demands the right to kill this little thief. Lay your plans, drow, for the hounds draw near. Alone, you stand a better chance. Leave those two, and live!

"Then come, drow. Finish our business." He laughed one more time and spun away into the darkness of the final tunnel.

"He's out, then," said Catti-brie. "Bruenor named that passage as a straight run to a door out of the halls."

Drizzt looked all around, trying to find some means to get them across the chasm.

"By Bruenor's own words, there is another way," Catti-brie offered. She pointed down to her right, toward the south end of the cavern. "A ledge," she said, "but hours of walking."

"Then run," replied Drizzt, his eyes still fixed upon the tunnel across the gorge.

By the time the three companions reached the ledge, the echoes of howls and specks of light far to the north told them that Duergar and shadow hounds had entered the cavern. Drizzt led them across the narrow walkway, his back pressed against the wall as he inched his way toward the other side. All the gorge lay open before him, and the fires still burned below, a grim reminder of the fate of his bearded friend. Perhaps it was fitting that Bruenor died here, in the home of his ancestors, he thought. Perhaps the dwarf had finally satisfied the yearning that had dictated so much of his life.

The loss remained intolerable to Drizzt, though. His years with Bruenor had shown him a compassionate and respected friend, a friend he could rely upon at any time, in any circumstance. Drizzt could tell himself over and over that Bruenor was satisfied, that the dwarf had climbed his mountain and won his personal battle, but in the terrible immediacy of his death, those thoughts did little to dispel the drow's grief.

Catti-brie blinked away more tears, and Wulfgar's sigh belied his stoicism when they moved out across the gorge that had become Bruenor's grave. To Catti-brie, Bruenor was father and friend, who taught her toughness and touched her with tenderness. All of the constants of her world, her family and home, lay burning far below, on the back of a hell-spawned dragon.

A numbness descended over Wulfgar, the cold chill of mortality and the realization of how fragile life could be. Drizzt had returned to him, but now Bruenor was gone. Above any emotions of joy or grief came a wave of instability, a tragic rewriting of heroic images and bard-sung legends that he had not expected. Bruenor had died with courage and strength, and the story of his fiery leap would be told and retold a thousand times. But it would never fill the void that Wulfgar felt at that moment.

✕ ✕ ✕ ✕

They made their way across to the chasm's other side and raced back to the north to get to the final tunnel and be free of the shadows of Mithral Hall. When they came again into the wide end of the cavern, they were spotted. Duergar shouted and cursed at them; the great black shadow hounds roared their threats and scratched at the lip of the other side of the gorge. But their enemies had no way to get at them, short of going all the way around to the ledge, and Drizzt stepped unopposed into the tunnel that Entreri had entered a few hours earlier.

Wulfgar followed, but Catti-brie paused at the entrance and looked back across the gorge at the gathered host of gray dwarves.

"Come," Drizzt said to her. "There is nothing that we can do here, and Regis needs our help."

Catti-brie's eyes narrowed and the muscles in her jaw clenched tightly as she fitted an arrow to her bow and fired. The silver streak whistled into the crowd of Duergar and blasted one from life, sending the others scurrying for cover. "Nothing now," Catti-brie replied grimly, "but I'll be comin' back! Let the gray dogs know it for truth.

"I'll be back!"

EPILOGUE

Drizzt, Wulfgar, and Catti-brie came into Longsaddle a few days later, road weary and still wrapped in a shroud of grief. Harkle and his kin greeted them warmly and invited them to stay at the Ivy Mansion for as long as they desired. But though all three of them would have welcomed the opportunity to relax and recover from their trials, other roads summoned them.

Drizzt and Wulfgar stood at the exit of Longsaddle the very next morning, with fresh horses provided by the Harpells. Catti-brie walked down to them slowly, Harkle holding back a few steps behind her.

"Will you come?" Drizzt asked, but guessed by her expression that she would not.

"Would that I could," Catti-brie replied. "Ye'll get to the halfling, I don't fear. I've another vow to fulfill."

"When?" Wulfgar asked.

"In the spring, by me guess," said Catti-brie. "The magic of the Harpells has set the thing to going; already they've called out to the clan in the dale, and to Harbromm in Citadel Adbar. Bruenor's kin'll be marchin' out afore the tenday's end, with many allies from Ten-Towns. Harbromm promises eight thousand, and some of the Harpells have pledged their help."

Drizzt thought of the undercity he had viewed in his passage of the lower levels, and of the bustle of thousands of gray dwarves, all outfitted in shining mithral. Even with all of Clan Battlehammer and their friends from the dale, eight thousand battle-seasoned dwarves from Adbar, and the magical powers of the Harpells, the victory would be hard won if won at all.

Wulfgar also understood the enormity of the task that Catti-brie would face, and doubt came to him about his decision to set out with Drizzt. Regis needed him, but he could not turn away from Catti-brie in her need.

Catti-brie sensed his torment. She walked up to him and kissed him suddenly, passionately, then jumped back. "Get yer business done and over, Wulfgar, son of Beornegar," she said. "And get ye back to me!"

"I, too, was Bruenor's friend," Wulfgar argued. "I, too, shared in his vision of Mithral Hall. I should be beside you when you go to honor him."

"Ye've a friend alive that needs ye now," Catti-brie snapped at him. "I can set the plans to going. Ye get yerself after Regis! Pay Entreri all he's got coming and be quick. Mighten be that ye'll get back in time to march to the halls."

She turned to Drizzt, a most-trusted hero. "Keep him safe for me," she pleaded. "Show him a straight road, and show him the way back!"

On Drizzt's nod, she spun and ran back up to Harkle and toward the Ivy Mansion. Wulfgar did not follow. He trusted in Catti-brie.

"For the halfling and the cat," he said to Drizzt, clasping Aegis-fang and surveying the road before them.

Sudden fires glowed in the drow's lavender eyes, and Wulfgar took an involuntary step back. "And for other reasons," Drizzt said grimly, looking out over the wide southland that held the monster he might have become. It was his destiny to meet Entreri in battle again, he knew, the test of his own worth to defeat the killer.

"For other reasons."

⚔ ⚔ ⚔ ⚔

Dendybar's breath came hard to him as he viewed the scene—Sydney's corpse stuffed into a corner of a dark room.

The specter, Morkai, waved his arm and the image was replaced by a view of the bottom of Garumn's Gorge.

"No!" Dendybar screamed when he saw the remains of the golem, headless and lying among the rubble. The mottled wizard shook visibly. "Where is the drow?" he demanded of the specter.

Morkai waved the image away and stood silent, pleased at Dendybar's distress.

"Where is the drow?" Dendybar repeated, more loudly.

Morkai laughed at him. "Find your own answers, foolish mage. My service to you is ended!" The apparition puffed into fire and was gone.

Dendybar leaped wildly from his magic circle and kicked the burning brazier over. "I shall torment you a thousand times for your insolence!" he yelled into the emptiness of the room. His mind spun with the possibilities. Sydney dead. Bok dead. Entreri? The drow and his friends? Dendybar needed answers. He could not forsake his search for the Crystal Shard, could not be denied the power he sought.

Deep breaths steadied him as he concentrated on the beginnings of a spell. He saw the bottom of the gorge again, brought the image into sharp focus within his mind. As he chanted through the ritual, the scene became more real, more tangible. Dendybar experienced it fully; the darkness, the hollow emptiness of the shadowy walls and the almost imperceptible swish of air running through the ravine, the jagged hardness of the broken stone under his feet.

He stepped out of his thoughts and into Garumn's Gorge.

"Bok," he whispered as he stared down at the twisted and broken form of his creation, his greatest achievement.

The thing stirred. A rock rolled away from it as it shifted and struggled to rise before its creator. Dendybar watched in disbelief, amazed that the magical strength he had imbued upon the golem was so resilient as to survive such a drop, and such mutilation.

Bok stood in front of him, waiting.

Dendybar studied the thing for a long moment, pondering how he might begin to restore it. "Bok!" he greeted it emphatically, a hopeful grin coming to him. "Come, my pet. I shall take you back home and mend your wounds."

Bok took a step forward, crowding Dendybar against the wall. The wizard, still not understanding, started to order the golem away.

But Bok's remaining arm shot up and grasped Dendybar by the throat, lifting him into the air and choking off any further commands. Dendybar grabbed and flailed at the arm, helpless and confused.

A familiar laugh came to his ears. A ball of fire appeared above the torn stump of the golem's neck, transforming into a familiar face.

Morkai.

Dendybar's eyes bulged in terror. He realized that he had overstepped his limits, had summoned the specter too many times. He had never truly dismissed Morkai from this last encounter, and suspected rightly that he probably wouldn't have been strong enough to push the specter from the material plane even if he had tried. Now, outside of his magic circle of protection he was at the mercy of his nemesis.

"Come, Dendybar," Morkai grinned, his dominating will twisting the golem's arm. "Join me in the realm of death where we might discuss your treachery!"

A snap of bone echoed across the stones, the ball of fire puffed away, and wizard and golem tumbled down, lifeless.

Farther down the gorge, half buried in a pile of debris, the fires of the burning dragon had died to a smoky smolder.

Another rock shifted and rolled away.

THE HALFLING'S GEM

THE LEGEND OF DRIZZT BOOK VI

The wizard looked down upon the young woman with uncertainty. Her back was to him; he could see the thick mane of her auburn locks flowing around her shoulders, rich and vibrant. But the wizard knew, too, the sadness that was in her eyes. So young she was, barely more than a child, and so beautifully innocent.

PROLOGUE

Yet this beautiful child had put a sword through the heart of his beloved Sydney.

Harkle Harpell brushed away the unwanted memories of his dead love and started down the hill. "A fine day," he said cheerily when he reached the young woman.

"Do ye think they've made the tower?" Catti-brie asked him, her gaze never leaving the southern horizon.

Harkle shrugged. "Soon, if not yet." He studied Catti-brie and could find no anger against her for her actions. She had killed Sydney, it was true, but Harkle knew just by looking at her that necessity, not malice, had guided her sword arm. And now he could only pity her.

"How are you?" Harkle stammered, amazed at the courage she had shown in light of the terrible events that had befallen her and her friends.

Catti-brie nodded and turned to the wizard. Surely there was sorrow edging her deep blue eyes, but mostly they burned with a stubborn resolve that chased away any hints of weakness. She had lost Bruenor, the dwarf who had adopted her and had reared her as his own since the earliest days of her childhood. And Catti-brie's other friends even now were caught in the middle of a desperate chase with an assassin across the southland.

"How quickly things have changed," Harkle whispered under his breath, feeling sympathy for the young woman. He remembered a time, just a few tendays earlier, when Bruenor Battlehammer and his small company had come through Longsaddle in their quest to find Mithral Hall, the dwarf's lost homeland. That had been a jovial meeting of tales exchanged and promises of future friendships with the Harpell clan. None of them could have known that a second party, led by an evil assassin, and by Harkle's own Sydney, held Catti-brie hostage and was gathering to pursue the company. Bruenor had found Mithral Hall, and had fallen there.

And Sydney, the female mage that Harkle had so dearly loved, had played a part in the dwarf's death.

Harkle took a deep breath to steady himself. "Bruenor will be avenged," he said with a grimace.

Catti-brie kissed him on the cheek and started back up the hill toward the Ivy Mansion. She understood the wizard's sincere pain, and she truly admired his decision to help her fulfill her vow to return to Mithrall Hall and reclaim it for Clan Battlehammer.

But for Harkle, there had been no other choice. The Sydney that he had loved was a facade, a sugar coating to a power-crazed, unfeeling monster. And he himself had played a part in the disaster, unwittingly revealing to Sydney the whereabouts of Bruenor's party.

Harkle watched Catti-brie go, the weight of troubles

slowing her stride. He could harbor no resentment toward her. Sydney had brought about the circumstances of her own death, and Catti-brie had no choice but to play them out. The wizard turned his gaze southward. He, too, wondered and worried for the drow elf and the huge barbarian lad. They had slumped back into Longsaddle just three days before, a sorrow-filled and weary band in desperate need of rest.

There could be no rest, though, not now, for the wicked assassin had escaped with the last of their group, Regis the halfling, in tow.

So much had happened in those few tendays; Harkle's entire world had been turned upside down by an odd mixture of heroes from a distant, forlorn land called Icewind Dale, and by a beautiful young woman who could not be blamed.

And by the lie that was his deepest love.

Harkle fell back on the grass and watched the puffy clouds of late summer meander across the sky.

⚔ ⚔ ⚔ ⚔ ⚔

Beyond the clouds, where the stars shone eternally, Guenhwyvar, the entity of the panther, paced excitedly. Many days had passed since the cat's master, the drow elf named Drizzt Do'Urden, had summoned it to the material plane. Guenhwyvar was sensitive to the onyx figurine that served as a link to its master and that other world; the panther could sense the tingle from that far-off place even when its master merely touched the statuette.

But Guenhwyvar hadn't felt that link to Drizzt in some time, and the cat was nervous now, somehow understanding in its otherworldly intelligence that the drow no longer possessed the figurine. Guenhwyvar remembered the time before Drizzt, when another drow, an evil drow, had been its master. Though in essence an animal, Guenhwyvar possessed dignity, a quality that its original master had stolen away.

Guenhwyvar remembered those times when it had been forced to perform cruel, cowardly acts against helpless foes for the sake of its master's pleasure.

But things had been very different since Drizzt Do'Urden came to possess the figurine. Here was a being of conscience and integrity, and an honest bond of love had developed between Guenhwyvar and Drizzt.

The cat slumped against a star-trimmed tree and issued a low growl that observers to this astral spectacle might have taken as a resigned sigh.

Deeper still would the cat's sigh have been if it knew that Artemis Entreri, the killer, now possessed the figurine.

I am dying.

Every day, with every breath I draw, I am closer to the end of my life. For we are born with a finite number of breaths, and each one I take edges the sunlight that is my life toward the inevitable dusk.

It is a difficult thing to remember, especially while we are

HALFWAY TO EVERYWHERE

in the health and strength of our youth, and yet, I have come to know that it is an important thing to keep in mind—not to complain or to make melancholy, but simply because only with the honest knowledge that one day I will die can I ever truly begin to live. Certainly I do not dwell on the reality of my own mortality, but I believe that a person cannot help but dwell, at least subconsciously, on that most imposing specter until he has come to understand, to truly understand and appreciate, that he will one day die. That he will one day be gone from this place, this life, this consciousness and existence, to whatever it is that awaits. For only when a person completely and honestly accepts the inevitability of death is he free of the fear of it.

So many people, it seems, stick themselves into the same routines, going through each day's rituals with almost religious precision. They become creatures of simple habit. Part of that is the comfort afforded by familiarity, but there is another aspect to it, a deep-rooted belief that as long as they keep everything the same, everything will remain the same. Such rituals are a way to control the world about them, but in truth, they cannot. For even if they follow the exact routine day after day after day, death will surely find them.

I have seen other people paralyze their entire existence around that greatest of mysteries, shaping their every movement, their every word, in a desperate attempt to find the answers to the unanswerable. They fool themselves, either through their interpretations of ancient texts or through some obscure sign from a natural event, into believing that they have found the ultimate truth, and thus, if they behave accordingly concerning that truth, they will surely be rewarded in the afterlife. This must be the greatest manifestation of that fear of death, the errant belief that we can somehow shape and decorate eternity itself, that we can curtain its windows and place its furniture in accordance with our own desperate desires. Along the road that led me to Icewind Dale, I came upon a group of followers of Ilmater, the god of suffering, who were so fanatical in their beliefs that they would beat each other senseless, and welcomed torment, even death itself, in some foolish belief that by doing so they would pay the highest tribute to their god.

I believe them to be wrong, though in truth, I cannot know anything for certain concerning what mystery lies beyond this mortal coil. And so I, too, am but a creature of faith and hope. I hope that Zaknafein has found eternal peace and joy, and pray with all my heart that when I cross over the threshold into the next existence, I will see him again.

Perhaps the greatest evil I see in this existence is when supposedly holy men prey upon the basic fears of death of the common folk to take from them. "Give to the church!" they cry. "Only then will you find salvation!" Even more subtle are the many religions that do not directly ask for a person's coin, but insist that anyone of goodly and godly heart who is destined for their particular description of heaven, would willingly give that coin over.

And of course, Toril is ripe with "doomsdayers," people who claim that the end of the world is at hand, and cry for repentance and for almost slavish dedication.

I can only look at it all and sigh, for as death is the greatest mystery, so it is the most personal of revelations. We will not know, none of us, until the moment it is upon us, and we cannot truly and in good conscience convince another of our beliefs.

It is a road we travel alone, but a road that I no longer fear, for in accepting the inevitable, I have freed myself from it. In coming to recognize my mortality, I have found the secret to enjoying those centuries, years, months, days, or even hours, that I have left to draw breath. This is the existence I can control, and to throw away the precious hours over fear of the inevitable is a foolish thing indeed. And to subconsciously think ourselves immortal, and thus not appreciate those precious few hours that we all have, is equally foolish.

I cannot control the truth of death, whatever my desperation. I can only make certain that those moments of my life I have remaining are as rich as they can be.

—Drizzt Do'Urden

TOWER OF TWILIGHT

A day and more we have lost," the barbarian grumbled, reining in his horse and looking back over his shoulder. The lower rim of the sun had just dipped below the horizon. "The assassin moves away from us even now!"

"We do well to trust in Harkle's advice," replied Drizzt Do'Urden, the dark elf. "He would not have led us astray." With the sunshine fading, Drizzt dropped the cowl of his black cloak back onto his shoulders and shook free the locks of his stark white hair.

Wulfgar pointed to some tall pines. "That must be the grove Harkle Harpell spoke of," he said, "yet I see no tower, nor signs that any structure was ever built in this forsaken area."

His lavender eyes more at home in the deepening gloom, Drizzt peered ahead intently, trying to find some evidence to dispute his young friend. Surely this was the place that Harkle had indicated, for a short distance ahead of them lay the small pond, and beyond that the thick boughs of Neverwinter Wood. "Take heart," he reminded Wulfgar. "The wizard called patience the greatest aid in finding the home of Malchor. We have been here but an hour."

"The road grows ever longer," the barbarian mumbled, unaware that the drow's keen ears did not miss a word. There was merit in Wulfgar's complaints, Drizzt knew, for the tale of a farmer in Longsaddle—that of a dark, cloaked man and a halfling on a single horse—put the assassin fully ten days ahead of them, and moving swiftly.

But Drizzt had faced Entreri before and understood the enormity of the challenge before him. He wanted as much assistance as he could get in rescuing Regis from the deadly man's clutches. By the farmer's words, Regis was still alive, and Drizzt was certain that Entreri did not mean to harm the halfling before getting to Calimport.

Harkle Harpell would not have sent them to this place without good reason.

"Do we put up for the night?" asked Wulfgar. "By my word, we'd ride back to the road and to the south. Entreri's horse carries two and may have tired by now. We can gain on him if we ride through the night."

Drizzt smiled at his friend. "They have passed through the city of Waterdeep by now," he explained. "Entreri has acquired new horses, at the least." Drizzt let the issue drop at that, keeping his deeper fears, that the assassin had taken to the sea, to himself.

"Then to wait is even more folly!" Wulfgar was quick to argue.

But as the barbarian spoke, his horse, a horse raised by Harpells, snorted and moved to the small pond, pawing the air above the water as though searching for a place to step. A moment later, the last of the sun dipped under the western horizon and the daylight faded away. And in the magical dimness of twilight, an enchanted tower phased into view before them on the little island in the pond, its every point twinkling like starlight, and its many twisting spires reaching up into the evening sky. Emerald green it was, and mystically inviting, as if sprites and faeries had lent a hand to its creation.

And across the water, right below the hoof of Wulfgar's horse, appeared a shining bridge of green light.

Drizzt slipped from his mount. "The Tower of Twilight," he said to Wulfgar, as though he had seen the obvious logic from the start. He swept his arm out toward the structure, inviting his friend to lead them in.

But Wulfgar was stunned at the appearance of the tower. He clutched the reins of his horse even tighter, causing the beast to rear up and flatten its ears against its head.

"I thought you had overcome your suspicions of magic," said Drizzt sarcastically. Truly Wulfgar, like all the barbarians of Icewind Dale, had been raised with the belief that wizards were weakling tricksters and not to be trusted. His people, proud warriors of the tundra, regarded strength of arm, not skill in the black arts of wizardry, as the measure of a true man. But in their many tendays on the road, Drizzt had seen Wulfgar overcome his upbringing and develop a tolerance, even a curiosity, for the practices of wizardry.

With a flex of his massive muscles, Wulfgar brought his horse under control. "I have," he answered through gritted teeth. He slid from his seat. "It is Harpells that worry me!"

Drizzt's smirk widened across his face as he suddenly came to understand his friend's trepidations. He himself, who had been raised amidst many of the most powerful and frightening sorcerers in all the Realms, had shaken his head in disbelief many times when they were guests of the eccentric family in Longsaddle. The Harpells had a unique—and often disastrous—way of viewing the world, though no evil festered in their hearts, and they wove their magic in accord with their own perspectives—usually against the presumed logic of rational men.

"Malchor is unlike his kin," Drizzt assured Wulfgar. "He does not reside in the Ivy Mansion and has played advisor to kings of the northland."

"He is a Harpell," Wulfgar stated with a finality that Drizzt could not dispute. With another shake of his head and a deep breath to steady himself, Wulfgar grabbed his horse's bridle and started out across the bridge. Drizzt, still smiling, was quick to follow.

"Harpell," Wulfgar muttered again after they had crossed to the island and made a complete circuit of the structure.

The tower had no door.

"Patience," Drizzt reminded him.

They did not have to wait long, though, for a few seconds later they heard a bolt being thrown, and then the creak of a door opening. A moment later, a boy barely into his teens walked right through the green stone of the wall, like some translucent specter, and moved toward them.

Wulfgar grunted and brought Aegis-fang, his mighty warhammer, down off his shoulder. Drizzt grasped the barbarian's arm to stay him, fearing that his weary friend might strike in sheer frustration before they could determine the lad's intentions.

When the boy reached them, they could see clearly that he was flesh and blood, not some otherworldly specter, and Wulfgar relaxed his grip. The youth bowed low to them and motioned for them to follow.

"Malchor?" asked Drizzt.

The boy did not answer, but he motioned again and started back toward the tower.

"I would have thought you to be older, if Malchor you be," Drizzt said, falling into step behind the boy.

"What of the horses?" Wulfgar asked.

Still the boy continued silently toward the tower.

Drizzt looked at Wulfgar and shrugged. "Bring them in, then, and let our mute friend worry about them," the dark elf said.

They found one section of the wall—at least—to be an illusion, masking a door that led them into a wide, circular chamber that was the tower's lowest level. Stalls lining one wall showed that they had done right in bringing the horses, and they tethered the beasts quickly and rushed to catch up to the youth. The boy had not slowed and had entered another doorway.

"Hold for us," Drizzt called, stepping through the portal, but he found no guide inside. He had entered a dimly lit corridor that rose gently and arced around as it rose, apparently tracing the circumference of the tower. "Only one way to go," he told Wulfgar, who came in behind him, and they started off.

Drizzt figured that they had done one complete circle and were up to the second level—ten feet at least—when they found the boy waiting for them beside a darkened side passage that fell back toward the center of the structure. The lad ignored this passage, though, and started off higher into the tower along the main arcing corridor.

Wulfgar had run out of patience for such cryptic games. His only concern was that Entreri and Regis were running farther away every second. He stepped by Drizzt and grabbed the boy's shoulder, spinning him about. "Are you Malchor?" he demanded bluntly.

The boy blanched at the giant man's gruff tone but did not reply.

"Leave him," Drizzt said. "He is not Malchor. I am sure. We will find the master of the tower soon enough." He looked to the frightened boy. "True?"

The boy gave a quick nod and started off again.

"Soon," Drizzt reiterated to quiet Wulfgar's growl. He prudently stepped by the barbarian, putting himself between Wulfgar and the guide.

"Harpell," Wulfgar groaned at his back.

The incline grew steeper and the circles tighter, and both friends knew that they were nearing the top. Finally the boy stopped at a door, pushed it open, and motioned for them to enter.

Drizzt moved quickly to be the first inside the room, fearing that the angry barbarian might make less than a pleasant first impression with their wizard host.

Across the room, sitting atop a desk and apparently waiting for them, rested a tall and sturdy man with neatly trimmed salt-and-pepper hair. His arms were crossed on his chest. Drizzt began to utter a cordial greeting, but Wulfgar nearly bowled him over, bursting in from behind and striding right up to the desk.

The barbarian, with one hand on his hip and one holding Aegis-fang in a prominent display before him, eyed the man for a moment. "Are you the wizard named Malchor Harpell?" he demanded, his voice hinting at explosive anger. "And if not, where in the Nine Hells are we to find him?"

The man's laugh erupted straight from his belly. "Of course," he answered, and he sprang from the desk and clapped Wulfgar hard on the shoulder. "I prefer a guest who does not cover his feelings with rosy words!" he cried. He walked past the stunned barbarian toward the door—and the boy.

"Did you speak to them?" he demanded of the lad.

The boy blanched even more than before and shook his head emphatically.

"Not a single word?" Malchor yelled.

The boy trembled visibly and shook his head again.

"He said not a—" Drizzt began, but Malchor cut him off with an outstretched hand.

"If I find that you uttered even a single syllable . . ." he threatened. He turned back to the room and took a step away. Just when he figured that the boy might have relaxed a bit, he spun back on him, nearly causing him to jump from his shoes.

"Why are you still here?" Malchor demanded. "Be gone!"

The door slammed even before the wizard had finished the command. Malchor laughed again, and the tension eased from his muscles as he moved back to his desk. Drizzt came up beside Wulfgar, the two looking at each other in amazement.

"Let us be gone from this place," Wulfgar said to Drizzt, and the drow could see that his friend was fighting a desire to spring over the desk and throttle the arrogant wizard on the spot.

To a lesser degree, Drizzt shared those feelings, but he knew the tower and its occupants would be explained in time. "Our greetings, Malchor Harpell," he said, his lavender eyes boring into the man. "Your actions, though, do not fit the description your cousin Harkle mantled upon you."

"I assure you that I am as Harkle described," Malchor replied calmly. "And my welcome to you, Drizzt Do'Urden, and to you, Wulfgar, son of Beornegar. Rarely have I entertained such fine guests in my humble tower." He bowed low to them to complete his gracious and diplomatic—if not entirely accurate—greeting.

"The boy did nothing wrong," Wulfgar snarled at him.

"No, he has performed admirably," Malchor agreed. "Ah, you fear for him?" The wizard took his measure of the huge barbarian, Wulfgar's muscles still knotted in rage. "I assure you, the boy is treated well."

"Not by my eyes," retorted Wulfgar.

"He aspires to be a wizard," Malchor explained, not ruffled by the barbarian's scowl. "His father is a powerful land-owner and has employed me to guide the lad. The boy shows potential, a sharp mind, and a love for the arts. But understand, Wulfgar, that wizardry is not so very different from your own trade."

Wulfgar's smirk showed a difference of opinion.

"Discipline," Malchor continued, undaunted. "For whatever we do in our lives, discipline and control over our own actions ultimately measure the level of our success. The boy has high aspirations and hints of power he cannot yet begin to understand. But if he cannot keep his thoughts silent for a single month, then I shan't waste years of my time on him. Your companion understands."

Wulfgar looked to Drizzt, standing relaxed by his side.

"I do understand," Drizzt said to Wulfgar. "Malchor has put the youth on trial, a test of his abilities to follow commands and a revelation to the depth of his desires."

"I am forgiven?" the wizard asked them.

"It is not important," Wulfgar grunted. "We have not come to fight the battles of a boy."

"Of course," said Malchor. "Your business presses; Harkle has told me. Go back down to the stables and wash. The boy is setting supper. He shall come for you when it is time to eat."

"Does he have a name?" Wulfgar said with obvious sarcasm.

"None that he has yet earned," Malchor replied curtly.

⚔ ⚔ ⚔ ⚔ ⚔

Though he was anxious to be back on the road, Wulfgar could not deny the splendor of the table of Malchor Harpell. He and Drizzt feasted well, knowing this to be, most probably, their last fine meal for many days.

"You shall spend the night," Malchor said to them after they had finished eating. "A soft bed would do you well," he argued against Wulfgar's disgruntled look. "And an early start, I promise."

"We will stay, and thank you," Drizzt replied. "Surely this tower will do us better than the hard ground outside."

"Excellent," said Malchor. "Come along, then, I have some items which should aid your quest." He led them out of the room and back down the decline of the corridor to the lower levels of the structure. As they walked, Malchor told his guests of the tower's formation and features. Finally they turned down one of the darkened side passages and passed through a heavy door.

Drizzt and Wulfgar had to pause at the entrance for a long moment to digest the wondrous sight before them, for they had come to Malchor's museum, a collection of the finest items, magical and otherwise, that the mage had found during the many years of his travels. Here were swords and full suits of polished armor, a shining mithral shield, and the crown of a long dead king. Ancient tapestries lined the walls, and a glass case of priceless gems and jewels glittered in the flicker of the room's torches.

Malchor had moved to a cabinet across the room, and by the time Wulfgar and Drizzt looked back to him, he was sitting atop the thing, casually juggling three horseshoes. He added a fourth as they watched, effortlessly guiding them through the rise and fall of the dance.

"I have placed an enchantment upon these that will make your steeds run swifter than any beasts in the land," he explained. "For a short time only, but long enough to get you to Waterdeep. That alone should be worth your delay in coming here"

"Two shoes to a horse?" Wulfgar asked, ever doubting.

"That would not do," Malchor came back at him, tolerant of the weary young barbarian. "Unless you wish your horse to rear up and run as a man!" He laughed, but the scowl did not leave Wulfgar's face.

"Not to fear," Malchor said, clearing his throat at the failed joke. "I have another set." He eyed Drizzt. "I have heard it spoken that few are as agile as the drow elves. And I have heard, as well, by those who have seen Drizzt Do'Urden at fight and at play, that he is brilliant even considering the standards of his dark kin." Without interrupting the rhythm of his juggling, he flipped one of the horseshoes to Drizzt.

Drizzt caught it easily and in the same motion put it into the air above him. Then came the second and third shoes, and Drizzt, without ever taking his eyes off Malchor, put them into motion with easy movements.

The fourth shoe came in low, causing Drizzt to bend to the ground to catch it. But Drizzt was up to the task, and he never missed a catch or a throw as he included the shoe in his juggling.

Wulfgar watched curiously and wondered at the motives of the wizard in testing the drow.

Malchor reached down into the cabinet and pulled out the other set of shoes. "A fifth," he warned, launching one at Drizzt. The drow remained unconcerned, catching the shoe deftly and tossing it in line.

"Discipline!" said Malchor emphatically, aiming his remark at Wulfgar. "Show me, drow!" he demanded, firing the sixth, seventh, and eighth at Drizzt in rapid succession.

Drizzt grimaced as they came at him, determined to meet the challenge. His hands moving in a blur, he quickly had all eight horseshoes spinning and dropping harmoniously. And as he settled into an easy rhythm, Drizzt began to understand the wizard's ploy.

Malchor walked over to Wulfgar and clapped him again on the shoulder. "Discipline," he said again. "Look at him, young warrior, for your dark-skinned friend is truly a master of his movements and thus, a master of his craft. You do not yet understand, but we two are not so different." He caught Wulfgar's eyes squarely with his own. "We three are not so different. Different methods, I agree. But to the same ends!"

Tiring of his game, Drizzt caught the shoes one by one as they fell and hooked them over his forearm, all the while eyeing Malchor with approval. Seeing his young friend slump back in thought, the drow wasn't sure which was the greater gift, the enchanted shoes or the lesson.

"But enough of this," Malchor said suddenly, bursting into motion. He crossed to a section of the wall that held dozens of swords and other weapons.

"I see that one of your scabbards is empty," he said to Drizzt. Malchor pulled a beautifully crafted scimitar from its mount. "Perhaps this will fill it properly."

Drizzt sensed the power of the weapon as he took it from the wizard, felt the care of its crafting and the perfection of its balance. A single, star-cut blue sapphire glittered in its pommel.

"Its name is Twinkle," Malchor said. "Forged by the elves of a past age."

"Twinkle," echoed Drizzt. Instantly a bluish light limned the weapon's blade. Drizzt felt a sudden surge within it, and somehow sensed a finer edge to its cut. He swung it a few times, trailing blue light with each motion.

How easily it arced through the air; how easily it would cut down a foe! Drizzt slid it reverently into his empty scabbard.

"It was forged in the magic of the powers that all the surface elves hold dear," said Malchor. "Of the stars and the moon and the mysteries of their souls. You deserve it, Drizzt Do'Urden, and it will serve you well."

Drizzt could not answer the tribute, but Wulfgar, touched by the honor Malchor had paid to his oft-maligned friend, spoke for him. "Our thanks to you, Malchor Harpell," he said, biting back the cynicism that had dominated his actions of late. He bowed low.

"Keep to your heart, Wulfgar, son of Beornegar," Malchor answered him. "Pride can be a useful tool, or it can close your eyes to the truths about you. Go now and take your sleep. I shall awaken you early and set you back along your road."

✕ ✕ ✕ ✕ ✕

Drizzt sat up in his bed and watched his friend after Wulfgar had settled into sleep. Drizzt was concerned for Wulfgar, so far from the empty tundra that had ever been his home. In their quest for Mithral Hall, they had trudged halfway across the northland, fighting every mile of the way. And in finding their goal, their trials had only begun, for they had then battled their way through the ancient dwarven complex. Wulfgar had lost his mentor there, and Drizzt his dearest friend, and truly they had dragged themselves back to the village of Longsaddle in need of a long rest.

But reality had allowed no breaks. Entreri had Regis in his clutches, and Drizzt and Wulfgar were their halfling friend's only hope. In Longsaddle, they had come to the end of one road but had found the beginning of an even longer one.

Drizzt could deal with his own weariness, but Wulfgar seemed cloaked in gloom, always running on the edge of danger. He was a young man out of Icewind Dale—the land that had been his only home—for the first time in his life. Now that sheltered strip of tundra, where the eternal wind blew, was far to the north.

But Calimport was much farther still, to the south.

Drizzt lay back on his pillow, reminding himself that Wulfgar had chosen to come along. Drizzt couldn't have stopped him, even if he had tried.

The drow closed his eyes. The best thing that he could do, for himself and for Wulfgar, was to sleep and be ready for whatever the next dawn would bring.

⚔ ⚔ ⚔ ⚔ ⚔

Malchor's student awakened them—silently—a few hours later and led them to the dining room, where the wizard waited. A fine breakfast was brought out before them.

"Your course is south, by my cousin's words," Malchor said to them. "Chasing a man who holds your friend, this halfling, Regis, captive."

"His name is Entreri," Drizzt replied, "and we will find him a hard catch, by my measure of him. He flies for Calimport."

"Harder still," Wulfgar added, "we had him placed on the road." He explained to Malchor, though Drizzt knew the words to be aimed at him, "Now we shall have to hope that he did not turn from its course."

"There was no secret to his path," argued Drizzt. "He made for Waterdeep, on the coast. He may have passed by there already."

"Then he is out to sea," reasoned Malchor.

Wulfgar nearly choked on his food. He hadn't even considered that possibility.

"That is my fear," said Drizzt. "And I had thought to do the same."

"It is a dangerous and costly course," said Malchor. "The pirates gather for the last runs to the south as the summer draws to an end, and if one has not made the proper arrangements . . ." He let the words hang ominously before them.

"But you have little choice," the wizard continued. "A horse cannot match the speed of a sailing ship, and the sea route is straighter than the road. So take to the sea, is my advice. Perhaps I can make some arrangements to speed your accommodations. My student has already set the enchanted shoes on your mounts, and with their aid, you may get to the great port in short days."

"And how long shall we sail?" Wulfgar asked, dismayed and hardly believing that Drizzt would go along with the wizard's suggestion.

"Your young friend does not understand the breadth of this journey," Malchor said to Drizzt. The wizard laid his fork on the table and another a few inches from it. "Here is Icewind Dale," he explained to Wulfgar, pointing to the first fork. "And this other, the Tower of Twilight, where you now sit. A distance of nearly four hundred miles lies between."

He tossed a third fork to Drizzt, who laid it out in front of him, about three feet from the fork representing their present position.

"It is a journey you would travel five times to equal the road ahead of you," Malchor told Wulfgar, "for that last fork is Calimport, two thousand miles and several kingdoms to the south."

"Then we are defeated," moaned Wulfgar, unable to comprehend such a distance.

"Not so," said Malchor. "For you shall ride with sails full of the northern wind, and beat the first snows of winter. You will find the land and the people more accommodating to the south."

"We shall see," said the dark elf, unconvinced. To Drizzt, people had ever spelled trouble.

"Ah," agreed Malchor, realizing the hardships a drow elf would surely find among the dwellers of the surface world. "But I have one more gift to give to you: a map to a treasure that you can recover this very day."

"Another delay," said Wulfgar.

"A small price to pay," replied Malchor, "and this short trip shall save you many days in the populated South, where a drow elf may walk only in the night. Of this I am certain."

Drizzt was intrigued that Malchor so clearly understood his dilemma and was apparently hinting at an alternative. Drizzt would not be welcome anywhere in the South. Cities that would grant the foul Entreri free passage would throw chains upon the dark elf if he tried to cross through, for the drow had long ago earned their reputation as ultimately evil and unspeakably vile. Few in all the Realms would be quick to recognize Drizzt Do'Urden as the exception to the rule.

"Just to the west of here, down a dark path in Neverwinter Wood and in a cave of trees, dwells a monster that the local farmers have named Agatha," said Malchor. "Once an elf, I believe, and a fair mage in her own right, according to legend, this wretched thing lives on after death and calls the night her time."

Drizzt knew the sinister legends of such creatures, and he knew their name. "A banshee?" he asked.

Malchor nodded. "To her lair you should go, if you are brave enough, for the banshee has collected a fair hoard of treasure, including one item that would prove invaluable to you, Drizzt Do'Urden."

He saw that he had the drow's full attention. Drizzt leaned forward over the table and weighed Malchor's every word.

"A mask," the wizard explained. "An enchanted mask that will allow you to hide your heritage and walk freely as a surface elf—or as a man, if that suits you."

Drizzt slumped back, a bit unnerved at the threat to his very identity.

"I understand your hesitancy," Malchor said to him. "It is not easy to hide from those who accuse you unjustly, to give credibility to their false perceptions. But think of your captive friend and know that I make this suggestion only for his sake. You may get through the southlands as you are, dark elf, but not unhindered."

Wulfgar bit his lip and said nothing, knowing this to be Drizzt's own decision. He knew that even his concerns about further delay could not weigh into such a personal discussion.

"We will go to this lair in the wood," Drizzt said at last, "and I shall wear such a mask if I must." He looked at Wulfgar. "Our only concern must be Regis."

⋊ ⋊ ⋊ ⋊ ⋊

Drizzt and Wulfgar sat atop their mounts outside the Tower of Twilight, with Malchor standing beside them.

"Be wary of the thing," Malchor said, handing Drizzt the map to the banshee's lair and another parchment that generally showed their course to the far South. "Her touch is deathly cold, and the legends say that to hear her keen is to die."

"Her keen?" asked Wulfgar.

"An unearthly wail too terrible for mortal ears to bear," said Malchor. "Take all care!"

"We shall," Drizzt assured him.

"We will not forget the hospitality or the gifts of Malchor Harpell," added Wulfgar.

"Nor the lesson, I hope," the wizard replied with a wink, drawing an embarrassed smile from Wulfgar.

Drizzt was pleased that his friend had shaken at least some of his surliness.

Dawn came upon them then, and the tower quickly faded into nothingness.

"The tower is gone, yet the wizard remains," remarked Wulfgar.

"The tower is gone, yet the door inside remains," Malchor corrected. He took a few steps back and stretched his arm out, his hand disappearing from sight.

Wulfgar jerked in bewilderment.

"For those who know how to find it," Malchor added. "For those who have trained their minds to the properties of magic." He stepped through the extradimensional portal and was gone from sight, but his voice came back to them one last time. "Discipline!" he called, and Wulfgar knew himself to be the target of Malchor's final statement.

Drizzt kicked his horse into motion, unrolling the map as he started away. "Harpell?" be asked over his shoulder, imitating Wulfgar's derisive tone of the previous night.

"Would that all of the Harpells were like Malchor!" Wulfgar replied. He sat staring at the emptiness that had been the Tower of Twilight, fully understanding that the wizard had taught him two valuable lessons in a single night: one of prejudice and one of humility.

⚔ ⚔ ⚔ ⚔ ⚔

From inside the hidden dimension of his home, Malchor watched them go. He wished that he could join them, to travel along the road of adventure as he had so often in his youth, finding a just course and following it against any odds. Harkle had judged the principles of those two correctly, Malchor knew, and had been right in asking Malchor to help them.

The wizard leaned against the door to his home. Alas, his days of adventure, his days of carrying the crusade of justice on his shoulders, were fading behind him.

But Malchor took heart in the events of the last day. If the drow and his barbarian friend were any indication, he had just helped to pass the torch into able hands.

2
A Thousand Thousand Little Candles

The assassin, mesmerized, watched as the ruby turned slowly in the candle-light, catching the dance of the flame in a thousand thousand perfect miniatures—too many reflections; no gem could have facets so small and so flawless.

And yet the procession was there to be seen, a swirl of tiny candles drawing him deeper into the redness of the stone. No jeweler had cut it; its precision went beyond a level attainable with an instrument. This was an artifact of magic, a deliberate creation designed, he reminded himself cautiously, to pull a viewer into that descending swirl, into the serenity of the reddened depths of the stone.

A thousand thousand little candles

No wonder he had so easily duped the captain into giving him passage to Calimport. Suggestions that came from within the marvelous secrets of this gem could not easily be dismissed. Suggestions of serenity and peace, words spoken only by friends . . .

A smile cracked the usually grim set of his face. He could wander deep into the calm.

Entreri tore himself from the pull of the ruby and rubbed his eyes, amazed that even one as disciplined as he might be vulnerable to the gem's insistent tug. He glanced into the corner of the small cabin, where Regis sat huddled and thoroughly miserable.

"I can now understand your desperation in stealing this jewel," he said to the halfling.

Regis snapped out of his own meditation, surprised that Entreri had spoken to him—the first time since they had boarded the boat back in Waterdeep.

"And I know now why Pasha Pook is so desperate to get it back," Entreri continued, as much to himself as to Regis.

Regis cocked his head to watch the assassin. Could the ruby pendant take even Artemis Entreri into its hold? "Truly it is a beautiful gem," he offered hopefully, not quite knowing how to handle this uncharacteristic empathy from the cold assassin.

"Much more than a gemstone," Entreri said absently, his eyes falling irresistibly back into the mystical swirl of the deceptive facets.

Regis recognized the calm visage of the assassin, for he himself had worn such a look when he had first studied Pook's wonderful pendant. He had been a successful thief then, living a fine life in Calimport. But the promises of that magical stone outweighed the comforts of the thieves' guild. "Perhaps the pendant stole me," he suggested on a sudden impulse.

But he had underestimated the willpower of Entreri. The assassin snapped a cold look at him, with a smirk clearly revealing that he knew where Regis was leading.

But the halfling, grabbing at whatever hope he could find, pressed on anyway. "The power of that pendant overcame me, I think. There could be no crime; I had little choice—"

Entreri's sharp laugh cut him short. "You are a thief, or you are weak," he snarled. "Either way you shall find no mercy in my heart. Either way you deserve the wrath of Pook!" He snapped the pendant up into his hand from the end of its golden chain and dropped it into his pouch.

Then he took out the other object, an onyx statuette intricately carved into the likeness of a panther.

"Tell me of this," he instructed Regis.

Regis had wondered when Entreri would show some curiosity for the figurine. He had seen the assassin toying with it back at Garumn's Gorge in Mithral Hall, teasing Drizzt from across the chasm. But until this moment, that was the last Regis had seen of Guenhwyvar, the magical panther.

Regis shrugged helplessly.

"I'll not ask again," Entreri threatened, and that icy certainty of doom, the inescapable aura of dread that all of Artemis Entreri's victims came to know well, fell over Regis once more.

"It is the drow's," Regis stammered. "Its name is Guen—" Regis caught the word in his mouth as Entreri's free hand suddenly snapped out a jeweled dagger, readied for a throw.

"Calling an ally?" Entreri asked wickedly. He dropped the statuette back into his pocket. "I know the beast's name, halfling. And I assure you, by the time the cat arrived, you would be dead."

"You fear the cat?" Regis dared to ask.

"I take no chances," Entreri replied.

"But will you call the panther yourself?" Regis pressed, looking for some way to change the balance of power. "A companion for your lonely roads?"

Entreri's laugh mocked the very thought "Companion? Why would I desire a companion, little fool? What gain could I hope to make?"

"With numbers comes strength," Regis argued.

"Fool," repeated Entreri. "That is where you err. In the streets, companions bring dependence and doom! Look at yourself, friend of the drow. What strength do you bring to Drizzt Do'Urden now? He rushes blindly to your aid, to fulfill his responsibility as your companion." He spat the word out with obvious distaste. "To his ultimate demise!"

Regis hung his head and could not answer. Entreri's words rang true enough. His friends were coming into dangers they could not imagine, and all for his sake, all because of errors he had made before he had ever met them.

Entreri replaced the dagger in its sheath and leaped up in a rush. "Enjoy the night, little thief. Bask in the cold ocean wind; relish all the sensations of this trip as a man staring death in the face, for Calimport surely spells your doom—and the doom of your friends!" He swept out of the room, banging the door behind him.

He hadn't locked it, Regis noted. He never locked the door! But he didn't have to, Regis admitted in anger. Terror was the assassin's chain, as tangible as iron shackles. Nowhere to run; nowhere to hide.

Regis dropped his head into his hands. He became aware of the sway of the ship, of the rhythmic, monotonous creaking of old boards, his body irresistibly keeping time.

He felt his insides churning.

Halflings weren't normally fond of the sea, and Regis was timid even by the measures of his kind. Entreri could not have found a greater torment to Regis than passage south on a ship, on the Sea of Swords.

"Not again," Regis groaned, dragging himself to the small portal in the cabin. He pulled the window open and stuck his head out into the refreshing chill of the night air.

⚔ ⚔ ⚔ ⚔

Entreri walked across the empty deck, his cloak tight about him. Above him, the sails swelled as they filled with wind; the early winter gales pushed the ship along its southern route. A billion stars dotted the sky, twinkling in the empty darkness to horizons bordered only by the flat line of the sea.

Entreri took out the ruby pendant again and let its magic catch the starlight. He watched it spin and studied its swirl, meaning to know it well before his journey's end.

Pasha Pook would be thrilled to get the pendant back. It had given him such power! More power, Entreri now realized, than others had assumed. With the pendant, Pook had made friends of enemies and slaves of friends.

"Even me?" Entreri mused, enthralled by the little stars in the red wash of the gem. "Have I been a victim? Or shall I be?" He wouldn't have believed that he, Artemis Entreri, could ever be caught by a magic charm, but the insistence of the ruby pendant was undeniable.

Entreri laughed aloud. The helmsman, the only other person on the deck, cast him a curious glance but thought no more about it.

"No," Entreri whispered to the ruby. "You shan't have me again. I know your tricks, and I'll learn them better still! I will run the path of your tempting descent and find my way back out again!" Laughing, he fastened the pendant's golden chain around his neck and tucked the ruby under his leather jerkin.

Then he felt in his pouch, grasped the figurine of the panther, and turned his gaze back to the north. "Are you watching, Drizzt Do'Urden?" he asked into the night.

He knew the answer. Somewhere far behind, in Waterdeep or Longsaddle or somewhere in between, the drow's lavender eyes were turned southward.

They were destined to meet again; they both knew. They had battled once, in Mithral Hall, but neither could claim victory.

There had to be a winner.

Never before had Entreri encountered anyone with reflexes to match his own or as deadly with a blade as he, and memories of his clash with Drizzt Do'Urden haunted his every thought. They were so akin, their movements cut from the same dance. And yet, the drow, compassionate and caring, possessed a basic humanity that Entreri had long ago discarded. Such emotions, such weaknesses, had no place in the cold void of a pure fighter's heart, he believed.

Entreri's hands twitched with eagerness as he thought of the drow. His breath puffed out angrily in the chill air. "Come, Drizzt Do'Urden," he said through his clenched teeth. "Let us learn who is the stronger!"

His voice reflected deadly determination, with a subtle, almost imperceptive, hint of anxiety. This would be the truest challenge of both their lives, the test of the differing tenets that had guided their every actions. For Entreri, there could be no draw. He had sold his soul for his skill, and if Drizzt Do'Urden defeated him, or even proved his equal, the assassin's existence would be no more than a wasted lie.

But he didn't think like that.

Entreri lived to win.

⚔ ⚔ ⚔ ⚔

Regis, too, was watching the night sky. The crisp air had settled his stomach, and the stars had sent his thoughts across the long miles to his friends. How often they had sat together on such nights in Icewind Dale, to share tales of adventure or just sit quietly in each others' company. Icewind

Dale was a barren strip of frozen tundra, a land of brutal weather and brutal people, but the friends Regis had made there, Bruenor and Catti-brie, Drizzt and Wulfgar, had warmed the coldest of the winter nights and taken the sting out of the biting north wind.

In context, Icewind Dale had been but a short stopover for Regis on his extensive travels, where he had spent less than ten of his fifty years. But now, heading back to the southern kingdom where he had lived for the bulk of his life, Regis realized that Icewind Dale had truly been his home. And those friends he so often took for granted were the only family he would ever know.

He shook away his lament and forced himself to consider the path before him. Drizzt would come for him; probably Wulfgar and Catti-brie, too.

But not Bruenor.

Any relief that Regis had felt when Drizzt returned unharmed from the bowels of Mithral Hall had flown over Garumn's Gorge with the valiant dwarf. A dragon had them trapped while a host of evil gray dwarves had closed in from behind. But Bruenor, at the cost of his own life, had cleared the way, crashing down onto the dragon's back with a keg of burning oil, taking the beast—and himself—down into the deep gorge.

Regis couldn't bear to recall that terrible scene. For all of his gruffness and teasing, Bruenor Battlehammer had been the halfling's dearest companion.

A shooting star burned a trail across the night sky. The sway of the ship remained and the salty smell of the ocean sat thick in his nose, but here at the portal, in the sharpness of the clear night, Regis felt no sickness—only a sad serenity as he remembered all of those crazy times with the wild dwarf. Truly Bruenor Battlehammer's flame had burned like a torch in the wind, leaping and dancing and fighting to the very end.

Regis's other friends had escaped, though. The halfling was certain of it—as certain as Entreri. And they would come for him. Drizzt would come for him and set things right.

Regis had to believe that.

And for his own part, the mission seemed obvious. Once in Calimport, Entreri would find allies among Pook's people. The assassin would then be on his own ground, where he knew every dark hole and held every advantage. Regis had to slow him down.

Finding strength in the narrow vision of a goal, Regis glanced about the cabin, looking for some clue. Again and again, he found his eyes drawn to the candle.

"The flame," he muttered to himself, a smile beginning to spread across his face. He moved to the table and plucked the candle from its holder. A small pool of liquid wax glittered at the base of the wick, promising pain.

But Regis didn't hesitate.

He hitched up one sleeve and dripped a series of wax droplets along the length of his arm, grimacing away the hot sting.

He had to slow Entreri down.

⚔ ⚔ ⚔ ⚔ ⚔

Regis made one of his rare appearances on the deck the next morning. Dawn had come bright and clear, and the halfling wanted to finish his business before the sun got too high in the sky and created that unpleasant mixture of hot rays in the cool spray. He stood at the rail, rehearsing his lines and mustering the courage to defy the unspoken threats of Entreri.

And then Entreri was beside him! Regis clutched the rail tightly, fearing that the assassin had somehow guessed his plan.

"The shoreline," Entreri said to him.

Regis followed Entreri's gaze to the horizon and a distant line of land.

"Back in sight," Entreri continued, "and not too far." He glanced down at Regis and displayed his wicked smile once again for his prisoner's benefit.

Regis shrugged. "Too far."

"Perhaps," answered the assassin, "but you might make it, though your half-sized breed is not spoken of as the swimming sort. Have you weighed the odds?"

"I do not swim," Regis said flatly.

"A pity," laughed Entreri. "But if you do decide to try for the land, tell me first."

Regis stepped back, confused.

"I would allow you to make the attempt," Entreri assured him. "I would enjoy the show!"

The halfling's expression turned to anger. He knew that he was being mocked, but he couldn't figure the assassin's purpose.

"They have a strange fish in these waters," said Entreri, looking back to the water. "Smart fish. It follows the boats, waiting for someone to go over." He looked back to Regis to weigh the effect of his chiding.

"A pointed fin marks it," he continued, seeing that he had the halfling's full attention. "Cutting through the water like the prow of a ship. If you watch from the rail long enough, you will surely spy one."

"Why would I want to?"

"Sharks, these fish are called," Entreri went on, ignoring the question. He drew his dagger, putting its point against one of his fingers hard enough to draw a speck of blood. "Marvelous fish. Rows of teeth as long as daggers, sharp and ridged, and a mouth that could *bite* a man in half." He looked Regis in the eye. "Or take a halfling whole."

"I do not swim!" Regis growled, not appreciating Entreri's macabre, but undeniably effective, methods.

"A pity," chuckled the assassin. "But do tell me if you change your mind." He swept away, his black cloak flowing behind him.

"Bastard," Regis mumbled under his breath. He started back toward the rail, but changed his mind as soon as he saw the deep water looming before him; he turned on his heel and sought the security of the middle of the deck.

Again the color left his face as the vast ocean seemed to close in over him and the interminable, nauseating sway of the ship . . .

"Ye seem ripe fer de rail, little one," came a cheery voice. Regis turned to see a short, bowlegged sailor with few teeth and eyes scrunched in a permanent squint. "Ain't to findin' yer sea legs yet?"

Regis shuddered through his dizziness and remembered his mission. "It is the other thing," he replied.

The sailor missed the subtlety of his statement. Still grinning through the dark tan and darker stubble of his dirty face, he started away.

"But thank you for your concern," Regis said emphatically. "And for all of your courage in taking us to Calimport."

The sailor stopped, perplexed. "Many a time, we's to taking ones to the south," he said, not understanding the reference to "courage."

"Yes, but considering the danger—though I am sure it is not great!" Regis added quickly, giving the impression that he was trying not to emphasize this unknown peril. "It is not important. Calimport will bring our cure." Then under his breath but still loud enough for the sailor to hear, he said, "If we get there alive."

" 'Ere now, what do ye mean?" the sailor demanded, moving back over to Regis. The smile was gone.

Regis squeaked and grabbed his forearm suddenly as if in pain. He grimaced and pretended to battle against the agony, while deftly scratching the dried patch of wax, and the scab beneath it, away. A small trickle of blood rolled out from under his sleeve.

The sailor grabbed him on cue, pulling the sleeve up over Regis's elbow. He looked at the wound curiously. "Burn?"

"Do not touch it!" Regis cried in a harsh whisper. "That is how it spreads—I think."

The sailor pulled his hand away in terror, noticing several other scars. "I seen no fire! How'd ye git a burn?"

Regis shrugged helplessly. "They just happen. From the inside." Now it was the sailor's turn to pale. "But I will make it to Calimport," he stated unconvincingly. "It takes a few months to eat you away. And most of my wounds are recent." Regis looked down, then presented his scarred arm. "See?"

But when he looked back, the sailor was gone, rushing off toward the captain's quarters.

"Take that, Artemis Entreri," Regis whispered.

3
Conyberry's Pride

"Those are the farms that Malchor spoke of," Wulfgar said as he and Drizzt came around a spur of trees on the great forest's border. In the distance to the south, a dozen or so houses sat in a cluster on the eastern edge of the forest, surrounded on the other three sides by wide, rolling fields.

Wulfgar started his horse forward, but Drizzt abruptly stopped him.

"These are a simple folk," the drow explained. "Farmers living in the webs of countless superstitions. They would not welcome a dark elf. Let us enter at night."

"Perhaps we can find the path without their aid," Wulfgar offered, not wanting to waste the remainder of yet another day.

"More likely we would get lost in the wood," Drizzt replied, dismounting. "Rest, my friend. This night promises adventure."

"Her time, the night," Wulfgar remarked, remembering Malchor's words about the banshee.

Drizzt's smile widened across his face. "Not this night," he whispered.

Wulfgar saw the familiar gleam in the drow's lavender eyes and obediently dropped from his saddle. Drizzt was already preparing himself for the imminent battle; already the drow's finely toned muscles twitched with excitement. But as confident as Wulfgar was in his companion's prowess, he could not stop the shudder running through his spine when he considered the undead monster that lay before them.

In the night.

⚔ ⚔ ⚔ ⚔ ⚔

They passed the day in peaceful slumber, enjoying the calls and dances of the birds and squirrels, already preparing for winter, and the wholesome atmosphere of the forest. But when dusk crept over the land, Neverwinter Wood took on a very different aura. Gloom settled all too comfortably under the wood's thick boughs, and a sudden hush descended on the trees, the uneasy quiet of poised danger.

Drizzt roused Walfgar and led him off to the south at once, not even pausing for a short meal. A few minutes later, they walked their horses to the nearest farmhouse. Luckily the night was moonless, and only a close inspection would reveal Drizzt's dark heritage.

"State yer business or be gone!" demanded a threatening voice from the low rooftops before they got close enough to knock on the house's door.

Drizzt had expected as much. "We have come to settle a score," he said without any hesitation.

"What enemies might the likes of yerselves have in Conyberry?" asked the voice.

"In your fair town?" Drizzt balked. "Nay, our fight is with a foe common to you."

Some shuffling came from above, and then two men, bows in hand, appeared at the corner of the farmhouse. Both Drizzt and Wulfgar knew that still more sets of eyes—and no doubt more bows—were trained upon them from the roof, and possibly from their flanks. For simple farmers, these folk were apparently well organized for defense.

"A common foe?" one of the men at the corner—the same who had spoken earlier from the roof—asked Drizzt. "Surely we've seen none of yer likes before, elf, nor of yer giant friend!"

Wulfgar brought Aegis-fang down from his shoulder, drawing some uneasy shuffling from the roof. "Never have we come through your fair town," he replied sternly, not thrilled with being called a giant.

Drizzt quickly interjected. "A friend of ours was slain near here, down a dark path in the wood. We were told that you could guide us."

Suddenly the door of the farmhouse burst open and a wrinkled old woman popped her head out. "Hey, then, what do ye want with the ghost in the wood?" she snapped angrily. "Not fer to both'ring those that leaves her to peace!"

Drizzt and Wulfgar glanced at each other, perplexed by the old woman's unexpected attitude. But the man at the corner apparently felt the same way.

"Yeah, leave Agatha be," he said.

"Go away!" added an unseen man from the roof.

Wulfgar, fearing that these people might be under some evil enchantment, gripped his warhammer more tightly, but Drizzt sensed something else in their voices.

"I had been told that the ghost, this Agatha, was an evil spirit," Drizzt told them calmly. "Might I have heard wrong? For goodly folk defend her."

"Bah, evil! What be evil?" snapped the old woman, thrusting her wrinkled face and shell of a body closer to Wulfgar. The barbarian took a prudent step back, though the woman's bent frame barely reached his navel.

"The ghost defends her home," added the man at the corner. "And woe to those who go there!"

"Woe!" screamed the old woman, pushing closer still and poking a bony finger into Wulfgar's huge chest.

Wulfgar had heard enough. "Back!" he roared mightily at the woman. He slapped Aegis-fang across his free hand, a sudden rush of blood swelling his bulging arms and shoulders. The woman screamed and vanished into the house, slamming the door in terror.

"A pity," Drizzt whispered, fully understanding what Wulfgar had set into motion. The drow dived headlong to the side, turning into a roll, as an arrow from the roof cracked into the ground where he had been standing.

Wulfgar, too, started into motion, expecting an arrow. Instead, he saw the dark form of a man leaping down at him from the rooftop. With a single hand the mighty barbarian caught the would-be assailant in midair and held him at bay, his boots fully three feet off the ground.

At that same instant, Drizzt came out of his roll and into position in front of the two men at the corner, a scimitar poised at each of their throats. They hadn't even had time to draw their bowstrings back. To their further horror, they now recognized Drizzt for what he was, but even if his skin had been as pale as that of his surface cousins, the fire in his eyes would have taken their strength from them.

A few long seconds passed, the only movement being the visible shaking of the three trapped farmers.

"An unfortunate misunderstanding," Drizzt said to the men. He stepped back and sheathed his scimitars. "Let him down," he said to Wulfgar. "Gently!" the dark elf added quickly.

Wulfgar eased the man to the ground, but the terrified farmer fell to the dirt anyway, looking up at the huge barbarian in awe and fear.

Wulfgar kept the grimace on his face—just to keep the farmer cowed.

The farmhouse door sprang open again, and the little old woman appeared, this time sheepishly. "Ye won't be killing poor Agatha, will ye?" she pleaded.

"Sure that she's no harm beyond her own door," added the man at the corner, his voice quaking with each syllable.

Drizzt looked to Wulfgar. "Nay," the barbarian said. "We shall visit Agatha and settle our business with her. But be assured that we'll not harm her.

"Tell us the way," Drizzt asked.

The two men at the corner looked at each other and hesitated.

"Now!" Wulfgar roared at the man on the ground.

"To the tangle of birch!" the man replied immediately. "The path's right there, running back to the east! Twists and turns, it does, but clear of brush!"

"Farewell, Conyberry," Drizzt said politely, bowing low. "Would that we could remain a while and dispel your fears of us, but we have much to do and a long road ahead." He and Wulfgar hopped into their saddles and spun their mounts away.

"But wait!" the old woman called after them. Their mounts reared as

Drizzt and Wulfgar looked back over their shoulders. "Tell us, ye fearless—or ye stupid—warriors," she implored them, "who might ye be?"

"Wulfgar, son of Beornegar!" the barbarian shouted back, trying to keep an air of humility, though his chest puffed out in pride. "And Drizzt Do'Urden!"

"Names I have heard!" one of the farmers cried out in sudden recognition.

"And names you shall hear again!" Wulfgar promised. He paused a moment as Drizzt moved on, then turned to catch his friend.

Drizzt wasn't sure that it was wise to be proclaiming their identities, and consequently revealing their location, with Artemis Entreri looking back for them. But when he saw the broad and proud smile on Wulfgar's face, he kept his concerns to himself and let Wulfgar have his fun.

⚔ ⚔ ⚔ ⚔

Soon after the lights of Conyberry had faded to dots behind them, Wulfgar turned more serious "They did not seem evil," he said to Drizzt, "yet they protect the banshee, and have even named the thing! We may have left a darkness behind us!"

"Not a darkness," Drizzt replied. "Conyberry is as it appears: a humble farming village of good and honest folk."

"But Agatha," Wulfgar protested.

"A hundred similar villages line this countryside," Drizzt explained. "Many unnamed, and all unnoticed by the lords of the land. Yet all of the villages, and even the Lords of Waterdeep, I would guess, have heard of Conyberry and the ghost of Neverwinter Wood."

"Agatha brings them fame," Wulfgar concluded.

"And a measure of protection, no doubt," added Drizzt.

"For what bandit would lay out along the road to Conyberry with a ghost haunting the land?" Wulfgar laughed. "Still, it seems a strange marriage."

"But not our business," Drizzt said, stopping his horse. "The tangle the man spoke of." He pointed to a copse of twisted birch trees. Behind it, Neverwinter Wood loomed dark and mysterious.

Wulfgar's horse flattened its ears. "We are close," the barbarian said, slipping from the saddle. They tethered their mounts and started into the tangle, Drizzt as silent as a cat, but Wulfgar, too big for the tightness of the trees, crunching with every step.

"Do you mean to kill the thing?" he asked Drizzt.

"Only if we must," the drow replied. "We are here for the mask alone, and we have given our word to the people of Conyberry."

"I do not believe that Agatha will willingly hand us her treasures," Wulfgar reminded Drizzt. He broke through the last line of birch trees and stood beside the drow at the dark entrance to the thick oaks of the forest.

"Be silent now," Drizzt whispered. He drew Twinkle and let its quiet blue gleam lead them into the gloom.

The trees seemed to close in about them; the dead hush of the wood only made them more concerned with the resounding noise of their own footfalls. Even Drizzt, who had spent centuries in the deepest of caverns, felt the weight of this darkest corner of Neverwinter on his shoulders. Evil brooded here, and if either he or Wulfgar had any doubts about the legend of the banshee, they knew better now. Drizzt pulled a thin candle from his belt pouch and broke it in half, handing a piece to Wulfgar.

"Stuff your ears," he explained in a breathless whisper, reiterating Malchor's warning. "To hear her keen is to die."

The path was easy to follow, even in the deep darkness, for the aura of evil rolled down heavier on their shoulders with every step. A few hundred paces brought the light of a fire into sight. Instinctively they both dropped to a defensive crouch to survey the area.

Before them lay a dome of branches, a cave of trees that was the banshee's lair. Its single entrance was a small hole, barely large enough for a man to crawl through. The thought of going into the lighted area within while on their hands and knees did not thrill either of them. Wulfgar held Aegis-fang before him and indicated that he would open a bigger door. Boldly he strode toward the dome.

Drizzt crept up beside him, uncertain of the practicality of Wulfgar's idea. Drizzt had the feeling that a creature who had survived so successfully for so very long would be protected against such obvious tactics. But the drow didn't have any better ideas at the moment, so he dropped back a step as Wulfgar hoisted the warhammer above his head.

Wulfgar spread his feet wide for balance and took a steadying breath, then slammed Aegis-fang home with all his strength. The dome shuddered under the blow; wood splintered and went flying, but the drow's concerns soon came to light. For as the wooden shell broke away, Wulfgar's hammer drove down into a concealed mesh of netting. Before the barbarian could reverse the blow, Aegis-fang and his arms were fully entangled.

Drizzt saw a shadow move across the firelight inside, and recognizing his companion's vulnerability, he didn't hesitate. He dived through Wulfgar's legs and into the lair, his scimitars nipping and jabbing wildly as he came. Twinkle nicked into something for just a split second, something less than tangible, and Drizzt knew that he had hit the creature of the nether world. But dazed by the sudden intensity of the light as he came into the lair, Drizzt had trouble finding his footing. He kept his head well enough to discern that the banshee had scampered into the shadows off to the other side. He rolled up to a wall, put his back against it for support, and scrambled to his feet, deftly slicing through Wulfgar's bonds with Twinkle.

Then came the wail.

It cut through the feeble protection of the candle wax with bone-shivering intensity, sapping into Drizzt's and Wulfgar's strength and dropping a dizzying blackness over them. Drizzt slumped heavily against the wall, and Wulfgar, finally able to tug free of the stubborn netting, stumbled backward into the black night and toppled onto his back.

Drizzt, alone inside, knew that he was in deep trouble. He battled against the dizzying blur and the stinging pain in his head and tried to focus on the firelight.

But he saw two dozen fires dancing before his eyes, lights he could not shake away. He believed that he had come out of the keen's effects, and it took him a moment to realize the truth of the place.

A magical creature was Agatha, and magical protections, confusing illusions of mirror images, guarded her home. Suddenly Drizzt was confronted on more than twenty fronts by the twisted visage of a long-dead elven maiden, her skin withered and stretched along her hollowed face and her eyes bereft of color or any spark of life.

But those orbs could see more clearly than any other in this deceptive maze. And Drizzt understood that Agatha knew exactly where he was. She waved her arms in circular motions and smirked at her intended victim.

Drizzt recognized the banshee's movements as the beginnings of a spell. Still caught in the web of her illusions, the drow had only one chance. Calling on the innate abilities of his dark race—and desperately hoping that he had correctly guessed which was the real fire—he placed a globe of darkness over the flames. The inside of the tree cave went pitch black, and Drizzt fell to his belly.

A blue bolt of lightning cut through the darkness, thundering just above the lying drow and through the wall. The air sizzled around him; his stark white hair danced on its ends.

Bursting out into the dark forest, Agatha's ferocious bolt shook Wulfgar from his stupor. "Drizzt," he groaned, forcing himself to his feet. His friend was probably already dead, and beyond the entrance was a blackness too deep for human eyes. But fearlessly, without a thought for his own safety, Wulfgar stumbled back toward the dome.

Drizzt crept around the black perimeter, using the heat of the fire as his guide. He brought a scimitar to bear with every step, but caught nothing with his cuts but air and the side of the tree cave.

Then, suddenly, his darkness was no more, leaving him exposed along the middle of the wall to the left of the door. And the leering image of Agatha was all about him, already beginning yet another spell. Drizzt glanced around for an escape route, but realized that Agatha didn't seem to be looking at him.

Across the room, in what must have been a real mirror, Drizzt caught sight of another image: Wulfgar crawling in defenselessly through the low entrance.

Again Drizzt could not afford to hesitate. He was beginning to understand the layout of the illusion maze and could guess at the general direction of the banshee. He dropped to one knee and scooped up a handful of dirt, splaying it in a wide arc across the room.

All of the images reacted the same way, giving Drizzt no clue as to which was his foe. But the real Agatha, wherever she was, was spitting dirt; Drizzt had disrupted her spell.

Wulfgar regained his feet and immediately smashed his hammer through the wall to the right side of the door, then reversed his swing and heaved Aegis-fang at the image across from the door, directly over the fire. Again Aegis-fang crashed into the wall, knocking open a hole to the nighttime forest.

Drizzt, firing his dagger futilely at yet another image across the way, caught a telltale flicker in the area where he had seen the reflection of Wulfgar. As Aegis-fang magically returned to Wulfgar's hands, Drizzt sprinted for the back of the chamber. "Lead me!" he cried, hoping his voice was loud enough for Wulfgar to hear.

Wulfgar understood. Bellowing "Tempus!" to warn the drow of his throw, he launched Aegis-fang again.

Drizzt dived into a roll, and the hammer whistled over his back, exploding into the mirror. Half of the images in the room disappeared, and Agatha screamed in rage. But Drizzt didn't even slow. He sprang over the broken mirror stand and the remaining chunks of glass.

Right into Agatha's treasure room.

The banshee's scream became a keen, and the killing waves of sound dropped over Drizzt and Wulfgar once again. They had expected the blast this time, though, and they pushed its force away more easily. Drizzt scrambled to the treasure hoard, scooping baubles and gold into a sack. Wulfgar, enraged, stormed about the dome in a destructive frenzy. Soon kindling lined the area where walls had stood, and scratches dripping tiny streams of blood crisscrossed Wulfgar's huge forearms. But the barbarian felt no pain, only the savage fury.

His sack nearly full, Drizzt was about to turn and flee when one other item caught his eye: He had been almost relieved that he hadn't found it, and a big part of him wished that it wasn't here, that such an item did not exist. Yet here it lay, an unremarkable mask of bland features, with a single cord to hold it in place over a wearer's face. Drizzt knew that, as plain as it seemed, it must be the item Malchor had spoken of, and if he had any thoughts of ignoring it now, they were quickly gone. Regis needed him, and to get to Regis quickly, Drizzt needed the mask. Still, the drow could not belay his sigh when he lifted it from the treasure hoard, sensing its tingling power. Without another thought, he put it in his sack.

Agatha would not so easily surrender her treasures, and the specter that confronted Drizzt when he hopped back over the broken mirror was all too real. Twinkle gleamed wickedly as Drizzt parried away Agatha's frantic blows.

Wulfgar suspected that Drizzt needed him now, and he dismissed his savage fury, realizing that a clear head was necessary in this predicament. He scanned the room slowly, hoisting Aegis-fang for another throw. But the barbarian found that he had not yet sorted out the pattern of the illusionary spells, and the confusion of a dozen images, and the fear of hitting Drizzt, held him in check.

Effortlessly Drizzt danced around the crazed banshee and backed her up toward the treasure room. He could have struck her several times, but he had given his word to the farmers of Conyberry.

Then he had her in position. He thrust Twinkle out before him and waded in with two steps. Spitting and cursing, Agatha retreated, tripping over the broken mirror stand and falling back into the gloom. Drizzt spun toward the door.

Watching the real Agatha, and the other images, disappear from sight, Wulfgar followed the sound of her grunt and finally sorted out the layout of the dome. He readied Aegis-fang for the killing throw.

"Let it end!" Drizzt shouted at him as he passed, slapping Wulfgar on the backside with the flat of Twinkle to remind him of their mission and their promise.

Wulfgar turned to look at him, but the agile drow was already out into the dark night. Wulfgar turned back to see Agatha, her teeth bared and hands clenched, rise up on her feet.

"Pardon our intrusion," he said politely, bowing low—low enough to follow his friend outside to safety. He sprinted along the dark path to catch up to Twinkle's blue glow.

Then came the banshee's third keen, chasing them down the path.

Drizzt was beyond its painful range, but its sting caught up to Wulfgar and knocked him off balance. Blindly, with the smug smile suddenly wiped from his face, he stumbled forward.

Drizzt turned and tried to catch him, but the huge man bowled the drow over and continued on.

Face first into a tree.

Before Drizzt could get over to help, Wulfgar was up again and running, too scared and embarrassed, to even groan.

Behind them, Agatha wailed helplessly.

⚔ ⚔ ⚔ ⚔

When the first of Agatha's keens wafted on the night winds the mile or so to Conyberry, the villagers knew that Drizzt and Wulfgar had found her lair. All of them, even the children, had gathered outside of their houses and listened intently as two more wails had rolled through the night air. And now, most perplexing, came the banshee's continual, mournful cries.

"So much fer them strangers," chuckled one man.

"Nah, ye're wrong," said the old woman, recognizing the subtle shift in Agatha's tones. "Them's wails of losing. They beat her! They did, and got away!"

The others sat quietly, studying Agatha's cries, and soon realized the truth of the old woman's observations. They looked at each other incredulously.

"What'd they call themselves?" asked one man.

"Wulfgar," offered another. "And Drizzt Do'Urden. I heared o' them before."

4

THE CITY OF SPLENDORS

They were back to the main road before dawn, thundering to the west, to the coast and the city of Waterdeep. With the visit to Malchor and the business with Agatha out of the way, Drizzt and Wulfgar once again focused their thoughts on the road ahead, and they remembered the peril their halfling friend faced if they failed in the rescue. Their mounts, aided by Malchor's enchanted horseshoes, sped along at a tremendous clip. All the landscape seemed only a blur as it rolled by.

They did not break when dawn came behind them, nor did they stop for a meal as the sun climbed overhead.

"We will have all the rest we need when we board ship and sail to the south," Drizzt told Wulfgar.

The barbarian, determined that Regis would be saved, needed no prompting.

The dark of night came again, and the thunder of the hooves continued unbroken. Then, when the second morning found their backs, a salty breeze filled the air and the high towers of Waterdeep, the City of Splendors, appeared on the western horizon. The two riders stopped atop the high cliff that formed the fabulous settlement's eastern border. If Wulfgar had been stunned earlier that year when he had first looked upon Luskan, five hundred miles up the coast, he now was stricken dumb. For Waterdeep, the jewel of the North, the greatest port in all the Realms, was fully ten times the size of Luskan. Even within its high wall, it sprawled out lazily and endlessly down the coast, with towers and spires reaching high into the sea mist to the edges of the companions' vision.

"How many live here?" Wulfgar gasped at Drizzt.

"A hundred of your tribes could find shelter within the city," the drow explained. He noted Wulfgar's anxiety with concern of his own. Cities were beyond the experiences of the young man, and the time Wulfgar had ventured into Luskan had nearly ended in disaster. And now there was Waterdeep, with ten times the people, ten times the intrigue—and ten times the trouble.

Wulfgar settled back a bit, and Drizzt had no choice but to put his trust in the young warrior. The drow had his own dilemma, a personal battle that he now had to settle. Gingerly he took the magical mask out of his belt pouch.

Wulfgar understood the determination guiding the drow's hesitant motions, and he looked upon his friend with sincere pity. He did not know if he could be so brave—even with Regis's life hanging on his actions.

Drizzt turned the plain mask over in his hands, wondering at the limits of its magic. He could feel that this was no ordinary item; its power tingled to his sensitive touch. Would it simply rob him of his appearance? Or might it steal his very identity? He had heard of other, supposedly beneficial, magical items that could not be removed once worn.

"Perhaps they will accept you as you are," Wulfgar offered hopefully.

Drizzt sighed and smiled, his decision made. "No," he answered. "The soldiers of Waterdeep would not admit a drow elf, nor would any boat captain allow me passage to the south." Without any more delays, he placed the mask over his face.

For a moment, nothing happened, and Drizzt began to wonder if all of his concerns had been for naught, if the mask were really a fake. "Nothing," he chuckled uneasily after a few more seconds, tentative relief in his tone. "It does not—" Drizzt stopped in midsentence when he noticed Wulfgar's stunned expression.

Wulfgar fumbled in his pack and produced a shiny metal cup. "Look," he bade Drizzt and handed him the makeshift mirror.

Drizzt took the cup in trembling hands—hands that trembled more when Drizzt realized they were no longer black—and raised it to his face. The reflection was poor—even poorer in the morning light to the drow's night eyes—but Drizzt could not mistake the image before him. His features had not changed, but his black skin now held the golden hue of a surface elf. And his flowing hair, once stark white, showed lustrous yellow, as shiny as if it had caught the rays of the sun and held them fast.

Only Drizzt's eyes remained as they had been, deep pools of brilliant lavender. No magic could dim their gleam, and Drizzt felt some small measure of relief, at least, that his inner person had apparently remained untainted.

Yet he did not know how to react to this blatant alteration. Embarrassed, he looked to Wulfgar for approval.

Wulfgar's visage had turned sour. "By all the measures known to me, you appear as any other handsome elven warrior," he answered to Drizzt's inquiring gaze. "And surely a maiden or two will blush and turn her eyes when you stride by."

Drizzt looked to the ground and tried to hide his uneasiness with the assessment.

"But I like it not," Wulfgar continued sincerely. "Not at all." Drizzt looked back to him uncomfortably, almost sheepishly.

"And I like the look upon your face, the discomfort of your spirit, even less," Wulfgar continued, now apparently a bit perturbed. "I am a warrior who has faced giants and dragons without fear. But I would pale at the notion of battling Drizzt Do'Urden. Remember who you are, noble ranger."

A smile found its way onto Drizzt's face. "Thank you, my friend," he said. "Of all the challenges I have faced, this is perhaps the most trying."

"I prefer you without the thing," said Wulfgar.

"As do I," came another voice from behind them. They turned to see a middle-aged man, well muscled and tall, walking toward them. He seemed casual enough, wearing simple clothes and sporting a neatly trimmed black beard. His hair, too, was black, though speckles of silver edged it.

"Greetings, Wulfgar and Drizzt Do'Urden," he said with a graceful bow.

"I am Khelben, an associate of Malchor. That most magnificent Harpell bade me to watch for your arrival."

"A wizard?" Wulfgar asked, not really meaning to speak his thoughts aloud.

Khelben shrugged. "A forester," he replied, "with a love for painting, though I daresay that I am not very good at it."

Drizzt studied Khelben, not believing either of his disclaimers. The man had an aura of distinction about him, a distinguished manner and confidence befitting a lord. By Drizzt's measure, Khelben was more likely Malchor's peer, at least. And if the man truly loved to paint, Drizzt had no doubt that he had perfected the art as well as any in the North. "A guide through Waterdeep?" Drizzt asked.

"A guide to a guide," Khelben answered. "I know of your quest and your needs. Passage on a ship is not an easy thing to come by this late in the year, unless you know where to inquire. Come, now, to the south gate, where we might find one who knows." He found his mount a short distance away and led them to the south at an easy trot.

They passed the sheer cliff that protected the city's eastern border, a hundred feet high at its peak. And where the cliff sloped down to sea level, they found another city wall. Khelben veered away from the city at this point, though the south gate was now in sight, and indicated a grassy knoll topped by a single willow.

A small man jumped down from the tree as they breached the knoll, his dark eyes darting nervously about. He was no pauper, by his dress, and his uneasiness when they approached only added to Drizzt's suspicions that Khelben was more than he had presumed.

"Ah, Orlpar, so good of you to come," Khelben said casually. Drizzt and Wulfgar exchanged knowing smiles; the man had been given no choice in the matter.

"Greetings," Orlpar said quickly, wanting to finish the business as expediently as possible. "The passage is secured. Have you the payment?"

"When?" Khelben asked.

"A tenday," replied Orlpar. "The *Coast Dancer* puts out in a tenday."

Khelben did not miss the worried looks that Drizzt and Wulfgar now exchanged. "That is too long," he told Orlpar. "Every sailor in port owes you a favor. My friends cannot wait."

"These arrangements take time!" Orlpar argued, his voice rising. But then, as if he suddenly remembered who he was addressing, he shrank back and dropped his eyes.

"Too long," Khelben reiterated calmly.

Orlpar stroked his face, searching for some solution. "Deudermont," he said, looking hopefully to Khelben. "Captain Deudermont takes the *Sea Sprite* out this very night. A fairer man you'll not find, but I do not know how far south he will venture. And the price will be high."

"Ah," Khelben smiled, "but fear not, my little friend. I have wondrous barter for you this day."

Orlpar looked at him suspiciously. "You said gold."

"Better than gold," Khelben replied. "Three days from Longsaddle my friends have come, but their mounts have not broken even a sweat."

"Horses?" balked Orlpar.

"Nay, not the steeds," said Khelben. "Their shoes. Magical shoes that can carry a horse like the wind itself!"

"My business is with sailors!" Orlpar protested as vigorously as he dared. "What use would I find with horseshoes?"

"Calm, calm, Orlpar," Khelben said softly with a wink. "Remember your brother's embarrassment? You will find some way to turn magical horseshoes into profit, I know."

Orlpar took a deep breath to blow away his anger. Khelben obviously had him cornered. "Have these two at the Mermaid's Arms," he said. "I will see what I can do." With that, he turned and trotted off down the hill toward the south gate.

"You handled him with ease," Drizzt remarked.

"I held every advantage," Khelben replied. "Orlpar's brother heads a noble house in the city. At times, this proves a great benefit to Orlpar. Yet, it is also a hindrance, for he must take care not to bring public embarrassment to his family.

"But enough of that business," Khelben continued. "You may leave the horses with me. Off with you, now, to the south gate. The guards there will guide you to Dock Street, and from there you will have little trouble finding the Mermaid's Arms."

"You are not to come with us?" asked Wulfgar, slipping down from his saddle.

"I have other business," Khelben explained. "It is better that you go alone. You will be safe enough; Orlpar would not cross me, and Captain Deudermont is known to me as an honest seaman. Strangers are common in Waterdeep, especially down in the Dock Ward."

"But strangers wandering beside Khelben, the painter, might draw attention," Drizzt reasoned with good-humored sarcasm.

Khelben smiled but did not answer.

Drizzt dropped from big saddle. "The horses are to be returned to Longsaddle?"

"Of course."

"Our thanks to you, Khelben," said Drizzt. "Surely you have aided our cause greatly." Drizzt thought for a moment, eyeing his horse. "You must know that the enchantment Malchor put on the shoes will not remain. Orlpar will not profit from the deal he made this day."

"Justice," chuckled Khelben. "That one has turned many an unfair deal, let me assure you. Perhaps this experience will teach him humility and the error of his ways."

"Perhaps," said Drizzt, and with a bow, he and Wulfgar started down the hill.

"Keep your guard, but keep your calm," Khelben called after them. "Ruffians are not unknown on the docks, but the police are ever-present. Many a stranger spends his first night in the city dungeons!" He watched the two of them descend the knoll and remembered, as Malchor had remembered, those long-ago days when it was he who followed the roads to distant adventures.

"He had the man cowed," Wulfgar remarked when he and Drizzi were out of Khelben's earshot. "A simple painter?"

"More likely a wizard—a powerful wizard," Drizzt replied. "And our thanks again are owed to Malchor, whose influence has eased our way. Mark my words, 'twas no simple painter that tamed the likes of Orlpar."

Wulfgar looked back to the knoll, but Khelben and the horses were nowhere to be seen. Even with his limited understanding of the black arts, Wulfgar realized that only magic could have moved Khelben and the three horses from the area so quickly. He smiled and shook his head, and marveled again at the eccentric characters the wide world kept showing him.

⚔ ⚔ ⚔ ⚔ ⚔

Following the directions given to them by the guards at the south gate, Drizzt and Wulfgar were soon strolling down Dock Street, a long lane that ran the length of Waterdeep Harbor on the south side of the city. Fish smells and salty air filled their nostrils, gulls complained overhead, and sailors and mercenaries from every stretch of the Realms wandered about, some busy at work, but most ashore for their last rest before the long journey to points south.

Dock Street was well outfitted for such merrymaking; every corner held a tavern. But unlike the city of Luskan's dockside, which had been given over to the rabble by the lords of the city long ago, Dock Street in Waterdeep was not an evil place. Waterdeep was a city of laws, and members of the Watch, Waterdeep's famed city guard, seemed always in sight.

Hardy adventurers abounded here, battle-hardened warriors that carried their weapons with cool familiarity. Still, Drizzt and Wulfgar found many eyes focused upon them, with almost every head turning and watching as they passed. Drizzt felt for his mask, at first worrying that it had somehow slipped off and revealed his heritage to the amazed onlookers. A quick inspection dispelled his fears, for his hands still showed the golden luster of a surface elf.

And Drizzt nearly laughed aloud when he turned to ask Wulfgar for confirmation that the mask still disguised his facial features, for it was then the dark elf realized that he was not the object of the gawks. He had been so close to the young barbarian for the last few years that he was used to Wulfgar's physical stature. Nearly seven feet tall, with corded muscles that thickened every year, Wulfgar strode down Dock Street with the easy air of sincere confidence.

Aegis-fang bouncing casually on one shoulder. Even among the greatest warriors in the Realms, this young man would stand out.

"For once, it seems that I am not the target of the stares," said Drizzt.

"Take off the mask, drow," Wulfgar replied, his face reddening with a rush of blood. "And take their eyes from me!"

"I would, but for Regis," Drizzt answered with a wink.

The Mermaid's Arms was no different from any other of the multitude of taverns that laced this section of Waterdeep. Shouts and cheers drifted out of the place, on air heavily scented with cheap ale and wine. A group of rowdies, pushing and shoving each other and throwing curses to the men they called friends, had gathered in front of the door.

Drizzt looked at Wulfgar with concern. The only other time the young man had been in such a place—at the Cutlass in Luskan—Wulfgar had torn apart the tavern, and most of its patrons, in a brawl. Clinging to ideals of honor and courage, Wulfgar was out of place in the unprincipled world of city taverns.

Orlpar came out of the Mermaid's Arms then and sifted adeptly through the rowdy crowd. "Deudermont is at the bar," he whispered out of the corner of his mouth. He passed Drizzt and Wulfgar and appeared to take no notice of them. "Tall; blue jacket and yellow beard," added Orlpar.

Wulfgar started to respond, but Drizzt kept him moving forward, understanding Orlpar's preference for secrecy.

The crowd parted as Drizzt and Wulfgar strode through, all their stares squarely on Wulfgar. "Bungo'll have 'im," one of them whispered when the two companions had moved into the bar.

"Be worth the watchin', though," chuckled another.

The drow's keen ears caught the conversation, and he looked again at his huge friend, noting how Wulfgar's size always seemed to single the barbarian out for such trouble.

The inside of the Mermaid's Arms offered no surprises. The air hung thick with the smoke of exotic weeds and the stench of stale ale. A few drunken sailors lay facedown on tables or sat propped against walls while others stumbled about, spilling their drinks—often on more sober patrons, who responded by shoving the offenders to the floor. Wulfgar wondered how many of these men had missed the sailing of their ships. Would they stagger about in here until their coin ran out, only then to be dropped into the street to face the coming winter penniless and without shelter?

"Twice I have seen the bowels of a city," Wulfgar whispered to Drizzt. "And both times I have been reminded of the pleasures of the open road!"

"The goblins and the dragons?" Drizzt retorted lightheartedly, leading Wulfgar to an empty table near the bar.

"A far lot better than this," Wulfgar remarked.

A serving wench was upon them before they had even sat down. "What's yer pleasure?" she asked absently, having long ago lost interest in the patrons she served.

"Water," Wulfgar answered gruffly.

"And wine," Drizzt quickly added, handing over a gold piece to dispel the woman's sudden scowl.

"That must be Deudermont," Wulfgar said, deflecting any forthcoming scolding concerning his treatment of the wench. He pointed to a tall man leaning over the bar rail.

Drizzt rose at once, thinking it prudent to be done with their business and out of the tavern as quickly as possible. "Hold the table," he told Wulfgar

Captain Deudermont was not the average patron of the Mermaid's Arms. Tall and straight, he was a refined man accustomed to dining with lords and ladies. But as with all of the ship captains who put into Waterdeep Harbor, especially on the day of their departures, Deudermont spent most of his time ashore, keeping a watchful eye on his valued crew and trying to prevent them from winding up in Waterdeep's overfilled jails.

Drizzt squeezed in next to the captain, brushing away the inquiring look of the barkeep. "We have a common friend," Drizzt said softly to Deudermont.

"I would hardly number Orlpar among my friends," the captain replied casually. "But I see that he did not exaggerate about the size and strength of your young friend."

Deudermont was not the only one who had noticed Wulfgar. As did every other tavern in this section of Waterdeep—and most bars across the

Realms—the Mermaid's Arms had a champion. A bit farther down the bar rail, a massive, hulking slob named Bungo had eyed Wulfgar from the minute the young barbarian had walked through the door. Bungo didn't like the looks of this one, not in the least. Even more than the corded arms, Wulfgar's graceful stride and the easy way he carried his huge warhammer revealed a measure of experience beyond his age.

Bungo's supporters crowded around him in anticipation of the coming brawl, their twisted smiles and beer-reeking breath spurring their champion to action. Normally confident, Bungo had to work to keep his anxiety under control. He had taken many hits in his seven-year reign at the tavern. His frame was bent now, and dozens of bones had been cracked and muscles torn. Looking at the awesome spectacle of Wulfgar, Bungo honestly wondered if he could have won this match even in his healthier youth.

But the regulars of the Mermaid's Arms looked up to him. This was their domain, and he their champion. They provided his free meals and drinks—Bungo could not let them down.

He quaffed his full mug in a single gulp and pushed himself off the rail. With a final growl to reassure his supporters, and callously tossing aside anyone in his way, Bungo made his way toward Wulfgar.

Wulfgar had seen the group coming before it had ever started moving. This scene was all too familiar to the young barbarian, and he fully expected that he would once again, as had happened at the Cutlass in Luskan, be singled out because of his size.

"What're ye fer?" Bungo said with a hiss as he towered, hands on hips, over the seated man. The other ruffians spread out around the table, putting Wulfgar squarely within their ring.

Wulfgar's instincts told him to stand and drop the pretentious slob where he stood. He had no fears about Bungo's eight friends. He considered them cowards who needed their leader to spur them on. If a single blow put Bungo down—and Wulfgar knew it would—the others would hesitate before striking, a delay that would cost them dearly against the likes of Wulfgar.

But over the last few months, Wulfgar had learned to temper his anger, and he had learned a broader definition of honor. He shrugged, making no move that resembled a threat. "A place to sit and a drink," he replied calmly. "And who might you be?"

"Name's Bungo," said the slob, spittle spraying with every word. He thrust his chest out proudly, as if his name should mean something to Wulfgar.

Again Wulfgar, wiping Bungo's spray from his face, had to resist his fighting instincts. He and Drizzt had more important business, he reminded himself.

"Who said ye could come to my bar?" Bungo growled, thinking—hoping—that he had put Wijlfgar on the defensive. He looked around at his friends, who leaned closer over Wulfgar, heightening the intimidation.

Surely Drizzt would understand the necessity to put this one down, Wulfgar reasoned, his fists tightening at his sides. "One shot," he muttered silently, looking around at the wretched group—a group that would look better sprawled out unconscious in the corners of the floor.

Wulfgar summoned an image of Regis to ward off his welling rage, but he could not ignore the fact that his hands were now clenched on the rim of the table so tightly that his knuckles had whitened for lack of blood.

$$\times \quad \times \quad \times \quad \times \quad \times$$

"The arrangements?" Drizzt asked.

"Secured," replied Deudermont. "I've room on the *Sea Sprite* for you, and I welcome the added hands—and blades—especially of such veteran adventurers. But I've a suspicion that you might be missing our sailing." He grasped Drizzt's shoulder to turn him toward the trouble brewing at Wulfgar's table.

"Tavern champion and his cronies," Deudermont explained, "though my bet would be with your friend."

"Coin well placed," Drizzt replied, "but we have no time. . ."

Deudermont guided Drizzt's gaze across to a shadowy corner of the tavern and to four men sitting calmly watching the growing tumult with interest. "The Watch," Deudermont said. "A fight will cost your friend a night in the dungeons. I cannot hold port!"

Drizzt searched the tavern, looking for some out. All eyes seemed to be closing in on Wulfgar and the ruffians, eagerly anticipating the fight. The drow realized that if he went to the table now, he would probably ignite the whole thing.

✕ ✕ ✕ ✕

Bungo thrust his belly forward, inches from Wulfgar's face, to display a wide belt notched in a hundred places. "Fer every man I beat," he boasted. "Give me somethin' to do on my night in jail." He pointed at a large cut to the side of the buckle. "Killed that one there. Squashed 'is head real good. Cost me five nights."

Wulfgar eased his grip, not impressed, but wary now of the potential consequences of his actions. He had a ship to catch.

"Perhaps it was Bungo I came to see," he said, crossing his arms and leaning back in his chair.

"Get 'im, then?" growled one of the ruffians.

Bungo eyed Wulfgar wickedly. "Come lookin' fer a fight?"

"Nay, I think not," Wulfgar retorted. "A fight? Nay, I am but a boy out to see the wide world!"

Bungo could not hide his confusion. He looked around to his friends, who could only shrug in response.

"Sit," Wulfgar offered. Bungo made no move.

The ruffian behind Wulfgar poked him hard in the shoulder and growled, "What're ye fer?"

Wulfgar had to consciously catch his own hand before it shot across and squashed the ruffian's filthy fingers together. But he had control now. He leaned closer to the huge leader. "Not to fight; to watch," he said quietly. "One day, perhaps, I might deem myself worthy to challenge the likes of Bungo, and on that day I will return, for I have no doubt that you will still be the champion of this tavern. But that day is many years away, I fear. I have so much to learn."

"Then why've ye come?" Bungo demanded, his confidence brimming over. He leaned over Wulfgar, threateningly close.

"I have come to learn," Wulfgar replied. "To learn by watching the toughest fighter in Waterdeep. To see how Bungo presents himself and goes about his affairs."

Bungo straightened and looked around at his anxious friends, who were leaning nearly to the point of falling over the table. Bungo flashed his toothless grin, customary before he clobbered a challenger, and the ruffians tensed. But then their champion surprised them, slapping Wulfgar hard on the shoulder—the clap of a friend.

Audible groans issued throughout the tavern as Bungo pulled up a chair to share a drink with the impressive stranger.

"Get ye gone!" the slob roared at his companions. Their faces twisted in disappointment and confusion, but they did not dare disobey. The one behind Wulfgar poked him again for good measure, then followed the others back to the bar.

⚔ ⚔ ⚔ ⚔

"A wise move," Deudermont remarked to Drizzt.

"For both of them," the drow replied, relaxing against the rail.

"You have other business in the city?" the captain asked.

Drizzt shook his head. "No. Get us to the ship," he said. "I fear that Waterdeep can bring only trouble."

⚔ ⚔ ⚔ ⚔

A million stars filled the sky that cloudless night. They reached down from the velvety canopy to join with the distant lights of Waterdeep, setting the northern horizon aglow. Wulfgar found Drizzt above decks, sitting quietly in the rolling serenity offered by the sea.

"I should like to return," Wulfgar said, following his friend's gaze to the now distant city.

"To settle a score with a drunken ruffian and his wretched friends," Drizzt concluded.

Wulfgar laughed but stopped abruptly when Drizzt wheeled on him.

"To what end?" Drizzt asked. "Would you then replace him as the champion of the Mermaid's Arms?"

"That is a life I do not envy," Wulfgar replied, chuckling again, though this time uncomfortably.

"Then leave it to Bungo," Drizzt said, turning back to the glow of the city.

Again Wulfgar's smile faded.

Seconds, minutes perhaps, slipped by, the only sound the slapping of the waves against the prow of the *Sea Sprite*. On an impulse, Drizzt slid Twinkle from its sheath. The crafted scimitar came to life in his hand, the blade glowing in the starlight that had given Twinkle its name and its enchantment.

"The weapon fits you well," Wulfgar remarked.

"A fine companion," Drizzt acknowledged, examining the intricate designs etched along the curving blade. He remembered another magical scimitar he had once possessed, a blade he had found in the lair of a dragon that he and Wulfgar had slain. That blade, too, had been a fine companion. Wrought of ice magic, the scimitar was forged as a bane to creatures of fire, impervious, along with its wielder, to their flames. It had served Drizzt well, even saving him from the certain and painful death of a demon's fire.

Drizzt cast his gaze back to Wulfgar. "I was thinking of our first dragon," he explained to the barbarian's questioning look. "You and I alone in the ice cave against the likes of Icingdeath, an able foe."

"He would have had us," Wulfgar added, "had it not been for the luck of that huge icicle hanging above the dragon's back."

"Luck?" Drizzt replied. "Perhaps. But more often, I dare to say, luck is simply the advantage a true warrior gains in executing the correct course of action."

Wulfgar took the compliment in stride; he had been the one to dislodge the pointed icicle, killing the dragon.

"A pity I do not have the scimitar I plundered from Icingdeath's lair to serve as a companion for Twinkle," Drizzt remarked.

"True enough," replied Wulfgar, smiling as he remembered his early adventures beside the drow. "But, alas, that one went over Garumn's Gorge with Bruenor."

Drizzt paused and blinked as if cold water had been thrown in his face. A sudden image flooded through his mind, its implications both hopeful and frightening. The image of Bruenor Battlehammer drifting slowly down into the depths of the gorge on the back of a burning dragon.

A burning dragon!

It was the first time Wulfgar had ever noted a tremble in the voice of his normally composed friend, when Drizzt rasped out, "Bruenor had my blade?"

ASHES

The room was empty, the fire burning low. The figure knew that there were gray dwarves, duergar, in the side chamber, through the partly opened door, but he had to chance it. This section of the complex was too full of the scum for him to continue along the tunnels without his disguise.

He slipped in from the main corridor and tiptoed past the side door to get to the hearth. He knelt before it and laid his fine mithral axe at his side The glow of the embers made him flinch instinctively, though he felt no pain as he dipped his finger into the ash.

He heard the side door swing open a few seconds later and rubbed a final handful of the ash over his face, hoping that he had properly covered his telltale red beard and the pale flesh of his long nose ail the length to its tip.

"What ye be doin'?" came a croak behind him.

The ash-covered dwarf blew into the embers, and a small flame came to life. "Bit o' chill," he answered. "Be needin' rest" He rose and turned, lifting the mithral axe beside him.

Two gray dwarves walked across the room to stand before him, their weapons securely sheathed. "Who ye be?" one asked. "Not o' Clan McUduck, an' not belongin' in these tunnels!"

"Tooktook o' Clan Trilk," the dwarf lied, using the name of a gray dwarf he had chopped down just the morning before. "Been patrollin', and been lost! Glad I be to find a room with a hearth!"

The two gray dwarves looked at each other, and then back to the stranger suspiciously. They had heard the reports over the last few tendays—since Shimmergloom, the shadow dragon that had been their god-figure, had fallen—tales of slaughtered duergar, often beheaded, found in the outer tunnels. And why was this one alone? Where was the rest of his patrol? Surely Clan Trilk knew enough to keep out of the tunnels of Clan McUduck.

And, why, one of them noticed, was there a patch of red on this one's beard?

The dwarf realized their suspicion immediately and knew that he could not keep this charade going for long. "Lost two o' me kin," he said. "To a drow." He smiled when he saw the duergar's eyes go wide. The mere mention of a drow elf always sent gray dwarves rocking back on their heels—and bought the dwarf a few extra seconds. "But worth it, it were!" he proclaimed, holding the mithral axe up beside his head. "Found me a wicked blade! See?"

Even as one of the duergar leaned forward, awed by the shining weapon, the red-bearded dwarf gave him a closer look, putting the cruel blade deep into his face. The other duergar just managed to get a hand to his sword hilt when he got hit with a backhand blow that drove the butt of the axe handle into his eye He stumbled back, reeling, but knew through the blur of pain that he was finished a full second before the mithral axe sliced the side of his neck.

Two more duergar burst in from the anteroom, their weapons drawn. "Get help!" one of them screamed, leaping into the fight. The other bolted for the door.

Again, luck was with the red-bearded dwarf. He kicked hard at an object on the floor, launching it toward the fleeing duergar, while parrying the first blow of his newest opponent with his golden shield.

The fleeing duergar was only a couple of strides from the corridor when something rolled between his feet, tripping him up and sending him sprawling to the floor, He got back to his knees quickly but hesitated, fighting back a gush of bile, when he saw what he had stumbled over.

The head of his kin.

The red-bearded dwarf danced away from another strike, rushing across the room to shield-slam the now-kneeling duergar, smashing the unfortunate creature into the stone wall.

But the dwarf, overbalanced in the fury of his rush, was down on one knee when the remaining duergar caught up to him. The intruder swung his shield back above him to block a downward thrust of the duergar's sword, and countered with a low sweep of his axe, aiming for the knees.

The duergar sprang back just in time, taking a nick on one leg, and before he could fully recover and come back with a counter, the red-bearded dwarf was up and at the ready.

"Yer bones are for carrion-eaters!" the dwarf growled.

"Who ye be?" the duergar demanded. "Not o' me kin, fer sure!"

A white smile spread across the dwarf's ash-covered face. "Battlehammer's me name," he growled, displaying the standard emblazoned upon his shield—the foaming mug emblem of Clan Battlehammer. "Bruenor Battlehammer, rightful king of Mithral Hall!"

Bruenor chuckled softly to see the gray dwarf's face blanch to white. The duergar stumbled back toward the door of the anteroom, understanding now that he was no match for this mighty foe. In desperation, he spun and fled, trying to slam the door shut behind him.

But Bruenor guessed what the duergar had in mind, and he got his heavy boot through the door before it could close. The mighty dwarf slammed his shoulder into the hard wood, sending the duergar flying back into the small room and knocking aside a table and chair.

Bruenor strode in confidently, never fearing even odds.

With no escape, the gray dwarf rushed back at him wildly, his shield leading and his sword above his head. Bruenor easily blocked the downward thrust, then smashed his axe into the duergar's shield. It, too, was of mithral, and the axe could not cut into it. But so great was Bruenor's blow that the leather strappings snapped apart and the duergar's arm went numb and drooped helplessly. The duergar screamed in terror and brought his short sword across his chest to protect his opened flank

Bruenor followed the duergar's swordarm with a shield-rush, shoving into his opponent's elbow and causing the duergar to overbalance. In a lightning combination with his axe, Bruenor slipped the deadly blade over the duergar's dipped shoulder.

A second head dropped free to the floor.

Bruenor grunted at the job well done and moved back into the larger room. The duergar beside the door was just regaining consciousness when Bruenor came up to him and shield-slammed him back into the wall. "Twenty-two," he mumbled to himself, keeping count of the number of gray dwarves he had cut down during these last few tendays.

Bruenor peeked out into the dark corridor. All was clear. He closed the door softly and went back to the hearth to touch up his disguise.

Following the wild descent to the bottom of Garumn's Gorge on the back of a flaming dragon, Bruenor had lost consciousness. Truly he was amazed when he managed to open his eyes. He knew the dragon to be dead as soon as he looked around, but he couldn't understand why he, still lying atop the smoldering form, had not been burned.

The gorge had been quiet and dark around him; he could not begin to guess how long he had remained unconscious. He knew, though, that his friends, if they had escaped, would probably have made their way out through the back door, to the safety of the surface.

And Drizzt was alive! The image of the drow's lavender eyes staring at him from the wall of the gorge as the dragon had glided past in its descent remained firmly etched in Bruenor's mind. Even now, tendays later as far as he could figure, he used that image of the indomitable Drizzt Do'Urden as a litany against the hopelessness of his own situation. For Bruenor could not climb from the bottom of the gorge, where the walls rose straight and sheer. His only option had been to slip into the sole tunnel running off the chasm's base and make his way though the lower mines.

And through an army of gray dwarves—duergar even more alert, for the dragon Bruenor had killed, Shimmergloom, had been their leader.

He had come far, and each step he took brought him a little closer to the freedom of the surface. But each step also brought him closer to the main host of the duergar. Even now he could hear the thrumming of the furnaces of the great undercity, no doubt teeming with the gray scum. Bruenor knew that he had to pass through there to get to the tunnels connecting the higher levels.

But even here, in the darkness of the mines, his disguise could not hold out to close scrutiny. How would he fare in the glow of the undercity, with a thousand gray dwarves milling all about him?

Bruenor shook away the thought and rubbed more ash onto his face. No need to worry now; he'd find his way through. He gathered up his axe and shield and headed for the door.

He shook his head and smiled as he approached, for the stubborn duergar beside the door was awake again—barely—and struggling to find his feet.

Bruenor slammed him into the wall a third time and casually dropped the axe blade onto his head as he slumped, this time never to awaken. "Twenty-two," the mighty dwarf reiterated grimly as he stepped into the corridor.

The sound of the closing door echoed through the darkness, and when it died away, Bruenor heard again the thrumming of the furnaces.

The undercity, his only chance.

He steadied himself with a deep breath, then slapped his axe determinedly against his shield and started stomping along the corridor toward the beckoning sound.

It was time to get things done.

The corridor twisted and turned, finally ending in a low archway that opened into a brightly fit cavern.

For the first time in nearly two hundred years, Bruenor Battlehammer looked down upon the great undercity of Mithral Hall. Set in a huge chasm, with walls tiered into steps and lined with decorated doorways, this massive chamber had once housed the entirety of Clan Battlehammer with many rooms to spare.

The place had remained exactly as the dwarf remembered it, and now, as in those distant years of his youth, many of the furnaces were bright with fire and the floor level teemed with the hunched forms of dwarven workers.

How many times had young Bruenor and his friends looked down upon the magnificence of this place and heard the chiming of the smithies' hammers and the heavy sighing of the huge bellows? he wondered.

Bruenor spat away the pleasant memories when he reminded himself that these hunched workers were evil duergar, not his kin. He brought his mind back into the present and the task at hand. Somehow he had to get across the open floor and up the tiers on the far side, to a tunnel that would take him higher in the complex.

A shuffle of boots sent Bruenor back into the shadows of the tunnel. He gripped his axe tightly and didn't dare to breathe, wondering if the time of his last glory had finally caught up to him. A patrol of heavily armed duergar marched up to the archway then continued past, giving only a casual glance down the tunnel.

Bruenor sighed deeply and scolded himself for his delay. He could not afford to tarry; every moment he spent in this area was a dangerous gamble. Quickly he searched for options. He was about halfway up one wall, five tiers from the floor. One bridge, at the highest tier, traversed the chasm, but no doubt it would be heavily guarded. Walking alone up there, away from the bustle of the floor, would make him too conspicuous.

Across the busy floor seemed a better route. The tunnels halfway up the other wall, almost directly across from where he now stood, would lead him to the western end of the complex, back to the hall he had first entered on his return to Mithral Hall, and to the open valley of Keeper's Dale beyond. It was his best chance, by his estimation—if he could get across the open floor.

He peeked out under the archway for any signs of the returning patrol. Satisfied that all was clear, he reminded himself that he was a king, the rightful king of the complex, and boldly stepped out onto the tier. The closest steps down were to the right, but the patrol had headed that way and Bruenor thought it wise to keep clear of them.

His confidence grew with each step. He passed a couple of gray dwarves, answering their casual greetings with a quick nod and never slowing his stride.

He descended one tier and then another, and before he even had time to consider his progress, Bruenor found himself bathed in the bright light of the huge furnaces at the final descent, barely fifteen feet from the floor. He crouched instinctively at the glow of the light, but he realized on a rational level that the brightness was actually his ally. Duergar were creatures of the dark, not accustomed to, nor liking, the light. Those on the floor kept their hoods pulled low to shield their eyes, and Bruenor did likewise, only improving his disguise. With the apparently unorganized movements on the floor, he began to believe that the crossing would be easy.

He moved out slowly at first, gathering speed as he went, but staying in a crouch, the collar of his cloak pulled up tightly around his cheeks, and his battered, one-horned helmet dipped low over his brow. Trying to maintain an air of easiness, Bruenor kept his shield arm at his side, but his other hand rested comfortably on his belted axe. If it came to blows, Bruenor was determined to be ready.

He passed by the three central forges—and the cluster of duergar they attracted—without incident, then waited patiently as a small caravan of ore-filled wheelbarrows were carted by. Bruenor, trying to keep the easy, cordial atmosphere, nodded to the passing band, but bile rose in his throat as he saw the mithral load in the carts—and at the thought of the gray scum extracting the precious metals from the walls of his hallowed homeland.

"Ye'll be paid for yer troubles," he mumbled under his breath. He rubbed a sleeve over his brow. He had forgotten how very hot the bottom area of the undercity became when the furnaces were burning. As with everyone else there, streaks of sweat began to make their way down his face.

Bruenor thought nothing of the discomfort at first, but then the last of the passing miners gave him a curious side-long glance.

Bruenor hunched even lower and quickly stepped away, realizing the effect his sweating would have on his feeble disguise. By the time he reached the first stair on the other side of the chasm, his face was fully streaked and parts of his whiskers were showing their true hue.

Still, he thought he might make it. But halfway up the stair, disaster struck. Concentrating more on hiding his face, Bruenor stumbled and bumped into a duergar soldier standing two steps above him. Reflexively Bruenor looked up, and his eyes met with the duergar's.

The dumbfounded stare of the gray dwarf told Bruenor beyond any doubt that the ploy was over. The gray dwarf went for his sword, but Bruenor didn't have time for a pitched battle. He drove his head between the duergar's knees—shattering one kneecap with the remaining horn of his helmet—and heaved the duergar behind him and down the stairs

Bruenor glanced around. Few had noticed, and fights were commonplace among the duergar ranks. Casually he started again up the stairs.

But the soldier was still conscious after he crashed to the floor and still coherent enough to point a finger up to the tier and shout, "Stop 'im!"

Bruenor lost all hope of remaining inconspicuous. He pulled out his mithral axe and tore along the tier toward the next stair. Cries of alarm sprang up throughout the chasm. A general commotion of spilled wheelbarrows, the clanging of weapons being drawn, and the thumping of booted feet closed in around Bruenor. Just as he was about to turn onto the next stairway, two guards leaped down in front of him.

"What's the trouble?" one of them cried, confused and not understanding that the dwarf they now faced had been the cause of the commotion. In horror, the two guards recognized Bruenor for what he was just as his axe tore the face off one and he shoulder-blocked the other off the tier.

Then up the stairs he sprinted, only to reverse his tracks as a patrol appeared at the top. Hundreds of gray dwarves rushed all about the undercity, their focus increasing on Bruenor.

Bruenor found another stair and got to the second tier.

But he stopped there, trapped. A dozen duergar soldiers came at him from both directions, their weapons drawn.

Bruenor scanned the area desperately. The tumult had brought more than a hundred of the gray dwarves on the floor rushing over to, and up, the original stair he had climbed.

A broad smile found the dwarf's face as he considered a desperate plan. He looked again at the charging soldiers and knew that he had no choice. He saluted the groups, adjusted his helmet and dropped suddenly from the tier, crashing down into the crowd that had assembled on the tier below him. Without losing his momentum, Bruenor continued his roll to the ledge, dropping along with several unfortunate gray dwarves onto another group on the floor.

Bruenor was up in a flash, chopping his way through. The surprised duergar in the crowd climbed over each other to get out of the way of the wild dwarf and his deadly axe, and in seconds, Bruenor was sprinting unhindered across the floor.

Bruenor stopped and looked all around. Where could he go now? Dozens of duergar stood between him and any of the exits from the undercity, and they grew more organized with every second.

One soldier charged him, only to be chopped down in a single blow. "Come on, then!" Bruenor shouted defiantly, figuring to take a fair share and more of the duergar down with him. "Come on, as many as will! Know the rage of the true king o' Mithral Hall!"

A crossbow quarrel clanked into his shield, taking a bit of the bluster out of his boastings. More on instinct than conscious thought, the dwarf darted suddenly for the single unguarded path—the roaring furnaces. He dropped the mithral axe into his belt loop and never slowed. Fire hadn't harmed him on the back of the falling dragon, and the warmth of the ashes he'd rubbed off his face never seemed to touch his skin.

And once again, standing in the center of the open furnace, Bruenor found himself impervious to the flames. He didn't have time to ponder this mystery and could only guess the protection from fire to be a property of the magical armor he had donned when he had first entered Mithral Hall.

But in truth, it was Drizzt's lost scimitar, neatly strapped under Bruenor's pack and almost forgotten by the dwarf, that had once again saved him.

The fire hissed in protest and started to burn low when the magical blade came in. But it roared back to life as Bruenor quickly started up the chimney. He heard the shouts of the astonished duergar behind him, along with cries to get the fire out. Then one voice rose above the others in a commanding tone. "Smoke 'im!" it cried.

Rags were wetted and thrown into the blaze, and great bursts of billowing gray smoke closed in around Bruenor. Soot filled his eyes and he could find no breath, still he had no choice but to continue his ascent.

Blindly he searched for cracks into which he could wedge his stubby fingers and pulled himself along with all of his strength.

He knew that he would surely die if he inhaled, but he had no breath left, and his lungs cried out in pain.

Unexpectedly he found a hole in the wall and nearly fell in from his momentum. A side tunnel? he wondered, astonished. He then remembered that all of the chimneys of the undercity had been interconnected to aid in their cleaning.

Bruenor pulled himself away from the rush of smoke and curled up inside the new passage. He tried to wipe the soot from his eyes as his lungs mercifully took in a deep draft, but he only aggravated the sting with his soot-covered sleeve. He couldn't see the blood flowing over his hands, but could guess at the extent of his wounds from the sharp ache along his fingernails.

As exhausted as he was, he knew that he could afford no delays. He crawled along the little tunnel, hoping that the furnace below the next chimney he came to was not in use.

The floor dropped away in front of him, and Bruenor almost tumbled down another shaft. No smoke, he noted, and with a wall as broken and climbable as the first. He tightened down all of his equipment, adjusted his helmet one more time, and inched out, blindly seeking a handhold and ignoring the aches in his shoulders and fingers. Soon he was moving steadily again.

But seconds seemed like minutes, and minutes like hours, to the weary dwarf, and he found himself resting as much as climbing, his breaths coming in heavy labored gasps. During one such rest, Bruenor thought he heard a shuffle above him. He paused to consider the sound. These shafts should not connect to any higher side passages, or to the overcity, he thought. Their ascent is straight to the open air of the surface. Bruenor strained to look upward through his soot-filled eyes. He knew that he had heard a sound.

The riddle was solved suddenly, as a monstrous form shuffled down the shaft beside Bruenor's precarious perch and great, hairy legs began flailing at him. The dwarf knew his peril at once.

A giant spider.

Venom-dripping pincers tore a gash into Bruenor's forearm. He ignored the pain and the possible implications of the wound and reacted with matched fury. He drove himself up the shaft, butting his head into the bulbous body of the wretched thing, and pushed off from the walls with all his strength.

The spider locked its deadly pincers onto a heavy boot and flailed with as many legs as it could spare while holding its position.

Only one course of attack seemed feasible to the desperate dwarf: dislodge the spider. He grasped at the hairy legs, twisting himself to snap them as he caught them, or at least to pull them from their hold on the wall. His arm burned with the sting of poison, and his foot, though his boot had repelled the pincers, was twisted and probably broken.

But he had no time to think of the pain. With a growl, he grabbed another leg and snapped it apart.

Then they were falling.

The spider—stupid thing—curled up as best it could and released its hold on the dwarf. Bruenor felt the rush of air and the closeness of the wall as they sped along. He could only hope that the shaft was straight enough to keep them clear of any sharp edges. He climbed as far over the spider as he could, putting the bulk of its body between himself and the coming impact.

They landed in a great splat. The air blasted from Bruenor's lungs, but with the wet explosion of the spider beneath him, he sustained no serious wounds. He still could not see, but he realized that he must again be on the floor level of the undercity, though luckily—for he heard no cries of alarm—in a less busy section. Dazed but undaunted, the stubborn dwarf picked himself up and wiped the spider fluid from his hands.

"Sure to be a mother's mother of a rainstorm tomorrow," he muttered, remembering an old dwarven superstition against killing spiders. And he started back up the shaft, dismissing the pain in his hands, the ache in his ribs and foot, and the poisoned burn of his forearm.

And any thoughts of more spiders lurking up ahead.

He climbed for hours, stubbornly putting one hand over the other and pulling himself up. The insidious spider venom swept through him with waves of nausea and sapped the strength from his arms. But Bruenor was tougher than mountain stone. He might die from his wound, but he was determined that it would happen outside, in the free air, under the stars or the sun.

He would escape Mithral Hall.

A cold blast of wind shook the exhaustion from him. He looked up hopefully but still could not see—perhaps it was nighttime outside. He studied the whistle of the wind for a moment and knew that he was only yards from his goal. A burst of adrenaline carried him to the chimney's exit—and the iron grate that blocked it.

"Damn ye by Moradin's hammer!" Bruenor spat. He leaped from the walls and grasped the bars of the grate with his bloodied fingers. The bars bent under his weight but held fast.

"Wulfgar could break it," Bruenor said, half in exhausted, delirium. "Lend me yer strength, me big friend," he called out to the darkness as he began tugging and twisting.

Hundreds of miles away, caught up in nightmares of his lost mentor, Bruenor, Wulfgar tossed uneasily in his bunk on the *Sea Sprite*. Perhaps the spirit of the young barbarian did come to Bruenor's aid at that desperate moment, but more likely the dwarf's unyielding stubbornness proved stronger than the iron. A bar of the grate bent low enough to slip out of the stone wall, and Bruenor held it free.

Hanging by one hand, Bruenor dropped the bar into the emptiness below him. With a wicked smile he hoped that some duergar scum might, at that instant, be at the bottom of the chimney, inspecting the dead spider and looking upward to find the cause.

Bruenor pulled himself halfway through the small hole he had opened, but had not the strength to squeeze his hips and belt through. Thoroughly drained, he accepted the perch, though his legs were dangling freely over a thousand-foot drop.

He put his head on the iron bars and knew no more.

6

BALÐUR'S GATE

"To de rail! To de rail!" cried one voice.

"Toss 'em over!" agreed another. The mob of sailors crowded closer, brandishing curved swords and clubs.

Entreri stood calmly in the midst of the storm, Regis nervously beside him. The assassin did not understand the crew's sudden fit of anger, but he guessed that the sneaky halfling was somehow behind it. He hadn't drawn weapons; he knew he could have his saber and dagger readied whenever he needed them, and none of the sailors, for all their bluster and threats, had yet come within ten feet of him.

The captain of the ship, a squat, waddling man with stiff gray bristles, pearly white teeth, and eyes lightened in a perpetual squint, made his way out from his cabin to investigate the ruckus.

"To me, Redeye," he beckoned the grimy sailor who had first brought to his ears the rumor that the passengers were infected with a horrible disease—and who had obviously spread the tale to the other members of the crew. Redeye obeyed at once, following his captain through the parting mob to stand before Entreri and Regis.

The captain slowly took out his pipe and tamped down the weed, his eyes never releasing Entreri's from a penetrating gaze.

"Send 'em over!" came an occasional cry, but each time, the captain silenced the speaker with a wave of his hand. He wanted a full measure of these strangers before he acted, and he patiently let the moments pass as he lit the pipe and took a long drag.

Entreri never blinked and never looked away from the captain. He brought his cloak back behind the scabbards on his belt and crossed his arms, the calm and confident action conveniently putting each of his hands in position barely an inch from the hilts of his weapons.

"Ye should have told me, sir," the captain said at length.

"Your words are as unexpected as the actions of your crew," Entreri replied evenly.

"Indeed," the captain answered, drawing another puff.

Some of the crew were not as patient as their skipper. One barrel-chested man, his arms heavily muscled and tattooed, grew weary of the drama. He boldly stepped behind the assassin, meaning to toss him overboard and be done with him.

Just as the sailor started to reach out for the assassin's slender shoulders, Entreri exploded into motion, spinning and returning to his cross-armed pose so quickly that the sailors watching him tried to blink the sun out of their eyes and figure out whether he had moved at all.

The barrel-chested man slumped to his knees and fell facedown on the deck, for in that blink of an eye, a heel had smashed his kneecap, and even more insidious, a jeweled dagger had come out of its sheath, poked his heart, and returned to rest on the assassin's hip.

"Your reputation precedes you," the captain said, not flinching.

"I pray that I do it justice," Entreri replied with a sarcastic bow.

"Indeed," said the captain. He motioned to the fallen man. "Might his friends see to his aid?"

"He is already dead," Entreri assured the captain. "If any of his friends truly wish to go to him, let them, too, step forward."

"They are scared," the captain explained. "They have witnessed many terrible diseases in ports up and down the Sword Coast."

"Disease?" Entreri echoed.

"Your companion let on to it," said the captain.

A smile widened across Entreri's face as it all came clear to him.

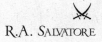

Lightning quick, he tore the cloak from Regis and caught the halfling's bare wrist, pulling him up off his feet and shooting a glare into the half-ling's terror-filled eyes that promised a slow and painful death. Immediately Entreri noticed the scars on Regis's arm.

"Burns?" He gawked.

"Aye, that's how the little one says it happens," Redeye shouted, sinking back behind his captain when Entreri's glare settled upon him. "Burns from the inside, it does!"

"Burns from a candle, more likely," Entreri retorted. "Inspect the wounds for yourself," he said to the captain. "There is no disease here, just the desperate tricks of a cornered thief." He dropped Regis to the deck with a thud.

Regis lay very still, not even daring to breathe. The situation had not evolved quite as he had hoped.

"Toss 'em over!" cried an anonymous voice.

"Not fer chancin'!" yelled another

"How many do you need to sail your ship?" Entreri asked the captain. "How many can you afford to lose?"

The captain, having seen the assassin in action and knowing the man's reputation, did not for a moment consider the simple questions as idle threats. Furthermore, the stare Entreri now fixed upon him told him without doubt that he would be the initial target if his crew moved against the assassin.

"I will trust in your word," he said commandingly, silencing the grumbles of his nervous crew. "No need to inspect the wounds. but disease or no, our deal is ended." He looked pointedly to his dead crewman.

"I do not mean to swim to Calimport," Entreri said in a hiss.

"Indeed," replied the captain. "We put in at Baldur's Gate in two days. You shall find other passage there."

"And you shall repay me," Entreri said calmly, "every gold piece."

The captain drew another long drag from his pipe. This was not a battle he would choose to fight. "Indeed," he said with equal calm. He turned toward his cabin and ordered his crew back to their stations as he went.

✕ ✕ ✕ ✕ ✕

He remembered the lazy summer days on the banks of Maer Dualdon in Icewind Dale. How many hours he had spent there, fishing for the elusive knucklehead trout, or just basking in the rare warmth of Icewind Dale's summer sun. Looking back on his years in Ten-Towns, Regis could hardly believe the course fate had laid out for him.

He thought he had found his niche, a comfortable existence—more comfortable still with the aid of the stolen ruby pendant—in a lucrative career as a scrimshander, carving the ivorylike bone of the knucklehead into marvelous little trinkets. But then came that fateful day, when Artemis Entreri showed up in Bryn Shander, the town Regis had come to call home, and sent the halfling scampering down the road to adventure with his friends.

But even Drizzt, Bruenor, Catti-brie, and Wulfgar had not been able to protect him from Entreri.

The memories provided small comfort to him as several grueling hours of solitude in the locked cabin slipped by. Regis would have liked to hide away in pleasant recollections of his past, but invariably his thoughts led back to the awful present, and he found himself wondering how he would be punished for his failed deception. Entreri had been composed, even amused, after the incident on the deck, leading Regis down to the cabin and then disappearing without a word.

Too composed, Regis thought.

But that was part of the assassin's mystique. No man knew Artemis Entreri well enough to call him friend, and no enemy could figure the man out well enough to gain an even footing against him.

Regis shrank back against the wall when Entreri at last arrived, sweeping through the door and over to the room's table without so much as a sidelong glance at the halfling. The assassin sat, brushing back his ink-black hair and eyeing the single candle burning on the table.

"A candle," he muttered, obviously amused. He looked at Regis. "You have a trick or two, halfling," he chuckled.

Regis was not smiling. No sudden warmth had come into Entreri's heart, he knew, and he'd be damned if he let the assassin's jovial facade take his guard down.

"A worthy ploy," Entreri continued. "And effective. It may take us a tenday to gain passage south from Baldur's Gate. An extra tenday for your friends to close the distance. I had not expected you to be so daring."

The smile left his face suddenly, and his tone was noticeably more grim when he added, "I did not believe that you would be so ready to suffer the consequences."

Regis cocked his head to study the man's every movement. "Here it comes," he whispered under his breath.

"Of course there are consequences, little fool. I commend your attempt—I hope you will give me more excitement on this tedious journey! But I cannot belay punishment. Doing so would take the dare, and thus the excitement, out of your trickery."

He slipped up from his seat and started around the table. Regis sublimated his scream and closed his eyes; he knew that he had no escape.

The last thing he saw was the jeweled dagger turning over slowly in the assassin's hand.

⚔ ⚔ ⚔ ⚔ ⚔

They made the River Chionthar the next afternoon and bucked the currents with a strong sea breeze filling their sails. By nightfall, the upper tiers of the city of Baldur's Gate lined the eastern horizon, and when the last hints of daylight disappeared from the sky, the lights of the great port marked their course as a beacon. But the city did not allow access to the docks after sunset, and the ship dropped anchor a half-mile out.

Regis, finding sleep impossible, heard Entreri stir much later that night. The halfling shut his eyes tightly and forced himself into a rhythm of slow, heavy breathing. He had no idea of Entreri's intent, but whatever the assassin was about, Regis didn't want him even suspecting that he was awake.

Entreri didn't give him a second thought. As silent as a cat—as silent as death—the assassin slipped through the cabin door. Twenty-five crewmen manned the ship, but after the long day's sail, and with Baldur's Gate awaiting the first light of dawn, only four of them would likely be awake.

The assassin slipped through the crew's barracks, following the light of a single candle at the rear of the ship. In the galley, the cook busily prepared the morning's breakfast of thick soup in a huge cauldron. Singing as he always did when he was at work, the cook paid no attention to his surroundings. But even if he had been quiet and alert, he probably would not have heard the slight footfalls behind him.

He died with his face in the soup.

Entreri moved back through the barracks, where twenty more died without a sound. Then he went up to the deck.

The moon hung full in the sky that night, but even a sliver of a shadow was sufficient for the skilled assassin, and Entreri knew well the routines of the watch. He had spent many nights studying the movements of the lookouts, preparing himself, as always, for the worst possible scenario. Timing the steps of the two watchmen on deck, he slithered up the mainmast, his jeweled dagger in his teeth.

An easy spring of his taut muscles brought him into the crow's nest.

Then there were two.

Back down on deck, Entreri moved calmly and openly to the rail. "A ship!" he called, pointing into the gloom. "Closing on us!"

Instinctively the two remaining watchmen rushed to the assassin's side and strained their eyes to see the peril in the dark —until the flash of a dagger told them of the deception.

Only the captain remained.

Entreri could easily have picked the lock on his cabin door and killed the man in his sleep, but the assassin wanted a more dramatic ending to his work; he wanted the captain to fully understand the doom that had befallen his ship that night. Entreri moved to the door, which opened onto the deck, and took out his tools and a length of fine wire.

A few minutes later, he was back at his own cabin, rousing Regis. "One sound, and I'll take your tongue," he warned the halfling.

Regis now understood what was happening. If the crew got to the docks at Baldur's Gate, they would no doubt spread the rumors of the deadly killer and his "diseased" friend, making Entreri's search for passage south impossible to fulfill.

The assassin wouldn't allow that at any cost, and Regis could not help but feel responsible for the carnage that night.

He moved quietly, helplessly, beside Entreri through the barracks, noting the absence of snores, and the quiet of the galley beyond. Surely the dawn was approaching; surely the cook would be hard at work preparing the morning meal. But no singing floated through the half-closed galley door.

The ship had stocked enough oil in Waterdeep to last the entire journey to Calimport, and kegs of the stuff still remained in the hold. Entreri pulled open the trap door and hoisted out two of the heavy barrels. He broke the seal on one and kicked it into a roll through the barracks, spewing oil as it went. Then he carried the other—and half-carried Regis, who was limp with fear and revulsion—topside, spreading the oil out more quietly and concentrating the spill in a tight arc around the captain's door.

"Get in," he told Regis, indicating the single rowboat hanging in a jigger off the starboard side of the ship. "And carry this." He handed the halfling a tiny pouch.

Bile rose in Regis's throat when he thought of what was inside the bag, but he took the pouch anyway and held it securely, knowing that if he lost it, Entreri would only get another.

The assassin sprang lightly across the deck, preparing a torch as he went. Regis watched him in horror, shuddering at the cold appearance of his shadowed face as he tossed the torch down the ladder to the oil-soaked barracks. Grimly satisfied as the flames roared to life, Entreri raced back across the deck to the captain's door.

"Good-bye!" was the only explanation he offered as he banged on the door. Two strides took him to the rowboat.

The captain leaped from his bed, fighting to orient himself. The ship was strangely calm, except for a telltale crackle and a wisp of smoke that slipped up through the floorboards.

Sword in hand, the captain threw the bolt back and pulled open the door. He looked around desperately and called for his crew. The flames had not reached the deck yet, but it was obvious to him—and should have been to his lookouts—that the ship was on fire. Beginning to suspect the awful truth, the captain rushed out, clad only in his nightshift.

He felt the tug of the trip-wire, then grimaced in further understanding as the wire noose bit deeply into his bare ankle. He sprawled face down, his sword dropping out in front of him. An aroma filled his nostrils, and he fully realized the deadly implications of the slick fluid drenching his nightshirt. He stretched out for his sword's hilt and clawed futilely at the wooden deck until his fingers bled.

A lick of flame jumped through the floorboards.

Sounds rolled eerily across the open expanse of water, especially in the empty dark of night. One sound filled the ears of Entreri and Regis as the assassin pulled the little rowboat against the currents of the Chionthar. It even cut through the din of the taverns lining the docks of Baldur's Gate, a half-mile away.

As if enhanced by the unspoken cries of protest of the dead crew—and by the dying ship itself—a singular, agonized voice screamed for all of them.

Then there was only the crackle of fire.

⚔ ⚔ ⚔ ⚔

Entreri and Regis entered Baldur's Gate on foot soon after daybreak. They had put the little rowboat into a cove a few hundred yards downriver, then sank the thing. Entreri wanted no evidence linking him to the disaster of the night before.

"It will be good to get home," the assassin chided Regis as they made their way along the extensive docks of the lower city. He led Regis's eye to a large merchant ship docked at one of the outer piers. "Do you remember the pennant?"

Regis looked to the flag flying atop the vessel, a gold field cut by slanted blue lines, the standard of Calimport. "Calimshan merchants never take passengers aboard," he reminded the assassin, hoping to diffuse Entreri's cocky attitude.

"They will make an exception," Entreri replied. He pulled the ruby pendant out from under his leather jacket and displayed it beside his wicked smile.

Regis fell silent once more. He knew well the power of the ruby and could not dispute the assassin's claim.

With sure and direct strides revealing that he had often before been in Baldur's Gate, Entreri led Regis to the harbormaster's office, a small shack just off the piers. Regis followed obediently, though his thoughts were hardly focused on the events of the present. He was still caught in the nightmare of the tragedy of the night before, trying to resolve his own part in the deaths of twenty-six men. He hardly noticed the harbormaster and didn't even catch the man's name.

But after only a few seconds of conversation, Regis realized that Entreri had fully captured the man under the hypnotic spell of the ruby pendant. The halfling faded out of the meeting altogether, disgusted with how well Entreri had mastered the powers of the pendant. His thoughts drifted again to his friends and his home, though now he looked back with lament, not hope. Had Drizzt and Wulfgar escaped the horrors of Mithral Hall, and were they now in pursuit? Watching Entreri in action and knowing that he would soon be back within the borders of Pook's realm, Regis almost hoped that they wouldn't come after him. How much more blood could stain his little hands?

Gradually Regis faded back in, half-listening to the words of the conversation and telling himself that there might be some important knowledge to be gained.

"When do they sail?" Entreri was saying.

Regis perked up his ears. Time was important. Perhaps his friends could get to him here, still a thousand miles from the stronghold of Pasha Pook.

"A tenday," replied the harbormaster, his eyes never blinking nor turning from the spectacle of the spinning gemstone.

"Too long," Entreri muttered under his breath. Then to the harbormaster, "I wish a meeting with the captain."

"Can be arranged."

"This very night . . . here."

The harbormaster shrugged his accord.

"And one more favor, my friend," Entreri said with a mock smile. "You track every ship that comes into port?"

"That is my job," said the dazed man.

"And surely you have eyes at the gates as well?" Entreri inquired with a wink.

I have many friends," the harbormaster replied. "Nothing happens in Baldur's Gate without my knowledge."

Entreri looked to Regis. "Give it to him," he ordered,

Regis, not understanding, responded to the command with a blank stare.

"The pouch," the assassin explained, using the same light-hearted tone that had marked his casual conversation with the duped harbormaster.

Regis narrowed his eyes and did not move, as defiant an act as he had ever dared to show his captor.

"The pouch," Entreri reiterated, his tone now deadly serious. "Our gift for your friends." Regis hesitated for just a second, then threw the tiny pouch to the harbormaster.

"Enquire of every ship and every rider that comes through Baldur's Gate," Entreri explained to the harbormaster. "Seek out a band of travelers—two at the least, one an elf, likely to be cloaked in secrecy, and the other a giant, yellow-haired barbarian. Seek them out, my friend. Find the adventurer who calls himself Drizzt Do'Urden. That gift is for his eyes alone. Tell him that I await his arrival in Calimport." He sent a wicked glance over at Regis. "With more gifts."

The harbormaster slipped the tiny pouch into his pocket and gave Entreri his assurances that he would not fail the task.

"I must be going," Entreri said, pulling Regis to his feet. "We meet tonight," he reminded the harbormaster. "An hour after the sun is down."

⨯ ⨯ ⨯ ⨯ ⨯

Regis knew that Pasha Pook had connections in Baldur's Gate, but he was amazed at how well the assassin seemed to know his way around. In less than an hour, Entreri had secured their room and enlisted the services of two thugs to stand guard over Regis while the assassin went on some errands.

"Time for your second trick?" he asked Regis slyly just before leaving. He looked at the two thugs leaning against the far wall of the room, engrossed in some less-than-intellectual debate about the reputed virtues of a local "lady."

"You might get by them," Entreri whispered.

Regis turned away, not enjoying the assassin's macabre sense of humor.

"But, remember, my little thief, once outside, you are on the streets—in the shadow of the alleyways, where you will find no friends, and where I shall be waiting." He spun away with an evil chuckle and swept through the door.

Regis looked at the two thugs, now locked in a heated argument. He probably could have walked out the door at that very moment.

He dropped back on his bed with a resigned sigh and awkwardly locked his hands behind his head, the sting in one hand pointedly reminding him of the price of bravery.

⚔ ⚔ ⚔ ⚔

Baldur's Gate was divided into two districts: the lower city of the docks and the upper city beyond the inner wall, where the more important citizens resided. The city had literally burst its bounds with the wild growth of trade along the Sword Coast. Its old wall set a convenient boundary between the transient sailors and adventurers who invariably made their way in and the long-standing houses of the land. "Halfway to everywhere" was a common phrase there, referring to the city's roughly equal proximity to Waterdeep in the North and Calimport in the South, the two greatest cities of the Sword Coast.

In light of the constant bustle and commotion that followed such a title, Entreri attracted little attention as he slipped through the lanes toward the inner city. He had an ally, a powerful wizard named Oberon, there who was also an associate of Pasha Pook's. Oberon's true loyalty, Entreri knew, lay with Pook, and the wizard would no doubt promptly contact the guild-master in Calimport with news of the recovered pendant, and of Entreri's imminent return.

But Entreri cared little whether Pook knew he was coming or not. His intent was behind him, to Drizzt Do'Urden, not in front, to Pook, and the wizard could prove of great value to him in learning more of the whereabouts of his pursuers.

After a meeting that lasted throughout the remainder of the day, Entreri left Oberon's tower and made his way back to the harbormaster's for the arranged rendezvous with the captain of the Calimport merchant ship. Entreri's visage had regained its determined confidence; he had put the unfortunate incident of the night before behind him, and everything was going smoothly again. He fingered the ruby pendant as he approached the shack.

A tenday was too long a delay.

✕ ✕ ✕ ✕

Regis was hardly surprised later that night when Entreri returned to the room and announced that he had "persuaded" the captain of the Calimport vessel to change his schedule.

They would leave in three days.

EPILOGUE

Wulfgar heaved and strained on the ropes, trying to keep the mainsail full of the scant ocean wind as the crew of the *Sea Sprite* looked on in amazement. The currents of the Chionthar pushed against the ship, and a sensible captain would normally have dropped anchor to wait for a more favorable breeze to get them in. But Wulfgar, under the tutelage of an old sea dog named Mirky, was doing a masterful job. The individual docks of Baldur's Gate were in sight, and the *Sea Sprite*, to the cheers of several dozen sailors watching the monumental pull, would soon put in.

"I could use ten of him on my crew," Captain Deudermont remarked to Drizzt.

The drow smiled, ever amazed at the strength of his young friend. "He seems to be enjoying himself. I would never have put him as a sailor."

"Nor I," replied Deudermont. "I only hoped to profit from his strength if we engaged with pirates. But Wulfgar found his sea legs early on."

"And he enjoys the challenge," Drizzt added. "The open ocean, the pull of the water, and of the wind, tests him in ways different than he has ever known."

"He does better than many," Deudermont replied. The experienced captain looked back downriver to where the open ocean waited. "You and your friend have been on but one short journey, skirting a coastline.

You cannot yet appreciate the vastness and the power of the open sea."

Drizzt looked at Deudermont with sincere admiration and even a measure of envy. The captain was a proud man, but he tempered his pride with a practical rationale. Deudermont respected the sea and accepted it as his superior. And that acceptance, that profound understanding of his own place in the world, gave the captain as much of an advantage as any man could gain over the untamed ocean. Drizzt followed the captain's longing stare and wondered about this mysterious allure the open waters seemed to hold over so many.

He considered Deudermont's last words. "One day, perhaps," he said quietly.

They were close enough now, and Wulfgar released his hold and slumped, exhausted, to the deck. The crew worked furiously to complete the docking, but each stopped at least once to slap the huge barbarian across the shoulder. Wulfgar was too tired to even respond.

"We will be in for two days," Deudermont told Drizzt. "It was to be a tenday, but I am aware of your haste. I spoke with the crew last night, and they agreed—to a man—to put right back out again."

"Our thanks to them, and to you," Drizzt replied sincerely.

Just then, a wiry, finely dressed man hopped down to the pier. "What ho, *Sea Sprite?*" he called. "Is Deudermont at your reins?"

"Pellman, the harbormaster," the captain explained to Drizzt. "He is!" he called to the man. "And glad to see Pellman, as well!"

"Well met, Captain," Pellman called. "And as fine a pull as I've ever seen! How long are you in port?"

"Two days," Deudermont replied. "Then off to the sea and the south."

The harbormaster paused for a moment, as if trying to remember something. Then he asked, as he had asked to every ship that had put in over the last few days, the question Entreri had planted in his mind. "I seek two adventurers," he called to Deudermont. "Might you have seen them?"

Deudermont looked to Drizzt, somehow guessing, as had the drow, that this inquiry was more than a coincidence.

"Drizzt Do'Urden and Wulfgar, by name," Pellman explained. "Though they may be using others. One's small and mysterious—elflike—and the other's a giant and as strong as any man alive!"

"Trouble?" Deudermont called.

"Not so," answered Pellman. "A message."

Wulfgar had moved up to Drizzt and heard the latter part of the conversation. Deudermont looked to Drizzt for instructions. "Your decision."

Drizzt didn't figure that Entreri would lay any serious traps for them; he knew that the assassin meant to fight with them, or at least with him, personally. "We will speak with the man," he answered.

"They are with me," Deudermont called to Pellman. " 'Twas Wulfgar," he looked at the barbarian and winked, then echoed Pellman's own description, "as strong as any man alive, who made the pull!"

Deudermont led them to the rail. "If there is trouble, I shall do what I can to retrieve you," he said quietly. "And we can wait in port for as long as two tendays if the need arises."

"Again, our thanks," Drizzt replied. "Surely Orlpar of Waterdeep set us aright."

"Leave that dog's name unspoken," Deudermont replied. "Rarely have I had such fortunate outcomes to my dealings with him! Farewell, then. You may take sleep on the ship if you desire."

Drizzt and Wulfgar moved cautiously toward the harbormaster, Wulfgar in the lead. Drizzt searched for any signs of ambush.

"We are the two you seek," Wulfgar said sternly, towering over the wiry man.

"Greetings," Pellman said with a disarming smile. He fished in his pocket. "I have met with an associate of yours," he explained, "a dark man with a halfling lackey."

Drizzt moved beside Wulfgar, and the two exchanged concerned glances.

"He left this," Pellman continued, handing the tiny pouch to Wulfgar. "And bade me to tell you that he will await your arrival in Calimport."

Wulfgar held the pouch tentatively, as if expecting it to explode in his face.

"Our thanks," Drizzt told Pellman. "We will tell our associate that you performed the task admirably."

Pellman nodded and bowed, turning away as he did so, to return to his duties. But first, he realized suddenly, he had another mission to complete, a subconscious command that he could not resist. Following Entreri's orders, the harbormaster moved from the docks and toward the upper level of the city.

Toward the house of Oberon.

Drizzt led Wulfgar off to the side, out of plain view. Seeing the barbarian's paling look, he took the tiny pouch and gingerly loosened the draw string, holding it as far away as possible. With a shrug to Wulfgar, who had moved a cautious step away, Drizzt brought the pouch down to his belt level and peeked in.

Wulfgar moved closer, curious and concerned when he saw Drizzt's shoulders droop. The drow looked to him in helpless resignation and inverted the pouch, revealing its contents.

A halfling's finger.

PART TWO

ALLIES

The world is full of ruffians. The world is full of people of good character. Both of these statements are true, I believe, because within most of the people I have known lies the beginning points of both seemingly disparate paths.

Some people are too timid to ever be ruffians, of course, and others too kindhearted, and similarly, some folk are too hard-tempered to ever let their good qualities show. But the emotional make-up of most people lies somewhere in the middle, a shade of gray that can be easily darkened or lightened by simple interaction. Race can certainly alter the shade—how well I have seen that since my road led me to the surface! An elf might noticeably flinch at the approach of a dwarf, while a dwarf might do likewise, or even spit upon the ground, if the situation is reversed.

Those initial impressions are sometimes difficult to overcome, and sometimes become lasting, but beyond race and appearance and other things that we cannot control, I have learned that there are definite decisions that I can make concerning which reaction I will edge someone else toward.

The key to it all, I believe, is respect.

When I was in Luskan with Wulfgar, we crossed through a tavern full of ruffians, men who used their fists and weapons on an almost daily basis. Yet, another friend of mine, Captain Deudermont of the Sea Sprite, often frequents such taverns, and rarely, very rarely, ever gets into so much as a verbal argument. Why is this? Why would a man such as Deudermont, obviously (as is shown by his dress and manner) a man of some wealth, and a man of respectable society, as well, not find himself immersed in brawls as regularly as the others? He often goes in alone, and stands quietly at the bar, but though he hardly says a word, he surely stands out among the more common patrons.

Is it fear that holds the ruffians from the man? Are they afraid that if they tangle with Deudermont, they will find retribution at the hands of his crew? Or has Deudermont simply brought with him such a reputation for ferocity as to scare off any potential challengers?

Neither, I say. Certainly the captain of the Sea Sprite must be a fine warrior, but that is no deterrent to the thugs of the taverns; indeed, the greatest fighting reputation only invites challenges among those folk. And though Deudermont's crew is formidable, by all accounts, more powerful and connected men than he have been found dead in the gutters of Luskan.

No, what keeps Captain Deudermont safe is his ability to show respect for anyone he meets. He is a man of charm, who holds well his personal pride. He grants respect at the outset of a meeting and continues that respect until the person forfeits it. This is very different than the way most people view the world. Most people insist that respect has to be earned, and with many, I have come to observe, earning it is no easy task! Many, and I include Bruenor and Wulfgar in this group, demand that anyone desiring their friendship first earn their respect, and I can understand their point of view, and once believed that I held one similar.

On my journey south on the Sea Sprite, Captain Deudermont taught me better, made me realize, without ever uttering a word on the subject, that demanding of another that he earns your respect is, in of itself, an act of arrogance, a way of self-elevation, implying by its very nature that your respect is worth earning.

Deudermont takes the opposite approach, one of acceptance and one lacking initial judgment. This may seem a subtle alternative, but it most certainly is not. Would that the man be anointed a king, I say, for he has learned the secret of peace. When Captain Deudermont, dressed in his finery, enters a tavern of common peasant thugs, most within the place, and society at large, would view him as superior.

And yet, in his interactions with these people, there is no air of superiority about the man at all. In his eyes and in his heart, he is among peers, among other intelligent creatures whose paths have led them to a different—and not better or worse—place than his own. And when Deudermont grants respect to men who would think nothing of cutting his heart out, he disarms them, he takes away whatever reason they might have found to fight with him.

There is much more to it than that, Captain Deudermont is able to do this because he can honestly attempt to see the world through the eyes of another. He is a man of empathy, a man who revels in the differences of people rather than fearing those differences.

How rich is his life! How full of wonder and how wide of experience!

Captain Deudermont taught these things to me, by example. Respect is one of the most basic needs of reasoning creatures, particularly among men. An insult is just that because it is an assault upon respect, upon esteem, and upon that most dangerous of qualities: pride.

So when I meet people now, they do not have to earn my respect. I grant it, willingly and happily, expecting that in doing so I will come to learn even more about this beautiful world around me, that my experiences will widen.

Certainly some people will see this as weakness or cowardice, will misconstrue my intentions as sublimation, rather than an acceptance of equal worth. But it is not fear that guides my actions—I have seen far too much of battle to fear it any longer—it is hope.

The hope that I will find another Bruenor, or another Catti-brie, for I have come to know that I can never have too many friends.

So I offer you respect, and it will take much for you to lose it. But if you do, if you choose to see it as weakness and seize upon your perceived advantage, well . . .

Perhaps I'll then let you talk with Guenhwyvar.

—Drizzt Do'Urden

7
STIRRINGS

The first thing he noticed was the absence of the wind. He had lain long hour after hour on his perch at the top of the chimney, and through it all, even in his semiconscious state, there had been the unceasing presence of the wind. It had taken his mind back to Icewind Dale, his home for nearly two centuries. But Bruenor had felt no comfort in the gale's forlorn moan, a continual reminder of his predicament and the last sound he thought he would ever hear.

But it was no more. Only the crackle of a nearby fire broke the quiet stillness. Bruenor lifted a heavy eyelid and stared absently into the flames, trying to discern his condition and his whereabouts. He was warm and comfortable, with a heavy quilt pulled up tightly around his shoulders. And he was indoors—the flames burned in a hearth, not in the open pit of a campfire.

Bruenor's eye drifted to the side of the hearth and focused on a neatly stacked pile of equipment.

His equipment!

The one-horned helm, Drizzt's scimitar, the mithral armor, and his new battle-axe and shining shield. And he was stretched out under the quilt, wearing only a silken night-shirt.

Suddenly feeling very vulnerable, Bruenor pulled himself up to his elbows.

A wave of blackness rolled over him and sent his thoughts reeling in nauseous circles. He dropped heavily to his back.

His vision returned for just a moment, long enough to register the form of a tall and beautiful woman kneeling over him. Her long hair, gleaming silver in the firelight, brushed across his face.

"Spider's poison," she said softly. "Would have killed anything but a dwarf."

Then there was only the blackness.

Bruenor awoke again a few hours later, stronger and more alert. Trying not to stir and bring any attention, he half-opened one eye and surveyed the area, glancing at the pile first. Satisfied that all of his equipment was there, he slowly turned his head over.

He was in a small chamber, apparently a one-roomed structure, for the only door seemed to lead outside. The woman he had seen earlier—though Bruenor wasn't really sure until now if that image had been a dream—stood beside the door, staring out the room's single window to the night sky beyond. Her hair was indeed silver. Bruenor could see that its hue was no trick of the firelight. But not silver with the graying of age; this lustrous mane glowed with vibrant life.

"Yer pardon, fair lady," the dwarf croaked, his voice cracking on every syllable. The woman twirled and looked at him curiously.

"Might I be getting a bit o' food?" asked Bruenor, never one to mix up his priorities.

The woman floated across the room and helped Bruenor up into a sitting position. Again a wave of blackness swirled over the dwarf, but he managed to shrug it away.

"Only a dwarf!" the woman muttered, astonished that Bruenor had come through his ordeal.

Bruenor cocked his head up at her. "I know ye, lady, though I cannot find yer name in me thoughts."

"It is not important," the woman replied. "You have come through much, Bruenor Battlehammer." Bruenor cocked his head further and leaned away at the mention of his name, but the woman steadied him and continued. "I attended to your wounds as best I could, though I feared that

I had come upon you too late to mend the hurts of the spider's poison."

Bruenor looked down at his bandaged forearm, reliving those terrible moments when he had first encountered the giant spider. "How long?"

"How long you lay atop the broken grate, I do not know," the woman answered. "But here you have rested for three days and more—too long for your stomach's liking! I will prepare some food." She started to rise, but Bruenor caught her arm.

"Where is this place?"

The lady's smile eased his grip. "In a clearing not far from the grate. I feared to move you."

Bruenor didn't quite understand. "Yer home?"

"Oh, no," the woman laughed, standing. "A creation, and only temporary. It will be gone with the dawn's light if you feel able to travel."

The tie to magic flickered recognition. "Ye're the Lady of Silverymoon!" Bruenor spouted suddenly.

"Clearmoon Alustriel," the woman said with a polite bow. "My greetings, noble King."

"King?" Bruenor echoed in disgust. "Suren me halls are gone to the scum."

"We shall see," said Alustriel.

But Bruenor missed the words altogether. His thoughts were not on Mithral Hall, but on Drizzt and Wulfgar and Regis, and especially on Catti-brie, the joy of his life. "Me friends," he begged to the woman. "Do ye know o' me friends?"

"Rest easy," Alustriel answered. "They escaped the halls, each of them."

"Even the drow?"

Alustriel nodded. "Drizzt Do'Urden was not destined to die in the home of his dearest friend."

Alustriel's familiarity with Drizzt triggered another memory in the dwarf. "Ye met him before," he said, "on our road to Mithral Hall. Ye pointed the way for us. And that is how ye knew me name."

"And knew where to search for you," Alustriel added. "Your friends think you dead, to their ultimate grief. But I am a wizard of some talent and can speak to worlds that oft bring surprising revelations. When the specter of Morkai, an old associate who passed from this world a few years ago, imparted to me an image of a fallen dwarf, half out of a hole on the side of a mountain, I knew the truth of the fate of Bruenor Battlehammer. I only hoped that I would not be too late."

"Bah! Fit as ever!" Bruenor huffed, thumping a fist into his chest. As he shifted his weight, a stinging pain in his seat made him wince.

"A crossbow quarrel," Alustriel explained.

Bruenor thought for a moment. He had no recollection of being hit, though the memory of his flight from the undercity was perfectly clear. He shrugged and attributed it to the blindness of his battle-lust. "So one o' the gray scum got me," he started to say, but then he blushed and turned his eyes away at the thought of this woman plucking the quarrel from his backside.

Alustriel was kind enough to change the subject. "Dine and then rest," she instructed. "Your friends are safe . . . for the present."

"Where—"

Alustriel cut him off with an outstretched palm. "My knowledge in this matter is not sufficient," she explained. "You shall find your answers soon enough. In the morning, I will take you to Longsaddle and Catti-brie. She can tell you more than I."

Bruenor wished that he could go right now to the human girl he had plucked from the ruins of a goblin raid and reared as his daughter, that he could crush her against him in his arms and tell her that everything was all right. But he reminded himself that he had never truly expected to see Catti-brie again, and he could suffer through one more night.

Any fears he had of anxious restlessness were washed away in the serenity of exhausted sleep only minutes after he had finished the meal. Alustriel watched over him until contented snores resounded throughout the magical shelter.

Satisfied that only a healthy sleeper could roar so loudly, the Lady of Silverymoon leaned back against the wall and closed her eyes.

It had been a long three days.

⚔ ⚔ ⚔ ⚔ ⚔

Bruenor watched in amazement as the structure faded around him with the first light of dawn, as if the dark of night had somehow lent the place the tangible material for its construction. He turned to say something to Alustriel but saw her in the midst of casting a spell, facing the pinkening sky and reaching out as though trying to grab the rays of light.

She clenched her hands and brought them to her mouth, whispering the enchantment into them. Then she flung the captured light out before her, crying out the final words of the dweomer, "Equine aflame!" A glowing ball of red struck the stone and burst into a shower of fire, forming almost instantly into a flaming chariot and two horses. Their images danced with the fire that gave them shape, but they did not burn the ground.

"Gather your things," the lady instructed Bruenor. "It is time we leave."

Bruenor stood motionless a moment longer. He had never come to appreciate magic, only the magic that strengthened weapons and armor, but neither did he ever deny its usefulness. He collected his equipment, not bothering to don armor or shield, and joined Alustriel behind the chariot. He followed her onto it, somewhat reluctantly, but it did not burn and it felt as tangible as wood.

Alustriel took a fiery rein in her slender hand and called to the team. A single bound lifted them into the morning sky, and they shot away, west around the bulk of the mountain and then south.

The stunned dwarf dropped his equipment to his feet—his chin to his chest—and clutched the side of the chariot. Mountains rolled out below him; he noted the ruins of Settlestone, the ancient dwarven city, now far below, and only a second later, far behind. The chariot roared over the open grassland and skimmed westward along the northern edge of the Trollmoors. Bruenor had relaxed enough to spit a curse as they soared over the town of Nesmé, remembering the less-than-hospitable treatment he and his friends had received at the hands of a patrol from the place. They passed over the Dessarin River network, a shining snake writhing through the fields, and Bruenor saw a large encampment of barbarians far to the north.

Alustriel swung the fiery chariot south again, and only a few minutes later, the famed Ivy Mansion of Harpell Hill, Longsaddle, came into view.

A crowd of curious wizards gathered atop the hill to watch the chariot's approach, cheering somberly—trying to maintain a distinguished air—as they always did when Lady Alustriel graced them with her presence. One face in the crowd blanched to white when the red beard, pointed nose, and one-horned helm of Bruenor Battlehammer came into view.

"But . . . you . . . uh . . . dead . . . fell," stammered Harkle Harpell as Bruenor jumped from the back of the chariot.

"Nice to see yerself, too," Bruenor replied, clad only in his nightshirt and helm. He scooped his equipment from the chariot and dropped the pile at Harkle's feet. "Where's me girl?"

"Yes, yes . . . the girl . . . Catti-brie . . . oh, where? Oh, there," he rambled, the fingers of one hand nervously bouncing on his lower lip. "Do come, yes do!" He grabbed Bruenor's hand and whisked the dwarf off to the Ivy Mansion.

They intercepted Catti-brie, barely out of bed and wearing a fluffy robe, shuffling down a long hall. The young woman's eyes popped wide when she spotted Bruenor rushing at her, and she dropped the towel she was holding, her arms falling limply to her side. Bruenor buried his face into her, hugging her around the waist so tightly that he forced the air from her lungs. As soon as she recovered from her shock, she returned the hug tenfold.

"Me prayers," she stammered, her voice quaking with sobs. "By the gods, I'd thought ye dead!"

Bruenor didn't answer, trying to hold himself steady. His tears were soaking the front of Catti-brie's robe, and he felt the eyes of a crowd of Harpells behind him. Embarrassed, he pushed open a door to his side, surprising a half-clad Harpell who stood naked to the waist.

"Excuse—" the wizard began, but Bruenor grabbed his shoulder and pulled him out into the hall, at the same time leading Catti-brie into the room. The door slammed in the wizard's face as he turned back to his chamber. He looked helplessly to his gathered kin, but their wide smiles and erupting laughter told him that they would be of no assistance. With a shrug, the wizard moved on about his morning business as though nothing unusual had happened.

It was the first time Catti-brie had ever seen the stoic dwarf truly cry. Bruenor didn't care and couldn't have done a thing to prevent the scene anyway. "Me prayers, too," he whispered to his beloved daughter, the human child he had taken in as his own more than a decade and a half before.

"If we'd have known," Catti-brie began, but Bruenor put a gentle finger to her lips to silence her. It was not important; Bruenor knew that Catti-brie and the others would never have left him if they had even suspected that he might be alive.

"Suren I know not why I lived," the dwarf replied. "None o' the fire found me skin." He shuddered at the memories of his tendays alone in the mines of Mithral Hall. "No more talk o' the place," he begged. " Behind me it is. Behind me to stay!"

Catti-brie, knowing of the approach of armies to reclaim the dwarven homeland, started to shake her head, but Bruenor didn't catch the motion.

"Me friends?" he asked the young woman. "Drow eyes I saw as I fell."

"Drizzt lives," Catti-brie answered, "as does the assassin that chased Regis. He came up to the ledge just as ye fell and carried the little one away."

"Rumblebelly?" Bruenor gasped.

"Aye, and the drow's cat as well."

"Not dead . . ."

"Nay, not to me guess," Catti-brie was quick to respond. "Not yet. Drizzt and Wulfgar have chased the fiend to the south, knowing his goal to be Calimport."

"A long run," Bruenor muttered. He looked to Catti-brie, confused. "But I'd have thought ye'd be with them."

"I have me own course," Catti-brie replied, her face suddenly stern. "A debt for repaying."

Bruenor understood at once. "Mithral Hall?" he choked out. "Ye figured to return, avengin' meself?"

Catti-brie nodded, unblinking.

"Ye're bats, girl!" Bruenor said. "And the drow would let ye go alone?"

"Alone?" Catti-brie echoed. It was time for the rightful king to know. "Nay, nor would I so foolishly end me life. A hundred kin make their way from the north and west," she explained. "And a fair number of Wulfgar's folk beside 'em."

"Not enough," Bruenor replied. "An army of duergar scum holds the halls."

"And eight thousand more from Citadel Adbar to the north and east," Catti-brie continued grimly, not slowing a beat. "King Harbromme of the dwarves of Adbar says he'll see the halls free again! Even the Harpells have promised their aid."

Bruenor drew a mental image of the approaching armies—wizards, barbarians, and a rolling wall of dwarves—and with Catti-brie at their lead. A thin smile cut the frown from his face. He looked upon his daughter with even more than the considerable respect he had always shown her, his eyes wet with tears once more.

"They wouldn't beat me," Catti-brie growled. "I meant to see yer face carved in the Hall of Kings, and meant to put yer name in its proper place o' glory!"

Bruenor grabbed her close and squeezed with all his strength. Of all the mantles and laurels he had found in the years gone by, or might find in the years ahead, none fit as well or blessed him as much as "Father."

✗ ✗ ✗ ✗ ✗

Bruenor stood solemnly on the southern slope of Harpell Hill that evening, watching the last colors fade out of the western sky and the emptiness of the rolling plain to the south. His thoughts were on his friends, particularly Regis—Rumblebelly—the bothersome halfling that had undeniably found a soft corner in the dwarf's stone heart.

Drizzt would be all right—Drizzt was always all right—and with mighty Wulfgar walking beside him, it would take an army to bring them down.

But Regis.

Bruenor never had doubted that the halfling's carefree manner of living, stepping on toes with a half-apologetic and half-amused shrug, would eventually get him in mud too deep for his little legs to carry him through. Rumblebelly had been a fool to steal the guildmaster's ruby pendant.

But "just desserts" did nothing to dispel the dwarf's pity at his halfling friend's dilemma, nor Bruenor's anger at his own inability to help. By his station, his place was here, and he would lead the gathering armies to victory and glory, crushing the duergar and bringing a level of prosperity back to Mithral Hall. His new kingdom would be the envy of the North, with crafted items that rivaled the works of the ancient days flowing out into the trade routes all across the Realms.

It had been his dream, the goal of his life since that terrible day nearly two centuries before, when Clan Battlehammer had been nearly wiped out and those few who had survived, mostly children, had been chased out of their homeland to the meager mines of Icewind Dale.

Bruenor's lifelong dream was to return, but how hollow it seemed to him now, with his friends caught in a desperate chase across the southland.

The last light left the sky, and the stars blinked to life. Nighttime, Bruenor thought with a bit of comfort.

The time of the drow.

The first hints of his smile dissipated, though, as soon as they began, as Bruenor suddenly came to view the deepening gloom in a different perspective. "Nighttime," he whispered aloud.

The time of the assassin.

8

A PLAIN BROWN WRAPPER

The simple wooden structure at the end of Rogues Circle seemed under-stated even for the decrepit side of the sprawling southern city of Calimport. The building had few windows, all boarded or barred, and not a terrace or balcony to speak of. Similarly, no lettering identified the building, not even a number on the door to place it. But everyone in the city knew the house and marked it well, for beyond either of its iron-bound doors, the scene changed dramatically. Where the outside showed only the weathered brown of old wood, the inside displayed a myriad of bright colors and tapestries, thickly woven carpets, and statues of solid gold. This was the thieves' guild, rivaling the palace of Calimshan's ruler himself in riches and decor.

It rose three floors from the street level, with two more levels hidden below. The highest level was the finest, with five rooms—an octagonal central hall and four antechambers off it—all designed for the comfort and convenience of one man: Pasha Pook. He was the guildmaster, the architect of an intricate thieving network. And he made certain that he was the first to enjoy the spoils of his guild's handiwork.

Pook paced the highest level's central hall, his audience chamber, stopping every circuit to stroke the shining coat of the leopard that lay beside his great chair. An uncharacteristic anxiety was etched upon the guildmaster's round face, and he twiddled his fingers nervously when he was not petting his exotic pet.

His clothes were of the finest silk, but other than the brooch that fastened his wrappings, he wore none of the abundant jewelry customary among others of his station—though his teeth did gleam of solid gold. In truth, Pook seemed a half-sized version of one of the four hill giant eunuchs that lined the hall, an inconspicuous appearance for a silver-tongued guild-master who had brought sultans to their knees and whose name sent the sturdiest of the ruffian street dwellers scurrying for dark holes.

Pook nearly jumped when a loud knock resounded off the room's main door, the one to the lower levels. He hesitated for a long moment, assuring himself that he would make the other man squirm for waiting—though he really needed the time to compose himself. Then he absently motioned to one of the eunuchs and moved to the overstuffed throne on the raised platform opposite the door and dropped a hand again to his pampered cat.

A lanky fighter entered, his thin rapier dancing to the swagger of his stride. He wore a black cape that floated behind him and was bunched at his neck. His thick brown hair curled into and around it. His clothes were dark and plain but crisscrossed by straps and belts, each with a pouch or sheathed dagger or some other unusual weapon hanging from it. His high leather boots, worn beyond any creases, made no sound other than the timed clump of his agile stride.

"Greetings, Pook," he said informally.

Pook's eyes narrowed immediately at the sight of the man. "Rassiter," he replied to the wererat.

Rassiter walked up to the throne and bowed halfheartedly, throwing the reclining leopard a distasteful glance. Flashing a rotted smile that revealed his lowly heritage, he put one foot upon the chair and bent low to let the guildmaster feel the heat of his breath.

Pook glanced at the dirty boot on his beautiful chair, then back at the man with a smile that even the uncouth Rassiter noticed was a bit too disarming. Figuring that he might be taking his familiarity with his partner a bit too far, Rassiter removed his foot from its perch and shuffled back a step.

Pook's smile faded, but he was satisfied. "It is done?" he asked the man.

Rassiter danced a circle and nearly laughed out loud. "Of course," he answered, and he pulled a pearl necklace from his pouch.

Pook frowned at the sight, just the expression the sly fighter had expected. "Must you kill them all?" the guildmaster said in a hiss.

Rassiter shrugged and replaced the necklace. "You said you wanted her removed. She is removed."

Pook's hands clutched the arms of the throne. "I said I wanted her taken from the streets until the job was completed!"

"She knew too much," Rassiter replied, examining his fingernails.

"She was a valuable wench," Pook said, back in control now. Few men could anger Pasha Pook as did Rassiter, and fewer still would have left the chamber alive.

"One of a thousand," chuckled the lanky fighter.

Another door opened, and an older man entered, his purple robes embroidered with golden stars and quarter-moons and a huge diamond fastening his high turban. "I must see—"

Pook cast him a sidelong glance. "Not now, LaValle."

"But Master—"

Pook's eyes went dangerously thin again, nearly matching the lines of his lipless grimace. The old man bowed apologetically and disappeared back through the door, closing it carefully and silently behind him.

Rassiter laughed at the spectacle. "Well done!"

"You should learn LaValle's manners," Pook said to him.

"Come, Pook, we are partners," Rassiter replied. He skipped over to one of the room's two windows, the one that looked south to the docks and the wide ocean. "The moon will be full tonight," he said excitedly, spinning back on Pook. "You should join us, Pasha! A grand feasting there will be!"

Pook shuddered to think of the macabre table that Rassiter and his fellow wererats planned to set. Perhaps the wench was not yet dead. . . .

He shook away such thoughts. I am afraid I must decline," he said quietly.

Rassiter understood—and had purposely enticed—Pook's disgust. He danced back over and put his foot on the throne, again showing Pook that foul smile. "You do not know what you are missing," he said. "But the choice is yours; that was our deal." He spun away and bowed low. "And you are the master."

"An arrangement that does well by you and yours," Pook reminded him.

Rassiter turned his palms out in concession, then clapped his hands together. "I cannot argue that my guild fares better since you brought us in." He bowed again. "Forgive my insolence, my dear friend, but I can hardly contain the mirth of my fortunes. And tonight the moon will be full!"

"Then go to your feast, Rassiter."

The lanky man bowed again, cast one more glare at the leopard, and skipped from the room.

When the door had closed, Pook ran his fingers over his brow and down through the stylishly matted remains of what once had been a thick tousle of black hair. Then he dropped his chin helplessly into a plump palm and chuckled at his own discomfort in dealing with Rassiter, the wererat.

He looked to the harem door, wondering if he might take his mind off his associate. But he remembered LaValle. The wizard would not have disturbed him, certainly not with Rassiter in the room, unless his news was important.

He gave his pet a final scratch on the chin and moved through the chamber's southeast door, into the wizard's dimly lit quarters. LaValle, staring intehtly into his crystal ball, did not notice him as he entered. Not wanting to disturb the wizard, Pook quietly took the seat across the small table and waited, amusing himself with the curious distortions of LaValle's scraggly gray beard through the crystal ball as the wizard moved this way and that.

Finally LaValle looked up. He could clearly see the lines of tension still on Pook's face, not unexpected after a visit from the wererat. "They have killed her, then?" he asked, already knowing the answer.

"I despise him," said Pook.

LaValle nodded in agreement. "But you cannot dismiss the power that Rassiter has brought you."

The wizard spoke the truth. In the two years since Pook had allied himself with the wererats, his guild had become the most prominent and powerful in the city. He could live well simply from the tithes that the dockside merchants paid him for protection—from his own guild. Even the captains of many of the visiting merchant ships knew enough not to turn away Pook's collector when he met them on the docks.

And those who didn't know better learned quickly.

No, Pook couldn't argue about the benefits of having Rassiter and his fellows around. But the guildmaster had no love for the wretched lycanthropes, human by day and something beastly, half rat and half man, by night. And he wasn't fond of the way they handled their business.

"Enough of him," Pook said, dropping his hands to the velvety black tablecloth. "I am certain that I shall need a dozen hours in the harem to get over our meeting!" His grin showed that the thought did not displease him. "But what did you want?"

A wide smile spread over the wizard's face. "I have spoken with Oberon in Baldur's Gate this day," he said with some pride. "I have learned of something that may make you forget all about your discussion with Rassiter."

Pook waited curiously, allowing LaValle to play out his dramatics. The wizard was a fine and loyal aide, the closest thing the guildmaster had to a friend.

"Your assassin returns!" LaValle proclaimed suddenly.

It took Pook a few moments to think through the meaning and implications of the wizard's words. But then it hit him, and he sprang up from the table. "Entreri?" he gasped, barely finding his breath.

LaValle nodded and nearly laughed out loud.

Pook ran his hand through his hair. Three years. Entreri, deadliest of the deadly, was returning to him after three long years. He looked curiously at the wizard.

"He has the halfling," LaValle answered to his unspoken question. Pook's face lit up in a broad smile. He leaned forward eagerly, his golden teeth shining in the candlelight.

Truly LaValle was glad to please his guildmaster, to give him the news he had waited so very long to hear. "And the ruby pendant!" the wizard proclaimed, banging a fist on the table.

"Yes!" Pook snarled, exploding into laughter. His gem, his most prized possession. With its hypnotic powers, he could rise to even greater heights of prosperity and power. Not only would he dominate all he met, but he would make them glad for the experience. "Ah, Rassiter," Pook muttered, suddenly thinking of the upper hand he could gain on his associate. "Our relationship is about to change, my rodent friend."

"How much will you still need him?" LaValle asked.

Pook shrugged and looked to the side of the room, to a small curtain. The Taros Hoop.

LaValle blanched at the thought of the thing. The Taros Hoop was a mighty relic capable of displacing its owner, or his enemies, through the very planes of existence. But the power of this item was not without price. Thoroughly evil it was, and every one of the few times LaValle had used it, he had felt a part of himself drain away, as though the Taros Hoop gained its power by stealing his life force. LaValle hated Rassiter, but he hoped that the guildmaster would find a better solution than the Taros Hoop.

The wizard looked back to find Pook staring at him. "'Tell me more!" Pook insisted eagerly.

LaValle shrugged helplessly and put his hand on the crystal ball. "I have not been able to glimpse them myself," he said. "Ever has Artemis Entreri been able to dodge my scrying. But by Oberon's words, they are not too far. Sailing the waters north of Calimshan, if not already within the borders. And they fly on a swift wind, Master. A tenday or two, no more."

"And Regis is with him?" Pook asked.

"He is."

"Alive?"

"Very much alive," said the wizard.

"Good!" Pook sneered. How he longed to see the treacherous halfling again! To have his plump hands around Regis's little neck! The guild had fallen on tough times after Regis had run off with the magical pendant. In truth, the problems had come mostly from Pook's own insecurity in dealing with people without the gem, so long had he been using it, and from the guildmaster's obsessive—and expensive—hunt to find the halfling. But to Pook, the blame fell squarely upon Regis. He even blamed the halfling for the alliance with the wererats' guild, for certainly he wouldn't have needed

Rassiter if he had had his pendant.

But now everything would work out for the best, Pook knew. Possessing the pendant and dominating the wererats, perhaps he could even think of expanding his power outside Calimport, with charmed associates and lycanthrope allies heading guilds throughout the southland.

LaValle seemed more serious when Pook looked back at him. "How do you believe Entreri will feel about our new associates?" he asked grimly.

"Ah, he does not know," said Pook, realizing the implications. "He has been gone too long." He thought for a moment then shrugged. "They are in the same business, after all. Entreri should accept them."

"Rassiter disturbs everyone he meets," the wizard reminded him. "Suppose that he crosses Entreri?"

Pook laughed at the thought. "I can assure you that Rassiter will cross Artemis Entreri only once, my friend."

"And then you shall make arrangements with the new head of the wererats," LaValle snickered.

Pook clapped him on the shoulder and headed for the door. "Learn what you can," he instructed the wizard. "If you can find them in your crystal ball, call to me. I cannot wait to glimpse the face of Regis the halfling again. So much I owe to that one."

"And you shall be?"

"In the harem," Pook answered with a wink. "Tension, you know."

LaValle slumped back in his chair when Pook had gone and considered again the return of his principal rival. He had gained much in the years since Entreri had left, even rising to this room on the third level as Pook's chief assistant.

This room, Entreri's room.

But the wizard never had any problems with the assassin. They had been comfortable associates, if not friends, and had helped each other many times in the past. LaValle couldn't count the number of times he had shown Entreri the quickest route to a target.

And there was that nasty situation with Mancas Tiveros, a fellow mage. "Mancas the Mighty," the other wizards of Calimport had called him, and they had pitied LaValle when he and Mancas fell into dispute concerning the origins of a particular spell. Both had claimed credit for the discovery, and everyone waited for an expected war of magic to erupt. But Mancas suddenly and inexplicably went away, leaving a note disclaiming his role in the spell's creation and giving full credit to LaValle. Mancas had never been seen again—in Calimport or anywhere else.

"Ah, well," LaValle sighed, turning back to his crystal ball. Artemis Entreri had his uses.

The door to the room opened, and Pook stuck his head back in. "Send a messenger to the carpenter's guild," he said to LaValle. "Tell them that we shall need several skilled men immediately."

LaValle tilted his head in disbelief.

"The harem and treasury are to stay," Pook said emphatically, feigning frustration over his wizard's inability to see the logic. "And certainly I am not conceding my chamber!"

LaValle frowned as he thought he began to understand.

"Nor am I about to tell Artemis Entreri that he cannot have his own room back," said Pook. "Not after he has performed his mission so excellently!"

"I understand," said the wizard glumly, thinking himself relegated once again to the lower levels.

"So a sixth room must be built," laughed Pook, enjoying his little game. "Between Entreri's and the harem." He winked again at his valued assistant. "You may design it yourself, my dear LaValle. And spare no expense!" He shut the door and was gone.

The wizard wiped the moisture from his eyes. Pook always surprised him, but never disappointed him. "You are a generous master, my Pasha Pook," he whispered to the empty room.

And truly Pasha Pook was a masterful leader as well, for LaValle turned back to his crystal ball, his teeth gritted in determination. He would find Entreri and the halfling. He wouldn't disappoint his generous master.

9

FIERY RIDDLES

Now running with the currents of the Chionthar, and with the breeze at enough of an angle from the north for the sails to catch a bit of a push, the *Sea Sprite* cruised away from Baldur's Gate at a tremendous rate, spitting a white spray despite the concurrent movement of the water.

"The Sword Coast by midafternoon," Deudermont said to Drizzt and Wulfgar. "And off the coast, with no land in sight until we make Asavir's Channel. Then a southern journey around the edge of the world and back east to Calimport.

"Calimport," he said again, indicating a new pennant making its way up the mast of the *Sea Sprite*, a golden field crossed by slanted blue lines.

Drizzt looked at Deudermont suspiciously, knowing that this was not an ordinary practice of sailing vessels.

"We run Waterdeep's flag north of Baldur's Gate," the captain explained. "Calimport's south."

"An acceptable practice?" Drizzt asked.

"For those who know the price," chuckled Deudermont. "Waterdeep and Calimport are rivals, and stubborn in their feud. They desire trade with each other—they can only profit from it—but do not always allow ships flying the other's flag to dock in their harbors."

"A foolish pride," Wulfgar remarked, painfully reminded of some similar traditions his own clannish people had practiced only a few years before.

"Politics," Deudermont said with a shrug. "But the lords of both cities secretly desire the trade, and a few dozen ships have made the connections to keep business moving. The *Sea Sprite* has two ports to call home, and everyone profits from the arrangement."

"Two markets for Captain Deudermont," Drizzt remarked slyly. "Practical."

"And it makes good sailing sense as well," Deudermont continued, his smile still wide. "Pirates running the waters north of Baldur's Gate respect the banner of Waterdeep above all others, and those south of here take care not to rouse the anger of Calimport and her massive armada. The pirates along Asavir's Channel have many merchant ships to pick from in the straights, and they are more likely to raid one that carries a flag of less weight."

"And you are never bothered?" Wulfgar couldn't help but ask, his voice tentative and almost sarcastic, as though he hadn't yet figured out if he approved of the practice.

"Never?" echoed Deudermont. "Not 'never,' but rarely. And on those occasions that pirates come at us, we till our sails and run. Few ships can catch the *Sea Sprite* when her sails are full of wind."

"And if they do catch you?" asked Wulfgar.

"That is where you two can earn your passage," Deudermont laughed. "My guess is that those weapons you carry might soften a looting pirate's desire to continue the pursuit."

Wulfgar brought Aegis-fang up in front of him. "I pray that I have learned the movements of a ship well enough for such a battle," he said. "An errant swing might send me over the rail!"

"Then swim to the side of the pirate ship," Drizzt mused, "and tip her over!"

⋊ ⋊ ⋊ ⋊ ⋊

From a darkened chamber in his tower in Baldur's Gate, the wizard Oberon watched the *Sea Sprite* sail out. He probed deeper into the crystal ball to scry the elf and huge barbarian standing beside the ship's captain on the deck. They were not from these parts, the wizard knew. By his dress and his coloring, the barbarian was more likely from one of those distant tribes far to the north, beyond even Luskan and around the Spine of the World mountains, in that desolate stretch of land known as Icewind Dale. How far he was from home, and how unusual to see one of his kind sailing the open sea!

"What part could these two play in the return of Pasha Pook's gem?" Oberon wondered aloud, truly intrigued. Had Entreri gone all the way to that distant strip of tundra in search of the halfling? Were these two pursuing him south?

But it was not the wizard's affair. Oberon was just glad that Entreri had called in the debt with so easy a favor. The assassin had killed for Oberon—more than once—several years ago, and though Entreri had never mentioned the favors in his many visits to Oberon's tower, the wizard had always felt as if the assassin held a heavy chain around his neck. But this very night, the long-standing debt would be cleared in the puff of a simple signal.

Oberon's curiosity kept him tuned to the departing *Sea Sprite* a bit longer. He focused upon the elf—Drizzt Do'Urden, as Pellman, the harbormaster, had called him. To the wizard's experienced eye, something seemed amiss about this elf. Not out of place, as the barbarian seemed. Rather something in the way Drizzt carried himself or looked about with those unique, lavender orbs.

Those eyes just did not seem to fit the overall persona of that elf, Drizzt Do'Urden.

An enchantment, perhaps, Oberon guessed. Some magical disguise. The curious wizard wished that he had more information to report to Pasha Pook. He considered the possibilities of whisking himself away to the deck of the ship to investigate further, but he hadn't the proper spells prepared for such an undertaking. Besides, he reminded himself again, this was not his affair.

And he did not want to cross Artemis Entreri.

⚔ ⚔ ⚔ ⚔ ⚔

That same night, Oberon flew out of his tower and climbed into the night sky, a wand in hand. Hundreds of feet above the city, he loosed the proper sequence of fireballs.

⚔ ⚔ ⚔ ⚔ ⚔

Riding the decks of a Calimport ship named *Devil Dancer,* two hundred miles to the south, Artemis Entreri watched the display. "By sea," he muttered, noting the sequence of the bursts. He turned to the halfling standing beside him.

"Your friends pursue us by sea," he said. "And less than a tenday behind! They have done well."

Regis's eyes did not flicker in hope at the news. The climate change was very evident now, every day and every night. They had left the winter far behind, and the hot winds of the southern Realms had settled uneasily on the halfling's spirits. The trip to Calimport would not be interrupted by any other stops, and no ship—even one less than a tenday behind—could hope to catch the speedy *Devil Dancer.*

Regis wrestled against an inner dilemma, trying to come to terms with the inevitability of his meeting with his old guildmaster.

Pasha Pook was not a forgiving man. Regis had personally witnessed Pook dealing out severe punishments to those thieves who dared to steal from other members of the guild. And Regis had gone even a step further than that; he had stolen from the guildmaster himself. And the item he had plucked, the magical ruby pendant, was Pook's most treasured possession. Defeated and despairing, Regis put his head down and walked slowly back toward his cabin.

The halfling's somber mood did nothing to quell the tingle running through Entreri's spine. Pook would get the gem and the halfling, and Entreri would be paid well for the service. But in the assassin's mind, Pook's gold was not the true reward for his efforts.

Entreri wanted Drizzt Do'Urden.

⚔ ⚔ ⚔ ⚔

Drizzt and Wulfgar also watched the fireworks over Baldur's Gate that night. Back in the open sea, but still more than a hundred and fifty miles north of the Devil Dancer, they could only guess at the display's significance.

"A wizard," Deudermont remarked, coming over to join the two. "Perhaps he does battle with some great aerial beast," the captain offered, trying to draw up some entertaining story. "A dragon or some other monster of the sky!"

Drizzt squinted to gain a closer look at the fiery bursts. He saw no dark forms weaving around the flares, nor any hint that they were aimed at a particular target. But possibly the *Sea Sprite* was simply too far away for him to discern such detail.

"Not a fight—a signal," Wulfgar blurted, recognizing a pattern to the explosions. "Three and one. Three and one.

"It seems a bit of trouble for a simple signal," Wulfgar added. "Would not a rider carrying a note serve better?"

"Unless it is meant as a signal to a ship," offered Deudermont.

Drizzt had already entertained that very thought, and he was becoming more than a little suspicious of the display's source, and of its purpose.

Deudermont studied the display a moment longer. "Perhaps it is a signal," he conceded, recognizing the accuracy of Wulfgar's observations of a pattern. "Many ships put in to and out of Baldur's Gate each day. A wizard greeting some friends or saying farewell in grand fashion."

"Or relaying information," Drizzt added, glancing up at Wulfgar. Wulfgar did not miss the drow's point; Drizzt could tell by the barbarian's scowl that Wulfgar was entertaining similar suspicions.

"But for us, a show and nothing more," Deudermont said, bidding them good night with a pat on the shoulder. "An amusement to be enjoyed."

Drizzt and Wulfgar looked at each other, seriously doubting Deudermont's assessment.

⚔ ⚔ ⚔ ⚔

"What game does Artemis Entreri play?" Pook asked rhetorically, speaking his thoughts aloud.

Oberon, the wizard in the crystal ball, shrugged. "Never have I pretended to understand the motives of Artemis Entreri."

Pook nodded his accord and continued to pace behind LaValle's chair.

"Yet I would guess that these two have little to do with your pendant," said Oberon.

"Some personal vendetta Entreri acquired along his travels," agreed Pook.

"Friends of the halfling?" wondered Oberon. "Then why would Entreri lead them in the right direction?"

"Whoever they may be, they can only bring trouble," said LaValle, seated between his guildmaster and the scrying device.

"Perhaps Entreri plans to lay an ambush for them," Pook suggested to Oberon. "That would explain his need for your signal."

"Entreri instructed the harbormaster to tell them that he would meet them in Calimport," Oberon reminded Pook.

"To throw them off," said LaValle. "To make them believe that the way would be clear until they arrived in the southern port."

"That is not the way of Artemis Entreri," said Oberon, and Pook was thinking the same thing. "I have never known the assassin to use such obvious tricks to gain the upper hand in a contest. It is Entreri's deepest pleasure to meet and crush challengers face to face."

The two wizards and the guildmaster who had survived and thrived by his ability to react to such puzzles appropriately all held their thoughts for a moment to consider the possibilities. All that Pook cared about was the return of his precious pendant. With it he could expand his powers ten times, perhaps even gaining the favor of the ruling Pasha of Calimshan himself.

"I do not like this," Pook said at length. "I want no complications to the return of the halfling, or of my pendant."

He paused to consider the implications of his decided course, leaning over LaValle's back to get close to Oberon's image. "Do you still have contact with Pinochet?" he asked the wizard slyly.

Oberon guessed the guildmaster's meaning. "The pirate does not forget his friends," he answered in the same tone. "Pinochet contacts me every time he finds his way to Baldur's Gate. He inquires of you as well, hoping that all is well with his old friend."

"And is he now in the isles?"

"The winter trade is rolling down from Waterdeep," Oberon replied with a chuckle. "Where else would a successful pirate be?"

"Good," muttered Pook.

"Should I arrange a welcome for Entreri's pursuers?" Oberon asked eagerly, enjoying the intrigue and the opportunity to serve the guildmaster.

"Three ships—no chances," said Pook. "Nothing shall interfere with the halfling's return. He and I have so very much to discuss!"

Oberon considered the task for a moment. "A pity," he remarked. "The *Sea Sprite* was a fine vessel."

Pook echoed a single word for emphasis, making it absolutely clear that he would tolerate no mistakes.

"Was."

The Weight of a King's Mantle

The halfling hung by his ankles, suspended upside down with chains above a cauldron of boiling liquid. Not water, though, but something darker. A red hue, perhaps.

Blood, perhaps.

The crank creaked, and the halfling dropped an inch closer. His face was contorted, his mouth wide, as if in a scream.

But no screams could be heard. Just the groans of the crank and a sinister laugh from an unseen torturer.

The misty scene shifted, and the crank came into view, worked slowly by a single hand that seemed unattached to anything else.

There was a pause in the descent.

Then the evil voice laughed one final time. The hand jerked quickly, sending the crank spinning.

A scream resounded, piercing and cutting, a cry of agony—a cry of death.

✕ ✕ ✕ ✕ ✕

Sweat stung Bruenor's eyes even before he had fully opened them. He wiped the wetness from his face and rolled his head, trying to shake away the terrible images and adjust his thoughts to his surroundings.

He was in the Ivy Mansion, in a comfortable bed in a comfortable room. The fresh candles that he had set out burned low. They hadn't helped; this night had been like the others: another nightmare.

Bruenor rolled over and sat up on the side of his bed. Everything was as it should be. The mithral armor and golden shield lay across a chair beside the room's single dresser. The axe that he had used to cut his way out of the duergar lair rested easily against the wall beside Drizzt's scimitar, and two helmets sat atop the dresser, the battered, one-horned helm that had carried the dwarf through the adventures of the last two centuries, and the crown of the king of Mithral Hall, ringed by a thousand glittering gemstones.

But to Bruenor's eyes, all was not as it should be. He looked to the window and the darkness of the night beyond. Alas, all he could see was the reflection of the candlelit room, the crown and armor of the king of Mithral Hall.

It had been a tough tenday for Bruenor. All the days had been filled with the excitement of the times, of talk of the armies coming from Citadel Adbar and Icewind Dale to reclaim Mithral Hall. The dwarf's shoulders ached from being patted so many times by Harpells and other visitors to the mansion, all anxious to congratulate him in advance for the impending return of his throne.

But Bruenor had wandered through the last few days absently, playing a role thrust upon him before he could truly appreciate it. It was time to prepare for the adventure Bruenor had fantasized about since his exile nearly two centuries before. His father's father had been king of Mithral Hall, his father before him, and back to the beginnings of Clan Battlehammer. Bruenor's birthright demanded that he lead the armies and retake Mithral Hall, that he sit in the throne he had been born to possess.

But it was in the very chambers of the ancient dwarven homeland that Bruenor Battlehammer had realized the truth of what was important to him. Over the course of the last decade, four very special companions had come into his life, not one of them a dwarf. The friendship the five had forged was bigger than a dwarven kingdom and more precious to Bruenor than all the mithral in the world. The realization of his fantasy conquest seemed empty to him.

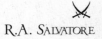

The moments of the night now held Bruenor's heart and his concentration. The dreams, never the same but always with the same terrible conclusion, did not fade with the light of day.

"Another one?" came a soft call from the door. Bruenor looked over his shoulder to see Catti-brie peeking in on him. Bruenor knew that he didn't have to answer. He put his head down in one hand and rubbed his eyes.

"About Regis again?" asked Catti-brie, moving closer. Bruenor heard the door softly close.

"Rumblebelly," Bruenor softly corrected, using the nickname he had tagged on the halfling who had been his closest friend for nearly a decade.

Bruenor swung his legs back up on the bed. "I should be with him," he said gruffly, "or at least with the drow and Wulfgar, lookin' for him!"

"Yer kingdom awaits," Catti-brie reminded him, more to dispel his guilt than to soften his belief in where he truly belonged—a belief that the young woman wholeheartedly shared. "Yer kin from Icewind Dale'll be here in a month, the army from Adbar in two."

"Aye, but we can't be going to the halls till the winter's past."

Catti-brie looked around for some way to deflect the sinking conversation. "Ye'll wear it well," she said cheerfully, indicating the bejeweled crown.

"Which?" Bruenor retorted, a sharp edge to his tongue.

Catti-brie looked at the dented helm, pitiful beside the glorious one, and nearly snorted aloud. But she turned to Bruenor before she commented, and the stern look stamped upon the dwarf's face as he studied the old helmet told her that Bruenor had not asked in jest. At that moment, Catti-brie realized, Bruenor saw the one-horned helmet as infinitely more precious than the crown he was destined to wear.

"They're halfway to Calimport," Catti-brie remarked, sympathizing with the dwarf's desires. "Maybe more."

"Aye, and few boats'll be leaving Waterdeep with the winter coming on," Bruenor muttered grimly, echoing the same arguments Catti-brie had leveled on him during his second morning in the Ivy Mansion, when he had first mentioned his desire to go after his friends.

"We've a million preparations before us," said Catti-brie, stubbornly holding her cheerful tone. "Suren the winter'll pass quickly, and we'll get the halls in time for Drizzt and Wulfgar and Regis's return."

Bruenor's visage did not soften. His eyes locked on the broken helmet, but his mind wandered beyond the vision, back to the fateful scene at Garumn's Gorge. He had at least made peace with Regis before they were separated . . .

Bruenor's recollections blew away from him suddenly. He snapped a wry glance upon Catti-brie. "Ye think they might be back in time for the fighting?"

Catti-brie shrugged "If they put right back out," she replied, curious at the question, for she knew that Bruenor had more in mind than fighting beside Drizzt and Wulfgar in the battle for Mithral Hall. "They can be coverin' many miles over the southland—even in the winter."

Bruenor bounced off the bed and rushed for the door, scooping up the one-horned helmet and fitting it to his head as he went.

"Middle o' the night?" Catti-brie gawked after him. She jumped up and followed him into the hall.

Bruenor never slowed. He marched straight to Harkle Harpell's door and banged on it loudly enough to wake everyone in that wing of the house. "Harkle!" he roared.

Catti-brie knew better than to even try to calm him. She just shrugged apologetically to each curious head that popped into the hall to take a look.

Finally, Harkle, clad only in a nightshirt and ball-tipped cap, and holding a candle, opened his door.

Bruenor shoved himself into the room, Catti-brie in tow. "Can ye make me a chariot?" the dwarf demanded.

"A what?" Harkle yawned, trying futilely to brush his sleep away. "A chariot?"

"A chariot!" Bruenor growled. "Of fire. Like the Lady Alustriel bringed me here in! A chariot of fire!"

"Well," Harkle stammered. "I have never—"

"Can ye do it?" Bruenor roared, having no patience now for unfocused blabbering.

"Yes . . . uh, maybe," Harkle proclaimed as confidently as he could. "Actually, that spell is Alustriel's specialty. No one here has ever . . ." He stopped, feeling Bruenor's frustrated glare boring into him. The dwarf stood straight-legged, one bare heel grinding into the floor, and his gnarled arms crossed over his chest, the stubby fingers of one hand tapping an impatient rhythm on his knotted biceps.

"I shall speak to the lady in the morning," Harkle assured him. "I am certain—"

"Alustriel's still here?" Bruenor interrupted

"Why, yes," Harkle replied. "She stayed on a few extra—"

"Where is she?" Bruenor demanded.

"Down the hall."

"Which room?"

"I shall take you to her in the morn—" Harkle began.

Bruenor grabbed the front of the wizard's nightshirt and brought him down to a dwarf's eye level. Bruenor proved the stronger even with his nose, for the long, pointy thing pressed Harkle's nose flat against one of his cheeks. Bruenor's eyes did not blink, and he spoke each word of his question slowly and distinctly, just the way he wanted the answer. "Which room?"

"Green door, beside the bannister." Harkle gulped.

Bruenor gave the wizard a goodhearted wink and let him go. The dwarf turned right past Catti-brie, returning her amused smile with a determined shake of his head, and burst into the hall.

"Oh, he should not disturb the Lady Alustriel at this late hour!" Harkle protested.

Catti-brie could not help but laugh. "So stop him yerself!

Harkle listened to the dwarf's heavy footsteps resounding down the hall; Bruenor's bare feet thudded on the wooden floor like bouncing stones. "No," Harkle answered her offer, his smile widening to match her own. "I think not."

Abruptly awakened in the night, the Lady Alustriel appeared no less beautiful, her silvery mane somehow mystically connected to the soft glow of the evening. Bruenor composed himself when he saw the lady, remembering her station and his manners.

"Uh, begging the lady's pardon," he stammered, suddenly very embarrassed by his actions.

"It is late, good King Bruenor," Alustriel said politely, an amused smile on her face as she viewed the dwarf, dressed only in his nightshirt and broken helmet. "What might have brought you to my door at this hour?"

"What with all that's going on about, I did not even know ye were still in Longsaddle," Bruenor explained.

"I would have come to see you before I left," Alustriel replied, her tone still cordial. "No need to disturb your sleep—or mine."

"Me thoughts weren't for good-byes," Bruenor said. "I be needing a favor."

"Urgently?"

Bruenor nodded emphatically. "A favor I should've asked afore we e'er got here."

Alustriel led him into her room and closed the door behind them, realizing the seriousness of the dwarf's business.

"I need another one of them chariots," said Bruenor. "To take me to the south."

"You mean to catch your friends and aid in the search for the halfling," Alustriel reasoned.

"Aye, I know me place."

"But I cannot accompany you," Alustriel said. "I have a realm to rule; it is not my place to journey unannounced to other kingdoms."

"I wouldn't be askin' ye to go," replied Bruenor.

"Then who will drive the team? You have no experience with such magic."

Bruenor thought for just a moment. "Harkle'll take me!" he blurted.

Alustriel couldn't hide a smirk as she thought of the possibilities for disaster. Harkle, like so many of his Harpell kin, usually hurt himself when spellcasting. The lady knew that she would not sway the dwarf, but she felt it her duty to point out all of the weaknesses of his plan.

"Calimport is a long way indeed," she told him. "The trip there on the chariot will be speedy, but the return could take many months. Will not the true king of Mithral Hall lead the gathering armies in the fight for his throne?"

"He will," Bruenor replied, "if it be possible. But me place's with me friends. I owe them at least that!"

"You risk much."

"No more than they've risked for me—many the times."

Alustriel opened the door. "Very well," she said, "and my respect on your decision. You will prove a noble king, Bruenor Battlehammer."

The dwarf, for one of the few times in his life, blushed.

"Now go and rest," said Alustriel. "I will see what I may learn this night. Meet me on the south slope of Harpell Hill before the break of dawn."

Bruenor nodded eagerly and found his way back to his room. For the first time since he had come to Longsaddle, he slept peacefully.

⚔ ⚔ ⚔ ⚔

Under the lightening sky of predawn, Bruenor and Harkle met Alustriel at the appointed spot. Harkle had eagerly agreed to the journey; he had always wanted a crack at driving one of Lady Alustriel's famed chariots. He seemed out of place next to the battle-charged dwarf, though, wearing his wizard's robe—tucked into leather hip boots—and an oddly shaped silver helmet with fluffy white fur wings and a visor that kept flopping down over his eyes.

Alustriel had not slept the rest of that night. She had been busy staring into the crystal ball the Harpells had provided her, probing distant planes in search of clues to the whereabouts of Bruenor's friends. She had learned much in that short time and had even made a connection to the dead mage Morkai in the spirit world to garner further information.

And what she had learned disturbed her more than a little.

She stood now, components in hand and awaiting the break of dawn, quietly facing the east. As the first rays of the sun peeked over the horizon, she swept them into her grasp and executed the spell. Minutes later, a flaming chariot and two fiery horses appeared on the hillside, magically suspended an inch from the ground. The licks of their flames sent tiny streams of smoke rising from the bedewed grass.

"To Calimport!" Harkle proclaimed, rushing over to the enchanted carriage.

"Nay," Alustriel corrected. Bruenor turned a confused glance on her.

"Your friends are not yet in the Empire of the Sands," the lady explained. "They are at sea and will find grave danger this day. Set your course to the southwest, to the sea, then true south with the coast in sight." She tossed a heart-shaped locket to Bruenor. The dwarf fumbled it open and found a picture of Drizzt Do'Urden inside.

"The locket will warm when you approach the ship that carries your friends," Alustriel said. "I created it many tendays ago, that I might have known if your group approached Silverymoon on your return from Mithral Hall." She avoided Bruenor's probing gaze, knowing the myriad of questions that must have been going through the dwarf's mind. Quietly, almost as if embarrassed, she added, "I should like it returned."

Bruenor kept his sly remarks to himself. He knew of the growing connection between Lady Alustriel and Drizzt. It became clearer and clearer every day. "Ye'll get it back," he assured her. He scooped the locket up in his fist and moved to join Harkle.

"Tarry not," Alustriel told them. "Their need is pressing this day!"

"Wait!" came a call from the hill. All three turned to see Catti-brie, fully outfitted for the road, with Taulmaril, the magical bow of Anariel that she had recovered from the ruins of Mithral Hall, slung easily over her shoulder. She ran down to the back of the chariot. "Ye weren't meaning to leave me so?" she asked Bruenor.

Bruenor couldn't look her in the eye. He had indeed meant to leave without so much as a good-bye to his daughter. "Bah!" he snorted. "Ye'd have only tried to stop me going!"

"Never I would!" Catti-brie growled right back at him. "Me thinkin's that yer doing right. But ye'd do righter if ye'd move over and make room for me!"

Bruenor shook his head emphatically.

"I've as much the right as yerself!" Catti-brie protested.

"Bah!" Bruenor snorted again. "Drizzt and Rumblebelly are me truest friends!"

"And mine!"

"And Wulfgar's been akin to a son to me!" Bruenor shot back, thinking he had won the round.

"And a mite bit more than that to me," Catti-brie retorted, "if he gets back from the South!" Catti-brie didn't even need to remind Bruenor that she had been the one who introduced him to Drizzt. She had defeated all of the dwarf's arguments. "Move aside, Bruenor Battlehammer, and make room! I've as much at stake as yerself, and I'm meaning to come along!"

"Who'll be seeing to the armies?" Bruenor asked.

"The Harpells'll put them up. They won't be marching to the halls until we're back, or until the spring at least."

"But if both of you go and do not return," Harkle interjected, letting the thought hang over them for a moment. "You are the only ones who know the way."

Bruenor saw Catti-brie's crestfallen look and realized how deeply she desired to join him on his quest. And he knew she was right in coming, for she had as much at stake in the chase across the southland as he. He thought for a moment, suddenly shifting to Catti-brie's side in the debate. "The lady knows the way," he said, indicating Alustriel.

Alustriel nodded. "I do," she replied. "And I would gladly show the armies to the halls. But the chariot will carry only two riders."

Bruenor's sigh was as loud as Catti-brie's. He shrugged helplessly at his daughter. "Better that ye stay," he said softly. "I'll bring 'em back for ye."

Catti-brie wouldn't let it go so easily. "When the fighting starts," she said, "and suren it will, would ye rather ye had Harkle and his spells beside ye, or me and me bow?"

Bruenor glanced casually at Harkle and immediately saw the young woman's logic. The wizard stood at the reins of the chariot, trying to find some way to keep the visor of his helmet up on his brow. Finally Harkle gave up and just tilted his head back far enough so he could see under the visor.

"Here, ye dropped a piece of it," Bruenor said to him. "That's why it won't stay up!"

Harkle turned and saw Bruenor pointing to the ground off the back of the chariot. He shuffled around beside Bruenor and bent over, trying to see what the dwarf was pointing at.

As Harkle bent to look, the weight of his silver helmet—which actually belonged to a cousin much larger than he—toppled him over and left him sprawled face down on the lawn. In the same moment, Bruenor swept Catti-brie into the chariot beside him.

"Oh, drats!" Harkle whined. "I would have so loved to go!"

"The lady'll make ye another one to fly," Bruenor said to comfort him. Harkle looked to Alustriel.

"Tomorrow morning," Alustriel agreed, quite amused by the whole scene. Then to Bruenor she asked, "Can you guide the chariot?"

"As well as he, by me guess!" the dwarf proclaimed, grabbing up the fiery reins. "Hold on, girl. We've half a world to cross!" He snapped the reins, and the chariot lifted into the morning sky, cutting a fiery streak across the blue-gray haze of dawn.

The wind rushed past them as they shot into the west, the chariot rocking wildly from side to side, up and down. Bruenor fought frantically to hold his course; Catti-brie fought frantically just to hold on. The sides wobbled, the back dipped and climbed, and once they even spun in a complete vertical circle, though it happened so fast—luckily—that neither of the riders had time to fall out!

A few minutes later, a single thundercloud loomed ahead of them. Bruenor saw it, and Catti-brie yelled a warning, but the dwarf hadn't mastered the subtleties of driving the chariot well enough to do anything about their course. They blew through the darkness, leaving a hissing steam tail in their wake, and rocketed out above the cloud.

And then Bruenor, his face glistening with wetness, found the measure of the reins. He leveled off the chariot's course and put the rising sun behind his right shoulder. Catti-brie, too, found her footing, though she still clung tightly to the chariot's rail with one hand, and to the dwarf's heavy cloak with the other.

⚔ ⚔ ⚔ ⚔

The silver dragon rolled over onto its back lazily, riding the morning winds with its legs—all four—crossed over it and its sleepy eyes half closed. The good dragon loved its morning glide, leaving the bustle of the world far below and catching the sun's untainted rays above the cloud level.

But the dragon's marvelous orbs popped open wide when it saw the fiery streak rushing at it from the east. Thinking the flames to be the fore-running fires of an evil red dragon, the silver swooped around into a high cloud and poised to ambush the thing. But the fury left the dragon's eyes when it recognized the strange craft, a fiery chariot, with just the helm of the driver, a one-horned contraption, sticking above the front of the carriage and a young human woman standing behind, her auburn locks flying back over her shoulders.

Its huge mouth agape, the silver dragon watched as the chariot sped past. Few things piqued the curiosity of this ancient creature, who had lived so very many years, but it seriously considered following this unlikely scene.

A cool breeze wafted in then and washed all other thoughts from the silver dragon's mind. "Peoples," it muttered, rolling again onto its back and shaking its head in disbelief.

⚔ ⚔ ⚔ ⚔

Catti-brie and Bruenor never even saw the dragon. Their eyes were fixed squarely ahead, where the wide sea was already in sight on the western horizon, blanketed by a heavy morning mist. A half-hour later, they saw the high towers of Waterdeep to the north and moved out from the Sword Coast and over the water. Bruenor, getting a better feel of the reins, swung the chariot to the south and dropped it low.

Too low.

Diving into the gray shroud of mist, they heard the lapping of the waves below them and the hiss of steam as the spray hit their fiery craft.

"Bring her up!" Catti-brie yelled. "Ye're too low!"

"Need to be low!" Bruenor gasped, fighting the reins. He tried to mask his incompetence, but he fully realized that they were indeed too close to the water. Struggling with all his might, he managed to bring the chariot up a few more feet and level it off. "There," he boasted. "Got it straight, and got it low."

He looked over his shoulder at Catti-brie. "Need to be low," he said again into her doubting expression. "We have to see the durn ship to find it!"

Catti-brie only shook her head.

But then they did see a ship. Not *the* ship, but a ship nonetheless, looming up in the mist barely thirty yards ahead.

Catti-brie screamed—Bruenor did, too—and the dwarf fell back with the reins, forcing the chariot upward at as steep an angle as possible. The ship's deck rolled out below them.

And the masts still towered above them!

If all the ghosts of every sailor who had ever died on the sea had risen from their watery graves and sought vengeance on this particular vessel, the lookout's face would not have held a truer expression of terror. Possibly he leaped from his perch—more likely he toppled in fright—but either way, he missed the deck and dropped safely into the water at the very last second before the chariot streaked past his crow's nest and nipped the top of the mainmast.

Catti-brie and Bruenor composed themselves and looked back to see the tip of the ship's mast burning like a single candle in the gray mist.

"Ye're too low," Catti-brie reiterated.

II
HOT WINDS

The *Sea Sprite* cruised easily under clear blue skies and the lazy warmth of the southern Realms. A strong trade wind kept its sails filled, and only six days after their departure from Baldur's Gate, the western tip of the Tethyr Peninsula was already in sight—a journey that normally took more than a tenday.

But a wizard's call traveled faster still.

Captain Deudermont took the *Sea Sprite* down the center of Asavir's Channel, trying to keep a safe distance from the peninsula's sheltered bays—bays that often held pirates poised for passing merchant vessels—and also cautious to keep a healthy gap of water between his ship and the islands on his west: the Nelanther, the infamous Pirate Isles. The captain felt safe enough in the crowded sea lane, with the banner of Calimport flying above his craft and the sails of several other merchant ships dotting the horizon every so often both in front of and behind the *Sea Sprite*.

Using a common merchant's trick, Deudermont closed in on a vessel and shadowed its course, keeping the *Sea Sprite* in its wake. Less maneuverable and slower than the *Sea Sprite* and flying the flag of Murann, a lesser city on the Sword Coast, this second ship would provide a much easier target to any pirates in the area.

Eighty feet above the water, taking a turn in the crow's nest, Wulfgar had the clearest view of the deck of the ship ahead. With his strength and agility, the barbarian was fast becoming quite a sailor, eagerly taking his turn at every job alongside the rest of the crew. His favorite duty was the crow's nest, though it was a tight fit for a man of his size. He was at peace in the warm breeze and solitude. He rested against the mast, using one hand to block out the daytime glare, and studied the crew's activities on the ship ahead.

He heard the front ship's lookout call something down, though he couldn't make out the words, then saw the crew rushing about frantically, most heading for the prow to watch the horizon. Wulfgar jolted upright and leaned over the nest, straining his eyes to the south.

⚔ ⚔ ⚔ ⚔ ⚔

"How do they feel, having us in tow?" Drizzt, standing beside Deudermont on the bridge, asked the captain. While Wulfgar had been building a rapport working beside the crew, Drizzt had struck a solid friendship with the captain. And realizing the value of the elf's opinions, Deudermont gladly shared his knowledge of his station, and of the sea, with Drizzt. "Do they understand their role as fodder?"

"They know our purpose in shadowing them, and their captain—if he is an experienced sailor—would do the same if our positions were reversed," Deudermont replied. "Yet we bring them an extra measure of safety as well. Just having a ship from Calimport in sight will deter many of the pirates."

"And perhaps they feel that we would come to their aid in the face of such an attack?" Drizzt was quick to ask.

Deudermont knew that Drizzt was interested in discovering if the *Sea Sprite* would indeed go to the other ship's aid. Drizzt had a strong streak of honor in him, Deudermont understood, and the captain, of similar morals, admired him for it. But Deudermont's responsibilities as the captain of a vessel were too involved for such a hypothetical situation. "Perhaps," he replied.

Drizzt let the line of questioning end, satisfied that Deudermont kept the scales of duty and morality in proper balance.

"Sails to the south!" came Wulfgar's call from above, bringing many of the *Sea Sprite's* crew to the forward rail.

Deudermont's eyes went to the horizon, then to Wulfgar. "How many?"

"Two ships!" Wulfgar called back. "Running north and even, and wide apart!"

"Port and starboard?" Deudermont asked.

Wulfgar took a close measure of the intercepting course, then affirmed the captain's suspicions. "We will pass between them!"

"Pirates?" Drizzt asked, knowing the answer.

"So it would seem," the captain replied. The distant sails came into view to the men on the deck.

"I see no flag," one of the sailors near the bridge called to the captain.

Drizzt pointed to the merchant ship ahead. "Are they the target?"

Deudermont nodded grimly. "So it would seem," he said again.

"Then let us close up with them," the drow said. "Two against two seems a fairer fight."

Deudermont stared into Drizzt's lavender eyes and was almost stunned by their sudden gleam. How could the captain hope to make this honorable warrior understand their place in the scenario? The *Sea Sprite* flew Calimport's flag, the other ship, Murann's. The two were hardly allies.

"The encounter may not come to blows," he told Drizzt. "The Murann vessel would be wise to surrender peacefully."

Drizzt began to see the reasoning. "So flying Calimport's flag holds responsibilities as well as benefits?"

Deudermont shrugged helplessly "Think of the thieves' guilds in the cities you have known," he explained. "Pirates are much the same—an unavoidable nuisance. If we sail in to fight, we would dispel any self-restraint the pirates hold upon themselves, most probably bringing more trouble than need be."

"And we would mark every ship under Calimport's flag sailing the Channel," Drizzt added, no longer looking at the captain, but watching the spectacle unfold before him. The light dropped from his eyes.

Deudermont, inspired by Drizzt's grasp of principles—a grip that would not allow such acceptance of rogues—put a hand on the elf's shoulder. "If the encounter comes to blows," the captain said, drawing Drizzt's gaze back to his own, "the *Sea Sprite* will join the battle."

Drizzt turned back to the horizon and clapped Deudermont's hand with his own. The eager fire returned to his eyes as Deudermont ordered the crew to stand ready.

The captain really didn't expect a fight. He had seen dozens of engagements such as this, and normally when the pirates outnumbered their intended victim, the looting was accomplished without bloodshed. But Deudermont, with so many years of experience on the sea, soon realized that something was strange this time. The pirate ships kept their course wide, passing too far abreast of the Murann ship to board it. At first, Deudermont thought the pirates meant to launch a distance strike—one of the pirate vessels had a catapult mounted to its afterdeck—to cripple their victim, though the act seemed unnecessary.

Then the captain understood the truth. The pirates had no interest in the Murann ship. The *Sea Sprite* was their target.

From his high perch, Wulfgar, too, realized that the pirates were sailing right by the lead ship. "Take up arms!" he cried to the crew. "They aim for us!"

"You may indeed get your fight," Deudermont said to Drizzt. "It seems that Calimport's flag will not protect us this time."

To Drizzt's nightattuned eyes, the distant ships appeared as no more than tiny black dots in the glare of the shining water, but the drow could make out what was happening well enough. He couldn't understand the logic of the pirates' choice, though, and he had a strange feeling that he and Wulfgar might be somehow connected to the unfolding events. "Why us?" he asked Deudermont.

The captain shrugged. "Perhaps they have heard a rumor that one of Calimport's ships will be laden with a valuable cargo."

The image of the fireballs exploding in the night sky over Baldur's Gate flashed in Drizz's mind. A signal? he wondered again. He couldn't yet put all of the pieces together, but his suspicions led him invariably to the theory that he and Wulfgar were somehow involved in the pirates' choice of ships.

"Do we fight?" he started to ask Deudermont, but he saw that the captain was already laying the plans.

"Starboard!" Deudermont told the helmsman. "Put us west to the Pirate Isles. Let us see if these dogs have a belly for the reefs!" He motioned another man to the crow's nest, wanting Wulfgar's strength for the more important duties on the deck.

The *Sea Sprite* bit into the waves and bowed low in a sharp right turn. The pirate vessel on the east, now the farthest away, cut its angle to pursue directly while the other, the bulkier of the two, kept its course straight, each second bringing the *Sea Sprite* closer for a shot of its catapult.

Deudermont pointed to the largest of the few islands visible in the west. "Skim her close," he told the helmsman, "but ware the single reef. Tide's low, and she should be visible."

Wulfgar dropped to the deck beside the captain.

"On that line," Deudermont ordered him. "You've the mainmast. If I bid you to pull, then heave for all your strength! We shan't get a second chance."

Wulfgar took up the heavy rope with a grunt of determination, wrapping it tightly around his wrists and hands.

"Fire in the sky!" one of the crewmen yelled, pointing back to the south, toward the bulky pirate ship. A ball of flaming pitch soared through the air, splashing harmlessly into the ocean with a hiss of protest, many yards short of the *Sea Sprite*.

"A tracing shot," Deudermont explained, "to give them our range."

Deudermont estimated the distance and figured how much closer the pirates would get before the *Sea Sprite* put the island between them.

"We'll slip them if we make the channel between the reef and the island," he told Drizzt, nodding to indicate that he thought the prospects promising.

But even as the drow and the captain began to comfort themselves with thoughts of escape, the masts of a third vessel loomed before them in the west, slipping out of the very channel that Deudermont had hoped to enter. This ship had its sails furled and was prepared for boarding.

Deudermont's jaw dropped open. "They were lying for us," he said to Drizzt. He turned to the elf helplessly. "They were lying for us."

"But we've no cargo of particular value," the captain continued trying to reason through the unusual turn of events. "Why would pirates run three vessels in a strike against a single ship?"

Drizzt knew the answer.

⚔ ⚔ ⚔ ⚔ ⚔

The ride was easier for Bruenor and Catti-brie now. The dwarf had settled comfortably at the reins of the fiery chariot, and the morning haze had burned away. They cruised down the Sword Coast, amused by the ships they passed over and the astonished expressions of every sailor who turned his eyes heavenward.

Soon after, they crossed the entrance to the River Chionthar, the gateway to Baldur's Gate. Bruenor paused a moment to consider a sudden impulse, then veered the chariot away from the coast.

"The lady bid us to stay to the coast," said Catti-brie as soon as she realized the shift in course

Bruenor grabbed Alustriel's magical locket, which he had strung around his neck, and shrugged his shoulders. "It's tellin' me different," he replied.

⚔ ⚔ ⚔ ⚔ ⚔

A second load of burning pitch hit the water, this time dangerously close to the *Sea Sprite*.

"We can run by her," Drizzt said to Deudermont, for the third ship still had not raised its sails.

The experienced captain recognized the flaw in the reasoning. The primary purpose of the ship coming out from the island was to block the channel's entrance. The *Sea Sprite* could indeed sail past that ship, but Deudermont would have to take his ship outside the dangerous reef and back into open water. And by then, they would be well within the catapult's range.

Deudermont looked over his shoulder. The remaining pirate ship, the one farthest to the east, had its sails full of wind and was cutting the water even more swiftly than the *Sea Sprite*. If a ball of pitch came in on the mark and the *Sea Sprite* took any damage at all to its sails, it would be quickly overtaken.

And then a second problem dramatically grabbed the captain's attention. A bolt of lightning blasted across the *Sea Sprite*'s deck, severing some lines and splintering off pieces of the mainmast. The structure leaned and groaned against the strain of the full sails. Wulfgar found a foothold and tugged against the pull with all his strength.

"Hold her!" Deudermont cheered him. "Keep us straight and strong!"

"They've a wizard," Drizzt remarked, realizing that the blast had come from the ship ahead of them.

"I feared as much," Deudermont replied grimly.

The seething fire in Drizzt's eyes told Deudermont that the elf had already decided upon his first task in the fight. Even in their obvious disadvantage, the captain felt a tug of pity for the wizard.

A sly expression came over Deudermont's face as the sight of Drizzt inspired a desperate plan of action. "Take us right up on her port," he told the helmsman. "Close enough to spit on them!"

"But, Captain," the sailor protested, "that'd put us in line for the reef!"

"Just what the dogs had hoped," Deudermont came back. "Let them think that we do not know these waters; let them think that the rocks will do their business for them!"

Drizzt felt comfortable with the security in the captain's tone. The wily old sailor had something in mind.

"Steady?" Deudermont called to Wulfgar.

The barbarian nodded.

"When I call for you, pull, man, as if your life depends on it!" Deudermont told him.

Next to the captain, Drizzt made a quiet observation. "It does."

⚔ ⚔ ⚔ ⚔ ⚔

From the bridge of his flagship, the fast-flying vessel on the east, Pinochet the pirate watched the maneuvering of the *Sea Sprite* with concern. He knew Deudermont's reputation well enough to know that the captain would not be so foolish as to put his ship onto a reef under a bright midday sun at low tide. Deudermont meant to fight.

Pinochet looked to the bulky ship and measured the angle to the *Sea Sprite*. The catapult would get two more shots, maybe three, before their target ran alongside the blocking ship in the channel. Pinochet's own ship was still many minutes behind the action, and the pirate captain wondered how much damage Deudermont would inflict before he could aid his allies.

But Pinochet quickly put thoughts of the cost of this mission out of his mind. He was doing a personal favor for the guildmaster of the largest gang of thieves in all of Calimport. Whatever the price, Pasha Pook's payment would surely outweigh it!

⚔ ⚔ ⚔ ⚔

Catti-brie watched eagerly as each new ship came into view, but Bruenor, confident that the magical locket was leading him to the drow, paid them no heed. The dwarf snapped the reins, trying to urge the flaming horses on faster. Somehow—perhaps it was another property of the locket—Bruenor felt that Drizzt was in trouble and that speed was essential.

The dwarf then snapped a stubby finger in front of him. "There!" he cried as soon as the *Sea Sprite* came into view.

Catti-brie did not question his observation. She quickly surveyed the dramatic situation unfolding below her.

Another ball of pitch soared through the air, slapping into the tail of the *Sea Sprite* at water level but catching too little of the ship to do any real damage.

Catti-brie and Bruenor watched the catapult being pulled back for another shot; they watched the brutish crew of the ship in the channel, their swords in hand, awaiting the approach of the *Sea Sprite*; and they watched the third pirate ship, rushing in from behind to close the trap.

Bruenor veered the chariot to the south, toward the bulkiest of the ships. "First for the catapult!" the dwarf cried in rage.

Pinochet, as well as most of the crewmen on the back two pirate ships, watched the fiery craft cutting a streak down from the northern sky, but the captain and crew of the *Sea Sprite* and the other ship were too enmeshed in the desperation of their own situation to worry about events behind them. Drizzt did give the chariot a second look, though, noticing a glistening reflection that might have been a single horn of a broken helmet peeking above the flames, and a form in back of that with flowing hair that seemed more than vaguely familiar.

But perhaps it was just a trick of the light and Drizzt's own undying hopes. The chariot moved away into a fiery blur and Drizzt let it go, having no time now to give it further thought.

The *Sea Sprite*'s crew lined the foredeck, firing crossbows at the pirate ship, hoping, more than anything else, to keep the wizard too engaged to hit them again.

A second lightning bolt did roar in, but the *Sea Sprite* was rocking wildly in the breakers rolling off the reef, and the wizard's blast cut only a minor hole in the mainsail.

Deudermont looked hopefully to Wulfgar, tensed and ready for the command.

And then they were crossing beside the pirates, barely fifteen yards from the other ship, and apparently heading on a deadly course into the reef.

"Pull!" Deudermont cried, and Wulfgar heaved, every muscle in his huge body reddening with a sudden influx of blood and adrenaline.

The mainmast groaned in protest, beams creaked and cracked, and the wind-filled sails fought back as Wulfgar looped the rope over his shoulder and drove himself forward. The *Sea Sprite* verily pivoted in the water, its front end lifting over the roll of a wave and lurching at the pirate vessel. Deudermont's crew, though they had witnessed Wulfgar's power in the River Chionthar, grabbed desperately at the rail and held on, awestruck.

And the stunned pirates, never suspecting that a ship under full sail could possibly cut so tight a turn, reacted not at all. They watched in blank amazement as the prow of the *Sea Sprite* smashed into their port flank, entangling the two ships in a deadly embrace.

"Take it to them!" Deudermont cried. Grapples soared through the air, further securing the *Sea Sprite*'s hold, and boarding planks were thrown down and fastened into place.

Wulfgar scrambled to his feet and pulled Aegis-fang off his back. Drizzt drew his scimitars but made no immediate move, instead scanning the deck of the enemy ship. He quickly focused on one man, not dressed like a wizard, but unarmed as far as Drizzt could tell.

The man went through some motions, as if in spellcasting, and the telltale magical sprinkles dusted the air around him.

But Drizzt was quicker. Calling on the innate abilities of his heritage, the drow limned the wizard's form in harmless purplish flames. The wizard's corporeal body faded from sight as his invisibility spell took effect.

But the purple outline remained.

"Wizard, Wulfgar!" Drizzt called.

The barbarian rushed to the rail and surveyed the pirate ship, easily spotting the magical outline.

The wizard, realizing his predicament, dived behind some casks.

Wulfgar didn't hesitate. He sent Aegis-fang hurtling end over end. The mighty warhammer drove through the casks, sending wood and water exploding into the air, and then found its mark on the other side.

The hammer blasted the wizard's broken body—still visible only by the outline of the drow's faerie fire—into the air and over the far rail of the pirate ship.

Drizzt and Wulfgar nodded to each other, grimly satisfied. Deudermont slapped a hand across his unbelieving eyes.

Perhaps they did have a chance.

⚔ ⚔ ⚔ ⚔

The pirates on the two back ships paused in their duties to consider the flying chariot. As Bruenor swung around the back of the bulky catapult ship and came in from behind, Catti-brie pulled the Taulmaril's bowstring tight.

"Think o' yer friends," Bruenor comforted her, seeing her hesitation. Only a few tendays earlier, Catti-brie had killed a human out of necessity, and the act had not set well with her. Now, as they closed on the ship from above, she could rain death among the exposed sailors.

She huffed a deep breath to steady herself and took a bead on a sailor, standing mouth agape, not even realizing that he was about to die.

There was another wav.

Out of the corner of her eye, Catti-brie spotted a better target. She swung the bow toward the back of the ship and sent a silver arrow streaking down. It blasted into the arm of the catapult, cracking the wood, the arrow's magical energy scorching a black hole as the silver shaft ripped through.

"Taste me flames!" Bruenor cried, steering the chariot downward. The wild dwarf drove his flaming horses straight through the mainsail, leaving a tattered rag in his wake.

And Catti-brie's aim was perfect; again and again the silver arrows whistled into the catapult. As the chariot rushed past a second time, the ship's gunners tried to respond with a ball of burning pitch, but the catapult's wooden arm had taken too much damage to retain any strength, and the ball of pitch lobbed weakly, a few feet up and a few feet out.

And dropped onto the deck of its own ship!

"One more pass!" Bruenor growled, looking back over his shoulder at the fires now roaring on the mast and the deck.

But Catti-brie's eyes were forward, to where the *Sea Sprite* had just crashed onto one vessel, and where the second pirate ship would soon join the fray. "No time!" she yelled. "They be needin'us up ahead!"

⚔ ⚔ ⚔ ⚔

Steel rang against steel as the crew of the *Sea Sprite* locked against the pirates. One rogue, seeing Wulfgar launch the warhammer, crossed over to the *Sea Sprite* and made for the unarmed barbarian, thinking him easy prey. He rushed in, thrusting his sword ahead.

Wulfgar easily sidestepped the blow, caught the pirate by the wrist, and slapped his other hand into the man's crotch. Changing the pirate's direction slightly but not breaking his momentum, Wulfgar hoisted him into the air and heaved him over the back rail of the *Sea Sprite*. Two other pirates, having the same initial response to the unarmed barbarian as their unfortunate comrade, stopped in their tracks and sought out better armed, but less dangerous, opponents.

Then Aegis-fang magically returned to Wulfgar's waiting grasp, and it was his turn to charge.

Three of Deudermont's crew, trying to cross over, were cut down on the central boarding plank, and now the pirates came rushing back across the opening to flood the *Sea Sprite*'s deck.

Drizzt Do'Urden stemmed the tide. Scimitars in hand—Twinkle glowing an angry blue light—the elf sprang lightly onto the wide boarding plank.

The group of pirates, seeing only a single, slender enemy barring the way, expected to bowl right through.

Their momentum slowed considerably when the first rank of three stumbled down in a whirring blur of blades, grasping at slit throats and bellies.

Deudermont and the helmsman, rushing to support Drizzt, slowed and watched the display, Twinkle and its companion scimitar rose and dipped with blinding speed and deadly accuracy. Another pirate went down, and yet another had his sword struck from his hand, so he dived into the water to escape the terrible elven warrior.

The remaining five pirates froze as if paralyzed, their mouths hanging open in silent screams of terror.

Deudermont and the helmsman also jumped back in surprise and confusion, for with Drizzt absorbed in the concentration of battle, the magical mask had played a trick of its own. It had slipped from the drow's face, revealing his dark heritage to all around.

✕ ✕ ✕ ✕

"Even if ye flame the sails, the ship'll get in," Catti-brie observed, noting the short distance between the remaining pirate ship and the tangled ships at the entrance to the channel.

"The sails?" Bruenor laughed. "Suren I mean to get more than that!"

Catti-brie stood back from the dwarf, digesting his meaning. "Ye're daft!" She gawked as Bruenor brought the chariot down to deck level.

"Bah! I'll stop the dogs! Hang on, girl!"

"The demons, I will!" Catti-brie shouted back. She patted Bruenor on the head and went with an alternate plan, dropping from the back of the chariot and into the water.

"Smart girl," Bruenor chuckled, watching her splash safely. Then his eyes went back to the pirates. The crew at the rear of the ship had seen him coming and were diving every which way to get clear.

Pinochet, at the front of the ship, looked back at the unexpected commotion just as Bruenor crashed in.

"Moradin!"

⚔ ⚔ ⚔ ⚔ ⚔

The dwarf's war cry resounded to the decks of the *Sea Sprite* and the third pirate vessel, above all the din of battle. Pirates and sailors alike on the embattled ships glanced back at the explosion on Pinochet's flagship, and Pinochet's crew answered Bruenor's cry with one of terror.

Wulfgar paused at the plea to the dwarven god, remembering a dear friend who used to shout such names at his enemies.

Drizzt only smiled.

⚔ ⚔ ⚔ ⚔ ⚔

As the chariot crashed to the deck, Bruenor rolled off the back and Alustriel's dweomer came apart, transforming the chariot into a rolling ball of destruction. Flames swept across the deck, licked at the masts, and caught the bottoms of the sails.

Bruenor regained his feet, his mithral axe poised in one hand and shining golden shield strapped across his other. But no one cared to challenge him at that moment. Those pirates who had escaped the initial devastation were concerned only with escape.

Bruenor spat at them and shrugged. And then, to the amazement of those few who saw him, the crazy dwarf walked straight into the flames, heading forward to see if any of the pirates up front wanted to play.

Pinochet knew at once that his ship was lost. Not the first time, and probably not the last, he consoled himself as he calmly motioned his closest officer to help him loose a small rowboat. Two of his other crewmen had the same idea and were already untying the little boat when Pinochet got there.

But in this disaster, it was every man for himself, and Pinochet stabbed one of them in the back and chased the other away.

Bruenor emerged, unbothered by the flames, to find the front of the ship nearly deserted. He grinned happily when he saw the little boat, and the pirate captain, touch down in the water. The other pirate was bent over the rail, untying the last of the lines.

And as the pirate hoisted one leg over the rail, Bruenor helped him along, putting a booted foot into his rear and launching him clear of the rail, and of the little rowboat.

"Turn yer back, will ye?" Bruenor grunted at the pirate captain as the dwarf dropped heavily into the rowboat. "I've a girl to pick out of the water!"

Pinochet gingerly slid his sword out of its sheath and peeked back over his shoulder.

"Will ye?" Bruenor asked again.

Pinochet swung about, chopping down viciously at the dwarf.

"Ye could've just said no," Bruenor taunted, blocking the blow with his shield and launching a counter at the man's knees.

✕ ✕ ✕ ✕

Of all the disasters that had befallen the pirates that day, none horrified them more than when Wulfgar went on the attack. He had no need for a boarding plank; the mighty barbarian leaped the gap between the ships. He drove into the pirate ranks, scattering rogues with powerful sweeps of his warhammer.

From the central plank, Drizzt watched the spectacle. The drow had not noticed that his mask had slipped, and he wouldn't have had time to do anything about it anyway. Meaning to join his friend, he rushed the five remaining pirates on the plank. They parted willingly, preferring the water below to the killing blades of a drow elf.

Then the two heroes, the two friends, were together, cutting a swath of destruction across the deck of the pirate ship. Deudermont and his crew, trained fighters themselves, soon cleared the *Sea Sprite* of pirates and had won over every boarding plank. Now knowing victory to be at hand, they waited at the rail of the pirate ship, escorting the growing wave of willing prisoners back to the *Sea Sprite's* hold while Drizzt and Wulfgar finished their task.

☒ ☒ ☒ ☒ ☒

"You will die, bearded dog!" Pinochet roared, slashing with his sword.

Bruenor, trying to settle his feet on the rocking boat, let the man keep the offensive, holding his own strikes for the best moments.

One came unexpectedly as the pirate Bruenor had booted from the burning ship caught up to the drifting rowboat. Bruenor watched his approach out of the corner of his eye.

The man grabbed the side of the little boat and hoisted himself up—only to be met with a blow to the top of the head by Bruenor's mithral axe.

The pirate dropped back down beside the rowboat, turning the water crimson.

"Friend o' yers?" Bruenor taunted.

Pinochet came on even more furiously, as Bruenor had hoped. The man missed a wild swing, overbalancing to Bruenor's right. The dwarf helped Pinochet along, shifting his weight to heighten the list of the boat and slamming his shield into the pirate captain's back.

"On yer life," Bruenor called as Pinochet bobbed back above the water a few feet away, "lose the sword!" The dwarf recognized the importance of the man, and he preferred to let someone else row.

With no options open to him, Pinochet complied and swam back to the little boat. Bruenor dragged him over the side and plopped him down between the oars. "Turn 'er back!" the dwarf roared. "And be pullin' hard!"

☒ ☒ ☒ ☒ ☒

"The mask is down," Wulfgar whispered to Drizzt when their business was finished. The drow slipped behind a mast and replaced the magical disguise.

"Do you think they saw?" Drizzt asked when he returned to Wulfgar's side. Even as he spoke, he noticed the *Sea Sprite's* crew lining the deck of the pirate ship and eyeing him suspiciously, their weapons in hand.

"They saw," Wulfgar remarked. "Come," he bade Drizzt, heading back toward the boarding plank. "They will accept this!"

Drizzt wasn't so certain. He remembered other times when he had rescued men, only to have them turn on him when they saw under the cowl of his cloak and learned the true color of his skin.

But this was the price of his choice to forsake his own people and come to the surface world.

Drizzt grabbed Wulfgar by the shoulder and stepped by him, resolutely leading the way back to the *Sea Sprite*. Looking back at his young friend, he winked and pulled the mask off his face. He sheathed his scimitars and turned to confront the crew.

"Let them know Drizzt Do'Urden," Wulfgar growled softly behind him, lending Drizzt all the strength he would ever need.

12

COMRADES

Bruenor found Catti-brie treading water beyond the carnage of Pinochet's ship. Pinochet paid the young woman no attention, though. Far in the distance, the crew on his remaining ship, the bulky artillery vessel, had brought the fires under control, but had turned tail and sailed away with all the speed it could muster.

"I thought ye had forgot me," Catti-brie said as the rowboat approached.

"Ye should've stayed by me side," the dwarf laughed at her.

"I've not the kinship with fire as yerself," Catti-brie retorted with a bit of suspicion.

Bruenor shrugged. "Been that way since the halls," he replied. "Mighten be me father's father's armor."

Catti-brie grabbed the side of the low-riding boat and started up, then paused in a sudden realization as she noticed the scimitar strapped across Bruenor's back. "Ye've got the drow's blade!" she said, remembering the story Drizzt had told her of his battle with a fiery demon. The magic of the ice-forged scimitar had saved Drizzt from the fire that day. "Suren that's yer salvation!"

"Good blade," Bruenor muttered, looking at its hilt over his shoulder. "The elf should find it a name!"

"The boat will not hold the weight of three," Pinochet interrupted.

Bruenor turned an angry glare on him and snapped, "Then swim!"

Pinochet's face contorted, and he started to rise threateningly.

Bruenor recognized that he had taunted the proud pirate too far. Before the man could straighten, the dwarf slammed his forehead into Pinochet's chest, butting him over the back of the rowboat. Without missing a beat, the dwarf grabbed Catti-brie's wrist and hoisted her up by his side.

"Put yer bow on him, girl," he said loudly enough for Pinochet, once again bobbing in the water, to hear. He threw the pirate the end of a rope. "If he don't keep up, kill 'im!"

Catti-brie set a silver-shafted arrow to Taulmaril's string and took a bead on Pinochet, playing through the threat, though she had no intention of finishing off the helpless man. "They call me bow the Heartseeker," she warned "Suren ye'd be wise to swim."

The proud pirate pulled the rope around him and paddled.

⚔ ⚔ ⚔ ⚔

"No drow's coming back to this ship!" one of Deudermont's crewmen growled at Drizzt.

The man took a slap on the back of the head for his words, and then sheepishly moved aside as Deudermont stepped up to the boarding plank. The captain studied the expressions of his crewmen as they surveyed the drow who had been their companion for tendays.

"What'll ye do with him?" one sailor dared to ask.

"We've men in the water," the captain replied, deflecting the pointed question. "Get them out and dry, and throw the pirates in chains." He waited a moment for his crewmen to disperse, but they held their positions, entranced by the drama of the dark elf.

"And get these ships untangled!" Deudermont roared.

He turned to face Drizzt and Wulfgar, now only a few feet from the plank. "Let us retire to my cabin," he said calmly. "We should talk."

Drizzt and Wulfgar did not answer. They went with the captain silently, absorbing the curious, fearful, and outraged stares that followed them.

Deudermont stopped halfway across the deck, joining a group of his crew as they looked to the south, past Pinochet's burning ship, to a small rowboat pulling hard in their direction.

"The driver of the fiery chariot that rushed across the sky," one of the crewman explained.

"He took down that ship!" another exclaimed, pointing to the wreckage of Pinochet's flagship, now listing badly and soon to sink. "And sent the third one running!"

"Then a friend of ours, he is indeed!" the captain replied.

"And of ours," Drizzt added, turning all eyes back upon him. Even Wulfgar looked curiously at his companion. He had heard the cry to Moradin, but had not dared to hope that it was indeed Bruenor Battlehammer rushing to their aid.

"A red-bearded dwarf, if my guess is correct," Drizzt continued. "And with him, a young woman."

Wulfgar's jaw dropped open. "Bruenor?" he managed to whisper. "Catti-brie?"

Drizzt shrugged. "That is my guess."

"We shall know soon enough," Deudermont assured them. He instructed his crewmen to bring the passengers of the rowboat to his cabin as soon as they came aboard, then he led Drizzt and Wulfgar away, knowing that on the deck the drow would prove a distraction to his crew. And at this time, with the ships fouled, they had important work to complete.

"What do you mean to do with us?" Wulfgar demanded when Deudermont shut the cabin door. "We fought for—"

Deudermont stopped the growing tirade with a calming smile. "You certainly did," he acknowledged. "I only wish that I had such mighty sailors on every voyage south. Surely then the pirates would flee whenever the *Sea Sprite* broke the horizon!"

Wulfgar eased back from his defensive posture.

"My deception was not intended to bring harm," Drizzt said somberly. "And only my appearance was a lie. I require passage to the south to rescue a friend—that much remains true."

Deudermont nodded, but before he could answer, a knock came on the door and a sailor peeked in. "Beggin' yer pardon," he began.

"What is it?" asked Deudermont.

"We follow yer every step, Captain, ye know that," the sailor stammered. "But we thought we should let ye know our feelings on the elf."

Deudermont considered the sailor, and then Drizzt, for a moment. He had always been proud of his crew; most of the men had been together for many years, but he seriously wondered how they would come through this dilemma.

"Go on," he prompted, stubbornly holding his trust in his men.

"Well, we know he's a drow," the sailor began, "and we know what that means." He paused, weighing his next words carefully. Drizzt held his breath in anticipation; he had been down this route before.

"But them two, they pulled us through a bad jam there," the sailor blurted all of a sudden. "We wouldn't a gotten through without 'em!"

"So you want them to remain aboard?" Deudermont asked, a smile growing across his face. His crew had come through once again.

"Aye!" the sailor replied heartily. "To a man! And we're proud to have 'em!"

Another sailor, the one who had challenged Drizzt at the plank just a few minutes before, poked his head in. "I was scared, that's all," he apologized to Drizzt.

Overwhelmed, Drizzt hadn't found his breath yet. He nodded his acceptance of the apology.

"See ye on deck, then," said the second sailor, and he disappeared out the door.

"We just thought ye should know," the first sailor told Deudermont, and then he, too, was gone.

"They are a fine crew," Deudermont said to Drizzt and Wulfgar when the door had closed.

"And what are your thoughts?" Wulfgar had to ask.

"I judge a man—elf—by his character, not his appearance," Deudermont declared. "And on that subject, keep the mask off, Drizzt Do'Urden. You are a far handsomer sort without it!"

"Not many would share that observation," Drizzt replied.

"On the *Sea Sprite*, they would!" roared the captain. "Now, the battle is won, but there is much to be done. I suspect that your strength would be appreciated at the prow, mighty barbarian. We have to get these ships unfouled and moving before that third pirate comes back with more of his friends!

"And you," he said to Drizzt with a sneaky smile. "I would think that no one could keep a shipload of prisoners in line better than you."

Drizzt pulled the mask off his head and tucked it in his pack. "There are advantages to the color of my skin," he agreed, shaking the gnarls out of his white locks. He turned with Wulfgar to leave, but the door burst in before them.

"Nice blade, elf!" said Bruenor Battlehammer, standing in a puddle of seawater. He tossed the magical scimitar to Drizzt. "Find a name for it, will ye? Blade like that be needing a name. Good for a cook at a pig roastin'!"

"Or a dwarf hunting dragons," Drizzt remarked. He held the scimitar reverently, remembering again the first time he had seen it, lying in the dead dragon's horde. Then he gave it a new home in the scabbard that had held his normal blade, thinking his old one a fitting companion for Twinkle.

Bruenor walked up to his drow friend and clasped his wrist firmly. "When I saw yer eyes lookin' out at me from the gorge," the dwarf began softly, fighting back a choke that threatened to break his voice apart, "suren then I knew that me other friends would be safe!"

"But they are not," Drizzt replied. "Regis is in dire peril."

Bruenor winked. "We'll get him back, elf! No stinkin' assassin's going to put an end to Rumblebelly!" He clenched the drow's arm tightly one final time and turned to Wulfgar, the lad he had ushered into manhood.

Wulfgar wanted to speak but could find no path for the words beyond the lump in his throat. Unlike Drizzt, the barbarian had no idea that Bruenor might still be alive, and seeing his dear mentor, the dwarf who had become as a father to him, back from the grave and standing before him was simply too much for him to digest. He grabbed Bruenor by the shoulders just as the dwarf was about to say something, and hoisted him up, locking him in a great bear hug.

It took Bruenor a few seconds of wiggling to get loose enough to draw breath. "If ye'd squeezed the dragon like that," the dwarf coughed, "I wouldn't've had to ride it down the gorge!"

Catti-brie walked through the door, soaking wet, with her auburn hair matted to her neck and shoulders. Behind her came Pinochet, drenched and humbled.

Her eyes first found the gaze of Drizzt, locking the drow in a silent moment of emotion that went deeper than simple friendship. "Well met," she whispered. "Good it is to look upon Drizzt Do'Urden again. Me heart's been with ye all along."

Drizzt cast her a casual smile and turned his lavender eyes away. "Somehow I knew that you would join our quest before it was through," he said. "Well met, then, and welcome along."

Catti-brie's gaze drifted past the drow to Wulfgar. Twice she had been separated from the man, and both times when they again had met, Catti-brie was reminded how much she had come to love him.

Wulfgar saw her, too. Droplets of seawater sparkled on her face, but they paled next to the shine of her smile. The barbarian, his stare never leaving Catti-brie, eased Bruenor back to the floor.

Only the embarrassment of youthful love kept them apart at that moment, with Drizzt and Bruenor looking on.

"Captain Deudermont," said Drizzt, "I give you Bruenor Battlehammer and Catti-brie, two dear friends and fine allies."

"And we brought ye a present," Bruenor chuckled. "Seeing as we got no coin to pay ye for passage." Bruenor walked over, grabbed Pinochet by the sleeve, and pulled the man front and center. "Captain o' the ship I burned, by me guess."

"Welcome to both of you," Deudermont replied. "And I assure you that you have more than earned your passage." The captain moved to confront Pinochet, suspecting the man's importance.

"Do you know who I am?" the pirate said in a huff, thinking that he now had a more reasonable person to deal with than the surly dwarf.

"You are a pirate," Deudermont replied calmly.

Pinochet cocked his head to study the captain. A sly smile crossed his face. "You have perhaps heard of Pinochet?"

Deudermont had thought, and feared, that he had recognized the man when Pinochet had first entered the cabin. The captain of the *Sea Sprite* had indeed heard of Pinochet—every merchant along the Sword Coast had heard of Pinochet.

"I demand that you release me and my men!" the pirate blustered.

"In time," Deudermont replied. Drizzt, Bruenor, Wulfgar, and Catti-brie, not understandingthe extent of the influence of the pirates, all looked at Deudermont in disbelief.

"I warn you that the consequences of your actions will be dire!" Pinochet continued, suddenly gaining the upper hand in the confrontation. "I am not a forgiving man, nor are my allies."

Drizzt, whose own people commonly bent the tenets of justice to fit rules of station, understood the captain's dilemma at once. "Let him go," he said. Both of his magical scimitars came out in his hands, Twinkle glowing dangerously. "Let him go and give him a blade. Neither am I forgiving."

Seeing the horrified look the pirate gave the drow, Bruenor was quick to join in. "Ayuh, Captain, let the dog free," the dwarf scowled. "I only kept his head on his shoulders to give ye a livin' gift. If ye don't want him . . ." Bruenor pulled his axe from his belt and swung it easily at the end of his arm.

Wulfgar didn't miss the point. "Bare hands and up the mast!" the barbarian roared, flexing his, muscles so they seemed they would burst. "The pirate and me! Let the winner know the glory of victory. And let the loser drop to his death!"

Pinochet looked at the three crazed warriors. Then, almost pleading for help, he turned back to Deudermont.

"Ah, ye're all missing the fun." Catti-brie grinned, not to be left out. "Where's the sport in one of ye tearin' the pirate apart? Give him the little boat and set him off." Her spritely face turned suddenly grim, and she cast a wicked glare at Pinochet. "Give him a boat," she reiterated, "and let him dodge me silver arrows!"

"Very well, Captain Pinochet," Deudermont began, barely hiding a chuckle. "I would not invoke the rage of the pirates. You are a free man and may go when you choose."

Pinochet snapped around, face to face with Deudermont.

"Or," continued the captain of the *Sea Sprite*, "you and your crew can remain in my hold, under my personal protection, until we reach port."

"You cannot control your crew?" the pirate spat.

"They are not my crew," Deudermont replied. "And if these four chose to kill you, I daresay that I could do little to deter them."

"It is not the way of my people to let our enemies live!" Drizzt interjected in a tone so callous that it sent shivers through the spines of even his closest friends. "Yet I need you, Captain Deudermont, and your ship." He sheathed his blades in a lightning-quick movement. "I will let the pirate live in exchange for the completion of our arrangements."

"The hold, Captain Pinochet?" Deudermont asked, waving two of his crewmen in to escort the pirate leader.

Pinochet's eyes were back on Drizzt. "If you ever sail this way again . . ." the stubborn pirate began ominously.

Bruenor kicked him in the behind. "Wag yer tongue again dog," the dwarf roared, "and suren I'll cut it out!"

Pinochet left quietly with Deudermont's crewmen.

⚔ ⚔ ⚔ ⚔

Later that day, while the crew of the *Sea Sprite* continued its repairs, the reunited friends retired to Drizzt and Wulfgar's cabin to hear of Bruenor's adventures in Mithral Hall. Stars twinkled in the evening sky and still the dwarf went on, talking of the riches he had seen, of the ancient and holy places he had come across in his homeland, of his many skirmishes with duergar patrols, and of his final, daring escape through the great undercity.

Catti-brie sat directly across from Bruenor, watching the dwarf through the swaying flame of the single candle burning on the table. She had heard his story before, but Bruenor could spin a tale as well as any, and she leaned forward in her chair, mesmerized once again. Wulfgar, with his long arms draped comfortably over her shoulders, had pulled his chair up behind her.

Drizzt stood by the window and gazed at the dreamy sky. How like the old times it all seemed, as if they had somehow brought a piece of Icewind Dale along with them. Many were the nights that the friends had gathered to swap tales of their pasts or to just enjoy the quiet of the evening together. Of course, a fifth member had been with the group then and always with an outlandish tale that outdid all the others.

Drizzt looked at his friends and then back to the night sky, thinking—hoping—of a day when the five friends would be rejoined.

A knock on the door made the three at the table jump, so engrossed were they—even Bruenor—in the dwarf's story. Drizzt opened the door, and Captain Deudermont walked in.

"Greetings," he said politely. "I would not interrupt, but I have some news."

"Just getting to the good part," Bruenor grumbled, "but it'll get better with a bit o' waiting!"

"I have spoken with Pinochet once again," said Deudermont. "He is a very prominent man in this land, and it does not fit well that he set up three ships to stop us. He was after something."

"Us," Drizzt reasoned.

"He said nothing directly," replied Deudermont, "but I believe that to be the case. Please understand that I cannot press him too far."

"Bah! I'll get the dog a barkin'!" Bruenor buffed.

"No need," said Drizzt. "The pirates had to be looking for us."

"But how would they know?" Deudermont asked.

"Balls of fire over Baldur's Gate," Wulfgar reasoned.

Deudermont nodded, remembering the display. "It would seem that you have attracted some powerful foes."

"The man we seek knew that we would come into Baldur's Gate," said Drizzt. "He even left a message for us. It would not have been difficult for the likes of Artemis Entreri to arrange a signal detailing how and when we left."

"Or to arrange the ambush," Wulfgar said grimly.

"So it would seem," said Deudermont.

Drizzt kept quiet, but suspected differently. Why would Entreri lead them all this way, only to have them killed by pirates? Someone else had entered the picture, Drizzt knew, and he could only guess that that person was Pasha Pook himself.

"But there are other matters we must discuss," said Deudermont. "The *Sea Sprite* is seaworthy, but we have taken serious damage as has the pirate ship we have captured."

"Do you mean to sail both out of here?" Wulfgar asked.

"Aye," replied the captain. "We shall release Pinochet and his men when we get to port. They will take the vessel from there."

"Pirates deserve worse," Bruenor grumbled.

"And will this damage slow our journey?" Drizzt asked, more concerned with their mission.

"It will," Deudermont replied. "I am hoping to get us to the kingdom of Calimshan, to Memnon, just beyond the Tethyr border. Our flag will aid us in the desert kingdom. There, we may dock and repair."

"For how long?"

Deudermont shrugged. "A tenday, perhaps, maybe longer. We'll not know until we can properly assess the damage. And another tenday after that to sail around the horn to Calimport."

The four friends exchanged disheartened and worried glances. How many days did Regis have left to live? Could the halfling afford the delay?

"But there is another option," Deudermont told them. "The journey from Memnon to Calimport by ship, around the city of Teshburl and into the Shining Sea, is much longer than the straight land route. Caravans depart for Calimport nearly every day, and the journey, though a hard one through the Calim Desert, takes but a few days."

"We have little gold for passage," said Catti-brie.

Deudermont waved the problem away. "A minor cost," he said. "Any caravan heading through the desert would be glad to have you along as guards. And you have earned ample reward from me to get you through." He jiggled a bag of gold strapped to his belt. "Or, if you choose, you may remain with the *Sea Sprite* for as long as you wish."

"How long to Memnon?" Drizzt asked.

"It depends on how much wind our sails can hold," replied Deudermont.

"Five days; perhaps a tenday."

"Tell us of this Calim Desert," said Wulfgar. "What is a desert?"

"A barren land," replied Deudermont grimly, not wanting to understate the challenge that would be before them if they chose that course. "An empty wasteland of blowing, stinging sands and hot winds. Where monsters rule over men, and many an unfortunate traveler has crawled to his death to be picked clean by vultures."

The four friends shrugged away the captain's grim description. Except for the temperature difference, it sounded like home.

13

PAYING THE PIPER

The docks rolled away beyond sight in either direction, the sails of a thousand ships speckled the pale blue waters of the Shining Sea, and it would take them hours to walk the breadth of the city before them, no matter which gate they sought.

Calimport, the largest city in all the Realms, was a sprawling conglomeration of shanties and massive temples, of tall towers springing from plains of low wooden houses. This was the hub of the southern coast, a vast marketplace several times the area of Waterdeep.

Entreri moved Regis off the docks and into the city. The halfling offered no resistance; he was too caught up in the striking emotions that the unique smells, sights, and sounds of the city brought over him. Even his terror at the thought of facing Pasha Pook became buried in the jumble of memories invoked by his return to his former home.

He had spent his entire childhood here as an orphaned waif, sneaking meals on the streets and sleeping curled up beside the trash fires the other bums set in the alleys on chilly nights. But Regis had an advantage over the other vagabonds of Calimport. Even as a young lad, he had undeniable charm and a lucky streak that always seemed to land him on his feet. The grubby bunch he had run with just shook their heads knowingly on the day their halfling comrade was taken in by one of the many brothels of the city.

The "ladies" showed Regis much kindness, letting him do minor cleaning and cooking tasks in exchange for a high lifestyle that his old friends could only watch and envy. Recognizing the charismatic halfling's potential, the ladies even introduced Regis to the man who would become his mentor and who would mold him into one of the finest thieves the city had ever known: Pasha Pook.

The name came back to Regis like a slap in the face, reminding him of the terrible reality he now faced. He had been Pook's favorite little cutpurse, the guildmaster's pride and joy, but that would only make things worse for Regis now. Pook would never forgive him for his treachery.

Then a more vivid recollection took Regis's legs out from under him as Entreri turned him down Rogues Circle. At the far end, around the cul-de-sac and facing back toward the entrance to the lane, stood a plain-looking wooden building with a single, unremarkable door. But Regis knew the splendors hidden within that unpretentious facade.

And the horrors.

Entreri grabbed him by the collar and dragged him along, never slowing the pace.

"Now, Drizzt, now," Regis whispered, praying that his friends were about and ready to make a desperate, last minute rescue. But Regis knew that his prayers would not be answered this time. He had finally gotten himself stuck in the mud too deeply to escape.

Two guards disguised as bums moved in front of the pair as they approached the door. Entreri said nothing but shot them a murderous stare.

Apparently the guards recognized the assassin. One of them stumbled out of the way, tripping over his own feet, while the other rushed to the door and rapped loudly. A peephole opened, and the guard whispered something to the doorman inside. A split second later, the door swung wide.

Looking in on the thieves'guild proved too much for the halfling. Blackness swirled about him, and he fell limp in the assassin's iron grasp. Showing neither emotion nor surprise, Entreri scooped Regis up over his shoulder and carried him like a sack into the guildhouse, and down the flight of stairs beyond the door.

Two more guards moved in to escort him, but Entreri pushed his way past them. It had been three long years since Pook had sent him on the road after Regis, but the assassin knew the way. He passed through several rooms, down another level, and then started up a long, spiral staircase. Soon he was up to street level again and still climbing to the highest chambers of the structure.

Regis regained consciousness in a dizzy blur. He glanced about desperately as the images came clearer and he remembered where he was. Entreri had him by the ankles, the halfling's head dangling halfway down the assassin's back and his hand just inches from the jeweled dagger. But even if he could have gotten to the weapon quickly enough, Regis knew that he had no chance of escape—not with Entreri holding him, two armed guards following, and curious eyes glaring at them from every doorway.

The whispers had traveled through the guild faster than Entreri.

Regis hooked his chin around Entreri's side and managed to catch a glimpse of what lay ahead. They came up onto a landing, where four more guards parted without question, opening the way down a short corridor that ended in an ornate, ironbound door.

Pasha Pook's door.

The blackness swirled over Regis once again.

⚔ ⚔ ⚔ ⚔ ⚔

When he entered the chamber, Entreri found that he had been expected. Pook sat comfortably on his throne, LaValle by his side and his favorite leopard at his feet, and none of them flinched at the sudden appearance of the two long-lost associates.

The assassin and the guildmaster stared silently at each other for a long time. Entreri studied the man carefully. He hadn't expected so formal a meeting.

Something was wrong.

Entreri pulled Regis off his shoulder and held him out—still upside down—at arm's length, as if presenting a trophy. Convinced that the halfling was oblivious to the world at that moment, Entreri released his hold, letting Regis drop heavily to the floor.

That drew a chuckle from Pook. "It has been a long three years," the guildmaster said, breaking the tension.

Entreri nodded. "I told you at the outset that this one might take time. The little thief ran to the corners of the world."

"But not beyond your grasp, eh?" Pook said, somewhat sarcastically. "You have performed your task excellently, as always, Master Entreri. Your reward shall be as promised." Pook sat back on his throne again and resumed his distant posture, rubbing a finger over his lips and eyeing Entreri suspiciously.

Entreri didn't have any idea why Pook, after so many difficult years and a successful completion of the mission, would treat him so badly. Regis had eluded the guildmaster's grip for more than half a decade before Pook finally sent Entreri on the chase. With that record preceding him, Entreri did not think three years such a long time to complete the mission.

And the assassin refused to play such cryptic games. "If there is a problem, speak it," he said bluntly.

"There was a problem," Pook replied mysteriously, emphasizing the past tense of his statement.

Entreri rocked back a step, now fully at a loss—one of the very few times in his life.

Regis stirred at that moment and managed to sit up, but the two men, engaged in the important conversation, paid him no notice.

"You were being followed," Pook explained, knowing better than to play a teasing game for too long with the killer. "Friends of the halfling?"

Regis's ears perked up.

Entreri took a long moment to consider his response. He guessed what Pook was getting at, and it was easy for him to figure out that Oberon must have informed the guildmaster of more than his return with Regis. He made a mental note to visit the wizard the next time he was in Baldur's Gate, to explain to Oberon the proper limits of spying and the proper restraints of loyalty. No one ever crossed Artemis Entreri twice.

"It does not matter," Pook said, seeing no answer forthcoming. "They will bother us no more."

Regis felt sick. This was the southland, the home of Pasha Pook. If Pook had learned of his friends' pursuit, he certainly could have eliminated them.

Entreri understood that, too. He fought to maintain his calm while a burning rage reared up inside him. "I tend to my own affairs," he growled at Pook, his tone confirming to the guildmaster that he had indeed been playing a private game with his pursuers.

"And I to mine!" Pook shot back, straightening in his chair. "I know not what connection this elf and barbarian hold to you, Entreri, but they have nothing to do with my pendant!" He collected himself quickly and sat back, realizing that the confrontation was getting too dangerous to continue. "I could not take the risk."

The tension eased out of Entreri's taut muscles. He did not wish a war with Pook and he could not change what was past. "How?" he asked.

"Pirates," Pook replied. "Pinochet owed me a favor."

"It is confirmed?"

"Why do you care?" Pook asked. "You are here. The halfling is here. My pen—" He stopped suddenly, realizing that he hadn't yet seen the ruby pendant.

Now it was Pook's turn to sweat and wonder. "It is confirmed?" Entreri asked again, making no move toward the magical pendant that hung, concealed, about his neck.

"Not yet," Pook stammered, "but three ships were sent after the one. There can be no doubt."

Entreri hid his smile. He knew the powerful drow and barbarian well enough to consider them alive until their bodies had been paraded before him. "Yes, there can indeed be doubt," he whispered under his breath as he pulled the ruby pendant over his head and tossed it to the guildmaster.

Pook caught it in trembling hands, knowing immediately from its familiar tingle that it was the true gem. What power he would wield now! With the magical ruby in his hands, Artemis Entreri returned to his side, and Rassiter's wererats under his command, he would be unstoppable!

LaValle put a steadying hand on the guildmaster's shoulder. Pook, beaming in anticipation of his growing power, looked up at him.

"Your reward shall be as promised," Pook said again to Entreri as soon as he had caught his breath. "And more!"

Entreri bowed. "Well met, then, Pasha Pook," he replied. "It is good to be home."

"Concerning the elf and barbarian," Pook said, suddenly entertaining second thoughts about ever mistrusting the assassin.

Entreri stopped him with outstretched palms. "A watery grave serves them as well as Calimport's sewers," he said "Let us not worry about what is behind us."

Pook's smile engulfed his round face. "Agreed, and well met, then," he beamed. "Especially when there is such pleasurable business ahead of us." He turned an evil eye upon Regis, but the halfling, sitting stooped over on the floor beside Entreri, didn't notice.

Regis was still trying to digest the news about his friends. At that moment, he didn't care how their deaths might affect his own future—or lack of one. He only cared that they were gone. First Bruenor in Mithral Hall, then Drizzt and Wulfgar, and possibly Catti-brie, as well. Next to that, Pasha Pook's threats seemed hollow indeed. What could Pook ever do to him that would hurt as much as those losses?

"Many sleepless nights I have spent fretting over the disappointment you have caused me," Pook said to Regis. "And many more I have spent considering how I would repay you!"

The door swung open, interrupting Pook's train of thought. The guildmaster did not have to look up to know who had dared to enter without permission. Only one man in the guild would have such nerve.

Rassiter swept into the room and cut an uncomfortably close circle as he inspected the newcomers. "Greetings, Pook," he said offhandedly, his eyes locking onto the assassin's stern gaze.

Pook said nothing but dropped his chin into his hand to watch. He had anticipated the meeting for a long time.

Rassiter stood nearly a foot taller than Entreri, a fact that only added to the wererat's already cocky attitude. Like so many simpleton bullies, Rassiter often confused size with strength, and looking down at this man who was a legend on the streets of Calimport—and thus his rival—made him think that he had already gained the upper hand. "So, you are the great Artemis Entreri," he said, contempt evident in his voice.

Entreri didn't blink. Murder was in his eyes as his gaze followed Rassiter, who still circled. Even Regis was dumbfounded at the stranger's boldness. No one ever moved so casually around Entreri.

"Greetings," Rassiter said at length, satisfied with his scan. He bowed low. "I am Rassiter, Pasha Pook's closest advisor and controller of the docks."

Still Entreri did not respond. He looked over to Pook for an explanation.

The guildmaster returned Entreri's curious gaze with a smirk and lifted his palms in a helpless gesture.

Rassiter carried his familiarity even further. "You and I," he half-whispered to Entreri, "we can do great things together." He started to place a hand on the assassin's shoulder, but Entreri turned him back with an icy glare, a look so deadly that even cocky Rassiter began to understand the peril of his course.

"You may find that I have much to offer you," Rassiter said, taking a cautious step back. Seeing no response forthcoming, he turned to Pook. "Would you like me to take care of the little thief?" he asked, grinning his yellow smile.

"That one is mine, Rassiter," Pook replied firmly. "You and yours keep your furry hands off him!"

Entreri did not miss the reference.

"Of course," Rassiter replied. "I have business, then. I will be going." He bowed quickly and spun to leave, meeting Entreri's eyes one final time. He could not hold that icy stare—could not match the sheer intensity of the assassin's gaze—with his own.

Rassiter shook his head in disbelief as he passed, convinced that Entreri still had not blinked.

"You were gone. My pendant was gone," Pook explained when the door closed again. "Rassiter has helped me retain, even expand, the strength of the guild."

"He is a wererat," Entreri remarked, as if that fact alone ended any argument.

"Head of their guild," Pook replied, "but they are loyal enough and easy to control." He held up the ruby pendant. "Easier now."

Entreri had trouble coming to terms with that, even in light of Pook's futile attempt at an explanation. He wanted time to consider the new development, to figure out just how much things had changed around the guildhouse. "My room?" he asked.

LaValle shifted uncomfortably and glanced down at Pook. "I have been using it," the wizard stammered, "but quarters are being built for me." He looked to the door newly cut into the wall between the harem and Entreri's old room. "They should be completed any day. I can be out of your room in minutes."

"No need," Entreri replied, thinking the arrangements better as they were. He wanted some space from Pook for a while, anyway, to better assess the situation before him and plan his next moves. "I will find a room below, where I might better understand the new ways of the guild."

LaValle relaxed with an audible sigh.

Entreri picked Regis up by the collar. "What am I to do with this one?"

Pook crossed his arms over his chest and cocked his head. "I have thought of a million tortures befitting your crime," he said to Regis. "Too many, I see, for truly, I have no idea of how to properly repay you for what you have done to me." He looked back to Entreri. "No matter," he chuckled. "It will come to me. Put him in the Cells of Nine."

Regis went limp again at the mention of the infamous dungeon. Pook's favorite holding cell, it was a horror chamber normally reserved for thieves who killed other members of the guild. Entreri smiled to see the halfling so terrified at the mere mention of the place. He easily lifted Regis off the floor and carried him out of the room.

"That did not go well," LaValle said when Entreri had left.

"It went splendidly!" Pook disagreed. "I have never seen Rassiter so unnerved, and the sight of it proved infinitely more pleasurable than I ever imagined!"

"Entreri will kill him if he is not careful," LaValle observed grimly.

Pook seemed amused by the thought. "Then we should learn who is likely to succeed Rassiter." He looked up at LaValle. "Fear not, my friend. Rassiter is a survivor. He has called the street his home for his entire life and knows when to scurry into the safety of shadows. He will learn his place around Entreri, and he will show the assassin proper respect."

But LaValle wasn't thinking of Rassiter's safety—he had often entertained thoughts of disposing of the wretched wererat himself. What concerned the wizard was the possibility of a deeper rift in the guild. "What if Rassiter turns the power of his allies against Entreri?" he asked in a tone even more grim. "The street war that would ensue would split the guild in half."

Pook dismissed the possibility with a wave of his hand. "Even Rassiter is not that stupid," he answered, fingering the ruby pendant, an insurance policy he might just need.

LaValle relaxed, satisfied with his master's assurances and with Pook's ability to handle the delicate situation. As usual, Pook was right, LaValle realized. Entreri had unnerved the wererat with a simple stare, to the possible benefit of all involved. Perhaps now, Rassiter would act more appropriately for his rank in the guild. And with Entreri soon to be quartered on this very level, perhaps the intrusions of the filthy wererat would come less often.

Yes, it was good to have Entreri back.

⚔ ⚔ ⚔ ⚔ ⚔

The Cells of Nine were so named because of the nine cells cut into the center of a chamber's floor, three abreast and three long. Only the center cell was ever unoccupied; the other eight held Pasha Pook's most treasured collection: great hunting cats from every corner of the Realms.

Entreri handed Regis over to the jailor, a masked giant of a man, then stood back to watch the show. Around the halfling the jailor tied one end of a heavy rope, which made its way over a pulley in the ceiling above the center cell then back to a crank off to the side.

"Untie it when you are in," the jailor grunted at Regis. He pushed Regis forward. "Pick your path."

Regis walked gingerly along the border of the outer cells. They all were roughly ten feet square with caves cut into the walls, where the cats could go to rest. But none of the beasts rested now, and all seemed equally hungry.

They were always hungry.

Regis chose the plank between a white lion and a heavy tiger, thinking those two giants the least likely to scale the twenty-foot wall and claw his ankle out from under him as he crossed. He slipped one foot onto the wall—which was barely four inches wide—separating the cells and then hesitated, terrified.

The jailor gave a prompting tug on the rope that nearly toppled Regis in with the lion.

Reluctantly he started out, concentrating on placing one foot in front of the other and trying to ignore the growls and claws below. He had nearly made the center cell when the tiger launched its full weight against the wall, shaking it violently. Regis overbalanced and tumbled in with a shriek.

The jailor pulled the crank and caught him in midfall, hoisting him just out of the leaping tiger's reach. Regis swung into the far wall, bruising his ribs but not even feeling the injury at that desperate moment. He scrambled over the wall and swung free, eventually stopping over the middle of the center cell, where the jailor let him down.

He put his feet to the floor tentatively and clutched the rope as his only possible salvation, refusing to believe that he must stay in the nightmarish place.

"Untie it!" the jailor demanded, and Regis knew by the man's tone that to disobey was to suffer unspeakable pain. He slipped the rope free.

"Sleep well," the jailor laughed, pulling the rope high out of the halfling's reach. The hooded man left with Entreri, extinguishing all the room's torches and slamming the iron door behind him, leaving Regis alone in the dark with the eight hungry cats.

The walls separating the cats' cells were solid, preventing the animals from harming each other, but the center cell was lined with wide bars—wide enough for a cat to put its paws through. And this torture chamber was circular, providing easy and equal access from all eight of the other cells.

Regis did not dare to move. The rope had placed him in the exact center of the cell, the only spot that kept him out of reach of all eight cats. He glanced around at the feline eyes, gleaming wickedly in the dim light. He heard the scraping of lunging claws and even felt a swish of air whenever one of them managed to squeeze enough leg through the bars to get a close swipe.

And each time a huge paw slammed into the floor beside him, Regis had to remind himself not to jump back—where another cat waited.

Five minutes seemed like an hour, and Regis shuddered to think of how many days Pook would keep him there. Maybe it would be better just to get it over with, Regis thought, a notion that many shared when placed in the chamber.

Looking at the cats, though, the halfling dismissed that possibility. Even if he could convince himself that a quick death in a tiger's jaws would be better than the fate he no doubt faced, he would never have found the courage to carry it through. He was a survivor—had always been—and he couldn't deny that stubborn side of his character that refused to yield no matter how bleak his future seemed.

He stood now, as still as a statue, and consciously worked to fill his mind with thoughts of his recent past, of the ten years he had spent outside Calimport. Many adventures he had seen on his travels, many perils he had come through. Regis replayed those battles and escapes over and over in his mind, trying to recapture the sheer excitement he had experienced—active thoughts that would help to keep him awake.

For if weariness overtook him and he fell to the floor, some part of him might get too close to one of the cats.

More than one prisoner had been clawed in the foot and dragged to the side to be ripped apart.

And even those who survived the Cells of Nine would never forget the ravenous stares of those sixteen gleaming eyes.

14
DANCING SNAKES

L uck was with the damaged *Sea Sprite* and the captured pirate vessel, for the sea held calm and the wind blew steadily but gently. Still, the journey around the Tethyr Peninsula proved tedious and all too slow for the four anxious friends, for every time the two ships seemed to be making headway, one or the other would develop a new problem.

South of the peninsula, Deudermont took his ships through a wide stretch of water called the Race, so named for the common spectacle there of merchant vessels running from pirate pursuit. No other pirates bothered Deudermont or his crew, however. Even Pinochet's third ship never again showed its sails.

"Our journey nears its end," Deudermont told the four friends when the high coastline of the Purple Hills came into view early on the third morning. "Where the hills end, Calimshan begins."

Drizzt leaned over the forward rail and looked into the pale blue waters of the southern seas. He wondered again if they would get to Regis in time.

"There is a colony of your people farther inland," Deudermont said to him, drawing him out of his private thoughts, "in a dark wood called Mir." An involuntary shudder shook the captain. "The drow are not liked in this region; I would advise you to don your mask."

Without thinking, Drizzt drew the magical mask over his face, instantly assuming the features of a surface elf. The act bothered the drow less than it shook his three friends, who looked on in resigned disdain. Drizzt was only doing what he had to do, they reminded themselves, carrying on with the same uncomplaining stoicism that had guided his life since the day he had forsaken his people.

The drow's new identity did not fit in the eyes of Wulfgar and Catti-brie. Bruenor spat into the water, disgusted at a world too blinded by a cover to read the book inside.

By early afternoon, a hundred sails dotted the southern horizon and a vast line of docks appeared along the coast, with a sprawling city of low clay shacks and brightly colored tents rolling out behind them. But as vast as Memnon's docks were, the number of fishing and merchant vessels and warships of the growing Calimshan navy was greater still. The *Sea Sprite* and its captured ship were forced to drop anchor offshore and wait for appropriate landings to open—a wait, the harbormaster soon informed Deudermont, of possibly a tenday.

"We shall next be visited by Calimshan's navy," Deudermont explained as the harbormaster's launch headed away, "coming to inspect the pirate ship and interrogate Pinochet."

"They'll take care o' the dog?" Bruenor asked.

Deudermont shook his head. "Not likely. Pinochet and his men are my prisoners and my trouble. Calimshan desires an end to the pirate activities and is making bold strides toward that goal, but I doubt that it would yet dare to become entangled with one as powerful as Pinochet."

"What's for him, then?" Bruenor grumbled, trying to find some measure of backbone in all the political double talk.

"He will sail away to trouble another ship on another day," Deudermont replied.

"And to warn that rat, Entreri, that we've slipped the noose," Bruenor snapped back.

Understanding Deudermont's sensitive position, Drizzt put in a reasonable request. "How long can you give us?"

"Pinochet cannot get his ship in for a tenday, and" the captain added with a sly wink, "I have already seen to it that it is no longer seaworthy.

I should be able to stretch that tenday out to two. By the time the pirate finds the wheel of his ship again, you will have told this Entreri of your escape personally."

Wulfgar still did not understand. "What have you gained?" he asked Deudermont. "You have defeated the pirates, but they are to sail free, tasting vengeance on their lips. They will strike at the *Sea Sprite* on your next passage. Will they show as much mercy if they win the next encounter?"

"It is a strange game we play," Deudermont agreed with a helpless smile. "But, in truth, I have strengthened my position on the waters by sparing Pinochet and his men. In exchange for his freedom, the pirate captain will swear off vengeance. None of Pinochet's associates shall ever bother the *Sea Sprite* again, and that group includes most of the pirates sailing Asavir's Channel!"

"And ye're to trust that dog's word?" Bruenor balked.

"They are honorable enough," replied Deudermont, "in their own way. The codes have been drawn and are held to by the pirates; to break them would be to invite open warfare with the southern kingdoms."

Bruenor spat into the water again. It was the same in every city and kingdom and even on the open water: organizations of thieves tolerated within limits of behavior. Bruenor was of a different mind. Back in Mithral Hall, his clan had custom-built a closet with shelving especially designed to hold severed hands that had been caught in pockets where they didn't belong.

"It is settled, then," Drizzt remarked, seeing it time to change the subject. "Our journey by sea is at an end."

Deudermont, expecting the announcement, tossed him the pouch of gold. "A wise choice," the captain said. "You will make Calimport a full tenday and more more before the *Sea Sprite* finds her docks. But come to us when you have completed your business. We shall put back for Waterdeep before the last of the winter's snows have melted in the North. By all of my reckoning, you have earned your passage."

"We're for leaving long afore that," replied Bruenor, "but thanks for yer offer!"

Wulfgar stepped forward and clasped the captain's wrist. "It was good to serve and fight beside you," he said. "I look forward to the day when next we will meet."

"As do we all," Drizzt added. He held the pouch high "And this shall be repaid."

Deudermont waved the notion away and mumbled, "A pittance." Knowing the friends' desire for haste, he motioned for two of his crewmen to drop a rowboat.

"Farewell!" he called as the friends pulled away from the *Sea Sprite*. "Look for me in Calimport!

✕ ✕ ✕ ✕ ✕

Of all the places the companions had visited, of all the lands they had walked through and fought through, none had seemed as foreign to them as Memnon in the kingdom of Calimshan. Even Drizzt, who had come from the strange world of the drow elves, stared in amazement as he made his way through the city's open lanes and marketplaces. Strange music, shrill and mournful—as often resembling wails of pain as harmony—surrounded them and carried them on.

People flocked everywhere. Most wore sand-colored robes, but others were brightly dressed, and all had some sort of head covering: a turban or a veiled hat. The friends could not guess at the population of the city, which seemed to go on forever, and doubted that anyone had ever bothered to count. But Drizzt and his companions could envision that if all the people of the cities along the northern stretches of the Sword Coast, Waterdeep included, gathered in one vast refugee camp, it would resemble Memnon.

A strange combination of odors wafted through Memnon's hot air: that of a sewer that ran through a perfume market, mixed with the pungent sweat and malodorous breath of the ever-pressing crowd. Shacks were thrown up randomly, it seemed, giving Memnon no apparent design or structure. Streets were any way that was not blocked by homes, though the four friends had all come to the conclusion that the streets themselves served as homes for many people.

At the center of all the bustle were the merchants. They lined every lane, selling weapons, foodstuffs, exotic pipe weeds—even slaves—shamelessly displaying their goods in whatever manner would attract a crowd. On one corner, potential buyers test-fired a large crossbow by shooting down a boxed-in range, complete with live slave targets. On another, a woman showing more skin than clothing—and that being no more than translucent veils—twisted and writhed in a synchronous dance with a gigantic snake, wrapping herself within the huge reptilian coils and then slipping teasingly back out again.

Wide-eyed and with his mouth hanging open, Wulfgar stopped, mesmerized by the strange and seductive dance, drawing a slap across the back of his head from Catti-brie and amused chuckles from his other two companions.

"Never have I so longed for home," the huge barbarian sighed, truly overwhelmed.

"It is another adventure, nothing more," Drizzt reminded him. "Nowhere might you learn more than in a land unlike your own."

"True enough," said Catti-brie. "But by me eyes, these folk be making decadence into society."

"They live by different rules," Drizzt replied. "They would, perhaps, be equally offended by the ways of the North."

The others had no response to that, and Bruenor, never surprised but always amazed by eccentric human ways, just wagged his red beard.

Outfitted for adventure, the friends were far from a novelty in the trading city. but being foreigners, they attracted a crowd, mostly naked, black-tanned children begging for tokens and coins. The merchants eyed the adventurers, too—foreigners usually brought in wealth—and one particularly lascivious set of eyes settled onto them firmly.

"Well, well?" the weaseling merchant asked his hunchbacked companion.

"Magic, magic everywhere, my master," the broken little goblin lisped hungrily, absorbing the sensations his magical wand imparted to him. He replaced the wand on his belt. "Strongest on the weapons—elf's swords, both, dwarf's axe, girl's bow, and especially the big one's hammer!" He thought of mentioning the odd sensations his wand had imparted about the elf's face, but decided not to make his excitable master any more nervous than was necessary.

"Ha ha ha ha ha," cackled the merchant, waggling his fingers. He slipped out to intercept the strangers.

Bruenor, leading the troupe, stopped short at the sight of the wiry man dressed in yellow-and-red striped robes and a flaming pink turban with a huge diamond set in its front.

"Ha ha ha ha ha. Greetings!" the man spouted at them, his fingers drumming on his own chest and his ear-to-ear smile showing every other tooth to be golden and those in between to be ivory. "I be Sali Dalib, I do be, I do be! You buy, I sell. Good deal, good deal!" His words came out too fast to be immediately sorted, and the friends looked at each other, shrugged, and started away.

"Ha ha ha ha ha," the merchant pressed, wiggling back in their path. "What you need, Sali Dalib got. In plenty, too, many. Tookie, nookie, bookie."

"Smoke weed, women, and tomes in every language known to the world," the lisping little goblin translated. "My master is a merchant of anything and everything!"

"Bestest o' de bestest!" Sali Dalib asserted. "What you need—"

"Sali Dalib got," Bruenor finished for him. The dwarf looked to Drizzt, confident that they were thinking the same thing: The sooner they were out of Memnon, the better. One weird merchant would serve as well as another.

"Horses," the dwarf told the merchant.

"We wish to get to Calimport," Drizzt explained.

"Horses, horses? Ha ha ha ha ha," replied Sali Dalib without missing a beat. "Not for long ride, no. Too hot, too dry. Camels de thing!"

"Camels. . . desert horses," the goblin explained, seeing the dumbfounded expressions. He pointed to a large dromedary being led down the street by its tan-robed master. "Much better for ride across the desert."

"Camels, then," snorted Bruenor, eyeing the massive beast tentatively. "Or whatever'll do!"

Sali Dalib rubbed his hands together eagerly. "What you need—"

Bruenor threw his hand out to stop the excited merchant. "We know, we know."

Sali Dahb sent his assistant away with some private instructions and led the friends through the maze of Memnon at great speed, though he never seemed to lift his feet from the ground as he shuffled along. All the while, the merchant held his hands out in front of him, his fingers twiddling and tap-tapping. But he seemed harmless enough, and the friends were more amused than worried. ,

Sali Dalib pulled up short before a large tent on the western end of the city, a poorer section even by Memnon's paupers' standards. Around the back, the merchant found what he was looking for. "Camels!" he proclaimed proudly.

"How much for four?" Bruenor huffed, anxious to get the dealings over with and get back on the road. Sali Dalib seemed not to understand.

"The price?" the dwarf asked.

"De price?"

"He wants an offer," Catti-brie observed.

Drizzt understood as well. Back in Menzoberranzan, the city of drow, merchants used the same technique. By getting the buyer—especially a buyer not familiar with the goods for sale—to make the first mention of price, they often received many times the value of their goods. And if the bid came in too low, the merchant could always hold out for the proper market value.

"Five hundred gold pieces for the four," Drizzt offered, guessing the beasts to be at least twice that value.

Sali Dalib's fingers began their tap dance again, and a sparkle came into his pale gray eyes. Drizzt expected a tirade and then an outlandish counter, but Sali Dalib suddenly calmed and flashed his gold-and-ivory smile.

"Agreed!" he replied.

Drizzt caught his tongue before his planned retort left his mouth in a meaningless gurgle. He cast a curious look at the merchant, then turned to count out the gold from the sack Deudermont had given him.

"Fifty more for ye if ye can get us hooked with a caravan for Calimport," Bruenor offered.

Sali Dalib assumed a contemplative stance, tapping his fingers against the dark bristles on his chin. "But there is one out dis very now," he replied.

"You can catch it with little trouble. But you should. Last one to Calimport for de tenday."

"To the south!" the dwarf cried happily to his companions.

"De south? Ha ha ha ha ha!" Sali Dalib blurted. "Not de south. De south is for thief bait!"

"Calimport is south," Bruenor retorted suspiciously. "And so's the road, by me guessing."

"De road to Calimport is south," Sali Dalib agreed, "but those who be smart start to de west, on de bestest road."

Drizzt handed a pouch of gold to the merchant. "How do we catch the caravan?"

"De west," Sali Dalib replied, dropping the pouch into a deep pocket without even inspecting the contents. "Only out one hour. Easy catch, dis. Follow de signposts on de horizon. No problem."

"We'll need supplies," Catti-brie remarked.

"Caravan is well-stocked," answered Sali Dalib. "Bestest place to buy. Now be going. Catch dem before dey turn south to de Trade Way!" He moved to help them select their mounts: a large dromedary for Wulfgar, a two-humper for Drizzt, and smaller ones for Catti-brie and Bruenor.

"Remember, good friends," the merchant said to them when they were perched upon their mounts. "What you need—"

"Sali Dalib got!" they all answered in unison. With one final flash of his gold-and-ivory smile, the merchant shuffled into the tent.

"He was more to bargaining, by me guess," Catti-brie remarked as they headed tentatively on the stiff-legged camels toward the first signpost. "He could've gotten more for the beasts."

"Stolen, o' course!" Bruenor laughed, stating what he considered the obvious.

But Drizzt wasn't so certain. "A merchant such as he would have sought the best price even for stolen goods," he replied, "and by all my knowledge of the rules of bargaining, he most certainly should have counted the gold."

"Bah!" Bruenor snorted, fighting to keep his mount moving straight. "Ye probably gave him more than the things are worth!"

"What, then?" Catti-brie asked Drizzt, agreeing more with his reasoning.

"Where?" Wulfgar answered and asked all at once. "He sent his goblin sneak away with a message."

"Ambush," said Catti-brie.

Drizzt and Wulfgar nodded. "It would seem," said the barbarian.

Bruenor considered the possibility. "Bah!" He snorted at the notion. "He didn't have enough wits in his head to pull it off."

"That observation might only make him more dangerous," Drizzt remarked, looking back a final time toward Memnon.

"Turn back?" the dwarf asked, not so quick to dismiss the drow's apparently serious concerns.

"If our suspicions prove wrong and we miss the caravan . . ." Wulfgar reminded them ominously.

"Can Regis wait?" asked Catti-brie.

Bruenor and Drizzt looked to each other.

"Onward," Drizzt said at length. "Let us learn what we may."

"Nowhere might you learn more than in a land unlike your own," Wulfgar remarked, echoing Drizzt's thoughts of that morning.

When they had passed the first signpost, their suspicions did not diminish. A large board nailed to the post named their route in twenty languages, all reading the same way: "De bestest road." Once again, the friends considered their options, and once again they found themselves trapped by the lack of time. They would continue on, they decided, for one hour. If they had found no signs of the caravan by then, they would return to Memnon and "discuss" the matter with Sali Dalib.

The next signpost read the same way, as did the one after that. By the time they passed the fifth, sweat drenched their clothes and stung their eyes, and the city was no longer in sight, lost somewhere in the dusty heat of the rising dunes. Their mounts didn't make the journey any better. Camels were nasty beasts, and nastier still when driven by an inexperienced rider. Wulfgar's, in particular, had a bad opinion of its rider, for camels preferred to pick their own route, and the barbarian, with his powerful legs and arms, kept forcing his mount through the motions he chose. Twice, the camel had arched its head back and launched a slobbery wad of spittle at Wulfgar's face.

Wulfgar took it all in stride, but he spent more than a passing moment fantasizing of flattening the camel's hump with his hammer.

"Hold!" Drizzt commanded as they moved down into a bowl between dunes. The drow extended his arm, leading the surprised glances skyward, where several buzzards had taken up a lazy, circular flight.

"There's carrion about," Bruenor noted.

"Or there is soon to be," Drizzt replied grimly.

Even as he spoke, the lines of the dunes encircling them transformed suddenly from the hazy flat brown of hot sands to the ominous silhouettes of horsemen, curved swords raised and gleaming in the bright sunlight.

"Ambush," Wulfgar stated flatly.

Not too surprised, Bruenor glanced around to take a quick measure of the odds. "Five to one," he whispered to Drizzt.

"It always seems to be," Drizzt answered. He slowly slid his bow from his shoulder and strung it.

The horsemen held their position for a long while, surveying their intended prey.

"Ye think they be wantin' to talk?" Bruenor asked, trying to find some humor in the bleak situation.

"Nah," the dwarf answered himself when none of the other three cracked a smile.

The leader of the horsemen barked a command, and the thunderous charge was on.

"Blast and bebother the whole damned world," Catti-brie grumbled, pulling Taulmaril from her shoulder as she slid from her mount. "Everyone wants a fight.

"Come on, then!" she shouted at the horsemen. "But let's get the fight a bit fairer!" She set the magical bow into action, sending one silver arrow after another streaking up the dunes into the horde, blasting rider after rider out of his saddle.

Bruenor gawked at his daughter, suddenly so grim-faced and savage. "The girl's got it right!" he proclaimed, sliding down from his camel. "Can't be fightin' up on one of them things!" As soon as he hit the ground, the dwarf grabbed at his pack and pulled out two flasks of oil.

Wulfgar followed his mentor's lead, using the side of his camel as a barricade. But the barbarian found his mount to be his first foe, for the ill-tempered beast turned back on him and clamped its flat teeth onto his forearm.

Drizzt's bow joined in on Taulmaril's deadly song, but as the horsemen closed in, the drow decided upon a different course of action. Playing on the terror of the reputation of his people, Drizzt tore off his mask and pulled back the cowl of his cloak, leaping to his feet atop the camel and straddling the beast with one foot on each hump. Those riders closing in on Drizzt pulled up short at the unnerving appearance of a drow elf.

The other three flanks collapsed quickly, though, as the horsemen closed in, still outnumbering the friends.

Wulfgar stared at his camel in disbelief, then slammed his huge fist between the wretched beast's eyes. The dazed camel promptly let go of its hold and turned its woozy head away.

Wulfgar wasn't finished with the treacherous beast. He noticed three riders bearing down on him, so he decided to pit one enemy against another. He stepped under the camel and lifted it clear off the ground, his muscles rippling as he heaved the thing into the charging pack. He just managed to dodge the tumbling mass of horses, riders, camels, and sand.

Then he had Aegis-fang in his hands, and he leaped into the jumble, crushing the bandits before they ever realized what had hit them.

Two riders found a channel through the riderless camels to get at Bruenor, but it was Drizzt, standing alone, who got in the first strike. Summoning his magical ability, the drow conjured a globe of darkness in front of the charging bandits. They tried to pull up short, but plunged in headlong.

That gave Bruenor all the time he needed. He struck a spark off his tinderbox onto the rags he had stuffed into the oil flasks, then tossed the flaming grenades into the ball of darkness.

Even the fiery lights of the ensuing explosions could not be seen within the globe of Drizzt's spell, but from the screams that erupted inside, Bruenor knew he had hit the mark.

"Me thanks, elf!" the dwarf cried. "Glad to be with ye again!"

"Behind you!" was Drizzt's reply, for even as Bruenor spoke, a third rider cut around the globe and galloped at the dwarf. Bruenor instinctively dropped into a ball, throwing his golden shield above him.

The horse trampled right over Bruenor and stumbled into the soft sand, throwing its rider.

The tough dwarf sprang to his feet and shook the sand out of his ears. That stomping would surely hurt when the adrenaline of battle died away, but right now, all Bruenor felt was rage. He charged the rider—now also rising to his feet—with his mithral axe raised above his head.

Just as Bruenor got there and started his overhead chop, a line of silver flashed by his shoulder, dropping the bandit dead. Unable to stop his momentum, the dwarf went head-long over the suddenly prostrate body and flopped facedown onto the ground.

"Next time, tell me, girl!" Bruenor roared at Catti-brie and spitting sand with every word.

Catti-brie had her own troubles. She had dropped low, hearing a horse thundering up behind her as she loosed the arrow. A curved sword swooshed past the side of her head, nicking her ear, and the rider went past.

Catti-brie meant to send out another arrow to follow the man, but while she was stooped, she saw yet another bandit bearing down on her from behind, this one with a poised spear and heavy shield leading the way.

Catti-brie and Taulmaril proved the swifter. In an instant, another arrow was on the magical bow's string and sent away. It exploded into the bandit's heavy shield and tore through, tossing the helpless man off the back of his mount and into the realm of death.

The riderless horse broke stride. Catti-brie caught its reins as it trotted by and swung up into the saddle to pursue the bandit who had cut her.

Drizzt still stood atop his camel, towering above his foes and deftly dancing away from the strikes of riders rushing by, all the while weaving his two magical scimitars into a dance of mesmerizing death. Again and again, bandits thought they had an easy shot at the standing elf, only to find their swords or spears catching nothing but air, and then to suddenly discover Twinkle or the other magical scimitar slicing a clean line across their throats as they started to gallop away.

Then two came in together, broadside to the camel and behind Drizzt. The agile drow leaped about, still comfortably holding his perch. Within mere seconds, he had both of his foes on the defensive.

Wulfgar finished the last of the three he had dropped, then sprang away from the mess, only to find his stubborn camel rising in front of him again. He slammed the nasty thing again, this time with Aegis-fang, and it dropped to the ground beside the bandits.

With that battle at an undeniable end, the first thing the barbarian noticed was Drizzt. He marveled at the magnificent dance of the drow's blades, snapping down to deflect a curved sword or to keep one of the drow's two opponents off balance. Drizzt would dispose of both of them in a matter of seconds.

Then Wulfgar looked past the drow, to where another rider quietly trotted in, his spearhead angled to catch Drizzt in the back.

"Drizzt!" the barbarian screamed as he heaved Aegis-fang at his friend.

At the sound of the shout, Drizzt thought Wulfgar was in trouble, but when he looked and saw the warhammer spinning toward his knees, he understood immediately. Without hesitation, he leaped out and over his foes in a twisting somersault.

The charging spearman didn't even have time to lament his victim's escape, for the mighty warhammer spun in over the camel's humps and smashed his face flat.

Drizzt's dive proved beneficial in his fight up front as well, for he had caught both swordsmen by surprise. In the split second of their hesitation, the drow, though he was upside down in midair, struck hard, thrusting his blades downward.

Twinkle dug deeply into a chest. The other bandit managed to dodge the second scimitar, but it came close enough for Drizzt to lock its hilt under the man's arm. Both riders came tumbling down with the drow, and only Drizzt landed on his feet. His blades crossed twice and dived again, this time ending the struggle.

Seeing the huge barbarian unarmed, another rider went after him. Wulfgar saw the man coming and poised himself for a desperate strike. As the horse charged in, the barbarian feinted to his right, away from the rider's sword arm and as the rider had expected. Then Wulfgar reversed direction, throwing himself squarely in the horse's path.

Wulfgar accepted the stunning impact and locked his arms about the horse's neck and his legs onto the beast's front legs, rolling backward with the momentum and causing the horse to stumble. Then the mighty barbarian yanked with all his might, bringing horse and rider right over him.

The shocked bandit could not react, though he did manage to scream as the horse drove him into the ground. When the horse finally rolled away, the bandit remained, buried upside down to the waist in the sand, his legs lolling grotesquely to one side.

His boots and beard filled with sand, Bruenor eagerly looked for someone to fight. Among the tall mounts, the short dwarf had been overlooked by all but a handful of the bandits. Now, most of them were already dead!

Bruenor rushed away from the protection of the riderless camels, banging his axe on his shield to draw attention to himself. He saw one rider turning to flee from the disastrous scene.

"Hey!" Bruenor barked at him. "Yer mother's an ore-kissin' harlot!"

Thinking he had every advantage over the standing dwarf, the bandit couldn't pass up the opportunity to answer the insult. He rushed over to Bruenor and chopped down with his sword.

Bruenor brought his golden shield up to block the blow, then stepped around the front of the horse. The rider swung about to meet the dwarf on the other side, but Bruenor used his shortness to his advantage. Barely bending, he slipped under the horse's belly, back to the original side, and thrust his axe up over his head, catching the confused man on the hip. As the bandit lurched over in pain, Bruenor brought his shield arm up, caught turban and hair in his gnarled fingers, and tore the man from his seat. With a satisfied grunt, the dwarf chopped into the bandit's neck

"Too easy!" the dwarf grumbled, dropping the body to the ground. He looked for another victim, but the battle was over. No more bandits

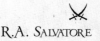

remained in the bowl, and Wulfgar, Aegis-fang back in his hands, and Drizzt were standing easily.

"Where's me girl?" Bruenor cried.

Drizzt calmed him with a look and a pointing finger.

On the top of a dune to the side, Catti-brie sat atop the horse she had commandeered, Taulmaril taut in her hands as she looked out over the desert.

Several riders galloped across the sand in full flight and another lay dead on the other side of the dune. Catti-brie put one of them in her sights, then realized that the fighting had ended behind her.

"Enough," she whispered, moving the bow an inch to the side and sending the arrow over the fleeing bandit's shoulder.

There has been enough killing this day, she thought.

Catti-brie looked at the carnage of the battle scene and at the hungry buzzards circling patiently overhead. She dropped Taulmaril to her side. The firm set of her grim visage melted away.

THE GUIDE

See the pleasure it promises," the guildmaster teased, scraping his hand over the barbed tip of a single spike sticking out of a block of wood on the center of the room's little table.

Regis purposely curled his lips into a stupid smile, pretending to see the obvious logic of Pook's words.

"Just drop your palm onto it," Pook coaxed, "then you will know the joy and will again be part of our family."

Regis searched for a way out of the trap. Once before he had used the ruse, the lie within a lie, pretending to be caught under the magical charm's influence. He had worked his act to perfection then, convincing an evil wizard of his loyalty, then turning on the man at a critical moment to aid his friends.

This time, though, Regis had even surprised himself, escaping the ruby pendant's insistent, hypnotizing pull. Now, though, he was caught: A person truly duped by the gem would gladly impale his hand on the barbed spike.

Regis brought his hand above his head and closed his eyes, trying to keep his visage blank enough to carry out the dupe. He swung his arm down, meaning to follow through on Pook's suggestion.

At the last moment, his hand swerved away and banged harmlessly on the table.

Pook roared in rage, suspecting all along that Regis had somehow escaped the pendant's influence. He grabbed the halfling by the wrist and smashed his little hand onto the spike, wiggling it as the spike went through. Regis's scream multiplied tenfold when Pook tore his hand back up the barbed instrument.

Then Pook let him go and slapped him across the face as Regis clutched his wounded hand to his chest.

"Deceiving dog!" the guildmaster shouted, more angry with the pendant's failure than with Regis's façade. He lined up for another slap but calmed himself and decided to twist the halfling's stubborn will back on Regis.

"A pity," he teased, "for if the pendant had brought you back under control, I might have found a place for you in the guild. Surely you deserve to die, little thief, but I have not forgotten your value to me in the past. You were the finest thief in Calimport, a position I might have offered you once again."

"Then no pity for the failure of the gem," Regis dared to retort, guessing the teasing game that Pook was playing, "for no pain outweighs the disgust I would feel at playing lackey to Pasha Pook!"

Pook's response was a heavy slug that knocked Regis off his chair and onto the floor. The halfling lay curled up, trying to stem the blood from both his hand and his nose.

Pook rested back in his chair and clasped his hands behind his head. He looked at the pendant, resting on the table in front of him. Only once before had it failed him, when he had tried it on a will that would not be captured. Luckily, Artemis Entreri had not realized the attempt that day, and Pook had been wise enough not to try the pendant on the assassin again.

Pook shifted his gaze to Regis, now passed out from the pain. He had to give the little halfling credit. Even if Regis's familiarity with the pendant had given him an edge in his battle, only an iron will could resist the tempting pull.

"But it will not help you," Pook whispered at the unconscious form. He sat back in his chair again and closed his eyes, trying to envision still another torture for Regis.

⚔ ⚔ ⚔ ⚔ ⚔

The tan-robed arm slipped in through the tent's flap and held the limp body of the red-bearded dwarf upside down by the ankle. Sali Dalib's fingers started their customary twiddle, and he flashed the gold-and-ivory smile so wide that it seemed as if it would take in his ears. His little goblin assistant jumped up and down at his side, squealing, "Magic, magic, magic!"

Bruenor opened one eye and lifted an arm to push his long beard out of his face. "Ye be likin' what ye're seeing?" the dwarf asked slyly.

Sali Dalib's smile disappeared, and his fingers got all tangled together.

Bruenor's bearer—Wulfgar, wearing the robe of one of the bandits— walked into the tent. Catti-brie came in behind him.

"So 'twas yerself that set the bandits upon us," the young woman growled.

Sali Dalib's exclamation of shock came out as so much gibberish, and the wily merchant spun away to flee. . . only to find a neat hole sliced into the back of his tent and Drizzt Do'Urden standing within it, leaning on one scimitar while the other rested easily on his shoulder. Just to heighten the merchant's terror, Drizzt had again taken off the magical mask.

"Uh . . . um, de bestest road?" the merchant stammered

"Bestest for yerself and yer friends!" Bruenor growled.

"So they thought," Catti-brie was quick to put in.

Sali Dalib curled his smile sheepishly, but he had been in tight spots a hundred times before and had always weaseled his way out. He lifted his palms, as if to say, "You caught me," but then jerked into a dizzying maneuver, pulling several small ceramic globes out of one of his robe's many pockets. He slammed them to the floor at his feet. Explosions of multi-colored light left a thick, blinding smoke in their wake, and the merchant dashed for the side of the tent.

Instinctively Wulfgar dropped Bruenor and jumped ahead, catching an armful of emptiness. The dwarf plopped onto the floor headfirst and rolled to a sitting position, his one-horned helm tilted to the side of his head. As the smoke thinned, the embarrassed barbarian looked back to the dwarf, who just shook his head in disbelief and mumbled, "Suren to be a long adventure."

Only Drizzt, ever alert, had not been caught unawares. The drow had shielded his eyes from the bursts, then watched the smoky silhouette of the merchant darting to the left. Drizzt would have had him before he got out of the hidden flap in the tent, but Sali Dalib's assistant stumbled into the drow's way. Barely slowing, Drizzt slammed Twinkle's hilt into the little goblin's forehead, dropping the creature into unconsciousness, then slipped the mask back on his face and jumped out to the streets of Memnon.

Catti-brie rushed by to follow Drizzt, and Bruenor leaped to his feet. "After 'im, boy!" the dwarf shouted at Wulfgar. The chase was on.

Drizzt caught sight of the merchant slipping into the throng of the streets. Even Sali Dalib's loud robe would blend well in the city's myriad of colors, so Drizzt added a touch of his own. As he had done to the invisible mage on the deck of the pirate ship, the drow sent a purplish glowing outline of dancing flames over the merchant.

Drizzt sped off in pursuit, weaving in and out of the crowd with amazing ease and watching for the bobbing line of purple ahead.

Bruenor was less graceful. The dwarf cut ahead of Catti-brie and plunged headlong into the throng, stomping toes and using his shield to bounce bodies out of his way. Wulfgar, right behind, cut an even wider swath, and Catti-brie had an easy time following in their wake.

They passed a dozen lanes and crashed through an open market, Wulfgar accidentally overturning a cart of huge yellow melons. Shouts of protest erupted behind them as they passed, but they kept their eyes ahead, each watching the person in front and trying not to get lost in the overwhelming bustle.

Sali Dalib knew at once that he was too conspicuous with the fiery outline to ever escape in the open streets. To add to his disadvantage, the eyes and pointing fingers of a hundred curious onlookers greeted him at every turn, signposts for his pursuers. Grabbing at the single chance before him, the merchant cut down one lane and scrambled through the doors of a large stone building.

Drizzt turned to make certain that his friends were still behind, then rushed through the doors, skidding to a stop on the steam-slicked marble floor of a public bathhouse. Two huge eunuchs moved to block the clothed elf, but as with the merchant who had come in just before, the agile Drizzt regained his momentum too quickly to be hindered. He skated through the short entry corridor and into the main room, a large open bath, thick with steam and smelling of sweat and perfumed soaps. Naked bodies crossed his path at every step, and Drizzt had to he careful where he placed his hands as he slipped through.

Bruenor nearly fell as he entered the slippery chamber, and the eunuchs, already out of their positions, got in front of him.

"No clothes!" one of them demanded, but Bruenor had no time for idle discussions. He stamped a heavy boot onto one of the giant's bare feet, then crunched the other foot for good measure. Wulfgar came in then and heaved the remaining eunuch aside.

The barbarian, leaning forward to gain speed, had no chance to stop or turn on the slippery floor, and as Bruenor turned to make his way along the perimeter of the bath, Wulfgar slammed into him, knocking them both to the floor and into a slide they could not brake.

They bounced over the rim of the bath and plunged into the water, Wulfgar coming up, waist deep, between two voluptuous and naked, giggling women.

The barbarian stammered an apology, finding his tongue twisted within the confines of his mouth. A slap across the back of his head shook him back to his senses.

"Ye're looking for the merchant, ye remember?" Catti-brie reminded him.

I am looking!" Wulfgar assured her.

"Then be lookin' for the one lined in purple!" Catti-brie shot back.

Wulfgar, his eyes freed with the expectation of another smack, noticed the single horn of a helmet poking out of the water at his side. Frantically he plunged his hand under, catching Bruenor by the scruff of the neck and hoisting him out of the bath. The not-too-happy dwarf came up with his arms crossed over his chest and shaking his head in disbelief once again.

Drizzt got out the back door of the bathhouse and found himself in an empty alley, the only unpopulated stretch he had seen since entering

Memnon. Seeking a better vantage, the drow scaled the side of the bathhouse and jogged along the roof.

Sali Dalib slowed his pace, thinking he had slipped the pursuit. The drow's purple fire died away, further adding to the merchant's sense of security. He wound his way through the back-alley maze. Not even the usual drunks leaned against the walls to inform his pursuers. He moved a hundred twisting yards, then two, and finally down an alley that he knew would turn onto the largest marketplace in Memnon, where anyone could become invisible in the blink of an eye.

As Sali Dalib approached the end of the alley, however, an elven form dropped in front of him and two scimitars flashed out of their sheaths, crossing before the stunned merchant, coming to rest on his collarbones, then drawing lines on either side of his neck.

When the four friends returned to the merchant's tent with their prisoner, they found, to their relief, the little goblin lying where Drizzt had bopped him. Bruenor none too gently pulled the unfortunate creature up behind Sali Dalib and tied the two back to back. Wulfgar moved to help and wound up hooking a loop of the rope over Bruenor's forearm. The dwarf wiggled free and pushed the barbarian away.

"Should've stayed in Mithral Hall," Bruenor grumbled. "Safer with the gray ones than beside yerself and the girl!"

Wulfgar and Catti-brie looked to Drizzt for support, but the drow just smiled and moved to the side of the tent.

"Ha ha ha ha ha," Sali Dalib giggled nervously "No problem here. We deal? Many riches, I have. What you need—"

"Shut yer mouth!" Bruenor snapped at him. The dwarf winked at Drizzt, indicating that he meant to play the bad guy role in the encounter.

"I don't be lookin' for riches from one what's tricked me," Bruenor growled. "Me heart's for revenge!" He looked around at his friends. "Ye all saw his face when he thought me dead. Suren was him that put the riding bandits on us."

"Sali Dalib never—" the merchant stammered.

"I said, 'Shut yer mouth!'" Bruenor shouted in his face, cowing him. The dwarf brought his axe up and ready on his shoulder.

The merchant looked to Drizzt, confused, for the drow had replaced the mask and now appeared as a surface elf once again. Sali Dalib guessed the truth of Drizzt's identity, figuring the black skin to be more fitting on the deadly elf, and he did not even think of begging for mercy from Drizzt.

"Wait on it, then," Catti-brie said suddenly, grabbing the handle of Bruenor's weapon. "May that there be a way for this dog to save his neck."

"Bah! What would we want o' him?" Bruenor shot back, winking at Catti-brie for playing her part to perfection.

"He'll get us to Calimport," Catti-brie replied. She cast a steely gaze at Sali Dalib, warning him that her mercy was not easily gotten. "Suren this time he'll take us down the true bestest road."

"Yes, yes, ha ha ha ha ha," Sali Dalib blurted. "Sali Dalib show you de way!"

"Show?" balked Wulfgar, not to be left out. "You will lead us all the way to Calimport."

"Very long way," grumbled the merchant. "Five days or more. Sali Dalib cannot—"

Bruenor raised his axe.

"Yes, yes, of course," the merchant erupted. "Sali Dalib take you there. Take you right to de gate . . . through de gate," he corrected quickly. "Sali Dalib even get de water. We must catch de caravan."

"No caravan," Drizzt interrupted, surprising even his friends. "We will travel alone."

"Dangerous," Sali Dalib replied. "Very, very. De Calim Desert be very full of monsters. Dragons and bandits."

"No caravan," Drizzt said again in a tone that none of them dared question. "Untie them, and let them get things ready."

Bruenor nodded, then put his face barely an inch from Sali Dalib's. "And I mean to be watchin' them meself," he said to Drizzt, though he sent the message more pointedly to Sali Dalib and the little goblin. "One trick and I'll cut 'em in half!"

Less than an hour later, five camels moved out of southern Memnon and into the Calim Desert with ceramic water jugs clunking on their sides.

Drizzt and Bruenor led the way, following the signposts of the Trade Way. The drow wore his mask, but kept the cowl of his cloak as low as he could, for the sizzling sunlight on the white sands burned at his eyes, which had once been accustomed to the absolute blackness of the underworld.

Sali Dalib, his assistant sitting on the camel in front of him, came in the middle, with Wulfgar and Catti-brie bringing up the rear. Catti-brie kept Taulmaril across her lap, a silver arrow notched as a continual reminder to the sneaky merchant.

The day grew hotter than anything the friends had ever experienced, except for Drizzt, who had lived in the very bowels of the world. Not a cloud hindered the sun's brutal rays, and not a wisp of a breeze came to offer any relief. Sali Dalib, more used to the heat, knew the lack of wind to be a blessing, for wind in the desert meant blowing and blinding sand, the most dangerous killer of the Calim.

The night was better, with the temperature dropping comfortably and a full moon turning the endless line of dunes into a silvery dreamscape, like the rolling waves of the ocean. The friends set a camp for a few hours, taking turns watching over their reluctant guides.

Catti-brie awoke sometime after midnight. She sat and stretched, figuring it to be her turn on watch. She saw Drizzt, standing on the edge of the firelight, staring into the starry heavens.

Hadn't Drizzt taken the first watch? she wondered.

Catti-brie studied the moon's position to make certain of the hour. There could be no doubt; the night grew long.

"Trouble?" she asked softly, going to Drizzt's side. A loud snore from Bruenor answered the question for Drizzt.

"Might I spell ye, then?" she asked. "Even a drow elf needs to sleep."

"I can find my rest under the cowl of my cloak," Drizzt replied, turning to meet her concerned gaze with his lavender eyes, "when the sun is high."

"Might I join ye, then?" Catti-brie asked. "Suren a wondrous night."

Drizzt smiled and turned his gaze back to the heavens, to the allure of the evening sky with a mystical longing in his heart as profound as any surface elf had ever experienced.

Catti-brie slipped her slender fingers around his and stood quietly by his side, not wanting to disturb his enchantment further, sharing more than mere words with her dearest of friends.

⚔ ⚔ ⚔ ⚔ ⚔

The heat was worse the next day, and even worse the following, but the camels plodded on effortlessly, and the four friends, who had come through so many hardships, accepted the brutal trek as just one more obstacle on the journey they had to complete.

They saw no other signs of life and considered that a blessing, for anything living in that desolate region could only be hostile. The heat was enemy enough, and they felt as if their skin would simply shrivel and crack away.

Whenever one of them felt like quitting, like the relentless sun and burning sand and heat were simply too much to bear, he or she just thought of Regis.

What terrible tortures was the halfling now enduring at the hands of his former master?

Epilogue

From the shadows of a doorway, Entreri watched Pasha Pook make his way up the staircase to the exit of the guildhouse. It had been less than an hour since Pook had regained his ruby pendant and already he was off to put it to use. Entreri had to give the guildmaster credit; he was never late for the dinner bell.

The assassin waited for Pook to clear the house altogether, then made his way stealthily back to the top level. The guards outside the final door made no move to stop him, though Entreri did not remember them from his earlier days in the guild. Pook must have prudently put out the word of Entreri's station in the guild, according him all the privileges he used to enjoy.

Never late for the dinner bell.

Entreri moved to the door to his old room, where LaValle now resided, and knocked softly.

"Come in, come in," the wizard greeted him, hardly surprised that the assassin had returned.

"It is good to be back," Entreri said.

"And good to have you back," replied the wizard sincerely. "Things have not been the same since you left us, and they have only become worse in recent months."

Entreri understood the wizard's point. "Rassiter?"

LaValle grimaced. "Keep your back to the wall when that one is about." A shudder shook through him, but he composed himself quickly. "But with you back at Pook's side, Rassiter will learn his place."

"Perhaps," replied Entreri, "though I am not so certain that Pook was as glad to see me."

"You understand Pook," LaValle chuckled. "Ever thinking as a guild-master! He desired to set the rules for your meeting with him to assert his authority. But that incident is far behind us already."

Entreri's look gave the wizard the impression that he was not so certain.

"Pook will forget it," LaValle assured him,

"Those who pursued me should not so easily be forgotten," Entreri replied.

"Pook called upon Pinochet to complete the task," said LaValle. "The pirate has never failed."

"The pirate has never faced such foes," Entreri answered. He looked to the table and LaValle's crystal ball. "We should be certain."

LaValle thought for a moment, then nodded his accord. He had intended to do some scrying anyway. "Watch the ball," he instructed Entreri. "I shall see if I can summon the image of Pinochet."

The crystal ball remained dark for a few moments, then filled with smoke. LaValle had not dealt often with Pinochet, but he knew enough of the pirate for a simple scrying. A few seconds later, the image of a docked ship came into view—not a pirate vessel, but a merchant ship. Immediately Entreri suspected something amiss.

Then the crystal probed deeper, beyond the hull of the ship, and the assassin's guess was confirmed, for in a sectioned corner of the hold sat the proud pirate captain, his elbows on his knees and his head in his hands, shackled to the wall.

LaValle, stunned, looked to Entreri, but the assassin was too intent on the image to offer any explanations. A rare smile had found its way onto Entreri's face.

LaValle cast an enhancing spell at the crystal ball. "Pinochet," he called softly.

The pirate lifted his head and looked around.

"Where are you?" LaValle asked.

"Oberon?" Pinochet asked. "Is that you, wizard?"

"Nay, I am LaValle, Pook's sorcerer in Calimport. Where are you?"

"Memnon," the pirate answered. "Can you get me out?"

"What of the elf and the barbarian?" Entreri asked LaValle, but Pinochet heard the question directly.

"I had them!" the pirate hissed. "Trapped in a channel with no escape. But then a dwarf appeared, driving the reins of a flying chariot of fire, and with him a woman archer—a deadly archer." He paused, fighting off his distaste as he remembered the encounter.

"To what outcome?" LaValle prompted, amazed at the development.

"One ship went running, one ship—my ship—sank, and the third was captured," groaned Pinochet. He locked his face into a grimace and asked again, more emphatically, "Can you get me out?"

LaValle looked helplessly to Entreri, who now stood tall over the crystal hall, absorbing every word. "Where are they?" the assassin growled, his patience worn away.

"Gone," answered Pinochet. "Gone with the girl and the dwarf into Memnon."

"How long?"

"Three days."

Entreri signaled to LaValle that he had heard enough.

"I will have Pasha Pook send word to Memnon immediately," LaValle assured the pirate. "You shall be released."

Pinochet sank into his original, despondent position. Of course he would be released; that had already been arranged. He had hoped that LaValle could somehow magically get him out of the *Sea Sprite's* hold, thereby releasing him from any pledges he would be forced to make to Deudermont when the captain set him free.

"Three days," LaValle said to Entreri as the crystal darkened. "They could be halfway here by now."

Entreri seemed amused at the notion. "Pasha Pook is to know nothing of this," he said suddenly.

LaValle sank back in his chair. "He must be told."

"No!" Entreri snapped. "This is none of his affair."

"The guild may be in danger," LaValle replied.

"You do not trust that I am capable of handling this?" Entreri asked in a low, grim tone. LaValle felt the assassin's callous eyes looking through him, as though he had suddenly become just another barrier to be overcome.

But Entreri softened his glare and grinned. "You know of Pasha Pook's weakness for hunting cats," he said, reaching into his pouch. "Give him this. Tell him you made it for him." He tossed a small black object across the table to the wizard. LaValle caught it, his eyes widening as soon as he realized what it was.

Guenhwyvar.

⚔ ⚔ ⚔ ⚔ ⚔

On a distant plane, the great cat stirred at the wizard's touch upon the statuette and wondered if its master meant to summon it, finally, to his side.

But, after a moment, the sensation faded, and the cat put its head down to rest.

So much time had gone by.

⚔ ⚔ ⚔ ⚔

"It holds an entity," the wizard gasped, sensing the strength in the onyx statuette.

"A powerful entity," Entreri assured him. "When you learn to control it, you will have brought a new ally to the guild."

"How can I thank—" LaValle began, but he stopped as he realized that he had already been told the price of the panther. "Why trouble Pook with details that do not concern him?" The wizard laughed, tossing a cloth over his crystal ball.

Entreri clapped LaValle on the shoulder as he passed toward the door. Three years had done nothing to diminish the understanding the two men had shared.

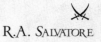

But with Drizzt and his friends approaching, Entreri had more pressing business. He had to go to the Cells of Nine and pay a visit to Regis.

The assassin needed another gift.

PART THREE

It is like looking into a mirror that paints the world with opposing colors: white hair to black; black skin to white, light eyes to dark. What an intricate mirror it is to replace a smile with a frown, and an expression of friendship with a seemingly perpetual scowl.

DESERT EMPIRES

For that is how I view Artemis Entreri, this warrior who can compliment every movement I make with similar precision and grace, the warrior who, in every way but one, I would regard as my equal.

How difficult it was for me to stand with him in the depths of Mithral Hall, fighting side by side for both our lives! Strangely, it was not any moral imperative that bothered me about fighting in that situation. It was no belief that Entreri should die, had to die, and that I, if I was not such a coward, would have killed him then and there, even if the action cost me my own life as I tried to escape the inhospitable depths. No, nothing like that.

What made it all so difficult for me was watching that man, that human assassin, and knowing, without the slightest shred of doubt, that I very well might have been looking at myself.

Is that who I would have become had I not found Zaknafein in those early years in Menzoberranzan? Had I not discovered the example of one who so validated my own beliefs that the ways of the drow were not right, morally and practically? Is that cold-hearted killer who I would have become had it been my vicious sister Briza training me instead of the more gentle Vierna?

I fear that it is, that I, despite all that I know to be true within the depths of my very heart, would have been overwhelmed by the situation about me, would have succumbed to the despair to a point where there remained little of compassion and justice. I would have become an assassin, holding strong within my own code of ethics, but with that code so horribly warped that I could no longer understand the truth of my actions, that I could justify them with the sheerest cynicism.

I saw all of that when I looked upon Entreri, and thanked Mielikki profoundly for those in my life, for Zaknafein, for Belwar Dissengulp and for Montolio, who helped me to steer the correct course. And if I saw a potential for myself within Entreri, then I must admit that there once was a potential for Entreri to become as I have become, to know compassion and community, to know friends, good friends, and to know love.

I think about him a lot, as he, no doubt, thinks about me. While his obsession is based in pride, in the challenge of overcoming me in battle, mine own is wrought of curiosity, of seeking answers within myself by observing the actions of who I might have become.

Do I hate him?

Strangely, I do not. That lack of hatred is not based on the respect that I give the man for his fighting prowess, for that measure of respect ends right there, at the edge of the battlefield. No, I do not hate Artemis Entreri because I pity him, the events that led to the wrong decisions he has made. There is true strength within him, and there is, or once was, a substantial potential to do good in a world so in need of heroes. For, despite his actions, I have come to understand that Entreri operates within a very strict code. In his own warped view of the world, I believe that Entreri honestly believes that he never killed anyone who did not deserve it. He held Catti-brie captive but did not rape her.

As for his actions concerning Regis . . . well, Regis was, in reality, a thief, and though he stole from another thief that does not excuse that crime. In Luskan, as in most cities in the Realms, thieves lose their hands, or worse, and certainly a bounty hunter sent to retrieve a stolen item, and the person who stole it, is well within the law to kill that person, and anyone else who hinders his task.

In Calimport, Artemis Entreri operates among thieves and thugs, among the very edge of civilization. In that capacity, he deals death, as did Zaknafein in the alleys of Menzoberranzan. There is a difference—certainly!—between the two, and I do not in any way mean to excuse Entreri from his crimes. Neither will I consider him the simple killing monster that was, say, Errtu.

No, there was once potential there, I know, though I fear he is far gone from that road, for when I look upon Artemis Entreri, I see myself, I see the capacity to love, and also the capacity to lose all of that and become cold.

So very cold.

Perhaps we will meet again and do battle, and if I kill him, I will shed no tears for him. Not for who he is, at least, but quite possibly, I will cry for who this marvelous warrior might have become.

If I kill him, I will be crying for myself.

—Drizzt Do'Urden

16
NEVER A FOULER PLACE

Entreri slipped through the shadows of Calimport's bowels as quietly as an owl glided through a forest at twilight. This was his home, the place he knew best, and all the street people of the city would mark the day when Artemis Entreri again walked beside them—or behind them.

Entreri couldn't help but smile slightly whenever the hushed whispers commenced in his wake—the more experienced rogues telling the newcomers that the king had returned. Entreri never let the legend of his reputation—no matter how well earned—interfere with the constant state of readiness that had kept him alive through the years. In the streets, a reputation of power only marked a man as a target for ambitious second-rates seeking, reputations of their own.

Thus, Entreri's first task in the city, outside of his responsibilities to Pasha Pook, was to reestablish the network of informants and associates that entrenched him in his station. He already had an important job for one of them, with Drizzt and company fast approaching, and he knew which one.

"I had heard you were back," squeaked a diminutive chap appearing as a human boy not yet into adolescence when Entreri ducked and entered his abode. "I guess most have."

Entreri took the compliment with a nod. "What has changed, my halfling friend?"

"Little," replied Dondon, "and lots." He moved to the table in the darkest corner of his small quarters, the side room, facing the ally, in a cheap inn called the Coiled Snake. "The rules of the street do not change, but the players do." Dondon looked up from the table's unlit lamp to catch Entreri's eyes with his own.

"Artemis Entreri was gone, after all," the halfling explained, wanting to make sure that Entreri fully understood his previous statement. "The royal suite had a vacancy."

Entreri nodded his accord, causing the halfling to relax and sigh audibly.

"Pook still controls the merchants and the docks," said Entreri. "Who owns the streets?"

"Pook, still," replied Dondon, "at least in name. He found another agent in your stead. A whole horde of agents." Dondon paused for a moment to think. Again he had to be careful to weigh every word before he spoke it. "Perhaps it would be more accurate to say that Pasha Pook does not control the streets, but rather that he still has the streets controlled."

Entreri knew, even before asking, what the little halfling was leading to. "Rassiter," he said grimly.

"There is much to be said about that one and his crew," Dondon chuckled, resuming his efforts to light the lantern.

"Pook loosens his reins on the wererats, and the ruffians of the street take care to stay out of the guild's way," Entreri reasoned.

"Rassiter and his kind play hard."

"And fall hard."

The chill of Entreri's tone brought Dondon's eyes back up from the lantern, and for the first time, the halfling truly recognized the old Artemis Entreri, the human street fighter who had built his shadowy empire one ally at a time. An involuntary shudder rippled up Dondon's spine, and he shifted uncomfortably on his feet.

Entreri saw the effect and quickly switched the subject. "Enough of this," he said. "Let it not concern you, little one. I have a job for you that is more in line with your talents."

Dondon finally got the lantern's wick to take, and he pulled up a chair, eager to please his old boss.

They talked for more than an hour, until the lantern became a solitary defense against the insistent blackness of the night. Then Entreri took his leave, through the window and into the ally. He didn't believe that Rassiter would be so foolish as to strike before taking full measure of the assassin, before the wererat could even begin to understand the dimensions of his enemy.

Then again, Entreri didn't mark Rassiter high on any intelligence scale.

Perhaps it was Entreri, though, who didn't truly understand his enemy, or how completely Rassiter and his wretched minions had come to dominate the streets over the last three years. Less than five minutes after Entreri had gone, Dondon's door swung open again.

And Rassiter stepped through.

"What did he want?" the swaggering fighter asked, plopping comfortably into a chair at the table.

Dondon moved away uneasily, noticing two more of Rassiter's cronies standing guard in the hall. After more than a year, the halfling still felt uncomfortable around Rassiter.

"Come, come now," Rassiter prompted. He asked again, his tone more grim, "What did he want?"

The last thing Dondon wanted was to get caught in a crossfire between the wererats and the assassin, but he had little choice but to answer Rassiter. If Entreri ever learned of the double-cross, Dondon knew that his days would swiftly end.

Yet, if he didn't spill out to Rassiter, his demise would be no less certain, and the method less swift.

He sighed at the lack of options and spilled his story, detail by detail, to Rassiter.

Rassiter gave no countermand to Entreri's instructions. He would let Dondon play out the scenario exactly as Entreri had devised it. Apparently, the wererat believed he could twist it into his own gains. He sat quietly for a long moment, scratching his hairless chin and savoring the anticipation of the easy victory, his broken teeth gleaming even a deeper yellow in the lamplight.

"You will run with us this night?" he asked the halfling, satisfied that the assassin business was completed. "The moon will be bright." He squeezed one of Dondon's cherublike cheeks. "The fur will be thick, eh?"

Dondon pulled away from the grasp. "Not this night," he replied, a bit too sharply.

Rassiter cocked his head, studying Dondon curiously. He always had suspected that the halfling was not comfortable with his new station. Might this defiance be linked to the return of his old boss? Rassiter wondered.

"Tease him and die," Dondon replied, drawing an even more curious look from the wererat.

"You have not begun to understand this man you face," Dondon continued, unshaken. "Artemis Entreri is not to be toyed with—not by the wise. He knows everything. If a half-sized rat is seen running with the pack, then my life is forfeit and your plans are ruined." He moved right up, in spite of his revulsion for the man, and set a grave visage barely an inch from Rassiter's nose.

"Forfeit," he reiterated, "at the least."

Rassiter spun out of the chair, sending it bouncing across the room. He had heard too much about Artemis Entreri in a single day for his liking. Everywhere he turned, trembling lips uttered the assassin's name.

Don't they know? he told himself once again as he strode angrily to the door. It is Rassiter they should fear!

He felt the telltale itching on his chin, then the crawling sensation of tingling growth swept through his body. Dondon backed away and averted his eyes, never comfortable with the spectacle.

Rassiter kicked off his boots and loosened his shirt and pants. The hair was visible now, rushing out of his skin in scraggly patches and clumps. He fell back against the wall as the fever took him completely. His skin bubbled and bulged, particularly around his face. He sublimated his scream as his snout elongated, though the wash of agony was no less intense this time—perhaps the thousandth time—than it had been during his very first transformation.

He stood then before Dondon on two legs, as a man, but whiskered and furred and with a long pink tail that ran out the back of his trousers, as a rodent.

"Join me?" he asked the halfling.

Hiding his revulsion, Dondon quickly declined. Looking at the ratman, the halfling wondered how he had ever allowed Rassiter to bite him, infecting him with his lycanthropic nightmare. "It will bring you power!" Rassiter had promised.

But at what cost? Dondon thought. To look and smell like a rat? No blessing this, but a disease.

Rassiter guessed at the halfling's distaste, and he curled his rat snout back in a threatening hiss, then turned for the door.

He spun back on Dondon before exiting the room. "Keep away from this!" he warned the halfling. "Do as you were bid and hide away!"

"No doubt to that," Dondon whispered as the door slammed shut.

✕ ✕ ✕ ✕ ✕

The aura that distinguished Calimport as home to so very many Calishites came across as foul to the strangers from the North. Truly, Drizzt, Wulfgar, Bruenor, and Catti-brie were weary of the Calim Desert when their five-day trek came to an end, but looking down on the city of Calimport made them want to turn around and take to the sands once again.

It was wretched Memnon on a grander scale, with the divisions of wealth so blatantly obvious that Calimport cried out as ultimately perverted to the four friends. Elaborate houses, monuments to excess and hinting at wealth beyond imagination, dotted the cityscape. Yet, right beside those palaces loomed lane after lane of decrepit shanties of crumbling clay or ragged skins. The friends couldn't guess how many people roamed the place—certainly more than Waterdeep and Memnon combined!—and they knew at once that in Calimport, as in Memnon, no one had ever bothered to count.

Sali Dalib dismounted, bidding the others do likewise, and led them down a final hill and into the unwalled city. The friends found the sights of Calimport no better up close. Naked children, their bellies bloated from lack of food, scrambled out of the way or were simply trampled as gilded, slave-drawn carts rushed through the streets. Worse still were the sides of those avenues, ditches mostly, serving as open sewers in the city's poorest sections. There were thrown the bodies of the impoverished, who had fallen to the roadside at the end of their miserable days.

"Suren Rumblebelly never told of such sights when he spoke of home," Bruenor grumbled, pulling his cloak over his face to deflect the awful stench. "Past me guessing why he'd long for this place!"

"De greatest city in de world, dis be!" Sali Dalib spouted, lifting his arms to enhance his praise.

Wulfgar, Bruenor, and Catti-brie shot him incredulous stares. Hordes of people begging and starving was not their idea of greatness. Drizzt paid the merchant no heed, though. He was busy making the inevitable comparison between Calimport and another city he had known, Menzoberranzan. Truly there were similarities, and death was no less common in Menzoberranzan, but Calimport somehow seemed fouler than the city of the drow. Even the weakest of the dark elves had the means to protect himself, with strong family ties and deadly innate abilities. The pitiful peasants of Calimport, though, and more so their children, seemed helpless and hopeless indeed.

In Menzoberranzan, those on the lowest rungs of the power ladder could fight their way to a better standing. For the majority of Calimport's multitude, though, there would only be poverty, a day-to-day squalid existence until they landed on the piles of buzzard-pecked bodies in the ditches.

"Take us to the guildhouse of Pasha Pook," Drizzt said, getting to the point, wanting to be done with his business and out of Calimport, "then you are dismissed."

Sali Dalib paled at the request. "Pasha Poop?" he stammered. "Who is dis?"

"Bah!" Bruenor snorted, moving dangerously close to the merchant. "He knows him."

"Suren he does," Catti-brie observed, "and fears him."

"Sali Dalib not—" the merchant began.

Twinkle came out of its sheath and slipped to a stop under the merchant's chin, silencing the man instantly. Drizzt let his mask slip a bit, reminding Sali Dalib of the drow's heritage. Once again, his suddenly grim demeanor unnerved even his own friends. "I think of my friend," Drizzt said in a calm, low tone, his lavender eyes absently staring into the city, "tortured even as we delay."

He snapped his scowl at Sali Dalib. "As you delay! You will take us to the guildhouse of Pasha Pook," he reiterated, more insistently, "and then you are dismissed."

"Pook? Oh, Pook," the merchant beamed. "Sali Dalib know dis man, yes, yes. Everybody know Pook. Yes, yes, I take you dere, den I go."

Drizzt replaced the mask but kept the stern visage. "If you or your little companion try to flee," he promised so calmly that neither the merchant nor his assistant doubted his words for a moment, "I will hunt you down and kill you."

The drow's three friends exchanged confused shrugs and concerned glances. They felt confident that they knew Drizzt to his soul, but so grim was his tone that even they wondered how much of his promise was an idle threat.

✕ ✕ ✕ ✕ ✕

It took more than an hour for them to twist and wind their way through the maze that was Calimport, to the dismay of the friends, who wanted nothing more than to be off the streets and away from the fetid stench. Finally, to their relief, Sali Dalib turned a final corner, to Rogues Circle, and pointed to the unremarkable wooden structure at its end: Pasha Pook's guildhouse.

"Dere be de Pook," Sali Dalib said. "Now, Sali Dalib take his camels and be gone, back to Memnon."

The friends were not so quick to be rid of the wily merchant. "More to me guessin' that Sali Dalib be heading for Pook to sell some tales o' four friends," Bruenor growled.

"Well, we've a way beyond that," said Catti-brie. She shot Drizzt a sly wink, then moved up to the curious and frightened merchant, reaching into her pack as she went.

Her look went suddenly grim, so wickedly intense that Sali Dalib jerked back when her hand came up to his forehead. "Hold yer place!" Catti-brie snapped at him harshly, and he had no resistance to the power of her tone. She had a powder, a flourlike substance, in her pack. Reciting some gibberish that sounded like an arcane chant, she traced a scimitar on Sali Dalib's forehead. The merchant tried to protest but couldn't find his tongue for his terror.

"Now for the little one," Catti-brie said, turning to Sali Dalib's goblin assistant. The goblin squeaked and tried to dash away, but Wulfgar caught it in one hand and held it out to Catti-brie, squeezing tighter and tighter until the thing stopped wiggling.

Catti-brie performed the ceremony again then turned to Drizzt. "They be linked to yer spirit now," she said. "Do ye feel them?"

Drizzt, understanding the bluff, nodded grimly and slowly drew his two scimitars.

Sali Dalib paled and nearly toppled over, but Bruenor, moving closer to watch his daughter's games, was quick to prop the terrified man up.

"Ah, let them go, then. Me witchin's through," Catti-brie told both Wulfgar and Bruenor. "The drow'll feel yer presence now," she hissed at Sali Dalib and his goblin. "He'll know when ye're about and when ye've gone. If ye stay in the city, and if ye've thoughts o' going to Pook, the drow'll know, and he'll follow yer feel—hunt ye down." She paused a moment, wanting the two to fully comprehend the horror they faced.

"And he'll kill ye slow."

"Take yer lumpy horses, then, and be gone!" Bruenor roared. "If I be seein' yer stinkin' faces again, the drow'll have to get in line for his cuts!"

Before the dwarf had even finished, Sali Dalib and the goblin had collected their camels and were off, away from Rogues Circle and back toward the northern end of the city.

"Them two're for the desert," Bruenor laughed when they had gone. "Fine tricks, me girl."

Drizzt pointed to the sign of an inn, the Spitting Camel, halfway down the lane. "Get us rooms," he told his friends. "I will follow them to make certain they do indeed leave the city."

"Wastin' yer time," Bruenor called after him. "The girl's got 'em running, or I'm a bearded gnome!"

Drizzt had already started padding silently into the maze of Calimport's streets.

Wulfgar, caught unawares by her uncharacteristic trickery and still not quite sure what had just happened, eyed Catti-brie carefully. Bruenor didn't miss his apprehensive look.

"Take note, boy," the dwarf taunted. "Suren the girl's got herself a nasty streak ye'll not want turned on yerself!"

Playing through for the sake of Bruenor's enjoyment, Catti-brie glared at the big barbarian and narrowed her eyes, causing Wulfgar to back off a cautious step. "Witchin' magic," she cackled. "Tells me when yer eyes be filled with the likings of another woman!" She turned slowly, not releasing him from her stare until she had taken three steps down the lane toward the inn Drizzt had indicated.

Bruenor reached high and slapped Wulfgar on the back as he started after Catti-brie. "Fine lass," he remarked to Wulfgar. "Just don't be gettin' her mad!"

Wulfgar shook the confusion out of his head and forced out a laugh, reminding himself that Catti-brie's "magic" had been only a dupe to frighten the merchant.

But Catti-brie's glare as she had carried out the deception, and the sheer strength of her intensity, followed him as he walked down Rogues Circle. Both a shudder and a sweet tingle spread down his spine.

⚔ ⚔ ⚔ ⚔ ⚔

Half the sun had fallen below the western horizon before Drizzt returned to Rogues Circle. He had followed Sali Dalib and his assistant far out into the Calim Desert, though the merchant's frantic pace gave no indications that he had any intentions of turning back to Calimport. Drizzt simply wouldn't take the chance; they were too close to finding Regis and too close to Entreri.

Masked as an elf—Drizzt was beginning to realize how easily the disguise now came to him—he made his way into the Spitting Camel and to the innkeeper's desk. An incredibly skinny, leather-skinned man, who kept his back always to a wall and his head darting nervously in every direction, met him.

"Three friends," Drizzt said gruffly. "A dwarf, a woman, and a golden-haired giant."

"Up the stairs," the man told him. "To the left. Two gold if you mean to stay the night." He held out his bony hand.

"The dwarf already paid you," Drizzt said grimly, starting away.

"For himself, the girl, and the big the innkeeper started, grabbing Drizzt by the shoulder. The look in Drizzt's lavender eves, though, stopped the innkeeper cold.

"He paid," the frightened man stuttered. "I remember. He paid."

Drizzt walked away without another word.

He found the two rooms on opposite sides of the corridor at the far end of the structure. He had meant to go straight in with Wulfgar and Bruenor and grab a short rest, hoping to be out on the street when night fully fell, when Entreri would likely be about. Drizzt found, instead, Catti-brie in her doorway, apparently waiting for him. She motioned him into her chamber and closed the door behind him.

Drizzt settled on the very edge of one of the two chairs in the center of the room, his foot tapping the floor in front of him.

Catti-brie studied him as she walked around to the other chair. She had known Drizzt for years but never had seen him so agitated.

"Ye seem as though ye mean to tear yerself into pieces," she said.

Drizzt gave her a cold look, but Catti-brie laughed it away. "Do ye mean to strike me, then?"

That prompted the drow to settle back in his chair.

"And don't ye be wearing that silly mask," Catti-brie scolded.

Drizzt reached for the mask but hesitated.

"Take it off!" Catti-brie ordered, and the drow complied before he had time to reconsider

"Ye came a bit grim in the street afore ye left," Catti-brie remarked, her voice softening.

"We had to make certain," Drizzt replied coldly. I do not trust Sali Dalib."

"Nor meself," Catti-brie agreed, "but ye're still grim, by me seeing."

"You were the one with the witching magic," Drizzt shotback, his tone defensive. "It was Catti-brie who showed herself grim then."

Catti-brie shrugged. "A needed act," she said. "An act I dropped when the merchant had gone. But yerself," she said pointedly, leaning forward and placing a comforting hand on Drizzt's knee. "Ye're up for a fight."

Drizzt started to jerk away but realized the truth of her observations and forced himself to relax under her friendly touch. He looked away, for he found that he could not soften the sternness of his visage.

"What's it about?" Catti-brie whispered.

Drizzt looked back to her then and remembered all the times he and she had shared back in Icewind Dale. In her sincere concern for him now, Drizzt recalled the first time they had met, when the smile of the girl—for she was then but a girl—had given the displaced and disheartened drow a renewed hope for his life among the surface dwellers.

Catti-brie knew more about him than anyone alive, about those things that were important to him, and made his stoic existence bearable. She alone recognized the fears that lay beneath his black skin, the insecurity masked by the skill of his sword arm.

"Entreri," he answered softly.

"Ye mean to kill him?"

"I have to."

Catti-brie sat back to consider the words. "If ye be killing Entreri to free Regis," she said at length, "and to stop him from hurting anyone else, then me heart says it's a good thing." She leaned forward again, bringing her face close to Drizzt's, "but if ye're meaning to kill him to prove yerself or to deny what he is, then me heart cries."

She could have slapped Drizzt and had the same effect. He sat up straight and cocked his head, his features twisted in angry denial. He let Catti-brie continue but he could not dismiss the importance of the observant woman's perceptions.

"Suren the world's not fair, me friend. Suren by the measure of hearts, ye been wronged. But are ye after the assassin for yer own anger? Will killing Entreri cure the wrong?

Drizzt did not answer, but his look turned stubbornly grim again.

"Look in the mirror, Drizzt Do'Urden," Catti-brie said, "without the mask. Killin' Entreri won't change the color of his skin—or the color of yer own."

Again Drizzt had been slapped, and this time it brought an undeniable ring of truth with it. He fell back in his chair, looking upon Catti-brie as he had never looked upon her before. Where had Bruenor's little girl gone? Before him loomed a woman, beautiful and sensitive and laying bare his soul with a few words. They had shared much, it was true, but how could she know him so very well? And why had she taken the time?

"Ye've truer friends than ever ye'll know," Catti-brie said, "and not for the way ye twirl a sword. Ye've others who would call themselves friend if only they could get inside the length of yer arm—if only ye'd learn to look."

Drizzt considered the words. He remembered the *Sea Sprite* and Captain Deudermont and the crew, standing behind him even when they knew his heritage.

"And if only ye'd ever learned to love," Catti-brie continued, her voice barely audible. "Suren ye've let things slip past, Drizzt Do'Urden."

Drizzt studied her intently, weighing the glimmer in her dark, saucerlike eyes. He tried to fathom what she was getting at, what personal message she was sending to him.

The door burst open suddenly, and Wulfgar bounded into the room, a smile stretching the length of his face and the eager look of adventure gleaming in his pale blue eyes. "Good that you are back," he said to Drizzt. He moved behind Catti-brie and dropped an arm comfortably across her shoulders. "The night has come, and a bright moon peeks over the eastern rim. Time for the hunt!"

Catti-brie put her hand on Wulfgar's and flashed him an adoring smile. Drizzt was glad they had found each other. They would grow together in a blessed and joyful life, rearing children that would no doubt be the envy of all the northland.

Catti-brie looked back to Drizzt. "Just for yer thoughts, me friend," she said quietly, calmly. "Are ye more trapped by the way the world sees ye or by the way ye see the world seein' ye?"

The tension eased out of Drizzt's muscles. If Catti-brie was right in her observations, he would have a lot of thinking to do.

"Time to hunt!" Catti-brie cried, satisfied that she had gotten her point across. She rose beside Wulfgar and headed for the door, but she turned her head over her shoulder to face Drizzt one final time, giving him a look that told him that perhaps he should have asked for more from Catti-brie back in Icewind Dale, before Wulfgar had entered her life.

Drizzt sighed as they left the room and instinctively reached for the magical mask.

Instinctively? he wondered.

Drizzt dropped the thing suddenly and fell back in the chair in thought, clasping his hands behind his head. He glanced around, hoping, but the room had no mirror.

17

IMPOSSIBLE LOYALTIES

LaValle held his hand within the pouch for a long moment, teasing Pook. They were alone with the eunuchs, who didn't count, in the central chamber of the top level. LaValle had promised his master a gift beyond even the news of the ruby pendant's return, and Pook knew that the wizard would offer such a promise with great care. It was not wise to disappoint the guildmaster.

LaValle had great confidence in his gift and had no trepidations about his grand claims. He slid it out and presented it to Pook, smiling broadly as he did so.

Pook lost his breath, and sweat thickened on his palms at the onyx statuette's touch. "Magnificent," he muttered, overwhelmed. "Never have I seen such craftsmanship, such detail. One could almost pet the thing!"

"One can," LaValle whispered under his breath. The wizard did not want to let on to all of the gift's properties at once, however, so he replied, "I am pleased that you are pleased."

"Where did you get it?"

LaValle shifted uneasily. "That is not important," he answered. "It is for you, Master, given with all of my loyalty." He quickly moved the conversation along to prevent Pook from pressing the point. "The workmanship of the statuette is but a fraction of its value," he teased, drawing a curious look from Pook.

"You have heard of such figurines," LaValle went on, satisfied that the time to overwhelm the guildmaster had come once again. "They can be magical companions to their owners."

Pook's hands verily trembled at the thought. "This," he stammered excitedly, "this might bring the panther to life?"

LaValle's sly smile answered the question.

"How? When might I—"

"Whenever you desire," LaValle answered.

"Should we prepare a cage?" Pook asked.

"No need."

"But at least until the panther understands who its master—"

"You possess the figurine," LaValle interrupted. "The creature you summon is wholly yours. It will follow your every command exactly as you desire."

Pook clutched the statuette close to his chest. He could hardly believe his fortune. The great cats were his first and foremost love, and to have in his possession one with such obedience, an extension of his own will, thrilled him as he had never been thrilled before.

"Now," he said. "I want to call the cat now. Tell me the words."

LaValle took the statue and placed it on the floor, then whispered into Pook's ear, taking care that his own uttering of the cat's name didn't summon Guenhwyvar and ruin the moment for Pook.

"Guenhwyvar," Pook called softly. Nothing happened at first, but both Pook and LaValle could sense the link being completed to the distant entity.

"Come to me, Guenhwyvar!" Pook commanded.

His voice rolled through the tunnel gate in the Planes of existence, down the dark corridor to the Astral Plane, the home of the entity of the panther. Guenhwyvar awakened to the summons. Cautiously the cat found the path.

"Guenhwyvar," the call came again, but the cat did not recognize the voice. It had been many tendays since its master had brought it to the Prime Material Plane, and the panther had had a well-deserved and much-needed rest, but one that had brought with it a cautious trepidation. Now, with an unknown voice summoning it, Guenhwyvar understood that something had definitely changed.

Tentatively, but unable to resist the summons, the great cat padded off down the corridor.

Pook and LaValle watched, mesmerized, as a gray smoke appeared, shrouding the floor around the figurine. It swirled lazily for a few moments then took definite shape, solidifying into Guenhwyvar. The cat stood perfectly still, seeking some recognition of its surroundings.

"What do I do?" Pook asked LaValle. The cat tensed at the sound of the voice—its master's voice.

"Whatever pleases you," LaValle answered. "The cat will sit by you, hunt for you, walk at your heel—kill for you."

Some ideas popped into the guildmaster's head at the last comment. "What are its limits?"

LaValle shrugged. "Most magic of this kind will fade after a length of time, though you can summon the cat again once it has rested," he quickly added, seeing Pook's disheartened look. "It cannot be killed; to do so would only return it to its plane, though the statue could be broken."

Again Pook's look soured. The item had already become too precious for him to consider losing it.

"I assure you that destroying the statue would not prove an easy task," LaValle continued. "Its magic is quite potent. The mightiest smith in all the Realms could not scratch it with his heaviest hammer!"

Pook was satisfied. "Come to me," he ordered the cat, extending his hand.

Guenhwyvar obeyed and flattened its ears as Pook gently stroked the soft black coat.

"I have a task," Pook announced suddenly, turning an excited glance at LaValle, "a memorable and marvelous task! The first task for Guenhwyvar."

LaValle's eyes lit up at the pure pleasure stamped across Pook's face.

"Fetch me Regis," Pook told LaValle. "Let Guenhwyvar's first kill be the halfling I most despise!"

⚔ ⚔ ⚔ ⚔ ⚔

Exhausted from his ordeal in the Cells of Nine, and from the various tortures Pook had put him through, Regis was easily shoved flat to his face before Pook's throne. The halfling struggled to his feet, determined to accept the next torture—even if it meant death—with dignity.

Pook waved the guards out of the room. "Have you enoyed your stay with us?" he teased Regis.

Regis brushed the mop of hair back from his face. "Acceptable," he replied. "The neighbors are noisy, though, growling and purring all the night through."

"Silence!" Pook snapped He looked at LaValle, standing beside the great chair. "He will find little humor here," the guildmaster said with a venomous chuckle.

Regis had passed beyond fear, though, into resignation. "You have won," he said calmly, hoping to steal some of the pleasure from Pook. "I took your pendant and was caught. If you believe that crime is deserving of death, then kill me."

"Oh, I shall!" Pook hissed. "I had planned that from the start, but I knew not the appropriate method."

Regis rocked back on his heels. Perhaps he wasn't as composed as he had hoped.

"Guenhwyvar," Pook called.

"Guenhwyvar?" Regis echoed under his breath.

"Come to me, my pet."

The halfling's jaw dropped to his chest when the magical cat slipped out of the half-opened door to LaValle's room.

"Wh-where did you get him?" Regis stuttered.

"Magnificent, is he not?" Pook replied. "But do not worry, little thief. You shall get a closer look." He turned to the cat.

"Guenhwyvar, dear Guenhwyvar," Pook purred, "this little thief wronged your master. Kill him, my pet, but kill him slowly. I want to hear his screams."

Regis stared into the panther's wide eyes. "Calm, Guenhwvvar," he said as the cat took a slow, hesitant stride his way. Truly it pained Regis to see the wondrous panther under the command of one as vile as Pook. Guenhwyvar belonged with Drizzt.

But Regis couldn't spend much time considering the implications of the cat's appearance. His own future became his primary concern.

"He is the one," Regis cried to Guenhwyvar, pointing at Pook. "He commands the evil one who took us from your true master, the evil one your true master seeks!"

"Excellent!" Pook laughed, thinking Regis to be grasping at a desperate lie to confuse the animal. "This show may yet be worth the agony I have endured at your hands, thief Regis!

LaValle shifted uneasily, understanding more of the truth to Regis's words.

"Now, my pet!" Pook commanded. "Bring him pain!"

Guenhwyvar growled lowly, eyes narrowed.

"Guenhwyvar," Regis said again, backing away a step. "Guenhwyvar, you know me."

The cat showed no indication that it recognized the halfling. Compelled by its master's voice, it crouched and inched across the floor toward Regis.

"Guenhwyvar!" Regis cried, feeling along the wall for an escape.

"That is the cat's name," Pook laughed, still not realizing the halfling's honest recognition of the beast. "Good-bye, Regis. Take comfort in knowing that I shall remember this moment for the rest of my life!"

The panther flattened its ears and crouched lower, tamping down its back paws for better balance. Regis rushed to the door, though he had no doubt that it was locked, and Guenhwyvar leaped, impossibly quick and accurate. Regis barely realized that the cat was upon him.

Pasha Pook's ecstacy, though, proved short-lived. He jumped from his chair, hoping for a better view of the action, as Guenhwyvar buried Regis. Then the cat vanished, slowly fading away.

The halfling, too, was gone.

"What?" Pook cried. "That is it? No blood?" He spun on LaValle. "Is that how the thing kills?"

The wizard's horrified expression told Pook a different tale. Suddenly the guildmaster recognized the truth of Regis's banterings with the cat. "It took him away!" Pook roared. He rushed around the side of the chair and pushed his face into LaValle's. "Where? Tell me!"

LaValle nearly fell from his trembling. "Not possible." He gasped. "The cat must obey its master, the possessor."

"Regis knew the cat!" Pook cried.

"Impossible loyalties," LaValle replied, truly dumbfounded.

Pook composed himself and settled back in his chair. "Where did you get it?" he asked LaValle.

"Entreri," the wizard replied immediately, not daring to hesitate.

Pook scratched his chin. "Entreri," he echoed. The pieces started failing into place. Pook understood Entreri well enough to know that the assassin would not give away so valuable an item without getting something in return. "It belonged to one of the halfling's friends," Pook reasoned, remembering Regis's references to the cat's true master.

"I did not ask," replied LaValle.

"You did not have to ask!" Pook shot back. "It belonged to one of the halfling's friends—perhaps one of those Oberon spoke of. Yes. And Entreri gave it to you in exchange for . . ." He tossed a wicked look LaValle's way.

"Where is the pirate, Pinochet?" he asked slyly.

LaValle nearly fainted, caught in a web that promised death wherever he turned.

"Enough said," said Pook, understanding everything from the wizard's paled expression "Ah, Entreri," he mused, "ever you prove a headache, however well you serve me. And you," he breathed at LaValle. "Where have they gone?"

LaValle shook his head. "The cat's plane," he blurted, "the only possibility."

"And can the cat return to this world?"

"Only if summoned by the possessor of the statue."

Pook pointed to the statue lying on the floor in front of the door. "Get that cat back," he ordered. LaValle rushed for the figurine.

"No, wait." Pook reconsidered. "Let me first have a cage built for it. Guenhwyvar will be mine in time. She will learn discipline."

LaValle continued over and picked up the statue, not really knowing where to begin. Pook grabbed him as he passed the throne.

"But the halfling," Pook growled, pressing his nose flat against LaValle's.

"On your life, wizard, get that halfling back to me!"

Pook shoved LaValle back and headed for the door to the lower levels. He would have to open some eyes in the streets, to learn what Artemis Entreri was up to and to learn more about those friends of the halfling, whether they still lived or had died in Asavir's Channel.

If it had been anyone other than Entreri, Pook would have put his ruby pendant to use, but that option was not feasible with the dangerous assassin.

Pook growled to himself as he exited the chamber. He had hoped, on Entreri's return, that he would never have to take this route again, but with LaValle so obviously tied into the assassin's games, Pook's only option was Rassiter.

⚔ ⚔ ⚔ ⚔ ⚔

"You want him removed?" the wererat asked, liking the beginnings of this assignment as well as any that Pook had ever given him.

"Do not flatter yourself," Pook shot back. "Entreri is none of your affair, Rassiter, and beyond your power."

"You underestimate the strength of my guild."

"You underestimate the assassin's network—probably numbering many of those you errantly call comrades," Pook warned. "I want no war within my guild."

"Then what?" the wererat snapped in obvious disappointment.

At Rassiter's antagonistic tone, Pook began to finger the ruby pendant hanging around his neck. He could put Rassiter under its enchantment, he knew, but he preferred not to. Charmed individuals never performed as well as those acting of their own desires, and if Regis's friends had truly escaped Pinochet, Rassiter and his cronies would have to be at their very best to defeat them.

"Entreri may have been followed to Calimport," Pook explained. "Friends of the halfling, I believe, and dangerous to our guild."

Rassiter leaned forward, feigning surprise. Of course, the wererat had already learned from Dondon of the Northerners' approach.

"They will be in the city soon," Pook continued. "You haven't much time."

They are already here, Rassiter answered silently, trying to hide his smile. "You want them captured?"

"Eliminated," Pook corrected. "This group is too mighty. No chances."

"Eliminated," Rassiter echoed. "Ever my preference."

Pook couldn't help but shudder. "Inform me when the task is complete," he said, heading for the door.

Rassiter silently laughed at his master's back. "Ah, Pook," he whispered as the guildmaster left, "how little you know of my influences." The wererat rubbed his hands together in anticipation. The night grew long, and the Northerners would soon be on the streets—where Dondon would find them.

18
DOUBLE TALKER

Perched in his favorite corner, across Rogues Circle from the Spitting Camel, Dondon watched as the elf, the last of the four, moved into the inn to join his friends. The halfling pulled out a little pocket mirror to check his disguise—all the dirt and scruff marks seemed in the right places; his clothes were far too large, like those a waif would pull off an unconscious drunk in an ally; and his hair was appropriately tousled and snarled, as if it hadn't been combed in years.

Dondon looked longingly to the moon and inspected his chin with his fingers. Still hairless but tingling, he thought. The halfling took a deep breath, and then another, and fought back the lycanthropic urges. In the year he had joined Rassiter's ranks, he had learned to sublimate those fiendish urges fairly well, but he hoped that he could finish his business quickly this night. The moon was especially bright.

People of the street, locals, gave an approving wink as they passed the halfling, knowing the master con artist to be on the prowl once more. With his reputation, Dondon had long become ineffective against the regulars of Calimport's streets, but those characters knew enough to keep their mouths shut about the halfling to strangers. Dondon always managed to surround himself with the toughest rogues of the city, and blowing his cover to an intended victim was a serious crime indeed!

The halfling leaned back against the corner of a building to observe as the four friends emerged from the Spitting Camel a short time later.

For Drizzt and his companions, Calimport's night proved as unnatural as the sights they had witnessed during the day. Unlike the northern cities, where nighttime activities were usually relegated to the many taverns, the bustle of Calimport's streets only increased after the sun went down. Even the lowly peasants took on a different demeanor, suddenly mysterious and sinister.

The only section of the lane that remained uncluttered by the hordes was the area in front of the unmarked structure on the back side of the circle: the guildhouse. As in the daylight, bums sat against the building's walls on either side of its single door, but now there were two more guards farther off to either side.

"If Regis is in that place, we've got to find our way in," Catti-brie observed.

"No doubt that Regis is in there," Drizzt replied. "Our hunt should start with Entreri."

"We've come to find Regis," Catti-brie reminded him, casting a disappointed glance his way. Drizzt quickly clarified his answer to her satisfaction.

"The road to Regis lies through the assassin," he said. "Entreri has seen to that. You heard his words at the chasm of Garumn's Gorge. Entreri will not allow us to find Regis until we have dealt with him."

Catti-brie could not deny the drow's logic. When Entreri had snatched Regis from them back in Mithral Hall, he had gone to great pains to bait Drizzt into the chase, as though his capture of Regis was merely part of a game he was playing against Drizzt.

"Where to begin?" Bruenor huffed in frustration. He had expected the street to be quieter, offering them a better opportunity to scope out the task before them. He had hoped that they might even complete their business that very night.

"Right where we are," Drizzt replied, to Bruenor's amazement.

"Learn the smell of the street," the drow explained. "Watch the moves of its people and hear their sounds. Prepare your mind for what is to come."

"Time, elf!" Bruenor growled back. "Me heart tells me that Rumble-belly's liken to have a whip at his back as we stand here smelling the stinkin' street!"

"We need not seek Entreri," Wulfgar cut in, following Drizzt's line of thinking. "The assassin will find us."

Almost on cue, as if Wulfgar's statement had reminded them all of their dangerous surroundings, the four of them turned their eyes outward from their little huddle and watched the bustle of the street around them. Dark eyes peered at them from every corner; each person that ambled past cast them a sidelong glance. Calimport was not unaccustomed to strangers—it was a trading port, after all—but these four would stand out clearly on the streets of any city in the Realms. Recognizing their vulnerability, Drizzt decided to get them moving. He started off down Rogues Circle, motioning for the others to follow.

Before Wulfgar, at the tail of the forming line, had even taken a step, however, a childish voice called out to him from the shadows of the Spitting Camel.

"Hey," it beckoned, "are you looking for a hit?"

Wulfgar, not understanding, moved a bit closer and peered into the gloom. There stood Dondon, seeming a young, disheveled human boy.

"What're yer fer?" Bruenor asked, moving beside Wulfgar.

Wulfgar pointed to the corner.

"What're yer fer?" Bruenor asked again, now targeting the diminutive, shadowy figure.

"Looking for a hit?" Dondon reiterated, moving out from the gloom.

"Bah!" Bruenor snorted, waving his hand "Just a boy. Get ye gone, little one. We've no time for play!" He grabbed Wulfgar's arm and turned away.

"I can set you up," Dondon said after them.

Bruenor kept right on walking, Wulfgar beside him, but now Drizzt had stopped, noticing his companions' delay, and had heard the boy's last statement.

"Just a boy!" Bruenor explained to the drow as he approached.

"A street boy," Drizzt corrected, stepping around Bruenor and Wulfgar and starting back, "with eyes and ears that miss little."

"How can you set us up?" Drizzt whispered to Dondon while moving close to the building, out of sight of the too curious hordes.

Dondon shrugged. "There is plenty to steal; a whole bunch of merchants came in today. What are you looking for?"

Bruenor, Wulfgar, and Catti-brie took up defensive positions around Drizzt and the boy, their eyes outward to the streets but their ears trained on the suddenly interesting conversation.

Drizzt crouched low and led Dondon's gaze with his own toward the building at the end of the circle.

"Pook's house," Dondon remarked offhandedly. "Toughest house in Calimport."

"But it has a weakness," Drizzt prompted.

"They all do," Dondon replied calmly, playing perfectly the role of a cocky street survivor.

"Have you ever been in there?"

"Maybe I have."

"Have you ever seen a hundred gold pieces?"

Dondon let his eyes light up, and he purposely and pointedly shifted his weight from one foot to the other.

"Get him back in the rooms," Catti-brie said. "Ye be drawing too many looks out here."

Dondon readily agreed, but he shot Drizzt a warning in the form of an icy stare and proclaimed, "I can count to a hundred!"

When they got back to the room, Drizzt and Bruenor fed Dondon a steady stream of coins while the halfling laid out the way to a secret back entrance to the guildhouse. "Even the thieves," Dondon proclaimed, "do not know of it!"

The friends gathered closely, eager for the details.

Dondon made the whole operation sound easy.

Too easy.

Drizzt rose and turned away, hiding his chuckle from the informant. Hadn't they just been talking about Entreri making contact? Barely minutes before this enlightening boy so conveniently arrived to guide them.

"Wulfgar, take off his shoes," Drizzt said. His three friends turned to him curiously. Dondon squirmed in his chair.

"His shoes," Drizzt said again, turning back and pointing to Dondon's feet. Bruenor, so long a friend of a halfling, caught the drow's reasoning and didn't wait for Wulfgar to respond. The dwarf grabbed at Dondon's left boot and pulled it off, revealing a thick patch of foot hair—the foot of a halfling.

Dondon shrugged helplessly and sank back in his chair. The meeting was taking the exact course that Entreri had predicted.

"He said he could set us up," Catti-brie remarked sarcastically, twisting Dondon's words into a more sinister light.

"Who sent ye?" Bruenor growled.

"Entreri," Wulfgar answered for Dondon. "He works for Entreri, sent here to lead us into a trap." Wulfgar leaned over Dondon, blocking out the candlelight with his huge frame.

Bruenor pushed the barbarian aside and took his place. With his boyish looks, Wulfgar simply could not be as imposing as the pointy-nosed, red-bearded, fire-eyed dwarven fighter with the battered helm. "So, ye little sneakster," Bruenor growled into Dondon's face. "Now we deal for yer stinkin' tongue! Wag it the wrong way, and I'll be cutting it out!"

Dondon paled—he had that act down pat—and began to tremble visibly.

"Calm yerself," Catti-brie said to Bruenor, playing out a lighter role this time. "Suren ye've scared the little one enough."

Bruenor shoved her back, turning enough away from Dondon to toss her a wink. "Scared him?" the dwarf balked. He brought his axe up to his shoulder. "More than scarin' him's in me plans!"

"Wait! Wait!" Dondon begged, groveling as only a halfling could. "I was just doing what the assassin made me do, and paid me to do."

"You know Entreri?" Wulfgar asked.

"Everybody knows Entreri," Dondon replied. "And in Calimport, everybody heeds Entreri's commands!"

"Forget Entreri!" Bruenor growled in his face. "Me axe'll stop that one from hurting yerself."

"You think you can kill Entreri?" Dondon shot back, though he knew the true meaning of Bruenor's claim.

"Entreri can't hurt a corpse," Bruenor replied grimly. "Me axe'll beat him to yer head!"

"It is you he wants," Dondon said to Drizzt, seeking a calmer situation.

Drizzt nodded, but remained silent. Something came across as out of place in this out of place meeting.

"I choose no sides," Dondon pleaded to Bruenor, seeing no relief forthcoming from Drizzt. "I only do what I must to survive."

"And to survive now, ye're going to tell us the way in," Bruenor said. "The safe way in."

"The place is a fortress," Dondon shrugged. "No way is safe." Bruenor started slipping closer, his scowl deepening.

"But, if I had to try," the halfling blurted, "I would try through the sewers."

Bruenor looked around at his friends.

"It seems correct," Wulfgar remarked.

Drizzt studied the halfling a moment longer, searching for some clue in Dondon's darting eyes. "It is correct," the drow said at length.

"So he saved his neck," said Catti-brie, "but what are we to do with him? Take him along?"

"Ayuh," said Bruenor with a sly look. "He'll be leading!"

"No," replied Drizzt, to the amazement of his companions. "The halfling did as we bade. Let him leave."

"And go straight off to tell Entreri what has happened?" Wulfgar said.

"Entreri would not understand," Drizzt replied. He looked Dondon in the eye, giving no indication to the halfling that he had figured out his little ploy within a ploy. "Nor would he forgive."

"Me heart says we take him," Bruenor remarked.

"Let him go," Drizzt said calmly. "Trust me."

Bruenor snorted and dropped his axe to his side, grumbling as he moved to open the door. Wulfgar and Catti-brie exchanged concerned glances but stepped out of the way.

Dondon didn't hesitate, but Bruenor stepped in front of him as he reached the door. "If I see yer face again," the dwarf threatened, "or any face ye might be wearin', I'll chop ye down!"

Dondon slipped around and backed into the hall, never taking his eyes off the dangerous dwarf, then he darted down the hall, shaking his head at how perfectly Entreri had described the encounter, at how well the assassin knew those friends, particularly the drow.

Suspecting the truth about the entire encounter, Drizzt understood that Bruenor's final threat carried little weight to the wily halfling. Dondon had faced them down through both lies without the slightest hint of a slip.

But Drizzt nodded approvingly as Bruenor, still scowling, turned back into the room, for the drow also knew that the threat, if nothing else, had made Bruenor feel more secure.

On Drizzt's suggestion, they all settled down for some sleep. With the clamor of the streets, they would never be able to slip unnoticed into one of the sewer grates. But the crowds would likely thin out as the night waned and the guard changed from the dangerous rogues of evening to the peasants of the hot day.

Drizzt alone did not find sleep. He sat propped by the door of the room, listening for sounds of any approach and lulled into meditations by the rhythmic breathing of his companions. He looked down at the mask hanging around his neck. So simple a lie, and he could walk freely throughout the world.

But would he then be trapped within the web of his own deception? What freedom could he find in denying the truth about himself?

Drizzt looked over at Catti-brie, peacefully slumped in the room's single bed, and smiled. There was indeed wisdom in innocence, a vein of truth in the idealism of untainted perceptions.

He could not disappoint her.

Drizzt sensed a deepening of the outside gloom. The moon had set. He moved to the room's window and peeked out into the street. Still the night people wandered, but they were fewer now, and the night neared its end. Drizzt roused his companions; they could not afford any more delays. They stretched away their weariness, checked their gear, and moved back down to the street.

Rogues Circle was lined with several iron sewer grates that looked as though they were designed more to keep the filthy things of the sewers underground than as drains for the sudden waters of the rare but violent rainstorms that hit the city. The friends chose one in the alley beside their inn, out of the main way of the street but close enough to the guildhouse that they could probably find their underground way without too much trouble.

"The boy can lift it," Bruenor remarked, waving Wulfgar to the spot. Wulfgar bent low and grasped the iron.

"Not yet," Drizzt whispered, glancing around for suspicious eyes. He motioned Catti-brie to the end of the ally, back along Rogues Circle, and he darted off down the darker side. When he was satisfied that all was clear, he waved back to Bruenor. The dwarf looked to Catti-brie, who nodded her approval.

"Lift it, boy," Bruenor said, "and be quiet about it!"

Wulfgar grasped the iron tightly and sucked in a deep draft of air for balance. His huge arms pumped red with blood as he heaved, and a grunt escaped his lips. Even so, the grate resisted his tugging.

Wulfgar looked at Bruenor in disbelief, then redoubled his efforts, his face now flushing red. The grate groaned in protest, but came up only a few inches from the ground.

"Suren somethings holdin' it down," Bruenor said, leaning over to inspect it.

A "clink" of snapping chain was the dwarf's only warning as the grate broke free, sending Wulfgar sprawling backward. The lifting iron clipped Bruenor's forehead, knocking his helmet off and dropping him on the seat of his pants. Wulfgar, still clutching the grate, crashed heavily and loudly into the wall of the inn.

"Ye blasted, foolheaded . . ." Bruenor started to grumble, but Drizzt and Catti-brie, rushing to his aid, quickly reminded him of the secrecy of their mission.

"Why would they chain a sewer grate?" Catti-brie asked.

Wulfgar dusted himself off. "From the inside," he added. "It seems that something down there wants to keep the city out."

"We shall know soon enough," Drizzt remarked. He dropped down beside the open hole, slipping his legs in. "Prepare a torch," he said. "I will summon you if all is clear."

Catti-brie caught the eager gleam in the drow's eyes and looked at him with concern.

"For Regis," Drizzt assured her, "and only for Regis." Then he was gone, into the blackness. Black like the lightless tunnels of his homeland.

The other three heard a slight splash as he touched down, then all was quiet.

Many anxious moments passed. "Put a light to the torch," Bruenor whispered to Wulfgar.

Catti-brie caught Wulfgar's arm to stop him. "Faith," she said to Bruenor.

"Too long," the dwarf muttered. "Too quiet."

Catti-brie held on to Wulfgar's arm for another second, until Drizzt's soft voice drifted up to them. "Clear," the drow said. "Come down quickly."

Bruenor took the torch from Wulfgar. "Come last," he said, "and slide the grate back behind ye. No need in tellin' the world where we went!"

✕ ✕ ✕ ✕ ✕

The first thing the companions noticed when the torchlight entered the sewer was the chain that had held the grate down. It was fairly new, without doubt, and fastened to a locking box constructed on the sewer's wall.

"Me thinking's that we're not alone," Bruenor whispered.

Drizzt glanced around, sharing the dwarf's uneasiness. He dropped the mask from his face, a drow again in an environ suited for a drow. "I will lead," he said, "at the edge of the light. Keep ready." He padded away, picking his silent steps along the edge of the murky stream of water that rolled slowly down the center of the tunnel.

Bruenor came next with the torch, then Catti-brie and Wulfgar. The barbarian had to stoop low to keep his head clear of the slimy ceiling. Rats squeaked and scuttled away from the strange light, and darker things took silent refuge under the shield of the water. The tunnel meandered this way and that, and a maze of side passages opened up every few feet. Sounds of trickling water only worsened the confusion, leading the friends for a moment, then coming louder at their side, then louder still from across the way.

Bruenor shook the diversions clear of his thoughts, ignored the muck and the fetid stench, and concentrated on keeping his track straight behind the shadowy figure that darted in and out at the front edge of his torchlight. He turned a confusing, multicornered intersection and caught sight of the figure suddenly off to his side.

Even as he turned to follow, he realized that Drizzt still had to be up front.

"Ready!" Bruenor called, tossing the torch to a dry spot beside him and taking up his axe and shield. His alertness saved them all, for only a split second later, not one, but two cloaked forms emerged from the side tunnel, swords raised and sharp teeth gleaming under twitching whiskers.

They were man-sized, wearing the clothes of men and holding swords. In their other form, they were indeed humans and not always vile, but on the nights of the bright moon they took on their darker form, the lycanthrope side. They moved like men but were mantled with the trappings—elongated snout, bristled brown fur, and pink tail—of sewer rats.

Lining them up over the top of Bruenor's helm, Catti-brie launched the first strike. The silvery flash of her killing arrow illuminated the side tunnel like a lightning bolt, showing many more sinister figures making their way toward the friends.

A splash from behind caused Wulfgar to spin about to face a rushing gang of the ratmen. He dug his heels into the mud as well as he could and slapped Aegis-fang to a ready position.

"They was layin' on us, elf!" Bruenor shouted.

Drizzt had already come to that conclusion. At the dwarf's first shout, he had slipped farther from the torch to use the advantage of darkness. Turning a bend brought him face to face with two figures, and he guessed their sinister nature before he ever got the blue light of Twinkle high enough to see their furry brows.

The wererats, though, certainly did not expect what they found standing ready before them. Perhaps it was because they believed that their enemies were solely in the area with the torchlight, but more likely it was the black skin of a drow elf that sent them back on their heels.

Drizzt didn't miss the opportunity, slicing them down in a single flurry before they ever recovered from their shock. The drow then melted again into the blackness, seeking a back route to ambush the ambushers.

Wulfgar kept his attackers at bay with long sweeps of Aegis-fang. The hammer blew aside any wererat that ventured too near, and smashed away chunks of the muck on the sewer walls every time it completed an arc. But as the wererats came to understand the power of the mighty barbarian, and came in at him with less enthusiasm, the best that Wulfgar could accomplish was a stalemate—a deadlock that would only last as long as the energy in his huge arms.

Behind Wulfgar, Bruenor and Catti-brie fared better. Catti-brie's magical bow—loosing arrows over the dwarf's head—decimated the ranks of the approaching wererats, and those few that reached Bruenor, off-balance and ducking the deadly arrows of the woman behind him, proved easy prey for the dwarf.

But the odds were fully against the friends, and they knew that one mistake would cost them dearly.

The wererats, hissing and spitting, backed away from Wulfgar. Realizing that he had to initiate more decisive fighting, the barbarian strode forward.

The ratmen parted ranks suddenly, and down the tunnel, at the very edge of the torchlight, Wulfgar saw one of them level a heavy crossbow and fire.

Instinctively the big man flattened against the wall, and he was agile enough to get out of the missile's path, but Catti-brie, behind him and facing the other way, never saw the bolt coming.

She felt a sudden searing burst of pain, then the warmth of her blood pouring down the side of her head. Blackness swirled about the edges of her vision, and she crumbled against the wall.

⚔ ⚔ ⚔ ⚔

Drizzt slipped through the dark passages as silently as death. He kept Twinkle sheathed, fearing its revealing light, and led the way with his other magical blade. He was in a maze, but figured that he could pick his route well enough to rejoin his friends. Every tunnel he picked, though, lit up at its other end with torchlight as still more wererats made their way to the fighting.

The darkness was certainly ample for the stealthy drow to remain concealed, but Drizzt got the uneasy feeling that his moves were being monitored, even anticipated. Dozens of passages opened up all around him, but his options came fewer and fewer as wererats appeared at every turn. The circuit to his friends was growing wider with each step, but Drizzt quickly realized that he had no choice but to go forward. Wererats had filled the main tunnel behind him, following his route.

Drizzt stopped in the shadows of one dark nook and surveyed the area about him, recounting the distance he had covered and noting the passages behind him that now flickered in torchlight. Apparently there weren't as many wererats as he had originally figured; those appearing at every turn were probably the same groups from the previous tunnels, running parallel to Drizzt and turning into each new passage as Drizzt came upon it at the other end.

But the revelation of wererat numbers came as little comfort to Drizzt. He had no doubts to his suspicions now. He was being herded.

⚔ ⚔ ⚔ ⚔

Wulfgar turned and started toward his fallen love, his Catti-brie, but the wererats came in on him immediately. Fury now drove the mighty barbarian. He tore into his attackers' ranks, smashing and squashing them with bone-splitting chops of his warhammer or reaching out with a bare hand to twist the neck of any who had slipped in beside him. The ratmen managed a few retreating stabs, but nicks and little wounds wouldn't slow the enraged barbarian.

He stomped on the fallen as he passed, grinding his booted heels into their dying bodies. Other wererats scrambled in terror to get out of his way.

At the end of their line, the crossbowman struggled to reload his weapon, a job made more difficult by his inability to keep his eyes off the spectacle of the approaching barbarian and made doubly difficult by his knowledge that he was the focus of the powerful man's rage.

Bruenor, with the wererat ranks dissipated in front of him, had more time to tend to Catti-brie. He bent over the young woman, his face ashen as he pulled her thick mane of auburn hair, thicker now with the wetness of her blood, from her fair face.

Catti-brie looked up at him through stunned eyes. "But an inch more, and me life'd be at its end," she said with a wink and a smile.

Bruenor scrambled to inspect the wound, and found, to his relief, that his daughter was correct in her observations. The quarrel had gouged her wickedly, but it was only a grazing shot.

"I'm all right," Catti-brie insisted, starting to rise.

Bruenor held her down. "Not yet," he whispered.

The fight's not done," Catti-brie replied, still trying to plant her feet under her. Bruenor led her gaze down the tunnel, to Wulfgar and the bodies piling all about him.

"There's our chance," he chuckled "Let the boy think ye're down."

Catti-brie bit her lip in astonishment of the scene. A dozen ratmen were down and still Wulfgar pounded through, his hammer tearing away those unfortunates who couldn't flee out of his way.

Then a noise from the other direction turned Catti-brie away. With her bow down, the wererats from the front had returned.

"They're mine," Bruenor told her. "Keep yerself down!"

"If ye get into trouble—"

"If I need ye, then be there," Bruenor agreed, "but for now, keep yerself down! Give the boy something to fight for!"

ⅹ ⅹ ⅹ ⅹ ⅹ

Drizzt tried to double back along his route, but the ratmen quickly closed off all of the tunnels. Soon his options had been cut down to one, a wide, dry side passage moving in the opposite direction from where he had hoped to go.

The ratmen were closing on him fast, and in the main tunnel he would have to fight them off from several different directions. He slipped into the passage and flattened against the wall.

Two ratmen shuffled up to the tunnel entrance and peered into the gloom, calling a third, with a torch, to join them. The light they found was not the yellow flicker of a torch, but a sudden line of blue as Twinkle came free of its scabbard. Drizzt was upon them before they could raise their weapons in defense, thrusting a blade clean through one wererat's chest and spinning his second blade in an arc across the other's neck.

The torchlight enveloped them as they fell, leaving the drow standing there, revealed both his blades dripping blood. The nearest wererats shrieked; some even dropped their weapons and ran, but more of them came up, blocking all of the tunnel entrances in the area, and the advantage of sheer numbers soon gave the ratmen a measure of confidence. Slowly, looking to each other for support with every step, they closed in on Drizzt.

Drizzt considered rushing a single, group, hoping to cut through their ranks and be out of the ring of the trap, but the ratmen were at least two deep at every passage, three or even four deep at some. Even with his, skill and agility, Drizzt could never get through them fast enough to avoid attacks at his back.

He darted back into the side passage and summoned a globe of darkness inside its entrance, then he sprinted beyond the area of the globe to take up a ready position just behind it.

The ratmen, quickening their charge as Drizzt disappeared back into the tunnel, stopped short when they turned into the area of unbreakable darkness. At first, they thought that their torches must have gone out, but so deep was the gloom that they soon realized the truth of the drow's spell. They regrouped out in the main tunnel, then came back in, cautiously.

Even Drizzt, with his night eyes, could not see into the pitch blackness of his spell, but positioned clear of the other side, he did make out a sword tip, and then another, leading the two front ratmen down the passage. They hadn't even broken from the darkness when the drow struck, slapping their swords away and reversing the angle of his cuts to drive his scimitars up the lengths of their arms and into their bodies. Their agonized screams sent the other ratmen scrambling back out into the main corridor, and gave Drizzt another moment to consider his position.

✕ ✕ ✕ ✕ ✕

The crossbowman knew his time was up when the last two of his companions shoved him aside in their desperate flight from the enraged giant. He at last fumbled the quarrel back into position and brought his bow to bear.

But Wulfgar was too close. The barbarian grabbed the crossbow as it swung about and tore it from the wererat's hands with such ferocity that it broke apart when it slammed into the wall. The wererat meant to flee, but the sheer intensity of Wulfgar's glare froze him in place. He watched, horrified, as Wulfgar clasped Aegis-fang in both hands.

Wulfgar's strike was impossibly fast. The wererat never comprehended that the death blow had even begun. He only felt a sudden explosion on top of his head.

The ground rushed up to meet him; he was dead before he ever splatted into the muck. Wulfgar, his eyes rimmed with tears, hammered on the wretched creature viciously until its body was no more than a lump of undefinable waste.

Spattered with blood and muck and black water, Wulfgar finally slumped back against the wall. As he released himself from the consuming rage, he heard the fighting behind and spun to find Bruenor beating back two of the ratmen, with several more lined up behind them.

And behind the dwarf, Catti-brie lay still against the wall. The sight refueled Wulfgar's fire. "Tempus!" he roared to his god of battle, and he pounded through the muck, back down the tunnel. The wererats facing Bruenor tripped over themselves trying to get away, giving the dwarf the opportunity to cut down two more of them—he was happy to oblige. They fled back into the maze of tunnels.

Wulfgar meant to pursue them, to hunt each of them down and vent his vengeance, but Catti-brie rose to intercept him. She leaped into his chest as he skidded in surprise, wrapped her arms around his neck, and kissed him more passionately than he had ever imagined he could be kissed.

He held her at arm's length, gawking and stuttering in confusion until a joyful smile spread wide and took all other emotions out of his face. Then he hugged her back for another kiss.

Bruenor pulled them apart. "The elf?" he reminded them. He scooped up the torch, now halfcovered with mud and burning low, and led them off down the tunnel.

They didn't dare turn into one of the many side passages, for fear of getting lost. The main corridor was the swiftest route, wherever it might take them, and they could only hope to catch a glimpse or hear a sound that would direct them to Drizzt.

Instead they found a door.

"The guild?" Catti-brie whispered.

"What else could it be?" Wulfgar replied." Only a thieves' house would keep a door to the sewers."

Above the door, in a secret cubby, Entreri eyed the three friends curiously. He had known that something was amiss when the wererats had begun to gather in the sewers earlier that night. Entreri had hoped they would move out into the city, but it had soon become apparent that the wererats meant to stay.

Then these three showed up at the door without the drow.

Entreri put his chin in his palm and considered his next course of action.

Bruenor studied the door curiously. On it, at about eye level for a human, was nailed a small wooden box. Having no time to play with riddles, the dwarf boldly reached up and tore the box free, bringing it down and peeking over its rim.

The dwarf's face twisted with even more confusion when he saw inside. He shrugged and held the box out to Wulfgar and Catti-brie.

Wulfgar was not so confused. He had seen a similar item before, back on the docks of Baldur's Gate. Another gift from Artemis Entreri—another halfling's finger.

"Assassin!" he roared, and he slammed his shoulder into the door. It broke free of its hinges, and Wulfgar stumbled into the room beyond, holding the door out in front of him. Before he could even toss it aside, he heard the crash behind him and realized how foolish the move had been. He had fallen right into Entreri's trap.

A portcullis had dropped in the entranceway, separating him from Bruenor and Catti-brie.

⚔ ⚔ ⚔ ⚔ ⚔

The tips of long spears led the wererats back through Drizzt's globe of darkness. The drow still managed to take one of the lead ratmen down, but he was backed up by the press of the group that followed. He gave ground freely, fighting off their thrusts and jabs with defensive swordwork. Whenever he saw an opening, he was quick enough to strike a blade home.

Then a singular odor overwhelmed even the stench of the sewer. A syrupy sweet smell that rekindled distant memories in the drow. The ratmen pressed him on even harder, as if the scent had renewed their desire to fight.

Drizzt remembered. In Menzoberranzan, the city of his birth, some drow elves had kept as pets creatures that exuded such an odor. Sundews, these monstrous beasts were called, lumpy masses of raglike, sticky tendrils that simply engulfed and dissolved anything that came too near.

Now Drizzt fought for every step. He had indeed been herded, to face a horrid death or perhaps to be captured, for the sundew devoured its victims so very slowly, and certain liquids could break its hold.

Drizzt felt a flutter and glanced back over his shoulder. The sundew was barely ten feet away, already reaching out with a hundred sticky fingers.

Drizzt's scimitars weaved and dived, spun and cut, in as magnificent a dance as he had ever fought. One wererat was hit fifteen times before it even realized that the first blow had struck home.

But there were simply too many of the ratmen for Drizzt to hold his ground, and the sight of the sundew urged them on bravely.

Drizzt felt the tickle of the flicking tendrils only inches from his back. He had no room to maneuver now; the spears would surely drive him into the monster.

Drizzt smiled, and the eager fires burned brighter in his eyes. "Is this how it ends?" he whispered aloud. The sudden burst of his laughter startled the wererats.

With Twinkle leading the way, Drizzt spun on his heels and dived at the heart of the sundew.

19

TRICKS AND TRAPS

Wulfgar found himself in a square, unadorned room of worked stone. Two torches burned low in wall sconces, revealing another door before him, across from the portcullis. He tossed aside the broken door and turned back to his friends. "Guard my back," he told Catti-brie, but she had already figured her part out and had brought her bow up level with the door across the room.

Wulfgar rubbed his hands together in preparation for his attempt to lift the portcullis. It was a massive piece indeed, but the barbarian did not think it beyond his strength. He grasped the iron, then fell back, dismayed, even before he had attempted to lift.

The bars had been greased.

"Entreri, or I'm a bearded gnome," Bruenor grumbled. "Ye put yer face in deep, boy."

"How are we to get him out?" Catti-brie asked.

Wulfgar looked back over his shoulder at the unopened door. He knew that they could accomplish nothing by standing there, and he feared that the noise of the dropping portcullis must have attracted some attention—attention that could only mean danger for his friends.

"Ye can't be thinking to go deeper," Catti-brie protested.

"What choice have I?" Wulfgar replied. "Perhaps there is a crank in there."

"More likely an assassin," Bruenor retorted, "but ye have to try it."

Catti-brie pulled her bowstring tight as Wulfgar moved to the door. He tried the handle but found it locked. He looked back to his friends and shrugged, then spun and kicked with his heavy boot. The wood shivered and split apart, revealing yet another room, this one dark.

"Get a torch," Bruenor told him.

Wulfgar hesitated. Something didn't feel right, or smell right. His sixth sense, that warrior instinct, told him he would not find the second room as empty as the first, but with no other place to go, he moved for one of the torches.

Intent on the situation within the room, Bruenor and Catti-brie did not notice the dark figure drop from the concealed cubby on the wall a short distance down the tunnel. Entreri considered the two of them for a moment. He could take them out easily, and perhaps quietly, but the assassin turned away and disappeared into the darkness.

He had already picked his target.

⚔ ⚔ ⚔ ⚔ ⚔

Rassiter stooped over the two bodies lying in front of the side passage. Reverting halfway through the transformation between rat and human, they had died in the excruciating agony that only a lycanthrope could know. Just like the ones farther back down the main tunnel, these had been slashed and nipped with expert precision, and if the line of bodies didn't mark the path clearly enough, the globe of darkness hanging in the side passage certainly did. It appeared to Rassiter that his trap had worked, though the price had certainly been high.

He dropped to the lower corner of the wall and crept along, nearly tripping over still more bodies of his guildmates as he came through the other side.

The wererat shook his head in disbelief as he moved down the tunnel, stepping over a wererat corpse every few feet. How many had the master swordsman killed?

"A drow!" Rassiter balked in sudden understanding as he turned the final bend. Bodies of his comrades were piled deep there, but Rassiter looked beyond them. He would willingly pay such a price for the prize he saw before him, for now he had the dark warrior in hand, a drow elf for a prisoner! He would gain Pasha Pook's favor and rise above Artemis Entreri once and for all.

At the end of the passage, Drizzt leaned silently against the sundew, draped by a thousand tendrils. He still held his two scimitars, but his arms hung limply at his sides and his head drooped down, his lavender eyes closed.

The wererat moved down the passage cautiously, hoping the drow was not already dead. He inspected his waterskin, filled with vinegar, and hoped he had brought enough to dissolve the sundew's hold and free the drow. Rassiter dearly wanted this trophy alive.

Pook would appreciate the present more that way.

The wererat reached out with his sword to prod at the drow, but recoiled in pain as a dagger flashed by, slicing across his arm. He spun back around to see Artemis Entreri, his saber drawn and a murderous look in his dark eyes.

Rassiter found himself caught in his own trap; there was no other escape from the passage. He fell flat against the wall, clutching his bleeding arm, and started inching his way back up the passage.

Entreri followed the ratman's progress without a blink.

"Pook would never forgive you," Rassiter warned.

"Pook would never know," Entreri hissed back.

Terrified, Rassiter darted past the assassin, expecting a sword in his side as he passed. But Entreri cared nothing about Rassiter; his eyes had shifted down the passage to the specter of Drizzt Do'Urden, helpless and defeated.

Entreri moved to recover his jeweled dagger, undecided as to whether to cut the drow free or let him die a slow death in the sundew's clutches.

"And so you die," he whispered at length, wiping the slime from his dagger.

✕ ✕ ✕ ✕

With a torch out before him, Wulfgar gingerly stepped into the second room. Like the first, it was square and unadorned, but one side was blocked halfway across by a floor-to-ceiling screen. Wulfgar knew that danger lurked behind the screen, knew it to be a part of the trap Entreri had set out and into which he had blindly rushed.

He didn't have the time to berate himself for his lack of judgment. He positioned himself in the center of the room, still in sight of his friends, and laid the torch at his feet, clutching Aegis-fang in both hands.

But when the thing rushed out, the barbarian still found himself gawking, amazed.

Eight serpentlike heads interwove in a tantalizing dance, like the needles of frenzied women knitting at a single garment. Wulfgar saw no humor in the moment, though, for each mouth was filled with row upon row of razor-sharp teeth.

Catti-brie and Bruenor understood that Wulfgar was in trouble when they saw him shuffle back a step. They expected Entreri, or a host of soldiers, to confront him. Then the hydra crossed the open doorway.

"Wulfgar!" Catti-brie cried in dismay, loosing an arrow. The silver bolt blasted a deep hole into a serpentine neck, and the hydra roared in pain and turned one head to consider the stinging attackers from the side.

Seven other heads struck out at Wulfgar.

✕ ✕ ✕ ✕

"You disappoint me, drow," Entreri continued. I had thought you my equal, or nearly so. The bother, and risks, I took to guide you here so we could decide whose life was the lie! To prove to you that those emotions you cling to so dearly have no place in the heart of a true warrior.

"But now I see that I have wasted my efforts," the assassin lamented. "The question has already been decided, if it ever was a question. Never would I have fallen into such a trap!"

Drizzt peeked out from one half-opened eye and raised his head to meet

Entreri's gaze. "Nor would I," he said, shrugging off the limp tendrils of the dead sundew. "Nor would I!"

The wound became apparent in the monster when Drizzt moved out. With a single thrust, the drow had killed the sundew.

A smile burst across Entreri's face. "Well done!" he cried, readying his blades. "Magnificent!"

"Where is the halfling?" Drizzt snarled.

"This does not concern the halfling," Entreri replied, "or your silly toy, the panther."

Drizzt quickly sublimated the anger that twisted his face.

"Oh, they are alive," Entreri taunted, hoping to distract his enemy with anger. "Perhaps, though perhaps not."

Unbridled rage often aided warriors against lesser foes, but in an equal battle of skilled swordsmen, thrusts had to be measured and defenses could not be let down.

Drizzt came in with both blades thrusting. Entreri deflected them aside with his saber and countered with a jab of his dagger.

Drizzt twirled out of danger's way, coming around a full circle and slicing down with Twinkle. Entreri caught the weapon with his saber, so that the blades locked hilt to hilt and brought the combatants close.

"Did you receive my gift in Baldur's Gate?" the assassin chuckled.

Drizzt did not flinch. Regis and Guenhwyvar were out of his thoughts now. His focus was Artemis Entreri.

Only Artemis Entreri.

The assassin pressed on. "A mask?" he questioned with a wide smirk. "Put it on, drow. Pretend you are what you are not!"

Drizzt heaved suddenly, throwing Entreri back.

The assassin went with the move, just as happy to continue the battle from a distance. But when Entreri tried to catch himself, his foot hit a mud-slicked depression in the tunnel floor and he slipped to one knee.

Drizzt was on him in a flash, both scimitars wailing away. Entreri's hands moved equally fast, dagger and saber twisting and turning to parry and deflect. His head and shoulders bobbed wildly, and remarkably, he worked his foot back under him.

Drizzt knew that he had lost the advantage. Worse, the assault had left him in an awkward position with one shoulder too close to the wall. As Entreri started to rise, Drizzt jumped back.

"So easy?" Entreri asked him as they squared off again. "Do you think that I sought this fight for so long, only to die in its opening exchanges?"

"I do not figure anything where Artemis Entreri is concerned," Drizzt came back. "You are too foreign to me, assassin. I do not pretend to understand your motives, nor do I have any desire to learn of them."

"Motives?" Entreri balked. "I am a fighter—purely a fighter. I do not mix the calling of my life with lies of gentleness and love!" He held the saber and dagger out before him. "These are my only friends, and with them—"

"You are nothing," Drizzt cut in. "Your life is a wasted lie."

"A lie?" Entreri shot back. "You are the one who wears the mask, drow. You are the one who must hide."

Drizzt accepted the words with a smile. Only a few days before, they might have stung him, but now, after the insight Catti-brie had given him, they rang hollowly in Drizzt's ears. "You are the lie, Entreri," he replied calmly. "You are no more than a loaded crossbow, an unfeeling weapon, that will never know life." He started walking toward the assassin, jaw firm in the knowledge of what he must do.

Entreri strode in with equal confidence.

"Come and die, drow," he spat.

✕ ✕ ✕ ✕ ✕

Wulfgar backed quickly, snapping his warhammer back and forth in front of him to parry the hydra's dizzying attacks. He knew that he couldn't hold the incessant thing off for long. He had to find a way to strike back against its offensive fury.

But against the seven snapping maws, weaving a hypnotic dance and lunging out singly or all together, Wulfgar had no time to prepare an attack sequence.

With her bow, beyond the range of the heads, Catti-brie had more success. Tears rimmed her eyes in fear for Wulfgar, but she held them back with a grim determination not to surrender. Another arrow blasted into the lone head that had turned her way, scorching a hole right between the eyes. The head shuddered and jerked back, then dropped to the floor with a thud, quite dead.

The attack, or the pain from it, seemed to paralyze the rest of the hydra for just a second, and the desperate barbarian did not miss the opportunity. He rushed forward a step and slammed Aegis-fang with all of his might into the snout of another head, snapping it back. It, too, dropped lifelessly to the floor.

"Keep it in front of the door!" Bruenor called. "And don't ye be coming through without a shout. Suren the girl'd cut' ye down!"

If the hydra was a stupid beast, it at least understood hunting tactics. It turned its body at an angle to the open door, preventing any chance for Wulfgar to get by. Two heads were down, and another silver arrow, and then another, sizzled in, this time catching the bulk of the hydra's body. Wulfgar, working frantically and just finished with the furious battle against the wererats, was beginning to tire.

He missed the parry as one head came in, and powerful jaws closed around his arm, cutting gashes just below his shoulder.

The hydra attempted to shake its neck and tear the man's arm off, its usual tactic, but it had never encountered one of Wulfgar's strength before. The barbarian locked his arm tight against his side, grimacing away the pain, and held the hydra in place. With his free hand Wulfgar grasped Aegis-fang just under the hammer's head and jabbed the butt end into the hydra's eye. The beast loosened its grip and Wulfgar tore himself free and fell back, just in time to avoid five other snapping attacks.

He could still fight, but the wound would slow him even more.

"Wulfgar!" Catti-brie cried again, hearing his groan.

"Get out o' there, boy!" Bruenor yelled.

Wulfgar was already moving. He dived toward the back wall and rolled around the hydra. The two closest heads followed his movement and dipped in to snap him up.

Wulfgar rolled right to his feet and reversed his momentum, splitting one jaw wide open with a mighty chop. Catti-brie, witnessing Wulfgar's desperate flight, put an arrow into the other head's eye.

The hydra roared in agony and rage and spun about, now having four lifeless heads bouncing across the floor.

Wulfgar, backing across to the other side of the room, got an angle to see what lay behind the screen. "Another door!" he cried to his friends.

Catti-brie got in one more shot as the hydra crossed over to pursue Wulfgar. She and Bruenor heard the crack as the door split free of its hinges, then a sliding bang as yet another portcullis dropped behind the big man.

✕ ✕ ✕ ✕

Entreri carried the latest attack, whipping his saber across at Drizzt's neck while simultaneously thrusting low with his dagger. A daring move, and if the assassin had not been so skilled with his weapons, Drizzt would surely have found an opening to drive a blade through Entreri's heart. The drow had all he could handle, though, just raising one scimitar to block the saber and lowering the other to push the dagger aside.

Entreri went through a series of similar double attack routines, and Drizzt turned him away each, time, showing only one small cut on the shoulder before Entreri finally was forced to back away.

"First blood is mine," the assassin crowed. He ran a finger down the blade of his saber, pointedly showing the drow the red stain.

"Last blood counts for more," Drizzt retorted as he came in with blades leading. The scimitars cut at the assassin from impossible angles, one dipping at a shoulder, the other rising to find the ridge under the rib cage.

Entreri, like Drizzt, foiled the attacks with perfect parries.

✕ ✕ ✕ ✕

"Are ye alive, boy?" Bruenor called. The dwarf heard the renewed fighting back behind him in the corridors, to his relief, for the sound told him that Drizzt was still alive.

"I am safe," Wulfgar replied, looking around the new room he had entered. It was furnished with several chairs and one table which had been

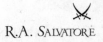

recently used, it appeared, for gambling. Wulfgar had no doubt now that he was under a building, most probably the thieves' guildhouse.

"The path is closed behind me," he called to his friends. "Find Drizzt and get back to the street. I will find my way to meet you there!"

"I'll not leave ye!" Catti-brie replied.

"I shall leave you," Wulfgar shot back.

Catti-brie glared at Bruenor. "Help him," she begged.

Bruenor's look was equally stern.

"We have no hope in staying where we are," Wulfgar called. "Surely I could not retrace my steps, even if I managed to lift this portcullis and defeat the hydra. Go, my love, and take heart that we shall meet again!"

"Listen to the boy," Bruenor said. "Yer heart's telling ye to stay, but ye'll be doing no favors for Wulfgar if ye follow that course. Ye have to trust in him."

Grease mixed with the blood on Catti-brie's head as she leaned heavily on the bars before her. Another demolished door sounded from deeper within the complex of rooms, like a hammer driving a stake into her heart. Bruenor grabbed her elbow gently. "Come, girl," he whispered. "The drow's afoot and needin' our help. Trust in Wulfgar."

Catti-brie pulled herself away and followed Bruenor down the tunnel.

⚔ ⚔ ⚔ ⚔ ⚔

Drizzt pressed the attack, studying the assassin's face as he went. He had succeeded in sublimating his hatred of the assassin, heeding Catti-brie's words and remembering the priorities of the adventure. Entreri became to him just another obstacle in the path to freeing Regis. With a cool head, Drizzt focused on the business at hand, reacting to his opponent's thrusts and counters as calmly as if he were in a practice gym in Menzoberranzan.

The visage of Entreri, the man who proclaimed superiority as a fighter because of his lack demotions, often twisted violently, bordering on explosive rage. Truly Entreri hated Drizzt. For all of the warmth and friendships the drow had found in his life, he had attained perfection with his weapons. Every time Drizzt foiled Entreri's attack routine and countered with an equally skilled sequence, he exposed the emptiness of the assassin's existence.

Drizzt recognized the boiling anger in Entreri and sought a way to exploit it. He launched another deceptive sequence but was again deterred.

Then he came in a straight double-thrust, his scimitars side by side and only an inch apart.

Entreri blew them both off to the side with a sweeping saber parry, grinning at Drizzt's apparent mistake. Growling wickedly, Entreri launched his dagger arm through the opening, toward the drow's heart.

But Drizzt had anticipated the move—had even set the assassin up. He dipped and angled his front scimitar even as the saber came in to parry it, sliding it under Entreri's blade and cutting back a reverse swipe. Entreri's dagger arm came thrusting out right in the scimitar's path, and before the assassin could poke his blade into Drizzt's heart, Drizzt's scimitar gashed into the back of his elbow.

The dagger dropped to the muck. Entreri grabbed his wounded arm, grimaced in pain, and rushed back from the battle. His eyes narrowed on Drizzt, angry and confused.

"Your hunger blurs your ability," Drizzt said to him, taking a step forward. "We have both looked into a mirror this night. Perhaps you did not I enjoy the sight it showed to you."

Entreri fumed but had no retort. "You have not won yet," he spat defiantly, but he knew that the drow had gained an overwhelming advantage.

"Perhaps not," Drizzt shrugged, "but you lost many years ago."

Entreri smiled evilly and bowed low, then took flight back through the passage.

Drizzt was quick to pursue, stopping short, though, when he reached the edge of the globe of blackness. He heard shuffling on the other side and braced himself. Too loud for Entreri, he reasoned, and he suspected that some wererat had returned.

"Are ye there, elf?" came a familiar voice.

Drizzt dashed through the blackness and side-stepped his astonished friends. "Entreri?" he asked, hoping that the wounded assassin had not escaped unseen.

Bruenor and Catti-brie shrugged curiously and turned to follow as Drizzt ran off into the darkness.

20

BLACK AND WHITE

Wulfgar, nearly overcome by exhaustion and by the pain in his arm, leaned heavily against the smooth wall of an upward-sloping passage. He clutched the wound tightly, hoping to stem the flow of his lifeblood.

How alone he felt.

He knew that he had been right in sending his friends away. They could have done little to help him, and standing there, in the open of the main corridor right in front of the very spot Entreri had chosen for his trap, left them too vulnerable. Wulfgar now had to move along by himself, probably into the heart of the infamous thieves' guild.

He released his grip on his biceps and examined the wound. The hydra had bitten him deeply, but he found that he could still move his arm. Gingerly he took a few swings with Aegis-fang.

He then leaned back against the wall once more, trying to figure a course of action in a cause that seemed truly hopeless.

✕ ✕ ✕ ✕ ✕

Drizzt slipped from tunnel to tunnel, sometimes slowing his pace to listen for faint sounds that would aid his pursuit. He didn't really expect to hear anything; Entreri could move as silently as he. And the assassin, like Drizzt, moved along without a torch, or even a candle.

But Drizzt felt confident in the turns he took, as if he were being led along by the same reasoning that guided Entreri. He felt the assassin's presence, knew the man better than he cared to admit, and Entreri could no more escape him than he could Entreri. Their battle had begun in Mithral Hall months before—or perhaps theirs was only the present embodiment in the continuation of a greater struggle that was spawned at the dawn of time—but, for Drizzt and Entreri, two pawns in the timeless struggle of principles, this chapter of the war could not end until one claimed victory.

Drizzt noted a glimmer down to the side—not the flickering yellow of a torch, but a constant silvery stream. He moved cautiously and found an open grate, with the moonlight streaming in and highlighting the wet iron rungs of a ladder bolted into the sewer wall. Drizzt glanced around quickly—too quickly—and rushed to the ladder.

The shadows to his left exploded into motion, and Drizzt caught the telltale shine of a blade just in time to turn his back from the angle of the blow. He staggered forward, feeling a burning across his shoulder blades and then the wetness of his blood rolling down under his cloak.

Drizzt ignored the pain, knowing that any hesitation would surely result in his death, and spun around, slamming his back into the wall and sending the curved blades of both his scimitars into a defensive spin before him.

Entreri issued no taunts this time. He came in furiously, cutting and slicing with his saber, knowing that he had to finish Drizzt before the shock of the ambush wore off. Viciousness replaced finesse, engulfing the injured assassin in a frenzy of hatred.

He leaped into Drizzt, locking one of the drow's arms under his own wounded limb and trying to use brute strength to drive his saber into his opponent's neck.

Drizzt steadied himself quickly enough to control the initial assault. He surrendered his one arm to the assassin's hold, concentrating solely on getting his free scimitar up to block the strike. The blade's hilt again locked with that of Entreri's saber, holding it motionless in midswing halfway between the combatants.

Behind their respective blades, Drizzt and Entreri eye-balled each other with open hatred, their grimaces only inches apart.

"How many crimes shall I punish you for, assassin?" Drizzt growled. Reinforced by his own proclamation, Drizzt pushed the saber back an inch, shifting the angle of his own deadly blade down more threateningly toward Entreri.

Entreri did not answer, nor did he seem alarmed at the slight shift in the blades' momentum. A wild, exhilarated look came into his eyes, and his thin lips widened into an evil grin.

Drizzt knew that the killer had another trick to play.

Before the drow could figure the game, Entreri spat a mouthful of filthy sewer water into his lavender eyes.

⚔ ⚔ ⚔ ⚔

The sound of renewed fighting led Bruenor and Catti-brie along the tunnels. They caught sight of the moonlit forms struggling just as Entreri played his wicked card.

"Drizzt!" Catti-brie shouted, knowing that she couldn't get to him, even get her bow up, in time to stop Entreri.

Bruenor growled and bolted forward with only one thought on his mind: If Entreri killed Drizzt, he would cut the dog in half!

⚔ ⚔ ⚔ ⚔

The sting and shock of the water broke Drizzt's concentration, and his strength, for only a split second, but he knew that even a split second was too long against Artemis Entreri. He jerked his head to the side desperately.

Entreri snapped his saber down, slicing a gash across Drizzt's forehead and crushing the drow's thumb between the twisting hilts. "I have you!" he squealed, hardly believing the sudden turn of events.

At that horrible moment, Drizzt could not disagree with the observation, but the drow's next move came more on instinct than on any calculations, and with agility that surprised even Drizzt. In the instant of a single, tiny hop, Drizzt snapped one foot behind Entreri's ankle and tucked the other under him against the wall. He pushed away and twisted as he went. On the slick floor, Entreri had no chance to dodge the trip, and he toppled backward into the murky stream, Drizzt splashing down on top of him.

The weight of Drizzt's heavy fall jammed the crosspiece of his scimitar into Entreri's eye. Drizzt recovered from the surprise of his own movement faster than Entreri, and he did not miss the opportunity. He spun his hand over on the hilt and reversed the flow of the blade, pulling it free of Entreri's and swinging a short cut back and down, with the tip of the scimitar diving in at the assassin's ribs. In grim satisfaction, Drizzt felt it begin to cut in.

It was Entreri's turn for a move wrought of desperation. Having no time to bring his saber to bear, the assassin punched straight out, slamming Drizzt's face with the butt of his weapon. Drizzt's nose splattered onto his cheek, flashes of color exploded before his eyes, and he felt himself lifted and dropped off to the side before his scimitar could finish its work.

Entreri scrambled out of reach and pulled himself from the murky water. Drizzt, too, rolled away, struggling against the dizziness to regain his feet. When he did, he found himself facing Entreri once again, the assassin even worse off than he.

Entreri looked over the drow's shoulder, to the tunnel and the charging dwarf and to Catti-brie and her killer bow, coming up level with his face. He jumped to the side, to the iron rungs, and started up to the street.

Catti-brie followed his motion in a fluid movement, keeping him dead in her sights. No one, not even Artemis Entreri, could escape once she had him cleanly targeted.

"Get him, girl!" Bruenor yelled.

Drizzt had been so involved in the battle that he hadn't even noticed the arrival of his friends. He spun around to see Bruenor rolling in, and Catti-brie just about to loose her arrow.

"Hold!" Drizzt growled in a tone that froze Bruenor in his tracks and sent a shiver through Catti-brie's spine. They both gawked, open-mouthed, at Drizzt.

"He is mine!" the drow told them.

Entreri didn't hesitate to consider his good fortune. Out in the open streets, his streets, he might find his sanctuary.

With no retort forthcoming from either of his unnerved friends, Drizzt slapped the magical mask up over his face and was just as quick to follow.

⨯ ⨯ ⨯ ⨯ ⨯

The realization that his delay might bring danger to his friends—for they had gone rushing off to search for some way to meet him back on the street—spurred Wulfgar to action. He clasped Aegis-fang tightly in the hand of his wounded arm, forcing injured muscles to respond to his commands.

Then he thought of Drizzt, of that quality his friend possessed to completely sublimate fear in the face of impossible odds and replace it with pointed fury.

This time, it was Wulfgar's eyes that burned with an inner fire. He stood wide-legged in the corridor, his breath rasping out as low growls, and his muscles flexing and relaxing in a rhythmic pattern that honed them to fighting perfection.

The thieves' guild, the strongest house in Calimport, he thought.

A smile spread over the barbarian's face. The pain was gone now, and the weariness had flown from his bones. His smile became a heartfelt laugh as he rushed off.

Time to fight.

He took note of the ascending slope of the tunnel as he jogged along and knew the next door he went through would be at or near street level. He soon came upon, not one, but three doors: one at the end of the tunnel and one on either side. Wulfgar hardly slowed, figuring the direction he was traveling to be as good as any, and barreled through the door at the corridor's end, crashing into an octagonal-shaped guard room complete with four very surprised guards.

"Hey!" the one in the middle of the room blurted as Wulfgar's huge fist slammed him to the floor. The barbarian spotted another door directly across from the one he had entered, and cut a beeline for it, hoping to get through the room without a drawn-out fight.

One of the guards, a puny, dark-haired little rogue, proved the quickest. He darted to the door, inserted a key, and flipped the lock, then he turned to face Wulfgar, holding the key out before him and grinning a broken-toothed smile.

"Key," he whispered, tossing the device to one of his comrades to the side.

Wulfgar's huge hand grabbed his shirt, taking out more than a few chest hairs, and the little rogue felt his feet leave the floor.

With one arm, Wulfgar threw him through the door.

"Key," the barbarian said, stepping over the kindling—and thief pile.

Wulfgar hadn't nearly outrun the danger, though. The next room was a great meeting hall, with dozens of chambers directly off it. Cries of alarm followed the barbarian as he sprinted through, and a well-rehearsed defense plan went into execution all around him. The human thieves, Pook's original guild members, fled for the shadows and the safety of their rooms, for they had been relieved of the responsibilities of dealing with intruders more than a year before—since Rassiter and his crew had joined the guild.

Wulfgar rushed to a short flight of stairs and leaped up them in a single bound, smashing through the door at the top. A maze of corridors and open chambers loomed before him, a treasury of artworks—statues, paintings, and tapestries—beyond any collection the barbarian had ever imagined. Wulfgar had little time to appreciate the artwork. He saw the forms chasing him. He saw them off to the side and gathering down the corridors before him to cut him off. He knew what they were; he had just been in their sewers.

He knew the smell of wererats.

⚔ ⚔ ⚔ ⚔ ⚔

Entreri had his feet firmly planted, ready for Drizzt as he came up through the open grate. When the drow's form began to exit onto the street, the assassin cut down viciously with his saber.

Drizzt, running up the iron rungs in perfect balance, had his hands free, however. Expecting such a move, he had crossed his scimitars up over his head as he came through. He caught Entreri's saber in he wedge and pushed it harmlessly aside.

Then they were faced off on the open street.

The first hints of dawn cracked over the eastern horizon, the temperature had already begun to soar, and the lazy city awakened around them.

Entreri came in with a rush, and Drizzt fought him back with wicked counters and sheer strength. The drow did not blink, his features locked in a determined grimace. Methodically he moved at the assassin, both scimitars cutting with even, solid strokes.

His left arm useless and his left eye seeing no more than a blur, Entreri knew that he could not hope to win. Drizzt saw it, too, and he picked up the tempo, slapping again and again at the slowing saber in an effort to further weary Entreri's only defense.

But as Drizzt pressed into the battle, his magical mask once again loosened and dropped from his face.

Entreri smirked, knowing that he had once again dodged certain death. He saw his out.

"Caught in a lie?" he whispered wickedly.

Drizzt understood.

"A drow!" Entreri shrieked to the multitude of people he knew to be watching the battle from nearby shadows. "From the Forest of Mir! A scout, a prelude to an army! A drow!"

Curiosity now pulled a throng from their concealments. The battle had been interesting enough before, but now the street people had to come closer to verify Entreri's claims. Gradually a circle began to form around the combatants, and Drizzt and Entreri heard the ring of swords coming free of scabbards.

"Good-bye, Drizzt Do'Urden," Entreri whispered under the growing tumult and the cries of "drow!" springing up throughout the area. Drizzt could not deny the effectiveness of the assassin's ploy. He glanced around nervously, expecting an attack from behind at any moment.

Entreri had the distraction he needed. As Drizzt looked to the side again, he broke away and stumbled off through the crowd, shouting, "Kill the drow! Kill him!"

Drizzt swung around, blades ready, as the anxious mob cautiously moved in. Catti-brie and Bruenor came up onto the street then and saw at once what had happened, and what was about to happen. Bruenor rushed to Drizzt's side and Catti-brie notched an arrow.

"Back away!" the dwarf grumbled. "Suren there be no evil here, except for the one ye fools just let get away!"

One man approached boldly, his spear leading the way.

A silver explosion caught the weapon's shaft, severing its tip. Horrified, the man dropped the broken spear and looked to the side, to where Catti-brie had already notched another arrow.

"Get away," she growled at him. "Leave the elf in peace, or me next shot won't be lookin' for yer weapon!"

The man backed away, and the crowd seemed to lose its heart for the fight as quickly as it had found it. None of them ever really wanted to tangle with a drow elf anyway, and they were more than happy now to believe the dwarf's words, that this one wasn't evil.

Then a commotion down the lane turned all heads. Two of the guards posing as bums outside the thieves' guild pulled open the door—to the sound of fighting—and charged inside, slamming the door behind them.

"Wulfgar!" shouted Bruenor, roaring down the road. Catti-brie started to follow but turned back to consider Drizzt.

The drow stood as if torn, looking one way, to the guild, and the other, to where the assassin had run. He had Entreri beaten; the injured man could not possibly stand up against him.

How could he just let Entreri go?

"Yer friends need ye," Catti-brie reminded him. "If not for Regis, then for Wulfgar."

Drizzt shook his head in self-reproach. How could he even have considered abandoning his friends at that critical moment? He rushed past Catti-brie, chasing Bruenor down the road.

✕ ✕ ✕ ✕ ✕

Above Rogues Circle, the dawn's light had already found Pasha Pook's lavish chambers. LaValle moved cautiously toward the curtain at the side of his room and pushed it aside. Even he, a practiced wizard, would not dare to approach the device of unspeakable evil before the sun had risen, the Taros Hoop, his most powerful—and frightening—device.

He grasped its iron frame and slid it out of the tiny closet. On its stand and rollers, it was taller than he, with the worked hoop, large enough for a man to walk through, fully a foot off the floor. Pook had remarked that it was similar to the hoop the trainer of his great cats had used.

But any lion jumping through the Taros Hoop would hardly land safely on the other side.

LaValle turned the hoop to the side and faced it fully, examining the symmetrical spider web that filled its interior. So fragile the webbing appeared, but LaValle knew the strength in its strands, a magical power that transcended the very planes of existence.

LaValle slipped the instrument's trigger, a thin scepter capped with an enormous black pearl, into his belt and wheeled the Taros Hoop out into the central room of the level. He wished that he had the time to test his plan, for he certainly didn't want to disappoint his master again, but the sun was nearly full in the eastern sky and Pook would not be pleased with any delay.

Still in his nightshirt, Pook dragged himself out into the central chamber at LaValle's call. The guildmaster's eyes lit up at the sight of the Taros Hoop, which he, not a wizard and not understanding the dangers involved with such an item, thought a simply wonderful toy.

LaValle, holding the scepter in one hand and the onyx figurine of Guenhwyvar in the other, stood before the device. "Hold this," he said to Pook, tossing him the statuette. "We can get the cat later; I'll not need the beast for the task at hand."

Pook absently dropped the statuette into a pocket.

"I have scoured the planes of existence," the wizard explained. I knew the cat to be of the Astral Plane, but I wasn't certain that the halfling would remain there—if he could find his way out. and of course, the Astral Plane is very extensive."

"Enough!" ordered Pook. "Be on with it! What have you to show me?"

"Only this," LaValle replied, waving the scepter in front of the Taros Hoop. The webbing tingled with power and lit up in tiny flashes of lightning. Gradually the light became more constant, filling in the area between strands, and the image of the webbing disappeared into the background of cloudy blue.

LaValle spoke a command word, and the hoop focused in on a bright, well-lit grayness, a scene in the Astral Plane. There sat Regis, leaning comfortably against the limned image of a tree, a starlight sketch of an oak, with his hands tucked behind his head and his feet crossed out in front of him.

Pook shook the grogginess from his head. "Get him," he coughed. "How can we get him?"

Before LaValle could answer, the door burst open and Rassiter stumbled into the room. "Fighting, Pook," he gasped, out of breath, "in the lower levels. A giant barbarian."

"You promised me that you would handle it," Pook growled at him.

"The assassin's friends—" Rassiter began, but Pook had no time for explanations. Not now.

"Shut the door," he said to Rassiter.

Rassiter quieted and did as he was told. Pook was going to be angry enough with him when he learned of the disaster in the sewers—no need to press the point.

The guildmaster turned back to LaValle, this time not asking. "Get him," he said.

LaValle chanted softly and waved the scepter in front of the Taros Hoop again, then he reached through the glassy curtain separating the planes and caught the sleepy Regis by the hair.

"Guenhwyvar!" Regis managed to shout, but then LaValle tugged him through the portal and he tumbled on the floor, rolling right up to the feet of Pasha Pook.

"Uh . . . hello," he stammered, looking up at Pook apologetically. "Can we talk about this?"

Pook kicked him hard in the ribs and planted the butt of his walking

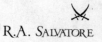

stick on Regis's chest. "You will cry out for death a thousand times before I release you from this world," the guildmaster promised.

Regis did not doubt a word of it.

21

WHERE NO SUN SHINES

Wulfgar dodged and ducked, slipping into the midst of lines of statues or behind heavy tapestries as he went. There were simply too many of the wererats, closing in all about him, for him to even hope to escape.

He passed one corridor and saw a group of three ratmen rushing down toward him. Feigning terror, the barbarian sprinted beyond the opening, then pulled up short and put his back tight against the corner. When the ratmen rushed into the room, Wulfgar smashed them down with quick chops of Aegis-fang.

He then retraced their steps back down the passage, hoping that he might confuse the rest of his pursuers.

He came into a wide room with rows of chairs and a high ceiling—a stage area for Pook's private showings by performing troupes. A massive chandelier, thousands of candles burning within its sconces, hung above the center of the room, and marble pillars, delicately carved into the likenesses of famed heroes and exotic monsters, lined the walls. Again Wulfgar had no time to admire the decorations. He noticed only one feature in the chamber: a short staircase along one side that led up to a balcony.

Ratmen poured in from the room's numerous entrances. Wulfgar looked back over his shoulder, down the passage, but saw that it, too, was blocked.

He shrugged and sprinted up the stairs, figuring that that route would at least allow him to fight off his attackers in a line rather than a crowd.

Two wererats rushed up right on his heels, but when Wulfgar made the landing and turned on them, they realized their disadvantage. The barbarian would have towered over them on even footing. Now, three steps up, his knees ran level with their eyes.

It wasn't such a bad position for offense; the wererats could poke at Wulfgar's unprotected legs. But when Aegis-fang descended in that tremendous arc, neither of the ratmen could possibly slow its momentum. And on the stairs, they didn't have much room to move out of the way.

The warhammer cracked onto the skull of one ratman with enough force to break his ankles, and the other, blanching under his brown fur, leaped over the side of the staircase.

Wulfgar nearly laughed aloud.

Then he saw the spears being readied.

He rushed into the balcony for the cover the railings and the chairs might provide and hoping for another exit. The wererats flooded onto the staircase in pursuit.

Wulfgar found no other doors. He shook his head, realizing that he was trapped, and slapped Aegis-fang to the ready.

What was it that Drizzt had told him about luck? That a true warrior always seemed to find the proper route—the one open path that casual observers might consider lucky?

Now Wulfgar did laugh out loud. He had killed a dragon once by dislodging an icicle above its back. He wondered what a huge chandelier with a thousand burning candles might do to a room full of ratmen.

"Tempus!" the barbarian roared to his battle god, seeking a measure of deity-inspired luck to aid his way—Drizzt did not know everything, after all! He launched Aegis-fang with all his strength, breaking into a dead run after the warhammer.

Aegis-fang twirled across the room as precisely as every throw Wulfgar had ever made with it. It blasted through the chandelier's supports, bringing a fair measure of the ceiling down with it. Ratmen scrambled and dived off to the side as the massive ball of crystal and flames exploded onto the floor.

Wulfgar, still in stride, planted a foot atop the balcony railing and leaped.

⚔ ⚔ ⚔ ⚔

Bruenor growled and brought his axe up over his head, meaning to chop the door to the guildhouse down in a single stroke, but as the dwarf pounded through the final strides to the place, an arrow whistled over his shoulder, scorching a hole around the latch, and the door swung free.

Unable to break his momentum, Bruenor barreled through the opening and tumbled head over heels down the stairs inside, taking the two surprised guards along with him.

Dazed, Bruenor pulled himself to his knees and looked back up the stairs, to see Drizzt sprinting down five steps at a stride and Catti-brie just cresting the top to follow.

"Durn ye, girl!'" the dwarf roared. "I told ye to tell me when ye was meaning to do that!"

"No time," Drizzt interrupted. He leaped the last seven steps—and clear over the kneeling dwarf—to intercept two wererats coming in on Bruenor's back.

Bruenor scooped up his helmet, plopped it back in place, and turned to join the fun, but the two wererats were long dead before the dwarf ever got back to his feet, and Drizzt was rushing away to the sounds of a larger battle farther in the complex. Bruenor offered Catti-brie his arm as she came charging past, so that he could profit from her momentum in the pursuit.

⚔ ⚔ ⚔ ⚔

Wulfgar's huge legs brought him clear over the mess of the chandelier, and he tucked his head under his arms as he dropped into a group of ratmen, knocking them every which way. Dazed but still coherent enough to mark his direction, Wulfgar barreled through a door and stumbled into another wide chamber. An open door loomed before him, leading into yet another maze of chambers and corridors.

But Wulfgar couldn't hope to get there with a score of wererats blocking his way. He slipped over to the side of the room and put his back to a wall.

Thinking him unarmed, the ratmen rushed in, shrieking in glee. Then Aegis-fang magically returned to Wulfgar's hands and he swatted the first two aside. He looked around, searching for another dose of luck.

Not this time.

Wererats hissed at him from every side, nipping with their ravaging teeth. They didn't need Rassiter to explain the power such a giant—a wererat giant—could add to their guild.

The barbarian suddenly felt naked in his sleeveless tunic as each bite narrowly missed its mark. Wulfgar had heard enough legends concerning such creatures to understand the horrid implications of a lycanthrope's bite, and he fought with every ounce of strength he could muster.

Even with his adrenaline pumping in his terror, the big man had spent half the night in battle and had suffered many wounds, most notably the gash on his arm from the hydra, opened again by his leap from the balcony. His swipes were beginning to slow.

Normally Wulfgar would have fought to the end with a song on his lips as he racked up a pile of dead enemies at his feet and smiled in the knowledge that he had died a true warrior. But now, knowing his cause to be hopeless, with implications much worse than death, he scanned the room for a certain method of killing himself.

Escape was impossible. Victory even more so. Wulfgar's only thought and desire at that moment was to be spared the indignity and anguish of lycanthropy.

Then Drizzt entered the room.

He came in on the back of the wererat ranks like a sudden tornado dropping onto an unprepared village. His scimitars flashed blood red in seconds; and patches of fur flew about the room. Those few ratmen in his path who managed to escape put their tails between themselves and the killer drow and fled from the room.

One wererat turned and got his sword up to parry, but Drizzt lopped off his arm at the elbow and drove a second blade through the beast's chest. Then the drow was beside his giant friend, and his appearance gave Wulfgar renewed courage and strength. Wulfgar grunted in exhilaration, catching one attacker full in the chest with Aegis-fang and driving the wretched beast right through a wall. The ratman lay, quite dead, on his back in one room, but his legs, looped at the knees through the room's newest window, twitched grotesquely for his comrades to witness.

The ratmen glanced nervously at each other for support and came at the two warriors tentatively.

If their morale was sinking, it flew away altogether a moment later, when the roaring dwarf pounded into the room, led by a volley of silver-streaking arrows that cut the rats down with unerring accuracy. For the ratmen, it was the sewer scenario all over again, where they had lost more than two dozen of their comrades earlier that same night. They had no heart to face the four friends united, and those that could flee, did.

Those that remained had a difficult choice: hammer, blade, axe, or arrow.

⚔ ⚔ ⚔ ⚔ ⚔

Pook sat back in his great chair, watching the destruction through an image in the Taros Hoop. It did not pain the guildmaster to see wererats dying—a few well-placed bites out in the streets could replenish the supply of the wretched things—but Pook knew that the heroes cutting their way through his guild would eventually wind up in his face.

Regis, held off the ground by the seat of his pants by one of Pook's hill giant eunuchs, watched, too. The mere sight of Bruenor, whom Regis had believed killed in Mithral Hall, brought tears to the halfling's eyes. And the thought that his dearest friends had traveled the breadth of the Realms to rescue him and were now fighting for his sake as mightily as he had ever witnessed, overwhelmed him. All of them bore wounds, particularly Catti-brie and Drizzt, but all of them ignored the pain as they tore into Pook's militia. Watching them felling foes with every cut and thrust, Regis had little doubt that they would win through to get to him.

Then the halfling looked to the side of the Taros Hoop, where LaValle stood, unconcerned, his arms crossed over his chest and his pearl-tipped scepter tapping on one shoulder.

"Your followers do not fare so well, Rassiter," the guildmaster remarked. "One might even note their cowardice."

Rassiter shuffled uneasily from one foot to the other.

"Is it that you cannot hold to your part of our arrangement?"

"My guild fights mighty enemies this night," Rassiter stammered. "They . . . we have not been able . . . the fight is not yet lost!"

"Perhaps you should see to it that your rats fare better," Pook said calmly, and Rassiter did not miss the command's—the threat's—tone. He bowed low and rushed out of the chamber, slamming the door behind him.

Even the demanding guildmaster could not hold the wererats wholly responsible for the disaster at hand.

"Magnificent," he muttered as Drizzt fought off two simultaneous thrusts and sliced down both wererats with individual, yet mystically intertwined counters. "Never have I seen such grace with a blade." He paused for a moment to consider that thought. "Perhaps once!"

Surprised at the revelation, Pook looked at LaValle, who nodded in accord.

"Entreri," LaValle inferred. "The resemblance is unmistakable. We know now why the assassin coaxed this group to the south."

"To fight the drow?" Pook mused. "At last, a challenge for the man without peer?"

"So it would seem."

"But, where is he, then? Why has he not made his appearance?"

"Perhaps he already has," LaValle replied grimly.

Pook paused to consider the words for a long moment; they were too unconscionable for him to believe. "Entreri beaten?" He gasped. "Entreri dead?"

The words rang like sweet music to Regis, who had watched the rivalry between the assassin and Drizzt with horror from its inception. All along, Regis had suspected that those two would fall into a duel that only one could survive. And all along, the halfling had feared for his drow friend.

The thought of Entreri gone put a new perspective on the battle at hand for Pasha Pook. Suddenly he needed Rassiter and his cohorts again;

suddenly the carnage he watched through the Taros Hoop had a more direct impact on his guild's immediate power.

He leaped from his seat and ambled over to the evil device. "We must stop this," he snarled at LaValle. "Send them away to a dark place!"

The wizard grinned wickedly and shuffled off to retrieve a huge book, bound in black leather. Opening it to a marked page, LaValle walked before the Taros Hoop and began the initial chantings of an ominous incantation.

⚔ ⚔ ⚔ ⚔ ⚔

Bruenor was first out of the room, searching for a likely route to Regis— and for more wererats to chop down. He stormed along a short corridor and kicked open a door, finding, not wererats, but two very surprised human thieves. Holding a measure of mercy in his battle-hardened heart—after all, he was the invader—Bruenor held back his twitching axe hand and shield-slammed the two rogues to the ground. He then rushed back out into the corridor and fell in line with the rest of his friends.

"Watch yer right!" Catti-brie cried out, noting some movement behind a tapestry near the front of the line, beside Wulfgar. The barbarian pulled the heavy tapestry down with a single heave, revealing a tiny man, barely more than a halfling, crouched and poised to spring. Exposed, the little thief quickly lost his heart for the fight and just shrugged apologetically as Wulfgar slapped his puny dagger away.

Wulfgar caught him up by the back of the neck, hoisting the little man into the air and putting his nose to the thief's. "What manner are you?" Wulfgar scowled. "Man or rat?"

"Not a rat!" the terrified thief shrieked. He spat on the ground to emphasize his point. "Not a rat!"

"Regis?" Wulfgar demanded. "You know of him?"

The thief nodded eagerly.

"Where can I find Regis?" Wulfgar roared, his bellow draining the blood from the thief's face.

"Up," the little man squeaked. "Pook's rooms. All the way up." Acting solely on instinct for survival, and having no real intentions to do anything but get away from the monstrous barbarian, the thief slipped one hand to a hidden dagger tucked in the back of his belt.

Bad judgment.

Drizzt slapped a scimitar against the thief's arm, exposing the move to Wulfgar.

Wulfgar used the little man to open the next door.

Again the chase was on. Wererats darted in and out of the shadows to the sides of the four companions, but few stood to face them. Those that did wound up in their path more often by accident than design!

More doors splintered and more rooms emptied, and a few minutes later, a stairway came into view. Broad and lavishly carpeted, with ornate banisters of shining hardwood, it could only be the ascent to the chambers of Pasha Pook.

Bruenor roared in glee and charged on. Wulfgar and Catti-brie eagerly followed. Drizzt hesitated and looked around, suddenly fearful.

Drow elves were magical creatures by nature, and Drizzt now sensed a strange and dangerous tingle, the beginnings of a spell aimed at him. He saw the walls and floor around him waver suddenly, as if they had become somehow less tangible.

Then he understood. He had traveled the Planes before, as companion to Guenhwyvar, his magical cat, and he knew now that someone, or something, was pulling him from his place on the Prime Material Plane. He looked ahead to see Bruenor and the others now similarly confused.

"Join hands!" the drow cried, rushing to get to his friends before the dweomer banished them all.

⚔ ⚔ ⚔ ⚔ ⚔

In hopeless horror, Regis watched his friends huddle together. Then the scene in the Taros hoop shifted from the lower levels of the guildhouse to a darker place, a place of smoke and shadows, of ghouls and demons.

A place where no sun shone.

"No!" the halfling cried out, realizing the wizard's intent. LaValle paid him no heed, and Pook only snickered at him. Seconds later, Regis saw his friends in their huddle again, this time in the swirling smoke of the dark plane.

Pook leaned heavily on his walking stick and laughed. "How I love to foil hopes!" he said to his wizard. "Once more you prove your inestimable worth to me, my precious LaValle!"

Regis watched as his friends turned back to back in a pitiful attempt at defense. Already, dark shapes swooped about them or hovered over them—beings of great power and great evil.

Regis dropped his eyes, unable to watch.

"Oh, do not look away, little thief," Pook laughed at him. "Watch their deaths and be happy for them, for I assure you that the pain they are about to suffer will not compare to the torments I have planned for you."

Regis, hating the man and hating himself for putting his friends in such a predicament, snapped a vile glare at Pook. They had come for him. They had crossed the world for him. They had battled Artemis Entreri and a host of wererats, and most probably many other adversaries. All of it had been for him.

"Damn you," Regis spat, suddenly no longer afraid. He swung himself down and bit the eunuch hard on the inner thigh. The giant shrieked in pain and loosened his grip, dropping Regis to the floor.

The halfling hit the ground running. He crossed before Pook, kicking out the walking stick the guildmaster was using for support, while very deftly slipping a hand into Pook's pocket to retrieve a certain statuette. He then went on to LaValle.

The wizard had more time to react and had already begun a quick spell when Regis came at him, but the halfling proved the quicker. He leaped up, putting two fingers into LaValle's eyes, disrupting the spell, and sending the wizard stumbling backward.

As the wizard struggled to hold his balance, Regis jerked the pearl-tipped scepter away and ran up to the front of the Taros Hoop. He glanced around at the room a final time, wondering if he might find an easier way.

Pook dominated the vision. His face blood red and locked into a grimace, the guildmaster had recovered from the attack and now twirled his walking stick as a weapon, which Regis knew from experience to be deadly.

"Please give me this one," Regis whispered to whatever god might be listening. He gritted his teeth and ducked his head, lurching forward and letting the scepter lead him into the Taros Hoop.

THE RIFT

Smoke, emanating from the very ground they stood upon, wafted by drearily and rolled around their feet. By the angle of its roll, the way it fell away below them only a foot or two off to either side, only to rise again in another cloud, the friends saw that they were on a narrow ledge, a bridge across some endless chasm.

Similar bridges, none more than a few feet wide, criss-crossed above and below them, and for what they could see, those were the only walkways in the entire plane. No solid land mass showed itself in any direction, only the twisting, spiraling bridges.

The friends' movements were slow, dreamlike, fighting against the weight of the air. The place itself, a dim, oppressive world of foul smells and anguished cries, exuded evil. Vile, misshapen monsters swooped over their heads and around the gloomy emptiness, crying out in glee at the unexpected appearance of such tasty morsels. The four friends, so indomitable against the perils of their own world, found themselves without courage.

"The Nine Hells?" Catti-brie whispered in a tiny voice, afraid that her words might shatter the temporary inaction of the multitudes gathering in the ever-present shadows.

"Hades," Drizzt guessed, more schooled in the known planes. "The domain of Chaos." Though he was standing right beside his friends, his words rang out as distant as had Catti-brie's.

Bruenor started to growl out a retort, but his voice faded away when he looked at Catti-brie and Wulfgar, his children, or so he considered them. Now there was nothing he could possibly do to help them.

Wulfgar looked to Drizzt for answers. "How can we escape?" he pressed bluntly. "Is there a door? A window back to our own world?"

Drizzt shook his head. He wanted to reassure them, to keep their spirits up in the face of the danger. This time, though, the drow had no answers for them. He could see no escape, no hope.

A bat-winged creature, doglike, but with a face grotesquely and unmistakably human, dived at Wulfgar, putting a filthy talon in line with the barbarian's shoulder.

"Drop!" Catti-brie yelled to Wulfgar at the last possible second. The barbarian didn't question the command. He fell to his face, and the creature missed its mark. It swerved around in a loop and hung in midair for a split second as it made a tight turn, then it came back again, hungry for living flesh.

Catti-brie was ready for it this time, though, and as it neared the group, she loosed an arrow. It reached out lazily toward the monster, cutting a dull gray streak instead of the usual silver. The magic arrow blasted in with the customary strength, though, scorching a wicked hole in the dog fur and unbalancing the monster's flight. It rolled in just above them, trying to right itself, and Bruenor chopped it down, dropping it in a spiraling descent into the gloom below them.

The friends could hardly be pleased with the minor victory. A hundred similar beasts flitted in and out of their vision above, below, and to the sides, many of them ten times larger than the one Bruenor and Catti-brie had felled.

"We can't be staying here," Bruenor muttered. "Where do we go, elf?"

Drizzt would have been just as content staying where they were, but he knew that marching out a course would comfort his friends and give them at least some feeling that they were making progress against their dilemma. Only the drow understood the depth of the horror they now faced. Only

Drizzt knew that wherever they might travel on the dark plane, the situation would prove to be the same: no escape.

"This way," he said after a moment of mock contemplation. "If there is a door, I sense that it is this way." He took a step down the narrow bridge but stopped abruptly as the smoke heaved and swirled before him.

Then it rose in front of him.

Humanoid in shape, it was tall and slender, with a bulbous, froglike head and long, three-fingered hands that ended in claws. Taller even than Wulfgar, it towered over Drizzt. "Chaos, dark elf?" it lisped in a guttural, foreign voice. "Hades?"

Twinkle glowed eagerly in Drizzt's hand, but his other blade, the one forged with ice-magic, nearly leaped out at the monster.

"Err, you do," the creature croaked.

Bruenor rushed up beside Drizzt. "Get yerself back, demon," he growled.

"Not demon," said Drizzt, understanding the creature's references and remembering more of the many lessons he had been taught about the Planes during his years in the city of drow. "Demodand."

Bruenor looked up at him curiously.

"And not Hades," Drizzt explained. "Tarterus."

"Good, dark elf," croaked the demodand. "Knowing of the lower planes are your people."

"Then you understand of the power of my people," Drizzt bluffed, "and you know how we repay even demon lords who cross us."

The demodand laughed, if that's what it was, for it sounded more like the dying gurgle of a drowning man. "Dead drow avenge do not. Far from home are you!" It reached a lazy hand toward Drizzt.

Bruenor rushed by his friend. "Moradin!" he cried, and he swiped at the demodand with his mithral axe. The demodand was faster than the dwarf had expected, though, and it easily dodged the blow, countering with a clubbing blow of its arm that sent Bruenor skidding on his face farther down the bridge.

The demodand reached down at the passing dwarf with its wicked claws.

Twinkle cut the hand in half before it ever reached Bruenor.

The demodand turned on Drizzt in amazement. "Hurt me you did, dark elf," it croaked, though no hint of pain rang out in its voice, "but better you must do!" It snapped the wounded hand out at Drizzt, and as he reflexively dodged it, the demodand sent its second hand out to finish the task of the first, cutting a triple line of gashes down the sprawled dwarf's shoulder.

"Blast and bebother!" Bruenor roared, getting back to his knees. "Ye filthy, slime-covered . . ." he grumbled, launching a second unsuccessful attack.

Behind Drizzt, Catti-brie bobbed and ducked, trying to get a clear shot with Taulmaril. Beside her, Wulfgar stood at the ready, having no room on the narrow bridge to move up beside the drow.

Drizzt moved sluggishly, his scimitars awkwardly twisting through an uneven sequence. Perhaps it was because of the weariness of a long night of fighting or the unusual weight of the air in the plane, but Catti-brie, looking on curiously, had never seen the drow so lackluster in his efforts.

Still on his knees farther down the bridge, Bruenor swiped more with frustration than his customary lust for battle.

Catti-brie understood. It wasn't weariness or the heavy air. Hopelessness had befallen the friends.

She looked to Wulfgar, to beg him to intervene, but the sight of the barbarian beside her gave her no comfort. His wounded arm hung limply at his side, and the heavy head of Aegis-fang dipped below the low-riding smoke. How many more battles could he fight? How many of these wretched demodand would he be able to put down before he met his end?

And what end would a victory bring in a plane of unending battles? she wondered.

Drizzt felt the despair most keenly. For all the trials of his hard life, the drow had held faith for ultimate justice. He had believed, though he never dared to admit it, that his unyielding faith in his precious principles would bring him the reward he deserved. Now, there was this, a struggle that could only end in death, where one victory brought only more conflict.

"Damn ye all!" Catti-brie cried. She didn't have a safe shot, but she fired anyway. Her arrow razed a line of blood across Drizzt's arm, but then exploded into the demodand, rocking it back and giving Bruenor the chance to scramble back to Drizzt's side.

"Have ye lost yer fight, then?" Catti-brie scolded them.

"Easy, girl," Bruenor replied somberly, cutting low at the demodand's knees. The creature hopped over the blade gingerly and started another attack, which Drizzt deflected.

"Easy yerself, Bruenor Battlehammer!" Catti-brie shouted. "Ye've the gall to call yerself king o' yer clan. Ha! Garumn'd be tossin' in his grave to see ye fightin' so!"

Bruenor turned a wicked glare on Catti-brie, his throat too choked for him to spit out a reply.

Drizzt tried to smile. He knew what the young woman, that wonderful young woman, was up to. His lavender eyes lit up with the inner fire. "Go to Wulfgar," he told Bruenor. "Secure our backs and watch for attacks from above."

Drizzt eyed the demodand, who had noted his sudden change in demeanor.

"Come, farastu," the drow said evenly, remembering the name given to that particular type of creature. "Farastu," he taunted, "the least of the demodand kind. Come and feel the cut of a drow's blade."

Bruenor backed away from Drizzt, almost laughing. Part of him wanted to say, "What's the point?" but a bigger part, the side of him that Catti-brie had awakened with her biting references to his proud history, had a different message to speak. "Come on and fight, then!" he roared into the shadows of the endless chasm. "We've enough for the whole damn world of ye!"

In seconds, Drizzt was fully in command. His movements remained slowed with the heaviness of the plane, but they were no less magnificent. He feinted and cut, sliced and parried, in harmony to offset every move the demodand made.

Instinctively Wulfgar and Bruenor started in to help him, but stopped to watch the display.

Catti-brie turned her gaze outward, plucking off a bowshot whenever a foul form flew from the hanging smoke. She took a quick bead on one body as it dropped from the darkness high above.

She pulled Taulmaril away at the last second in absolute shock.

"Regis!" she cried.

The halfling ended his half-speed plummet, plopping with a soft puff into the smoke of a second bridge a dozen yards across the emptiness from friends. He stood and managed to hold his ground against a wave of dizziness and disorientation.

"Regis!" Catti-brie cried again. "How did ye get yerself here?"

"I saw you in that awful hoop," the halfling explained. "Thought you might need my help."

"Bah! More that ye got yerself thrown here, Rumblebelly," Bruenor replied.

"Good to see you, too," Regis shot back, "but this time you are mistaken. I came of my own choice." He held the pearl-tipped scepter up for them to see. "To bring you this."

Truly Bruenor had been glad to see his little friend even before Regis had refuted his suspicion. He admitted his error by bowing low to Regis, his beard dipping under the smoky swirl.

Another demodand rose up, this one across the way, on the same bridge as Regis. The halfling showed his friends the scepter again. "Catch it," he begged, winding up to throw. "This is your only chance to get out of here!" He mustered up his nerve—there would only be one chance—and heaved the scepter as powerfully as he could. It spun end over end, tantalizingly slow in its journey toward the three sets of outstretched hands.

It could not cut a swift enough path through the heavy air, though, and it lost its speed short of the bridge.

"No!" Bruenor cried, seeing their hopes falling away.

Catti-brie growled in denial, unhitching her laden belt and dropping Taulmaril in a single movement.

She dived for the scepter.

Bruenor dropped flat to his chest desperately to grab her ankles, but she was too far out. A contented look came over her as she caught the scepter. She twisted about in midair and threw it back to Bruenor's waiting hands, then she plummeted from sight without a word of complaint.

✕ ✕ ✕ ✕ ✕

LaValle studied the mirror with trembling hands. The image of the friends and the plane of Tarterus had faded into a dark blur when Regis had jumped through with the scepter. But that was the least of the wizard's concerns now. A thin crack, detectable only at close inspection, slowly etched its way down the center of the Taros Hoop.

LaValle spun on Pook, charging his master and grabbing at the walking stick. Too surprised to fight the wizard off, Pook surrendered the cane and stepped back curiously.

LaValle rushed back to the mirror. "We must destroy its magic!" he screamed and he smashed the cane into the glassy image.

The wooden stick, sundered by the device's power, splintered in his hands, and LaValle was thrown across the room. "Break it! Break it!" he begged Pook, his voice a pitiful whine.

"Get the halfling back!" Pook retorted, still more concerned with Regis and the statuette.

"You do not understand!" LaValle cried. "The halfling has the scepter! The portal cannot be closed from the other side!"

Pook's expression shifted from curiosity to concern as the gravity of his wizard's fears descended over him. "My dear LaValle," he began calmly, "are you saying that we have an open door to Tarterus in my living quarters?"

LaValle nodded meekly.

"Break it! Break it!" Pook screamed at the eunuchs standing beside him. "Heed the wizard's words! Smash that infernal hoop to pieces!"

Pook picked up the broken end of his walking stick, the silver-shod, meticulously crafted cane he had been given personally by the Pasha of Calimshan.

The morning sun was still low in the eastern sky, but already the guild-master knew that it would not be a good day.

✕ ✕ ✕ ✕ ✕

Drizzt, trembling with anguish and anger, roared toward the demodand, his every thrust aimed at a critical spot. The creature, agile and experienced, dodged the initial assault, but it could not stay the enraged drow. Twinkle cut a blocking arm off at the elbow, and the other blade dived into the demodand's heart. Drizzt felt a surge of power run through his arm as his scimitar sucked the life-force out of the wretched creature, but the drow contained the strength, burying it within his own rage, and held on stubbornly.

When the thing lay lifeless, Drizzt turned to his companions.

"I did not . . ." Regis stammered from across the chasm. "She . . . I . . ."

Neither Bruenor nor Wulfgar could answer him. They stood frozen, staring into the empty darkness below.

"Run!" Drizzt called, seeing a demodand closing in behind the halfling. "We shall get to you!"

Regis tore his eyes from the chasm and surveyed the situation. "No need!" he shouted back. He pulled out the statuette and held it up for Drizzt to see. "Guenhwyvar will get me out of here, or perhaps the cat could aid—"

"No!" Drizzt cut him short, knowing what he was about to suggest. "Summon the panther and be gone!"

"We will meet again in a better place," Regis offered, his voice breaking in sniffles. He placed the statuette down before him and called out softly.

Drizzt took the scepter from Bruenor and put a comforting hand on his friend's shoulder. He then held the magic item to his chest, attuning his thoughts to its magical emanations.

His guess was confirmed; the scepter was indeed the key to the portal back to their own plane, a gate that Drizzt sensed was still open. He scooped up Taulmaril and Catti-brie's belt. "Come," he told his two friends, still staring at the darkness. He pushed them along the bridge, gently but firmly.

✕ ✕ ✕ ✕ ✕

Guenhwyvar sensed the presence of Drizzt Do'Urden as soon as it came into the plane of Tarterus. The great cat moved with hesitancy when Regis asked it to take him away, but the halfling now possessed the statuette and Guenhwyvar had always known Regis as a friend. Soon Regis found himself in the swirling tunnel of blackness, drifting toward the distant light that marked Guenhwyvar's home plane.

Then the halfling knew his error.

The onyx statuette, the link to Guenhwyvar, still lay on the smoky bridge in Tarterus.

Regis turned himself about, struggling against the pull of the planar tunnel's currents. He saw the darkness at the back end of the tunnel and could guess the risks of reaching through. He could not leave the statuette, not only for fear of losing his magnificent feline friend, but in revulsion at the thought of some foul beast of the lower planes gaining control over Guenhwyvar. Bravely he poked his three-fingered hand through the closing portal.

All of his senses jumbled. Overwhelming bursts of signals and images from two planes rushed at him in a nauseating wave. He blocked them away, using his hand as a focal point and concentrating all of his thoughts and energies on the sensations of that hand.

Then his hand dropped upon something hard, something vividly tangible. It resisted his tug, as though it were not meant to pass through such a gate.

Regis was fully stretched now, his feet held straight down the tunnel by the incessant pull, and his hand stubbornly latched to the statuette he would not leave behind. With a final heave, with all the strength the little halfling had ever summoned—and just a tiny bit more—he pulled the statuette through the gate.

The smooth ride of the planar tunnel transformed into a nightmarish bounce and skip, with Regis hurtling head over heels and deflecting off the walls, which twisted suddenly, as if to deny him passage. Through it all, Regis clutched at only one thought: keep the statuette in his grasp.

He felt he would surely die. He could not survive the beating, the dizzying swirl.

Then it died away as abruptly as it had begun, and Regis, still holding the statuette, found himself sitting beside Guenhwyvar with his back to an astral tree. He blinked and looked around, hardly believing his fortune.

"Do not worry," he told the panther. "Your master and the others will get back to their world." He looked down at the statuette, his only link to the Prime Material Plane. "But how shall I?"

While Regis floundered in despair, Guenhwyvar reacted differently. The panther spun about in a complete circuit and roared mightily into the starry vastness of the plane. Regis watched the cat's actions in amazement as Guenhwyvar leaped about and roared again, then bounded away into the astral nothingness.

Regis, more confused than ever, looked down at the statuette. One thought, one hope overrode all others at that moment.

Guenhwyvar knew something.

⋇ ⋇ ⋇ ⋇ ⋇

With Drizzt taking a ferocious lead, the three friends charged along, cutting down everything that dared to rise in their path. Bruenor and Wulfgar fought wildly, thinking that the drow was leading them to Catti-brie.

The bridge wound along a curving and rising route, and when Bruenor realized its ascending grade, he grew concerned. He was about to protest, to remind the drow that Catti-brie had fallen below them, but when he looked back, he saw that the area they had started from was clearly above them. Bruenor was a dwarf accustomed to lightless tunnels, and he could detect the slightest grade unerringly.

They were going up, more steeply now than before, and the area they had left continued to rise above them.

"How, elf?" he cried. "Up and up we go, but down by what me eyes be telling me."

Drizzt looked back and quickly understood what Bruenor was talking about. The drow didn't have time for philosophical inquiries; he was merely following the emanations of the scepter that would surely lead them to a gate. Drizzt did pause, though, to consider one possible quirk of the directionless, and apparently circular, plane.

Another demodand rose up before them, but Wulfgar swatted it from the bridge before it could even ready a strike. Blind rage drove the barbarian now, a third burst of adrenaline that denied his wounds and his weariness. He paused every few steps to look about, searching for something vile to hit, then he rushed back to the front, beside Drizzt, to get the first whack at anything trying to block their path.

The swirling smoke parted before them suddenly, and they faced a lighted image, blurry, but clearly of their own plane.

"The gate," Drizzt said. "The scepter has kept it open. Bruenor will pass through first."

Bruenor looked at Drizzt in blank amazement. "Leave?" he asked breathlessly. "How can ye ask me to leave, elf? Me girl's here."

"She is gone, my friend," Drizzt said softly.

"Bah!" Bruenor snorted, though it sounded as more of a sniffle. "Don't ye be so quick to make such a claim!"

Drizzt looked upon him with sincere sympathy, but refused to relinquish the point or change his course.

"And if she were gone, I'd stay as well," Bruenor proclaimed, "to find her body and carry it from this eternal hell!"

Drizzt grabbed the dwarf by the shoulders and squared up to face him. "Go, Bruenor, back to where we all belong," he said. "Do not diminish the sacrifice that Catti-brie has made for us. Do not steal the meaning from her fall."

"How can ye ask me to leave?" Bruenor said with a sniffle that he did not mask. Wetness glistened the edges of his gray eyes. "How can ye—"

"Think not of what has passed!" Drizzt said sharply. "Beyond that gate is the wizard that sent us here, the wizard that sent Catti-brie here!"

It was all Bruenor Battlehammer needed to hear. Fire replaced the tears in his eyes, and with a roar of anger he dived through the portal, his axe leading the way.

"Now—" Drizzt began, but Wulfgar cut him short.

"You go, Drizzt," the barbarian replied. "Avenge Catti-brie and Regis.

Finish the quest we undertook together. For myself, there will be no rest. My emptiness will not fade."

"She is gone," Drizzt said again.

Wulfgar nodded. "As am I," he said quietly.

Drizzt searched for some way to refute the argument, but truly Wulfgar's grief seemed too profound for him to ever recover.

Then Wulfgar's gaze shot up, and his mouth gaped in horrified—and elated—disbelief. Drizzt spun about, not as surprised, but still over-whelmed, by the sight before him.

Catti-brie fell limply and slowly from the dark sky above them.

It was a circular plane.

Wulfgar and Drizzt leaned together for support. They could not determine if Catti-brie was alive or dead. She was wounded gravely, at the least, and even as they watched, a winged demodand swooped down and grabbed at her leg with its huge talons.

Before a conscious thought had time to register in Wulfgar's mind, Drizzt had Taulmaril bent and sent a silver arrow into flight. It thundered into the side of the demodand's head just as the creature took hold of the young woman, blasting the thing from life.

"Go!" Wulfgar yelled at Drizzt, taking one stride. "I see my quest now! I know what I must do!"

Drizzt had other ideas. He slipped a foot through Wulfgar's legs and dropped in a spin, driving his other leg into the back of the barbarian's knees and tripping Wulfgar down to the side, toward the portal. Wulfgar understood the drow's intentions at once, and he scrambled to regain his balance.

Again Drizzt was the quicker. The point of a scimitar nicked in under Wulfgar's cheekbone, keeping him moving in the desired direction. As he neared the portal, just when Drizzt expected him to try some desperate maneuver, the drow drove a boot under his shoulder and kicked him hard.

Betrayed, Wulfgar tumbled into Pasha Pook's central chamber. He ignored his surroundings, grabbed at the Taros Hoop and shook it with all his strength.

"Traitor!" he yelled. "Never will I forget this, cursed drow!"

"Take your place!" Drizzt yelled back at him from across the planes. "Only Wulfgar has the strength to hold the gate open and secure. Only Wulfgar! Hold it, son of Beornegar. If you care for Drizzt Do'Urden, and if ever you loved Catti-brie, hold the gate!"

Drizzt could only pray that he had appealed to the small part of rationale accessible in the enraged barbarian. The drow turned from the portal, tucking the scepter into his belt and slinging Taulmaril over his shoulder. Catti-brie was below him now, still falling, still unmoving.

Drizzt drew out both his scimitars. How long would it take him to pull Catti-brie to a bridge and find his way back to the portal? he wondered. Or would he, too, be caught in an endless, doomed, fall?

And how long could Wulfgar hold the gate open?

He brushed away the questions. He had no time to speculate on their answers.

The fires gleamed in his lavender eyes, Twinkle glowed in one hand, and he felt the urgings of his other blade, pleading for a demodand's heart to bite.

With all the courage that had marked Drizzt Do'Urden's existence coursing through his veins, and with all the fury of his perceptions of injustice focused on the fate of that beautiful and broken woman failing endlessly in a hopeless void, he dived into the gloom.

23

IF EVER YOU LOVED
CATTI-BRIE

Bruenor had come into Pook's chambers cursing and swinging, and by the time his initial momentum had worn away, he was far across the room from the Taros Hoop and from the two hill giant eunuchs that Pook had on guard. The guildmaster was closest to the raging dwarf, looking at him more in curiosity than terror.

Bruenor paid Pook no mind whatsoever. He looked beyond the plump man, to a robed form sitting against a wall: the wizard who had banished Catti-brie to Tarterus.

Recognizing the murderous hate in the red-bearded dwarf's eyes, LaValle rolled to his feet and scrambled through the door to his own room. His racing heart calmed when he heard the click of the door behind him, for it was a magic doorway with several holding and warding spells in place. He was safe—or so he thought.

Often wizards were blinded by their own considerable strength to other—less sophisticated, perhaps, but equally strong—forms of power. LaValle could not know the boiling cauldron that was Bruenor Battlehammer, and could not anticipate the brutality of the dwarf's rage.

His surprise was complete when a mithral axe, like a bolt of his own lightning, sundered his magically barred door to kindling and the wild dwarf stormed in.

Wulfgar, oblivious to the surroundings and wanting only to return to Tarterus and Catti-brie, came through the Taros Hoop just as Bruenor exited the room. Drizzt's call from across the planes, though, begging him to hold the portal open, could not be ignored. However the barbarian felt at that moment, for Catti-brie or Drizzt, he could not deny that his place was in guarding the mirror.

Still, the image of Catti-brie falling through the eternal gloom of that horrid place burned at his heart, and he wanted to spring right back through the Taros Hoop to rush to her aid.

Before the barbarian could decide whether to follow his heart or his thoughts, a huge fist slammed into the side of his head, dropping him to the floor. He flopped facedown between the tree trunk legs of two of Pook's hill giants. It was a difficult way to enter a fight, but Wulfgar's rage was every bit as intense as Bruenor's.

The giants tried to drop their heavy feet on Wulfgar, but he was too agile for such a clumsy maneuver. He sprang up between them and slammed one square in the face with a huge fist. The giant stared blankly at Wulfgar for a long moment, disbelieving that a human could deliver such a punch, then it hopped backward weirdly and dropped limply to the floor.

Wulfgar spun on the other, shattering its nose with the butt end of Aegis-fang. The giant clutched its face in both hands and reeled. For it, the fight was already over.

Wulfgar couldn't take the time to ask. He kicked the giant in the chest, launching it halfway across the room.

"Now, there is only me," came a voice. Wulfgar looked across the room to the huge chair that served as the guildmaster's throne, and to Pasha Pook, standing behind it.

Pook reached down behind the chair and pulled out a neatly concealed heavy crossbow, loaded and ready. "And I may be fat like those two," Pook chuckled, "but I am not stupid." He leveled the crossbow on the back of the chair.

Wulfgar glanced around. He was caught, fully, with no chance to dodge away.

But maybe he didn't have to.

Wulfgar firmed his jaw and puffed out his chest. "Right here, then," he said without flinching, tapping his finger over his heart. "Shoot me down." He cast a glance over his shoulder, to where the image in the Taros Hoop now showed the shadows of gathering demodands. "And you defend the entrance to the plane of Tarterus."

Pook eased his finger off the trigger.

If Wulfgar's point had made an impression, it was driven home a second later when the clawed hand of a demodand reached through the portal and latched onto Wulfgar's shoulder.

⚔ ⚔ ⚔ ⚔ ⚔

Drizzt moved as if swimming in his descent through the gloom, the pumping actions gaining him ground on Catti-brie. He was vulnerable, though, and he knew it.

So did a winged demodand watching him fall by.

The wretched creature hopped off its perch as soon as Drizzt had passed, flapping its wings at an awkward angle to gain momentum in its dive. Soon it was overtaking the drow, and it reached out its razor-sharp claws to tear at him as it passed.

Drizzt noticed the beast at the last moment. He twisted over wildly and spun about, trying to get out of the diving thing's path and struggling to ready his scimitars.

He should have had no chance. It was the demodand's environment, and it was a winged creature, more at home in flight than on the ground.

But Drizzt Do'Urden never played the odds.

The demodand strafed past, its wicked talons ripping yet another tear in Drizzt's fine cloak. Twinkle, as steady as ever even in midfall, lopped off one of the creature's wings. The demodand fluttered helplessly to the side and continued down in a tumble. It had no heart left for battle against the drow elf, and no wing left to catch him anyway.

Drizzt paid it no heed. His goal was in reach.

He caught Catti-brie in his arms, locking her tightly against his chest.

She was cold, he noted grimly, but he knew that he had too far to go to even think about that. He wasn't certain if the planar gate was still open, and he had no idea of how he could stop his eternal fall.

A solution came to him in the form of another winged demodand, one that cut an intercepting path at him and Catti-brie. The creature did not mean to attack yet, Drizzt could see; its route seemed more of a flyby, where it would pass under them to better inspect its foe.

Drizzt didn't let the chance go. As the creature passed under, the dark elf snapped himself downward, extending to his limit with one blade-wielding hand. Not aimed to kill, the scimitar found its mark, digging into the creature's backside. The demodand shrieked and dived away, pulling free of the blade.

Its momentum, though, had tugged Drizzt and Catti-brie along, angling their descent enough to line them up with one of the intersecting smoky bridges.

Drizzt twisted and turned to keep them in line, holding out his cloak with his free arm to catch a draft, or tucking it in tightly to lessen the drag. At the last moment, he spun himself under Catti-brie to shield her from the impact. With a heavy thud and a whoosh of smoke, they landed.

Drizzt crawled out and forced himself to his knees, trying to find his breath.

Catti-brie lay below him, pale and torn, a dozen wounds visible, most vividly the gash from the wererat's quarrel. Blood soaked much of her clothing and matted her hair, but Drizzt's heart did not drop at the gruesome sight, for he had noted one other event when they had plopped down.

Catti-brie had groaned.

꙾ ꙾ ꙾ ꙾ ꙾

LaValle scrambled behind his little table. "Keep you back, dwarf," he warned, "I am a wizard of great powers."

Bruenor's terror was not apparent. He drove his axe through the table, and a blinding explosion of smoke and sparks filled the room.

When LaValle recovered his sight a moment later, he found himself

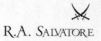

facing Bruenor, the dwarf's hands and beard trailing wisps of gray smoke, the little table broken flat, and his crystal ball severed clean in half.

"That the best ye got?" Bruenor asked.

LaValle couldn't get any words past the lump in his throat.

Bruenor wanted to cut him down, to drive his axe right between the man's bushy eyebrows, but it was Catti-brie, his beautiful daughter, who truly abhorred killing with all of her heart, whom he meant to avenge. Bruenor would not dishonor her memory.

"Drats!" he groaned, slamming his forehead into LaValle's face. The wizard thumped up against the wall and stayed there, dazed and motionless, until Bruenor closed a hand on his chest, tearing out a few hairs for good measure, and threw him facedown on the floor. "Me friends might be needin' yer help, wizard," the dwarf growled, "so crawl! And know in yer heart that if ye make one turn I don't be liking, me axe'll cleave yer head down the middle!"

In his semiconscious state, LaValle hardly heard the words, but he fathomed the dwarf's meaning well enough and forced himself to his hands and knees.

$$\times \quad \times \quad \times \quad \times \quad \times$$

Wulfgar braced his feet against the iron stand of the Taros Hoop and locked his own iron grip onto the demodand's elbow, matching the creature's mighty pull. In his other hand the barbarian held Aegis-fang ready, not wanting to swing through the planar portal but hoping for something more vulnerable than an arm to come through to his world.

The demodand's claws cut deep wounds in his shoulder, filthy wounds that would be long in healing, but Wulfgar shrugged away the pain. Drizzt had told him to hold the gate if ever he had loved Catti-brie.

He would hold the gate.

Another second passed and Wulfgar saw his hand slipping dangerously close to the portal. He could match the demodand's strength, but the demodand's power was magical, not physical, and Wulfgar would grow weary long before his foe.

Another inch, and his hand would cross through to Tarterus, where other hungry demodands no doubt waited.

A memory flashed in Wulfgar's mind, the final image of Catti-brie, torn and falling. "No!" he growled, and he forced his hand back, pulling savagely until he and the demodand were back to where they had started. Then Wulfgar dropped his shoulder suddenly, tugging the demodand down instead of out.

The gamble worked. The demodand lost its momentum altogether and stumbled down, its head poking through the Taros Hoop and into the Prime Material Plane for just a second, long enough for Aegis-fang to shatter its skull.

Wulfgar jumped back a step and slapped his warhammer into both hands. Another demodand started through, but the barbarian blasted it back into Tarterus with a powerful swipe.

Pook watched it all from behind his throne, his crossbow still aimed to kill. Even the guildmaster found himself mesmerized by the sheer strength of the giant man, and when one of his eunuchs recovered and stood up, Pook waved it away from Wulfgar, not wanting to disturb the spectacle before him.

A shuffle off to the side forced him to look away, though, as LaValle came crawling out of his room, the axe-wielding dwarf walking right behind.

Bruenor saw at once the perilous predicament that Wulfgar faced and knew that the wizard would only complicate things. He grabbed LaValle by the hair and pulled him up to his knees, walking around to face the man.

"Good day for sleepin'," the dwarf commented, and he slammed his forehead again into the wizard's, knocking LaValle into blackness. He heard a click behind him as the wizard slumped, and he reflexively swung his shield between himself and the noise, just in time to catch Pook's crossbow quarrel. The wicked dart drove a hole through the foaming mug standard and barely missed Bruenor's arm as it poked through the other side.

Bruenor peeked over the rim of his treasured shield, stared at the bolt, and then looked dangerously at Pook. "Ye shouldn't be hurtin' me shield!" he growled, and he started forward.

The hill giant was quick to intercept.

Wulfgar caught the action out of the corner of his eye, and would have loved to join in—especially with Pook busy reloading his heavy crossbow—but the barbarian had troubles of his own. A winged demodand swooped through the gate in a sudden rush and flashed by Wulfgar.

Fine-tuned reflexes saved the barbarian, for he snapped a hand out and caught the demodand by a leg. The monster's momentum staggered Wulfgar backward, but he managed to hold on. He slammed the demodand down beside him and drove it into the floor with a single chop of his warhammer.

Several arms reached through the Taros Hoop, shoulders and heads poked through, and Wulfgar, swinging Aegis-fang furiously, had all he could handle simply keeping the wretched things at bay.

⚔ ⚔ ⚔ ⚔ ⚔

Drizzt ran along the smoky bridge, Catti-brie draped limply over one shoulder. He met no further resistance for many minutes and understood why when he at last reached the planar gate.

Huddled around it, and blocking his passage, was a score of demodands.

The drow, dismayed, dropped to one knee and laid Catti-brie gently beside him. He considered putting Taulmaril to use, but realized that if he missed, if an arrow somehow found its way through the horde, it would pass through the gate and into the room where Wulfgar stood. He couldn't take that chance.

"So close," he whispered helplessly, looking down to Catti-brie. He held her tightly in his arms and brushed a slender hand across her face. How cool she seemed. Drizzt leaned low over her, meaning only to discern the rhythm of her breathing, but he found himself too close to her, and before he even realized his actions, his lips were to hers in a tender kiss. Catti-brie stirred but did not open her eyes.

Her movement brought new courage to Drizzt. "Too close," he muttered grimly, "and you'll not die in this foul place!" He scooped Catti-brie up over his shoulder, wrapping his cloak tightly around her to secure her to him. Then he took up his scimitars in tight grips, rubbing his sensitive fingers across the intricate craftings of their hilts, becoming one with his weapons, making them the killing extensions of his black arms. He took a deep breath and set his visage.

He charged, as silently as only a drow elf could be, at the back of the wretched horde.

⚔ ⚔ ⚔ ⚔

Regis rose uncomfortably as the black silhouettes of hunting cats darted in and out of the starlight surrounding him. They did not seem to threaten him—not yet—but they were gathering. He knew beyond doubt that he was their focal point.

Then Guenhwyvar bounded up and stood before him, the great cat's head level with his own.

"You know something," Regis said, reading the excitement in the panther's dark eyes. Regis held up the statuette and examined it, noting the cat's tenseness at the sight of the figurine.

"We can get back with this," the halfling said in sudden revelation. "This is the key to the journey, and with it, we can go wherever we desire!" He glanced around and considered some very interesting possibilities. "All of us?"

If cats could smile, Guenhwyvar did.

24
INTERPLANAR GOO

O utta me way, ye overstuffed bag o' blubber!" Bruenor roared.

The giant eunuch planted its legs wide apart and reached down at the dwarf with a huge hand—which Bruenor promptly bit.

"They never listen," he grumbled, He stooped low and dashed between the giant's legs, then straightened quickly, the single horn on his helmet putting the poor eunuch up on its toes. For the second time that day, its eyes crossed and it tumbled, this time its hands low to hold its newest wound.

A killing rage evident in his gray eyes, Bruenor turned back to Pook. The guildmaster, though, seemed unconcerned, and in truth, the dwarf hardly, noticed the man. He concentrated instead on the crossbow again, which was loaded and leveled at him.

⚔ ⚔ ⚔ ⚔ ⚔

Drizzt's single emotion as he came in was anger, anger at the pain the wretched creatures of Tarterus had caused to Catti-brie.

His goal, too, was singular: the little patch of light in the gloom, the planar gate back to his own world.

His scimitars led the way, and Drizzt grinned at the thought of tearing through the demodand flesh, but the drow slowed as he came in, his anger tempered by the sight of his goal. He could whirl in on the demodand horde in an attacking frenzy and probably manage to slip through the gate, but could Catti-brie take the punishment the mighty creatures would surely inflict before Drizzt got her through?

The drow saw another way. As he inched in on the back of the demodand line, he reached out wide to either side with his blades, tapping the back two demodands on their outside shoulders. As the creatures reflexively turned to look back over their shoulders, Drizzt darted between them.

The drow's blades became a whirring prow, nicking away the hands of any other demodands that tried to catch him. He felt a tug on Catti-brie and whirled quickly, his rage doubled. He couldn't see his target, but he knew that he had connected on something when he brought Twinkle down and heard a demodand shriek.

A heavy arm clubbed him on the side of the head, a blow that should have felled him, but Drizzt spun back again and saw the light of the gate only a few feet ahead—and the silhouette of a single demodand, standing to block his passage.

The dark tunnel of demodand flesh began to close about him. Another large arm wheeled in, but Drizzt was able to duck beneath its arc.

If the demodand delayed him a single second, he would be caught and slaughtered.

Again it was instinct, faster than thought, that carried Drizzt through. He slapped the demodand's arms wide apart with his scimitars and ducked his head, slamming into the demodand's chest, his momentum forcing the creature backward through the gate.

⚔ ⚔ ⚔ ⚔ ⚔

The dark head and shoulders came through into Wulfgar's sights, and he hammered Aegis-fang home. The mighty blow snapped the demodand's backbone and jolted Drizzt, who pushed from the other side.

The demodand fell dead, half in and half out of the Taros Hoop, and the stunned drow rolled limply to the side and out, tumbling into Pook's room, beneath Catti-brie.

Wulfgar paled at the sight and hesitated, but Drizzt, realizing that more creatures would soon rush through, managed to lift his weary head from the floor. "Close the gate," he gasped.

Wulfgar had already discerned that he could not shatter the glassy image within the hoop—striking at it only sent his warhammer's head into Tarterus. Wulfgar started to drop Aegis-fang to his side.

Then he noticed the action across the room.

✕ ✕ ✕ ✕

"Are you quick enough with that shield?" Pook teased, wiggling the crossbow.

Intent on the weapon, Bruenor hadn't even noticed Drizzt and Catti-brie's grand entrance. "So ye've one shot to kill me, dog," he spat back, unafraid of death, "and one alone." He took a determined step forward.

Pook shrugged. He was an expert marksman, and his crossbow was as enchanted as any weapon in the Realms. One shot would be enough.

But he never got it off.

A twirling warhammer exploded into the throne, knocking the huge chair over into the guildmaster and sending him sprawling heavily into the wall.

Bruenor turned with a grim smile to thank his barbarian friend, but his smile washed away and the words died in his throat when he saw Drizzt and Catti-brie lying beside the Taros Hoop.

The dwarf stood as if turned to stone, his eyes not blinking, his lungs not drawing breath. The strength went out of his legs, and he fell to his knees. He dropped his axe and shield and scrambled, on all fours, to his daughter's side.

Wulfgar clasped the iron edges of the Taros Hoop in his hands and tried to force them together. His entire upper body flushed red, and the veins and sinewy muscles stood out like iron cords in his huge arms. But if there was any movement in the gate, it was slight.

A demodand arm reached through the portal to prevent the closing, but the sight of it only spurred Wulfgar on. He roared to Tempus and pushed with all his strength, driving his hands together, bending the edges of hoop in to meet each other.

The glassy image bowed with the planar shift, and the demodand's arm dropped to the,floor, cleanly severed. Likewise, the demodand that lay dead at Wulfgar's feet, with half its body still inside the gate, twitched and turned.

Wulfgar averted his eyes at the horrid spectacle of a winged demodand caught within the warping planar tunnel, bent and bowed until its skin began to rip apart.

The magic of the Taros Hoop was strong, and Wulfgar, for all of his strength, could not hope to bend the thing far enough to complete the job. He had the gate warped and blocked, but for how long? When he tired, and the Taros Hoop returned to its normal shape, the portal would open once again. Stubbornly the barbarian roared and drove on, turning his head to the side in anticipation of the shattering of the glassy surface.

✕ ✕ ✕ ✕ ✕

How pale she seemed, her lips almost blue and her skin dry and chill. Her wounds were vicious, Bruenor saw, but the dwarf sensed that the most telling injury was neither cut nor bruise. Rather, his precious girl seemed to have lost her spirit, as though she'd given up her desire for life when she had fallen into the darkness.

She now lay limp, cold, and pale in his arms. On the floor, Drizzt instinctively recognized the dangers. He lolled over to the side, pulling his cloak out wide, shielding Bruenor, who was quite oblivious to his surroundings, and Catti-brie with his own body.

Across the room, LaValle stirred, shaking the grogginess out of his head. He rose to his knees and surveyed the room, immediately recognizing Wulfgar's attempt to close the gate.

"Kill them," Pook whispered to the wizard but not daring to crawl out from under the overturned chair.

LaValle wasn't listening; he had already begun a spell.

⚔ ⚔ ⚔ ⚔ ⚔

For the first time in his life, Wulfgar found his strength inadequate. "I cannot!" he grunted in dismay, looking to Drizzt—as he always looked to Drizzt—for an answer.

The wounded drow was barely coherent.

Wulfgar wanted to surrender. His arm burned from the gashes of the hydra bite; his legs seemed barely able to hold him; his friends were helpless on the floor.

And his strength was not enough!

He shot his gaze to and fro, searching for some alternate method. The hoop, however powerful, had to have a weakness. Or, at least, to hold out any hope, Wulfgar had to believe that it did.

Regis had gotten through it, had found a way to circumvent its power.

Regis.

Wulfgar found his answer.

He gave a final heave on the Taros Hoop, then released it quickly, sending the portal into a momentary wobble. Wulfgar didn't hesitate to watch the eerie spectacle. He dived down and snatched the pearl-tipped scepter from Drizzt's belt, then leaped up straight and slammed the fragile device onto the top of the Taros Hoop, shattering the black pearl into a thousand tiny shards.

At that same moment, LaValle uttered the last syllable of his spell, releasing a mighty bolt of energy. It ripped past Wulfgar, searing the hairs on his arm, and blasted into the center of the Taros Hoop. The glassy image, cracked into the circular design of a spider's web by Wulfgar's cunning strike, broke apart altogether.

The ensuing explosion rocked the foundations of the guildhouse.

Thick patches of darkness swirled about the room; the onlookers perceived the whole place to be spinning, and a sudden wind whistled and howled in their ears, as though they had all been caught in the tumult of a rift in the very planes of existence. Black smoke and fumes rushed in upon them. The darkness became total.

Then, as quickly as it had begun, it passed away and daylight returned to the battered room. Drizzt and Bruenor were the first to their feet, studying the damage and the survivors.

The Taros Hoop lay twisted and shattered, a bent frame of worthless iron with a sticky, weblike substance clinging stubbornly in torn patches. A winged demodand lay dead on the floor, the severed arm of another creature beside it, and half the body of yet another beside that, still twitching in death, with thick, dark fluids spilling onto the floor.

A dozen feet back sat Wulfgar, propped up on his elbows and looking perplexed, one arm bright red from LaValle's energy bolt, his face blackened by the rush of smoke, and his entire frame matted in the gooey webbing. A hundred little dots of blood dotted the barbarian's body. Apparently the glassy image of the planar portal had been more than just an image.

Wulfgar looked at his friends distantly, blinked his eyes a few times, and dropped flat on his back.

LaValle groaned, catching the notice of Drizzt and Bruenor. The wizard started to struggle back to his knees, but realized that he would only be exposing himself to the victorious invaders. He slumped back to the floor and lay very still.

Drizzt and Bruenor looked at each other, wondering what to do next.

"Fine to see the light again," came a soft voice below them. They looked down to meet the gaze of Catti-brie, her deep blue eyes opened once again.

Bruenor, in tears, dropped to his knees and huddled over her. Drizzt started to follow the dwarf's lead, but sensed that theirs should be a private moment. He gave a comforting pat on Bruenor's shoulder and walked away to make sure that Wulfgar was all right.

A sudden burst of movement interrupted him as he knelt over his barbarian friend. The great throne, torn and scorched against the wall, toppled forward. Drizzt held it away easily, but while he was engaged, he saw Pasha Pook dart out from behind the object and bolt for the room's main door.

"Bruenor!" Drizzt called, but he knew even as he said it that the dwarf was too caught up with his daughter to be bothered. Drizzt pushed the great chair away and pulled Taulmaril off his back, stringing it as he started in pursuit.

Pook rushed through the door, swinging around to slam it behind him.

"Rassit—" he started to yell as he turned back toward the stairs, but the word stuck in his throat when he saw Regis, arms crossed, standing before him at the top of the stairway.

"You!" Pook roared, his face twisting and his hands clenching in rage.

"No, him," Regis corrected, pointing a finger above as a sleek black form leaped over him.

To the stunned Pook, Guenhwyvar appeared as no more than a flying ball of big teeth and claws.

By the time Drizzt got through the door, Pook's reign as guildmaster had come to a crashing end.

"Guenhwyvar!" the drow called, within reach of his treasured companion for the first time in many tendays. The big panther loped over to Drizzt and nuzzled him warmly, every bit as happy with the reunion.

Other sights and sounds kept the meeting short, however. First there was Regis, reclining comfortably on the decorated banister, his hands locked behind his head and his furry feet crossed. Drizzt was glad to see Regis again, as well, but more disturbing to the drow were the sounds echoing up the stairs: screams of terror and throaty growls.

Bruenor heard them, too, and he came out of the room to investigate. "Rumblebelly!" he hailed Regis, following Drizzt to the halfling's side.

They looked down the great stairway at the battles below. Every now and then, a wererat crossed by, pursued by a panther. One group of ratmen formed a defensive circle, their blades flashing about to deter Guenhwyvar's feline friends, right below the friends, but a wave of black fur and gleaming teeth buried them where they stood.

"Cats?" Bruenor gawked at Regis. "Ye brought cats?"

Regis smiled and shifted his head in his hands. "You know a better way to get rid of mice?"

Bruenor shook his head and couldn't hide his own smile. He looked back at the body of the man who had fled the room. "Dead, too," he remarked grimly.

"That was Pook," Regis told them, though they had already guessed the guildmaster's identity. "Now he is gone, and so, I believe, will his wererats associates be."

Regis looked at Drizzt, knowing an explanation to be necessary. "Guenhwyvar's friends are only hunting the ratmen," he said. "And him, of course." He pointed to Pook. "The regular thieves are hiding in their rooms—if they're smart—but the panthers wouldn't hurt them anyway."

Drizzt nodded his approval at the discretion Regis and Guenhwyvar had chosen. Guenhwyvar was not a vigilante.

"We all came through the statue," Regis continued. "I kept it with me when I went out of Tarterus with Guenhwyvar. The cats can go back through it to their own plane when their work is done." He tossed the figurine back to its rightful owner.

A curious look came over the halfling's face. He snapped his fingers and hopped down from the banister, as if his last action had given him an idea. He ran to Pook, rolled the former guildmaster's head to the side—trying to ignore the very conspicuous wound in Pook's neck—and lifted off the ruby pendant that had started the whole adventure. Satisfied, Regis turned to the very curious stares of his two friends.

"Time to make some allies," the haffling explained, and he darted off down the stairs.

Bruenor and Drizzt looked at each other in disbelief.

"He'll own the guild," Bruenor assured the drow.

Drizzt didn't argue the point.

✕ ✕ ✕ ✕

From an alley on Rogues Circle, Rassiter, again in his human form, heard the dying screams of his fellow ratmen. He had been smart enough to understand that the guild was overmatched by the heroes from the North, and when Pook sent him down to rally the fight, he had slipped instead back into the protection of the sewers.

Now he could only listen to the cries and wonder how many of his lycanthrope kin would survive the dark day. "I will build a new guild," he vowed to himself, though he fully understood the enormity of the task, especially now that he had achieved such notoriety in Calimport. Perhaps he could travel to another city—Memnon or Baldur's Gate—farther up the coast.

His ponderings came to an abrupt end as the flat of a curving blade came to rest on his shoulder, the razor edge cutting a tiny line across the side of his neck.

Rassiter held up a jeweled dagger. "This is yours, I believe," he said, trying to sound calm. The saber slipped away and Rassiter turned to face Artemis Entreri.

Entreri reached out with a bandaged arm to pull the dagger away, at the same time slipping the saber back into its scabbard.

"I knew you had been beaten," Rassiter said boldly. "I feared you dead."

"Feared?" Entreri grinned. "Or hoped?"

"It is true that you and I started as rivals," Rassiter began.

Entreri laughed again. He had never figured the ratman worthy enough to be considered a rival.

Rassiter took the insult in stride. "But we then served the same master." He looked to the guildhouse, where the screaming had finally begun to fade. "I think Pook is dead, or at least thrown from power."

"If he faced the drow, he is dead," Entreri spat, the mere thought of Drizzt Do'Urden filling his throat with bile.

"Then the streets are open," Rassiter reasoned. He gave Entreri a sly wink. "For the taking."

"You and I?" Entreri mused.

Rassiter shrugged. "Few in Calimport would oppose you," the wererat said, "and with my infectious bite, I can breed a host of loyal followers in mere tendays. Certainly none would dare stand against us in the night."

Entreri moved beside him, joining him in his scan of the guildhouse. "Yes, my ravenous friend," he said quietly, "but there remain two problems."

"Two?"

"Two," Entreri reiterated. "First, I work alone."

Rassiter's body jolted straight as a dagger blade cut into his spine.

"And second," Entreri continued, without missing a breath, "You are dead." He jerked the bloody dagger out and held it vertical, to wipe the blade on Rassiter's cloak as the wererat fell lifeless to the ground.

Entreri surveyed his handiwork and the bandages on his wounded elbow.

"Stronger already," he muttered to himself, and he slipped away to find a dark hole. The morning was full and bright now, and the assassin, still with much healing to do, was not ready to face the challenges he might come across on the daytime streets.

25

A WALK IN THE SUN

Bruenor knocked lightly on the door, not expecting a response. As usual, no reply came back. This time, though, the stubborn dwarf did not walk away. He turned the latch and entered the darkened room.

Stripped to the waist and running his slender fingers through his thick mane of white hair, Drizzt sat on his bed with his back to Bruenor. Even in the dimness, Bruenor could clearly see the scab line sliced across the drow's back. The dwarf shuddered, never imagining in those wild hours of battle that Drizzt had been so viciously wounded by Artemis Entreri.

"Five days, elf," Bruenor said quietly. "Do ye mean to live yer life in here?"

Drizzt turned slowly to face his dwarven friend. "Where else would I go?" he replied.

Bruenor studied the lavender eyes, twinkling to reflect the light of the hallway beyond the open door. The left one had opened again, the dwarf noted hopefully. Bruenor had feared that the demodand's blow had forever closed Drizzt's eye.

Clearly it was healing, but still those marvelous orbs worried Bruenor. They seemed to him to have lost a good bit of their luster.

"How is Catti-brie?" Drizzt asked, sincerely concerned about the young woman, but also wanting to change the subject.

Bruenor smiled. "Not for walkin' yet," he replied, "but her fighting's back and she's not caring for lyin' quiet in a bed!" He chuckled, recalling the scene earlier in the day, when one attendant had tried to primp his daughter's pillow. Catti-brie's glare alone had drained the blood from the man's face. "Cuts her servants down with her blade of a tongue when they fuss over her."

Drizzt's smile seemed strained. "And Wulfgar?"

"The boy's better," Bruenor replied. "Took four hours scraping the spider gook off him, and he'll be wearin' wrappings on his arm for a month to come, but more'n that's needed to bring that boy down! Tough as a mountain, and nearen as big!"

They watched each other until the smiles faded and the silence grew uncomfortable. "The halfling's feast is about to begin," Bruenor said. "Ye going? With a belly so round, me guess is that Rumblebelly will set a fine table."

Drizzt shrugged noncommittally.

"Bah!" Bruenor snorted. "Ye can't be living yer life between dark walls!" He paused as a thought suddenly popped into his head. "Or are ye out at night?" he asked slyly.

"Out?"

"Hunting," explained Bruenor. "Are ye out hunting Entreri?"

Now, Drizzt did laugh—at the notion that Bruenor linked his desire for solitude to some obsession with the assassin.

"Ye're burning for him," Bruenor reasoned, "and he for yerself if he's still for drawing breath."

"Come," Drizzt said, pulling a loose shirt over his head. He picked up the magical mask as he started around the bed, but stopped to consider the item. He rolled it over in his hands, then dropped it back to the dressing table. "Let us not be late for the feast."

Bruenor's guess about Regis had not missed the mark; the table awaiting the two friends was splendidly adorned with shining silver and porcelain, and the aromas of delicacies had them unconsciously licking their lips as they moved to their appointed seats.

Regis sat at the long table's head, the thousand gemstones he had sewn into his tunic catching the candlelight in a glittering burst every time he shifted in his seat. Behind him stood the two hill giant eunuchs who had guarded Pook at the bitter end, their faces bruised and bandaged

At the halfling's right sat LaValle, to Bruenor's distaste, and at his left, a narrow-eyed halfling and a chubby young man, the chief lieutenants in the new guild.

Farther down the table sat Wulfgar and Catti-brie, side by side, their hands clasped between them, which, Drizzt guessed—by the pale and weary looks of the two—was as much for mutual support as genuine affection.

As weary as they were, though, their faces lit with smiles, as did Regis's, when they saw Drizzt enter the room, the first time any of them had seen the drow in nearly a tenday.

"Welcome, welcome!" Regis said happily. "It would have been a shallow feast if you could not join us!"

Drizzt slid into the chair beside LaValle, drawing a concerned look from the timid wizard. The guild's lieutenants, too, shifted uneasily at the thought of dining with a drow elf.

Drizzt smiled away the weight of their discomfort; it was their problem, not his. "I have been busy," he told Regis.

"Brooding," Bruenor wanted to say as he sat next to Drizzt, but he tactfully held his tongue.

Wulfgar and Catti-brie stared at their black friend from across the table.

"You swore to kill me," the drow said calmly to Wulfgar, causing the big man to sag back in his chair.

Wulfgar flushed a deep red and tightened his grip on Catti-brie's hand.

"Only the strength of Wulfgar could have held that gate," Drizzt explained. The edges of his mouth turned up in a wistful smile.

"But, I—" Wulfgar began, but Catti-brie cut him short.

"Enough said about it, then," the young woman insisted, banging her fist into Wulfgar's thigh. "Let us not be talking about troubles we've past. Too much remains before us!"

"Me girl's right," spouted Bruenor. "The days walk by us as we sit and heal! Another tenday, and we might be missing a war."

"I am ready to go," declared Wulfgar.

"Ye're not," retorted Catti-brie. "Nor am I. The desert'd stop us afore we ever got on the long road beyond."

"Ahem," Regis began, drawing their attention. "About your departure . . ." He stopped to consider their stares, nervous about presenting his offer in just the right way. "I . . . uh . . . thought that . . . I mean . . ."

"Spit it," demanded Bruenor, guessing what his little friend had in mind.

"Well, I have built a place for myself here," Regis continued.

"And ye're to stay," reasoned Catti-brie. "We'll not blame ye, though we're sure to be missing ye!"

"Yes," said Regis, "and no. There is room here, and wealth. With the four of you by my side . . ."

Bruenor halted him with an upraised hand. "A fine offer," he said, "but me home's in the North."

"We've armies waiting on our return," added Catti-brie.

Regis realized the finality of Bruenor's refusal, and he knew that Wulfgar would certainly follow Catti-brie back to Tarterus if she so chose. So the halfling turned his sights on Drizzt, who had become an unreadable puzzle to them all in the last few days.

Drizzt sat back and considered the proposition, his hesitancy to deny the offer drawing concerned stares from Bruenor, Wulfgar, and particularly, Catti-brie. Perhaps life in Calimport would not be so bad, and certainly the drow had the tools to thrive in the shadowy realm Regis planned to operate within. He looked Regis square in the eye.

"No," he said. He turned at the audible sigh from Catti-brie across the table, and their eyes locked. "I have walked through too many shadows already," he explained. "A noble quest stands before me, and a noble throne awaits its rightful king."

Regis relaxed back in his chair and shrugged. He had expected as much. "If you are all so determined to go back to a war, then I would be a sorry friend if I did not aid your quest."

The others eyed him curiously, never amazed at the surprises the little one could pull.

"To that end," Regis continued, "one of my agents reported the arrival of an important person—from the tales Bruenor has told me of your journey south—in Calimport this morning." He snapped his fingers, and a young attendant entered from a side curtain, leading Captain Deudermont.

The captain bowed low to Regis, and lower still to the dear friends he had made on the perilous journey from Waterdeep. "The wind was at our backs," he explained, "and the *Sea Sprite* runs swifter than ever. We can depart on the morrow's dawn; surely the gentle rock of a boat is a fine place to mend weary bones!"

"But the trade," said Drizzt. "The market is here in Calimport. And the season. You did not plan to leave before spring."

"I may not be able to get you all the way to Waterdeep," said Deudermont. "The winds and ice will tell. But you surely will find yourself closer to your goal when you take to land once again." He looked over at Regis, then back to Drizzt. "For my losses in trade, accommodations have been made."

Regis tucked his thumbs into his jeweled belt. "I owed you that, at the least!"

"Bah!" snorted Bruenor, an adventurous gleam in his eye. "Ten times more, Rumblebelly, ten times more!"

✕ ✕ ✕ ✕ ✕

Drizzt looked out of his room's single window at the dark streets of Calimport. They seemed quieter this night, hushed in suspicion and intrigue, anticipating the power struggle that would inevitably follow the downfall of a guildmaster as powerful as Pasha Pook.

Drizzt knew that there were other eyes out there, looking back at him, at the guildhouse, waiting for word of the drow elf—waiting for a second chance to battle Drizzt Do'Urden.

The night passed lazily, and Drizzt, unmoving from his window, watched it drift into dawn. Again, Bruenor was the first to his room.

"Ye ready, elf?" the eager dwarf asked, closing the door behind him as he entered.

"Patience, good dwarf," Drizzt replied. "We cannot leave until the tide is right, and Captain Deudermont assured me that we had the bulk of the morning to wait."

Bruenor plopped down on the bed. "Better," he said at length. "Gives me more time to speak with the little one."

"You fear for Regis," observed Drizzt.

"Ayuh," Bruenor admitted. "The little one's done well by me." He pointed to the onyx statuette on the dressing table. "And by yerself. Rumblebelly said it himself: There's wealth to be taken here. Pook's gone, and it's to be grab-as-grab-can. And that Entreri's about—that's not to me likin'. And more of them ratmen, not to doubt, looking to pay the little one back for their pain. And that wizard! Rumblebelly says he's got him by the gemstones, if ye get me meaning, but it seems off to me that a wizard's caught by such a charm."

"To me, as well," Drizzt agreed.

"I don't like him, and I don't trust him!" Bruenor declared. "Rumblebelly's got him standing right by his side."

"Perhaps you and I should pay LaValle a visit this morning," Drizzt offered, "that we might judge where he stands."

⚔ ⚔ ⚔ ⚔ ⚔

Bruenor's knocking technique shifted subtly when they arrived at the wizard's door, from the gentle tapping he had laid on Drizzt's door, to a battering-ram crescendo of heavy slugs. LaValle jumped from his bed and rushed to see what was the matter, and who was beating upon his brand new door.

"Morning, wizard," Bruenor grumbled, pushing into the room as soon as the door cracked open.

"So I guessed," muttered LaValle, looking to the hearth and beside it to the pile of kindling that was once his old door.

"Greetings, good dwarf," he said as politely as he could muster. "And Master Do'Urden," he added quickly when he noticed Drizzt slipping in behind. "Were you not to be gone by this late hour?"

"We have time," said Drizzt.

"And we're not for leaving till we've seen to the safety of Rumblebelly," Bruenor explained.

"Rumblebelly?" echoed LaValle.

"The halfling!" roared Bruenor. "Yer master."

"Ah, yes, Master Regis," said LaValle wistfully, his hands going together over his chest and his eyes taking on a distant, glossy look.

Drizzt shut the door and glared, suspicious, at him.

LaValle's faraway trance faded back to normal when he considered the unblinking drow. He scratched his chin, looking for somewhere to run. He couldn't fool the drow, he realized. The dwarf, perhaps, the halfling, certainly, but not this one. Those lavender eyes burned holes right through his facade. "You do not believe that your little friend has cast his enchantment over me," he said.

"Wizards avoid wizards' traps," Drizzt replied.

"Fair enough," said LaValle, slipping into a chair.

"Bah! Then ye're a liar, too!" growled Bruenor, his hand going to the axe on his belt. Drizzt stopped him.

"If you doubt the enchantment," said LaValle, "do not doubt my loyalty. I am a practical man who has served many masters in my long life. Pook was the greatest of these, but Pook is gone. LaValle lives on to serve again."

"Or mighten be that he sees a chance to make the top," Bruenor remarked, expecting an angry response from LaValle.

Instead, the wizard laughed heartily. "I have my craft," he said. "It is all that I care for. I live in comfort and am free to go as I please. I need not the challenges and dangers of a guildmaster." He looked to Drizzt as the more reasonable of the two. "I will serve the halfling, and if Regis is thrown down, I will serve he that takes the halfling's place."

The logic satisfied Drizzt, and convinced him of the wizard's loyalty beyond any enchantment the ruby could have induced. "Let us take our leave," he said to Bruenor, and he started out the door.

Bruenor could trust Drizzt's judgment, but he couldn't resist one final threat. "Ye crossed me, wizard," he growled from the doorway. "Ye nearen killed me girl. If me friend comes to a bad end, ye'll pay with yer head."

LaValle nodded but said nothing.

"Keep him well," the dwarf finished with a wink, and he slammed the door with a bang.

"He hates my door," the wizard lamented.

The troupe gathered inside the guildhouse's main entrance an hour later, Drizzt, Bruenor, Wulfgar, and Catti-brie outfitted again in their adventuring gear, and Drizzt with the magical mask hanging loose around his neck.

Regis, with attendants in tow, joined them. He would make the trip to the *Sea Sprite* beside his formidable friends. Let his enemies see his allies in all their splendor, the sly new guildmaster figured, particularly a drow elf.

"A final offer before we go," Regis proclaimed.

"We're not for staying," Bruenor retorted.

"Not to you," Regis said. He turned squarely to Drizzt. "To you."

Drizzt waited patiently for the pitch as the halfling rubbed his eager hands together.

"Fifty thousand gold pieces," Regis said at length, "for your cat."

Drizzt's eyes widened to double their size.

"Guenhwyvar will be well cared for, I assure—"

Catti-brie slapped Regis on the back of the head. "Find yer shame," she scolded. "Ye know the drow better than that!"

Drizzt calmed her with a smile. "A treasure for a treasure?" he said to Regis. "You know I must decline. Guenhwyvar cannot be bought, however good your intentions may be."

"Fifty thousand," Bruenor huffed. "If we wanted it, we'd take it afore we left!"

Regis then realized the absurdity of the offer, and he blushed in embarrassment.

"Are you so certain that we came across the world to your aid?" Wulfgar asked him. Regis looked at the barbarian, confused.

"Perhaps 'twas the cat we came after," Wulfgar continued seriously.

The stunned look on Regis's face proved more than any of them could bear, and a burst of laughter like none of them had enjoyed in many months erupted, infecting even Regis.

"Here," Drizzt offered when things had quieted once again. "Take this instead." He pulled the magical mask off his head and tossed it to the halfling.

"Should ye keep it until we get to the boat?" Bruenor asked.

Drizzt looked to Catti-brie for an answer, and her smile of approval and admiration cast away any remaining doubts he might have had.

"No," he said. "Let the Calishites judge me for what they will." He swung open the doors, allowing the morning sun to sparkle in his lavender eyes.

"Let the wide world judge me for what it will," he said, his look one of genuine contentment as he dropped his gaze alternately into the eyes of each of his four friends.

"You know who I am."

EPILOGUE

The *Sea Sprite* cut a difficult course northward up the Sword Coast, into the wintry winds, but Captain Deudermont and his grateful crew were determined to see the four friends safely and swiftly back to Waterdeep.

Stunned expressions from every face on the docks greeted the resilient vessel as it put into Waterdeep Harbor, dodging the breakers and the ice floes as it went. Mustering all the skill he had gained through years of experience, Deudermont docked the *Sea Sprite* safely.

The four friends had recovered much of their health, and their humor, during those two months at sea, despite the rough voyage. All had turned out well in the end—even Catti-brie's wounds appeared as if they would fully heal.

But if the sea voyage back to the North was difficult, the trek across the frozen lands was even worse. Winter was on the wane but still thick in the land, and the friends could not afford to wait for the snows to melt. They said their good-byes to Deudermont and the men of the *Sea Sprite*, tightened heavy cloaks and boots, and trudged off through Waterdeep's gate along the Trade Way on the northeastern course to Longsaddle.

Blizzards and wolves reared up to stop them. The path of the road, its plentiful markings buried under a year's worth of snow, became no more than the guess of a drow elf reading the stars and the sun.

Somehow they made it, though, and they stormed into Longsaddle, ready to retake Mithral Hall. Bruenor's kin from Icewind Dale were there to greet them, along with five hundred of Wulfgar's people. Less than two tendays later, General Dagnabit of Citadel Adbar led his eight thousand dwarven troops to Bruenor's side.

Battle plans were drawn and redrawn. Drizzt and Bruenor put their memories of the undercity and mine caverns together to create models of the place and estimate the number of duergar the army would face.

Then, with spring defeating the last blows of winter, and only a few days before the army was to set out to the mountains, two more groups of allies came in, quite unexpectedly: contingents of archers from Silverymoon and Nesme. Bruenor at first wanted to turn the warriors from Nesme away, remembering the treatment he and his friends had received at the hands of a Nesme patrol on their initial journey to Mithral Hall, and also because the dwarf wondered how much of the show of allegiance was motivated in the hopes of friendship, and how much in the hopes of profit!

But, as usual, Bruenor's friends kept him on a wise course. The dwarves would have to deal extensively with Nesme, the closest settlement to Mithral Hall, once the mines were reopened, and a smart leader would patch the bad feelings there and then.

⚔ ⚔ ⚔ ⚔

Their numbers were overwhelming, their determination unrivaled, and their leaders magnificent. Bruenor and Dagnabit led the main assault force of battle-hardened dwarves and wild barbarians, sweeping out room after room of the duergar scum. Catti-brie, with her bow, the few Harpells who had made the journey, and the archers from the two cities, cleared the side passages along the main force's thrust.

Drizzt, Wulfgar, and Guenhwyyar, as they had so often in the past, forged out alone, scouting the areas ahead of and below the army, taking out more than their share of duergar along the way.

In three days, the top level was cleared. In two tendays, the undercity. By the time spring had settled fully onto the northland, less than a month after

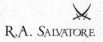

the army had set out from Longsaddle, the hammers of Clan Battlehammer began their smithing song in the ancient halls once again.

And the rightful king took his throne.

✕ ✕ ✕ ✕ ✕

Drizzt looked down from the mountains to the distant lights of the enchanted city of Silverymoon. He had been turned away from that city once before—a painful rejection—but not this time.

He could walk the land as he chose, now, with his head held high and the cowl of his cloak thrown back. Most of the world did not treat him any differently; few knew the name of Drizzt Do'Urden. But Drizzt knew now that he owed no apologies, or excuses, for his black skin, and to those who placed unfair judgment upon him, he offered none.

The weight of the world's prejudice would still fall upon him heavily, but Drizzt had learned, by the insights of Catti-brie, to stand against it.

What a wonderful friend she was to him. Drizzt had watched her grow into a special young woman, and he was warmed now by the knowledge that she had found her home.

The thought of her with Wulfgar, and standing beside Bruenor, touched the dark elf, who had never experienced the closeness of family.

"How much we all have changed," the drow whispered to the empty mountain wind.

His words were not a lament.

✕ ✕ ✕ ✕ ✕

The autumn saw the first crafted goods flow from Mithral Hall to Silverymoon, and by the time winter turned again to spring, the trade was in full force, with the barbarians from Icewind Dale working as market bearers for the dwarven goods.

That spring, too, a carving was begun in the Hall of Kings: the likeness of Bruenor Battlehammer.

To the dwarf who had wandered so far from his home and had seen so many marvelous—and horrible—sights, the reopening of the mines, and even the carving of his bust, seemed of minor importance when weighed against another event planned for that year.

"I told ye he'd be back," Bruenor said to Wulfgar and Catti-brie, who both sat beside him in his audience hall. "Th' elf'd not be missing such a thing as yer wedding!"

General Dagnabit—who, with blessings from King Harbromme of Citadel Adbar, had stayed on with two thousand other dwarves, swearing allegiance to Bruenor—entered the room, escorting a figure who had become less and less noticeable in Mithral Hall over the last few months.

"Greetings," said Drizzt, moving up to his friends

"So ye made it," Catti-brie said absently, feigning disinterest.

"We had not planned for this," added Wulfgar in the same casual tone. "I pray that there may be an extra seat at the table."

Drizzt only smiled and bowed low in apology. He had been absent quite often—for tendays at a time—lately. Personal invitations to visit the Lady of Silverymoon and her enchanted realm were not so easily refused.

"Bah!" Bruenor snorted. "I told ye he'd come back! And back to stay, this time!"

Drizzt shook his head.

Bruenor cocked his in return, wondering what was getting into his friend. "Ye hunting for that assassin, elf?" he could not help but ask.

Drizzt grinned and shook his bead again "I've no desire to meet that one again," he replied. He looked at Catti-brie—she understood—then back to Bruenor. "There are many sights in the wide world, dear dwarf, that cannot be seen from the shadows. Many sounds more pleasant than the ring of steel, and many smells preferable to the stench of death."

"Cook another feast," Bruenor grumbled. "Suren the elf has his eyes fixed on another wedding!"

Drizzt let it go at that. Maybe there was a ring of truth in Bruenor's words, for some distant date. No longer did Drizzt limit his hopes and desires. He would see the world as he could and draw his choices from his wishes, not from limitations he might impose upon himself. For now, though, Drizzt had found something too personal to be shared.

For the first time in his life, the drow had found peace.

Another dwarf entered the room and scurried up to Dagnabit. They both took their leave, but Dagnabit returned a few moments later.

"What is it?" Bruenor asked him, confused by all the bustle.

"Another guest," Dagnabit explained, but before he could launch a proper introduction, a halfling figure slipped into the room.

"Regis!" Catti-brie cried. She and Wulfgar rushed to meet their old friend.

"Rumblebelly!" Bruenor yelled. "What in the Nine Hells—"

"Did you believe that I would miss this occasion?" Regis huffed. "The wedding of two of my dearest friends?"

"How'd ye know?" Bruenor asked.

"You underestimate your fame, King Bruenor," Regis said, dropping into a graceful bow.

Drizzt studied the halfling curiously. He wore his gem-studded jacket and more jewelry, including the ruby pendant, than the drow had ever seen in one place. And the pouches hanging low on Regis's belt were sure to be filled with gold and gems.

"Might ye be staying long?" Catti-brie asked.

Regis shrugged. "I am in no hurry," he replied. Drizzt cocked an eyebrow. A master of a thieves' guild did not often leave his place of power; too many were usually ready to steal it out from under him.

Catti-brie seemed happy with the answer and happy with the timing of the halfling's return. Wulfgar's people were soon to rebuild the city of Settlestone, at the base of the mountains. She and Wulfgar, though, planned to remain in Mithral Hall, at Bruenor's side. After the wedding, they planned to do a bit of traveling they'd had in mind, maybe back to Icewind Dale, maybe along with Captain Deudermont later in the year, when the *Sea Sprite* sailed back to the southlands.

Catti-brie dreaded telling Bruenor that they would be leaving, if only for a few months. With Drizzt so often on the road, she feared that the dwarf would be miserable. But if Regis planned to stay on for a while . . .

"Might I have a room," Regis asked, "to put my things and to rest away the weariness of a long road?"

"We'll see to it," Catti-brie offered.

"And for your attendants?" Bruenor asked.

"Oh," stammered Regis, searching for a reply. "I . . . came alone. The southerners do not take well to the chill of a northern spring, you know."

"Well, off with ye, then," said Bruenor. "Suren it be me turn to set out a feast for the pleasure of yer belly."

Regis rubbed his hands together eagerly and left with Wulfgar and Catti-brie, the three of them breaking into tales of their latest adventures before they had even left the room.

"Suren few folk in Calimport have ever heared o' me name, elf," Bruenor said to Drizzt after the others had gone. "And who south o' Longsaddle would be knowing of the wedding?" He turned a sly eye on his dark friend. "Suren the little one brings a bit of his treasure along with him, eh?"

Drizzt had come to the same conclusion the moment Regis had entered the room. "He is running."

"Got himself into trouble again," Bruenor snorted, "or I'm a bearded gnome!"